PENGUIN BOO
SACRED GAM

PART I

Vikram Chandra's first novel, *Red Earth and Pouring Rain*, won the Commonwealth Writers' Prize for Best First Book and the David Higham Prize. His collection of short stories, *Love and Longing in Bombay*, won the Commonwealth Writers' Prize for Best Book (Eurasia Region). *Sacred Games* was awarded the Hutch Crossword Award for English Fiction and the Salon Book Award. His latest book is *Mirrored Mind: My Life in Letters and Code*, a non-fiction *New York Times* Editor's Choice selection. Chandra is a recipient of the Guggenheim fellowship, and his work has been translated into nineteen languages.

See www.vikramchandra.com.

Critical Acclaim for *Sacred Games*

'Vikram Chandra's *Sacred Games* wins the Hutch Crossword prize for English Fiction because in a crowded field filled with really first rate writing, the jury unanimously felt it was the outstanding novel of this year.'—Anita Roy, Mukul Kesavan, Shoma Chaudhury (judges, 2006 Crossword Book Award for Fiction)

'This is a ravishing, over-exuberant stab at the Great Indian Novel, an extraordinary work of fiction that will reward you in full for your investment of time...There's a superabundance of tumultuous narrative, acres of magnificent prose, and maybe a dozen too many characters. Yet these unruly parts ultimately fit together into a chaotic and luminous whole, one that mirrors Chandra's capacious vision of his homeland.'—Jennifer Reese, *Entertainment Weekly* (USA)

'This is a moment worth marking. It's a landmark in the history of Indian English literature. Decades from now, we'll be looking back at the roster of great contemporary novels, and the title *Sacred Games* will trip off our tongues blithely and reverentially...Then there's the setting. Bombay. It's more than a setting. It's the book itself. Chandra brings it brilliantly, deeply alive—in all her foulness, filth and stained beauty...This is a great novel, perhaps the greatest book on Bombay ever written.'—Ashok Banker, *Hindustan Times*

'"All human life is here" was the old newspaper boast, and so it is in *Sacred Games*, delineated with a master's grandeur and scope and a miniaturist's precision and tenderness. Seven years it took Chandra to write, and such is the haunting precision of its observation and the resonant authority of its narrative voice that one could read it seven times over and still be finding new treasures; missed flourishes of virtuosity. One uses the terms "epic" and "classic" with caution. But if eloquence, confidence, humanity, grace and fine observation are their raw materials, perhaps *Sacred Games* deserves those epithets.'—Jane Shilling, *The Daily Telegraph* (UK)

'It may have taken him three books, but *Sacred Games* is where Chandra really finds humour through his mastery of irony. This is a brutal and passionate tale, always, but Chandra throughout tempts you to seek meaning above and below the narrative, to smile with pleased recognition…Best of all, he effortlessly draws the reader into a tale that actually isn't particularly straightforward at all. The story line is determinedly non-linear, the structure episodically jump-cut, very evocative of Donald Barthelme. That master of spare prose might have taken 380 pages to write a comparable tale, but that's not the point. Don de Lillo might have needed 1,500, and in neither case would these two literary giants have written this gargantuan tale of Bombay/Mumbai and all its little Indias in quite the same heartbreaking, sardonic, funny and violent way…Buy this Rabelaisian masterpiece of mordant homage to Bombay today. Vikram Chandra has set the benchmark for the Bombay novel very high indeed.'—Hari Menon, *Tehelka*

'Like a sculptor making small, delicate chips in stone, Chandra moves things along at a measured pace, building his characters, finding glorious little details in the minutiae of everyday Bombay life, yet remaining sharply focused on the main thrust of his detective story…*Sacred Games* quakes with seismic historical shocks, as if Chandra were intent on blasting open India's historically amnesiac present, a time when India (or at least its media and its political class) is intoxicated by its glorious future. Chandra telescopes the past through the present with a series of historical insets into the narrative, reminding readers, as if he were an adept in palmistry, that "the shape of the future" lies "in the lines of the past…" What we get here is an occult history worthy of Borges. The last hours of Gaitonde's life—his final dialogue with the murdered woman before their deaths, the last of a series of fabulous exchanges between them—are electrifying, a baroque distillation of all that has gone on before. *Sacred Games*'s legacy might prove similar to that of Chandra's brother-in-law's film *Parinda*: By extending the territory of Indian literary fiction, it will allow others to tell crime stories of their own. Chandra's ultimate achievement is both as a genre novelist and as a novelist who uses genre elements. Solving the crime is important, but he also hands us the keys to the city and reveals its sordid mysteries.'—Carl Bromley, *The Nation* (USA)

'Vikram Chandra's masterly new novel—exactly 900 pages long—starts with a white Pomeranian, Fluffy, flying out of the window in upper-middle-class Mumbai...The spare, Hitchcockian funniness of the writing—the sense that it creates of schoolgoing ordinariness and urban kitsch erupting into bizarre and brutal catastrophe, and yet the ordinariness somehow managing to hold it all in eventually, in feats of epic-cinematic, divinely comic inclusiveness—is just one of the many ways in which Chandra's virtuosity unfolds in the novel...Yet, what holds the novel most profoundly and vitally together, and enables its mastery of the actual as well as the fabulous, the real and the surreal, is the cinema of Mumbai. Bollywood is to *Sacred Games* what chivalric romance is to Don Quixote—a living, self-perpetuating mythology, a shimmering universe of images and meanings by which people live and die, make, re-make and know (or resist knowing) themselves and the worlds and stories they inhabit.'—Aveek Sen, *The Telegraph*

'[Chandra] immerses the reader in a rich and utterly convincing world...A monumental portrait of interwoven lives that lingers with a reader long after the case is closed.'—Thomas Wharton, *The Globe and Mail* (Canada)

'For my money, this is the great Bombay book of the last decade. It gets the city's corrosive heat, the absolute knockdown democratic fever of it; and it goes some way to explaining why Bombay engenders loyalty among all those who live or have lived there...And one of the delights, for this reader at least, is the Bambaiyya Hindi, presented without italics, explanation, or apology: the apradhis, khabaris and pocket-maars, the bhais and boys, the gullels and ghodas...These are words that occur so often in Bombay they can be plucked out of the city's dirty air. But Chandra has done more. He uses them with such unerring gusto that they become celebratory, incantatory, not a code for insiders but something shared, like a song on the radio.'—Jeet Thayil, *Outlook*

'*Sacred Games*, though often suspenseful, is never filmi. Although the meat of this novel clings to the bones of a crime story, and there's certainly plenty of crime in it, the book is really a passionate tribute to contemporary India in all its vigor and vulgarity. Because it's not a family saga, it blessedly avoids what have become the clichés of the Indian literary novel.'—Laura Miller, Salon.com (USA)

'Chandra casts an enchanting and enthralling spell that documents two tales of two worlds—the Mumbai police and the Mumbai underworld. And garnishes it with many other tales...In doing so, he takes the enigma of Bombay to a new unparalleled high...This is a novelist at the height of his prowess almost sneering at all the academics who would no doubt try to construct and deconstruct this great Indian fable...Reportedly, Chandra took seven years to pen this epic masterpiece. The effort has well been worth it. For *Sacred Games* does the impossible. It makes an unwieldy hardcover unputdownable without missing a single literary beat.'—Vijay Nair, *Deccan Herald*

'Vikram Chandra's narrative is greater than a gangster story or a cinematic rendering of Indian life, or even an epic battle of good against evil...This is a work that can not only suck a reader in, but also turn an outlaw who should be thoroughly despicable into a heroic figure...The resulting web, intricate and large, comes together in the novel's startling, unexpected climax...[This is] a grand story that is carefully and passionately told. The final chapters, leading to the reason for Gaitonde's death, are breathtaking, as is Chandra's attention to the detail of character and circumstance. The work is so lovely, and so subtle, that it's well worth the cover price.'—Robin Vidimos, *The Denver Post* (USA)

'*Sacred Games* is storytelling at its very peak. Characters leap off the page to punch one in the gut, the narrative keeps the reader panting to know what happens next for every one of its 900 pages...If you've been underwhelmed by recent writing from India that, with a few exceptions, seems all too predictable in image and language, writing that wears its post-colonial heart on its sleeve and its reliance on the plot devices of arranged marriage and East-meets-West on its dust jacket—then run, don't walk towards *Sacred Games*. This thrilling, epic work is nothing less than a kick to the seat of the pants of recent Indian literature.'—Niranjana Iyer, *Asian Review of Books*

'An astonishingly engaging tome...[*Sacred Games*] can be easily acknowledged as a literary masterpiece.'—*Indulge Magazine* (USA)

'There's a vicarious excitement that you feel through the blood and gore of *Sacred Games*. A bewildering feeling that violence, poetry, hope, destruction and love all come together in this epic-of-sorts, to create a throbbing portrait of a city caught in the swirl of history...You grow into the story, and the stories coiled within it, into the restlessness of the characters, trapped as they are by some ghost, some vulnerability. The language is remarkably elastic, bringing a grainy, coarse texture to the narrative, as well as a moving poetry. In the end, *Sacred Games* is a "hard-boiled" thriller with razor-sharp edges, asking questions that unsettle and then don't let you go. In the same way that fears grip both Sartaj and Ganesh, control them, don't let them sleep.'—*First City* magazine

'Bold, fresh and big...Best of all, not only does *Sacred Games* deserve praise for its ambitions but also for its terrific achievement...When, as a reader, you reach the last page of *Sacred Games*, you feel as though you've been expelled from a world that, over weeks of reading, has come to feel like a second home.'—Maureen Corrigan, 'Fresh Air', NPR (USA)

'Vikram Chandra never fails to astonish. Almost like a magician conjuring up his latest trick, Chandra, the writer, has once again shown his ability to move ahead. Not afraid to experiment, he has drawn a variety of characters to build and share his story...Chandra has pulled off a coup of sorts with a masterpiece that dazzles as it races along the Mumbai skyline.'—*The Hindu*

'The novel oscillates splendidly between its two central characters...Chandra makes an enormous meal of Mumbai, the metropolis once called Bombay, each ingredient sharp and memorable...The imagery can be stunning...Submerging in [*Sacred Games*], like the Ganges itself, can restore your wonder.'—Karen Long, *The Plain Dealer* (USA)

'In a colossal romp, Chandra offers a view of Mumbai that many suspect, perhaps have even spoken of, but never confronted...Chandra's virtuosity of language that alternately thrills and repels, gets down to the basics of life in Mumbai. His skills as a storyteller are intact as are those of his minute and painstaking research into the hearts and minds of his characters. *Sacred Games* will tempt even the most reluctant reader with the incredible enthusiasm of its huge cast, the energy of its characters and the plots and subplots that make this many-layered story so memorable. Written with a rare combination of humour and anger, it is easy to see why this will become a popular book bordering on the classic.'—Suchitra Behal, *The Hindu*

'*Sacred Games* becomes much more than the sum of its spiraling parts...Then there's the structure, spider-webbed like a crack in a window across time and space..."If you want to live in the city you have to think ahead three turns, and look behind a lie to see the truth and then behind that truth to see a lie," says Gaitonde, recalling one of the lessons of his youth. One could say as much about the ample splendor of *Sacred Games*. Much more than a simple exercise in crime fiction, Chandra's tour de force is ambitious in all its facets. With its striking prose, ruthless capacity for violence and Gordian composition, *Sacred Games* offers up a world worthy of the effort required to take it all in.'—Clayton Moore, *Rocky Mountain News* (USA)

'One of *Sacred Games*' strengths is that Chandra goes well beyond the headlines, or for that matter, even the body copy of what has appeared in newspapers. His research is phenomenal, his insights, for the most part, extremely perspicacious…On balance *Sacred Games* is a ripping good read. At 900 pages, isn't it too long and bulky? It seems bulky only so long as the hard cover edition is held unopened in a single palm—the wrist may start to ache after a while. Once the book is put down, and the reading begins, it doesn't seem bulky at all…Yeh dil mange still more.'—Debashish Mukerji, *The Week*

'Epic it is, though, in scale and scope and in the quality of the writing, which is superb…*Sacred Games* is a stunning novel and one of the best crime novels of the year.'—Mike Ripley, *Birmingham Post* (UK)

'Meticulously structured and tautly told, it is the kind of novel that one reads hungrily, turning the pages but lingering over every paragraph and sentence, wanting to get to the end but not wanting the book to end at all…The narrative is not only about moves and countermoves. It is sustained by its moments of intense feeling—the suddenness of loss, the pain of having to betray a friend—but the melancholy wisdom that it offers is that the losses and betrayals are also part of the game. Meanwhile, other disparate characters wash up on the shores of the story like migrants to this island city by the sea, and the novel manages to hold them all together. Teeming with people and their individual histories, the book races back and forth between past and present, darkness and daylight, like the trains that whip across the cityscape…With notable effortlessness, the novel traverses the history of the Subcontinent, recalling not only the many griefs but also the steady struggle forward…[A] splendid novel.'—Uma Mahadevan-Dasgupta, *Himal Southasian* (Nepal)

'The ultimate subcontinental noir…Even as Chandra digresses to depict the horrors of partition, he stays in the skin of his characters, never resorting to DeLillo-ish atmospherics…Any book that makes palpable a very foreign city, explores deep moral questions, and teaches you lots of dirty Hindi is well worth lugging around.'—*New York Magazine* (USA)

'Vikram Chandra has achieved the near-impossible. He has constructed a superbly realized world of alien languages, customs and styles, presented on the page without apologies or explanations, and has somehow created a wholly believable universe. Now, in a fiction cunningly disguised as a straightforward crime drama, Chandra comes into his own...Chandra might have been content to simply concentrate on the crime elements, resulting in a lean, bloody entertainment of blackmail, double-crosses and bullets, but there is a heft and passion at work that elevates the plot from its pulpy origins. The expansive breadth of *Sacred Games* reveals a truly Dickensian world view of events and people.'—Corey Redecop, *Winnipeg Free Press* (Canada)

'*Sacred Games* is also a cocky experiment with the conventions of a thriller, breaking every rule a film director tells Gaitonde is necessary for a successful formula film...*Sacred Games* is sweaty, bloody, and unapologetically melodramatic. It's raucous...It's comic...In the end, the book is about this city, the dream factory of India, which remakes everyone and no one is what he seems...In those few inches that separate the myth from the reality, Chandra gives a startling, blood-pumping fallible humanity to his characters.'—Sandip Roy, *San Francisco Chronicle* (USA)

'We read compulsively, unable to put the book down...Once you open it, it owns you...Dismissing this book as a crime novel is like calling *Crime and Punishment* a thriller...*Sacred Games* is huge—as big as ambition, as consuming as love, as deep as compassion and as grand as India itself.'—Erica Eisdorfer, *The Carrboro Citizen* (Canada)

'One of the remarkable achievements in Vikram Chandra's stunning new novel, *Sacred Games*, is its portrayal of the all-encompassing, ingrained nature of the corruption in Mumbai...[*Sacred Games*] is a landmark work, a novel so ambitious and fully achieved it makes most American crime novelists—the Lehanes, the Pelecanos, even the Ellroys—seem naive and timid by comparison...As much as it is a multi-lingual dazzler of ambitious fiction, it's a rich, riveting thriller...Here, there is family, faith, a romantic affair, a sexual obsession, blackmail, betrayal, a city on the brink of chaos, and all of it is lyrically, lovingly conveyed. *Sacred Games* is one of the very few 900-page novels of recent vintage that as I read it, I was always eager for more.'—Jerome Weeks, ArtsJournal.com (USA)

'*Sacred Games* is one of those books you immerse yourself in, a passport to an alien world and, like life, you imagine it could go on forever. It envisions a world—an underworld, actually—that is complete, persuasive and startlingly original.'—Tom Beer, *Newsday* (USA)

'A genre-bending, multilayered saga...Chandra's expertly paced and nuanced unfolding of Gaitonde's life is interwoven with narratives that delve into the lives of various satellite characters...While *Sacred Games* takes an all-encompassing look at crucial issues facing modern-day India...thanks to its muscular prose and Chandra's obvious fondness for even his most deeply flawed characters, the book also succeeds as an entertainment extravaganza: a detective novel in full, and then a good deal more.'—Jenny Feldman, *Elle Magazine* (USA)

'Like Chandra's book, Singh's investigation adds up to much more than appears on the surface, and we read eagerly.'—Francine Prose, 'Critics Choice', *People Magazine* (USA)

'Go ahead. Close the book, turn out the lights. Even then, Ganesh Gaitonde, Sartaj Singh, and their many friends and enemies will whisper in your ear, beckoning from Mumbai and its jarring, joyous madness. Talk about an offer you can't refuse.'—Erik Spanberg, *The Christian Science Monitor* (USA)

'It's hard to do justice to the richness and vitality of this story—it's a full-immersion experience, as if Dickens had written *The Godfather* and placed it in India...Those stories, those glimpses at the myriad subgroups that comprise the city and those uniquely individual people who are drawn into the investigation, give the story its great resonance and depth.'—Rick Sullivan, *The Grand Rapids Press* (USA)

'*Sacred Games*, despite its length, is compulsively readable...This is a novel of voices, each of which is unmistakable. For while stories link the characters, from the poor in their hovels to the rich in their high-rises, the smutty aura of Mumbai arises from the prose itself. To re-create a city Mr. Chandra has fashioned a language equal to it, a promiscuous English open to all comers, as greedy and as vivid as Mumbai itself.'—Eric Ormsby, *The New York Sun* (USA)

'Great books create their necessity, though, and if you can lift this tremendous story into your shopping cart, bring it home and read it, you'll probably wonder how you got by so long without it...It is a terrific, brilliant, earthmover of a book.'—John Freeman, *Newcity Chicago* (USA)

'Chandra pulls strings with a puppeteer's mastery, connecting each disclosure of a concealed affiliation or conspiracy with what has gone before, whetting our appetites for ever more mayhem, depravity, and intrigue. The combination of an elephantine plot with a clockmaker's precise deployment of its sinister particulars is certainly attention-getting...Yet it's the characters who haunt us. Sartaj's tarnished integrity and Ganesh's perverted organizational genius hover over the novel like imperiled twin peaks, and there's something almost Homeric in the fateful intensity of their opposition...Few readers will be un-enthralled...It's a rare pleasure to be arrested by this novel's thunderous momentum, and caught up in its web.'—Bruce Allen, *The Boston Globe* (USA)

'Chandra is a prodigiously talented wordsmith with passion and boundless aspiration, and his intent here is obvious: *Sacred Games* is his ambitious, ostentatious shot at the Great Indian Novel. It is an extraordinary work of fiction and a literary accomplishment of the highest order—artful, educational, and one-of-a-kind.'—Tim Robinson, *The Hamilton Spectator* (USA)

'What keeps the reader interested is Chandra's total mastery of character and atmosphere. Great sheets of characterization wash over the reader like monsoon rains, but all the characters, and there are dozens, ring absolutely true. They become real people, who the reader invests heavily in, even when they're unpleasant...If you're looking for a novel that you can get lost in for weeks at a time over these winter nights, this is the one.'—Barry Hammond, *Edmonton Journal* (Canada)

'In *Sacred Games*, Chandra has surpassed his previous works, both in beauty and in bulk...The splendor of Chandra's prose is quite enough to enrapture a reader for 900 pages.'—Skye K. Moody, *The Seattle Times* (USA)

'Mr. Chandra brilliantly evokes a diverse slice of the population of Mumbai, a city that comes alive in *Sacred Games* in all its vibrant chaos...Perhaps Mr. Chandra's greatest strength is the compassion and understanding he has for all his flawed and needy characters.'— Henny Sender, *The Wall Street Journal* (USA)

'When I'd finished all 900 pages, I felt bereft. From the first, savagely funny paragraph (it requires a health warning for dog lovers) it's a crackerjack, even if you're not familiar with Indian obscenities.'— Chris Patten, *New Statesman* (UK)

'Once in a while you find a book that sucks you so thoroughly into the world it creates that each time you slip your bookmark between the pages and close the cover, you come up blinking, surprised to find yourself in your own skin again. Vikram Chandra's intricate *Sacred Games* is just such a novel.'—Miriam Wolf, *The Sunday Oregonian* (USA)

'Vikram Chandra's Mumbai mammoth of a literary thriller about cops and thugs, film-stars and financiers, unspools with Dickensian brio and at Dickensian length, but seldom loses its touch for street-smart observation and suspense.'—Boyd Tonkin, 'Books of the Year', *Independent* (UK)

'Chandra takes you inside the world of a Bombay cop. After reading the book, you'll swear you know precisely how to collect a bribe from a nightclub owner, how to count the money in a glance, and where to find the smart fellow who will shift the loot to a Swiss bank account. Rarely entirely honest or entirely rotten, Chandra's Bombay exists in a penumbra of moral ambiguity—which is why *Sacred Games* is one of the best novels about India in a long time.'—Aravind Adiga, '10 Best Asian Books of 2006', *Time* (Asia edition)

'Epic, sprawling depiction of Bombay's seedy underworld by one of India's master storytellers. Its protagonist, inspector Sartaj Singh, has earned a place among the world's outstanding fictional detectives. One of the most exhilarating reads of 2006.'—'Books of the Year', *Financial Times* (UK)

'Chandra has captured that gritty, sickeningly sweet, perspiration-soaked, electrifying, addictive quality of India...Chandra has managed to weave the best and worst parts of Mumbai into an utterly spellbinding novel. Though the mafia angle always sells well, it's more than just "The Godfather in India"—Chandra's prose elevates it to a literary masterpiece.'—Julie Welter, *Publishers Weekly* (USA)

'This is an immense, brilliant and bewildering novel. The hardback edition has exactly 900 pages and not one of them is wasted. It took Vikram Chandra seven years to write. I can only hope he has already started on his next book.'—Esme Choonara, *The Socialist Review* (UK)

'Vikram Chandra's novel *Sacred Games* is a gutsy, well-crafted attempt at giving the city the kind of novel it deserves...[It] is a big, bustling...constantly engaging novel that, like the city it explores, inexplicably manages to work.'—Nirpal Dhaliwal, *The Evening Standard* (UK)

'This is no simple Holmes-Moriarty adventure or merely an entertaining read. It works on numerous levels, the most vibrant of which paints a realistic landscape of India and the intrinsic machinery that allows it to move forward, when the laws of sociology suggest the country should have collapsed long ago. It addresses crime, politics, religion, the caste system, history, business, the psychology of power, the juxtaposition of good and evil, and the effects of merging cultures on a nation—to name a few of its topics. It is against this setting that Chandra's stories-within-a-story spin, and what glorious diversions they are.'—Allen Pierleoni, *Sacramento Bee* (USA)

'Between them the two narratives add up to a kaleidoscopic vision of an immense city—glittering and squalid, pullulating with energy, grossly overpopulated, driven by the volatile forces of ambition, despair and religious ardour. That city is the real protagonist of Chandra's book, as well as the stage on which his Comedie Humaine is played out. Appropriately, the disaster, which both master criminal and policeman are struggling to avert, is one that threatens, not any particular person or group, but the whole reeking, noisy, beautiful place...Each of these characters and dozens of others add something—a piece of a glitter or a dark accent—to the immense mosaic Chandra is constructing...[A] hugely ambitious and dazzlingly energetic book.'—Lucy Hughes-Hallett, *Sunday Times* (UK)

'By telling his tale in popular form, Chandra has found a vehicle particularly suited to the New India—to its passions and poverty, its outsize dreams and insecurities. Gaitonde may be larger than life in his appetites but not in his ambitions. The reader can recognize the same desperate striving in him as in a lowly Bihari slum dweller, a cop on the make.'—Nisid Hajari, *Newsweek International*

'One thing Chandra does superbly well is give a sense of the changes and the continuities of modern India...*Sacred Games* conjures up a Mumbai that is far more convincing than others we've been offered, one that accurately portrays the recent changes in Indian society...I was grateful for my full-blooded lesson in Hindi curses. All are brilliantly embedded so that every meaning is clear, a remarkable achievement. Anthony Burgess once did a similar job for Russian in the teenage argot of *A Clockwork Orange*, but his publisher insisted on a glossary, against Burgess's better judgement. Chandra manages without.'—Kevin Rushby, *Guardian Unlimited* (UK)

'Chandra manages to forge an intimacy between the reader and the two often morally unattractive men who rage across these 900 pages...*Sacred Games* is both riveting and brilliantly vile.'—Ruby Lancaster, *Time Out* (UK)

SACRED 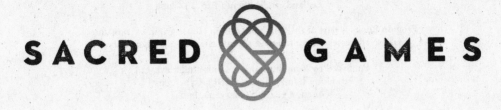 GAMES

PART I

VIKRAM CHANDRA

PENGUIN BOOKS

An imprint of Penguin Random House

PENGUIN BOOKS

USA | Canada | UK | Ireland | Australia
New Zealand | India | South Africa | China

Penguin Books is part of the Penguin Random House group of companies
whose addresses can be found at global.penguinrandomhouse.com

Published by Penguin Random House India Pvt. Ltd
7th Floor, Infinity Tower C, DLF Cyber City,
Gurgaon 122 002, Haryana, India

Penguin
Random House
India

First published in India in Viking by Penguin Books India 2006
Published in Penguin Books 2007

Copyright © Vikram Chandra 2006

ISBN 9780143445944

████████████████████████

Printed at Thomson Press India Ltd, New Delhi

www.penguin.co.in

MIX
Paper
FSC FSC® C010615

For
Anuradha Tandon
and
S. Hussain Zaidi

Contents

Acknowledgements

Some of the travel for this book was funded by a University Facilitating Fund grant from George Washington University.

I'm grateful to my erstwhile colleagues at George Washington University for their support and forbearance, especially my friends in the Creative Writing Program: Faye Moskowitz; David McAleavey; Jody Bolz; Jane Shore; Maxine Claire.

S. Hussain Zaidi has been extraordinarily generous with his vast knowledge, warm friendship and unstinting support. I am indebted to him.

Many others offered me aid, information and hospitality during the writing of this book:

Anuradha Tandon; Arup Patnaik, DIG, CBI; API Rajan Gule, CID; Fazal Irani; Akbar Irani; API Sanjay Rangnekar; Violet Monis; Iqbal Khan; Imtiaz Khan; Nisha Jamwal; Rajeev Samant; Rakesh Maria, DIG; Viral Mazumdar; Bandana Tewari; Shernaz Dinshaw; Nonita Kalra; A.D. Singh; Sabina Singh; Rajiv Somani; Aftab Khan; Rasna Behl; Ashutosh Sohni; Shruti Pandit; Kalpana Mhatre; Deepak Jog, DCP; Srila Chatterjee; Sherry Zutshi; Namita Waikar; Shashi Tharoor; Julia Eckert; Jaideep and Seema Mehrotra; Dr Ashok Gupta; Namrata Sharma Zakaria; Dr Amiq Gazdhar; Farzand Ahmed; Menaka Rao; Gyan Prakash.

In Delhi, Punjab and Jammu and Kashmir: Harinder Baweja; A.K. Sehgal; Amit Sehgal; Manohar Singh; Agha Shahid Ali; Shafi; Sumit (Surd) Nurpuri; Praveen Swami.

In Bihar: Sanjay Jha; Vinod Mishra; Ravinder Jadav; Ashok Kumar Singh, SP, Gaya; N.C. Dhoundial, DIG, Gaya; R.K. Prasad, Dy SP, Gaya; Sunit Kumar, IGP, Patna; Subnath Jha; Bibhuti Nath Jha 'Mastan'; Gopal Dubey; Surendra Trivedi; Sh. Shaiwal.

There are others I cannot name. They know who they are.

As always, I'm grateful to my parents, Navin and Kamna, and my sisters, Tanuja and Anupama; my friend and support, Margo True; Eric Simonoff; Julian Loose; David Davidar; Terry Karten; and Vidhu Vinod Chopra.

And to Melanie, who changed everything.

The hymns in the chapter 'Ganesh Gaitonde Explores the Self' are from the *Rig Vega*. I adapted Raimundo Pannikar's translations (*The Vedic Experience*, Motilal Banarsidass, 2001).

Dramatis Personae

Sartaj Singh: a Sikh police inspector in Mumbai

Katekar: a police constable who works with Sartaj Singh
  Shalini, Katekar's wife
  Mohit and **Rohit,** their sons

Mrs Kamala Pandey: a married woman and airline hostess with a lover, an airline pilot named Umesh

Kamble: an ambitious police sub-inspector who works with Sartaj Singh

Parulkar: a deputy commissioner of police in Mumbai

Ganesh Gaitonde: a notorious Hindu gangster and don, leader of the G-Company in Mumbai

Suleiman Isa: a much-feared Muslim gangster and don, leader of a rival gang in Mumbai

Paritosh Shah: a supremely gifted money handler for gangsters, including Ganesh Gaitonde

Kanta Bai: a businesswoman who deals with Paritosh Shah and Ganesh Gaitonde

Badriya: Paritosh Shah's bodyguard

Anjali Mathur: a government intelligence agent investigating Ganesh Gaitonde's death

Chotta Badriya: Ganesh Gaitonde's bodyguard, and the younger brother of Badriya

Juliet (Jojo) Mascarenas: a television producer/agent for aspiring actors and models . . . and a high class Madam

Mary Mascarenas: Jojo's sister who works as a hairdresser

Wasim Zafar Ali Ahmad: a social worker in a poor neighbourhood in Mumbai who has political aspirations

Prabhjot Kaur, 'Nikki': Sartaj Singh's mother, originally from the Punjab

Navneet, her beloved oldest sister

Ram Pari: the maidservant of Nikki's mother in the Punjab

Bunty: Ganesh Gaitonde's right hand man and organizer

Bipin Bhonsle: a Hindu fundamentalist politician whom Ganesh Gaitonde helps get elected to public office

Sharma (aka Trivedi): Bipin Bhonsle's ally who also works, through intermediaries, for Swami Shridhar Shukla

Swami Shridhar Shukla, 'Guru-ji': a Hindu guru and nationalist, a spiritual adviser of international renown, who becomes Ganesh Gaitonde's spiritual mentor

Subhadra Devalekar: Ganesh Gaitonde's wife and mother of his young son

K. D. Yadav (aka Mr Kumar): a pioneering Indian intelligence officer who 'ran' Ganesh Gaitonde and became a mentor to Anjali Mathur

Mr Kulkarni: the intelligence agent who runs Ganesh Gaitonde after K. D. Yadav

Major Shahid Khan: a Pakistani intelligence agent who masterminds a counterfeit money operation against India

Shambhu Shetty: proprietor of the Delite Dance Bar

Iffat-bibi: Suleiman Isa's maternal aunt who is one of his main controllers in Mumbai

Majid Khan: a police inspector in Mumbai, a colleague of Sartaj Singh

Zoya Mirza: an actress and a rising star in the Indian film industry

Aadil Ansari: an educated but poor man from a small rural town who flees to Mumbai to escape the violent conflicts of his native Bihar

Sharmeen Khan: the high-school-age daughter of Major Shahid Khan, who moves to the USA to work in Washington, DC, and brings his family – wife, daughter, and mother – with him

Daddi: Shahid Khan's mother, originally from the Punjab; to her family, she is a Muslim, but she hides a secret

SACRED GAMES

Policeman's Day

A white Pomeranian named Fluffy flew out of a fifth-floor window in Panna, which was a brand-new building with the painter's scaffolding still around it. Fluffy screamed in her little lap-dog voice all the way down, like a little white kettle losing steam, bounced off the bonnet of a Cielo, and skidded to a halt near the rank of schoolgirls waiting for the St Mary's Convent bus. There was remarkably little blood, but the sight of Fluffy's brains did send the conventeers into hysterics, and meanwhile, above, the man who had swung Fluffy around his head by one leg, who had slung Fluffy into the void, one Mr Mahesh Pandey of Mirage Textiles, that man was leaning on his windowsill and laughing. Mrs Kamala Pandey, who in talking to Fluffy always spoke of herself as 'Mummy', now staggered and ran to her kitchen and plucked from the magnetic holder a knife nine inches long and two wide. When Sartaj and Katekar broke open the door to apartment 502, Mrs Pandey was standing in front of the bedroom door, looking intensely at a dense circle of two-inch-long wounds in the wood, about chest-high. As Sartaj watched, she sighed, raised her hand and stabbed the door again. She had to struggle with both hands on the handle to get the knife out.

'Mrs Pandey,' Sartaj said.

She turned to them, the knife still in a double-handed grip, held high. She had a pale, tear-stained face and tiny bare feet under her white nightie.

'Mrs Pandey, I am Inspector Sartaj Singh,' Sartaj said. 'I'd like you to put down that knife, please.' He took a step, hands held up and palms forward. 'Please,' he said. But Mrs Pandey's eyes were wide and blank, and except for the quivering of her forearms she was quite still. The hallway they were in was narrow, and Sartaj could feel Katekar behind him, wanting to pass. Sartaj stopped moving. Another step and he would be comfortably within a swing of the knife.

3

'Police?' a voice said from behind the bedroom door. 'Police?'

Mrs Pandey started, as if remembering something, and then she said, 'Bastard, bastard,' and slashed at the door again. She was tired now, and the point bounced off the wood and raked across it, and Sartaj bent her wrist back and took the knife quite easily from her. But she smashed at the door with her hands, breaking her bangles, and her last wiry burst of anger was hard to hold and contain. Finally they sat her down on the green sofa in the drawing room.

'Shoot him,' she said. '*Shoot* him.' Then she put her head in her hands. There were green and blue bruises on her shoulder. Katekar was back at the bedroom door, murmuring.

'What did you fight about?' Sartaj said.

'He wants me not to fly any more.'

'What?'

'I'm an air hostess. He thinks . . .'

'Yes?'

She had startling light-brown eyes, and she was angry at Sartaj for asking. 'He thinks since I'm an air hostess, I keep hostessing the pilots on stopovers,' she said, and turned her face to the window.

Katekar was walking the husband over now, with a hand on his neck. Mr Pandey hitched up his silky red-and-black striped pyjamas, and smiled confidentially at Sartaj. 'Thank you,' he said. 'Thanks for coming.'

'So you like to hit your wife, Mr Pandey?' Sartaj barked, leaning forward. Katekar sat the man down, hard, while he still had his mouth open. It was nicely done. Katekar was a senior constable, an old subordinate, a colleague really – they had worked together for almost seven years now, off and on. 'You like to hit her, and then you throw a poor puppy out of a window? And then you call us to save you?'

'She said I hit her?'

'I have eyes. I can see.'

'Then look at this,' Mr Pandey said, his jaw twisting. 'Look, look, look at this.' And he pulled up his left pyjama jacket sleeve, revealing a shiny silver watch and four evenly spaced scratches, livid and deep, running from the inside of the wrist around to the elbow. 'More, I've got more,' Mr Pandey said, and bowed low at the waist and lowered his head and twisted to raise his collar away from the skin. Sartaj got up and walked around the coffee table. There was a corrugated red

4

welt on Mr Pandey's shoulder blade, and Sartaj couldn't see how far down it went.

'What's that from?' Sartaj said.

'She broke a Kashmiri walking stick on my back. This thick, it was,' Mr Pandey said, holding up his thumb and forefinger circled.

Sartaj walked to the window. There was a group of uniformed boys clustering around the small white body below, pushing each other closer to it. The St Mary's girls were squealing, holding their hands to their mouths, and begging the boys to stop. In the drawing room, Mrs Pandey was gazing brightly at her husband, her chin tucked into her chest. 'Love,' Sartaj said softly. 'Love is a murdering gaandu. Poor Fluffy.'

'Namaskar, Sartaj Saab,' PSI Kamble called across the station house. 'Parulkar Saab was asking after you.' The room was some twenty-five feet across, with four desks lined up across the breadth of it. There was a six-foot poster of Sai Baba on the wall, and a Ganesha under the glass on Kamble's desk, and Sartaj had felt impelled to add a picture of Guru Gobind Singh on the other wall, in a somewhat twisted assertion of secularism. Five constables came jerkily to attention, and then subsided into their usual sprawl on white plastic chairs.

'Where is Parulkar Saab?'

'With a pack of reporters. He's giving them tea and telling them about our new initiative against crime.'

Parulkar was the deputy commissioner for Zone 13, and his office was next door, in a separate building that was the zonal headquarters. He loved reporters, and had a genius for being jovial with them, and a recent knack for declaiming couplets during interviews. Sartaj wondered sometimes if he sat up late with books of poetry, practising in front of a mirror. 'Good,' Sartaj said. 'Somebody has to tell them about all our hard work.'

Kamble let out a snort of laughter.

Sartaj sat at the desk next to Kamble and flipped open a copy of the *Indian Express*. Two members of the Gaitonde gang had been shot to death in an encounter with the Flying Squad in Bhayander. The police had acted on received intelligence and intercepted the two as they proceeded to a factory office in that locality; the two extortionists had been hailed and told to surrender, but they had instantly fired at the squad, who then retaliated, et cetera, et cetera. There was a colour photograph of plain-clothes men bending over two oblong red stains on the ground. In other news, there had been two break-ins in Andheri East, one in Worli, and this last one had ended in the fatal stabbing of a young couple. As Sartaj read, he could hear the elderly man sitting across from Kamble talking about slow death. His eighty-year-old mausi had fallen down a flight of stairs and broken her hip. They had checked her into the Shivsagar Polyclinic, where she had borne with her usual stoicism the unrelenting pain in her old bones. After all, she had marched with Gandhi-ji in forty-two and had suffered her first fracture then – of the collarbone from a mounted policeman's lathi – and also the bare floors of jail cells afterwards. She had an old-fashioned strength, which saw sacrifice of the self as one's duty in the world. But when the pressure ulcers flowered their deep red wounds on her arms and shoulders and back, even she had said, perhaps it is time for me to die. The elderly man had never heard her say anything of the like, but now she groaned, I want to die. And it took her twenty-two days to find relief, twenty-two days before blessed darkness. If you had seen her, the elderly man said, you too would have cried.

Kamble was flipping pages in a register. Sartaj completely believed the elderly man's story, and understood his problem: the Shivsagar Polyclinic wouldn't let him take the body without a No Objection Certificate endorsed by the police. The handwritten note on Brihanmumbai Municipal Corporation stationery would say that the police were satisfied that the death in question was natural, that there was no foul play involved, that the body could be released to relatives for disposal. This was supposed to prevent murders – dowry killings and suchlike – from being passed off as accidents, and Police Sub Inspector Kamble was supposed to sign it on behalf of the ever watchful, khaki-clad guardians of Mumbai, but he had it sitting next to his elbow and he was studiously scribbling in his register. The elderly man had his hands folded together, and his white hair fell over his forehead, and he was looking at the indifferent Kamble with moist eyes. 'Please, sir,' he said.

Sartaj thought it was on the whole a finely considered performance, and that the grief was genuine, but the bit about Gandhi-ji and broken collarbones quite excessively and melodramatically reproving. Both the elderly man and Kamble knew well that a payment would have to be made before the certificate was signed. Kamble would probably hold out for eight hundred rupees; the old man wanted to give only five hundred or so, but the sacrifices of the elders had been done to death in the movies, and Kamble was quite indifferent to the degeneration-of-India gambit. He now closed his red register and reached for a green one. He studied it closely. The old man began the whole story again, from the fall down the stairs. Sartaj got up, stretched, and walked out into the courtyard of the station. In the shade of the gallery that ran along the front of the building, and under the tin portico, there was the usual crowd of touts, hangers-on, relatives of those chained in the detection room inside, messengers and representatives from local businessmen, favour-seekers, and, here and there, those marked by misfortune and sudden misery, now looking up at him in mingled hope and bitterness.

Sartaj walked past them all. There was an eight-foot wall around the whole complex, of the same reddish-brown brick as the station house and the zonal headquarters. Both buildings were two storeys high, with identical red-tiled roofs and oval-topped windows. There was a promise in the grim arches, in the thickness of the walls and the uncompromising weight of the façades, there was the reassurance of bulky power, and so law and order. A sentry snapped to attention as Sartaj went up the stairs. Sartaj heard the laughter from Parulkar's cabin well before he could see it, while he was still twisting through the warren of cubicles piled high with paper. Sartaj knocked sharply on the lustrous wood of Parulkar's door, then pushed it open. There was a quick upturning of laughing faces, and Sartaj saw that even the national newspapers had come out for the story of Parulkar's initiative, or at least for his poetry. He was good copy.

'Gentlemen, gentlemen,' Parulkar said, raising one proud, pointing hand. 'My most daring officer, Sartaj Singh.' The correspondents lowered their teacups with a long clatter and looked at Sartaj sceptically. Parulkar walked around the desk, tugging at his belt. 'One minute, please. I'll talk to him outside for a moment, then he will tell you about our initiative.'

Parulkar shut the door, and led Sartaj around the back of the cabin, to a very small kitchen which now boasted a gleaming new Brittex water filter on its wall. Parulkar pressed buttons and a bright stream of water fell into the glass he held below.

'It tastes very pure, sir,' Sartaj said. 'Very good indeed.'

7

Parulkar was drinking deep draughts from a steel tumbler. 'I asked them for their best model,' he said. 'Because clean water is absolutely necessary.'

'Yes, sir.' Sartaj took a sip. 'Sir – "daring"?'

'They like daring. And you had better be daring if you want to stay in this job.'

Parulkar had sloping shoulders and a pear-shaped body that defeated the best tailors, and his uniform was crumpled already, but that was only usual. There was a sag in his voice, a resignation in his sideways glance that Sartaj had never known. 'Is something wrong, sir? Is there some complication with the initiative, sir?'

'No, no, no complication with the initiative. No, nothing to do with that at all. It is something else.'

'Yes, sir?'

'They are after me.'

'Who, sir?'

'Who else?' Parulkar said with unusual asperity. 'The government. They want me out. They think I've gone high enough.'

Parulkar was now a deputy commissioner of police, and he had once been a lowly sub-inspector. He had risen through the Maharashtra State Police, and he had made that near-impossible leap into the august Indian Police Service, and he had done it alone, with good police work, a sense of humour, and very long hours. It had been an astonishing and unparalleled career, and he had risen to become Sartaj's mentor. He emptied his glass, and poured more water from his new Brittex filter.

'Why, sir?' Sartaj said. 'Why?'

'I was too close to the previous government. They think I'm a Congress man.'

'So they may want you out. That doesn't mean anything. You have lots of years left before retirement.'

'You remember Dharmesh Mathija?'

'Yes, that's the fellow who built our wall.' Mathija was a builder, one of the more conspicuously successful ones in the northern suburbs, a man whose ambition showed like a sweaty fever on his forehead. He had built, in record time, the extension of the compound wall at the rear of the station, around the recently filled lowland. There was now a Hanuman temple and a small lawn and young trees that you could see from the offices to the rear of the building. Parulkar's passion was improvement. He said it often: we must improve. Mathija and Sons had improved the station, and of course they had done it for free. 'So what about Mathija, sir?'

Parulkar was taking little sips of water, swirling it about in his mouth. 'I was called to the DG's office yesterday, early.'

'Yes, sir.'

'The DG had a call from the home minister. Mathija has threatened to file a case. He said he was forced to do some work for me. Construction.'

'That's absurd, sir. He came himself. How many times he visited you here. We all saw that. He was happy to do it.'

'Not our wall here. At my home.'

'At your home?'

'The roof needed work urgently. As you know, it's a very old house. My ancestral abode really. Also, it needed a new bathroom. Mamta and my granddaughters have moved back home. As you know. So.'

'And?'

'Mathija did it. He did good work. But now he says he has me on tape threatening him.'

'Sir?'

'I remember phoning him to tell him to hurry up. Finish the work before the last monsoons. I may have used some strong language.'

'But so what, sir? Let him go to court. Let him do what he wants. Let him see what we do to his life here, sir. At his sites, all his offices . . .'

'Sartaj, that's just their excuse. It's a way to put pressure on me, and let me know I am not wanted. They're not satisfied with just transferring me, they want to get rid of me.'

'You will fight back, sir.'

'Yes.' Parulkar was the best player of the political game Sartaj had ever known: he was a grandmaster of the subtle art of contact and double-contact and back-channel, of ministers and corporators cultivated and kept happy, business interests allowed room for profits, backslapping and exchanges with commissioners of police, favours finely weighed and dispensed and remembered, deals made and forgotten – he was an aficionado of the subtle sport, he was simply the best. It was incredible that he was so tired. His collar sagged, and the swell of his belly was no longer jaunty, only weighted by regret. He drank another glass of water, fast. 'You had better get in there, Sartaj. They're waiting for you.'

'I'm sorry, sir.'

'I know you are.'

'Sir.' Sartaj thought he should say something else, something full of gratitude and somehow conclusive about what Parulkar had meant to him – the years together, the cases solved and the ones left and abandoned, the manoeuvres learnt, how to live and work and survive as a policeman in the city – and yet Sartaj was able only to come to rigid attention. Parulkar nodded. Sartaj was certain he understood.

Outside the cabin, Sartaj checked the tuck of his shirt, ran a hand over his turban. Then he stepped in, and told the reporters about more policemen on more streets, about community interaction, about strict supervision and transparency, about how things were going to get better.

For lunch Sartaj had an uttapam sent to the station from the next-door Udipi Restaurant. The keen kick of the chillies was invigorating, but when he was finished, Sartaj was unable to get up from his chair. It had been a very light meal but he was crushed, pulped by lassitude. He was barely able to get up and pull the bench from the wall, to slip off his shoes and lie flat and very straight on the wood. His arms were crossed on his chest. A deep breath, then another, and the edge cutting into the back of his thigh receded, and in the swimming drowsiness he was able to forget details, and the world became a receding white blur. Yet a sharp undertow flung him into anger, and after a moment he was able to remember what he was restless about. All of Parulkar's triumphs were going to be wiped away, made meaningless by an engineered disgrace. And once Parulkar was gone, what of Sartaj? What would become of him? Sartaj had begun recently to feel that he himself had accomplished nothing in his life. He was past forty, a divorced police inspector with middling professional prospects. Others from his batch had climbed past him, he was just pedalling along, doing his job. He looked into his future and saw that he would not achieve as much as his own father, and much less than the redoubtable Parulkar. I am quite useless, Sartaj thought, and felt very bleak. He sat up, rubbed his face, shook his head violently, and pulled on his shoes. He stalked into the front room, where PSI Kamble was rubbing his stomach lightly in circles. He looked quite satisfied.

'Good lunch?' Sartaj said.

'Absolute top first-class biryani from that new Laziz Restaurant on S.T. Road,' Kamble said. 'In a fancy clay pot, you know. We're getting very pish-posh in Kailashpada.' Kamble straightened up and leaned closer. 'Listen. You know those two gaandus who were encountered yesterday by the Flying Squad in Bhayander?'

'Gaitonde gang, yes?'

'Right. You know the Gaitonde gang and the Suleiman Isa gang have been stepping up their war again, right? So, I heard the two hits yesterday were a supari given by the S-Company. I heard that the Flying Squad boys made twenty lakhs.'

'You'd better get in the squad then.'

'Boss, what do you think I'm saving up for? I hear the going rate to get in is twenty-five lakhs.'

'Very expensive.'

'Very,' Kamble said. His face was aglow, every pore open and alight. 'But money makes it all happen, my friend, and to make money you have to spend money.'

Sartaj nodded, and Kamble sank into a register again. Sartaj had once heard it from a slumlord convicted of murder, the bitter secret of life in the metropolis: *paisa phek, tamasha dekh.* They had literally bumped into each other, walking round a corner in a basti in Andheri. They had recognized each other instantly, despite Sartaj's plain clothes and the slumlord's new paunch. Sartaj said, arre, Bahzad Hussain, aren't you supposed to be serving fifteen years for offing Anwar Yeda? And Bahzad Hussain laughed nervously, and said, Inspector saab, you know how it is, I got parole and now it says in my file that I'm absconding in Bahrain, *paisa phek, tamasha dekh.* Which was absolutely true: if you had money to throw, you could watch the spectacle – the judges and magistrates trapezing blithely, the hoop-jumping politicians, the happy, red-nosed cops. Bahzad Hussain had the grace and good sense to come quietly to the station, and he was very confident, and wanted only a cup of tea and a chance to make a few phone calls. He made jokes and laughed a lot. Yes, he had thrown his money and watched the spectacle. All of this police jhanjhat was only a slight waste of time, nothing more. *Paisa phek, tamasha dekh.*

Kamble now had a family standing in front of him, a mother and a father and a son in blue-uniform short pants. The father was a tailor who had come back home from the shop early in the afternoon, to get

11

some suiting material he had forgotten. On the way he had taken a short-cut and seen his son, who was supposed to be in school, playing marbles against the factory wall with some faltu street kids. The mother was doing the talking now. 'Saab, I beat him, his father shouts at him, nothing helps. The teachers have given up. He shouts back at us, my son. He thinks he's too smart. He thinks he doesn't need school. I'm tired of it, saab. You take him. You put him in jail.' She made the motion of emptying her hands, and dabbed at her eyes with the end of her blue pallu. Looking at her hands and finely muscled forearms, Sartaj was certain that she worked as a bai, that she washed dishes and clothes for the wives of executives in the Shiva Housing Colony. The son had his head down, and was scraping the side of one shoe against the other.

Sartaj crooked a finger. 'Come here.' The boy shuffled sideways. 'What's your name?'

'Sailesh.' He was about thirteen, quite wise, with a stylish floppy hair-do and flashing black eyes.

'Hello, Sailesh.'

'Hello.'

Sartaj smashed a hand down on to the table. It was very loud, and Sailesh started and backed away. Sartaj grabbed him by the collar and twisted him around the end of the desk. 'You think you're tough, Sailesh? You're so tough you're not scared of anyone, Sailesh? Let me show you what we do with tough taporis like you, Sailesh.' Sartaj walked him around the room and through a door and into the detection room, lifting him off the floor with every stride. Katekar was sitting with another constable at the end of the room, near the squatting line of chained prisoners.

'Katekar,' Sartaj called.

'Sir.'

'Which is the toughest of this lot?'

'This one, sir, thinks he's hard. Narain Swami, pickpocket.'

Sartaj shook Sailesh so that his head wobbled and snapped. 'This big man here thinks he's harder than all of us. Let him see. Give Narain Swami some dum and let the big man see.'

Katekar lifted the cringing Narain Swami and bent him over, and Swami struggled and jingled his chains, but when the first open-palmed blow landed on his back with an awful popping noise he got the idea. With the second one he howled quite creditably. After the third and fourth he was sobbing. 'Please, please, saab. No more.'

After the sixth, Sailesh was weeping fat tears. He turned his face away and Sartaj forced his chin around.

'Want to see more, Sailesh? You know what we do next?' Sartaj pointed at the thick white bar that ran from one wall to the other, close to the ceiling. 'We put Swami on the ghodi. We string him up on the bar, hands and feet, and give it to him with the patta. Show him the patta, Katekar.'

But Sailesh, looking at the thick length of the strap, whispered, 'No, don't.'

'What?'

'Please don't.'

'You want to end up here, Sailesh? Like Narain Swami?'

'No.'

'What's that?'

'No, saab. Please.'

'You will, you know. If you keep going like you are.'

'I won't, saab. I won't.'

Sartaj turned him around, both hands on his shoulders, and walked him towards the door. Narain Swami was still bent over, and flashing an upside-down grin. Outside, sitting on a metal chair with a Coke bottle clutched between his knees, Sailesh listened quietly to Sartaj. He sipped his Coke and Sartaj told him how people like Narain Swami ended up, beaten up, used up, addicted, in jail and out of it, wasted and tired and finally dead. All of it from not going to school and disobeying his mother.

'I'll go,' Sailesh said.

'Promise?'

'Promise,' Sailesh said and touched his throat.

'Better keep it,' Sartaj said. 'I hate people who break promises. I'll come after you.'

Sailesh nodded, and Sartaj led him out. At the station gate, the mother hung back. She came close to Sartaj and held up her fisted hands and opened them. In the right there was the twisted end of her pallu, and in the left a neatly folded hundred rupee note. 'Saab,' she said.

'No,' Sartaj said. 'No.'

She had oiled hair and reddened eyes. She smiled, barely, and held up her hands higher, and opened them further.

'No,' Sartaj said. He turned and walked away.

*

13

Katekar drove with an easy grace that found the gaps in the traffic with balletic timing. Sartaj pushed his seat back and drowsily watched him change gears and snake the Gypsy between trucks and autos with less than inches to spare. Sartaj had long ago learned to relax. He still anticipated a crash every few minutes, but he had learned from Katekar not to care. It was all confidence. You went forward, and someone always backed off at the last moment, and it was always the other gaandu. Katekar scratched at his crotch, growled 'Eh, bhenchod,' and stared down a double-decker driver, forced him to an absolute stop. They took a left, and Sartaj grinned at the wide swagger of the turn. 'Tell me, Katekar,' Sartaj said, 'who is your favourite hero?'

'Film hero?'

'What else?'

Katekar was embarrassed. 'When I do watch movies –' He jiggled the gear stick, and wiped a spot of dust from the windscreen. 'When there is some film on television,' – which was only all the time – 'I like to watch Dev Anand.'

'Dev Anand? Really?'

'Yes, sir.'

'But he's my favourite also.' Sartaj liked the old black-and-white ones where Dev Anand listed across the screen at an impossible angle, unbelievably dashing and sublimely suave. In his limp perfection there was an odd comfort, a nostalgia for a simplicity that Sartaj had never known. But he had expected Katekar to be an Amitabh Bachchan extremist, or an enthusiast of the muscle boys, Sunil Shetty or Akshay Kumar, who stood huge on the posters like some new gigantic and bulging species. 'Which Dev Anand film do you like best, Katekar?'

Katekar smiled, and tipped his head to the side. It was a perfect Dev Anand waggle. 'Why, sir, *Guide*, sir. Of course.'

Sartaj nodded. 'Of course.' *Guide* was in bright sixties colour, all the better to savour the intense and ecstatic love that Dev found for Waheeda, and the bitterness of his final tragedy. Sartaj had always found the long-drawn-out death of the guide almost unbearable to watch, all his loneliness and his withered love. But here was Katekar with his unexpected Dev-sympathies. Sartaj laughed, and sang, '*Gata rahe mera dil . . .*' Katekar bobbed his head, and when Sartaj forgot the lyrics after '*Tu hi meri manzil,*' he sang the next couplet, all the way until the antra. Now they were grinning at each other.

'They don't make movies like that any more,' Sartaj said.

'No, they don't, sir,' Katekar said. They had a clear stretch of road now, all the way up to the intersection at Karanth Chowk. They sped past clusters of apartment buildings to the right, ensconced behind a long grey wall, and on the left the untidy shacks of a basti opened doors directly on to the road. Katekar stopped at the light smoothly, coming from headlong velocity to an even halt.

'There are rumours about Parulkar Saab,' he said, wiping the inside of the steering wheel with his forefinger.

'What kind of rumours?'

'That he's ill, and is thinking of leaving the force.'

'What's his illness?'

'Heart.'

This was a good rumour, Sartaj thought, as rumours went. It might have been Parulkar himself who'd started this one, working from the basic operational principle that a secret was impossible to keep, that everybody would know something soon, and that it was better you should shape the wild theorizing that would take place, steer it and find advantage in it. 'I don't know about him leaving,' Sartaj said, 'but he is considering his options.'

'For his heart?'

'Something like that.'

Katekar nodded. He didn't seem too concerned. Sartaj knew that Katekar wasn't a great fan of Parulkar Saab, although he would never speak badly of him in front of Sartaj. He had said once, though, that he didn't trust Parulkar. He had offered no reasons, and Sartaj had put his suspicions down to enduring anti-Brahminism. Katekar didn't trust Brahmins, and he disliked Marathas for their middle-caste grabbiness and greed and kshatriya pretensions. Sartaj could see that from Katekar's OBC point of view, there was justification enough for his prejudices. Look at history, he had said more than once. And Sartaj had always accepted, without question, that the backward castes had been treated horribly for interminable centuries. But he argued the caste politics of the past and present with Katekar, and challenged his conclusions. They had always left those dangerous topics amiably enough. Finally, Sartaj was just glad that Katekar's history hadn't included uppity Jatt Sikhs in any immediate way. They had known each other for a long time, and Sartaj had come to depend on him.

They pulled into a narrow parking space in front of the Sindoor Restaurant, Fine Indian and Continental Dining. Sartaj reached back behind his seat for a white Air India bag. He squeezed out past a Peugeot, past a paan-wallah at the gate, and then waited for a line of white-shirted executives to pass. From where he was standing, he could see, at a diagonal across the road, a large white sign with red lettering: 'Delite Dance Bar and Restaurant'. Sartaj's shirt was drenched, plastered to his back from the shoulders to the belt. Inside Sindoor, the decor was altogether wedding-shamiana, down to the band instruments behind the cashier's booth and the mehndi-frills around the edges of the menu. Katekar sat across from Sartaj in a four-customer booth, and they both lowered their heads gratefully under the heavy wash of cold air from a vent just above. A waiter brought two Pepsis, and they both gulped fast, but before they were half-way through, Shambhu Shetty was with them. He slid smoothly in next to Sartaj, neat and trim as always in blue jeans and a blue denim shirt.

'Hello, saab.'

'All good, Shambhu?'

'Yes, saab.' Shambhu shook hands with both of them. Sartaj had his usual moment of envy for the iron of Shambhu's grip, for his taut shoulders and his smooth, twenty-four-year-old face. Once, the year before, he had leaned back in the booth and raised his shirt and shown them his biscuited belly, the little triangles of muscle rising up to his chest. A waiter brought Shambhu a fresh pineapple juice. He never drank aerated drinks, or anything with sugar in it.

'Been trekking, Shambhu?' Katekar said.

'Going early next week, my friend. To Pindari glacier.'

On the red rexine of the seat, between Sartaj and Shambhu, there was a heavy brown envelope. Sartaj slid it into his lap, and raised the flap. Inside, there were the usual ten stacks of hundred-rupee notes, stapled and rubber-banded by the bank into little ten-thousand-rupee bricks.

'Pindari?' Katekar said.

Shambhu was amazed. 'Boss, do you ever leave Bombay? Pindari is in the Himalayas. Above Nainital.'

'Ah,' Katekar said. 'Gone for how long?'

'Ten days. Don't worry, I'll be back by next time.'

Sartaj pulled the Air India bag from between his feet, unzipped it, and slid the envelope in. The station and the Delite Dance Bar had a monthly arrangement. Shambhu and he were merely representatives of the two organizations, dispensing and collecting. The money was not personal, and they had been seeing each other for a year and some months now, ever since Shambhu had taken over as manager of Delite, and they had grown to like each other. He was a good fellow, Shambhu, efficient, low-profile, and very fit. He was trying to persuade Katekar to climb mountains.

'It'll clear out your head,' Shambhu said. 'Why do you think the great yogis always did tapasya way up there? It's the air. It improves meditation, brings peace. It's good for you.'

Katekar raised his empty Pepsi glass. 'My tapasya is here, brother. Here only I find enlightenment every night.'

Shambhu laughed, and clinked glasses with Katekar. 'Don't burn us with your fierce austerities, O master. I'll have to send apsaras to distract you.'

They giggled together, and Sartaj had to smile at the thought of Katekar seated cross-legged on a deerskin, effulgent with pent-up energy. He tugged at the zipper on the bag, and nudged Shambhu with his elbow. 'Listen, Shambhu-rishi,' Sartaj said. 'We have to do a raid.'

'What, again? We just had one not five weeks ago.'

'About seven, I think. Almost two months. But, Shambhu, the government's changed. Things have changed.' Things had indeed changed. The Rakshaks were the new government in the state. What had once been a muscular right-wing organization, proud of its disciplined and looming cadres, was now trying to become a party of statesmen. As state ministers and cabinet secretaries, they had toned down their ranting nationalism, but they would not give up their battle against cultural degeneration and western corruption. 'They promised to reform the city.'

'Yes,' Shambhu said. 'That bastard Bipin Bhonsle. All those speeches about cleaning up corruption since he became minister. And what's all that noise about protecting Indian culture he's been throwing around lately? What are we but Indian? And aren't we protecting our culture also? Aren't the girls doing Indian dances?'

They were doing that exactly, spinning under disco lights to filmi music, quite respectably covered up in cholis and saris, while men held up fans of twenty and fifty-rupee notes for them to pick from, but the Delite Dance Bar as a temple of culture was an audacity that silenced Sartaj and Katekar completely. Then they both said 'Shambhu' together, and he held up his hands. 'Okay, okay. When?'

17

'Next week,' Sartaj said.

'Do it before I leave. Monday.'

'Fine. Midnight, then.' Under the new edict, the bars were supposed to close at eleven-thirty.

'Oh, come, come, saab. You're taking the rotis from the mouths of poor girls. That's too-too early.'

'Twelve-thirty.'

'At least one, please. Have some mercy. As it is, that's half the night's earning gone.'

'One, then. But you better still have some girls there when we come in. We'll have to arrest some.'

'That bastard Bhonsle. Close down the bars, but what is this new shosha of arresting girls? Why? What for? All they're trying to do is make a living.'

'The new shosha is ruthless discipline and honesty, Shambhu. Five girls in the van. Ask for volunteers. They can give whatever names they like. And it'll be short. Home by three, three-thirty. We'll drop them.'

Shambhu nodded. He did really seem to like his girls, and they him, and from what Sartaj heard, he never tried to push his take of the dancers' tips beyond the standard sixty per cent. From the really popular ones he took only forty. A happy girl is a better earner, he had once said to Sartaj. He was a good businessman. Sartaj had great hopes for him.

'Okay, boss,' Shambhu said. 'Will be organized. No problem.' Outside, he walked in front of the Gypsy as they backed out into the thickening traffic, grinning and grinning.

'What?' Sartaj said.

'Saab, you know, if I can tell the girls you are coming on the raid, you your very own self, I bet I'll get ten volunteers.'

'Listen, chutiya,' Sartaj said.

'Twelve even, if you escorted them in the van,' Shambhu said. 'That Manika asks about you all the time. So brave he is, she says. So handsome.'

Katekar was very serious. 'I know her. Nice home-loving girl.'

'Fair-complexioned,' Shambhu said. 'Good at cooking, embroidery.'

'Bastards,' Sartaj said. 'Bhenchods. Come on, Katekar, drive. We're late.'

Katekar drove, making no attempt to hide a smile as big as Shambhu's. A swarm of sparrows dipped crazily out of the sky, grazing the bonnet of the Gypsy. It was almost evening.

There was a murder waiting at the station for them. Majid Khan, who was the senior inspector on duty, said it had been half an hour since the call had come in from Navnagar, from the Bengali Bura. 'There's nobody else here to take it,' he said. 'Falls to you, Sartaj.'

Sartaj nodded. A murder case three hours before the end of the shift was something that the other officers would be happy to have missed, unless it was especially interesting. The Bengali Bura in Navnagar was very poor, and dead bodies there were just dead, devoid of any enlivening possibilities of professional praise, or press, or money.

'Have a cup of tea, Sartaj,' Majid said. He flipped through the stacks of Delite money, and then put them in the drawer on the right-hand side of the desk. Later he would move the money to the locker of the Godrej cupboard behind his desk, where the larger part of the operating budget of the station was kept. It was all cash, and none of it came from state funds, which weren't enough to pay for the paper the investigating officers wrote the panchanamas on, or the vehicles that they drove, or the petrol they used, or even for the cups of tea that they and a thousand visitors drank. Some of the Delite money Majid would keep, as part of his perquisites as senior inspector, and some of it would be passed on, upwards.

'No, I'd better not,' Sartaj said. 'Better get out there. Sooner there, sooner to sleep.'

Majid was stroking his moustache, which was a flamboyant handlebar like his army father's. He maintained it with faithful indulgence, with foreign unguents and delicate pruning, in the face of all mockery. 'Your bhabhi was remembering you,' he said. 'When are you coming to dinner?'

Sartaj stood up. 'Tell her I said thanks, Majid. And next week, yes? Wednesday? Khima, yes?' Majid's wife was actually not a very good cook, but her khima was not offensive, and so Sartaj professed a great passion for it. Since his divorce the officers' wives had been feeding him regularly, and he suspected that there was other scheming afoot. 'I'm off.'

'Right,' Majid said. 'Wednesday. I'll clear it with the general and let you know.'

In the jeep, Sartaj considered Majid and Rehana, happy couple. At their table, eating their food, he saw the economy of gesture between them, how each simple sentence contained whole histories of years together, and he watched Farah of sixteen and her exasperated teasing of Imtiaz, thirteen and impatient and sure of himself, and Sartaj was part of the easeful sprawl on the carpet afterwards, as they watched some favourite game show. They wanted him there, and most often he couldn't stop wanting to leave. He went each time eagerly, glad to be in a home, with a family, with family. But their happiness made his chest ache. He felt that he was getting used to being alone, he must be, but he also knew he would never be completely reconciled to it. I'm monstrous, he thought, not this and not that, and then he glanced around guiltily to the back of the Gypsy, where four constables sat in identical poses, their two rifles and two lathis hugged close to the chest. They were looking, all of them, at the dirty metal flooring, swaying gently one way and then the other. The sky behind was yellow and drifting rivulets of blue.

The dead man's father was waiting for them at the edge of Navnagar, below the gentle slope covered from nullah to road with hovels. He was small and nondescript, a man who had spent a lifetime effacing himself. Sartaj stepped after him through the uneven lanes. Although they were going up the slope, Sartaj had a feeling of descent. Everything was smaller, closer, the pathways narrow between the uneven walls of cardboard and cloth and wood, the tumbling roofs covered with plastic. They were well into the Bengali Bura, which was the very poorest part of Navnagar. Most of the shacks were less than a man's standing height, and the citizens of the Bengali Bura sat in their doorways, tattered and ragged, and the barefooted children ran before the police party. On Katekar's face there was furious contempt for jhopadpatti-dwellers who let dirt and filth and garbage pile up not two feet from their own doors, who let their little daughters squat to make a mess exactly where their sons played. These are the people who ruin Mumbai, he had said often to Sartaj, these ganwars who come from Bihar or Andhra or maderchod Bangladesh and live like animals here. These were indeed from maderchod Bangladesh, Sartaj thought, although they all no doubt had papers that said they were from Bengal, that each was a bona fide Indian citizen. Anyway, there was nowhere in their watery delta to send them back to, not half a bigha of land that was theirs, that would hold them all. They came in their thousands, to work as servants and on the roads and on the construction sites. And one of them was dead here.

He had fallen across a doorway, chest inside, feet splayed out. He was young, not yet out of his teens. He wore expensive keds, good jeans and a blue collarless shirt. The forearms were slashed deep, to the bone, which was common in assaults with choppers, when the victim typically tried to ward off the blows. The cuts were clean, and deeper at one end than the other. The left hand had only a small oozing stump where the little finger had been, and Sartaj knew there was no use looking for it. There were rats about. Inside the shack it was hard to see, hard to make out anything through the buzzing darkness. Katekar clicked on an Eveready torch, and in the circle of light Sartaj flapped the flies away. There were cuts on the chest and forehead, and a good strong one had gone nearly through the neck. He might have already been walking dead from the other wounds, but that one had killed him, dropped him down with a thud. The floor was dark, wet mud.

'Name?' Sartaj said.

'His, saab?' the father said. He was facing away from the door, trying not to look at his son.

'Yes.'

'Shamsul Shah.'

'Yours?'

'Nurul, saab.'

'They used choppers?'

'Yes, saab.'

'How many of them?'

'Two, saab.'

'You know them?'

'Bazil Chaudhary and Faraj Ali, saab. They live close by. They are friends of my son.'

Katekar was scribbling in a notebook, his lips moving tightly with the unfamiliar names.

'Where are you from?' Sartaj said.

'Village Duipara, Chapra block, district Nadia, West Bengal, saab.' It came out all in a little rush, and Sartaj knew he had rehearsed it many times at night, had studied it on the papers he had bought as soon as he had reached Bombay. A murder case involving Bangladeshis was unusual because they usually kept their heads low, worked, tried to make a living, and tried very hard to avoid attracting attention.

'And the others? Also from there?'

'Their parents are from Chapra.'

'Same village?'

'Yes, saab.' He had that Urdu-sprinkled Bangladeshi diction that Sartaj had learnt to recognize. He was lying about the country the village was in, that was all. The rest was all true. The fathers of the victim and the murderers had probably grown up together, splashing in the same rivulets.

'Are they related to you, those two?'

'No, saab.'

'You saw this?'

'No, saab. Some people shouted for me to come.'

'Which people?'

'I don't know, saab.' From down the lane there was a muttering, a rise and fall of voices, but there was nobody to be seen. None of the neighbours wanted to be caught up in police business.

'Whose house is this?'

'Ahsan Naeem, saab. But he wasn't here. Only his mother was in the house, she is with the neighbours now.'

'She saw this?'

Nurul Shah shrugged. Nobody wanted to be a witness, but the old woman would not be able to avoid it. Perhaps she would plead shortness of vision.

'Your son was running?'

'Yes, saab, from over there. They were sitting in Faraj's house.'

So the dead boy had been trying to get home. He must have tired, and tried to get into a house. The door was a piece of tin hung off the bamboo vertical with three pieces of wire. Sartaj stepped away from the body, away from the heavy smell of blood and wet clay. 'Why did they do this? What happened?'

'They all had been drinking together, saab. They had a fight.'

'What about?'

'I don't know. Saab, will you catch them?'

'We'll write it down,' Sartaj said.

At eleven Sartaj stood under a pounding stream of cold water, his face held up to it. The pressure in the pipes was very good, so he lingered under the shower, moving the sting from one shoulder to the other. He was thinking, despite himself and the rush of water in his ears, about

Kamble and money. When Sartaj had been married, he had taken a certain pride in never accepting cash, but after the divorce he had realized how much Megha's money had protected him from the world, from the necessities of the streets he lived in. A nine-hundred-rupee monthly transportation allowance hardly paid for three days of fuel for his Bullet, and of the many notes he dropped into the hands of informants every day, maybe one or two came from his minuscule khabari allowance, and there was nothing left for the investigation of a young man's death in Navnagar. So Sartaj took cash now, and was grateful for it. Saala Sardar is no longer the saala of rich bastards, so he's woken up: he knew the officers and men said this with satisfaction, and they were right. He had woken up. He took a breath and moved his head so that the solid thrust at the centre of the flow pummelled him between the eyes. The lashing noise of it filled his head.

Outside, in his drawing room, it was very quiet. That there was no sleep yet, however tired he was and despite his yearning for it, he knew. He lay on his sofa, with a bottle of Royal Challenge whisky and one of water on the table next to him. He drank in accurate little sips, timed regularly. He allowed himself two tall glasses at the end of working days, and had been resisting the urge recently to go to three. He lay with his head away from the window, so he could watch the sky, lit still by the city. To the left was a long grey sliver, the building next door, turned by the window frame into a crenellated abstraction, and to the right what was called darkness, what disintegrated softly under the eye into an amorphous and relentless yellow illumination. Sartaj knew where it came from, what made it, but as always he was awed by it. He remembered playing cricket on a Dadar street, the fast *pok* of the tennis ball and the faces of friends, and the feeling that he could hold the whole city in his heart, from Colaba to Bandra. Now it was too vast, escaped from him, each family adding to the next and the next until there was that cool and endless glow, impossible to know, or escape. Had it really existed, that small empty street, clean for the children's cricket games and dabba-ispies and tikkar-billa, or had he stolen it from some grainy black-and-white footage? Given it to himself in gift, the memory of a happier place?

Sartaj stood up. Leaning against the side of the window, he finished the whisky, tipping the glass far over to get the last drop. He leaned out, trying to find a breeze. The horizon was hazy and far, with lights burning hard underneath. He looked down, and saw a glint in the car park far below, a piece of glass, mica. He thought suddenly how easy it would be to keep leaning over, tipping until the weight carried him. He saw himself falling, the white kurta flapping frantically, the bare chest and stomach underneath, the nada trailing, a blue-and-white bathroom rubber chappal tumbling, the feet rotating, and before a whole circle was complete the crack of the skull, a quick crack and then silence.

Sartaj stepped back from the window. He put the glass down on the coffee table, very carefully. Where did that come from? He said it aloud, 'Where did that come from?' Then he sat on the floor, and found that it was painful to bend his knees. His thighs were aching. He put both his hands on the table, palms down, and looked at the white wall opposite. He was quiet.

Katekar was eating left-over Sunday mutton. There was a muscle in his back, to the right and low, that was fluttering, but there was the thick, hot consolation of the mutton with its simple richness of potato and rice, and the stinging pleasure of the green-chilli pickle – with his lips burning he could forget the spasms, or at least ignore them.

'More?' Shalini said.

He shook his head. He settled back in his chair and burped. 'You have some,' he said.

Shalini shook her head. 'I ate,' she said. She was able to resist mutton very late at night, but it was not this alone that kept her arms as thin as the day they had married, nineteen years ago almost to the day. Katekar watched her as she turned the knob on the stove to the left with a single clean movement, high burn to off. There was a pleasing accuracy in her movements as she scoured and stacked the utensils for the wash tomorrow, a clean efficiency that lived very functionally in the very small space that was her. She was a spare woman, inside and out, and she fed his appetites.

'Come, Shalu,' he said, wiping his mouth decisively. 'It's late. Let's sleep.'

He watched as she wiped the tabletop, hard, with her glass bangles clinking. The kholi was small but very clean on the inside. When she had finished, he unlatched the folding legs to the table and swung it up against the wall. The two chairs went in the corners. While she organized the kitchen, he unrolled two chatais where the table had been. Then one mattress on her chatai, and a pillow, and a pillow for himself, but his back would tolerate only the hard ground, and so then the beds were ready. He took a glass of water from the matka, and a box of Monkey tooth powder, and went outside and down the lane, stepping carefully. There was the crowded huddle of kholis, mostly pucca, with electrical wire strung over the roofs and through doorways. The municipal tap was dry at this hour, of course, but there was a puddle of water under the brick wall behind it. Katekar leaned on the wall, dabbed some tooth powder on his forefinger and cleaned his teeth, conserving the water precisely, so that the last mouthful he spat out left his mouth clean.

Shalini was lying on her side when he came into the kholi. 'Did you go?' she said, still facing away. He put the glass down on a shelf in the kitchen. 'Go,' Shalini said. 'Or you'll wake up in an hour.'

At the other end of the lane there was a turn, then another, and then a sudden opening out into an open slope falling to the highway. There was a dense smell rising from the ground, and Katekar squatted into it, and surprised himself with the furious stream that he sent down the tilt, and he sighed and watched the lights approach and vanish below. He came back to the kholi, clicked off the light bulb, took off his banian and pants and lowered himself to his chatai. He lay flat on his back, right leg spread wide, left arm and thigh against Shalini's mattress. After a moment she shifted her weight and settled slowly against him. He felt her shoulder blade on his chest, her hip against the rise of his stomach. She sank into him and he was still. Now, with the quiet and his own silence he could hear, on the other side of the black sheet that divided the kholi into two, the twinned breathing of his sons. They were nine and fifteen, Mohit and Rohit. Katekar listened to his family, and after a while, even in the darkness, he could see the shape of his home. On his side of the sheet there was a small colour television on a shelf, and next to it pictures of his parents and Shalini's parents, all garlanded, and also a large gold-framed photograph of the boys at the zoo. There was a Lux soap calendar turned to June and Madhubala. Under it, a green phone with a lock on the dial. At the foot of the chatais, a whirring table-fan. Behind his head, he knew, there was a two-in-one and his collection of tapes, songs from old Marathi films. Two black trunks stacked on top of each other. Clothes hanging on hooks, his shirt and pants on a hanger. Shalini's shelf with its brass figures of Ambabai and Bhavani, and a garlanded picture of Sai Baba. And the kitchen, with racks all the way to the roof and rows

25

and rows of gleaming steel utensils. And then on the other side of the black sheet, the shelves with schoolbooks, two posters of Sachin Tendulkar at bat, one small desk piled high with pens and notebooks and old magazines. A metal cupboard with two exactly equal compartments.

Katekar smiled. At night he liked to survey his possessions, to feel them solid and real under his heavy-lidded gaze. He lay poised on some twilight border, still far from sleep, the twitch moving up and down his back but not able to travel across the mass of his body to Shalini, and the things he had earned from life encircled him, and he knew how fragile this fortification was, but it was comfortable. In it he was calm. He felt the bulk of his arms and legs lighten, and he was floating in the streaming air, his eyes closed. He slept.

With the sleek little television remote in his hand, Sartaj flicked fast from a car race in Detroit to a dubbed American show about women detectives to a slug, slick and brown, in some huge winding river and then to a filmi countdown show. Two heroines in red miniskirts, smiling and curvy and neither more than eighteen, danced on top of the arches of the vine-wrapped ruin of a palace. Sartaj clicked again. Against a trembling background of news-file clips cut fast, a blonde VJ chattered fast about a bhangra singer from London and his new album. The VJ was Indian, but her name was Kit and her glittering blonde hair hung to her bare shoulders. She thrust a hand at the camera and now suddenly she was in a huge mirrored room filled from end to end with dancers moving together and happy. Kit laughed and the camera moved close to her face and Sartaj saw the lovely angular planes of her face and felt the delicious contentment of her slim legs. He snapped off the television and stood up.

Sartaj walked stiffly to the window. Beyond the fizzing yellow lamps in the compound of the neighbouring building, there was the darkness of the sea, and far ahead, a sprinkling of bright blue and orange that was Bandra. With a good pair of binoculars you could even see Nariman Point, not so far across the sea but at least an hour away on empty night-time roads, and very far from Zone 13. Sartaj felt a sudden ache in his chest. It was as if two blunt stones were grinding against each other, creating not fire but a dull, steady glow, a persistent and unquiet desire. It rose into his throat and his decision was made.

26

Twelve minutes of fast driving took him through the underpass and on to the highway. The open stretches of road and the wheel slipping easily through his fingers were exhilarating, and he laughed at the speed. But in Tardeo the traffic was backed up between the brightly-lit shops, and Sartaj was suddenly angry at himself, and wanted to turn around and go back. The question came to him with the drumming of his fingers on the dashboard: What are you doing? What are you doing? Where are you going in your ex-wife's car which she left you out of kindness, which might fall to pieces under your gaand on this pitted horror of a road? But it was too late, the journey half-done even though the first glad momentum was gone, and he drove on. By the time he pulled up, parked and walked to the Cave, it was almost one and now he was very tired. But here he was and he could see the crowd around the back door, which was the one open after closing time at eleven-thirty.

They parted for him and let him through. He was older, yes, maybe even much older, but there was no reason for the curious stares and the silence as he stepped through. They were dressed in loose shiny shirts, shorter dresses than he had ever seen, and they made him very nervous. He fumbled at the door, and finally a girl with a silver ring through her lower lip reached out and held it open for him. By the time it occurred to him that he should thank her, he was already inside and the door was closing. He squared his shoulders and found a corner at the bar. With a draught beer in his hand, he had something to do, and so he turned to face the room. He was hedged in close, and it was hard to see more than a few feet, and everywhere they were talking animatedly, leaning close to each other and shouting against the music. He drank his beer quickly, as if he were interested in it. Then his mug was empty and he ordered another one. There were women on all sides, and he looked at each in turn, trying to imagine himself with each one. No, that was too far ahead, so he tried to think of what he would say to any one of them. Hello. No, Hi. Hi, I'm Sartaj. Try to speak English only. And with a smile. Then what? He tried to listen to the conversation on his left. They were talking about music, an American band that he had never heard of, but that was only to be expected, and a girl with her back to Sartaj said, 'The last cut was too slow,' and Sartaj lost the response from the ponytailed boy facing her, but the other girl with the small upturned nose said, 'It was cool, bitch.' Sartaj upended his mug and wiped his mouth. The desire that had brought him across the city had vanished suddenly, leaving a dark residue of bitterness. It was very late and he was finished.

He paid quickly and left. There was a different lot near the door now, but again with the same silence, the same stares, the same beaded necklaces and piercings and practised dishevelment, and he understood that his elegant blue trousers marked him fatally as an outsider. By the time he reached the end of the lane he had no confidence in his white shirt with the button-down collar either. He navigated the right turn on to the main road carefully, stepping over two boys sleeping on the pavement, and walked towards the Crossroads Mall, where he had parked. His feet fell soundlessly on the littered pavement and the shuttered shop doors loomed above. I can't be this drunk on two beers, he thought, but the lampposts seemed very far away and he wanted very much to shut his eyes.

Sartaj went home. He fell into his bed. Now he was able to sleep, it slid heavily on to his shoulders like a choking black landslide. And then instantly it was morning and the shrill grinding of the telephone was in his ear. He groped his way to it.

'Sartaj Singh?' The voice was a man's, peremptory and commanding.

'Yes?'

'Do you want Ganesh Gaitonde?'

Siege in Kailashpada

❦

'You're never going to get in here,' the voice of Gaitonde said over the speaker after they had been working on the door for three hours. They had tried a cold chisel on the lock first, but what had looked like brown wood from a few feet away was in fact some kind of painted metal, and although it turned white under the blade and rang like a sharp temple bell, the door didn't give. Then they had moved to the lintels with tools borrowed from a road crew, but even when the road men took over, wielding the sledgehammers with long, expert swings and huffing breaths, the concrete bounced their blows off blithely, and the Sony speaker next to the door laughed at them. 'You're behind the times,' Gaitonde crackled.

'If I'm not getting in, you're not getting out,' Sartaj said.

'What? I can't hear you.'

Sartaj stepped up to the door. The building was a precise cube, white with green windows, on a large plot of land in Kailashpada, which was on the still-developing northern edge of Zone 13. Here, among the heavy machinery groping at swamp, edging Bombay out farther and wider, Sartaj had come to arrest the great Ganesh Gaitonde, gangster, boss of the G-Company and wily and eternal survivor.

'How long are you going to stay in there, Gaitonde?' Sartaj said, craning his neck up. The deep, round video eye of the camera above the door swivelled from side to side and then settled on him.

'You're looking tired, Sardar-ji,' Gaitonde said.

'I am tired,' Sartaj said.

'It's very hot today,' Gaitonde said sympathetically. 'I don't know how you sardars manage under those turbans.'

There were two Sikh commissioners on the force, but Sartaj was the only Sikh inspector in the whole city, and so was used to being

29

identified by his turban and beard. He was known also for the cut of his pants, which he had tailored at a very film-starry boutique in Bandra, and also for his profile, which had once been featured by *Modern Woman* magazine in 'The City's Best-Looking Bachelors'. Katekar, on the other hand, had a large paunch that sat on top of his belt like a suitcase, and a perfectly square face and very thick hands, and now he came around the corner of the building and stood wide-legged, with his hands in his pockets. He shook his head.

'Where are you going, Sardar-ji?' Gaitonde said.

'Just some matters I have to take care of,' Sartaj said. He and Katekar walked to the corner together, and now Sartaj could see the ladder they had going up to the ventilator.

'That's not a ventilator,' Katekar said. 'It only looks like one. There's just concrete behind it. All the windows are like that. What is this place, sir?'

'I don't know,' Sartaj said. It was somehow deeply satisfying that even Katekar, Mumbai native and practitioner of a very superior Bhuleshwar-bred cynicism, was startled by an impregnable white cube suddenly grown in Kailashpada, with a black, swivel-mounted Sony video camera above the door. 'I don't know. And he sounds very strange, you know. Sad almost.'

'What I have heard about him, he enjoys life. Good food, lots of women.'

'Today he's sad.'

'But what's he doing here in Kailashpada?'

Sartaj shrugged. The Gaitonde they had read about in police reports and in the newspapers dallied with bejewelled starlets, bankrolled politicians and bought them and sold them – his daily skim from Bombay's various criminal dhandas was said to be greater than annual corporate incomes, and his name was used to frighten the recalcitrant. Gaitonde Bhai said so, you said, and the stubborn saw reason, and all roads were smoothed, and there was peace. But he had been in exile for many years – on the Indonesian coast in a gilded yacht, it was rumoured – far but only a phone call away. Which meant that he might as well have been next door, or as it turned out, amazingly enough, in dusty Kailashpada. The early-morning man with the tip-off had hung up abruptly, and Sartaj had jumped out of bed and called the station while pulling on his pants, and the police party had come roaring to Kailashpada in a hasty caravan bristling with rifles. 'I don't know,' Sartaj said. 'But now that he's here, he's ours.'

'He's a prize, yes, sir,' Katekar said. He had that densely snobbish look he always assumed when he thought Sartaj was being naïve. 'But you're sure you want to make him yours? Why not wait for someone senior to arrive?'

'They'll be a long time getting here. They have other business going on.' Sartaj was hoping ardently that no commissioner would arrive to seize his prize. 'And anyway, Gaitonde's already mine, only he doesn't know it.' He turned to walk back towards the door. 'All right. Cut off his power.'

'Sardar-ji,' Gaitonde said, 'are you married?'

'No.'

'I was married once –'

And his voice stopped short, as if cut by a knife.

Sartaj turned from the door. Now it was a matter of waiting, and an hour or two under a hot June sun would turn the unventilated, unpowered building into a furnace that even Gaitonde, who was a graduate of many jails and footpaths and slums, would find as hard to bear as the corridors of hell. And Gaitonde had been lately very successful and thus a little softened, so perhaps it would be closer to an hour. But Sartaj had taken only two steps when he felt a deep hum rising through his toes and into his knees, and Gaitonde was back.

'What, you thought it would be so easy?' Gaitonde said. 'Just a power cut? What, you think I'm a fool?'

So there was a generator somewhere in the cube. Gaitonde had been the first man in any of the city's jails, perhaps the first man in all of Mumbai, to own a cellular phone. With it, safe in his cell, he had run the essential trades of drugs, matka, smuggling and construction. 'No, I don't think you're a fool,' Sartaj said. 'This, this building is very impressive. Who designed it for you?'

'Never mind who designed it, Sardar-ji. The question is, how are you going to get in?'

'Why don't you just come out? It'll save us all a lot of time. It's really hot out here, and I'm getting a headache.'

There was a silence, filled with the murmuring of the spectators who were gathering at the end of the lane.

'I can't come out.'

'Why not?'

'I'm alone. I'm only me by myself.'

'I thought you had friends everywhere, Gaitonde. Everyone every-where is a friend of Gaitonde Bhai's, isn't it? In the government, in the press, even in the police force? How is it then that you are alone?'

'Do you know I get applications, Sardar-ji? I probably get more applications than you police chutiyas. Don't believe me? Here, I'll read you one. Hold on. Here's one. This one's from Wardha. Here it is.'

'Gaitonde!'

'"Respected Shri Gaitonde." Hear that, Sardar-ji? "Respected." So then . . . "I am a twenty-two-year-old young man living in Wardha, Maharashtra. Currently I am doing my MCom, having passed my BCom exam with seventy-one per cent marks. I am also known in my college as the best athlete. I am captain of the cricket team." Then there's a lot of nonsense about how bold and strong he is, how every-one in town's scared of him. OK, then he goes on: "I am sure that I can be of use to you. I have for long followed your daring exploits in our newspapers, which print very often these stories of your great power and powerful politics. You are the biggest man in Mumbai. Many times when my friends get together, we talk about your famous adventures. Please, Shri Gaitonde, I respectfully submit to you my vita, and some small clippings about me. I will do whatever work you ask. I am very poor, Shri Gaitonde. I fully believe that you will give me a chance to make a life. Yours faithfully, Amit Shivraj Patil." Hear that, Sardar-ji?'

'Yes, Gaitonde,' Sartaj said, 'I do. He sounds like a fine recruit.'

'He sounds like a lodu, Sardar-ji,' Gaitonde said. 'I wouldn't hire him to wash my cars. But he would do well as a policeman.'

'I'm getting tired of this, Gaitonde,' Sartaj said. Katekar had his shoulders tensed, he was glowering at Sartaj, wanting him to curse Gaitonde, to shut him up by telling him exactly what kind of bhen-chod he was, that they were going to string him up and shove a lathi up his filthy gaand. But, it seemed to Sartaj, to shout abuse at an unhinged man inside an impregnable cube would be spectacularly use-less, if momentarily satisfying.

Gaitonde laughed bitterly. 'Are your feelings hurt, saab? Should I be more respectful? Should I tell you about the wonderful and aston-ishing feats of the police, our defenders who give their lives in service without a thought for their own profit?'

'Gaitonde?'

'What?'

'I'll be back. I need a cold drink.'

Gaitonde became avuncular, affectionate. 'Yes, yes, of course you do. Hot out there.'

'For you also? A Thums Up?'

'I've a fridge in here, chikniya. Just because you're so fair and so hero-like good looking doesn't mean you're extra smart. You get your drink.'

'I will. I'll be back.'

'What else would you do, Sardar-ji? Go, go.'

Sartaj walked down the street, and Katekar fell in beside him. The cracked black tarmac swam and shimmered in the heat. The street had emptied, the spectators bored by the lack of explosions and bullets and hungry for lunch. Between Bhagwan Tailors and Trimurti Music, they found the straightforwardly named Best Cafe, which had tables scattered under a neem tree and rattling black floor fans. Sartaj pulled desperately at a Coke, and Katekar sipped at fresh lime and soda, only slightly sweet. He was trying to lose weight. From where they sat they could see Gaitonde's white bunker. What was Gaitonde doing back in the city? Who was the informant who had given him to Sartaj? All these were questions for later. First catch the man, Sartaj thought, then worry about why and when and how, and he took another sip.

'Let's blow it up,' Katekar said.

'With what?' Sartaj said. 'And that'll kill him for sure.'

Katekar grinned. 'Yes, sir. So what, sir?'

'And what would the intelligence boys say?'

'Sahib, excuse me, but the intelligence boys are mainly useless bhadwas. Why didn't they know he was building this thing?'

'Now, that would have been very-very intelligent, wouldn't it?' Sartaj said. He leaned back in his chair and stretched. 'You think we can find a bulldozer?'

Sartaj had a metal chair brought to the front of the bunker, and he sat on it, patting his face with a cold, wet towel. He was sleepy. The video camera was unmoving and silent.

'Ay, Gaitonde!' Sartaj said. 'You there?'

The camera made its very small buzzing machine noise, nosed about blindly and found Sartaj. 'I'm here,' Gaitonde said. 'Did you get a drink? Shall I phone and order something for you to eat?'

Sartaj thought suddenly that Gaitonde had learned that big voice from the movies, from Prithviraj Kapoor in a smoking jacket being magnanimous to the lowly. 'I'm fine. Why don't you order something for yourself?'

'I don't want food.'

'You'll stay hungry?' Sartaj was trying to calculate the chances of starving Gaitonde out. But he remembered that Gandhi-ji had lasted for weeks on water and juice. The bulldozer would arrive in an hour, an hour and a half, at most.

'There's plenty of food in here, enough for months. And I've been hungry before,' Gaitonde said. 'More hungry than you could imagine.'

'Listen, it's too hot out here,' Sartaj said. 'Come out and back at the station you can tell me all about how hungry you were.'

'I can't come out.'

'I'll take care of you, Gaitonde. There are all sorts of people trying to kill you, I know. But no danger, I promise. This is not going to turn into an encounter. You come out now and we'll be back at the station in six minutes. You'll be absolutely safe. From there you can call your friends. Safe, ekdum safe. You have my promise.'

But Gaitonde wasn't interested in promises. 'Back when I was very young, I left the country for the first time. It was on a boat, you know. Those days, that was the business: get on a boat, go to Dubai, go to Bahrain, come back with gold biscuits. I was excited, because I had never left the country before. Not even to Nepal, you understand. Okay, Sardar-ji, establishing shot: there was the small boat, five of us on it, sea, sun, all that kind of chutmaari atmosphere. Salim Kaka was the leader, a six-foot Pathan with a long beard, good man with a sword. Then there was Mathu, narrow and thin everywhere, always picking his nose, supposed to be a tough boy. Me, nineteen and didn't know a thing. And there was Gaston, the owner of the boat, and Pascal, his assistant, two small dark men from somewhere in the south. It was Salim Kaka's deal, his contacts there, and his money that hired the boat, and his experience, when to go out, when to come back, everything was his. Mathu and I were his boys, behind him all the time. Got it?'

Katekar rolled his eyes. Sartaj said, 'Yes, Salim Kaka was the leader, you and Mathu were the guns and Gaston and Pascal sailed the boat. Got it.'

Katekar propped himself against the wall next to the door and spilled paan masala into his palm. The speaker gleamed a hard, metallic silver. Sartaj shut his eyes.

Gaitonde went on. 'I had never seen such a huge sky before. Purple and gold and purple. Mathu was combing his hair again and again into a Dev Anand puff. Salim Kaka sat on the deck with us. He had huge feet, square and blunt, each cracked like a piece of wood, and a beard that was smooth and red like a flame. That night he told us about his first job, robbing an angadia couriering cash from Surat to Mumbai. They caught the angadia as he got off the bus, tossed him in the back of an Ambassador and went roaring away to an empty chemical godown in the industrial estates at Vikhroli. In the godown they stripped him of his shirt, his banian, his pants, everything, and found sewn inside the pants, over the thighs, four lakhs in five-hundred-rupee notes. Also a money belt with sixteen thousand in it. He was standing there baby-naked, his big paunch shaking, holding his hands over his shrunken lauda, as they left. Clear?'

Sartaj opened his eyes. 'A courier, they got him, they made some money. So what?'

'So the story's not over yet, smart Sardar-ji. Salim Kaka was closing the door, but then he turned around and came back. He caught the guy by the throat, lifted him up and around and put a knee between his legs. "Come on, Salim Pathan," someone yelled to him. "This is no time to take a boy's gaand." And Salim Kaka, who was groping the angadia's bum, said, "Sometimes if you squeeze a beautiful ass, as you would a peach, it reveals all the secrets of the world," and he held up a little brown silk packet which the angadia had taped behind his balls. In it were a good dozen of the highest-quality diamonds, agleam and aglitter, which they fenced the next week at fifty per cent, and Salim Kaka's cut alone was one lakh, and this was in the days when a lakh meant something. "But," Salim Kaka said, "the lakh was the least of it, money is only money." But after that he was known as a lustrous talent, a sharp lad. "I'll squeeze you like a peach," he'd say, cocking a craggy eyebrow, and the poor unfortunate at the receiving end would spill cash, cocaine, secrets, anything.

'"How did you know with the angadia, Salim Kaka?" I asked, and Salim Kaka said, "It is very simple. I looked at him from the door and he was still afraid. When I had my knife at his throat he had said to me in a child's little trembling voice, 'Please don't kill me, my baap.' I hadn't killed him, he was still alive and holding his lauda, the money was gone, but it wasn't his, we were leaving, so why was he still afraid? A man who is afraid is a man who still has something to lose.'"

'Very impressive,' Sartaj said. He shifted in his chair, and regretted it immediately as his shoulder blade found a curve of heated metal. He adjusted his turban and tried to breathe slowly, evenly. Katekar was fanning himself with a folded afternoon newspaper, his eyes abstracted and his forehead slack, while into the slow stirring of the air came Gaitonde's voice with its cool electronic hiss.

'I resolved to be sharply watchful for ever after, for I was ambitious. That night I laid my body down along the bow, as close as I could get to the onrushing water, and I dreamed. Did I tell you I was nineteen? I was nineteen and I made myself stories about cars and a high house and myself entering a party and flashbulbs popping.

'Mathu came and sat beside me. He lit a cigarette for himself and gave me one. I drew hard on it like him. In the dark I could see the puff of his hair, his haggard shoulders, and I tried to remember his features, which were too bony to be anywhere close to Dev Anand's, but still every day he stroked talcum powder on to that pointy rat's face and tried. I felt suddenly kindly towards him. "Isn't this beautiful?" I said. He laughed. "Beautiful? We could drown," he said, "and nobody would know what happened to us. We would disappear, *phat*, gone." His cigarette made spirals in the dark. "What do you mean?" I asked. "Oh, you pitiful dehati idiot," he said. "Don't you know? Nobody knows we are out here." "But," I said, "Salim Kaka's people know, his boss knows." I could feel him laughing at me, his knee jogging against my shoulder. "No, they don't." He was leaning closer to me, whispering, and I could smell his banian and see the pale phosphorescence of his eyes. "Nobody knows, he didn't tell his boss. Don't you get it? This is his own deal. Why do you think we're on this little khatara of a boat, not a trawler? Why do you think we are with him, one dehati smelling of farm dirt and a very-very junior member of the company? Eh? Why? This is Salim Kaka's own little operation. He wants to go independent, and to go independent, what do you need? Capital. That's what. That's why we're out here slopping away in this chodu, wheezing tin trap, one pitch away from the big fishes. He thinks he's going to make enough to start himself all new and fresh and shiny. Capital, capital, you understand?"

'I sat up then. He put a hand on my shoulder and swung himself up. "Gaandu," he said, "if you want to live in the city you have to think ahead three turns, and look behind a lie to see the truth and then behind that truth to see the lie. And then, and then, if you want to live well, you need a bankroll. Think about it." Mathu patted my shoulder and drew back. I saw his face for a second in dim light as he lowered himself into the cabin. And I did think about it.'

Under the speaker Katekar turned his head, right and left, and Sartaj heard the small clicking noise of the bones in his neck. 'I remember this Salim Kaka,' Katekar said softly. 'I remember seeing him in Andheri, walking around in a red lungi and a silk kurta. The kurtas were of different colours, but the lungi was always red. He worked with Haji Salman's gang, and he had a woman in Andheri, I remember hearing.'

Sartaj nodded. Katekar's face was puffy, as if he had just woken from sleep. 'Love?' Sartaj said.

Katekar grinned. 'Judging by the silk, it must have been,' he said. 'Or maybe it was just that she was seventeen and had a rear like a prancing deer's. She was an auto mechanic's daughter, I think.'

'Don't believe in love, Katekar?'

'Saab, I believe in silk, and in everything that is soft, and everything else that is hard, but . . .'

Above their heads the speaker rumbled. 'What are you mumbling about, Sardar-ji?'

'Go on, go on,' Sartaj said. 'Just minor instructions.'

'So listen. The next afternoon, we started to see tree branches in the water, pieces of old crates, bottles bobbing down and up, tyres, once the whole wooden roof of a house floating upside down. Gaston stayed on deck the whole time now, one arm around the mast, looking this way and that with binoculars, never stopping. I asked Mathu, "Are we close?" He shrugged. Salim Kaka came up in a new kurta. He stood by the bow, looking to the north, and I saw his fingers dabbing at the silver taveez at his chest. I wanted to ask him where we were, but there was a seriousness on his face that kept me from speaking.'

Sartaj remembered the pictures of Gaitonde, the medium-sized body and the medium face, neither ugly nor handsome, all of it instantly forgettable despite the bright blue and red cashmere sweaters, everything quite commonplace. But now there was this voice, quiet and urgent, and Sartaj tipped his head towards the speaker.

'As night came, in the last failing light, there was a pinpoint of red winking steadily to the north. We dropped anchor, then headed towards it in a dinghy. Mathu rowed and Salim Kaka sat opposite, watching our beacon, and I between them. I was expecting a wall, like I had seen near the Gateway of India, but instead there were high rushes that towered above our heads. Salim Kaka took a pole and pushed us through the feathered banks that creaked and whispered, and although I wasn't told to, I had my ghoda in my hand, loaded and ready. Then the wood scraped under my feet, hard on ground. Flashlight in hand, Salim Kaka led us up the island – that's what it was, a soft wet rising in the swamp. We walked for a long time, half an hour maybe, Salim Kaka in front, under a rising moon. He had a brown canvas bag over his shoulder, big as a wheat sack. Then I saw the beacon again, over the top of the stalks. It was a torch tied to a pole. I could smell the tallow; the flames jumped two feet high. Under it there were three men. They were dressed like city people, and in the leaping light I could see their fair skin, their bushy black eyebrows, their big noses. Turks? Iranis? Arabs? I don't know still, but two of them had rifles, muzzles pointed just a little away from us. My trigger was cool and sweaty on my finger. I cramped and thought, You'll fire and finish us all. I took a breath, turned my wrist, feeling the butt against my thumb, and watched them. Salim Kaka and one of them spoke, their heads close together. Now the bag was offered, and a suitcase in return. I saw a gleam of yellow, and heard the clicks of locks shutting. My arm ached.

'Salim Kaka stepped backward, and we edged away from the foreigners. I felt the smooth, wet rim of a stalk against my neck, and I couldn't find a way out, only the yielding pressure of vegetation, and panic. Then Salim Kaka turned abruptly and slipped between the bushes, the faint beam of his flashlight marking his way, and then Mathu. I came last, sideways, my revolver hand held low, my neck taut. I can still see them watching, the three men. I see the gleam of the metal bands around the rifle muzzles, and their shaded eyes. We were walking fast. I felt as if we were flying, and the tall grass that had pulled and clawed at me at first now brushed softly along my sides. Salim Kaka turned his head, and I saw his frantic smile. We were happy, running.

'Salim Kaka paused at the edge of a little stream where water had cut a drop of three feet, maybe four, and he reached down with his right foot and found a place for his heel. Mathu looked at me, his face cut into angles by the gaunt moonlight, and I looked at him. Before Salim Kaka had completed his step, I knew where we were going. The report of the revolver bounced off the water into my belly. I knew the butt had bruised the base of my thumb. Only when the flare left my eyes could I see again, and my stomach was twisting and loosening and twisting, and at the bottom of the ditch Salim Kaka's feet were treading steadily, as if he were still finding his way to the boat. The water thrashed and boiled. "Fire, Mathu," I said. "Fire, maderchod." Those were the first words I had spoken since we'd come ashore. My voice was firm and strange, the sound of it alien. Mathu tilted his head and pointed his barrel. Again, a flash brought the weeds out from the shadows, but still those feet clambered away, going steadily somewhere. I aimed my revolver into the round, frothy turbulence, and at the first discharge all movement stopped, but I put another one in just to make sure. "Come on," I said, "let's go home." Mathu nodded, as if I were in charge, and he jumped into the ditch and scrabbled for the suitcase. The flashlight was glowing under the water, a luminous yellow bubble that embraced exactly half of Salim Kaka's head. I snapped it up as I went through, though all the way back to the dinghy the fat moon was low overhead and lit us to safety.'

Sartaj and Katekar heard Gaitonde drink now. They heard, clearly, every long gulp and the glass emptying. 'Whisky?' Sartaj whispered. 'Beer?'

Katekar shook his head. 'No, he doesn't drink. Doesn't smoke either. Very health-conscious don he is. Exercises every day. He's drinking water. Bisleri with a twist of lime in it.'

Gaitonde went on, hurrying now. 'When the sun came up on the boat the next day, Mathu and I were still awake. We had spent the night sitting in the cabin, across from each other, with the suitcase tucked under Mathu's bunk but still visible. I had my revolver in my lap, and I could see Mathu's under his thigh. The roof above my head creaked out a stealthy step. We had told Gaston and Pascal that we had been ambushed by the police, the police of whatever country we had been in. Pascal had wept, and they were both moving very gently now, in respect for our mourning. Behind Mathu's head there was the dark brown of the wood, and the white of his banian floating and dipping with the swell of the waves. There was the hazy distance between us, and I knew what he was thinking. So I decided. I put my revolver

39

on the pillow, put my feet up on the bunk. "I'm going to sleep," I said. "Wake me up in three hours and then you can rest." I turned to the wood, with my back towards Mathu, and shut my eyes. Very low down on my back there was a single circle on my skin which twitched and crawled. It expected a bullet. I could not calm it. But I kept my breathing steady, my knuckles against my lips. There are some things you can control.

'When I woke it was evening. There was a thick orange light pushing into the cabin from the hatch, colouring the wood like fire. My tongue filled my throat and mouth, and my hand when I tried to move it had become a loathsome bloated weight. I thought the bullet had found me, or I had found the bullet, but then I jerked once and my heart was thudding painfully and I sat up. My stomach was covered with sweat. Mathu was asleep, his face down on the pillow. I tucked my revolver into my waistband and went up. Pascal smiled at me out of his black little face. The clouds were piled above us, enormous and bulging, higher and higher into the red heaven. And this boat a twig on the water. My legs shook and I sat down and shook. I trembled and stopped and then trembled again. When it was dark, I asked Pascal for two strong bags. He gave me two white sacks made of canvas, with drawstrings.

'"Wake up," I said to Mathu when I went downstairs, and kicked his bunk. He came awake groping for his revolver, which he couldn't find until I pointed to it, between the mattress and the wall. "Calm down, you jumpy chut. Just calm down. We have to share." He said, "Don't ever do that again." He was growling, stretching his shoulders up like a rooster heaving its feathers. I smiled at him. "Listen," I said, "you bhenchod sleepy son of maderchod Kumbhkaran, do you want your half or what?" He calculated for a moment, still all swollen and angry, but then he subsided with a laugh. "Yes, yes," he said. "Half-half. Half-half."

'Gold is good. It moves and slips on your fingers with a satisfying smoothness. When it is near to pure it has that healthy reddish glow that reminds you of apple cheeks. But that afternoon, as we moved the bars from the suitcase into the sacks, one by one, one for one and then one for the other, what I liked best was the weight. The bars were small, a little longer than the breadth of my palm, much smaller than I had expected, but they felt so dense and plump I could hardly bear to put each in my sack. My face was warm and my heart congested

40

and I knew I had done right. When we got to the last bar, which was mine, I put it in my left pants pocket, where I could feel it always, slapping against me. Then the revolver on the other side, at the back of my waistband. Mathu nodded. "Almost home," he said. "How much do you think it's worth?" His smile was slow and faltering. He picked at his nose, as he always did when he was nervous, which was most of the time. I looked down at him and felt only contempt. I knew absolutely and for certain and in one instant that he would always be a tapori, nothing more, maybe even with ten or twelve people working for him, but always nothing more than a nerve-racked small-time local buffoon, jacked up into tottery brutishness with a gun and a chopper under his shirt, that's all. If you think in rupees, you're a sweep-carrying bhangi, nothing more. Because lakhs are dirt, and crores are shit. I thought, what is golden is the future in your pocket, the endless possibility of it. So I shoved the sack under my bunk, nudging the last of it under with my foot as Mathu watched with wide eyes. I turned my back on him and climbed up to the deck, laughing to myself. I was no longer afraid. I knew him now. That night I slept like a baby.'

Katekar snorted, and shook his head. 'And for years he slept a restful sleep every night, while the bodies fell right and left.' Sartaj held up a warning hand, and Katekar wiped the sweat from his face and muttered quietly, 'They're all of them the swinish same, maderchod greedy bastards. The trouble is, when one gets killed, five come up to take his place.'

'Quiet,' Sartaj said. 'I want to hear this.'

The speaker growled again. 'The day after the next, I saw, over the water, a faraway hillock. "What is that?" I asked Gaston. "Home," he said. From the bow Pascal called to another boat leaning out towards the horizon. "Aaa-hoooooooooo," he called, and the long cry and its echoing reply wrapped about my shoulders. I was home.

'We helped to beach the boat, and then took leave of Pascal and Gaston. Mathu was whispering threats at them, but I shouldered him aside, not too gently, and said, "Listen, boys, keep this quiet, very quiet, and we'll do business again." I gave them a gold bar each from my share, and shook hands with them, and they grinned and were my fellows for life. Mathu and I walked a little way down the road, to the bus stop, with our white sacks dragging over our shoulders. I waved down an auto-rickshaw and nodded at Mathu. I left him standing there, his finger at his nose, buffeted by exhaust. I knew he wanted to come with me, but he thought more of himself than he was, and he would've forced me to kill him, sooner or later. I had no time for him. I was going to Bombay.'

The speaker was silent. Sartaj stood up, turned and looked up and down the street. 'Eh, Gaitonde?' he said.

A moment passed, and then the answer came: 'Yes, Sartaj?'

'The bulldozer's here.'

Indeed it was there, a black leviathan that now appeared at the very end of the street with a throaty clanking that caused a crowd to appear instantly. The machine had a certain dignity, and the driver had a cap on his head, worn with the flair of a specialist.

'Get those people out of the road,' Sartaj said to Katekar. 'And that thing up here. Pointed this way.'

'I can hear it now,' Gaitonde said. The video lens moved in its housing restlessly.

'You'll see it soon,' Sartaj said. The policemen near the vans were checking their weapons. 'Listen, Gaitonde, this is all a farce that I don't like one bit. We've never met, but still we've spent the afternoon talking. Let's be gentlemen. There's no need for this. Just come out and we can go back to the station.'

'I can't do that,' Gaitonde said.

'Stop it,' Sartaj said. 'Stop acting the filmi villain, you're better than that. This isn't some schoolboy game.'

'It is a game, my friend,' Gaitonde said. 'It is only a game, it is leela.'

Sartaj turned away from the door. He wanted, with an excruciating desire, a cup of tea. 'All right. What's your name?' he said to the driver of the bulldozer, who was leaning against a gargantuan track.

'Bashir Ali.'

'You know what to do?'

Bashir Ali twisted his blue cap in his hands.

'It's my responsibility, Bashir Ali. I'm giving you an order as a police inspector, so you don't have to worry about it. Let's get that door down.'

Bashir Ali cleared his throat. 'But that's Gaitonde in there, Inspector sahib,' he said tentatively.

Sartaj took Bashir Ali by the elbow and walked him to the door.

'Gaitonde?'

42

'Yes, Sardar-ji?'

'This is Bashir Ali, the driver of the bulldozer. He's afraid of helping us. He's frightened of you.'

'Bashir Ali,' Gaitonde said. The voice was commanding, like an emperor's, sure of its consonants and its generosity.

Bashir Ali was looking at the middle of the door. Sartaj pointed up at the video camera, and Ali blinked up at it. 'Yes, Gaitonde Bhai?' he said.

'Don't worry. I won't forgive you –' Bashir Ali blanched '– because there's nothing to forgive. We are both trapped, you on that side of the door and me on this. Do what they tell you to do, get it over with and go home to your children. Nothing will happen to you. Not now and not later. I give you my word.' There was a pause. 'The word of Ganesh Gaitonde.'

By the time Bashir Ali had climbed up to his seat on top of the bulldozer he had understood, it seemed, his starring role in the situation. He put his cap on his head with a twirl and pointed it backward. The engine grunted and then settled into a steady roar. Sartaj leaned close to the speaker. The left side of his head, from the nape of the neck to the temples, was caught in a sweeping pulse of heat and pain.

'Gaitonde?'

'Speak, Sardar-ji, I'm listening.'

'Just open this door.'

'You want me to just open this door? I know, Sardar-ji, I know.'

'Know what?'

'I know what you want. You want me to just open this door. Then you want to arrest me and take me to the station. You want to be a hero in the newspapers. You want a promotion. Two promotions. Deep down you want even more. You want to be rich. You want to be an all-India hero. You want the President to give you a medal on Republic Day. You want the medal in full colour on television. You want to be seen with film stars.'

'Gaitonde . . .'

'But you know, I've had all that. And I'll beat you. Even in this last game I'll beat you.'

'How? You have some of your boys in there with you?'

'No. Not one. I told you, I'm alone.'

'A tunnel? A helicopter hidden inside?'

Gaitonde chuckled. 'No, no.'

'What then? You have a battery of Bofors guns?'

'No. But I'll beat you.'

The bulldozer was shimmering on the black road, flanked by grim-eyed policemen. Their choices were narrowing rapidly, leading them inevitably to this metal door, and they were determined, and helpless, and afraid.

'Gaitonde,' Sartaj said, rubbing his eyes. 'Last chance. Come on, yaar. This is stupid.'

'I can't do it. Sorry.'

'All right. Just stay back from the door when we come in. And have your hands up.'

'Don't worry,' Gaitonde said. 'I'm no danger.'

Sartaj stood up straight, his back to the door, and checked his revolver. He rotated the cylinder, and the yellow bullets sat fat and round in the metal. The heat came through the soles of his shoes, into his feet.

Suddenly the speaker came to life again against his shoulder blade. 'Sartaj, you called me yaar. So I'll tell you something. Build it big or small, there is no house that is safe. To win is to lose everything, and the game always wins.'

Sartaj could feel the tinny trembling in his chest from the speaker. The machine in front of him produced a blare that pressed him back against the door, and it was enough. He palmed the cylinder back into the revolver, and stepped off the porch. 'All right,' he shouted. 'Let's go, let's go, let's go.' He waved towards the door with the weapon. The speaker was buzzing again, but Sartaj wasn't listening. As he walked away, he thought that under the engine's roar he heard a last fragment, a question: 'Sartaj Singh, do you believe in God?'

Sartaj called, 'Come on, Bashir Ali, move.' Bashir Ali raised a hand, and Sartaj pointed a rigid finger at him. 'Get that thing moving.'

Bashir Ali crouched in his high seat, and the behemoth lurched forward, past Sartaj, and smashed against the building with a dull crunch, raising a soaring cloud of plaster. But after a moment, when the bulldozer pulled back, the building still stood complete and sacrosanct, the door not even dented. Only the video camera had been injured: it lay next to the door, flattened neatly half-way along its length. A long jeer rose from the crowd down the street. It grew louder when Bashir Ali switched off his engine.

'What was that?' Sartaj said when Bashir Ali stepped down into the bulldozer's shadow.

'What do you expect when you won't let me do it the way it should be done?'

They were both wiping plaster from their noses. On the sunlit side of the bulldozer the crowd was chanting, 'Jai Gaitonde.'

'Do you know the way to do it?'

Bashir Ali shrugged. 'I have an idea.'

'All right,' Sartaj said. 'Fine. Do it how you want.'

'Get out of my way then. And get your men back from the building.'

As Bashir Ali spun his steed on the gravel, Sartaj saw that he was an artist. He operated with flicks and thumps of his hands on the driving sticks, leaning into the direction of his turns, in sympathy with the groaning gears underneath. He raised and then lowered his blade, positioning it precisely, with its lower extended edge level with the door. He reversed ten feet, twenty, thirty, his arm jauntily on the back of his seat. He came at the building at a diagonal, and as he went past Sartaj he gleamed a white grin. This time there was a scream of metal, and when the violent juddering of the bulldozer had ceased, Sartaj saw that the door had been peeled back, inward. A crack ran three feet up into the masonry.

'Back!' Sartaj shouted. He was running forward, revolver held in front of him. 'Get back, get back.' Then Bashir Ali was gone, and Sartaj was leaning against one side of the doorway, and Katekar on the other. An icy wind came out and Sartaj felt it drying the sweat on his face and his forearms. Suddenly, for a moment, he envied Gaitonde all his air-conditioners, the frigid climate control won by his audacity. And for a moment, rising from somewhere deep in his hips, unbidden and nauseating, like a buoyant dribble of bile, was a tiny bubble of admiration. He took a deep breath. 'Do you think the building will hold?' he said.

Katekar nodded. He was looking in, through the door, and his face was dark with rage. Sartaj touched the tip of his tongue to his upper lip, felt the dryness, and then they went in. Sartaj went ahead, and at the first door inside Katekar went by him. Behind them followed the rustling of the others. Sartaj was trying to hear above the thunderous unclenching of his heart. He had done entries like this before, and it never got better. It was very cold inside the building, and the light was low and luxurious. There was carpet under their feet. There were four square rooms, all white, all empty. And at the exact centre of the building was a very steep, almost vertical, metal staircase going downward through the floor. Sartaj nodded at Katekar, and then followed him down. The metal door at the bottom opened easily, but it was very heavy, and when Katekar finally had it back Sartaj saw that it was as thick as a hatch to a bank vault. Inside it was dark. Sartaj was shivering uncontrollably. He moved past Katekar, and now he saw a bluish light on the left. Katekar slid past his shoulders and went out wide, and then they shuffled forward, weapons held rigidly before them. Another step and now in the new angle Sartaj saw a figure, shoulders, in front of a bank of haze-filled TV monitors, a brown hand near the controls on a black panel.

'Gaitonde!' Sartaj hadn't meant to shout – a gentle admonitory assertion was the preferred tone – and now he squeezed his voice down. 'Gaitonde, put your hands up very slowly.' There was no movement from the figure in the darkness. Sartaj tightened his finger painfully on his trigger, and fought the urge to fire, and fire again. 'Gaitonde. Gaitonde?'

From Sartaj's right, where Katekar was, came a very small click, and even as Sartaj turned his head the room was flooded with white neon radiance, generous and encompassing and clean. And in the universal illumination Gaitonde sat revealed, a black pistol in his left hand, and half his head gone.

Gaitonde's right eye bulged with a bloodshot and manic intensity. Sartaj could see the fragile tracery of pink lines, the hard black of the pupil, the shining seep of fluid from the inside corner, which despite himself he thought of as a tear. But it was only the body reacting to the gigantic blow which had sheared off everything from the chin up on the other side, slicing from the left nostril up into the forehead and spraying a creamy mess on to the white ceiling. A tooth winked pearl-like, whole and undamaged, from the raw red where Gaitonde's tight-lipped grimace stopped abruptly.

'Sir,' Katekar said. Sartaj jerked, and followed the rigidly pointing barrel of Katekar's revolver to a doorway in the white wall. Just where the boundary lay between sharp brightness and darkness, in that shadow, were two small bare feet, toes pointing up at the ceiling. Sartaj stepped up, and he couldn't see the body clearly, just the cuffs of white pants, but he knew somehow, from the indistinct spread of

46

the hips, that it was a woman. Again Katekar found a switch, and there she was, yes, a woman, wearing tight white pants, slung low – Sartaj knew they were called hipsters. She wore a tight pink top, it was elegant. It showed her belly, she must have been proud of the narrowness of her waist and the perfect navel. And there was a hole in her chest, just under the downy spot on her thorax where the top clipped shut.

'He shot her,' Sartaj said.

'Yes,' Katekar said. 'She must have been standing in the doorway.'

Her face was turned to the left, with long hair falling over her cheek.

'Check the rest,' Sartaj said. In the square room where the girl lay, there were three bare beds, in a row, with white night-stands next to each. It looked rather like a dormitory. Against the wall, an exercise cycle and a row of graduated weights on a rack. DVDs of old black-and-white movies. A steel cabinet with a row of AK-56 rifles, and pistols underneath. And there were showers and western-style toilets in a bathroom, and three cupboards full of men's clothing and shoes and boots. In the central room Katekar had finished his survey, and they stood together over Gaitonde.

There was a press of armed policemen behind Sartaj, jostling shoulders and clanking rifle butts as they craned forward to see what the great Gaitonde had come to, and his murdered girlfriend. 'Enough,' Sartaj said. 'What is this, a free tamasha? A film show? I want everyone up and out of here.' But he knew his voice was full of relief and released tension, and they grinned at him as they turned away. He propped himself on the edge of the long desk and waited for the strange liquid elasticity behind his kneecaps to subside. From the back of Gaitonde's chair there was a steady drip on to the floor.

Katekar was opening and shutting the white cabinets that lined the central room, with a blue handkerchief draped over his fingers. He was always methodical in the wake of gunshots, and Sartaj found comfort in the breadth and solidity of his shoulders and the serious set of his jaw.

'Nothing in here, sir,' Katekar said. 'Not one thing.'

Next to Sartaj's leg, there was a drawer in the desk. Sartaj found his own handkerchief and pulled at the handle. A small black book sat in the exact centre of the drawer, the edges lined up with the sides of the drawer.

'Diary?' Katekar said.

It was an album, black pages covered with sticky film, behind which photographs had been inserted. Sartaj flipped the pages by the very corners. Women, some very young, in posed studio shots, looking over shoulders and holding their faces and cocking their hips, decently dressed but all glamorous.

'All his women,' Sartaj said.

'All his randis,' Katekar said. He flipped his blue handkerchief over his index finger and edged open the waist-high filing cabinet that stood at the other end of the desk. Sartaj heard the intake of his breath even over the low hum of the generators. 'Sir.'

The filing cabinet was full of money. The money was new money, five-hundred-rupee notes in clean little bundles still in the Central Bank of India wrappers and rubber bands, and the bundles were held together in bricks of five by crisp shrink-wrapped plastic. Katekar pushed at the top layer, into the crack between the stacks. There was more underneath. And then more.

'How much?' Sartaj said.

Katekar thumped the side of the cabinet gently, thoughtfully. 'It's full all the way down. That's a lot of money. Fifty lakhs? More.'

It was more money than either had ever seen in one place before. There was a decision to be made, and they looked at each other frankly, and Sartaj decided. He nudged the cabinet shut with his knee. 'Too much money,' he said.

Katekar exhaled. He was unmistakably wistful for a second, that was all. But it had been him who had taught Sartaj this important lesson of survival, that to lunge for big prizes without enough information was to invite disaster. He shook himself loose now of the enchantment of big money with a huffing noise and a big grin. 'The big people will take care of Gaitonde's money,' he said. 'Now we wait?'

'We wait.'

The bunker was full. There were lab technicians and photographers, and senior officers from three zones and the Crime Branch. Gaitonde sat in the middle, well-lit and somehow shrunken. Sartaj watched as Parulkar leaned over Gaitonde, pointing something out to another zonal commissioner. Parulkar was in his element, discussing a successful operation with those who mattered, and Sartaj was grateful to him. He was sure that Parulkar would polish and improve the story, and give him more credit than he was due. This was a talent Parulkar had. Sartaj depended on him for it.

Three men came down the staircase, moving fast. Sartaj had never seen them before. The one in the lead had his hair cut so close to the skull that Sartaj could see the scalp under the neat grey. This one spoke to Parulkar, and flashed an ID card. Parulkar listened, and although he didn't give anything away, Sartaj saw him become very still. He nodded, and then led Flat-head and the other two over to Sartaj.

'This is the officer,' Parulkar said to Flat-head. 'Inspector Sartaj Singh.'

'I am SP Makand, CBI.' Flat-head was very curt. 'Did you find anything?'

'The money,' Sartaj said. 'An album. We didn't go through his pockets yet, we were waiting until . . .'

'Good,' Makand said. 'We will take over now.'

'Can we do anything?'

'No. We will be in touch. Have your men clear the location.' Makand's two flankers were already moving around the room, telling the technicians to pack up.

Sartaj nodded. That Gaitonde would be taken from him he had expected. That Gaitonde had appeared in Zone 13 was inexplicable, that his career had come to a sudden stop in Kailashpada was a professional gift altogether too perfect to be left to Sartaj alone. Life did not allow such undiluted felicities. But Makand's dismissal – even coming from a man from an elite central agency – was altogether too abrupt. And yet here was Parulkar being as bland as desi butter, with not a protest or small objection. So Sartaj followed his lead, summoned Katekar and got out.

It was evening. Sartaj stood in the lee of the metal door, in the shadows, and he could see the reporters waiting on the other side of the row of police jeeps. Parulkar was next to him, smartening himself up for the press. 'Sir,' Sartaj said, 'why did they kick us out? The CBI doesn't need local help any more?'

Parulkar tucked his shirt in, and tugged at his belt. 'They seemed very tense. My feeling was that they were afraid something in there would get exposed.'

'They're trying to cover something up?'

Parulkar tilted his head and allowed himself to look canny. 'Beta,' he said, 'when someone is willing to be that rude to us, it usually means they are trying to hide something. Come on. Let's go and tell our friends from the press how you brought down the great don Ganesh Gaitonde.'

So Sartaj stepped out into the flare of flashbulbs and told the journalists of his coup. He told them that he had talked to Gaitonde before they had knocked down the door, that Gaitonde had seemed unafraid and rational. He did not tell them Gaitonde's story about gold. And he did not tell them, or Katekar or Parulkar, about the question he thought Gaitonde had asked, at the last. He wasn't sure he had heard it, anyway. So he told the reporters about the anonymous tip that morning, and what had followed, and he said no, he had no idea why a mafia don would want to kill himself.

But later, at home that night, he remembered Gaitonde's grandiloquent voice, his rapid speech, his sadness. He had never met Ganesh Gaitonde, and now their lives had crossed and the man was dead. On the edge of sleep, Sartaj remembered all that he had heard and read about Gaitonde, the rumours and legends, the intelligence reports and the news-magazine interviews. He tried to connect the public image to the voice he had heard, and couldn't. There had been the famous gangster, and there was the man this afternoon. But what did it matter, any of it? Gaitonde was dead. Sartaj turned over, thumped his pillows determinedly, arranged them, and lay down his head and slept.

Ganesh Gaitonde Sells His Gold

❦

So, Sardar-ji, are you listening still? Are you somewhere in this world with me? I can feel you. What happened next, and what happened next, you want to know. I was walking under the whirling sky riven by clouds, with the unceasing tug of gold on my back and the city ahead. I was nineteen and I had gold on my back. Here I was, Ganesh Gaitonde, wearing a dirty blue shirt, brown pants, torn rubber-bottomed shoes and no socks, with forty-seven rupees in my pocket and a revolver in my belt and gold on my back. I had nowhere to go, because I couldn't go back to the building in Dadar where I had space to sleep outside the spice-smelling storage room of a restaurant. If Salim Kaka's people were going to look for me, or if anyone else was going to look for me, I would be gone, not found like a simpleton and given a dog's death. Since I had found the gold I had lost trust. I had the problems of a rich man. I thought: in all the world I have only forty-seven rupees and a revolver and this gigantic weight of metal. Gold is no good on my back, I must sell it. Gold is of no consequence until I sell it. How to sell gold, so much of it? Where to sell it? Until I sell it I am a poor man. A poor man with a rich man's problems.

I grinned, and then I laughed. There was a need to find a stash, now, quickly, but the situation was also funny. I sang: 'Mere desh ki dharti sona ugle, ugle heere moti.' But ten-thirty in the morning was no time to be walking around the outer edges of Borivali with a loaded ghoda and gold, bent by the weight and very tired. There were far fields and thickets of trees and buildings only here and there, small cottages clustered together very village-like, but sooner or later somebody was going to notice, to ask, to want. I had only three bullets left. Thirty or three hundred bullets wouldn't make a difference if someone found out what I was carrying.

There was a barbed-wire fence to the right, guarding a stand of

51

trees. I looked behind, ahead, and my decision was made. I slipped under the lowest strand, pulled the sack after and walked fast, no running, a fast walk to the trees. In the shade I squatted and settled into a wait. I flexed my hands, trying to work off the cramp that came from clutching my sack, from carrying its heavy burden. If anything happened it would happen now. I was enveloped all at once by tiny flying insects, and was willing to take the bites, but they moved in a shivering cloud around my shoulders, a tremble in the air. In the shimmering circle I was remembering the slope of a mountain seen through a window, a schoolbook fluttering in the breeze, my mother's endless weeping in the next room. Endless. Enough – I waved a hand in front of my face and came out of it. I moved forward in a crouch, through the dark under the branches, towards a sheet of water I could see now. A small pond, held in a saucer-like depression, edged around with yellowing weeds. I sat again, squatting with the sack in front. There were no footprints in the soft mud around the pond, no paths through the coarse grass, no man or woman all the way to the barbed wire on the far side of the water, or even beyond, on the road. But I wanted to give it another half an hour. I held firmly on to the smooth rectangle of the bar in my pocket and breathed in, out. I followed the quick iridescent dip of dragonflies on the water. I was determined not to slip again, never to fall gently into the slow whirlpool of the past. There had been a life, I had left it. For Ganesh Gaitonde there was only this day, this day's night and every day ahead.

When it was time, I backed away into the trees, into the darkest shade. I chose a tree and began to dig. The earth was loose, but dry, and it was slow going, and soon my fingers were raw. I should have first found something to dig with, a piece of tin, something. Bad planning. But it was started now, and I went on, moving the dirt in fistfuls. When I reached the harder layer under the topsoil I sat back and scraped at it with my heels until I had loosened it. The work was hard, and I was sweating, and when I stopped it wasn't really a hole, just a shallow depression really, under the dark trunk. I was tired, and hungry, and it would have to be enough. My chest was heaving. I tugged at the drawstring on the sack, and took out two biscuits of gold, and lost a minute or two in the soft bronze burn of them, under the dappled shadows. Then the sack went into the cranny, and I scraped earth back over it. It looked like a small mound, and I scurried about under the trees, finding tufts of grass to pat down over it, leaves and twigs. I stood back and looked down at the arrangement. It looked like an incidental rise under a tree, any tree, and in the dimness it would pass, unless somebody sat down on it maybe. But why would anyone come here, why wander, why sit? It was safe. I felt sure of it. But from the fence I had to come back once, just to make sure I could find my way back. But only once. After that I made myself roll under the fence, walk down the road, take the corner firmly, despite the plunging fall of loss in my stomach, a plummet that hurt so hard I had to hold my belly with both hands. Risk is risk and so comes profit. If it's gone it's gone. You have to make a deal. Make the deal.

All I had was a name: Paritosh Shah. I had heard it twice, once from a man named Azam Sheikh, who had just returned from a four-year sentence for burglary. He came out of prison and executed another clean job within two days, a daytime break-and-enter-and-grab on a newly-wed couple's apartment in Santa Cruz East. 'The good little wife went to the market to buy vegetables for her husband's dinner,' Azam said, 'and we got her gold necklace, and her bangles, and her earrings, and her nose-ring, everything except the mangalsutra, and Paritosh Shah cut us a good price for the lot.' I had been standing behind the kitchen door in the restaurant where I worked as a waiter, taking a break and listening to the boasting, and when Azam saw my feet under the door he cursed me and shut up. I moved away. Afterwards, his waiter told me Azam Sheikh had left a tip of three rupees, after an hour and a half of tangdis and shammi kebabs and beer, but within a month I had the satisfaction of hearing that Azam Sheikh was back in jail, caught in another Santa Cruz East job when a sleeping maidservant woke up and screamed. He was caught by neighbours and beaten bloody. Azam Sheikh walked funny now, there was that satisfaction – that and the name of Paritosh Shah.

Which I had heard again, after I had become close to Salim Kaka, after I had gained Kaka's trust. We had gone out, Mathu and Salim Kaka and me, to Borivali, for shooting practice. In a clearing in the jungle, Mathu and I had fired six shots each, and Salim Kaka had shown us the stance, the grip, and we had loaded and reloaded until it was fast and easy and I could do it without looking. That had pleased Salim Kaka, and he had thumped me on the shoulder. He let us fire two shots more each. The eruptions rolled along my forearms, louder than I had ever imagined, and down my spine, and I exulted, and the birds billowed above. 'Don't clutch your samaan,' Salim Kaka said. 'Hold it smooth, hold it firm, hold it with love.' There was a chalked target on a tree trunk, and I exploded the chips from its very centre. 'With love,' I said, and Salim Kaka laughed with me. On the long walk out of the jungle, under the bare brown branches, through the enveloping thorn bushes, Salim Kaka scared us with tales of leopards. A girl gathering wood had been killed in this very jungle not ten days ago. 'The leopard comes so fast you can't see him, all you feel is his teeth in your neck,' he said. 'I'll blow his eyes out,' I said, and twirled my revolver. Mathu said, 'Of course, maderchod, you're a gold-medal shooter after all.' I spat, and said, 'There'd be money from the leopard skin. I'd skin the bhenchod and sell it.' 'To whom, chutiya?' Mathu wanted to know. I pointed to Salim Kaka: 'To Kaka's receiver.' 'No,' Salim Kaka said. 'He's only interested in jewellery, diamonds, gold, high-price electronics.' 'Not your mangy leopard skin,' Mathu said, and laughed. Afterwards Mathu stood by the highway and waited for an auto-rickshaw, his arm up, and Salim Kaka squatted next to me, we hunkered side-by-side next to a wall, pissing. I stared at the wall, holding myself, impatient suddenly with the long train ride ahead, then the bus and walk to home and sleep. 'What's the matter, yaara?' Salim Kaka said. 'Still thinking about your leopard skin?' Salim Kaka's teeth were stained brown from tobacco, and they were strong and solid. 'Don't worry, you can take the skin to that Paritosh Shah, he'll take anything, I hear.' 'Who?' I said. 'Some new receiver in Goregaon. He's ambitious,' Salim Kaka said. Then Mathu had an auto-rickshaw stopped, and Salim Kaka shook himself and stood up, and I stood and zipped up, and Salim Kaka grinned at me and we walked over, rubbing shoulders. In the bouncing and jerking auto we were all squeezed together and Salim Kaka in the centre held the black bag containing the revolvers. They were his, belonged to him. He held the bag close.

So now I went to Goregaon, which was easy enough, but Paritosh Shah was one man in this locality of lakhs, and he was not advertised among the billboards for sex doctors and real-estate agents and cement dealers at the station. I bought a newspaper, found a vadapau-wallah outside the station and ate and considered the problem. With a glass of tea from the chai-wallah one booth down I began to see a possible solution. 'Bhidu,' I said to the chai-wallah, 'where's the police station here?'

I walked to the station, through narrow roads lined with shops and thelas on either side. I slipped through fast, bending and sliding shoulder-first through the crowds, revived by the tea and eager for the next turn. I found the station, and leaned against the bonnet of a car, facing the long, low, brown façade. I could actually see, even from this distance, through the front door into the receiving room with its long desks, and I knew what lay beyond, the crowded offices, the prisoners squatting in rows, the bare cells at the very back. The small crowd in front shifted and wandered and re-formed but was always there, and I flipped through the newspaper and watched. I could pick out the cops, even the plain-clothes ones, from the coil of their necks and a backward leaning, something like a cobra sprung straight in the middle of fresh furrows, hood fanned, quivering with power and arrogance. They had that glittery belligerence in their eyes. I was looking for something else.

It took until two-thirty and two false starts before I found my informant. There was one narrow-hipped man who sidled out of the side of the gate and angled down the road with the oily reticence of a born pickpocket, and I followed him for half a mile, and finally came to mistrust his long hands, which flexed and relaxed in hungry, doglike greediness. Back at the station, I watched again, and fixed on an older man, perhaps of fifty or so, who came out of the front doors, stood just outside the gate and opened a cigarette pack with a flick of his thumb. He tapped a cigarette on the pack three times, precise and deliberate, and then lit it and pulled at it, all with the same unhurried confidence. I walked behind him and liked the neat curve of the white hair across the back of his neck, and the inconspicuous grey bush-shirt. But at the street crossing, when I came around him and asked for a cigarette, please, the man looked at me with such open friendliness, with such lack of suspicion that I knew he was completely respectable. He was some office-goer who had come to the station to report a stolen bicycle, or loud neighbours, he would have no idea who Paritosh Shah was. I took a cigarette and thanked him and came back to my post.

I was crushing the cigarette butt with my heel when I heard her. It was a deep voice, unmistakably a woman's but bass and resonant, she was arguing with the auto-rickshaw driver, telling him she did the same trip every week and his meter was off and he could expect twelve-sixty from some chutiya fresh from UP, not her. I couldn't see much of her past the auto-rickshaw and the driver, only plump arms and a tight yellow blouse, and when the driver screeched off with nine rupees, I had a glimpse of a deep red sari, a fleshy back and plump waist, a quick and rolling stride, all of it somehow wholly disreputable. Now I was impatient. I no longer bothered to examine the others who went in and out, I was waiting for her. When she emerged forty-five minutes later I was rehearsed and ready.

She crossed the road and stood waiting for an auto-rickshaw, one large hand on her hip and the other waving imperiously at every blaring one that passed. I took a breath and stepped closer, and saw under the sweep of hennaed hair her pouchy cheeks, strong eyebrows, large lotus-shaped gold earrings. She was old, older, marked by time, forty years or fifty, far from youth. I liked her tubby, forward-leaning stance, her feet wide apart and strong. Her pallu hung carelessly from her shoulder, not very modest at all.

'The rickshaws are all full at this time,' I said.

'Go away, boy. I'm not a randi,' she growled. 'Although you don't look like you could afford one.'

I hadn't thought she had looked at me yet. 'I'm not looking for a randi.'

'So you say.' Now she turned her face to me, and her eyes bulged slightly out, not ugly but unusual, it made her face precarious, ready to fall on the world with some jolting surprise. 'What do you want, then?'

'I have a question to ask you.'

'Why would I answer?'

'I need help.'

'You look as if you do. You can't get your pants open and you want me to pull it out for you. Why should I get my hands dirty? Do I look like your mother to you?'

I laughed, and knew my teeth had bared. 'No, you don't. Not even a little bit. But still you might help.'

An auto-rickshaw going the other way slowed and came curvetting across the road towards us. The woman took hold of the iron bar above its meter before it stopped, and swung herself into the seat. 'Go,' she said to the driver.

'Paritosh Shah,' I said, hunching my shoulders and leaning forward into the rickshaw. Now I had her attention.

'What about him?'

'I need to find him.'

'You need to?'

'Yes.'

She slipped forward on the seat, and gave me fully the blank threat of her gaze. 'You look too dirty to be a khabari. They try to look clean and trustworthy.'

'I'm not,' I said. 'I wouldn't know who to inform to.'

'Get in,' she said. She made room on the cracked red rexine, gave instructions to the auto-rickshaw driver and we went put-putting away through unfamiliar lanes. The buildings came closer to each other now, jammed together wall against wall, and the streets were close with people who stepped aside for the auto to pass. I peered out on the left, and then through the oval window in the canvas at the rear.

'Calm down,' the woman said. 'You're safe. If I wanted to harm you, that big ghoda in your pants wouldn't save you.'

I looked down. I had been holding the revolver through stained blue cloth. I let go of it and massaged my right hand with the other. 'I've never been here before,' I said.

'I know,' she said. She leaned over to me. 'What's your name?'

'My name is Ganesh. And yours?'

'I am Kanta Bai. What do you have for Paritosh Shah?'

I said, close to her ear, 'I have gold.' I came closer. 'Biscuits.'

'Be quiet, Ganesh, until we get out of the auto.'

The auto stopped on a busy bazaar square full of wholesale clothing shops, and she led me through rapid turns in narrowing lanes. She was known well here, and people passing greeted her by name, but she hurried by without a pause. At the end of a lane there was a wall with a break in it, a jagged hole lined with shattered bricks, and on the other side there was a basti. I watched my feet and followed her rapid walk. The shacks were closer now, and in some places the pucca buildings were so close to each other across the lane that it was like walking through a tunnel. Men and women and children stood aside to let Kanta Bai pass. There were boys, young men, sitting on ledges and in doorways and I felt their eyes on my neck, and I kept my back straight and kept close to Kanta Bai.

I smelt the overpowering round richness of gur first, and then the vomit. We turned right and passed by a low doorway, and I saw metal tables, and men sitting around them drinking. A boy put a plate with two boiled eggs down on the table nearest the entrance, and his customer shook out the last milky drops from a glass into his mouth. Kanta Bai angled around the side of the building, and the whine of an electric turbine deepened its pitch. She left me in a dark room filled to the ceiling with sacks of gur. 'Wait here,' she said, and so I waited. The warm smell settled on my shoulders, brown as river-bottom earth. Through the unceasing grind of the motor I could hear the highest notes from a radio in the front room, the bar, just the tinny tops of the song, coming to me like froth, and I wondered about the quality of Kanta Bai's product. There had been customers enough, maybe twenty on a work-day afternoon, sipping steadily at the eight and ten-rupee glasses of saadi and satrangi they distilled in the back. It was a good business, raw materials cheap and legally available, overheads low. And the demand for good desi liquor was steady and constant, as continuous and vast as the tramp of feet in the lanes outside. I leaned forward and through the curtained doorway I could see just the bare feet of Kanta Bai's workers and the dragging bottoms of sacks, and occasionally the round gleam of bottles. I recognized her sari, and so was able to turn away and be standing at the furthest end of the room when she turned aside the curtain. When I saw her eyes, burning white despite the sloughy darkness of the gur sacks, I was afraid.

'I spoke to Paritosh Shah on the phone,' she said.

I was unable to speak, buried by the abrupt terror of being alone, inexperienced, alone with gold. I nodded, and in the same motion leaned my shoulder against the doorway, very casual. I put a hand on my hip and nodded again.

Kanta Bai was faintly amused. A very small ripple of pleasure passed through her jaw, and she said, 'Let's see your gold.'

I nodded. I was still very unsafe, queasy inside, but this was necessary. I groped in my right pocket, moved the bars to my left hand, and held them out, two of them weighty in my palm.

Kanta Bai took the bars, tested their heft and weight, and gave them back to me. Her eyes were steady on my face. 'He'll see you now. I'll have one of my boys take you.'

'Good,' I said, now able to find my voice and confidence. The biscuits went back to my pocket, and I fumbled out a thin roll of notes, and fanned them out.

'You can't pay me.'

'What?'

'How much do you have?'

I turned my hand to the side, to the light. 'Thirty-nine rupees.'

At this she gurgled out a laugh, and her cheeks bunched and her eyes squeezed almost shut. 'Bachcha, go and meet Paritosh Shah. He'll owe me a favour if things go well. Thirty-nine rupees doesn't make you Raja Bhoj of Bumbai.'

'I'll owe a favour, too,' I said. 'If things go well.'

'Very smart,' she said. 'Maybe you're a good boy after all.'

Paritosh Shah was a family man. I waited for him on a second-floor hallway, near a staircase that exhaled occasional blasts of sharp urine-stink. The building was six storeys tall and ancient, with a bamboo framework roped and nailed to its tottering façade, and worrisome gaps in the ornate scrollwork on the balconies. The second floor was full of male Shahs, who passed by where Kanta Bai's boy had left me on the landing, and they called each other Chachu and Mamu and Bhai, and ignored me entirely. They walked by my dirty shirt and ragged trousers with the barest of glances. They were a flashy, gold-ringed lot who wore mostly white safari suits. I could see their white shoes and white chappals lined up in untidy rows near the uniformed guard at the door. Somewhere inside was the sanctum of Paritosh Shah, guarded by a hoary old muchchad perched on a stool with an absurdly long-barrelled shotgun. He wore a blue uniform with yellow braid, and his moustache was enormous and curved at the ends. After twenty minutes of passing Shahs and piss-stench, I was starting to feel quite insulted, and somehow my resentment focused itself on the ammunition belt the old man wore around his chest, on its cracked leather and three cylindrical red cartridges. I imagined pulling my revolver and putting a hole in the centre of the ammunition belt, just above the saggy stomach. It was an absurd thought, but there was satisfaction in it.

Ten minutes more went by, and that was enough. It was either now or the bullet to his chest. I had a pulsing headache. 'Listen, mamu,' I said to the guard, who was now investigating his left ear with a pencil stub. 'Tell Paritosh Shah I came to do business, not to stand out here and smell his latrine.'

'What?' The pencil came out. 'What?'

'Tell Paritosh Shah I'm gone. Gone elsewhere. His loss.'

'Wait, wait.' The old man leaned back and pointed his moustachios through the doorway. 'Badriya, come and see what this fellow is saying.'

Badriya came, and he was younger by much, and very tall, a quiet-moving muscle-builder, with a deliberate padding way about him in his bare feet. He stood in the doorway with his arms hanging away from his chest, and I was sure he had a weapon tucked away in the small of his back, under the black bush-shirt. 'Is there a problem?'

It was a challenge, no question about it, and the man was blank-faced and hard, but I was riding now on the thin-drawn craziness of the moment, on the exhaustion from the long day and the bracing leap of anger. 'Yes, problem,' I said. 'I'm tired of waiting for your mader-chod Paritosh Shah.'

The old man bristled and started to climb down from his stool, but Badriya spoke quietly. 'He's a busy man.'

'So am I.'

'Are you?'

'I am.'

And that was all it took. The guard had panic in his shoulders. His grip on the shotgun was clumsy, far up the stock, and with one leg on the ground and the other on a cross-bar of the stool he was tilted wrong and unbalanced. I watched him and I watched Badriya. It was absurd to be near death in a sudden moment in a grimy corridor with nostrils full, unreasonable to be almost moneyed and not yet, ludicrous to be Ganesh Gaitonde, poor in the city and standing to the side always, there was no sense in any of it and so there was an exulting eagerness in me, a glad and crazy courage. Here. Now. Here I am. What of it?

Badriya raised his left hand slowly. 'All right,' he said. 'I'll go and see if he's free now.'

I shrugged. 'Okay,' I said, liking the English word, one of the very few I knew then. 'Okay. I'll wait.' I grinned at the muchchad for the next few minutes, frightening the old man more and more, setting his hands trembling on the shotgun. By the time Badriya appeared again, I was sure I could stare the ancient soldier and his martial whiskers straight into a heart attack. But there was business to be done.

'Come,' Badriya said, and I pulled off my shoes and followed. The annexe led into a warren of hallways lined with identical black doors. 'Raise your arms,' Badriya said. I nodded, and raised the front of my shirt, and sucked in my stomach as Badriya gently took up my revolver. Badriya gave it a professional flip back-and-forth of the wrist, looking along its barrel. He raised it to his nose, intent. He was barrel-chested, heavy-necked. 'Been fired not too long ago,' he said.

'Yes,' I said.

Badriya reversed the revolver in his hand, and although I couldn't tell quite how it was done, it was a very stylish move. 'Turn around,' Badriya said. He patted me down quickly, with a series of fluttering taps under my arms and up my thighs, and no more than a very slight pause on the bars in the pockets. It was professionally done, no animosity, and I thought better of Paritosh Shah for having Badriya on his team. 'Last door on the left,' Badriya said with the last pat.

Paritosh Shah was lying on his side on a white gadda, propped up on a round pillow. The room was quite bare, panelled brown walls, smooth and shiny, with frosted white glass high up near the ceiling, all of it air-conditioned to a chill that I found instantly painful. There was a tidy row of three black phones next to the gadda. Paritosh Shah was very relaxed, and he raised a languid hand at a low stool. 'Sit,' he said. I sat, aware of Badriya behind and to the left, and the small click of the black door as it shut. 'You're the boy,' Paritosh Shah said. He wasn't very old himself, maybe six, seven, at most ten years older than I was, but he had an air of tremendous and weary confidence. 'Name?' he said, and somehow his limp drape on the soft gadda, his one leg bent under, his stillness, all of it warned, don't try and fool me, boy.

'Ganesh.'

'You're a rash lad, Ganesh. Ganesh what?'

'Ganesh Gaitonde.'

'You're not a Bombay original. Ganesh Gaitonde from where?'

'Doesn't matter.' I leaned back and brought out two bars. I laid them side by side on the edge of Paritosh Shah's gadda.

'You could've tried selling those to any Marwari jeweller. Why come to me?'

'I want a fair price. And I can get you more.'

'How much more?'

'Many more. If I get fair price for these.'

Paritosh Shah tilted, toppling upright like a child's doll with a weight in the bottom. I saw then that he had thin arms and shoulders, but a round ball of a stomach that he folded his hands over. 'Fifty-gram biscuits. If they check out, seven thousand rupees each.'

'Market price is fifteen thousand for fifty grams.'

'That's the market price. This is why gold gets smuggled.'

61

'Below half is too much below. Thirteen thousand.'

'Ten. That's as much as I can do.'

'Twelve.'

'Eleven.'

I nodded. 'Done.'

Paritosh Shah whispered into one of the black phones, and with his free hand he held out a silver box filled with silver-flecked paan and supari and elaichi. I shook my head. Money is what I wanted, money to hold and grasp, money in my pocket, I wanted thick wads of notes, the thickness enough for silver boxes, for soft gaddas and red bed-spreads and record players and clean bathrooms and love, enough crisp paper for confidence and safety and life. My mouth was dry. I gripped my hands together tightly, and held them hard against each other through the discreet knock on the door, and then as it shut and Badriya put down a small scale and two stacks of currency, one fat and one thin.

'Just to check,' Paritosh Shah said. And he picked up the bars one by one, by the fingertips, and laid them on the scale against precise lit-tle weights. 'Fine.' He smiled. 'Very fine.' He was looking at me expectantly. The money lay on the gadda, and I moved my will like a vibrating steel spring and stilled myself and showed no sign of notic-ing it until Paritosh Shah stretched out slim fingers to slide the stack forward two inches. So I took it, with a hand that shook only slightly.

I stood up. The room swayed, the frosty oblongs of white light dipped into my eyes and there was a blinking flash of white sky, no horizon.

Then Paritosh Shah said, 'You don't talk very much.'

'I'll talk more next time.' Badriya had the door open, and the corri-dor was long, and I emerged from it with my cash in my pocket and dizziness tamped firmly down. I bent over easily to pull on my shoes, and when I came up I had the thin curl of thirty-nine rupees in my left hand. I tucked it behind the old guard's ammunition belt, put it in firmly with an extra little polishing motion on the leather. 'Here, mamu,' I said. 'And next time I come, don't keep me standing out-side.'

The man stuttered, and Badriya laughed out loud. He held out the revolver, and raised an eyebrow. 'You kept one gold bar back.'

I checked my chambers with a quick motion of my wrist, crisp as I could make it. 'That one's not for sale,' I said.

'Why?'

I laid away the revolver, and raised a hand in farewell. 'Not everything is.' On the street outside, I was still very alert. I stood in front of a Bata store and watched the glass on the shoe display, looking for lurkers. The chances were high that I was being followed, that Paritosh Shah had made his swift calculations and sent out someone, perhaps Badriya, to shadow and discover, to uncover much gold. It was only logical. But no reflected pursuers appeared, and I left the window and wandered, ambling slowly and pausing often behind blind corners to watch the faces that passed. I was ready but relaxed, at home in these city streets like I had never been. I felt a lordly compassion for the pretty little bungalows I was walking by now, lit up in the soft evening twilight, for the happy, rich children I could see running in and out. None of it was alien now. And I tried hard to resist comfort, to keep alive the sharp edge of distrust against the euphoria of a profitable deal, the ecstasy of flinging out into the world one throw of dice that rolled fluently to the inevitable condition of victory. Don't be careless. Watch, watch. The numbers fell right but the board moves. What is white will be black. Climb high and fast and the long snakes lie waiting. Play the game.

I stood in front of a temple. I looked left and right and had no idea of how I had got there. There were apartment buildings on one side of the road, lower constructions on the other, the sloping tiled roofs of mill workers, shipping clerks, postmen. The temple stood at a corner, and it must have been the reverberating pealing of the bell that had drawn me to the courtyard, under the high saffron peak of its roof. I leant on a pillar and checked again for followers, for lethal shadows amidst the auto-rickshaws and Ambassadors. If they were out there, smelling of malice and greed, the temple was as good a place as any to wait them out. I had no use for temples, I despised incense and comfortable lies and piety, I did not believe in gods or goddesses, but here was a haven. I took off my shoes and went in. The worshippers sat cross-legged on the smooth floor, crowded together through the length of the long hall. The walls were an austere white, lit up by tube-lights, but the dark heads swayed in a field of bright saris, purple and shining green and blue and deep red, all the way to the orange statue of Hanuman flying, suavely holding the mountain above his head. I found a place against the back wall and sat, instantly comfortable with my feet tucked in under. A man in saffron robes sat on a dais in front of Hanuman, and his discourse came easily and strongly to me, that old story about Bali and Sugreev, the conflict, the challenge, the duel, with the ambushing god waiting in the woods. I knew the turns and tricks well, and I nodded along with the old action and the rhythms of the lesson. When the priest recited couplets, holding out both his arms, the congregation chanted behind him and the women's voices rose high in the hall. The arrow flew and Bali lay writhing on the ground, pierced, his heels scraping the forest floor, and I raised my knees and rested my head on them, and I was comfortable.

I awoke to the shaking of the saffron-robed priest. 'Beta,' he said, 'time to go home.' He had white hair and an impish face. 'Time for lock-up here. Hanuman-ji has to go to sleep.'

I rubbed the crick from my neck, hard. 'Yes. I'll go.' I was the last one in the hall.

'Hanuman-ji understands. You were tired. Worked long. He sees everything.'

'Sure,' I said. What fantastic stories the old and the weak tell to each other, I thought. I stretched out my legs, stood and stumbled to the locked donation box in front of Hanuman. Peeling off a five-hundred-rupee note from the thinner wad, I remembered that I hadn't counted the notes when Paritosh Shah had given them. Amateur-like and not to be done again. I slipped the money into the slit, and found the priest ready to my right with a thali full of prasad. I held out my cupped right hand, and ate the small sugary peda on the way out. My mouth flooded painfully with saliva, and I was rested, and life was very sweet.

Now there was no multitude for assassins to hide in, and walking fast down the road, with the crunch of my shoes loud, I felt I was safe. The streetlights left no darkness on this long stretch, and I was completely alone. I waved down an auto-rickshaw, and was at the station three turns and five minutes later. I paid, and was almost at the ticket window when a man leaning against the iron fence raised his chin in inquiry: what do you want? I looked a moment too long, but kept moving, and now the man was walking beside me, with that cheery, insinuating tout's whisper: 'What you looking for, boss? You want some fun, haan? Charas, Calmpose, everything I got. You want a woman? Look at that auto there. All ready for you.' There was an auto parked across the road, pulled in deep at an angle in front of a shuttered shop. The driver was leaning on it, and I saw the glow of his bidi, and knew that the man was looking straight at me. The bidi moved, and the driver motioned against the back window of the auto, knocking, and a figure moved inside it, and a woman's head leaned out on the left side, into the lamplight. All I could see of her was the black shine of her hair, and the strong yellow of her sari, but I didn't need to see any more to know what sort of raddled randi sold her chut at stations in the back of an auto. I laughed, and paid for my ticket.

But the pimp stayed with me. 'Okay, boss,' he whispered chummily on the way to the platform gate. 'I misjudged you, saab. You want something better. You're a man of fine tastes, my mistake. You just look a little, you know . . . But I have the girl for you, boss.' He kissed his fingers. 'Her husband used to work in a bank, was a big saab, poor fellow, then he had an accident. Complete cripple he became. Can't work. So she has to make a living for both of them, what to do? Very exclusive. Only for some gentlemen, you see, in her own apartment. I can take you straight there. You'll see what a high-class cheez she is, boss. Completely convent-educated.'

I stopped. 'Is she fair?'

'Like Hema Malini, bhidu. You touch her skin and you'll get a current. Like fresh malai.'

'How much?'

'Five thousand.'

'I'm not a tourist. One thousand.'

'Two thousand. Don't say anything. You see the girl, and if you think she's not worth the money, you give me whatever you want and I'll leave quietly and not a word more. Believe me, if you saw her outside her husband's bank you wouldn't believe she has to do this, poor woman. Like one phataak memsaab she looks.'

'What's your name?'

'Raja.'

I put the train ticket in my back pocket. 'All right, Raja,' I said. 'Just don't make me angry.'

Raja giggled. 'No, saab, no. Please come.'

She was fair, no question. She opened the door and even in the bleary light from the lift I saw that she was fair, not quite Hema Malini-pale but light like afternoon wheat. She sat on a brown sofa while Raja counted his two thousand and bowed himself out. She wore a dull green sari with gold borders, and round gold earrings, and sat very respectable and contained with her shoulders high and hands in lap.

'What's your name?' I said.

'Seema,' she said, not meeting my stare.

'Seema.' I shifted from one foot to the other by the door, not sure of what to do next. I was experienced all right, but in a different kind of establishment, and the shiny glass table with its vase of flowers and the painting on the wall with just colours dashed together and the short brown carpet, all of these stopped me altogether. But she stood and went further into the apartment, and I stepped up manfully, taking it all in, the stretch of her blouse across the sunken river of her spine and the white phone in its alcove in the wall of the passageway. She clicked on a lamp in the bedroom, and when she flipped back the bedcover I tensed: it was altogether too professional. I had seen the same folding down of the sheets before, the same towel.

'Hold on,' I said, and went back out into the hallway. The bathroom was clean, and I pissed into the western-style commode with some satisfaction, at length. But then I saw that there was no soap near the tap, no bucket. I zipped. The cupboards in the kitchen were empty, not a plate, not a pot, not even a gas or a stove, only two glasses drying upside down next to the basin. Now I was sure that I had been fooled. The apartment was nobody's home, not a bank saab's, not a good wife's, there was no cripple and no memsaab, only a whore got up and powdered. She lay on the bed, naked but for the earrings, her arms crossed over her small breasts and her belly rising and falling under the thin shadow of her hipbone, and one ankle over another. I stood over her, breathing through my mouth.

'Speak English,' I said.

'What?'

In her eyes there was real surprise, and I grew more angry. 'I told you. Speak English.'

She had a sharp little nose and a small retreating chin, and she was puzzled for another moment, and then she laughed, just a very little bit and bitterly amused. 'Shall I speak?' she said. Then she spoke in English, and the words rattled around my head, and I knew that they were really English, I felt it in the crack of the consonants. 'Bas?' she said.

'No,' I said. I was hard, vibrating deep at the root. 'Don't stop.' She spoke English while I took off my clothes. I turned around to take off my pants and hide the revolver from her. When I turned back she was staring at the ceiling and speaking English. I nudged her ankles apart. 'Don't stop,' I said. I ground and bucked on top of her and she turned her face to the side and spoke. I reared up and the skin on her neck was sandy under the lamplight and I could hear her words. I understood none of it but the sound of it was an angry excitement inside my head. Then I felt a distant overflow, far below, and I was still.

I was very tired, Sardar-ji. I leaned forward into my walk. I was going back to my gold. The momentum of nearly falling over at every step kept me moving, but at every exhausted buckling of my knees I grew more afraid. I was very close to the gold now, I recognized every intersection and the shapes of particular buildings and shadowed trees. There was no moon but it was a light night, and out in this unbuilt open ground I saw clearly the black direction of the road and the white of a milestone. The gold was gone, taken, I felt a hole in my chest. It was gone, vanished out of my life. I should give up now. It would be easy for me to find a patch of grass by the road, tip over into it, sleep. Stop it. Ganesh Gaitonde, keep going. You have won every game today. Win again. You know exactly where you are.

The calculation of the precise section of barbed-wire fence was not a problem. I counted off the posts, looked up and down the way, and rolled under. Under the trees I passed into disastrous black, and was lost. With one hand extended I went gliding, rustling through space, not sure of the distances now, but I felt and reached and at the right moment I stopped and turned to the right. A step, and there was the tree. I passed a hand down the trunk and the ground below was flat. All around the trunk I went, feeling with both hands. After two circles, maybe three, I leaned a shoulder against it and made a long bleating sound. Ganesh Gaitonde, Ganesh Gaitonde. I scrabbled to the next tree, stopped when I grazed my head on it. Around it, around it. And then the next one. My cry was high now, a constant shriek under the canopy and darkness. It went without rise or fall in a half-circle. Stopped abruptly, because I had both hands on a fatness. The swelling rose out of the earth and filled both my palms. I traced it softly, up to the tree and down to the bottom of the mound, making out its shape. I moaned and dug both hands into it. I went rooting furiously into it, and welcomed the pain in my fingers. The cloth came first, and then the heavenly, familiar shape of a rectangle. My shoulders shook and I moved my hand and it was all there. All and undisturbed and mine. Up to my forearms in earth, I let my head drop and gulped in the smell of grass and my armpits and my body and knew that the world was mine. As dawn came I wrapped myself around the mound and slept with my revolver under my breast.

Going Towards Home

Sartaj was woken by a reporter who wanted to know what he thought of Ganesh Gaitonde's use of politicians, the corruption of the legal system and recent scandals in the police department. Sartaj cut off the stream of questions with a curt 'No comment' and slammed the phone down. He turned over, pushed his face into the pillow, but the light was seeping over his eyelids and his mind was turning. With a sigh he pushed himself up. Being a minor three-day celebrity was not going to be easy, he could see. He walked around the bed, his eyes half-shut, remembering how Gaitonde loved to give interviews. That bastard liked to talk, Sartaj thought, and pushed open the door to the bathroom.

For breakfast Sartaj had three pieces of toast with butter, a soggy orange and chai left too long on the burner. In the *Indian Express*, Gaitonde was front-page news, posing confidently on a mountain-top, and the story was three columns across and very deep, and Sartaj read it all, the sudden rise, the vast power, the intricate feuds and the executions and the ambushes, the whole game. Sartaj Singh was mentioned, of course, as the intrepid leader of the police party, but there was nothing about the dead woman, not a word. As far as the world knew, Gaitonde had died alone.

The phone rang. Sartaj let it go on, suffering its harsh rattle along the back of his neck. He was sure it was a journalist, but finally he gave in and picked up the receiver.

'Inspector Singh?'

It was Parulkar's PA, Sardesai, speaking in his very peculiar and very nasal half-whisper.

'Sardesai Saab,' Sartaj said. 'Everything all right?' Usually, calls from Parulkar's office were put through by the operator outside his cabin. Sardesai only called when there was urgent, confidential work to be done, or there was some departmental skulduggery afoot.

'Yes, there is no problem. But Parulkar Saab would like you to come into his office as soon as possible.'

'Now?'

'Now.'

There would be no more information forthcoming from Sardesai over the phone. Even in person, he was famously secretive, which was as a personal assistant should be. Sartaj hung up, hurried to the shower. He had known Parulkar for a long time, and had never known him to call a subordinate from home without good reason. There were other officers who did that, who treated their juniors as servants. But Parulkar had no arrogance, only proper pride in the work that his men did. That was why he had prospered. So when Parulkar called, Sartaj went, fast.

Katekar's sons were standing by him. He opened his eyes and they knelt, giggling, just off the chatai and tugging on his toes. They were both wearing pressed grey shorts, white shirts and striped blue-and-red ties. They both had the same razor-sharp parting in the hair, on the left and absolutely straight.

'Where's your mother?' Katekar mumbled. His mouth was full of onion gone caustic and unlovely.

'Off to the vegetable market,' Rohit said.

'Fall in outside in exactly five minutes.'

They fled from his growling rise and mock lunge, and in the kitchen he threw water on his face and shoulders. They were waiting for him outside, backs to the wall, feet apart and hands held behind. They came to attention and Katekar inspected their shoes, their shirts and the organization of the books in their blue school-bags. The ritual was complete when he gave them each ten rupees. Katekar dismissed the parade, and the two boys walked down the lane with Katekar follow-ing. Mohit was happy with his ten rupees, but Katekar knew that Rohit had started to think of it as only ten rupees, and to long for all the things in the world that ten rupees would not buy. A man edged a scooter slowly around the corner and the two brothers stood sideways to let him pass. Katekar saw the golden down on Mohit's cheek in the early sun, and looked away quickly, afraid of the future that pressed on his heart and made it full.

'Papa?'

'Fast, fast,' he said. 'Or we'll miss the bus.'

70

After he had waved them on to No 180, watched it nose into the traffic, Katekar bought a copy of *Loksatta* and folded it under his arm. He read it while queuing for the municipal lavatory, with a Dalda can full of water resting between his feet. Bomb blast in Israel, four dead. Exchange of fire across Line of Control, situation in Srinagar tense. Conwoman fools housewives out of jewellery in Ghatkopar. Congress party supremos deny rumours of infighting. There was a front-page story about Gaitonde, about his long career of close shaves and escapes. Why had Gaitonde killed himself, the reporter asked, and could construct no theory. Around Katekar neighbours gossiped and laughed, but everyone knew that he must be left to his paper. When the line jerked forward he moved the water can without looking up from his news.

After his turn in the lavatory, he strode past the line of men, relaxed and easy. He greeted each one expansively, but didn't stop to gossip. He went purposefully home, and was exactly in time. Shalini was sliding open the big steel padlock as he came around the corner. Katekar shut the door behind himself, pushed up the latch. He pulled off his kurta, put it on the last hook to the left, which was its accustomed place. 'There's enough water for your bath,' Shalini said from the kitchen. She handed him a green towel, but as she turned towards the kitchen he touched her neck, just where it curved into the shoulder. She shivered, and giggled. 'Don't,' she said, but when he lay on his chatai she curled over him tightly. He moved her hand – with a jangle of bangles – to his crotch. She had her head tightly pressed into his chest. Even after all these years, she wouldn't look at him, he knew she wouldn't let him turn her face to his, not yet, but he exhaled slowly as the glassy tinkling sounds between them speeded and became a small pealing. Shalini moved and with a quick motion she had her sari up, and they both stirred against each other, reaching, and then she found him. He settled his hands on her hips and shut his eyes. Then he felt her lips, small and warm and agile, against the line of his chin.

Shalini sent him away with a handful of prasad from the Devi Padmavati temple. Katekar ate the tender bits of coconut with particular pleasure. Religion was women's business and also the curse of the nation, but the milky flesh of the coconut was a voluptuous gift anyhow, and his shoulders tingled as he walked.

The lane was narrow, narrow enough in some sections that Katekar could have touched the walls on both sides of it with outstretched hands. Most of the doors of the homes were open, for the air. A grandmother sat on her front step, holding her darkly oiled, naked grandson in her lap, laughing into the toothless pink rosebud of his smile. Katekar came around a corner, past a tiny shop selling cigarettes, packets of shampoo, paan, batteries, and then he stood aside to let a row of young women go by, and the girls stepped tidily over the curve of the gutter, powdered and properly salwar-kameezed for shops and offices. Katekar watched the swish of red and yellow fabric. He had one foot propped up on a two-inch pipe that ran along the bottom of the wall. The mohalla committee had collected money for the laying of this secondary water pipe last year, but it worked only when the pressure in the main municipal pipe down near the main road was good. Now they were collecting money for a pump.

On Maganchand Road the thela-wallahs already had their fruit piled high, and the fishsellers were laying out bangda and bombil and paaplet on their slabs. The rush hour had packed the cars close. At the bus stop Katekar stood at the outskirts of a loose cluster of people. He opened his paper and read the editorial, which was about the failure of the civil state in Pakistan. When the double-decker came, Katekar let the crowd rush ahead of him. The conductor finally cut off the shoving influx and rang the bell. The bus lurched forward, and Katekar raised a hand, and the conductor made room for him on the step with a quick, respectful nod. Katekar had ridden on this bus for eight years, ever since he had bought the kholi, and all the conductors on the route knew that he was a policeman. This conductor, whose name was Pawle, moved past Katekar towards the rear of the bus, clicking his ticket-punch at the passengers, and then worked his way towards the front. Katekar listened to the fall of the small coins. Citizens loved to complain about the horror of the morning traffic, which surpassed itself every year, but Katekar loved the enormous bustle of millions on the move, the hurtling local trains with thick clusters of bodies hanging precariously from the doors, the sonorous tramp and hum of the crowd inside the tall hall of Churchgate Station. It made him feel alive. The impatient blare of the horns shivered up his forearms. He leaned out of the bus, stretching his weight against the metal bar he was holding on to. A group of college girls hurried and skipped through the cars, calling out to each other and laughing.

Katekar tapped his fingers on the side of the bus, and sang under his breath: '*Lat pat lat pat tujha chalana mothia nakhriyacha . . .*'

There was a woman in Parulkar's cabin. Makand, the CBI man who had taken over Gaitonde's bunker, was also sitting in front of Parulkar's desk, his head as smooth as grey steel. Sartaj stood very quietly at attention until Parulkar asked him to sit down.

'They need your help, Sartaj,' Parulkar said, 'in an aspect of the Gaitonde matter.'

'Sir,' Sartaj said, and kept his back straight.

'They will tell you what they need.'

Sartaj nodded. 'Yes, sir.' He shifted in his chair towards Makand, leaned forward with what he hoped was exactly the right degree of alert eagerness. But it was the woman who spoke.

'We wanted to talk to you about Gaitonde's death.' Her voice was dry, firm. She hadn't missed a thing, had seen his automatic assumption.

'Yes,' Sartaj said. 'Yes, um, madam.'

'This is DCP Mathur,' Parulkar said. 'DCP Anjali Mathur. She is in charge of the investigation.' Sartaj could see that Parulkar was amused by her and him, by them and the ironies of the new world they were living in.

Anjali Mathur nodded, and spoke without looking at Parulkar. 'You received a call yesterday calling you to the location where you found Gaitonde?'

'Yes, madam.'

'Why you, inspector?'

'Madam?'

'Why do you think you received the call?'

'I don't know, madam.'

'Do you know Gaitonde from before?'

'No, madam.'

'Never met him?'

'No, madam.'

'Did you recognize the voice on the phone?'

'No, madam.'

'You were talking to him a long time before you got into the house.'

'We were waiting for the bulldozer, madam.'

'What did you talk about?'

73

'He talked, madam. He told one long story about how he started his career.'

'Yes, his career. I read your report. Did he say why he was in Mumbai?'

'No, madam.'

'Are you sure?'

'Yes, madam.'

'Did he say anything else about his purpose, about that house? Anything else at all?'

'No, madam. I'm sure.'

DCP Anjali Mathur had an interest in Gaitonde, and she was looking for details, but Sartaj had none to give her. He looked blandly at her and waited.

Finally she spoke. 'What about the dead woman? Do you know her?'

'No, madam. I don't know who she is. I wrote that in the report. Unknown female.'

'Do you have any ideas?'

There was Katekar's ready theory about filmi randis, but it was based on nothing more substantial than the dead woman's clothes. Sartaj had seen the same clothes at some very expensive clubs in the city. There was no reason to assume that the woman was a whore. 'No, madam.'

'Are you sure?'

'Yes, madam.' She was sceptical, steady in her evaluation of him, and he bore her examination evenly. He felt her come to a decision.

'Inspector, I need you to do some work for us. But first, you need to know that we are not CBI. We are with RAW. But this information is only for you. Nobody else needs to know it. Clear?'

It was not at all clear why RAW, the famed Research and Analysis Wing – with its covert mystique and its exotic reputation – should be sitting here in Parulkar's office. Ganesh Gaitonde was a big criminal, so yes, the Central Bureau of Investigation should investigate him, that made sense. But RAW was supposed to fight foreign enemies of the state outside India's borders. Why were they here, interested in Kailashpada? And this Anjali Mathur was an unlikely international secret agent. But perhaps that was the point. She had a round face, smooth, fair skin. There was no sindoor in her hair, but women no longer signalled their happily married state, Sartaj's ex-wife never

74

had. Sartaj had the uneasy feeling of wading into swiftly pulling waters, of being spun by completely unknown currents, and so he practised Parulkar's principle of polite sarkari obsequiousness. 'Yes, madam,' he said. 'Very clear.'

'Good,' she said. 'Find out. Find out who this woman was.'

'Yes, madam.'

'You would have the local knowledge, so find out. But our interest in this is to be kept in the strictest confidence. We want you to work on this for us, you and that constable, Katekar. Only you two. And only the two of you are aware of this assignment. Nobody else in the station is to know anything. Security concerns at the highest level are involved. Is that clear?'

'Yes, madam.'

'Keep the investigation as quiet as you can. First priority, you are to find out who this woman was, what her relationship with Gaitonde was, what she was doing in that house. Second, we need to know what Gaitonde was doing in Mumbai – why he was here, how long he had been here, what he has done while he was here.'

'Yes, madam.'

'Find anyone you can who worked with him. But proceed with discretion. We can't afford a big noise about this. Keep it quiet, whatever you do. It's natural for you to have an interest in Gaitonde after you found him. So if someone asks, just say you are clearing up a few loose ends. Clear?'

'Yes, madam.'

She slid a thick envelope across the desk. It was plain white, with a phone number in black ink centred on it. 'You report to me, and only me. This envelope contains copies of the photographs from the album we found in Gaitonde's desk. And photographs of the dead woman. Also, these are keys that were in the dead woman's pocket. One looks like a door key, the other is a car key, Maruti. The third key, I don't know what it's for.' The keys were on a steel hoop.

'Yes, madam.'

'Any doubts? Any questions?'

'No, madam.'

'Call me at the number on the envelope if you have any queries, or information to report. Parulkar Saab has told me that you are one of his most dependable officers. I am sure you will produce good results.'

'Parulkar Saab is kind. I will do my best.'

'Shabash,' Parulkar said, looking quite expressionless and unreadable. 'You may leave.'

Sartaj stood up, saluted him, took the envelope and walked smartly out. Outside, in the brilliant light of the morning, he blinked and stood near the railing for a moment, hefting the envelope in his hand. So the Gaitonde incident was not yet closed. Perhaps there were coups to be counted yet, and laurels to be won. Perhaps the great Ganesh Gaitonde still had some gifts to give to Sartaj. This was all very good, being chosen to conduct this secret investigation in the interests of national security, but Sartaj was uneasy. Anjali Mathur's urgency had somehow smelt of fear. Gaitonde was dead, but his terror lived on.

Sartaj stretched, swung his shoulders from side to side and swatted away a fly that buzzed close to his face. He hurried down the staircase and went to work.

*

Majid Khan's office was crowded with representatives of a local traders' association. They were protesting about the shocking police inaction in the face of the flood of extortion calls their members had received in the last few months. Sartaj took a chair at the back of the room and listened to Majid soothe and calm them and ask for their help in return. 'We can't do anything if you don't call us in, if you give in and pay them,' he said. 'But tell us in a timely fashion, and we will do our best.' Fifteen minutes of this and the traders finally all rose together, shifted their paunches about and left, but not before their president, a particularly lardy paan-chewing type, managed to mention that in addition to the burden of constant fear, he had to carry so many weighty expenses for his daughter's wedding next month. Even in these hard times, the wedding was going to have to be respectably expensive, these days people expected so much, and after all, MLA Saab was coming, Ranade Saab was coming. The trader-president bowed low over Majid's hand as he shook it, but nevertheless left behind the fact of his closeness to MLA Saab, and therefore the strong possibility of his being able to cause policemen's transfers to distant and dry postings.

'Bastards,' Majid said dispassionately when the office was emptied of traders.

'Bastards,' Sartaj said, getting up to sit in a chair in front of the desk. The wood was still warm from a trader, and he shifted uncomfortably in it.

76

'So I hear you had a very important early meeting with important CBI people.'

'Yes, yes.' That Majid knew about the meeting was not surprising, but Sartaj was still sometimes surprised by the speed at which news got around the station. 'That is what I wanted to consult you about, boss. Here.' Sartaj spread the photographs from Gaitonde's album across Majid's desk. 'Do you know any of these women?'

Majid stroked his moustache with both hands, testing it for flair and neatness. 'Actresses? Models?'

'Yes. Or something like that.'

Majid leafed through the photographs. 'To do with Gaitonde?'

'Yes. I'm just curious.'

'You are trying to be discreet, my friend. But don't tell me. I don't want to know.' Majid shook his head. 'One or two look familiar, but I couldn't tell you names. Bombay is full of girls like this. One looks like the next one. They come and they go.'

'And this one?' This one was the dead one, caught in close-up. She looked unmistakably dead, with her blue lips and inert bare shoulders and complete indifference to the camera watching from up close.

'This is the woman inside Gaitonde's house?' Majid said softly. 'Who they are hiding from the papers?'

'Yes.'

Majid gathered up the photographs and slid them back to Sartaj. He leaned back, and folded his arms across his chest. 'No, baba, I don't know. I don't know anything. And you be careful, Sardar-ji. Don't be brave. Parulkar Saab will try to protect you, but he's in trouble himself. Poor fellow, he's not a good enough Hindu for the Rakshaks.'

'Where does that leave you and me?' Sartaj said. 'I'm not a very good Hindu.'

Majid smiled, a big, toothy widening of his face which made him look like a boy, in spite of the moustache's awful grandeur. 'Sartaj,' he said, 'you're not even a good Sikh.'

Sartaj stood up. 'I must be good at something. But I don't know what that is yet.'

Majid gurgled out his long, slow laughter. 'Arre, Sartaj, you used to be good with women. So if you want to know about these women, ask other women.'

Sartaj waved a dismissive hand and left. But he couldn't deny that Majid – lumbering big-footed Pathan that he was – had the right idea

77

about asking women about women. It was early in the day, though, and women and national security would have to wait till later. There was a murder to investigate first.

'This whole area stinks,' Katekar said as he pulled the Gypsy into a narrow parking space between two trucks.

There certainly was a heavy smell that he and Sartaj had to endure as they walked down the road, but Sartaj thought it was a bit unfair of Katekar to single out this locality as especially stinky. The whole city stank at some time or the other. And after all, the citizens of Navnagar had to pile their rubbish somewhere. It was not their fault that the municipality's collection trucks came by only once a fortnight, to make a dent in this undulating ridge of garbage to their left. 'Patience, Maharaj,' Sartaj said. 'We'll be out of the stench soon.'

Katekar refused to let go of his sourness. Sartaj understood that he was being sullen not about the smell, but about being here in Navnagar at all. So a Bangladeshi boy had been murdered by his yaars, but so what? It was a minor case with minor possibilities, and it could easily be investigated on paper, just like the municipality lorries which on paper ran punctually every morning. Nobody would mind too much if this case was left undetected, and so it was silly to be out here, suffering odours and the odiousness of these foreigners. But Sartaj wanted to investigate. He told himself that it was proper officerly ambition to solve cases and get ahead, if only a little, but he knew that it was also just stubbornness. He didn't like people getting killed on his beat, and he hated the thought that murderers could just walk away. He knew that Katekar knew this, that it wasn't even idealism that drove Sartaj through certain cases. It was just a keeda that he had. They had been through this several times, with Sartaj doggedly following a lead and Katekar disapproving but staying close behind. Sartaj sometimes wondered why Katekar didn't just ask to work with someone else, or even for a transfer to some wetter posting. He needed the money, surely. And yet Katekar always went through the ritual of displeasure, and came along anyway. Now Sartaj stepped off the road and started up the slope, and he was sure that Katekar was to his left, a little behind and flanking.

Navnagar in the morning was marginally less crowded, but Sartaj still felt the kholis pressing in on him as he manoeuvred his way through the lanes. People stood aside and pressed up against the walls when they saw his uniform, and still he had to turn his torso to avoid brushing into them. In this city, the rich had some room, and the middle class had less, and the poor had none. This is why Papa-ji had retired to Pune, he said he wanted to be able to wake up and look out long, to feel as if there was still some empty space in the world. Papa-ji had found his little piece of lawn, and a vegetable garden behind the house, but Sartaj suspected that he had sometimes missed these tunnel-like streets of Mumbai's slums, these shacks that crept forward every year, each added-on room seizing ground and holding on. He certainly never stopped reminiscing about them.

Papa-ji had never told a story specifically about Navnagar, perhaps because nothing spectacular or particularly grotesque had ever taken place here. But he had told Sartaj often enough that the way to an apradhi was through the family. Find the mother and father, he had said, and you will find the thief, the murderer, the forger. So Sartaj and Katekar were in Navnagar, looking for the relatives of Bazil Chaudhary and Faraj Ali, who had killed their friend Shamsul Shah. As expected, the immediate families of the killers had fled. They had packed up as many of their belongings as they could take, and had locked their kholis, and had decamped on the day of the murder. Sartaj and Katekar broke the locks, and inside the kholis they found old mattresses, empty gunny sacks and an old colour photograph of Bazil Chaudhary's family. In the picture, Bazil Chaudhary was only a ten-year-old boy in a bright red shirt, but now Sartaj knew what the parents looked like. He had no doubt he would find them, sooner or later. They were poor, they would have to sell the kholi, they would depend on their connections in Navnagar to survive. It was much harder to disappear than people ordinarily thought. The task, for the policeman, was to pick up the strands of their lives, and follow along.

The interviews in Navnagar that morning yielded some information, none of it case-breaking but all of it quite relevant. The Bangladeshi neighbours of the victim and the apradhis were sullen and secretive, and declared they knew nothing. After Katekar loomed over them, and Sartaj threatened a trip to the police station and quick deportation, they allowed that they maybe knew a little, a very insignificant little. Shamsul – the dead one – and Bazil both worked as couriers, and Faraj took temporary jobs here and there. Yet for the last few months they all three had a lot of money, and nobody knew why or how.

In the empty kholis Sartaj and Katekar had searched, there was scant evidence of money. The families of the apradhis had taken their luxuries with them. But in the dead boy's house, there was a brand-new colour television, and a large gas stove in the kitchen area, and shiny steel pots, and his father now confessed that the departed son had bought a new kholi a few days previously.

'He was a good boy,' Nurul Shah said.

This kholi was very small, only one room divided by a faded red sheet. Behind the curtain, Sartaj could hear women rustling and whispering. They needed more space, and the good boy had obtained it for them. The family had been about to move into the new kholi when their son had been cruelly taken from them. 'But,' Sartaj said, 'a big new place, that must have cost a lot of money.'

Nurul Shah lowered his head and watched the floor. He had thinning white hair and taut shoulders toughened by a lifetime of hard work.

'Your neighbours say your family is suddenly rich,' Sartaj said. 'They said your son treated his sisters well. They said he bought new spectacles for his mother.'

Nurul Shah's hands were clamped around each other, and the tips of the fingers now whitened from the pressure. He began to weep, making no sound at all.

'I think,' Sartaj said, 'if I look behind the curtain, I will find other expensive things. Where did your son get all this money from?'

'Eh,' Katekar rumbled, 'Inspector Saab asked you a question. Answer him.'

Sartaj put a hand on Nurul Shah's shoulder, and held on past the man's sudden panic at the touch. 'Listen,' he said very softly. 'Nothing is going to happen to you or your family. I am not interested in bothering you. But your son is dead. If you don't tell me everything, I can't help you. I can't find the bastards who did it.'

The man was scared of the policemen in his home, of what had happened and what could happen, but he was trying to find the courage to speak up.

'Your son was doing some business, some hera-pheri. If you tell me everything, I will find them. Otherwise they will escape.' Sartaj shrugged, and straightened up.

'I don't know, saab,' Nurul Shah said. 'I don't know.' He was shivering and bent over. 'I asked Shamsul what he was doing, but he never told me anything.'

'He and those two, Bazil and Faraj, were doing something together?'

'Yes, saab.'

'Was there anyone else?'

'There was Reyaz Bhai.'

'Another friend of theirs?'

'He was older.'

'Full name?'

'I only know that much: Reyaz Bhai.'

'What does he look like?'

'I never met him.'

'Where does he live?'

'Four lanes down, saab. On the main-road side.'

'He lives here in Navnagar, in the Bengali Bura, and you never met him?'

'No, saab. He didn't come out of his house much.'

'Why?'

'He is a Bihari, saab,' Nurul Shah said, as if that were an explanation.

But the Bihari was gone from his kholi as well, and there was already a new family living there. Sartaj and Katekar found the landlord, a portly Tamil who lived on the other side of Navnagar. He had found the room unoccupied on the day of the murder, and had promptly cleaned it out the next day and rented it again. No, he didn't know anything about this Reyaz except that he had paid in advance, and was no trouble. What did Reyaz look like? Tall, thin, young face but with full white hair. Yes, completely white hair. The man could be forty, fifty, anything. Spoke smoothly, was definitely educated. He had left nothing in the kholi except some books, which the landlord had sold that very afternoon to a paper and raddi shop on the main road. No, he didn't know what the books were.

So Sartaj and Katekar stood at the edge of Navnagar, below the small world it contained. 'All right,' Sartaj said, looking at the terraced, untidy descent of the rusted tin roofs. 'So this Bihari is the boss.'

'He plans everything. These three, these are his boys.' Katekar wiped his face with an enormous blue handkerchief, and then the back of his neck and his forearms. 'They make money.'

'Doing what? Fraud? Robbery? Or are they shooters for some gang?'

'Maybe. But I've never heard of that, Bangladeshis in a company.'

'These boys grew up here, maybe they're more Indian than anything else. But this Bihari is the key. He's older, he's professional. He lives quietly, doesn't show off his money, he clears out fast and first when there's trouble. Wherever he is, those boys are going to be.'

'Yes, saab,' Katekar said. He put away his handkerchief. 'So we find the Bihari.'

'We find the Bihari.'

Pursuing the Bihari had to wait while Sartaj fulfilled certain obligations. Policing was often a scattered business that required setting aside one job to attend to another. What Sartaj had to do now was strictly unofficial and had nothing to do with any case, and he had to do it alone. He dropped Katekar at the station and drove south to Santa Cruz. He was to meet Parulkar in a sparkling new building just off Linking Road, near Swaraj Ice-cream. Sartaj parked behind the building and marvelled at the green marble in the lobby, and the sleek steel lift. The apartment Parulkar was waiting in was supposed to belong to Parulkar's niece. This niece worked at a bank, and her husband was in import-export, but they were barely out of their twenties, and the apartment was very large and very expensive. The gold letters on the nameplate spelled out 'Namjoshi', but Sartaj was certain that the three-bedroom apartment actually belonged to Parulkar. Certainly, the ease with which he sat cross-legged on a huge sofa in the drawing room, like a rotund, khaki-clad sage, suggested a man in charge of his own prime real estate and his own destiny.

'Come, come, Sartaj,' Parulkar said. 'We must hurry.'

'Sorry, sir. The traffic is bad.'

'The traffic is bad all the time.' But Parulkar was not reprimanding Sartaj, he was fatherly and patient, and only mindful of his own hectic schedule. He pointed at a frosty glass of water on the table. Sartaj took off the silver cover and drank, and followed Parulkar across the shadowed breadth of the drawing room, to a bedroom.

Parulkar shut the door behind them and padded around the high white bed to the other side of the room. He opened a cupboard, and hefted out a black duffle-bag. 'It's forty today.'

'Yes, sir,' Sartaj said. Parulkar meant forty lakhs. These were Parulkar's recent unofficial earnings, which Sartaj would move over to Worli, and hand over to Parulkar's consultant, Homi Mehta, who would funnel it to a Swiss account and charge only a very reasonable commission. Sartaj ferried Parulkar's money every few weeks, and he had long ago stopped being surprised by the amounts. Parulkar was, after all, the commissioner for a very rich zone. It was a very wet posting, and Parulkar drank deep from its burbling fount of money. He was an avid earner, but not greedy, and he was very careful about the disposal of the money. His personal assistant, Sardesai, handled the collection of the money, but Sardesai knew nothing of what happened to the money once he had given it to Parulkar. Parulkar passed it over to Sartaj, who moved it to Mehta, the consultant. Sartaj only knew that then, somehow, the money disappeared from India and reappeared abroad, where it sat safe and accumulated interest in hard currency.

Parulkar emptied the cash on to the bedspread and handed the bag to Sartaj. 'Eighty bundles of five-hundred-rupee notes,' he said. They trusted each other completely, but this was their ritual each time money went to the consultant. Sartaj gathered up a hefty brick of money and put it into the bag. He would do this eighty times while Parulkar watched, and then they would have an agreed-upon count.

'What are you going to do about this Gaitonde business?' Parulkar said, watching Sartaj's hands.

'I was going to ask you about that, sir.'

Parulkar pulled his legs up on to the bed and took up his meditative posture again. 'I don't know that much about the Gaitonde company. There was a fellow called Bunty who ran their business in Mumbai. Smart fellow, Suleiman Isa's boys shot him, put him in a wheelchair, but he was Gaitonde's trusted man, he stayed in charge from his wheelchair. There was a time when you could just go to Gopalmath and meet Bunty, but after he got shot he went into hiding. Ask Mehta for this Bunty's number, he will have it.' Mehta, as a money manager, was neutral in the gang wars. All sides used his services impartially, and valued him equally.

'Yes, sir.'

'But of course your best intelligence on Gaitonde may come from his enemies. Let me make a couple of calls, and I will get you in touch with someone. Someone who is very, let us say, knowledgeable.'

'Thank you, sir.' What Parulkar meant was that he would use his links inside the Suleiman Isa company to get someone to talk to Sartaj. Since Parulkar's connections with that company went back years, even decades, the source he would provide for Sartaj would no doubt be a highly placed one. So this was a big favour, one more in a long string of kindnesses that Parulkar had bestowed on Sartaj. 'Forty, sir,' Sartaj said, putting the last stack into the bag. 'Sir, what is this all about? Gaitonde is dead, why do they want to know about him now?'

'I don't know, Sartaj. But be careful. What I understand from my sources is that the IB is also involved in this Gaitonde business.'

'IB, sir? Why?'

'Who knows? But it seems this whole investigation is actually a joint operation. IB is letting RAW handle the details, so RAW is talking to you and me. When these big agencies get involved in a case, mere policemen have to watch their backs. Do your work, but don't try to be a hero for them.'

Sartaj zipped the bag. So it was not only international agents who were interested in Gaitonde's demise. The Intelligence Bureau, with its domestic counter-intelligence purview, was also curious. It all made Sartaj feel quite small. 'Of course not, sir. I am never a hero. I don't have the height.'

Parulkar rocked back and forth, gurgling with laughter. 'Nowadays even very short people are becoming heroes, Sartaj. The world has changed, my dear fellow.'

Sartaj thought for a moment that Parulkar would recite a couplet, but Parulkar was in a hurry, and he left it at 'my dear fellow' and sent his cash and Sartaj on their way. He only said, 'My regards to Bhabhi-ji,' and raised a hand, and that was all.

As he drove to Worli, Sartaj thought about Papa-ji. Most people remembered Sartaj's father as a tall man, but he had been only five feet seven and a half. His ramrod posture, his muscular arms and glorious moustache and, above all, his always-perfect turban, all these gave him a stature that magnified him in memory. Sartaj, his son, was a full inch taller, but he knew that he was not nearly as impressive, in his person or reputation, as Papa-ji. Papa-ji had been honest. He had insisted always on the crispest turban, on the finest suit, but he had managed to maintain his style on his wages, and had worn the same blue double-breasted blazer for a decade's worth of weddings and official functions. After his death, Sartaj had found the blazer in a trunk, carefully mothballed and wrapped in crisp paper. And now, long after Papa-ji's death, strangers still said to Sartaj, 'Oh, you are

Sardar Saab's son? He was a good man.' A year ago, in Crawford Market, a diamond merchant had patted Sartaj sadly on his shoulder, and said, 'Beta, your father was the only honest policeman I have ever known.' Sartaj had nodded, and muttered, 'Yes, he was a good man,' and walked away, his shoulders stiff.

Now Sartaj wheeled right towards the sea-front, then pulled a fast U-turn in front of a bus and came coasting back to the pavement. The general provision store to his right was crowded with uniformed children buying ice-creams. They looked as if they were in the third or fourth, but their school-bags were huge and very heavy. They were too young to know yet that medical school positions were bought and sold, that entrance papers for management schools were leaked to those who could afford it. Sartaj pulled Parulkar's duffle-bag from behind the front seat and walked slowly through the kids. When he had been their age, he had known Parulkar already for a year and more. Parulkar had then been a young, slim sub-inspector, a favourite chela of Papa-ji's. Papa-ji had liked Parulkar, had thought him intelligent and hard-working and dedicated. He had often brought Parulkar home for dinner, he said, 'The boy is unmarried and needs to eat good home food once in a while.' But Ma had never really taken to Parulkar. She was civil enough, but she didn't trust him from the start. 'Just because he listens to your stories endlessly you think he's your devoted bhakt,' she said to Papa-ji. 'But mark my words, these Marathas are too clever.' It was no use telling her that Parulkar was not a Maratha, but in fact a Brahmin. She said, 'Whatever he is, he's a sharp one.' Her dislike for Parulkar had intensified with his steady ascent through the ranks, and when he had passed Papa-ji's rank and gone beyond, she had stopped talking about Parulkar altogether. She called him only 'that man', and didn't even argue when Papa-ji spoke about men's destinies, and how each one of us should be grateful with what Vaheguru had given.

Sartaj angled up the narrow stairs next to the general provision store, which led up to Mehta's tiny office. Mehta had worked in these four little cubicles all his life, and he lived close by, in a spacious but simple apartment overlooking the sea. He was a neat, discreet Parsi gent, dressed now, as always, in complete white. 'Arre, Sartaj, come, come,' he said, reaching across the table with a fragile hand for a quick, limp shake. He was thin, but elegant, and Sartaj always admired the cut of his fine grey hair. Homi Mehta reminded him somehow of the black-and-white movies that ran on television on Sunday afternoons, it was easy to imagine him sweeping down the seafront in a black Victoria.

'This is from Saab,' Sartaj said, and put the duffle-bag on the desk.

'Yes, yes,' Mehta said. 'But when are you going to bring me some of your own cash, young man? You need to save for the future.'

'I am a poor man, Uncle,' Sartaj said. 'What to save, when there is hardly enough to survive?'

This was a conversation that Sartaj and Mehta had every time Sartaj visited, but today Mehta wasn't willing to let it go so soon. 'Arre, what are you telling me? The man who got Ganesh Gaitonde has not got even a little money?'

'There was no reward.'

'Some people are saying that you got a good amount from Dubai to put a bullet in Gaitonde's head.'

'Uncle, I didn't kill Gaitonde. He shot himself. And nobody paid me.'

'All right, baba. I didn't say anything. People, you know, people are saying it.'

Mehta was counting Parulkar's money, laying the bricks in orderly stacks on the right-hand side of the desk. He was a meticulous man, and scrupulous in his accounting. A long time ago, during one of their first meetings, he had told Sartaj, 'In a world of dishonesty, I am an entirely honest man.' He had said it without pride, as just a statement of fact. He had explained to Sartaj that finally all the movement of money in and out of the country depended on the consultants. They were also called 'managers', in Delhi they were 'headmasters', but whatever name they were given, everything depended on their honesty. The money came from secret deals and graft, bribery and embezzlement, extortion and murder, and the managers took care of it with discretion and integrity. They made it vanish and they made it reappear. They were the secret magicians who were crucial to all business, and therefore they knew everyone.

'Uncle, I need some help,' Sartaj said.

'Tell me.'

'Parulkar Saab said you may know how I can get in touch with one of Gaitonde's men.'

'Which one?'

'Bunty.'

The old man gave nothing away. He wiped his fingers on a tissue, and started another stack. 'I will have to ask him,' he said. 'What should I tell him?'

'I just want to talk to him. I want to ask him some questions about Gaitonde.'

'You want to ask him some questions about Gaitonde.' Mehta nodded, and squared away the last stack of money. 'Okay. You have a new mobile, write down the number.'

Sartaj grinned, and wrote on a pad. Old man Mehta didn't miss a thing, even the small bulge in his breast pocket. Sartaj had finally succumbed and bought a mobile phone, after years of insisting they were too expensive and the rates were too high. He had paid too much, eventually, for a tiny Motorola because it was so silvery and stylish. The phone was still shiny and unused, and he hadn't given the number to anyone yet, but Homi Mehta was ancient and wise and keen-eyed.

'Here, Uncle,' Sartaj said. 'Thank you.'

'Okay. Forty total,' Mehta said, patting the money.

Sartaj stood up. 'Right. I will see you next time.'

'Next time, bring me something to save for you. Think of your old age.'

Sartaj raised a hand, and left Mehta and the money. There had been a time, when Sartaj had still been married to Megha, when Mehta always told him to save for his future children. After the divorce, Mehta had stopped doing that, and had started with these reminders of age and passing time. I must really be starting to look old, Sartaj thought.

There was a different group of children at the store now, older ones in their early teens, more sophisticated and self-conscious than the lot before. They drank Pepsis and Cokes and whispered to each other. Sartaj walked half-way to the jeep, then came back to the store and bought a Chocobar. There were other, fancier ice-creams available nowadays, but Sartaj liked that old Kwality taste of slightly oily chocolate with the vanilla underneath, it was the flavour of his childhood. The teenagers nudged each other: don't miss the funny sardar policeman chomping at a Chocobar. Sartaj smiled and walked on, and by the time he reached the jeep he was licking at the bare wooden stick. He crunched it between his teeth, as he had always done as a boy, flipped it away and drove.

The rush-hour traffic was coiling around the streets now, stiffening into a congealed mass. Sartaj settled himself in for the long ride. There was a violent shimmer in the air above the metal of the car roofs, and now a sudden quiet as the drivers switched off their engines to wait out the crush. Sartaj peeled his sweaty back away from the seat, and with his forearms on his knees and head hanging he stared at the dusty black of his shoes. The sun gathered its hard heat against his shoulder and neck, but there was nowhere to escape from it. Through the window a bus-driver watched him dispassionately, and when Sartaj met his glance he looked away, shifting in his high seat. Beyond him, a mannequin thrust her hip forward behind glass. Sartaj followed the shop windows, and they receded into the glare of the sky, and he imagined the immense length of the island, all of it stuck and still in this multitudinous evening rush, clogged and moving in jerks and ricocheting little jumps. He sighed, then took the phone out of his pocket and dialled.

'Ma?' he said.

'Sartaj.'

'Peri pauna, Ma.'

'Jite raho, beta. I read about you in the paper.'

'Yes, Ma.' The rumble of engines being switched on swept up the road, and Sartaj turned his ignition over.

'Such a big criminal you caught, why was there no picture of you?'

'Ma, the work is important,' Sartaj said, amused at her and at his own pomposity. 'Not photos in the paper.' He waited expectantly for her sharp retort, but she had already moved on.

'Where are you calling from?'

'Where? Mumbai, Ma.'

'No, I mean where in Bumbai?'

She didn't miss anything, this policeman's wife. Sartaj said, 'I'm driving back from Worli.'

'Oho, so you got a mobile at last.'

'Yes, Ma.' She herself was indifferent to technological advances, and said she didn't want a VCR because she wouldn't know how to work it, but she had long wanted Sartaj to have a mobile.

'What is the number?' she said.

Sartaj gave it to her, and added, 'Remember, no calls during duty hours.'

She laughed. 'I was doing duty before you were born. And always, you are the one who always calls me from work. Like now.'

'Yes, yes.' She would be sitting on the sofa in the small living room, her legs curled up under her, holding the large black handset up to her ear with a small hand. He could hear her smile. She had lost weight this last year, and despite the fine wrinkles and white hair, she sometimes looked like the slim young girl Sartaj had seen in photographs. 'But I'm not working now. I'm just caught in traffic.'

'That Bumbai is impossible to live in now. So expensive. And too many people.'

This was true, but where else was there to go? Maybe many years later, there would be a small house for Sartaj somewhere else. But right now he found it hard to imagine being away permanently from this messy, impossible city. A small holiday, now and then, was all Sartaj needed. 'This Saturday, Ma, I'll come to Pune.'

'Good. I haven't seen you for months.'

Sartaj had gone to Pune exactly four weeks ago, but he knew better than to argue. 'Do you need anything from here?'

She didn't want anything for herself, but she had a list of items for mausis and taus and nephews and nieces. It was no use telling Ma that these things were now surely available in a good-sized city like Pune, because she had specific Mumbai shops that were to be patronized, and instructions to be given to certain shopkeepers she had known for decades. Sartaj always arrived in Pune with a bag for his clothes and a suitcase full of child-sized clothes and mithai and salty snacks and shampoos for Ma to give away to her numerous near and dear. She lived close to family in Pune, and Sartaj trusted her to keep him updated on the network of relatives that stretched all the way up to Punjab and beyond. He thought of her as inextricably embedded in that family, while he himself was distanced from it, not quite separated but gone away somehow, like a planet that had spun out too far from its sun. He liked to listen to her stories of family feuds and ancient tragedies, as long as he could avoid being drawn into their fatal gravity and made a participant. Reminded by a book of nursery rhymes she wanted Sartaj to bring, she started a tale now, about her chacha who used to insist that he could speak English. Sartaj had heard it many times before, but he liked listening to it now, and laughed in all the proper places.

At Siddhi Vinayak he said goodbye to Ma, and settled back into the seat, smiling. It was good to look forward to the trip to Pune. A crowd swirled around the entrance to the Siddhi Vinayak lane, a host of worshippers bringing their entreaties and supplications and gratitude. The temple rose to its golden spire, carrying its huge symmetries easily to the sky. Sartaj wondered if Ganesh Gaitonde had some other place where he went to from the city, some town or village he called his native place. He would ask Katekar.

Ganesh Gaitonde had said something about God and belief at the end. By now Gaitonde would know for sure whether there was a God to believe in, or not. Sartaj didn't particularly care about Gaitonde's soul, but he knew it was time to go and look at his body, his and the dead woman's. He had been avoiding it, but he would have to go. Sartaj cursed Ganesh Gaitonde, and drove on.

The next morning, Katekar protested about the visit to Gaitonde, as Sartaj had expected. The man was dead, Katekar said, and he and the woman would remain dead, so there was no need to go near them now, none at all.

'You can stay outside,' Sartaj told him. 'But you should be used to dead bodies by now.'

The morgue was an ancient sandstone building, pitted and stained but still handsome with its tall arches and flowery stonework. It stood, green-shaded, under a huge banyan tree at the rear of KD Hospital. Sartaj dropped Katekar off at the gate of the hospital, drove around the building and parked near a paan-stained wall. For all his rationalism, Katekar had a horror of the morgue, its doctor and attendants, the emerald light under the banyan tree. He said the whole place smelt, that he could smell it from across the hospital compound, that there was a yellow miasma that slid into your clothes and sank into your pockets and stayed. Sartaj rather enjoyed this unexpected upsurge of superstition deep within the stolid frame of Ganpatrao Popat Katekar, man of science. It gave Sartaj something to point to when Katekar affected a superior sneer at Sartaj's various romanticisms.

Sartaj went past the enquiry window, with its small cluster of anxious men who had come looking for missing relatives and friends. He went down a dark corridor and through the double glass doors marked 'No Entrance'. An attendant in brown shorts and shirt sat behind a scratched metal desk, under muzzy tube-lights. He salaamed Sartaj, who took a deep breath, blinked once and went through another pair of swinging doors, of green-painted wood this time. The room on the other side was quite large, big as a good-sized wedding hall, well-lit from two square skylights and two rows of tube-lights. The floor was smooth brown stone, sloping inwards to a square drain. There were two brown bodies, both male, naked on the stone tables to the left. The top of the far one's skull had been removed, with a precise round cut that made him a cartoon character whose head had come unscrewed. His brain sat in a tidy grey mound on a tray next to his elbow. And here, on the right, was Dr Chopra, analyst at the abyss, working efficiently. He was scooping out intestines into a large tray. Sartaj turned his head away.

'Dr Chopra?'

'Ah, Sartaj. Wait, wait.'

Sartaj watched the wall, followed the cracks in the grey plaster up to the ceiling and then back down again. And then the rusted bars on the closed window, he counted them and examined their thickness. Meanwhile there were small sucking sounds to his right, and a little wet grinding. The first of the many times Sartaj had come in here, into Dr Chopra's dissection house, he had made himself look, on the principle that a policeman must gaze steadfastly at everything, anything, what the world is truly made of, you must know it all unflinchingly, without repugnance or perverse fascination. And he had seen what Dr Chopra had exposed, had been able to look at it, and it wasn't that horrifying after all, just the complicated inner clockwork of the body, a fluid machinery possessed of an intricate, severe harmony. But the surfaces of the corpses followed him and stayed with him into his sleep, the light ring of skin on the third finger of a fisted hand, the tribal tattoo on a woman's chin, the crimson flecks of lipstick on a lower lip, faint but unmistakable. He accumulated fragments of the dead, tiny memories of their lives that cost something to carry, and finally he decided he no longer had a young man's pride, that he would save his will for work, for his own cases. So he no longer looked.

'Done,' Dr Chopra said.

Sartaj heard the snap of rubber gloves, and he turned, keeping his head tilted up. He saw the dead man's face, and stared for a moment. Then he saw the thick thatch of Dr Chopra's hair. The doctor was the hairiest man Sartaj had ever met. It was just past twelve, and Dr Chopra's cheeks and jaw were already shaded dark, and there was a thick black mat of hair that came up from his chest, half-way up his neck. He was washing his hands in a basin.

91

'Doctor saab,' Sartaj said, 'I need to see Gaitonde and his female friend.'

'Fine,' said Dr Chopra. 'They're in the cold room.'

'Post-mortem done already?'

'Arre, Gaitonde was a big bhai, yes? He and his friend got jumped ahead in the queue.' Dr Chopra laughed, and it was quite genuine, full of pleasure. 'You want me to get the boys to haul them out of the cold room? Quicker if we go there.'

There was a challenge in his stance, in the raising of his bushy, overhanging eyebrow: if you can take it, Mr Policeman. The cold room was what Katekar absolutely hated. He had been inside only once, when he and Sartaj had been looking for the body of a khabari. Katekar had stepped into the cold room, put a hand to his mouth and turned and walked out, walked out to the banyan tree. Sartaj had stayed inside and found the body they were looking for. Sartaj had done it before, he could do it now. He shrugged. 'Cold room is fine.'

A shaded walkway led to the cold room, through the obliterating afternoon glare. Sartaj squinted, and walked, and now there was no avoiding the smell. They passed through a door, into a long dark passageway, and it pressed up against his cheeks. The windows were closed against the heat, against the throbbing of the sun, and the air inside the entryway was engorged with the ripe, round exhalations from the two rows of bodies stacked against the walls, in sheets on double racks. The sheets were damp and the ground below the racks was slimy, slick.

Sartaj nodded at the attendants sitting at the desk at the end of the corridor. He could feel a hiccup curling itself at the back of his throat, and he didn't want to open his mouth.

'Inspector saab,' one attendant said, rising. 'After a long time.' He had been reading a Hindi novel, and his friend was writing a letter. They both stood up.

Sartaj spoke carefully, enunciating. 'It smells worse than last time,' he said as he went past the desk.

'Arre, saab,' the attendant with the novel said, 'wait until the air-conditioners break again. Then you'll really smell something.'

'Wait until it rains and the leaks start coming through the walls,' the other one said with large satisfaction. 'Then you'll really have fun.'

There is a certain pleasure we take in thinking about how bad it gets, Sartaj thought, and then in imagining how it will inevitably get worse. And still we survive, the city stumbles on. Maybe one day it'll all just fall apart, and there was a certain gratification in that thought too. Let the maderchod blow.

Dr Chopra nodded at his attendants. The door to the cold room was shiny steel, very sleek and new and promising high technology and sterility. The fiction-reading attendant touched the heavy door-handle, touched his throat and mouthed a mantra. He grabbed the handle and leaned back, and the door swung open. 'Come,' Dr Chopra said.

And inside there were the jumbled rows of bodies that Sartaj remembered. They lay naked on the tiled floor, jammed up against each other, shoulder to shoulder, shoulder over shoulder, from one side of the long room to the other. Each was stitched up the front, in broad looping knots in thick black thread, where the long incision had been made for the post-mortem. Rusty, dark skin, gone as densely opaque as mud, spiky, petrified pubic hair. Sartaj was thinking, it's not really cold in here. They call it a cold room but there are restaurants that are colder, the upstairs room of the Delite Dance Bar is colder. He could hear the dull, halting rush of the air-conditioner.

'Ladies are over here,' Dr Chopra said.

In this channel, past all carnality, the decencies were preserved. The ladies were piled on top of each other in a kind of small cabin to the left, with its own metal door. The attendants reached in and shifted the bodies around, tugged and pulled, and something knocked on the door and made a happy bonging. Sartaj found himself concerned with the attendants' hands, they're handling all that without gloves, he hoped they washed their hands afterwards.

'Saab,' the letter-writer said. They had found her.

Sartaj stepped back. His shoes were sticking to the floor.

There was the usual long incision up her front. Her lips had turned the cracked pale blue of old candles, and had drawn back from her upper teeth. The autopsy photo in the file had flattened out her cheekbones, and had made invisible the sharp nose. But the nose had been broken once, there was a small dent in it. In death she was plain, but there was muscle on her shoulders and along her flanks, and Sartaj saw her in a dancer's jaunty stance, glowing and proud of her figure.

'Unknown female deceased,' Dr Chopra read from a long sheet. 'Five foot three and a half inches, 110 pounds, black hair to shoulder length, eyes black, four-inch scar on right knee, had last eaten about eight hours prior to death, cause of death single gunshot trauma to sternum, bullet passed upwards at an angle and exited at T4, causing extensive damage to lungs, spinal cord. Death was instantaneous.'

Instantaneous death. Sartaj wondered if she had seen it coming, the raised barrel and Gaitonde's reddened eye above. 'No distinguishing marks besides the scar?'

'None.'

'All right,' Sartaj said. Sometimes the body of the deceased taught you things that you didn't know before, but this had been a short history. She was unmarked by life, mainly.

'And Gaitonde?' Dr Chopra said, turning.

'Gaitonde. Yes.'

Sartaj followed Dr Chopra down the room, in the small lane between the bodies. There were flows of liquids across the floor, light albumen runs and thick blackish discharges. Sartaj carefully placed one foot, then the other. Gaitonde lay in the middle of a row, indistinguishable from the others but for the ruin of his head. The exposed inner flesh had turned black. 'Five foot six, 151 pounds, he's survived two bullet wounds.' Dr Chopra pointed. 'Interestingly enough, one was in his buttocks. The great Gaitonde must have been running when he got that one. The other wound was in his left shoulder, here.'

Sartaj bent over Gaitonde, and saw that he had a fine profile, with a noble brow. He was born to be a king, Sartaj thought, or maybe a sage. He must have looked in the mirror and wondered what he would become.

Dr Chopra was stroking the hair on the back of his right hand. An air-conditioner kicked itself on with a low rumble, and the fetid smell surged up from Gaitonde and the rest of them. 'Thanks, doctor saab,' Sartaj said, and he had had enough. He straightened and went, going fast. He turned sideways to go past the attendants, who were lifting the female deceased back through the cabin door. He went by them. Light seeped through the angles of the main doorway, and in the brightness Sartaj saw on the floor a tattered rind of black flesh, a small piece of jaw attached to three teeth. He stepped over it and fled into the sunlight.

'Are you all right?' Dr Chopra said.

Sartaj was standing by the banyan tree, one hand on its grainy bark, breathing. 'Why can't you keep that gaandu place cold? Why?'

'The air-conditioners break down, the wiring is old and the fuses blow, and the population is too large. The morgue is too small.'

Yes, it was unfair to blame the good Dr Chopra. It was in no way his fault, that there wasn't enough money, too little electricity, too small a space and far too many dead. 'Sorry, Doc,' Sartaj said. He made a large gesture in the air, an awkward movement that took in everything. Dr Chopra nodded and smiled. 'Thanks,' Sartaj said.

'I hope seeing them was useful.'

'Yes, yes. Very useful.' Sartaj said this, but as he was walking to the jeep he wasn't sure. Now the desire to see the bodies, which only a little while ago had seemed so coherent, seemed bizarre. What had he learnt? Sartaj had no idea. It had all been a waste of time. He was eager to be away, back at the station, but at the jeep he found himself unable to get in. He stepped over a border made of painted half-bricks into what was left of a garden, found a patch of dead brown grass and wiped the bottom of his shoes, rubbed them back and forth on the grass until the stalks broke with small clicking sounds and his grinding heart settled and calmed.

Shalini was cooking by the time Katekar got home. She cleaned at a doctor's house in Saat Bungla, but at only one house, unlike some others who had three jhadoo-katka jobs, or four. It was good to have the money from the doctor, but they had decided that she needed to be home when the boys came in, at home in the afternoons and early evenings so they could feel her presence and she could keep an eye out. But the money was very welcome. And it was good to know a doctor with a clinic, for times of special need. Katekar put down his mat and pillow. Shalini was cooking, and he liked the stir of her motions, they lulled him, the tinkle of the spoons, the flurrying back-and-forth rush of the knife, the fast bubbling of the flames on the stove, the leaping sizzle when she flung in a fistful of goda masala. He was comfortable, with the quiet stirring of air from the table-fan set on 'Low'. He napped easily in the day, stored sleep like a camel hoarded water. In the life of a constable, this was necessary. He took a long breath.

When he awoke it was dark inside the kholi, and there was the bustle of evening in the lane outside. He turned his wrist, and it was six-thirty. 'Where are the boys?' he said. He didn't need to turn his head to know Shalini was sitting in the doorway.

'Playing,' she said.

He sat up, rubbed his eyes. The stove rattled as she pumped it, and then he saw her face, suddenly bronzed out of the shade. 'They're fighting,' he said, and he didn't need to say that he didn't mean the boys.

'Yes.' Amritrao Pawar and his wife Arpana lived two kholis down, and they had been fighting continuously, as nearly as their neighbours could tell, for eleven years. Four years after their marriage, Pawar had acquired another woman. Arpana had left, gone back to her parents, and had been reassured that it was merely a passing thing, that Pawar had quit the other woman, and that it was all over. She had come back, but then the other woman had had a child, and now Pawar maintained two establishments. He and Arpana refused to part, refused to come closer or divide, they fought and fought. For Arpana's neighbours, the other woman was still the other woman, Arpana had not called her by name in eleven years, and Pawar never spoke about her.

Katekar and Shalini drank their tea seated across from each other. She had the kaande pohe he liked on a plate between them. 'I spoke to Bharti yesterday.'

Bharti was her younger sister, who was married to a scrap-metal dealer in Kurla. There was apparently much money in scrap metal, because Bharti always came to visit in a new sari. Last year, she had come the day before Gudi-Padwa, wearing new gold bangles of a conspicuous thickness and glow, and bearing not only batasha garlands but also large, fragrant boxes of puranpoli and chirote for the boys. Katekar had watched his sons lick their glistening, sweet fingers, and he had watched his wife's face as she had put away the boxes and the new sari for herself, and he had marvelled at how generosity can be the subtlest of all weapons, and especially between sisters. So now he took a long sip of his tea. 'Yes?' he said.

'They're buying the next kholi also,' Shalini said.

'In the chawl?'

'Where else?'

The retort had come quick and sharp, and she was not backing down from his quizzical look. So now her sister and brother-in-law would tear down walls, combine rooms, have a home that was expansive enough to contain their sense of themselves. 'They have three children,' Katekar said. 'They need the space.'

Shalini snorted and picked up the plate of biscuits. 'What, those little taporis need a palace to live in?' She got up and began to gather spoons, rattle the bowl about. 'Bharti has been a wastrel since she was this high. Those two never think about the future. Their children will turn out bad, you wait and see.'

She loved her nieces and nephew, smothered them with hugs and unbent more with them than with her own sons, and Katekar knew this well. So he put on his shirt, drew on his pants. She had the pot scoured and hung up already. Katekar grinned at her. 'I heard a joke yesterday,' he said.

'What?'

'Once Laloo Prasad Yadav met some Japanese businessmen who had come to Bihar. The Japanese businessmen said to him, "Chief-minister-ji, your state has great resources. Give us a free hand for three years and we'll turn Bihar into the next Japan." Laloo looked very surprised. He said, "And you Japanese are supposed to be efficient! Three years? Give me a free hand for three days and I'll turn Japan into the next Bihar."'

'Not very funny.' But she was smiling.

'Arre,' Katekar said, 'your family just never had a sense of humour.'

This was a theme they had explored for years: his family was extravagant but fun-loving, hers was thrifty but boring. Variations on this theory took in the boys, Rohit had gone on Katekar, Mohit on his mother. Now Shalini was thinking of her sons. 'Will you be done early enough to stop at Patil's?'

Patil was the tailor who had a shop two lanes down, tucked into a long narrow building that stood on what had once been a broken wall and an unused gutter. Patil had filled in the gutter, closed off the rear, put on a roof, and now he sat two full-time tailors at sewing machines. He made uniforms for the boys, good ones, strong enough that Mohit could wear what Rohit grew out of. 'Not today,' Katekar said. 'I'll pick it up tomorrow. One half-pant, one shirt, yes?'

'Yes,' Shalini said. Her irritation had melted away. She liked that he remembered, he could see that.

Outside, the clouds sat in luxurious orange tiers. It was too early for rain, but Katekar could feel it coming. The sky was histrionically spectacular, but nobody was stopping to look at it. Katekar walked briskly, cutting an efficient loop to go to the bus-stop by way of the play-ground. He was thinking about sex. He had been quite unfaithful in the years immediately after he and Shalini had been married, before Rohit had been born. Looking back now, it seemed like a feverish mad-ness, the visits he had made to dance bars and the money he had spent on girls, on grimy rooms, on taxis late at night. Shalini had been hardly more than a girl herself then, and he had lowered his head into the arc of her neck nightly, and found in the clutch of her hands on his shoul-ders an answering hunger, more carefully quiet than his own but as insistent, as fierce. And still he had gone to other women, randis. There was no reason for it but an urgency he felt at the offering of unknown, anonymous bellies under cheap, diaphanous nylon. It was a kind of common madness, accepted by the men of the world, and at least he had had the sense and the knowledge – even in those long-ago days when the girls themselves were surprised by this carefulness – to always wear a condom. After Rohit had been born, after he had held the tiny body of his son against his chest and felt the enormous, inescapable weight of his own love, it had become almost impossible to spend his hard-earned money elsewhere. There were these new urgencies, first among all desires: school uniforms, books, shoes, hair-oil, cricket bats, evenings at Chowpatty. Yet, it had happened even after he had come to know what amount of childish happiness was contained in a twenty-rupee note, in two kulfis as the sun set over a calm sea, he had still gone to women, despite his two sons and the two futures he was building. But it had happened rarely, the women countable on one hand in twice as many years. Men, Shalini said sometimes, there is madness in men. He always kept quiet, but he always wanted to say, the madness is in their bones, not in their hearts, not in their heads. Logic doesn't fail, it just gets worn down sometimes, a little tired, and it wants to lie down. But I struggle for you.

The maidan held what looked like a dozen games of cricket, with pitches angled to each other and very close. Fielders from various games ran past and behind each other. There must have been a couple of hundred boys racing past each other, on this narrow strip of packed yellow earth backed up between a sludgy nullah and the back wall of a municipal shamshan ghat. Katekar walked along the wall, his right shoulder brushing against its intricate whorls of graffiti and torn posters. He worried sometimes about children playing one wall away from burning bodies, about the billowing smoke depositing unclean ash on to the pitches. But you needed a place to cremate the dead, and the only alternative was to play at the edge of the basti, on the open road next to passing traffic. In any case, today there were no fires, no smoke. There were no more dead on this day. Mohit was sitting on a little rising mound, next to a cluster of chappals. He was looking seawards, dreamy and happy, and Katekar felt something squeeze inside his chest and give way. Rohit was the son just like his father, he was confident and practical, often funny, but it was Mohit, with his thoughtful inwardness, who made Katekar helpless with worry. Rohit's ambition and his anger might get him into trouble, but what would become of sensitive little Mohit? What would happen to such gentleness? Katekar squatted beside him.

'Not playing?' Katekar said.

'Papa.' Mohit shrugged. He looked away, and started biting his lower lip, which he did when he was embarrassed.

'It's all right,' Katekar said, with a pat on Mohit's shoulder. He had told them often, his sons, that sports developed character. 'You didn't feel like it?'

Mohit shook his head, fast. Katekar wanted to ask, what were you thinking about just now? What were you seeing in the little sliver of watery horizon between buildings? But he smiled and rubbed Mohit's head. 'Where's your brother?'

'There.'

Rohit was bowling. It was a fast ball, a little wild but with good speed. The batsman missed it altogether, hardly saw it, and the wicket-keeper took it smoothly and gave it back to Rohit in the same motion. Rohit jogged back to the wicket, easy and thinking about the next delivery. He was a good player, Katekar could tell that just from his effortless poise, from his confidence and his scientific precision as he waved his fielders in, you to the left, a little more, yes, there. Rohit saw his father then, stopped short. And there was just a small moment when Katekar saw him flinch, tighten into a resentful frown at being interrupted, invaded by his heavy-stepping father. Then he smiled and started forward. Katekar waved him back with an overhand motion: bowl. Rohit went back to his crease, stepped out his run-up and now his action was good but the ball was wide. The next one was short.

Katekar got up. 'Mohit,' he said. 'Don't be late going home. Study well. I'll see you tomorrow.'

'Yes, Papa,' Mohit said.

Katekar squeezed Mohit's shoulder, then walked away, fast. He was tempted, but he didn't turn his head to see Rohit playing.

PSI Kamble came along for the raid on the Delite Dance Bar. 'I'll be your undercover man,' he said, and laughed loudly at his own wit, because they knew him at the Delite better than they knew some of their own dancers. He sat always in a prime centre booth facing the dance floor, and there were always special dispensations in his bill. In the van, on the way to Delite, he was in a glorious mood, and he told them jokes. 'How do you fit thirty Marwaris in a Maruti 800? You throw a hundred-rupee note inside.' The constables in the back of the van, including two women, laughed.

Sartaj asked, 'Why so happy, Kamble? What was the score today?'

Kamble shook his head, and was silent and smug, and then jovial again. On they drove, to the sound of his laughter. At the Delite, after they had parked the van, and were waiting for the appointed time, Kamble came out of the building carrying a whisky and water. He drew Sartaj to the side, away from the constables, and walked him a little way down the road. He smelt powerfully of some musky after-shave, and was wearing a white Benetton T-shirt with striped green sleeves, tucked into blue jeans. He leaned back and raised one foot at a time, showing off an impressively complicated and colourful pair of running shoes. 'Very musst shoes, no?' he said.

'Very. Foreign?'

'Yes, boss. Nike.'

'Very expensive.'

'Expense is all relative. When there is money in your pocket, expenses get small. No money, expenses get big.'

'Money got in your pocket?'

Kamble considered Sartaj for a moment, head lowered over his glass. 'Suppose –' he said. 'Suppose a bright young police officer had a khabari, a very useful one who came up with information only once in a while, but ekdum solid information when he did.'

'What khabari is this? Who?'

'Never mind the khabari. Not important. What is important that the intelligent young officer got a tip this morning: that one local small-time thief called Ajay Mota had a stash of stolen mobile phones in his kholi. These are brand-new phones, you understand, taken during a break-in robbery three days ago, at a shop in Kurla.'

'Very good. So this officer goes and arrests Ajay Mota?'

'No, no, no. That is too simple, boss. No, the khabari knows where this Ajay Mota lives. But the officer doesn't reel the bastard in yet. No, he invests some time, he dresses in plain clothes, he takes the khabari, waits outside Ajay Mota's basti and gets the khabari to point out the bastard when he emerges with a bag on his shoulder. This is a risk, of course – what if Ajay Mota had gone another way? But he doesn't. The officer leaves the khabari behind, and follows Ajay Mota. Another risk, this following in busy traffic. It's not easy, but the officer has a motorbike, and Ajay Mota is in an auto. So the apradhi's auto goes along for ten minutes, then the apradhi gets off, goes into a shop. Comes out twenty minutes later, his bag over his shoulder. So now the officer takes him, khata-khat, grabs him by the collar, shows him a revolver, two slaps, you are under arrest, bhenchod, you want to co-operate? Then, without pause, the officer takes him inside the shop, shoves him through to the back, and there's the receiver, with the stolen phones in front of him. So, the officer has two arrests, the stolen goods are recovered and in Ajay Mota's bag is forty thousand rupees.'

'Only forty thousand? How many phones were there?'

Kamble laughed, and emptied his glass, and caught the last few drops on his extended tongue. He was very pleased. 'Never mind how many phones there were, Sartaj Saab. The important thing is, the bad men were caught,' he said, standing up very straight, wagging a finger. 'I need to refill my glass, boss. Again and again.' And he went, humming to himself.

Sartaj thought of Kamble's triumph as they executed the raid. Kamble was right, the bad men had been caught. Kamble himself had taken a good chunk of cash, probably about half of what was in the bag, and maybe one or two phones. The money was a reward for his excellent policing, for his alertness and his risk-taking. He had done well today, and he was celebrating. He deserved it.

The Delite raid itself was very orderly. Shambhu had the five girls waiting for arrest in an orderly row in his office. They were eating paya and making jokes about policemen and their sticks, while the rest of them went outside to their usual appointed cabbies for the ride home. They were a glittery, flashy bunch, mostly young, some of them quite lovely in their thick, big-screen make-up and their pride in the sleek curves of their waists.

Shambhu came walking towards Sartaj now, followed at a few yards by Kamble. They were friends, of a similar age, both body-builders, but where Shambhu was lean and chiselled, Kamble had bulk, rounded masses and bulges.

'All right, saab,' Shambhu said. 'Arrest away.'

One of the women constables stood by the van, and the other opened the Delite door and called. The arrestees trooped out on to the road and climbed into the back of the van, swaying up into it, their elegant heels glinting in the red light from the neon Delite sign.

'Going on that – that walk still?' Katekar said to Shambhu.

'An expedition,' Shambhu said. 'A walk is what you do when you go to the corner paan shop.'

'Expedition, yes, you're going?'

'Tomorrow.'

'Don't fall off a mountain.'

'Safer there than here, boss.'

Sartaj was watching Kamble, who was humming. He had his feet very wide apart and his shoulders thrown back and his elbows out. Sartaj walked around him. 'Tell the young officer I said, good job.'

Kamble grinned. 'I will, boss,' he said. He hummed again, and this time Sartaj could make out the song: *Kya se kya ho gaya, dekhte dekhte*'. Kamble raised his arms, ducked his head and danced a couple of steps. '*Tum pe dil aa gaya, dekhte dekhte.*'

'We're going,' Sartaj said. 'Are you coming?'

'No,' Kamble said. He shrugged his head over a shoulder, back towards the Delite. 'I have an appointment.'

Not all the girls at the Delite had been arrested, or had gone home. 'Have fun,' Sartaj said.

'Boss,' Kamble said, 'I always do.'

Sartaj thumped on the side of the van, and they pulled away. 'Sartaj Saab,' he heard Shambhu calling after him, 'you could have fun too, sir. You should have fun, once in a while. Fun is good.' Kamble was laughing, Sartaj could hear him.

It was only after they were back at the station that they discovered they had arrested six dancers, not five. The girls sat in a row on a bench in the Detection Room and Sartaj realized they were six, and that the extra sixth was Manika. She lowered her head and looked at him demurely with her chunni over her head, all enormous dark eyes and shyness, and the other girls burst out laughing. Sartaj took a deep breath and walked out of the room.

'This must be Kamble and Shambhu's idea of fun,' he said to Katekar.

'I didn't have anything to do with it, sir,' Katekar said.

Katekar had on a very serious face, and Sartaj believed him. He said, 'Send them in one by one. I'll sit there.'

'Yes, sir, one by one.'

Katekar stood by the door, and the women constables brought the girls in one by one, and also retreated to the door. Sartaj wrote down the names: Sunita Singh, Anita Pawar, Rekha Kumar, Neena Sanu, Shilpa Chawla. They had the names all ready for him, and were relaxed and not perturbed by him at all, and only became hesitant when he pulled the photographs from Gaitonde's album and flipped them over one by one. Then each of them shook their heads, determined and expressionless. 'No, no, no,' Shilpa Chawla said as he showed her the photographs of the young women, the smiling come-hither poses under soft lights.

'Look at the photo before you say no,' Sartaj said. He tapped his forefinger on a young woman in a blue hat. 'Look at her.'

'I don't know her,' Shilpa Chawla said, her jaw tight. When he showed her the dead woman, who he had kept till last, Shilpa Chawla sat back in her chair and crossed her arms across her chest. 'Why are you asking me? Why are you showing me all this? I don't know who this is.' Shilpa Chawla, with her doubly starry pseudonym, was disgusted and angry and frightened, and Sartaj had no evidence that she was lying.

'All right,' he said to Katekar. 'Send in Manika.'

She was older than the others, maybe in her early thirties, although you had to pay very close attention to see that, and even then the age was mainly in her slightly weary confidence, in the forthright straightness of her back and the blunt interest she directed at him. By the door, Katekar and the women constables were grinning at each other, and Sartaj was glad that they were too far away to hear Manika.

'How are you?' she said in English.

'I have some questions to ask you, madam,' Sartaj said, and his Hindi was clipped.

'Ask,' she said. She was dark, slim, very tall, maybe five eight, and not pretty exactly, but she had dimples and she thrust out her chin and her eyes were completely alive, and she made Sartaj uneasy.

'Do you know these women?'

She flipped over the photographs, paying close attention to each one. 'Oh,' she said at the third one, 'how *ugly* that blouse is! Look at those frills on the sleeves, she looks like a joker. Nice-looking girl at that. Someone needs to teach her how to dress.'

'Do you know her?'

'No,' Manika said, and she took the remaining photographs from his hand and leaned back in her chair. She was wearing a black ghagra-choli with silver on it everywhere, and the front of the choli was thick with it, like armour on the thin fabric. She was the only one who had come in her dance-floor clothes. 'Who are these women, inspector saab?' Now she was demure again. 'Girls you want to make friends with?'

'Do you know any of them?'

She was quiet, and her hands had stopped moving. Sartaj knew that she was looking at the dead woman. 'Do you know her?' She shook her head. 'It's very important that you tell me if you know.'

'No, I don't know. What happened to her?'

'She was murdered.'

'Murdered?'

'Shot.'

'By a man?'

'Yes, by a man.'

She put the photographs face-down on the desk. 'Of course by a man. Sometimes I don't know why we care about you. Really I don't know.'

Sartaj could hear the buzzing of the tube-light in the corridor outside, and distant footsteps at the front of the station. 'You are right,' he said. 'Most of the time I don't know either.'

There was an appraising scepticism in her raised eyebrow, not hostility, just a certain weary disbelief. 'Can I go now?' she said softly.

'Yes. What name shall I write down?'

'Whatever you want.'

He started to write, but stopped when she got up. The chunni slipped from her shoulder as she turned, and he saw that the choli was held together at the back by black strings, exposing the fine turns of her shoulder-blades and the long brown column of her back. On the dance floor she must pirouette, he thought, and blaze those eyes over a shoulder at the men in the booths, at the staring men in the darkness.

'I'll tell you,' she said from the door. In the four steps from the chair she had recovered her grin, her jaunty irony.

'Tell me what?'

She came back to the desk, turned the photographs face-up and went past the dead woman, flicked others aside with a long red fingernail, while she held her chunni close with the other hand. 'This one,' she said.

'What about her?'

'You'll have to be very nice to me,' she said. 'Her name is Kavita, or at least that's what she called herself when she danced at Pritam. She got parts in some videos and stopped dancing. Then I heard she was on some serial. After she got the serial she lived in Andheri East, in a PG. She was very lucky always, that Kavita. Not many girls like us get that far. Not one in a thousand. Ten thousand.'

'Kavita. Are you sure it's her? Is it her real name?'

'Of course I'm sure. And you'll have to ask her if it's her real name. Are you going to be nice?'

'Yes, of course I am.'

'You're lying, but you're a man, so I'll forgive you. Do you know why I told you?'

'No.'

'The man who did this is a rakshasa. And don't feel too good, you're a rakshasa also. But maybe you'll catch that rakshasa. And punish him.'

'Maybe,' Sartaj said. The man who did it had been caught, and yet had escaped, and Sartaj had never been sure about punishment, because it always seemed too much or too little. I catch them because that's what I do, and they run because that's what they do, and the world keeps turning. But there was no explaining this to Manika, and so he said, 'Thanks.'

After she had gone, after they had put the lot of them into a van and sent them home, Sartaj dropped Katekar at the corner of Sriram Road, which was within comfortable walking distance of Katekar's place. Katekar raised his hand to his chest, and turned, and then Sartaj said, 'What does a rakshasa look like?'

Katekar leaned down to the window. 'I don't know, sir. On television they have long black hair, horns. And pointy teeth sometimes.'

'And they go around eating people?'

'I think that's their main job, sir.'

They both laughed. They had spent the day working, and they had made small progress in their investigations, and so they were happy. 'That would be nice to have during some interrogations,' Sartaj said. 'Horns, and teeth like wolves.'

But on the way home it occurred to Sartaj that most people he interrogated were so frightened that he might already have oversized canines. It was the uniform that terrified them, that brought back all those tales of police brutality collected over many generations. Even the ones who wanted help spoke warily around policemen, and the ones who didn't need help tried to be overly friendly in case they ever did. Policemen were monsters, set aside from everyone else. But Parulkar had once told Sartaj, 'We are good men who must be bad to keep the worst men in control. Without us, there would be nothing left, there would only be a jungle.'

A low, yellow haze flitted behind the buildings as Sartaj drove. The streets were quiet. Sartaj imagined the citizens sleeping in their millions, safe for one more night. The image gave him some satisfaction, but not nearly as much as it used to. He couldn't tell if this was because he had become more of a rakshasa, or less so. Still, he had a job to do, and he did it. Now he needed to sleep. He went home.

Ganesh Gaitonde Acquires Land

I took the land between N.C. Road and the hill which overlooks it. You know Gopalmath basti, from N.C. Road all the way up the hill and four miles wide, from Sindh Chowk to G.T. Junction? All that was empty land then, nothing but a wasteland of weeds and bushes – it was municipal land. The government owned it, and so nobody owned it. I took it.

You know how it's done, Sartaj. It's easy. You pay off three chutiyas in the municipality, oil them up properly and then you kill the local dada who thinks he deserves a percentage on your action, like it's his bhenchod birthright. That's it. Then the land is yours. I took it, and it was mine.

I had sold my gold, and I had money. Paritosh Shah, fat Gujarati that he was, told me I should put all my cash into business: buy this, sell that. 'I can double it for you within a year,' he said. 'Triple it.' He knew exactly how much I had, since he had bought all my gold from me.

I listened to him, as he sprawled elegantly on his gadda, one cushion under his shoulder and another under his knees. I thought about it, but I knew it in my bones, if you don't own land you are nothing. You can die for love, you can die for friendship, you can die for money, but finally the only real thing in the world is land. You can depend on land. I said, 'Paritosh Bhai, I trust you, but let me follow my own road.' He thought I was a fool, but I had already seen the land, and had walked up and down it, and knew it was the right place, near the road and not so far from the railway station. So we gave money to the municipality, to one clerk and to two officers, and the land was mine to build on.

But then there was the problem of Anil Kurup. We had the scrub cleared, and my contractor had his men digging out the foundations for the kholis, and we were expecting a truckload of cement, and Anil Kurup's boys stopped the truck on the way down from the main road, and took it to Gopalmath village, which was about a mile up the road. We never saw any cement, and instead they sent a piece of paper with a phone number on it. 'You're a bachcha from nowhere,' Anil Kurup shouted at me when I called. 'And you think you're going to come into my village and spit into my face. Maderchod, one hen doesn't get sold here without me knowing about it. I'll put a truckload of cement up your gaand and send you back to whatever gutter you came out of.' I kept calm and quietly asked for a day to think about it. He cursed me some more and finally told me to call him the next day. He was right, of course. He had grown up in Gopalmath, and this area was his, no question about it, he ruled it like a king. There wasn't much in his raj, just some small shops, a garage or two, but it was all his.

Four days later I went to see him in Gopalmath. I went with Chotta Badriya. You remember that big muscleman Badriya who was Paritosh Shah's bodyguard? This Chotta Badriya was his little brother. He was actually Badrul-Ahmed, and his elder brother's name was Badruddin, their father had been told by some Sufi pir that he should give all his sons names beginning with 'Ba –' for their success and well-being. So they had their fancy long names, but to us they were just Badriya and Chotta Badriya. Badriya and I saw each other every time I went to see Paritosh Shah, and we liked each other, and when I started my project he asked me to take his younger brother with me, to make his life. This Chotta was bigger actually, bigger than his big brother, as big as a mountain. He was a good boy, well-mannered and obedient, so I was glad to have him along with me. I said to his brother, 'If you ask, I give.'

That afternoon, though, with Anil Kurup, I was trying to keep what was mine. Chotta Badriya and I went walking into Gopalmath, and a sad little rubbish dump it was then, one kuchcha road and clustering hovels surrounded by palm trees and fields, and a few shops on the main road. Anil Kurup was waiting for us in the back of a dhaba just off the main road, which in those days was the only place in Gopalmath which had a phone.

His boys searched us, took our ghodas from us, and they were very impressed, I don't think they'd expected us to be carrying pistols. There were five of them. They led us through a door into the back room, past the huge karhais filled with frying puris and bhajiyas. Anil

Kurup was sitting at a table, drinking beer. At two in the afternoon, the ugly bastard was red-eyed and burping. He had thick lips, hair falling over his forehead, white chappals. I put on the table in front of him a newspaper wrapped around twenty thousand in cash.

'Not enough,' he said.

'Bhai,' I said, 'I'll have the rest soon, next week, I promise. And I would have brought this earlier, only I didn't know.'

'What kind of brainless bhenchod are you?' he said. 'You don't find out about an area before you go into it and start digging it up?'

'Sorry,' I said. And I shrugged, small and helpless.

He laughed then, spitting beer on to the table. 'Sit,' he said. 'Both of you. Have some beer.'

I said, 'Just some chai, Anil Bhai.'

'If I offer, you have beer.'

'Yes, Anil Bhai.' And he laughed again, and his three boys who were in the room laughed. They got us beer, a bottle each and glasses, and we drank.

'Where are you from, bachcha?' he said.

'Nashik.'

'You have to grow up in this Mumbai to know how it works,' he said. 'You can't just come in and act like a chutiya, you'll end up with your brains out on the road.'

'Yes, Anil Bhai,' I said. 'He's absolutely right, Badriya,' I said. 'We have to listen to Anil Bhai.'

Anil Kurup was puffed up like an avuncular toad now. 'Arre, go and get us some bhajiyas to eat,' he said. 'And bring some eggs also.'

Two of the boys jumped to attention and hurried out. That left one leaning against the wall to my right.

'Bhai, I have to ask some advice from you,' I said.

'Ask, ask.'

'It's about the municipality and water,' I said. And I scratched my nose.

And right then Chotta Badriya nudged his beer bottle off the table. 'Maderchod,' he said, and bent down to the floor. He came up quick, stood up and leaned forward in one flash, and his arm went suddenly across the table too fast to see, and then Anil Kurup was rocking back in his chair with a wooden handle growing from his right eye.

I had a bottle in my hand, and I smashed it across the face of the boy on my right. He squealed and clutched at himself, and I went past him and slammed the door shut, I threw the bolt and put my shoulder against the wood. I knew none of Anil Kurup's boys had guns, and our own ghodas were unloaded, so there was no danger of a bullet coming through the door, just Anil Kurup's fools shouting and slamming against it.

'Stop,' I shouted. 'Stop! Prashant. Vinod. Amar. He's dead. Anil Kurup is dead. And my boys are outside, and you may kill us, but they'll kill every one of you. I know your names. I know all your names and my boys know who you are. You can get us, but they'll kill every one of you. Amar, just take a step back and think about it. He's dead.'

Anil Kurup was dead, with blood seeping over his cheek. When they found our pistols, they hadn't searched further, and what Chotta Badriya had under his trouser leg was one of those straight picks that you use to break ice, with the handle set crosswise, he had it on the inside of his left leg, held there with three pieces of white medical tape. He was too strong, that Chotta Badriya, and he had put it right into Anil Kurup's eyeball, smashed it in with all his weight and muscle behind it. Very fast he was, and there was nothing they could have done about it. Only afterwards, when he was dead, they could have tried to kill us. But I talked them down. I told them I'd make them rich, that Anil Kurup was a stupid bastard, that he had robbed them for years, and cheated them, and now that he was dead it was mad of them to die for him. Because if they tried to do anything to us, they would die for sure, my boys were sworn to avenge me. I told them to look outside, and sure enough, there were six of my boys, standing in a line across the road.

We walked out of there alive, Chotta Badriya and me, and with our pistols back under our shirts. 'What a speech you gave, Ganesh Bhai,' Chotta Badriya said when we were out and had left Gopalmath behind us. And then he laughed, and he had to stop in the middle of the path and lower his head and put his hands on his knees and laugh. I thumped him on the back, and smiled. We had done it. And we really did it, Sardar-ji. Ask anyone the story of Ganesh Gaitonde and they will begin it there, in that dhaba in Gopalmath. I know that how I killed Anil Kurup has been told so many times that it doesn't seem true any more. In five different movies they put it, and in the last one they had me doing it – the character based on me, that is – with a small pistol that he had strapped to his ankle. But this is really how it happened. And it happened, actually and truly like this, in spite of how untrue all the telling and retelling of it has made it.

News of my victory against Anil Kurup spread through the neighbouring localities, and people started to come to me to settle matters, to give them jobs and protection, to help them deal with the police and the local government. My war with him had been short and decisive, and I realized only after it was over that I had needed to fight it not only for territory, but for legitimacy. I was now recognized as Ganesh Gaitonde of Gopalmath, and nobody could dispute my right to stay in the city. I had succeeded in more ways than one.

But why had I succeeded? I had won because before I went walking into Anil Kurup's home, I knew everything about him. I knew his history, I knew his strength, I knew his weapons, I knew the names of his followers and how long they had been with him. I took the time to investigate him, to learn him, and he – the arrogant gaandu – knew nothing about me. So I had won. But why had Chotta Badriya followed me into the mouth of death itself? He hardly knew me, and he knew the insane risk of my plan, and yet he came with me. I tell you that he came with me because I commanded him to. Most men want to be led, and there are only a very few who can lead. I had a problem, I had a choice and I made a decision. I decided, and so Chotta Badriya and the others followed me. Those who cannot decide are pliable mud in the hands of those who can. I took my boys and made them into my diamond-hard weapon, and I built the basti of Gopalmath. I didn't skimp on the materials or the building itself, we made sturdy, spacious and very pucca kholis, laid them out according to plan. You could tell by looking at them, by feeling the solid brick and plaster that these were homes that would last, that these lanes would remain unflooded even during the heaviest of monsoons. The word spread: Ganesh Gaitonde doesn't dilute his cement with sand, he gives value for money.

Gopalmath filled up fast, there were citizens queuing up for the kholis even before we finished them, before we had the land cleared, before we even imagined the rows of houses. Up and down the road the basti spread, and it went climbing up the hill, it seemed to grow every day. Right from that beginning, we had Dalits and OBCs, Marathas and Tamils, Brahmins and Muslims. The communities tended to cluster together, lane by lane. People like to stay with those they know, like seeks like, and even in the thick crores of the city, in this jungle where a man can lose his name and become something else, the lowest of the low will seek his own kind, and live with them in proud public squalor. I saw this, and thought it strange, that not one man in thousands has the courage to be alone. But it was good, they crowded together, and from them I gathered the boys who made up my company. Gaitonde Company it was called, or G-Company, and we were quickly famous. Not yet in the papers, but in the north and east of Mumbai the basti-dwellers knew us, and the police, and the other companies.

Mothers came to me then. 'A job in the Post Office for my boy, Ganesh Bhai,' one said. 'Settle him somewhere, Ganesh Bhai,' another said. 'You know best.' They wanted jobs, and justice, and blessings. I gave them all that, and water, and electricity over wires pulled from the lines near the main road. I lived in a pucca house at the foot of Gopalmath hill, we had built it with two bedrooms and a big central hall, and on the steps outside every morning a crowd gathered, seekers, supplicants, applicants and yes, devotees. They came to ask for things and to lower their heads. 'We just wanted your darshan, Ganesh Bhai,' some said, and so I gave it to them, and they gazed and folded their hands and retreated, storing goodwill against the certain disasters of the future. And their blessings came to me, and money, cash from the shopkeepers and traders and garage-owners and dhaba-owners of the area, and we kept them and their establishments safe. Businessmen caught up in quarrels and wran-glings came to me, and I listened to all sides of the case and gave a decision, a fair and fast ruling that would be enforced by my boys, with force if necessary, and for this mandvali and for being able to avoid the endless and useless law courts, all the disputants paid me a percentage of the contested value as fee. Money came in and went out. In eight months I had a payroll of thirty-seven people, brawlers to break heads, yes, but not only that, also boys to run errands and others to take care of the police-wallahs and municipality-wallahs and the electricity-wallahs. In my bones I understood something that Paritosh Shah never had to teach me, that you have to spend money to make money. I had good relations with the inspector who had the charge of our area from G.T. station, Samant his name was, week by week we met his sub-inspectors and slipped them envelopes. We gave them many thousands, but it was only money. With a big heart I spent it and more came.

That year we celebrated Diwali with strings of electric lights along all the main lanes, a big dais at the central chowk with bhajan-singing and mithai, and finally, after dark, I stood at the gate of my house and gave basketfuls of atom bombs and rockets and phuljadis to the children of the basti. The sky over Gopalmath showered sparking streams of gold and silver, and the rising detonations sounded the return of good and the victory of virtue over death. My house was outlined in flickering points of light, in the darkness I couldn't see the walls but the flames from the hundreds of diyas told me that I had a place of my own, my earth, and I was home. Paritosh Shah came along then, with Kanta Bai and Bada Badriya, and he found me standing outside, and he drew me into the house. 'Let us welcome Lakshmi,' he said.

We sat on two gaddas pulled together, and we played cards. I said, 'I'm not very good at this.'

Kanta Bai laughed, and said, 'Ganesh Gaitonde, you are the wildest gambler I have ever met. And you're not good at teen-patti? How can that be? But I'll teach you.' She was sitting cross-legged with a pillow in her lap and her elbows resting on the pillow while she shuffled the cards, fast, fast. They made a whirring noise under her fingers. 'But, Paritosh Bhai, pull out some of the good stuff,' she said. Then we had to send out for ice, and three of the boys to Vyas Bazaar, where they took the owner of Parthiv Household Goods from his dinner and down to open his shop, because Paritosh Shah wouldn't drink Johnny Walker out of steel tumblers, which were all I had. He held up the sparkling new glasses my boys brought back, and said they weren't so bad. And when I held my glass in my hand, and ran my finger over the sharp edges patterned into its sides, and felt its solid weight, I had to admit that there was a rightness about it. I knew now that drinking the good stuff meant that you drank it out of good glasses. Paritosh Shah held up his glass and shook it gently, next to his grinning face. 'Listen to it, boss,' he said. 'Listen, listen.' I brought up my glass to my ear and shook it, and heard the small, perfect music the ice made against the glass. 'Cheers,' Paritosh Shah said. I hesitated, it was an English word I had heard before but had never said. 'Chee-yers,' Paritosh Shah said.

'Cheers,' I said. Kanta Bai laughed and dealt a hand. I sipped at Johnny Walker, and liked all of it, the taste of it, the ice against my teeth, the cold, smooth surface under my lower lip. 'Cheers,' I said again, and understood that for Johnny Walker you needed a whole different home, a brand-new setting.

We played cards. I lost and lost all night. The notes went from my side to theirs, but I was happy. I knew it would come back, let Lakshmi go with happiness, don't be afraid, and she comes back to lavish blessings on you, she takes you into her lap and holds you close, like a son. In this going and coming is Lakshmi's happiness. So we slapped the cards down, and the money went, but I was content, it would come back multiplied and grown, from Paritosh Shah and his businesses and his knowledge of all the businessmen in the area who made fortunes, who ate and drank in my kingdom and owed me tribute, from Kanta Bai and her satrangi hooch and the hundreds who drank it and the thousands more who would drink it if I helped her, and that Diwali night was golden. Somebody had put on a cassette recorder and the songs flowed – 'Jab tak hai jaan jaan-e-jahaan' – and outside there was the slam of bombs and the long, hysterical rattles of entire ladhis of crackers, and we played, and the circle of players got wider, and Paritosh Shah told jokes, and Inspector Samant arrived and joined the circle and showed us how to play paplu, and Kanta Bai's palloo slipped from her shoulder and she roared in amusement at Chotta Badriya, who shyly turned his face away from her bountiful brimming-over, her over-run over her blouse, and the cards flew, and I lost, and lost.

I awoke under a sheet pulled from the gadda. I must have dragged it over myself during the night, to protect against the hissing table-fan set on 'High'. The room was empty, filthy with cigarette butts and smeared plates and empty glasses. I stood up and pain pressed up through my neck and into my head. I looked around for my chappals, then gave up and walked outside in my bare feet. Chotta Badriya was asleep just outside the door, his shirt smeared with vomit, the reek of it made me choke, and I rushed to the gate and bent over and heaved endlessly, and brought up only a mouthful, and yet it was hot and bitter as poison. It was still before the first grey, and the road in both directions was completely empty, and anyone could have come into Gopalmath, walked into my house and killed me as I slept. It would've been easy. I turned and went back in, up the stairs to the roof. I sat on top of the water tank and waited for day. I was thirsty but wouldn't drink. I wanted to remember the pain and the disgust.

The shape of what I had built came slowly out of the darkness, in a series of slow leaps. The cement we had used was stained and brownish already, and the people who had moved into the kholis had added colour, the blue and green of their clothes strung up in doorways, the winking pearl of plastic on roofs; there were red slogans on the walls, and brightly coloured women in posters, and all the kholis close to each other, a dense patchwork of rectangles and squares strung over with electric wires, connections taken from here to there and knitting it all close. This was mine.

Chotta Badriya's head came through the roof. 'Bhai?' he said.

'Here.'

He came up, and I saw that his hair was slicked back, wet. He had washed himself, and put on a new shirt. He was a good boy.

'We will sell liquor,' I said, 'but we will never have another drop of it in this house.'

'Bhai?'

'Not satrangi, not narangi, not Johnny Walker, nothing.'

'Yes, bhai.'

'Now go and make some tea. And see if you can find something for us to eat.'

Business grows. I had the boys collecting hafta from the shopkeepers and businessmen around Gopalmath, all the way to Gaikwad Road, which was the border between my territory and the area belonging to the Cobra Gang. I'm not making this up, they were really called the Cobra Gang, like some outfit led by Pran and Ranjit in a movie from thirty years ago. They had the eastern area all the way to the fishing villages at Malad Creek, and so they had smuggling going also, and all in all they were strong, very strong, bigger than us and with a gushing cash-flow. I had never seen their top man, one Rajesh Parab, an old artiste, he had come up with Haji Mastan and must have been fifty, sixty by now. But I had seen his boys on the streets, and now and then in the bars. I went not for the drinking, you understand, after that first Johnny Walker night I never drank again, but for the women, the waitresses and the dancers. My boys followed me in this, none of them touched liquor, not so much as one beer. I never asked them for this, never made a rule, but when I stopped, Chotta Badriya stopped, and then it became a tradition in our ranks. I was glad of this: to give something up together brought the boys close, it made them a team. I hadn't thought of this when I stopped drinking, but I saw clearly how it worked, and I encouraged it. A man of the G-Company never loses his head, I told them, he keeps cold. He stays awake even when he sleeps. Have women, I said, that's a man's pleasure, a diversion worthy of a shooter, have five, have ten. But to pour poison down your own throat, to make yourself stupid and slow, that's a maderchod idiot's game. Let the Cobra Gang do that.

I knew a war was coming. It was inevitable. There had been some minor collisions between my boys and theirs, hard looks in passing on the streets, shoulders jostling in the lobby of a cinema, shoving, a whispered gali. But we were at peace. I sat on the roof at night, turning the future in my head, testing it. Whichever path I chose, and whichever one after that, the events led to conflict, and slaughter. They were big, we were small. The only peace we could keep was one in which they remained big and we small, and we took their leftovers, and stepped aside and bowed when they passed, and ate their shit, today and tomorrow and the day after. This was possible, this unequal calm, but then there was me. I was not made to be small. The G-Company was me, and I looked into myself, without deceit and without mercy, and I knew I could never be small. I was bigger than when I had been born, bigger than when I had come to this city, and I would grow bigger. So war would come. So, I thought, let us accept that fighting will come, and let us prepare for it. And when the day comes, we will fight without hate, without anger. We will prevail.

'Find me names, faces,' I told Chotta Badriya. 'I want to know who they are.' So we spent money, and in small ways helped small people, and before long we had our own network of khabaris, some deep in Cobra Gang territory. There was one paan-wallah who had his shop at the mouth of Nabbargali, where Rajesh Parab lived in the very highest apartment of a three-storey house, and this paan-wallah watched them going and coming all day long, and when in the evenings he walked home, one of our boys joined him for ten minutes, and so we had their daily roster. We paid the paan-wallah, but money alone was not why he did it. Six years before, very late one winter night, Rajesh Parab had driven up drunk in a brand-new Toyota, asked for paan and then told the paan-wallah that his maghai paan sat like a brick on the tongue, that he should go back to UP and relearn his trade. The next afternoon Rajesh Parab had stopped by again, sober and smiling, and had taken his paan as usual, and although he had forgotten what he had said when he was high on his new Japanese horse, an insult can live inside a man for a long time, burrowing like a tiny pin-headed worm and getting thicker and longer until it is wrapped through his gut and squeezing and squeezing. So the paan-wallah remembered, and he helped us, and others did as well.

Under Rajesh Parab there were four Number Twos, each handling different aspects of his business, and I knew their names and where they lived. In a black diary I had pages covered with the names of their controllers and their boys, who they were, their histories, and also listings of Rajesh Parab's business associates, his financiers, the builders aligned with him. I studied this black diary until my boys began to smile a little. 'Bhai is reading his Gita,' they whispered among themselves. I didn't mind. I was looking for an entrance, a chink where I could hurl an attack and break the Cobra Gang into fragments and eat it piecemeal. There was one name in my diary I didn't understand, one name I couldn't fit into the formation I saw arrayed against me. A man called Vilas Ranade had been with Rajesh Parab for a long time, nobody could tell how long, and yet this Vilas Ranade didn't do any-thing for Rajesh Parab. He didn't manage anything, not the smuggling, not the hafta, not the dealings with builders, and some-times he wasn't even seen close to Rajesh Parab's house for weeks, months. Nobody knew where he lived. Nobody could tell me if he was married, if he had children, if he had a taste for gambling, nothing. And yet when he came to the house he walked straight up to Rajesh Parab's apartment, no queuing for him, and even if there was an MLA in deep mid-discussion, Rajesh Parab came out to meet Vilas Ranade. Vilas Ranade had never been in jail, and had been only twice men-tioned in the newspapers. Finally I said to Chotta Badriya, 'I want to know what this bastard looks like. Get me a photograph.'

Meanwhile, there was the matter of weapons. I wouldn't trust my life to country-made guns, and those days a Chinese Star pistol cost ten, twelve thousand. I couldn't afford Glocks, of course, but we hid 9 mm ammunition and Stars in my house, in a dozen kholis in Gopalmath, and in Gopalmath temple, which at that time was just one small shrine and a room for the pujari. It took weeks, months, this slow build-up, and it took much thought, how much money to spend on arms, how much to pay the boys, how much for improve-ments in the basti so that the people were happy. So we prepared for war.

One evening Chotta Badriya came to tell me that we had success-fully negotiated for and taken delivery of a load of ammunition. I was sitting in a bar called Mahal, down by the Link Road in Jogeshwari, with four of my boys, I remember clearly it was Mohan Surve, Pradeep Pednekar, Krishna Gaikwad and Qariz Shaikh. Chotta Badriya came into the bar, came straight to us, we were sitting at our usual table. He was grinning as he squeezed in at the end of the booth. 'Good deal, bhai,' he said. 'Three hundred kanchas. All good and guaranteed.' Now this was our own language, kanchas and gullels for bullets and pistols. The Cobra Gang and all the other companies might say daane for bullets, and samaan for pistols, but we said kanche and gullels. This too I encouraged, it set us apart from the rest, made us belong to each other more because we spoke a private tongue, and to become one of us you had to learn it, and in learning it you were changed. I saw this in the new boys as they worked hard, trying to pass from being mere neighbourhood taporis to respected bhais. They learned the language, and then the walk, and they pre-tended to be something, and then they became it. And so for American dollars, we said choklete, not Dalda like the rest of our world; for British pounds, lalten, not peetal; for heroin and brown sugar, gulal, not atta; for police, Iftekar, not nau-number; a job gone wrong was ghanta, not fachchad; and a girl so impossibly ripe and round and tight that it hurt to look at her was not a chabbis, but a churi.

So we got Chotta Badriya a mango lassi, and Qariz Shaikh talked on. We were discussing the long-ago feud between Haji Mastan and Yusuf Patel, how they had been partners once, but how when betrayal and business rivalry had brought them to war, Haji Mastan had resolved to eliminate his friend. Qariz Shaikh had heard these tales from his father. 'Haji Mastan gave the supari on Yusuf Patel to Karim Lala,' he said. 'But Yusuf Patel survived the hit.'

'I saw that Karim Lala once,' Mohan Surve said. 'Near Grant Road Station. Two years ago.'

'Yes?' I said. 'What did he look like?'

'Big Pathan bastard,' Mohan Surve said. 'Real tall, and big. He has huge hands. He's retired now. Lives around there. But even now at this age he walks like a badshah. What a terror he must have been, in his days.'

I tried to imagine Karim Lala and his frontier swagger, that accent I remembered from the Pathan that Pran had played in *Zanjeer*. I had heard these old stories of bloodshed before, but now I listened to them with desperate attention. I was looking now for lessons, for principles about loss and victory, for the tactics that had been used by the ones who were still alive, those who had survived since those days when Haji Mastan and Yusuf Patel hunted each other through Mohammed Ali Road and Dongri. I listened to Qariz Shaikh, but I was restless. To be sitting and talking and thinking was not enough. I wanted to be back in Gopalmath, back in the lanes. I stood up.

'Chalo,' I said.

'Already, bhai?' Mohan Surve said. 'It's only eleven.'

Chotta Badriya upended his lassi glass and drank steadily and his throat bobbed up and down.

'I'm sick of this place,' I said. 'Let's go.'

I walked fast towards the door. Outside, the road sloped down to the darting lights of the highway. On the left, three rickshaws stood in a row. We were parked to the right, on the other side of the lamppost. It was a decrepit, ancient Ambassador taxi that Qariz Shaikh's father drove during the days. I wanted a better car, but we had money only for guns. Soon, some day, I thought. I started across the road, through the oval of light. I could hear the others behind me. I turned my head over my shoulder, and there was Chotta Badriya, stuffing a handker-chief in his pocket, and close behind him the others. They moved, walking, and their shoulders shifted as they walked, and through a chance gap in the figures I saw Mohan Surve under the neon sign, still near the door, his back against the wall and not moving. It was too far to see his eyes, but he was not walking, not moving. And then, in that instant, I hurled myself to the side, clawing towards the dark, lunging out of the light, and I felt a blow on my shoulder that took me along with it, nearly to the ground, but I found my feet and was running along the side of the building, and I knew I had been hit but I never heard the gunshots. At the corner I stopped myself with a hand on the wall, turned and saw movement in the passage, and twisted around the corner and ran again, and I had my pistol out. Now I heard the shots. I risked a look back, and it was Chotta Badriya, at the corner and firing at something on the other side of the corner.

'Badriya,' I called. 'Come.'

We went over a wall, through a building compound and out of its gate, and down a road. Two more turns and I had to stop. I leaned against a truck, and then bent over and spurted vomit on to the road.

My left arm was shuddering, squeezing in regular spasms of pain. 'Are you hit?' I said to Chotta Badriya.

'Not one touch,' he said. 'Not one. I'm fine.' He laughed, a thin crackling sound.

'Good,' I said, turning my head to look at him. 'I know it's not you.'

'What's not me?'

'The one who sold us to them. Because if you were, you wouldn't be here now. And if you were, you could kill me now.' The barrel of his pistol was six inches from my head, one quick movement from my death.

'Bhai,' he said. 'Really, bhai.' He was shocked. I loved him in that moment, loved him like a brother.

'Wipe your face,' I said. 'You still have mango lassi on it. And get me to a doctor.'

I made phone calls from the doctor's table, as he stitched and worried at my shoulder. I called Paritosh Shah and Kanta Bai and some others of my boys and told them to be ready. Paritosh Shah said that the police were already on the scene at the bar, and that three of my boys were dead. Pradeep Pednekar, Krishna Gaikwad and Qariz Shaikh had died. Pradeep Pednekar had been shot once through the hips, and then again at close range in the head. There was no news of Mohan Surve. And I had survived.

Being shot is a peculiar experience, quite unlike any other. When it first happened I didn't really recognize it, I was so eager to get away that it didn't occur to me that the thing I felt in my skin and muscle was a bullet ploughing in. I didn't feel the pain until later, until I had the possibility of life in my mouth, as succulent as a mango. Now my shoulder and chest were cold, like somebody had frozen my bones from the inside out and was stabbing me with a sliver of ice. I said to Chotta Badriya, 'Get me to Gopalmath.'

Three of our boys had brought a car to the doctors. They and Chotta Badriya took me to the car, surrounding me and shielding me with their own bodies. They followed me. We had once been strangers, but now we were bound together. We had been attacked, we had survived, so now they loved me a little. They asked me, Are you all right, bhai? Are you comfortable? We sped down the empty night road towards Gopalmath. I had made this velocity, and in its wake they came behind me. I was one lone man who had almost died that night, and they clung to me.

'What do we do now?' Chotta Badriya said.

'Find me Mohan Surve,' I said.

In Gopalmath my house had already been cleared, checked twice by my boys. I got in safely, and was back in my own room, sitting on the gadda. I put boys on the peripheries of Gopalmath, to watch for an attack, but I knew I was safe, at least for now. The crowded lanes were my guard, these children who wandered in the streets, the women who sat in the doorways. They all knew each other, up and down the alleys. There was no getting past them for the enemy, not without loss.

'You should sleep,' Chotta Badriya said. It was already morning.

'Yes,' I said. I knew I needed to rest, there was no use in exhausting myself. 'You also. But see to it that there is no gap in the guard.'

I lay in my bed, shaking under my sheet. Vibrations, little tremblings started in my stomach and spread into my chest and then my throat. The left side of my body was aching steadily. But it wasn't the pain that kept me awake. It was rage at myself, at my stupidity. Now, in looking back, it was obvious: you cannot watch someone without changing the world they live in, and if they are alert they will feel these shifts, sense the faint echo of your questions as they roll along the ground, and they will watch you in return. They had watched, and reached the same conclusions as I had, they had read me, they had predicted me and then they took my gaand. They had picked the place, and the time, and the method, and declared war. If not for a chance glance, a trick of time and my body, a bullet finding its way through space along one angle and not another, if not, if not, if not, I would have been dead on the road in front of Mahal, reduced to nothing again, a small man become smaller. The war would have started and been instantly over. This was what I couldn't bear, my foolishness, my blindness.

Finally, I laid aside the past, which cannot be changed but only left. I cut it from me as if with a scalpel. The future is what exists for you, I said. You are a man of the future. I planned. And I slept.

The next day I carried the war to them. They knew we had been watching, but they couldn't hide everything from us. We knew at least something, what business they did, where they went. On that next day we killed five of them. There were two separate attacks, and I led one of them. It was difficult for me to move, I couldn't raise my arm without a struggle, but the boys were watching me, and this was a crucial time. So I sat in the front seat of the car, next to Chotta Badriya, who was driving. There were three other boys in the back seat. We waited for the enemy outside Kamath's Hotel, where we knew they were meeting a builder for cash collection. It was six o'clock, and the road was full of workers coming home, trailing long evening shadows. When I closed my eyes I could still see the burning of the sun, it blazed inside my head.

'That's them,' Chotta Badriya said.

There were three, all young, wearing white shirts and good pressed trousers, like good businessmen making a living in the world. The middle one was carrying a plastic shopping bag in his left hand.

'Pass behind them,' I said.

We came up through the car park, turned right as they reached the bottom of the stairs in front of the hotel, and hummed slowly along, letting them pass directly in front of us. I let them take two more steps, then opened my door with my left hand, pushed it wide, took the pistol from my lap. We all came out at once. Chotta Badriya fired the first shot, and then it was one continual roar. They never even turned around. My hand was unsteady, and I don't think any of my shots hit. But I remember a gout of blood exploding like a momentary flower on the other side of a man's head, he must have seen it hanging in front of his eyes before he dropped down dead. It was all quick and easy. Chotta Badriya got back into the car.

'Get the money,' I said.

Two minutes later we were safely on S.V. Road. Inside the shopping bag there were three lakhs, and a new bottle of Halo anti-dandruff shampoo.

'Bhai, that's for me,' Chotta Badriya said. He was full of glee.

'Here,' I said, and tossed the bottle into his lap. 'You have dandruff?'

'No,' he said. 'And now I won't. I'll prevent it. You see?'

I had to laugh at that. 'You're one mad chutiya,' I said.

'I think I should grow my hair,' he said. 'I think long hair will look good on me.'

'Yes, yes, you'll look like bhenchod Tarzan himself,' I said. I managed a nap on the way back to Gopalmath, and when we got home I was given the news that the other mission – to ambush some of their boys who frequented a carrom club near Andheri station – had netted us two more wickets. So we were ahead of them for now, but the match wasn't over, it had barely begun yet. In the series that followed, we stayed ahead of them, but only just. By the end of the month, they had lost twelve players, and we eleven. Twelve to them was minor losses, they had many many more batsmen waiting to substitute, but we were almost half gone, vanished from Gopalmath. Samant the inspector laughed at me on the phone more than once. 'Gaitonde,' he said, 'they are bajaoing your baja, you better run away and hide, you'll get finished.'

After our thirteenth death, three of my boys just didn't appear for morning attendance the next day. I knew they hadn't been killed, but that they had just walked away from a losing game. I saw the logic of it. We were indeed brothers, and the battles we had suffered together had made us more so, but when defeat is certain, when you are hiding, exhausted and stripped of hope, and the strong enemy is coming to break your thighs, some men will just quit you. This was just another defeat among defeats, and I swallowed it, and looked to those who were still with me. We went on, kept our businesses going, the daily round of living, all the time moving in twos and threes, comforted by the hard metal we carried under our shirts, our weapons that we obsessively cleaned and oiled and caressed. I saw Sunny, one of my boys, raise his pistol to his head, touch it to his forehead in whispered prayer before he went out of the door, and I laughed and asked him if he lit diyas and did puja in front of it every morning, and he ducked his head and smiled, abashed. But we were desperately in need of blessings, and if I thought it would have helped, I would have prostrated myself in front of my garlanded Tokarev without a second's hesitation.

It was a woman who finally showed me the way. I went with Kanta Bai and the boys to Siddhi Vinayak, and we stood in the long queue that wound up the temple steps. It was all nonsense to me, all this praying and whining, but the boys believed and wanted to go, and it was good for morale, so I went along. Despite all her monstrous vulgarity and cynicism, Kanta Bai was a great devotee also. She held a thali in her hands, and had her pallu draped very respectably over her head. Ahead of us and behind us, in line, were my boys, shoulder to shoulder. There was that full, sweet temple smell of rose-water and agarbatties in my head, and I felt safe. Kanta Bai said, 'I know what you are going to ask for.'

'It's obvious,' I said. 'Even *he* already knows, if he exists and knows anything,' I said, with a jerk of my head up the stairs, where Ganesha sat, supposedly knowing everything.

She shook her head. 'He can't give you what you won't take with your own hands.'

'What do you mean?'

She had her head down to the thali, very low, as she neatened up the little piles of rice and sindoor and flower petals. Her neck was puffed up in round folds of flesh. 'They're going to kill you,' she said. 'You're going to die.'

We moved ahead three jerky steps now, up the stairs. On the other side of the passageway came a steady stream of worshippers, hurrying down the stairs, full of hope now, renewed now that they had confronted the god, seen him and shown themselves, shamelessly exposed their need and their pain. 'Why?' I said.

'Because you fight like a fool. All this hero-giri, shooting here and shooting there, you can't win like that. They will win. They've already won. You think war is about showing them you have a big lauda.'

My pistol was in my waistband, heavy against my belly, and as I looked at her, saying this and not even looking at me, I wanted to pull it out and shoot her. I could have done it easily, I saw it clearly, myself doing it, and the anger came up my throat into my head, like a hoarse humming, until it shadowed my eyes. I wiped at my tears with the back of my hand, and said, 'How then?'

'Fight the war to win it. It doesn't matter who kills more men. It doesn't matter if all of Mumbai thinks you are losing. The only thing that matters is victory.'

'But how to win?'

'Cut off their head.'

'Kill Rajesh Parab?'

'Yes. But really he's an old fool. He's the boss, but he's set in his ways.'

'It's Vilas Ranade then. He's the one.'

'Yes,' she said. 'If you get Vilas Ranade, you will leave them deaf and blind.'

Vilas Ranade was the one. He was Rajesh Parab's general, he had decimated us, tricked us, gone in front of us when we had expected him behind, and he had killed us. I knew now that he led them in war. But I still knew nothing about him, whether he had a wife, sons, what he looked like, where he went. He had no pattern, no habitation, no desires that I could see. I didn't know how to track a man who lived only for war. 'I don't even have a photo of him,' I said.

'They keep him out of town,' she said. 'Pune, Nashik, somewhere there. They bring him in only when there is trouble.'

'He sleeps until it's time to wake him up?'

'You don't waste a good shooter on trips to the municipality office. It's too risky. And he's the best of shooters. He's been around for a long time, ten, twelve years.'

'You've seen him?'

'Never.'

I was quiet for the rest of our time up the steps and into the temple, and when we finally got up to Ganesha, I didn't ask him for anything. I just watched him, examined his noose and his goad and laddoos and broken tusk, and wondered how he would scheme his army of ganas out of defeat, how the remover of obstacles would remove an obstacle he couldn't find and pin down. We had to move on then, the pressure of oncoming worshippers was huge and unrelenting, but I carried his image with me all the way home. We were stuck in a monstrous traffic jam in Juhu, and Kanta Bai fell asleep next to me, clutching her prasad from the temple on her lap, and I listened to her snoring, and thought and thought. My shoulder was burning, quiet little eddies of stinging fire, but the endless circling in my head was more painful: I could see the players of the game, the lanes and the buildings they moved from and to, Gopalmath, Nabargali, all of it laid out before me when I shut my eyes, and I went endlessly round and around, looking for an opening, a way to tear it all apart and put it together again. And the traffic growled and choked outside, and here we were, still alive, still breathing.

'Let me out,' I said. I leaned over and opened the door, and got out of the car. Chotta Badriya slid out from behind the wheel. 'No, no, get back in.'

'But, bhai . . .'

'Listen to me, just get back in. I want to walk for a bit.'

He was afraid of a coincidence, of somebody from the other side out for a stroll among the evening walkers and bhelpuri-eaters. It was possible, but I wanted suddenly to be alone. I raised a hand at him, and I think I must have frightened him with the look on my face, because he got right back in.

I walked down the curving road to the beach, past the chat-stalls and on to the sand. There were families walking with me, children excited into laughter by the horses trotting at the edge of the water, by the toy-wallahs and their hovering, silvery clouds of balloons, by the tantalizing kulfi-wallahs and their cool boxes all filmed over with tiny pearls of moisture. Here there was no war. Here was peace. I walked lightly amongst the old couples out for their evening walks, and the ranks of restless young men. The sea rushed steadily up the land, and finally I sat on a half-built brick platform, facing the waves. I was tired, empty-minded, and it was good to have my hair stirred gently by the water's slow breathing. There was a movement to my left. I looked, and under a pile of refuse, palm fronds and soggy paper packets and coconut husks, there was a jerky squirming, quick little dashings and then alert stillness. In the shadows there were more shadows, moving fast, and I saw a white cardboard box shift in a zigzag line, trembling with the urgency of hunger. I got up and walked over, and stood over the box, and I could now smell the strong rot, all the last leftover food, everything that had been thrown away. But there was no movement now. I laughed. 'Rats, I know you're here,' I said. 'I know you are.' But they were too clever for me. They lay still, and if I wanted I could probably kill some of them, but finally they would survive my attack and me.

'Bhai!' The shout came from down the beach. I raised my arm.

'Here,' I called. They came running up, Chotta Badriya and two others.

'Are you all right?' he said.

'I'm fine,' I said. I was, really. There was something moving inside me, a faint scurrying I could hardly see. I knew I had to wait for it to emerge. 'Let's go home,' I said.

I set up a meeting with Inspector Samant the next day. We met at a hotel in Sakinaka. 'This Vilas Ranade,' I said. 'I want his wicket. I have ten petis.'

He laughed in my face. He had a thick moustache, not very much hair on his head and big white teeth. He was sweating through his shirt, big wet dark patches. 'Ten lakhs!' he said. 'For Vilas Ranade. You're too hopeful.'

'Fifteen then.'

'Do you know who you're talking about? He was here when you were still drinking milk.'

I said, 'True. But can you do it?'

'It can be done.'

'You know something. What do you know?'

His eyes were steady, opaque. He was right, it had been a very stupid question. He had no reason to tell me what he knew. I was nervous, over-eager. Then he said, 'Why should I do it?'

'I will be here long after he's gone, Samant Saab. You know that. You've seen my progress. If we can work together, think of what lies in the future. Those Cobra Gang chutiyas have no future, no vision. What they do, they do, but they won't do anything new. The future is worth more than cash.'

He was listening. He wiped his shining takli with a handkerchief. 'Thirty,' he said.

'I can do twenty, saab. And once this is all over, there will be much much more.'

'Twenty-five. And I want it all in advance.'

Which was unprecedented, and insane. But – 'Yes, saab,' I said, 'I'll bring it to you in three days.'

He nodded, and took some saunf from the dish in the middle of the table. The bill he was leaving to me.

'Also, then, in three days,' I said, 'you had better arrest me.'

I didn't have any twenty-five lakhs in cash. I had five lakhs, maybe six and a half if I called in little loans I had made to citizens in Gopalmath, for medicine, for wedding saris. I couldn't do that, and I knew better than to ask Paritosh Shah for so bulky a loan. He was a businessman, and I was not currently a good risk, but he would find it very hard to say no to me, and it might have broken us apart. So I didn't ask that of him, but I did ask him for a big score. 'A target?' he said. 'Worth twenty-five lakhs? In three days?' I knew I was asking much, but he understood the urgency.

'Never mind the risk,' I told him. 'Just think about the prize.' He didn't have to think about it very long. Mahajan Jewellers, on Advani Road. It pleased me that it was right in the middle of Cobra Gang territory, a mile and a half from Rajesh Parab's house. We watched Mahajan Jewellers for one day and one night, and then I decided that we would do it during the day. Night might have been safer, but it would have meant getting in through the heavy sliding grille at the front, through the three locks, then through the shutter door they dropped down and locked also, and then through the glass doors. No, we went in at four in the afternoon, straight through the open door. There was one watchman out front, with the usual single-shot shotgun, and when he saw us coming with our seven pistols and choppers he dropped it without hesitation. On our way out, he held the door open for us. We had two stolen cars waiting outside, and getting away was smooth. No problems.

So now we had the money. The property itself wasn't enough, Paritosh Shah gave us fifteen lakhs for everything we had taken, and he loaned us the rest. I let him give me the money. I had confidence again, I could see my path, and I knew he felt it. It wasn't a favour he was doling out now, but an investment in future earnings. I was now full, and he was adding to my fullness. I was good for his cash, and for more. So I had the money, and straightaway, a day early, I called in Samant and gave it to him. And he arrested me.

Into the lock-up we went, myself and three of my boys. We were arrested for suspected complicity in the Mahajan Jewellers robbery and remanded to custody, that's what it said in the newspapers. On the outside, my boys disappeared from the streets, from Gopalmath, and the Cobra Gang celebrated. G-Company was finished, over and done with, all very quickly and no trouble at all, that was what they said. I sat in my cell and watched the wall. I had my back to one wall and I watched the other. My boys sat on all sides of me. I could stand the narrow space easily, the heat, I forced down the brittle rotis and the watery dal, but the repose of it, not moving and working, the rest and stillness of it crawled just under my skin and made me want to tear myself open. There were busy, buzzing insects in my veins. But I taught myself patience. I watched the wall. I felt it watching me, strong in its blankness. It wanted to outlast me. It knew it could. I stared it down. And I waited.

It took nine days. When the constables came to get us, my boys stood guard and I pissed on the wall. I wrote circles into its indifference while they watched, and then I let them lead me out. There was an advocate who had done the paperwork waiting in the senior inspector's room, and he led us out of the station. Our bail had been posted. It was dark outside, a moonless night and cloudy. Chotta Badriya was waiting outside with a car. He looked very tired, and he had his hair tied back, held back with one of those bands that girls wear.

'What's that in your hair, chutiya?' I said.

'Just like that, bhai,' he said, blushing like a girl and twisting his head down and to the side. And he smiled. When he smiled I knew it was all right.

He drove us fast into the thick of the city, up the spine and on to the highway, past Goregaon, and I felt revived by the crowds, by the weaving rows of trucks and cars, and the children running after a ball on the side of the road, and the ceaseless noise of it. I was quiet but completely awake, alert like a snake. Chotta Badriya wasn't talking, and I didn't want to ask him any questions, not yet. The promise sweltered in the air and it was delicious to hold in my mouth, the anticipation, the not knowing. We turned off the highway on to the slip road, and then off it, past a jhopadpatti, into darkness. Our beams conjured up a dusty road, trees sliding into existence and out again, it was like falling into a tunnel. I went eagerly into it. Then we took a sharp left, and the road changed, we crunched over dirt. There was a car parked at the end of the lane, and the hard black of a building through the overhanging branches, and we got out and walked towards it, around a corner, and now there was a single bulb above a door. And sitting on a crate next to the door, Samant, with his cigarette signalling red.

'Took too long,' he said. 'You're late.'

'It was the lawyers and everything,' Chotta Badriya said.

Samant tugged on the door, which opened with a long metallic squeak. Just inside, there was a man face-down on the floor. A blue shirt and black pants, and his hips cocked up and stiff.

'Vilas Ranade,' Samant said, with a little motion of his hand, palm up as if he was making introductions.

'You did it alone?' I said.

'He was a brown-sugar sniffer,' Samant said. 'The stupid bhenchod. He thought nobody knew. Used to go by himself to get it. I know the dealer who sold to him.'

'The dealer told you when Vilas Ranade would come to buy?'

'He had to, if he wanted to keep dealing.'

'You're sure this is Vilas Ranade?'

'I've seen him twice at the Mulund station when I was posted there. He had friends there.'

'I want to see his face.'

Chotta Badriya stepped over the body, tugged at the shoulder. Vilas Ranade's shirt was black at the front, soggy. Chotta Badriya got behind him, and then Vilas Ranade sat up into the light. He looked sleepy, eyelids half down. I know him, I thought. He looked just like me. I squatted in front of him, leaned closer. Yes, he was my duplicate. I waited for one of the others to remark on it, but nobody spoke.

'What's the matter, bhai?' Chotta Badriya said finally. 'Don't like his face?'

'No, I think the bastard's got an ugly face.' I tapped Vilas Ranade on the cheek lightly, and I stood up. 'What a game you played, Samant Saab,' I said. I took Samant by the hand and shook it violently. I thumped him on the shoulder, and I laughed, and all of them, every one of them, laughed with me. But in me it was all acting. I was making big motions and roaring and celebrating, but inside, inside I was bewildered: what did it mean that Vilas Ranade and I looked alike, and why did none of the others see it? What did it mean that he and I had hunted each other, like ghosts seen in mirrors, and then killed? Where did this coincidence point me, where was it taking me?

I was still dazzled when we got into the cars. Again we drifted through the long, unlit night, and by the time we were near the highway I had solved the conundrum. I had decided it had been a trick of the light. If he had looked so like me, Chotta Badriya would have seen it. Samant would have said something. I was tired from the days in the lock-up. I needed sleep, rest, good food. There was nothing to worry about.

Shooter Vilas Ranade Killed in Encounter, some of the afternoon papers reported the next day. Parab Gang Warlord Dies in Encounter. And then we destroyed the Cobra Gang. We ambushed their boys, we took their money, we intimidated their businessmen, we strolled down their streets. We lost four more of our boys, and one of them was my Sunny, who by now was so fervent in his worship of pistols that he carried two of them. A bullet fired from behind broke something in his back and left him pissing out his life into the road. But we shattered the Cobra Gang, and took their territories. We were still smaller, but now that seemed an advantage. We hit and ran, and then circled back and hit again. They were confused and old, like their Rajesh

Parab, who at the last tried to seek help from the bigger companies, he went here and there, to Dubai even, and everyone gave him assurances, and promises, and nothing else. We were the winning team, and we had a bright, burnished shine about us, and those watching the battle saw this, and placed their bets. They knew the practical lesson, had learnt it already: a small band of fighters, knit by hardship into brotherly love, will easily beat a large, unwieldy organization with its courage failing and its belief vanished.

Rajesh Parab died of a heart attack six weeks later, in his bed, in his sleep at night. Paritosh Shah said, 'He must have dreamed you coming through his door.' But I was glad I didn't have to kill him. I would have felt like a dog-catcher putting down a tired, yelping cur, and there was no pleasure even in the thought of it.

I caught a fever that winter. A dry, jittery whistling in my head and a jerky restlessness tossed me about my sweaty bed. Movies did not calm me, nor music, nor the girl Chotta Badriya brought in. I spat and spat, trying to rid myself of a rush of bitter saliva. I swallowed the pills, drank the salty water, ate the plain white rice. The fever stayed with me.

So I was wide awake at two in the morning when Chotta Badriya tapped at my door. 'We found Mohan Surve,' he said.

'You have him here?'

'Outside in the car.'

'Get him in.'

I got up and dressed. Since he had betrayed us, Mohan Surve had vanished from Bombay. After that night when I had seen his face outside the Mahal Bar, lit red by the neon, he had just gone, phut, away. Once the bullets had started flying, nobody had seen him, ever, not in Bombay and not in Wadgaon, where his sister stayed with her husband and children.

Chotta Badriya came in and helped me with my shoes. 'We watched the sister,' he said. 'The postman was showing us her letters.'

'Good. And then?'

'And then nothing much. Surve thought he was being very smart. Money orders every month from a Manmohan Pansare in Pune. Finding out which post office the money orders came from was simple enough. Then we just watched the post office. He had grown a beard.'

The beard was soft and very thin on Mohan Surve's face and didn't much disguise him. He still had fat cheeks, beady squirrel eyes. I would've known him from fifty feet. He began babbling as soon as he saw me.

'Bhai, I just got scared because of the shots and ran and hid,' he said. 'I didn't want to be part of all this any more, I can't take it, I'm a coward, forgive me, bhai, but that's how I am, forgive me. Sorry, bhai, sorry.'

He kept using that English word 'sorry', and that irritated me, angered me even more sharply than what he had already done.

'How much were his money orders?' I asked Chotta Badriya.

'Five thousand, six thousand, like that. The first one was ten thousand.'

And I looked at Mohan Surve. 'Don't try it, Mohan. Just don't try it.' My voice was a calm whisper, a surprise even to myself.

Then he broke, and threw himself on the ground, and clutched at my ankles, and fell loose. I smelt the piss spilling from him. Chotta Badriya had tied his wrists together with green electrical wire, and now as he twisted and turned, his skin chafed and blood seeped over the wire. On and on Mohan Surve went: the Cobra Gang had come to him first, he had said no to them, but they had threatened to kill his sister and her husband and the children, Vilas Ranade had threatened him personally with a sword. So he had told them I would be at Mahal that night, and they had prepared their ambush.

I had Chotta Badriya peel him away from my legs, and then I went back into my room. I sat on my bed. I thought of my boys who had died first, Krishna Gaikwad, Pradeep Pednekar and Qariz Shaikh with his stories, and I remembered how it felt to run down the side of the building, run from death with the shadows flailing towards me, and the pump of blood down my chest. Mohan Surve was making a wail in the next room now, it had all the force of a scream but not the loudness, and yet it penetrated the wall, this querulous long moan. I called Chotta Badriya in. 'Shut him up,' I said. 'I don't want him making noises. Make him calm. Give him something, whisky, something. And get the boys together. Anyone who is around or is available, tell them to be here in half an hour.'

So Chotta Badriya untied Mohan Surve's hands, gave him nimbu pani with three Calmpose crushed in. By the time the boys were together, Mohan Surve was lying curled on the ground, one arm over his head. The boys picked him up, hauled him up at the wrists and ankles and his head fell back and his eyes rolled, all glassy, dark and moving. I walked out of the house, and they followed. They carried Mohan Surve at four points, four of them, and brought him behind me. He was quiet now. We took him through the empty lanes and left the houses behind, and went up the hill above Gopalmath. I had a large Eveready torch, and I lit the way. I turned around only when we were at the top, at the small upturned bowl. While they all came up, the trailing line of my company, I was looking out at the haze of lights. My fever softened the diamond points into circling halos, and the horizon swam under this swarming, gleamy flux, the breathing of this undulating city.

'We're all here,' Chotta Badriya said.

I turned to them. 'Stretch him out,' I said. And they did. The four who had carried him sat above and below him and pulled him into a wide cross. Mohan Surve lay still, illuminated by the round beams from electric torches. 'You know what he did,' I said to the company. 'Many of us died.' I held out a hand to Chotta Badriya, who snuggled into it the cold handle of a sword. I walked around Mohan Surve until I stood directly over his head, facing the floating fire of the city, and hefted the blade in my hand. It was curiously heavy for such a slim, long thing. Good dense steel. There was a scar high on my shoulder, which I felt as a slight stiff tug sometimes, near my heart, but the strength was back in my arms. I widened my stance, raised the sword above my head, took a breath and dashed it down, into Mohan Surve's right arm, just below the shoulder. At this he raised his head and looked around, turning his eyes from side to side. I had the sword up again, and with the second stroke I separated his arm away from his body. The boy holding his right wrist fell backwards, and there was an immediate thick jet of black blood into the jiggling light. And a sound like a groan came from the company, and Mohan Surve began to talk. A confused jumble of syllables that sounded no sense, that's what it was. Mohan Surve babytalked even as Chotta Badriya took off his left arm with a single sweep of the sword, and I heard the clang of metal on the rock and saw a jumping shower of white sparks, and Mohan Surve's voice rose higher and his head was still up when somebody stepped up from the ranks and took the sword and attacked his left thigh. Then he screamed. But when it came to his right leg he was quiet, and his head was turned to the side. I think he was already dead.

'Take the pieces,' I said, 'and throw them somewhere. And I never want to hear his name again.'

Then I walked down my hill, to my basti, to my home. In the mirror in the alcove immediately to the right of the door, I saw that my shirt was ruined, splashed all over with blood. I took it off, and also my trousers, soggy to the front, and my damp shoes. I took a bath, with hot water. I ate a little sabudane ki khichdi, and drank a glass of milk with almonds in it. Then I slept.

Investigating Women

❧

The next day, Sartaj joined Parulkar on his morning constitutional. They walked in circles around Bradford Park, which was a small circle at the intersection of seven roads near Parulkar's house. It was five-thirty, and the grass underfoot was a little damp. Parulkar was wearing red keds under his flappy white pyjamas and speeding around the circumference, overtaking the other walkers and then lapping them. Sartaj was putting in serious effort to keep up.

'I don't understand the teaching at these new schools,' Parulkar said. 'How can Ajay be five and a half and not be able to read? They call themselves the best school in Mumbai. We had to use a dozen contacts to get the boy in, you know.'

Ajay was Parulkar's grandson, who was in upper KG at the very new and very modern Dalmia school. 'It's a new system of teaching, sir. They don't want to put pressure on the children.'

'Yes, yes, but at least teach them to read "cat" and "bat" by now. And you and I had pressure, and we didn't come out so badly.'

They went past Parulkar's bodyguards now, and then into another lap. 'I didn't do so well under all that pressure, sir. I was terrified by those exams.'

'Arre, you were not so bad. Only you had other things on your mind always, cricket and movies and then later, my God, girls.' Parulkar grinned. 'You remember that time I had to stand guard while you were studying?'

That was when Sartaj was fifteen. He had taken to jumping out of the window during mugging hours at home, and finally Parulkar had volunteered to keep a watch over him the night before his maths exam. They had a fine time actually, with regular dosages of whipped-up Nescafé, and oranges and small bananas, and Parulkar had shown a talent for reducing complex problems to simple questions. Sartaj had passed the exam with a fifty-eight per cent score, which was the highest he ever achieved in maths. 'Yes, sir. And we saw the chowkidar sleeping.'

They had thrown orange peels at the slumbering chowkidar, and now they laughed as they had then.

'Business now, Sartaj.'

'Yes, sir.' This meant they were coming to the end of the walk, which was meant to be mostly free of work distractions.

'I have a contact for you from the S-Company. Her name is Iffat-bibi. She is Suleiman Isa's maternal aunt. For a long time, she has been one of his main controllers here in Mumbai. She's old, but don't be fooled by that. She's very intelligent, very ruthless, she has been one of his main assets.'

'Yes, sir.'

'This is the number you can reach her at.' Parulkar slipped a folded note to Sartaj. 'She's always there in the afternoons. She will expect your call.'

'Thank you, sir. This is a big connection, sir.'

Parulkar shrugged, flapped a dismissive hand. 'And be careful. Whatever information she gives you, it's not for free. Sooner or later she'll ask something of you. So don't promise her anything you can't deliver.'

'Right, sir.'

'Interesting woman. There was a time, I was told, that men were killed over her. But when I first met her she was already old. And you know, I thought then that she may have been beautiful once, but she was never any man's trophy. If a man was killed over her, she made it happen. No doubt about that. No doubt at all.'

'I'll be careful, sir.'

Parulkar's walk was over, but he went to his car at the same speed. Sartaj watched him go, and thought that he had never truly repaid Parulkar for everything he had been given. 'Nothing in life is free' had been one of Parulkar's first lessons, but Sartaj had never felt that he had returned equal value. Maybe some day it would all become due.

That morning, Sartaj and Katekar followed Manika's lead to the glossy-pictured Kavita, who had once danced at a bar called Pritam but had made that very rare leap into the lower rungs of show business. Her name was actually Naina Aggarwal, and she was from Rae Bareli. The manager at Pritam Dance Bar looked at the photograph and told them the name of the serial she was acting in: *47 Breach Candy*. He watched it every Thursday, he was very proud of her, even though she had never contacted him once she had started appearing on television. The owner of Jazz Films, which produced *47 Breach Candy*, gave Sartaj her phone number and address and told him to watch the show, which was doing very well, very high TRPs, very good reviews, it was very entertaining, based on an American show but completely Indianized, completely of our culture. Naina Aggarwal lived not in Andheri East any more, but in an apartment in Lokhandwalla with three other girls, who all worked in television. She was small, prettier than her picture, and she started weeping even as Sartaj asked her where she was from, what her father did, if she had any brothers or sisters. Her mascara had blackened her face all the way to her chin by the time he said, 'We know you've been involved in some very bad activity. But we are not about to harass you. If you help us.'

She nodded fast, holding her hands clasped in front of her mouth. She sat on her bed, curled small, and she was very afraid of them, in that room she had managed to earn for herself. There was a shelf above the bed, bolted to the wall, and it was crowded with photographs of Rae Bareilly people in bright shirts, and Sartaj recognized her school-principal father. She came from a very respectable family, and she had danced at the bar only for two months, when she had first come to the city, when her money had rushed from her hands faster than she had imagined possible. She nodded eagerly. She was desperate to get the police away from her room before her flatmates and neighbours knew that she was involved in such nasty police business, that she had once danced in a sleazy bar.

'Here,' Sartaj said. He put the photograph of the dead woman on the bed next to Naina. 'You know this person?' She was terrified now, but couldn't look away from the photograph. 'It's all right. Just tell us her name.'

It took several swallows, three tries, before she could get it out. 'Jojo.'

'Jojo? J-o-j-o?'

'Yes. What has happened to her?'

'She is dead.'

Naina curled her legs up on the bed and looked very young. The serial she acted in was full of intrigue and adultery and murder, but Sartaj could see that she couldn't bring herself to ask how Jojo had died.

'Don't worry,' Sartaj said. 'We are not going to involve you in any of this, if you are honest with us. What was her surname?'

'Mascarenas.'

'Jojo Mascarenas. And you worked for her?'

'Yes.'

'How?'

Without raising her head from her knees, Naina tried a small shrug. 'She is a model co-ordinator and producer. She recommended me to agencies, she put me in videos.'

Sartaj was very soft and gentle now. 'But that wasn't everything, was it?'

Katekar was leaning against the door, letting Sartaj handle the interrogation. He and Sartaj had worked out, over the years, that in certain situations with women Sartaj's solicitousness and care worked better than the blunter tools of intimidation and loud voices. They used each skill impartially, depending on the context and the case. So now Katekar was shrinking himself into the corner and being very still.

'Naina-ji,' Sartaj said, 'this is very serious business. Murder. But I can't protect you if you are not completely honest with me. Don't worry. I promise I will not involve you in this at all, your name will never come up. I am just trying to find out about this Jojo. I am not interested in you at all, you are in no danger. So please, tell me.'

'She, she found clients for me.'

'Clients.'

She wept hard now, doubled over, shaking. They left ten minutes later, with Jojo Mascarenas's phone number and office address, and certain facts: Jojo was a model co-ordinator, and she also owned a TV production company, she produced programmes, and if there wasn't a production under way, roles and campaigns to go around, she could connect supply and demand, send the young, beautiful and needy to the rich and demanding, it was all a matter of a couple of glossies and a few phone calls, it was simple, it was efficient and everyone got what they wanted.

Sartaj and Katekar waited for the lift in a shadowed hallway. 'So crying Naina got the serial,' Katekar said. 'After all that dancing.'

'Yes,' Sartaj said. 'But what happens if the serial flops?'

'Back to Rae Bareilly.'

The unlit lift came and they stepped in, and after Katekar had rattled the folding metal gate shut three times, hard, they dropped, through fleeting bands of light. 'Nobody ever goes back to Rae Bareilly,' Sartaj said. And even if she went, Sartaj thought, would Rae Bareilly take her back? She had come all the way to Lokhandwalla, and to 47 *Breach Candy*, and to Jojo, and Jojo had sent her to other places.

'Time to call the Dilli-wali, sir?' Katekar said. Long bars of black were sliding up his face.

'Not quite yet,' Sartaj said. 'I want to know who this Jojo was.'

Jojo Mascarenas was neat. She had been dead for five days, but her apartment was clean, still shiny and scrubbed and polished. There was a row of gleaming steel ladles on the kitchen wall, hung on steel hooks in graduated order of size. The two phones and the answering machine on the counter next to the dining table were aligned precisely, and the tiled surfaces in the bathroom off the hallway shimmered a deep blue.

'This woman made money,' Katekar said.

But she was careful with it. The office address they had been given turned out to be her apartment, on the third floor of 'Nazara', on Yari Road. She made money but practised economies: the first small bedroom to the right of the hallway was her production office, crammed full with files and three desks and a computer and two phones and a fax machine, all in elegant order, all necessary to the work she did. Even her bedroom was not extravagant, just a simple double mattress on a low frame, no headboard. There was a tall mirror on the wall, and a table in front of it, lined with rows of cosmetics, and a black stool. There were no leather sofas, no chandeliers, no gold statues, none of the extravagances that Sartaj had come to expect from people who traded in images and bodies. When he had slid the key he had been carrying in his pocket into the lock, when it had turned smoothly, he had expected to see a red-satined filmi bordello, or a slattern's mess, but not this sober haven, this quiet home and workplace. It mystified him.

'All right,' Sartaj said. 'Let's search it.'

'What are we looking for?' Katekar said.

'Who this woman was.'

Katekar set to work, but he was impatient, quick, disapproving. Sartaj knew that he liked better the thin, pointed narrative of your ordinary murder case, where there was a corpse, an unknown killer or killers, and you were looking for a motive. Here there were two dead, one had obviously killed the other, and what did it matter what their relationship was? How would you know? Why would you care? Who cared about a gangster and a pimp? Katekar was quiet, but Sartaj knew he was cursing. Aaiyejhavnaya case it was according to Katekar, Sartaj was sure, and aaiyejhavnayi Delhi woman, this was all jhav-ed. 'Jhav-jhav-jhav,' Sartaj hummed as he worked. He did the bedroom first, because it was easy. Anything useful would be in the office, but the bedroom had to be done, and so he went at it. There was a cupboard built deep into the wall, along the entire length of the room, and it had two densely packed rows of hanging saris, blouses, ghagras, trousers, jeans, T-shirts, shirts. There was an order to it, a womanly and very personal logic that Sartaj couldn't quite understand, but it reminded him powerfully of the gradations of shirts in his cupboard by colour, from red to blue. Jojo's cupboard made him like her. He liked her love for shoes, her care for leather, her understanding of the different functions of footwear, why it was necessary to have three pairs of sneakers, from spare to super-technological, and he liked that she had them on the rightmost end of the lowest of three stepped rows of sandals and boots and chappals and stiletto heels. The apartment was simple, almost bare, but the clothes were flamboyant. Sartaj approved.

But, as expected, there was nothing in the bedroom of particular interest. A pink bathroom held a multiplicity of shampoos and soaps, and two pairs of panties and a bra hung on the curtain rod. There were more clothes and some dishes and old lamps in the high-up storage slots above the clothes cupboard, and make-up and various kinds of thread and sewing needles in the drawers of the dressing table, and a stack of *Femina* and *Cosmopolitan* and *Stardust* and *Elle* next to the bed, but that was all. Katekar was finishing up the drawing room when Sartaj came out into the hallway.

'Her big purse was behind the kitchen counter,' he said. 'On the floor. Just sitting there.'

'Anything in it?'

'Lipstick-shipstick, that's all. No driver's licence, but there is a voting card and a PAN card.'

He held the cards out. Juliet Mascarenas, they both said. But this was the first time Sartaj had seen her smile. She was very alive in both pictures, sparkling lazily at the camera, confident that she knew something about you.

'Anything else?' Sartaj said.

'Nothing. But there are no photos.'

'Photos?'

'Photos. There's not one in the entire house. I've never known a woman who didn't stick photos all over the place.'

Katekar was right. When Megha had left him, she had taken many photographs with her, and still Sartaj had spent a Sunday afternoon putting pictures in a shoe box, pulling them from the walls. And Ma had entire walls of them, histories of the family and the branches of it, all laid out, all its connections and losses. 'Maybe this Jojo keeps them in her files,' Sartaj said. And they went into her office. The files were in a black filing cabinet, four chambers high. They were neatly labelled: 'D'Souza Shoe Ad'; 'Sharmila Restaurant Campaign'. The bottom shelf was packed, heavy, it came outwards slowly.

'Actors?' Katekar said.

'Yes, and actresses.' The men were to the right, women to the left, in alphabetized rows of glossies, with résumés stapled to the back. Anupama, Anuradha, Aparna. Not quite actresses yet, but young and hopeful. Full of hope. And there was a fullness of them, there were just too many of them. Most would not be successful, but more kept coming to this city of gold. From this surplus and hunger, from this simple equation, came Jojo's business. They searched on, opening drawers and lifting files off shelves. There was a half-height metal cabinet, which the third key on Jojo's hoop opened, and inside they found her bank books, her cheque books, her bank statements, and jewellery in a metal box: two gold necklaces, three pairs of gold bracelets in different designs, a string of pearls, diamond earrings and a tangled pile of silver.

'Where's her cash?' Katekar said. 'Where does she keep her cash?'

Cash was how clients for a certain commodity paid their debts. There was some black money in Jojo's legitimate television business, but much of it was conducted with honest, above-board cheques. Her little side-business of prostitution generated only cash, this was certain, reams of it. But it wasn't in the metal cabinet. You couldn't keep it in a bank. Where was it? Sartaj went into the hallway, circled the kitchen and the drawing room. He lifted a framed print off the wall. It was a forest scene, but under the verdant glade there was only the wall. He stood on the edge of the tub in the bathroom and tapped the tiles on the ceiling. It was all solid, no hidden hollows, no secret compartments behind the water tank suspended above the door. Back into the hallway, and Sartaj saw that Katekar had moved the cabinets and tables in the office away from the walls and was on his knees testing the edges of the floor. In the past, they had found money in subtle hideaways, in precisely engineered hollows, there was an expertise in this city in hiding money, the builders had perfected the art of crafting shelves and headboards that slid away at the touch of a secret button to reveal money packed away. Once they had discovered gold bars in the pouchy bottoms of rich red brocade curtains. It was called black money, but Sartaj always thought of it as grey: it was illegal and a blight, but taxes were legal and a blight, and so he searched for it but never felt contempt for those who hoarded it. But Jojo made her cash from selling youngsters to the sticky appetites of men, and so her money was blacker than most, despite the cleanliness she practised in her life. Where was it, this reeking money, this pile of paper smelling of crusty hotel sheets and dried sweat? Where? Not in the pink bathroom, and not inside her mattress. Sartaj took her clothes from the cupboard and threw them on to the bed, making a luxurious pile of silky crimson and white and deep greens. He probed the walls of the cupboard, tapping and then pressing with his hands, and he took in her smell, the breath of her body and her perfumes. He stood for a moment with his palms on the roof of the cupboard, flat, and then he went and sat on the bed. Resting on a cascade of blouses and skirts, he asked, where have you hidden it? Where? The most likely place was the bathroom, because tiles were easy to build behind, but it was such an ancient cliché: Hema Malini and Meena Kumari and half a dozen other heroines had been caught with cash in their loos, and Jojo was more complicated than that. Sartaj was sure of it.

Leaning back, he started to see the sense of her shoes. There were three tiers of steps built at the bottom of the cupboard, in the same wood, stretching nearly across the entire width. Bottom step, extreme right, was the most informal, sneakers and bright Bata rubber chappals and then Kolhapuri chappals, a great variety of them. Second step was comfortable shoes, practical ones, professional but hardy, and easy to wear for an entire day of work. But the leftward end of the second step edged over into boots, chunky ones with long thick laces and lashings of attitude, and then the top shelf started on the right with a pair of black boots with needle-sharp heels and soft tops that must have risen half-way up Jojo's thighs. From there the heels were ever more delicate and dangerous, and the uppers and straps thin and thinner, and Sartaj saw how the leftmost and last pair on the top shelf, a diaphanous, burning amber nothing of a shoe, all tapering knife-heel and single diagonal thong, would make Jojo's foot naked even as it clothed it. 'Well done, Jojo,' he said. 'Those are shoes, Jojo.'

He got up, moved the shoes off the middle shelf, and took hold of the plank and tugged at it. It was solid. He bent his head and peered, and he could see the floor and the rear of the cupboard under the shelves. The top row swept down from the boots to the stilettos, and Sartaj said, 'You go from right to left, Jojo.' He leaned low, spread his arms wide, and grasped the sides of the top shelf, and pulled. Still solid, and then his fingers slipped and he felt a groove, two grooves, one on each side. They ran along the sides of the shelves, just under the overhanging lip of the top shelf, a finger-thickness high, a few inches long: handles. Sartaj's nose was an inch from one of Jojo's black stilettos, and his pulse was humming. Got you. Got you. He grasped the handles and pulled backwards. Nothing, no give. Still solid. But there was a little movement at the top of the right handle, a contraction under his fingers. He braced the heel of his hand against the top of the shelf and squeezed, as if he were pressing a very stiff brake on a motorcycle, and yes, yes, a definite movement, a catch gave way. He did it on both sides and pulled backwards and the whole thing, all of it, the three shelves with the shoes on top, the entire construction came away from the back of the cupboard. He went backwards, grinning, scattering chappals and boots and strappy sandals. 'Ay, Katekar,' he yelled. 'Katekar.'

Together, they peered happily into the two-foot-deep compartment that Jojo had hidden her secrets in. There was, of course, the cash: neat stacks of hundred-rupee and five-hundred-rupee bundles, pushed all the way back, to the left. Katekar was measuring it professionally between the outstretched thumb and forefinger of his left hand. 'Not much,' he said. 'Five or six lakhs. Some of it looks the same as Gaitonde's stash.' These five-hundred-rupee bundles were all new, in Central Bank of India wrappers, again stacked inside the same efficient shrink-wrapped plastic.

'Gaitonde must have paid her,' Sartaj said.

'For her randi services.'

On the right, also against the back of the niche, lay three black photo albums on top of each other. But Sartaj felt no urgency, no desire to take them, to flip them open and delve into Jojo's hidden life. He was concentrated on the money, and he knew Katekar was also. He could hear it in the slow drag of Katekar's breath, compressed by the awkward forward squat. The cash was very problematic: six lakhs in black money discovered in a dead woman's apartment was ordinarily a free gift for the good policemen. Not all of it – maybe five lakhs was the surprise present, and one lakh would have to go into the panchnama and therefore into the government's maw, and that was enough. Nobody would ask awkward questions about a dead madam's black money. The amount was small enough for nobody to notice its absence, and so Katekar's rules of prudence would not be violated. Nobody would notice, unless Jojo kept records, or had told somebody about her stash. Unlikely, but possible. In a high-pressure, Delhi-orientated case involving RAW this was too much risk, there was a single glance between them and it was decided.

'Albums,' Sartaj said briskly, and drew them out. The first photograph in the first album was a younger Jojo, younger by many years and much experience. She was wearing a red dress, a child's frock really, with a square neck and a high waist, and looked to be about sixteen. She was sitting on a black couch, her arms intertwined with an older girl's, a young woman with the same broad, toothy smile. The following few pages had the same pair, laughing on a bed, on the seashore, on a balcony against a rising Mumbai skyline.

'Sisters,' Katekar said.

'Right,' Sartaj said. 'But who is taking all the pictures?' He flipped on through the pages of happiness and love. Then there was a blank page, all white. But there had once been a photograph there, he could still see the impression it had made under the sheer plastic. The next page again had the two sisters, this time in the Hanging Gardens. But there had been a photograph removed every two pages or so, and about half-way through the album, the sisters were having a birthday. It wasn't a party really, just them, gifts on the dining table and a pink cake with lots of white icing.

'Seventeenth,' Katekar said. He had, with his quick head for numbers, assessed the bright candle flames.

Sartaj turned the page, and there was a blank, this time with no impression left by an image. The rest of the album was empty. The photography had stopped abruptly. Sartaj put the album aside, and turned to the next one. This one went backwards into childhood. The sisters were in white school shirts and dark skirts. And then they stood barefoot, their identical pigtails sticking straight out like wings, happy in front of a house with a heavy stone lintel and thick wooden doors and a sunlit courtyard inside. 'Village,' said Sartaj. 'But where?'

'South,' Katekar said. 'Somewhere south. Konkan.'

Now they were in a studio, the sisters, in identical blue frocks with puffy sleeves and enormous bursts of lace at the throat, and their mother was with them. She wore sober black, a dress with sleeves down to the wrists, and her head shone with streams of grey, and the lights picked out the crucifix she wore at her neck and made it blaze. She was smiling, but carefully. 'No father,' Sartaj said.

'No father at all,' Katekar said. 'What is it, a farm?'

The sisters played under trees, in groves brimming over with green light, they ran between long rows of plants with broad leaves curling at the edges. 'I don't know,' Sartaj said. He knew nothing about trees, or plants, or farms. This was another world.

The last album was of the old-fashioned type which nobody made any more, with thick black pages, and the first photograph was held on to the page by small black corners, elegant little tabs, Sartaj couldn't remember what they were called. But both he and Katekar said together, 'Father.' The father sat with that particular stiffness which men and women from a long-ago generation assumed in front of cameras, it was the formality owed to a rare event, and he wore a white uniform. His shoulders were thrown back, and his right hand was curled in a fist against his hip.

'Navy,' Katekar said.

'Merchant Navy.'

The father had his daughters' eyes, large and direct. Actually, for the next couple of pages he had only one daughter, who stood between him and his wife, holding both their hands. And then suddenly, on a fresh page, here was the new arrival. She reached out with both her hands and her feet towards the camera, grinning toothlessly, fine-haired and round-faced. She reached towards the name above the photo, the name hand-inked on to the black page in white writing edged with flourishes and decorative marks: Juliet.

'Ju-li-et?' Katekar said.

'Yes,' Sartaj said. 'Like with Romeo.'

Katekar's laugh was long and full. 'So Juliet became Jojo? And Gaitonde was her Romeo?' He pronounced it 'Rom-yo', and Sartaj found his pleasure unfair and ugly, and his guffaws scraped across the base of Sartaj's skull. He thought Katekar very coarse and ganwar and low-class in that moment, and didn't care to correct him. Sartaj was feeling protective of the Juliet-that-was, before Jojo ever existed. She grew up in the pages that followed, under the care of her sister and mother. Soon after Juliet began walking, the mother began to dress the two sisters alike, in identical frocks and the same hair and the same hair-band. This first photograph with the two of them in matching outfits was a studio portrait, in front of a backdrop of the Eiffel Tower. They stood holding hands under the graceful arc towards a red sky, and now there were two names in white ink under the picture: 'Mary' and 'Juliet' separated by a fancy curlicue.

'Mary Mascarenas,' Sartaj said. That was the sister.

This paired dressing ended when Juliet was ten, or maybe eleven, in the last pictures in the album. In that birthday photograph, she had her hair cut short in a smart little bob, much shorter than Mary's, and she had a necklace, bright, light-coloured beads. The frock was the same as her sister's, but it was somehow different. She carried it better. Juliet had started to assert herself, she knew who she was and she was resisting her mother. Sartaj liked the tip-toed exuberance of her stance, her impudence. And then there was the serious Mary.

In Jojo's fat address book, under 'M', Sartaj found 'Mary' and work and home phone numbers, and an address in Colaba. But the number was old, outdated, Sartaj knew that the Colaba exchange had been converted to digital at least seven, eight years ago. Had Jojo not talked to Mary for eight years? Sartaj pondered, and they put the apartment in order, things back to their original positions, everything but the bedroom cupboard. Then Sartaj made the call to the Delhi-walli.

They sat in Jojo's office and waited. Sartaj swivelled slowly on Jojo's office chair and thought about sisters and their quarrels. Ma spoke often about her own older sister, Mani-mausi, and of her stubbornness, her silly communistic refusal to get live-in help despite long illness and weakness, what if she has one of those fainting spells and falls down the stairs or something, how many times I've told her to come here and stay with me, but she's so stubborn. Sartaj could never bring himself to point out that she, Ma, the younger sister, was no less self-willed, no less protective of her own prickly independence, no less devoted to the house she had built, to its high walls, its lambent floors and familiar lights, its corridors of quiet.

Jojo had built herself a home also, and it had been hard-won. Next to the kitchen sink, in a small floor-level cupboard, they had found a box of tools, and two rows of cans of paint in various colours. She had painted the rooms herself. Inside the fridge, there were plastic containers full of left-over food. Jojo threw nothing away. Despite the extravagance of her shoes, she was frugal. She was energetic too, Sartaj thought. You could see that in the photos. She must have been good at what she did.

The Delhi-walli came quickly. She was there in twenty minutes, maybe even less, in a black Ambassador. From Jojo's drawing-room window, Sartaj and Katekar watched the car pull into the building's compound, fast. There was a fast rat-tat-tat of car doors slamming shut, and barely two minutes later there was a knock on the door.

Anjali Mathur led her people in, breathing hard. Today her salwar-kameez was dark brown. The man immediately behind her was Makand, who had thrown Sartaj out of Gaitonde's bunker. 'Bedroom?' Anjali Mathur said.

Sartaj pointed. On the phone, he had already told her Jojo's name, her profession, her professions, and about the secret niche in the cupboard, about the sister named Mary. The number he had called was a land line, but the call must have been forwarded to the mobile phone she carried in her left hand.

'Could you wait outside?' she threw over her shoulder as she marched across the room. One of her short-haired flunkies was already holding the door-knob, and Katekar was barely through the door when it shut firmly. He and Sartaj stood in the corridor, too baffled to be angry.

There was nothing to do but wait, and so they did. 'Those chutiyas with her were the same ones,' Katekar said, 'from that day with Gaitonde.'

Sartaj nodded. The three men with Anjali Mathur had been at Gaitonde's bunker, and they all had the same haircut and the same shoes. What shoes did she have on, with her brown salwaar-kameez?

He hadn't noticed, it had all been too quick. Something eminently sensible, he was sure, flat-heeled and sturdy. She was that sort, with her hair tied tightly back and her dupatta efficiently slung and the square brown leather bag with the strong straps, big enough to hold whatever an international agent carried on her missions. The air in front of the lift was stale and very hot, and Sartaj felt the sweat gather on his forearms. He began to breathe deeply, in a rhythm he had developed in a thousand stake-outs. If he could get it just right, heat and sweat would recede, and time would turn inward on itself until it whirlpooled into stillness, and he was relieved of the world while he was still in it. But he had to get it just right. He breathed, and he could hear Katekar on the other side of the door, trying also to find a repose in the pressing stillness. They perspired together, and after a while they were breathing together. Sartaj was floating, veering up and vanishing into rooms of his childhood where with anxious concentration he whitened his keds for PT in the morning, and showed them to Papa-ji, who was a stickler for perfect white, much more than any monitor at school, and who had impressed upon his son the urgent lesson that the best outfit could be ruined in its effect by a sloppy pair of shoes, and an ordinary one made glorious by soft, mirror-shined, deep brown tasselled loafers. What had Ma done with Papa-ji's shoes, those orderly columns of black and brown in the special narrow cupboard which always stood to the left of the clothes cupboard? And what had become of his suits, of that mothball-tinged wool smell of rain-laden mountainsides? Given away, packed away. Lost now, even a white Filipino shirt that a friend had brought back from Manila, that had set off Papa-ji's white upturned moustaches and the forward sweep of his beard, that he had worn with an entrancing flamboyance on his sixty-seventh birthday with grey twill trousers and a jet-black turban. Sartaj had burst out laughing in admiration when he had first seen him walking down the gravel path at the front of the house. But later that evening, on the way back from the restaurant, they had climbed up three flights of stairs in a new shopping mall, and Papa-ji had had to stop on the second landing to catch his breath, and Sartaj had faced away, looking steadfastly out of a window at neon signs and had listened to the small alternating, fluttering sound, life still finding itself, working on, and he had been afraid.

'Inspector Singh?' It was Makand, poking his grey bullet-head into the corridor. 'Come in, please.' The invitation was for Sartaj only.

Inside, Anjali Mathur was seated at the dining table. She pointed at the bottle of cold water and glasses on the table. 'Sorry about keeping you outside. The case is such that we have to be very careful.'

The rest of her little army was absent from the drawing room. Searching the bedroom, perhaps. Sartaj poured himself a glassful, drank, and waited. The water was deliciously cold. He was content to drink and be quiet because he had no idea what kind of case it was. Anjali Mathur had very direct eyes, very bright, and now she was waiting for him to say something. He poured himself another glass, and drank it slowly this time, sipping. If the case was such, whatever kind of such that was, he had nothing to gain by speaking. He sipped, and looked right back at her, not contesting her stare, but casual and drinking and yet not giving way.

She shifted slightly, and settled into the faintest of smiles. 'Do you want to know what the case is?'

'You'll tell me what I need to know,' Sartaj said.

'I can't tell you very much. But I can tell you that it's very big.'

'Yes.'

'What do you feel about that?'

'It scares me.'

'You don't feel excited that you've been picked to work on a big case?'

Sartaj threw his head back and laughed. 'Excitement is one thing. But big cases can eat up small inspectors.'

She was smiling broadly now. 'But you'll work on it?'

'I do what I'm told.'

'Yes. I'm sorry I can't tell you much more about it. But let us say that it involves national security, great danger to national security.' Again, she was waiting for him to say something. 'You understand what I'm saying?'

Sartaj shrugged. 'That kind of thing seems always filmi to me. Usually the most exciting thing I do is arrest local taporis for extortion. A murder here and there.'

'This is real.'

'Okay.'

'And very big.'

'I understand.' Sartaj didn't understand much at all, but if it was the right kind of big case, perhaps it wasn't bad to be attached to it.

Perhaps there was credit and commendations to be had from doing small things for a big case.

'We need more on what this Jojo and Gaitonde were doing together. What their business was together.'

'Yes.'

'You found this Jojo very fast. Shabash. But we need to know more. Press the investigation from the Gaitonde side. Follow up with his partners, his employees, anyone you can find. See what they say.'

'I'll do that.'

'I'll have this phone number for this sister checked out by someone in the Colaba station, and when we get a fix on her, you go and talk to her, see what you can get about Jojo from her.'

'I should talk to the sister?'

'Yes.'

It was impossible to investigate without changing what you were investigating, without the subjects becoming wary. And Anjali Mathur, for reasons she wasn't about to reveal, wanted very much to have her suspects think that this was a local investigation. Sartaj thought that she had a good investigator's face, curious but neutral, not giving away anything. 'Okay, madam,' he said. 'I can tell her where the sister died?'

'Yes. See if she knows anything about the sister's dealings with Gaitonde. And as before, report to me directly. Only to me. On that phone number.'

And that was it, as far as instructions and clarifications from Anjali Mathur went. Sartaj took the bottle and a glass from the table, and took it into the corridor for Katekar, who was by now quite drenched with sweat from the shoulders down the back. He was much less bothered by summer heat than Sartaj, he thought nothing of walking a couple of miles through a May afternoon, but he sweated much more. Sartaj put this heat-resistant stamina down to a lifetime of conditioning: Katekar had grown up without even fans, and so he survived heatwaves blithely. It was all a question of what you were used to. Katekar drank a glass of water. 'Are we finished with this now?' he said with a little tilt of his head over his left shoulder, towards the apartment, Jojo and Anjali Mathur.

'Not yet,' Sartaj said.

Katekar said nothing.

'Drink up,' Sartaj said, grinning. 'We have lots to do. National security depends on us.'

There was somebody else who wanted to talk about national security waiting for Sartaj at the station. His name was Wasim Zafar Ali Ahmad, and it was printed in Hindi, Urdu and English on the card that he handed to Sartaj. Under the name there was a title, 'Social Worker', and two phone numbers.

'I was surprised, inspector saab,' he said, 'when I heard that you had been twice to Navnagar and had not contacted me. I thought that maybe it was difficult to find me. I am usually not at my home. I move around a lot, for work.'

Sartaj turned the card over with his fingertips and laid it down. 'I went to Bengali Bura.' They were sitting at his desk, across from each other.

'Which is very much in Navnagar. I do a lot of work there.' He was about thirty, this long-named Ahmad, a little plump and a little tall and very confident. He had been waiting for Sartaj at the front of the station and had followed him inside, his card ready. He was wearing a black shirt with small white embroidery at the cuffs, spotless white pants and a determined expression.

'Do you know the boy who was killed?' Sartaj said.

'Yes, I had seen him sometimes.'

Sartaj had seen Ahmad too, he was sure of it. He looked familiar, and no doubt he came and went from the station, social workers often did. 'You live in Navnagar?'

'Yes. On the highway side. My family was one of the first ones there. That time, it was mostly people from UP, from Tamil Nadu. These Bangladeshis, they came later. Too many of them, but what can you do? So I work with them.'

'And you knew the apradhis? And this Bihari fellow who was their boss?'

'Only by face, inspector saab. Not enough to say hi-hello. But I know people who know them. And now this murder they have done. It is very bad. They come from outside and do bad things in our country. And they spoil the name of good people who are from here.'

He meant Indian Muslims, who suffered broad-brushed slander and hatred put abroad by Hindu fundamentalists. Sartaj sat back, rubbed at his beard. Wasim Zafar Ali Ahmad was definitely interesting.

Like most so-called social workers, he wanted to move ahead, to become a big man in the area, a man with connections who would attract a clientele, a man who would be noticed by the political parties as a local organizer and volunteer and finally a potential candidate. Social workers had become MLAs and even MPs, it took a long time but it had been done many times. Ahmad had the politician's gift of mouthing clichés without sounding ridiculous. He looked intelligent enough, and maybe he had the drive and the ruthlessness. 'So,' Sartaj said, 'for the sake of the country and good citizens, you want to help me with this case?'

'Of course, inspector saab, of course.' Ahmad's happiness at being understood came from his belly, his whole body. He put his elbows on the desk and leaned forward towards Sartaj. 'I know everyone in Navnagar, and even in Bengali Bura I have lots of connections, I work with those people, I know them. So I can quietly ask, you know. Try to find out what people are saying, what people know.'

'And what do you know now? Do you know anything?'

Ahmad chortled, 'Arre, no, no, inspector saab. But I have no doubt I can find out something here and there, some little thing.' And he sat back, chubby and self-contained.

Sartaj gave in. Ahmad wasn't stupid enough to give away good tips for nothing, or his sources. 'Good,' Sartaj said. 'I will be grateful if you can render any assistance. And is there anything I can do for you?'

They understood each other now. 'Yes, saab, actually there is.' Ahmad put away his charm and stated his terms quietly, plainly. 'In Navnagar there are two brothers, young boys, one is nineteen, another is twenty. Every day they bother the girls when they are leaving for work, they say this and that. I have asked them to stop, but then they threatened me. They have openly said that they will break my arms and legs. I could take action against them myself, but I have restrained myself. But when the water starts to rise above one's head, inspector saab . . .'

'Names? Age? Where do I find them?'

Ahmad already had the particulars neatly written out in his diary, and he tore the page out for Sartaj with fastidious care. He supplied descriptions and details of the family, and then excused himself. 'I have taken up enough of your time, saab,' he said. 'But please call me any time, day or night, if you need anything.'

'I'll call you after I see to these two,' Sartaj said.

'The citizens of Navnagar will be very happy, saab, if you can rescue their sisters and daughters from this daily trouble.'

With that, Wasim Zafar Ali Ahmad placed a hand on his chest and made his exit. He had invoked the people of Navnagar, but both he and Sartaj knew that the two brothers had to be disciplined because Ahmad wanted it so. This was the first offering in their deal, this test of trust and goodwill. Sartaj would pick up the roadside Romeos, whose main offence was undoubtedly not their harassment of passing women but their disrespect towards Ahmad. Sartaj would see to them, and Ahmad would give him some information. Ahmad would then be seen in the basti as a man who had police connections, and his name would be heard and more people would arrive at his door, seeking his patronage and help, and in turn inflate his influence. If all went well for him, maybe in a few years, Sartaj would be the one calling him 'Saab'. But all that was a long while away, and first there was this little task of the chastisement of the Eve-teasing brothers. All great careers began with these little exchanges and were sustained by them. Mutual interest was the lubricating oil that ran the great and small machinery of the world, and Sartaj would use it to send criminals skidding into captivity. He felt excitement prickle up his neck and through his forearms, that old thrill which came to him when he felt a case opening up. Good, good, this was good. It was foolish to expect success, but Sartaj couldn't help savouring the anticipation. He would find the killers, he would catch them, he would win: the thought of victory sparked in his chest like a tiny burn, and he took energy from it all day.

That evening, over a glass of Scotch, Sartaj told Majid Khan about his new long-named source. Majid wasn't a drinker, but he had a bottle of Johnny Walker Black for Sartaj. Sartaj drank from it every time he came for dinner, and this evening he was depending on it a little too much, gulping it down greedily. He was telling Majid about Wasim Zafar Ali Ahmad while Majid's kids put plates on the table and their mother rattled spoons in the kitchen.

'Yes, I know him, this Ahmad,' Majid said. 'Actually, I know his father.'

'How?'

'I found him during the riots, just next to the highway in Bandra. I was going to Mahim with four constables. From far away, I saw these three bastards standing over something. The streets were completely empty, you know, and there was just this empty road and these three. So I told the driver, go, go. And we sped up, and as soon as they saw the jeep, the three chutiyas ran off. Now I saw this man lying on the ground. You know, grey beard, clean white kurta, white topi, just an old Muslim gentleman. He had tried to run, they had caught up with him, pushed him down. He was very scared, but he wasn't hurt.'

'He would have been. If you hadn't saved him. Dead.'

'Arre, I didn't save him. We happened to come along.' Majid wasn't being falsely modest, he was stating flat facts. He scratched at his chest, and drank from his glass of nimbu pani. 'Anyway, we put him in the back of the jeep, took him along. He couldn't speak for an hour. But ever since then, he comes every Bakr'id to my office, he brings some gosht, I touch it and send him back with it. But he comes without fail. Nice old fellow.'

They were standing on the balcony of Majid's eighth-floor apartment, leaning on the parapet. There was a perfectly round moon hanging low over the staggered oblongs of the rooftops, over the dark rim of watery lowlands and the row of tin-roofed kholis and the sea beyond. Sartaj couldn't think of the last time he had seen this round moon. Maybe, he thought, you needed to be up this high to see it, high above the streets. 'His son never came with the old man? To thank you and ask you for help?'

'No.'

'Smart fellow.' Ahmad was demonstrating his intelligence by not presuming on the thread of gratitude that bound his father and Majid, tugging on it. He was proceeding in the proper manner, going through Sartaj, the local inspector. If Ahmad could make Sartaj and the constables happy, they would recommend him to Majid, who perhaps would make it possible for Ahmad to gain influence and conduct activities of questionable legality, bringing prosperity and further advancement.

'Yes,' Majid said. 'He's not an innocent like his father.'

'Innocents have very good luck sometimes, no?'

'Sometimes. The father said they had some relative who was killed in the riots. Cousin brother.'

'Close cousin?'

'No, far, it sounded like. The old man was making a big fuss about it the first time he came to see me. I told him he was lucky it was only one far cousin. In this country, if you look at any family long enough, you'll find some far cousin whose luck turned bad. If not in this riot, then in some other one.'

This was true. Sartaj had heard stories in his own family, about people fleeing homes in the middle of the night.

'Come on, you two,' Rehana called from inside. She had the familiar plastic bowl with its close-fitting top and red rose pattern in her hand. She had been making rotis in the kitchen. The khima would have been made earlier in the evening in collaboration with her all-purpose maidservant, and between the two of them they could produce delight or devastation. It was always a lottery, and Sartaj pulled up his chair glad of the whisky he had drunk. Imtiaz and Farah were elbowing each other as they settled in. He had known them since they had been toddlers, and now that they were almost grown up the small apartment seemed smaller.

Imtiaz passed him a bowl. 'Uncle, have you seen the CIA website?' he said.

'The CIA, like Americans?' Sartaj said.

'Yes, they have a site, and they let you look at their secret documents.'

Farah was serving raita into a bowl for Sartaj. 'If they let you read it, it's not secret, idiot. Uncle, he spends hours finding weird articles and talking to girls on the internet.'

'You shut up,' Imtiaz said. 'Nobody's talking to you.'

Majid was smiling. 'For this I spent thousands and thousands of rupees, so my son can talk to girls in America?'

'Europe,' Farah said. 'He has a girlfriend in Belgium, and another one in France.'

'You have girlfriends?' Sartaj said. 'How old are you?'

'Fifteen.'

'Fourteen,' Farah said. She was smiling. 'I bet he's told them he was eighteen.'

'At least I sound like I'm eighteen. Not like some people who behave as if they're eleven still.'

Farah reached under the table, and Imtiaz winced. He held up his arm. 'The fingernails of the female,' he said, looking very pleased with himself, 'are deadlier than the male.'

'Stop it, you two,' their mother said. 'Let Uncle eat.'

Sartaj ate and was relieved to find that this evening had somehow been saved from culinary havoc. 'New haircut?' he said to Farah.

'Yes! You are the only man in the world who would notice. My dear Papa didn't figure out for three days why I was looking different.'

'Very nice,' Sartaj said. She looked quite plumply pretty, and Sartaj wondered if she had boyfriends in Belgium, or even in Bandra. But he kept the question to himself, knowing that Majid was very liberal, but that his tolerance of light-hearted romance didn't extend to his daughter. He might spend hard-won cash on a computer for his children, for his son, but that fierce cavalry moustache wasn't just an affectation. Boys under the spell of Farah's new look would have to be madly brave to climb up her castle wall eight floors tall. She was beaming now, and Sartaj was sure that there were lads whose fear had been banished by that glow. He himself had done some wall-climbing in long-ago days, and had braved fierce fathers for a lovely face.

After dinner, Rehana brought Sartaj a cup of tea and sat next to him on the sofa. She had the same broad cheekbones as her children, and a comfortable heaviness. In the gold-framed photograph on the wall she was a slim, hennaed bride, but even then, even with the formally lowered head, she had had the same bright eyes. 'So, Sartaj. Got a girlfriend?'

'Yes,' Sartaj said. 'Yes.'

'Who? Tell me.'

'A girl.'

'So what would a girlfriend be, a pineapple? Sartaj, for a policeman, you're a very-very bad liar.'

'It's a boring topic, Bhabhi.'

'My son doesn't think so.' Her son had walked down to the corner shop with her husband and daughter for ice-cream. 'Sartaj, you're not that old yet. How are you going to get through life like this? You need a family.'

'You sound just like my mother.'

'Because we're both right. We both want you to be happy.'

'I am.'

'What?'

'Happy.'

'Sartaj, anybody looking at you knows exactly how happy you are.'

And looking at her in the haven of her contentment, Sartaj thought he could have said the same thing about her. He felt acutely now the sodden, sweaty weariness of his own body, the whisky misery of it. He was annoyed now, at having the professional momentum of the day dragged down into this useless discussion about happiness with happy Rehana. He was saved from further investigation of the nature of happiness by a knock on the door. 'Ice-cream,' he said. 'Ice-cream.'

He ate a bowl of the ice-cream, and fled.

A violent buzzing woke Sartaj out of a dream about flying across oceans to meet foreign women. There was a very intricate plot involving watchful mothers and speeding jeeps, but it was gone as soon as his eyes opened. He propped himself up, baffled, and couldn't think where the noise came from. For a moment he thought it was the doorbell gone wrong, but then he remembered the mobile phone. He groped for it on the bedside table, dropped it off the side and had to pull it back up by the charging wire. Finally he got it open.

'Sartaj Saab?'

'Who is this?' Sartaj barked.

'Bunty, saab. Somebody told me you wanted to talk to me.'

'Bunty, yes, yes. Good that you called.' Sartaj swung his feet to the ground and tried to collect himself, to recollect a strategy for talking to Gaitonde's man. But he couldn't remember if he had thought one through, and finally he just said, 'I want to meet you.'

'The rumour is that you shot Bhai.'

'I didn't shoot Gaitonde. Forget rumours. What do you think, Bunty?'

'My information is that he was dead when you got in.'

'You have good information, Bunty. It all was very strange. Why should a man like that kill himself?'

'That's what you want to talk about?'

'That and other things. I'll tell you when I see you.'

'What do I know about why he killed himself?'

'Listen, Bunty. I just want to talk to you. If you help me, I may be able to help you. Gaitonde is dead, Suleiman Isa's boys will be looking for you. I've heard that some of your own people have split away already.'

'That is a game I have played for years.'

'True, but now? Alone? How far will you run?'

'You mean in my wheelchair, saab?' Bunty's voice was gravelly, with a little hiss of effort at the end of each breath. Maybe it was how he had to sit, some constriction of the lungs. But he was not sad, only amused. 'I can go faster in this thing than most men can run.'

Sartaj sat up, glad of the chance to be curious and friendly. 'Really? I've never seen a wheelchair like that.'

'This is foreign, saab. It goes up and down stairs also. It can do all sorts of things.'

'That is amazing. It must have been very expensive.'

'Bhai gave it to me. He liked things like that, up to date.'

'So he was a modern man?'

'Yes, very modern. But it is very hard to keep this chair running, you know. Nobody knows how to repair it here, and spare parts and everything you have to bring from vilayat. It breaks down too much.'

'Not built for Indian conditions.'

'Yes. Like one of those new cars. They look good, but finally only an Ambassador can get you to any village you want to go.'

'Meet me, Bunty. Maybe I can get you to your village safely.'

'I was born here in Mumbai, in GTB Nagar only, saab. And you are too eager to meet me. Maybe Suleiman Isa has asked you to send me home.'

'Bunty, you ask anyone. I have no connections to Suleiman Isa or any of his men.'

'You are close to Parulkar Saab.'

'That may be. But I don't do such work for him, Bunty. You know that. I am just a simple man.' Sartaj stood up, walked around the bottom of the bed. He was pushing too hard, at a man who was trying to outmanoeuvre death on his speedy wheelchair. 'Listen, you don't want to meet, no problem. Just think about it, okay?'

'Yes, saab. I have to be careful, especially now.'

'Yes.'

'Saab, but I can help you over the phone. What did you want to know?'

So Bunty was keeping his options open with Sartaj, in case he himself needed help later. He had problems of his own, after all, and he wanted to stay alive. Sartaj relaxed, shook his shoulders loose and stretched his neck. Now they had the possibility of a relationship. 'Tell me, you really know nothing about why Gaitonde took his own wicket?'

'No, saab. I don't know. Really I don't know.'

'You knew he was back in Bombay?'

'I knew. But I hadn't seen him for weeks. We spoke only on the phone. He was hiding out in that thing.'

'That house?'

'Yes. He wouldn't come out.'

'Why?'

'I don't know. He was always careful.'

'What did he sound like on the phone?'

'Sound like? Like Bhai.'

'Yes, but was he sad? Happy?'

'He was a bit khiskela. But he was always like that.'

'Khiskela how?'

'Like his brain was full of things. Sometimes he would talk to me for an hour about something that had nothing to do with business, just talk and talk.'

'Like what?'

'I don't know. One day it was about computers in the old times. He said that there were computers and super-weapons in the *Mahabharata*, he went on and on about Ashwathamma. I didn't listen. Even before, when he was on his boat, he liked to talk long on the phone. It was a big waste of money. But he was Bhai, so you just kept saying, haan, haan, and he went on.'

'Who was that woman with him?'

'Jojo. She sent him items.'

'Sent him?'

'Yes. First-class items for Bhai. He used to have them flown out to Thailand or wherever he was. Virgins. Jojo was the supplier.'

'Virgins all the way from here?'

'Yes, he liked Indian virgins.'

'How many?'

'I don't know. Once a month maybe.'

'And Jojo was his woman also?'

'She was a bhadwi. He must have taken hers also. That was one of his hobbies.'

'Why did he come back to Mumbai, Bunty?'

'I don't know.'

'You were his main boss in Mumbai, Bunty. Of course you know.'

'I was just one of his Number Twos.'

'I was told you were the closest to him.'

'I stayed with him.'

'And the others left him? Why?'

There was a thin crackling on the line, of cellophane and card-board, and Sartaj waited as Bunty lit his cigarette and took in a drag.

'Some left. Business was down,' Bunty said.

'Why?'

'It doesn't matter now.'

This was the heart of the matter. Sartaj knew this from Bunty's reluctance to give it away, from his studied casualness. Carefully, very slowly, Sartaj said, 'You're right, Bunty. It doesn't matter now, so tell me.'

Bunty drew on his cigarette. He let the smoke out, wheezed a little. Sartaj waited.

'Saab, business is down for everyone.'

'But more for the Gaitonde company than all others. Bunty, don't be a chutiya. If you are honest with me, I can be straight with you. Tell me.'

'Bhai wasn't concentrating on business. He had us all running here, running there.'

'After what?'

Bunty laughed suddenly. 'He had us chasing a sadhu. He said we had to find a wise man.'

'What sadhu? Chasing where?'

'Three sadhus altogether, and one was the leader. Really, saab, I can't tell you more.'

'Why not?'

'I don't know much more.'

'Tell me what you know.'

'Not like this, saab.'

'So let us meet.'

'Saab, you talk to Parulkar Saab.'

'About what?'

'I want to surrender. But they will do an encounter on me, saab.'

It made sense, that Bunty wanted to come in. He would be safer in custody, and jail would shield him from his many enemies. But he was afraid of being executed before his name ever showed up on an arrest roster. 'If you have something good to give us,' Sartaj said, 'I am sure Parulkar Saab will look after you.'

'I have everything, saab. I was with Bhai for a long time.'

'Okay. I'll speak to Parulkar saab. Then I want to know who this sadhu was, this leader fellow.'

'Once I am safe, saab, I will tell everything I know. I will give you his name. I am the only one who knows.'

'All right. I will talk to Parulkar Saab, and tell you what he says. Give me a phone number.'

'I am calling from a PCO, saab. And I am not in Mumbai. I will call you.'

'Fine.' Bunty must be very afraid, to be this careful even as he searched for a way to secure shelter. 'When will you be back?'

'Monday, saab.'

'Call me on Monday evening, and I will tell you what Parulkar saab says.'

'Yes, saab. I will put down now.'

Bunty hung up, and Sartaj made chai and considered the vagaries of the gangster's life. That death could come suddenly was a given, but what struck Sartaj as poignant was that Bunty was trying to trust Parulkar, his most feared predator. Parulkar had over the years been responsible for the hunting down of many G-Company men. He had used his many sources to obtain intelligence and fix the whereabouts of Gaitonde's functionaries, and had sent out his teams to trap them and kill them. Unless the dead men were prime shooters or eminent Number Twos, the newspapers reported their deaths in one-paragraph stories at the bottom of back pages. Bunty might rate a front-page mention in the city sections, perhaps. For his special wheel-chair, maybe, if not his death.

Sartaj finished his chai, and then called the Delhi-walli, to tell her about Gaitonde's search.

'A sadhu was the leader of this group?' Anjali Mathur said.

'Yes, madam.'

'What sadhu? Was there a name?'

'No, madam. The source refused to release any other information at this time. I might know more in a few days.'

'All right. This is very strange. We knew that Gaitonde was very religious, that he conducted pujas quite often. But we don't know of any sadhus in connection with him. And why would he be looking for this man?'

'I don't know, madam.'

'Yes.'

She paused. Sartaj waited. He was getting used to Anjali Mathur's slow deliberation.

'I have an address for you,' she said. 'Write it down.'

'The sister?'

'Yes, the sister. She's moved. She's in Bandra now.'

Before going to see the sister in Bandra, Sartaj made a stop at the station. He had to make a phone call. The piece of paper that Parulkar had given him with the S-Company contact on it had only a phone number, no name. Sartaj had to make an effort to remember. Iffat-bibi. Yes, that was it. Iffat-bibi, who was Suleiman Isa's maternal aunt and criminal accomplice. Sartaj couldn't conjure up a face for her as he dialled, but when she answered her phone and he heard her voice, he instantly thought of Begum Akhtar. There was the same roughened sweetness about the voice, that old-world heartbreak that floated off worn vinyl albums, full of pain but strong as the edge of a curving Avadhi dagger. 'So you are Parulkar's man?' she said.

'Yes, madam.'

'Arre, don't call me that, you can't be so formal with me. After all, you are Sardar Saab's son.'

'You knew him?'

'Since when?' Iffat-bibi said. 'I knew him when he was a young rangroot, almost. He was so handsome, baap re.'

Papa-ji had never told Sartaj about Iffat-bibi, but maybe she was the sort of woman fathers didn't tell children about. 'Yes, he was very keen about his clothes.'

'Your father,' Iffat-bibi said, 'loved the reshmi kabab from a place we owned called Ashiana. But that restaurant no longer exists.'

Sartaj remembered the kababs, but he didn't know that Iffat-bibi had had anything to do with them. Iffat-bibi wanted to tell stories about Sardar Saab. She said he had once found a destitute twelve-year-old boy wandering around VT, and Sardar Saab had used his own money to buy him food and a reserved train ticket back to Punjab. 'Sardar Saab was a good man,' she sighed. 'Very straight and simple.'

Sartaj looked at his hand, at the steel kara on the wrist and the mark it had left over a lifetime, and nodded. 'Yes.' He waited.

'You should come and visit us some time. I will give you better reshmi kababs than the ones from Ashiana.'

'Yes, Iffat-bibi. I will come some time.'

Iffat-bibi had observed the proprieties, and now she was willing to get down to business. 'What can I do for you?'

'I need information about Gaitonde.'

'That maderchod?' It was a shock to hear the word in that voice which promised song, and now Sartaj understood how she could be counsellor and helpmeet to a bhai, and not just an indulgent grandmother offering food. 'For years he bothered us. Very good that you took care of him at last.'

'I didn't, Bibi,' Sartaj said. 'But tell me about him. What sort of man was he?'

He was a conniving, cowardly cur, she said. He ran from a fight, and he betrayed his own men. He was a sinful lecher who used and destroyed young girls.

'But he ran a big company, Bibi.'

She allowed that he was a good manager, and he had made some money in his day. No, she didn't know what he was doing back in the city. The last she had heard he was skulking off in Thailand or Indonesia, the bastard. She told stories about Gaitonde, about his perfidies. He had killed innocent people, saying they were Suleiman Isa's friends. He was an insect.

'Bibi, do you know of any sadhu in connection with him?'

'Sadhu? No. All that praying and piety, everything was a sham. He never did a bit of good for anyone in his life, may he burn.'

Sartaj thanked her, and said, 'Now I must go, Bibi.'

'You're talking to anyone on Gaitonde's side?'

'Here and there, Bibi.'

She laughed. 'Fine, don't tell me if you don't want to, beta. But if you have a problem, come to me. After all, you are Sardar Saab's son.'

'Yes, Bibi.'

'Phone me some time. I am an old woman, but keep in touch. I may be of use. This is my personal number, write it down.'

Sartaj put the number and name into his diary, but he thought she wouldn't be of much use, this garrulous old woman. She had nothing useful to give him, or perhaps he didn't have anything she thought worth trading good information for. He put the phone down, and went out into the station, looking for Katekar. Now they had to visit another woman.

Mary Mascarenas sat on her bed and shuddered. She held herself around the belly, arms tightly wrapped, and lowered her head and shook. Sartaj waited. Maybe she had quarrelled with Jojo, perhaps she had even wished her sister dead, but now it had happened, a part of her life had fallen away, and she was trembling from the amputation. There was no use trying to talk to her until the agitation was over, and so Sartaj and Katekar were waiting, looking around her very small apartment, one room with an attached kitchen really, and a cupboard of a bathroom. She had a green and black bedspread on the single bed, some small plants on the window-ledge, an ancient black rotary phone, two framed paintings on the wall, a grey-patterned dhurrie on the floor. Sitting on the single wooden chair at the foot of the bed, Sartaj saw how she had built a haven for herself. The walls were a pale green, and he was sure that she had painted them herself, to complement the darker green of the plants and the jungle emeralds of the paintings, where cottages sat amongst exuberant foliage and parrots fluttered through the treetops. Now the bright Mumbai sun slipped through the white blinds and ignited the hues that Mary Mascarenas had arranged for herself, and the shimmering, jerking fall of her hair hid her face.

Katekar rolled his eyes. He padded into the kitchen, and Sartaj could see his head craning, turning. He was taking inventory. He would go into the bathroom next, and take careful note of buckets, toothbrush, face creams. This was something they had in common, this faith in details, in particulars. Sartaj had noticed it the first time Katekar had reported to him, many years ago, about a pickpocket who worked the line from Churchgate to Andheri Station. Katekar had droned on about name, age, height, and then added that the bastard had married three times, and that he had a weakness for papri-chaat and falooda, in the basti where he had grown up this was well known. They'd caught him three weeks later, at the Mathura Dairy Farm near Santa Cruz station, with his head lowered over a plate of bhel-puri after a profitable evening rush-hour, sitting across from a cross-eyed girlfriend who was well on her way to becoming wife number four. Close observation didn't always bring arrests, and success, but what Sartaj appreciated was Katekar's essential understanding of the fact that there were many ways to describe a man, but to say that he was a Hindu, a poor man, a criminal, all of this gave no grip, no hold. Only when you knew which shampoo he favoured, what songs he listened to, who and how he liked to chodo, what paan he ate, only then you caught him, had him, even if you never arrested him. So Katekar was in Mary's bathroom now. Sartaj was sure he was sniffing at her soap.

'Why?' she said suddenly. She pushed the hair back from her face, tugged it back angrily. 'Why?'

She had her sister's cheekbones, and a plumper, round jawline, all blurred now by her loss. She wasn't weeping, but was still quivering, squeezing it down until Sartaj could see it only in the tips of her fingers, and in her chin.

'Miss Mascarenas was involved in nefarious activities with the mafia don Ganesh Gaitonde,' he said. 'This resulted in . . .'

'I heard you before,' she said. 'But why?'

Why everything? she wanted to know. Why a bullet hole in the chest, why a concrete floor, why Ganesh Gaitonde? Sartaj shrugged. 'I don't know,' he said. Why do men kill women? Why do they kill each other? These were questions that bit at him sometimes, but he drowned them in whisky. Otherwise why not ask, why life? That way lay hurtling chasms, the temptations of long heights. Better to do the job. Better to put one apradhi in jail, and then, when you could, another. Katekar was at the bathroom door, his eyes alive with sunlight. 'I don't know, miss,' Sartaj said.

'You don't know,' she said. She nodded heavily, as if this confirmed some great suspicion. 'I want her,' she said.

'Miss?'

'I want her,' she said slowly, with hard-strained patience, 'for burial.'

'Yes, of course. Handing over of body is sometimes difficult when the investigation is still ongoing, you understand. But we will arrange for the body to be released. But I need to ask you some questions.'

'I don't want to answer any questions just now.'

'But these are questions about your sister. You just said that you want to know what happened to her.'

She wiped her face and sat forward a little and suddenly he was the subject of study. Her eyes were a lighter brown than they first appeared, and in a moment he was able to see the flecks dusted through them. He was now very uncomfortable, her scrutiny was shameless, direct and long, and at least his position should have shielded him from the unexpected intimacy of that unending look. But he wouldn't drop his gaze. At last she said, 'What did you say your name was?'

'Inspector Sartaj Singh.'

'Sartaj Singh, have you ever lost a sister?' Her voice rose. 'Have you ever had a sister *murdered*?'

Her utter lack of fear was irritating. Citizens, and especially women, were always subdued with policemen, careful, scared, formal. Mary Mascarenas was dismissively casual. But she had just lost her sister, and so he took a breath and held down his annoyance. 'Miss, I'm sorry to ask you this kind of thing at a time like this . . .'

'Then don't.'

'This is a very important matter. This is a case that involves national security,' Sartaj said. And then he couldn't think of anything to say. He felt quite in the wrong, somehow, and therefore angry. Mary Mascarenas didn't look frightened, but she wasn't brave either. She was saddened, weary, and truly expecting nothing from him except more suffering. She was just going to be very stubborn, and shouting at her wasn't going to help. He took a breath. 'National security. Do you understand?'

'Are you going to hit me?'

'What?'

'Are you going to break my bones? Isn't that what you do?'

'No, we don't,' Sartaj snapped. He caught himself, steadied and held up a hand. 'Miss, we will arrange for the release of the body. Also, there were some possessions, and they are impounded currently, for the investigation. But those will be released to you eventually. I will phone when arrangements are complete. Here is the number at the station where you can get in touch with me.' He carefully put his card at the foot of the bed, at the very edge, and turned away.

On the stairway Katekar turned his head back up to Sartaj. 'She will talk, sir.'

'Why are you whispering?' Usually Katekar was the bulky threat, he was the looming promise of slaps and thumps and kicks, and Sartaj played the understanding friend, the unexpectedly benign and bearded face of authority. With women he was always kind. But Mary Mascarenas had been hostile, and Sartaj was irritated. From the bottom of the yard he looked up at her door, which was shutting as he watched. She had a good little PG at the back of an old house on a quiet residential street, shaded by the interlocked branches of two old trees. The house was one of those unexpected treasures that still survived in Bandra, an old grey cottage with slatted shutters and ironwork on the balconies and white trim on the doors and windows.

The yard was covered with leaves which crackled underfoot. All very pretty, and vexing.

But Katekar was right, she would talk. Sartaj walked down the street. She would feed her anger, tell herself what a beast that sardar inspector was, what a bastard, but finally she would be left with only her guilt, and she would need to tell him what had happened, what had become of Mary and Juliet Mascarenas. She would confess to him because she had to make him understand. Forgiveness was not what they really needed, the survivors, it was always too late for that. What they wanted was only that someone in a uniform, a robe, somebody with three lions on their shoulder should say, yes, I see how it came about, first this happened, and then that, and so you did this and then this. So she would talk. But now it was time to leave her alone. Now it was time to save the body from disposal by incineration, so that Mary Mascarenas could bury her sister. People set great store by small dignities, small illusions. Mary Mascarenas would never see the cold room, he would save her from seeing what really happened to dead sisters. Let her bury Jojo. Then she would talk.

Sartaj shaded his eyes and peered out at the sea, at the shifting sash of quicksilver visible through the trees and the two buildings below. It was late, time for him to go home, to his own family.

Prabhjot Kaur sat in an armchair in her bedroom and listened to her home. The house was black. At night it seemed bigger, the familiar contours pushed back by a moving dark, an absence of light that was somehow alive with ghostly slivers of colour. Prabhjot Kaur could hear Sartaj sleeping. It was a long way, across and down the hall, but at this time she could hear many things: the slow settling of the ancient dining table, the steady plit-tap, plit-tap of drops from the tap behind her neighbour's house, the shivery movement of small animals under the hedge at the front of the house, the hum of the night itself, that low and living vibration that made all other sounds larger. She heard all this, and loud in it, her son's breathing. She knew how he lay, straight on his back with his head turned to one side, and a pillow held against his chest. He had come late, carrying two overstuffed bags as usual, weary from the train ride but also from much else, she could see that. After a quick bath he had eaten the rajma-chawal she had waiting for him, he ate it silently, with relief. She sat across the table from him, warmed by the familiar way he had of eating the rice

167

from left to right, systematic, and patting the food with his fork often, making it neat. He had done that as a small boy, with the fork held crosswise in his fist. Rajma-chawal was his favourite food, his Sunday treat, and he liked the rice with plenty of fried onion.

She asked him questions every now and then, whether the slow leak in the Bombay bathroom wall had been fixed, whether he had written a letter to his Delhi Chacha-ji. It was not Sartaj's answers she wanted as much as the sound of his voice. When he was done, he sat back, stilled, both arms hanging limp at the sides of the chair, blinking slowly. She took his plate. 'Go to sleep, beta,' she said.

The armchair she sat in now was old, the oldest piece of furniture in the house. It had been patched, restrung, re-upholstered, QuickFixed, operated on, saved for her. Sartaj's father had brought it home one evening, tipped it slowly from the back of a tempo, smiling a glory of flashing teeth over her What-is-this? How-much-money-did-you-spend? It had taken him an hour to persuade her to sit in it, to admit it was not too uncomfortable. It was the first big thing they had bought together, the first piece of their small household that had not come in dowry. Now the night was a vast unknown territory she was exploring alone, a drifting plain that rolled its horizons back eternally, and she preferred to suffer it sitting back in her armchair, because it was lazy to be in bed when she was awake. But no, it wasn't true, suffering undiluted and pure it wasn't, even though sometimes loneliness spoke its iron hum of locusts behind her eyes, filled her stomach with blowing sand, gritty and grinding and cruel. There was something else that kept her from living with her son, or from moving into the capacious sprawl of her brother's house just down the street and to the right, into the tumbling warmth of nieces and nephews and shouted quarrels and kulfi-smeared faces. It was something so monstrous she kept it from herself. But she felt it, late at night, hidden under the contours of her face, which she touched and felt as if it were a mask, as she savoured, slowly, the unspeakable pleasure of being alone.

She shook her head angrily against this delight now, pushed it away. It took her a full minute to get up from the armchair, four separate movements of arm and hip and legs. There was no need to switch on the light for the walk into the hallway and down it. The bureau was to the left, good dishes in the first drawer and second, the expensive dishes with the lily pattern that she liked for its neat spiralling circles in a bright blue, and to her right shoulder, the glisten of the photographs she could recite and remember, a wedding picture laminated in hard plastic, the red of her sari darkened into a rich black, she could remember the photographer's two-toned shoes and his head hidden under a black cloth, and her younger devar with his red tie and cheeky smile, 'Come now, Pabi-ji, where's that lovely lovely laugh?' Then there had been an ecstatic glow of light, and she had managed a smile that lingered now, past all decay. And there was Sartaj at ten, in a blue turban too large for his head and a blue blazer with shiny new brass buttons, what you couldn't see in the photograph was his left knee under the flannel trousers, which he had sliced open that morning on a strand of barbed wire, climbing through a fence to short-cut through an empty plot on the way to the school bus, she had told him a hundred times not to. Then there had been the tetanus injections, and the ice-cream his father had bought him, a whole brick of Kwality vanilla, Sartaj's favourite. They had the same tastes, father and son, the same urgent need for a mirror glitter on shoe leather, for a new jacket every other year. At the end of the corridor, he, the father, stood against a grey studio backdrop in his last-but-one jacket, a tweed with a green and black weave, worn with a white shirt and a silky green scarf, his beard now a soft white that he finally no longer fought against with stains and dyes. A white beard looks fully distinguished, she had told him twice a day for months on end, until he had believed her, and now she left him behind and stood in a doorway, and Sartaj slept, breathing quickly.

He spoke now, muttering something into the sheet clumped at the side of his head. At the foot of the bed, she bent slowly and found, on the floor, his pants, shirt, underwear. Sartaj was saying something, she clearly heard the word 'boat' in it. She shut the door quietly because he would want to sleep late, and the servants came early. On the way to the bathroom she turned out his pockets and found a handkerchief, and it all went into the washing bucket for the bai.

In her armchair she listened for the tapping of the watchman's lathi at the very last turn of the road, it was time. He made a large circle around the clustered homes every hour. And listening, she heard the tiniest creak of resentment rising from her bones, a very small rub of resistance, barely heard amidst the larger music of happiness, of a life not without pain but lived well: home, husband, son, and her the wife. It was unseemly, after all these years and years, this unvanquished and sullen spark rising from clothes on the floor, this small spurt of anger at having to always do things for men, always. Yes, unseemly, especially with Sartaj so tired, seeking comfort, he had come to her. She knew this. He had told her he slept deeply in this house, slept better. He had slept bravely in his own bedroom that first night long ago, he must have been six, maybe a little older when they finally had an apartment with a room for him, with a little veranda that looked out into a small garden where she had grown roses and hung wet saris and uniforms on a line. How many clothes had she washed in those early days, how many blue days of Rin and torn blue short pants and matching socks, and had she on some mornings pressed down that same grating itch of annoyance, buried it firmly and deep under tumbling avalanches of love? Prabhjot Kaur pushed the thoughts back, put her hands on the old wood of the armrests and held them hard and rocked her head back and forward, and tried to think of a holiday time in the hills, she and Karamjeet and their son walking on a winding hilly ridge, but she was seeing instead a house in a city very far away, immeasurably further now that it lay on the other side of a new border and a long wire fence that flashed with murderous electricity, and this house had shutters painted green and a big baithak at the front with all new furniture in it and after you went through the dark passage leading from outside to in, there was a bricked courtyard surrounded by arches and rooms. In this courtyard were Prabhjot Kaur's father and mother, her two elder brothers and her two sisters. And one of these sisters was Navneet, beloved and best of all, and now lost for ever. Gone, Navneet-bhenji was gone. With both hands, Prabhjot Kaur wiped her forehead, her face. It was useless to remember. The histories had already been written, and what had happened, had happened. Being alive, having a family, came with its inevitable portion of pain. There was no running away from life, and trying to wish away suffering only made it more present. She took a deep breath: bear it. Carry it all, the small dissatisfactions of every day and the huge murderous tragedies of long ago, carry it all with the help and grace of Vaheguru. Carry it for those you love. Prabhjot Kaur took a deep breath and tried to think of the tasks for tomorrow.

Her breathing was even, slow. From across the garden outside came that steady tapping, the small explosive spatter of water on stones.

❦ INSET: *A House in a Distant City*

The courtyard was washed every morning, and in it sat Prabhjot Kaur, scrubbing a karhai with ash under the hand-pump. She was the best and youngest daughter of three: Navneet, Maninder and Prabhjot. Or actually Navneet-bhenji, Mani and then Prabhjot, or Nikki, for her smallness. Prabhjot Kaur liked to help their Mata-ji, who always said, 'Look at her, this Nikki of a girl, this Prabhjot Kaur, only ten and helping more than the rest of you all put together,' which usually meant that Nikki had to watch out for a pinch from Mani, who loved to catch up the flesh on the inner side of her upper arm with fingers as unrelenting and iron as a chimta and twist and twist, whispering, 'Little rat, I'll show you, rattie.' Nikki wore her bruises with forbearance, and even compassion for Mani, who had big ears and looked like an awestruck dehati scarecrow, after three sudden inches gained in her fourteenth year. Mani wandered around, shrieky and awkward and full of rage, not too good at studies, stuck inextricably in the middle of three sisters, which meant that she was not special even by virtue of position or age, always not here and not quite there. Nikki, on the other hand, was coddled by her two brothers, Iqbal-veerji and Alok-veerji, who at eighteen and seventeen were younger than Navneet-bhenji but more remote than her because of their hulking maleness and their passion for cricket. Her father liked to look at Nikki's notebooks, which she covered with plain brown paper folded into sharp, precise corners and edges, which she adorned with her full, proper name in green ink, with the initial letters of 'Prabhjot' and 'Kaur' especially elaborated and curled. Her Punjabi and Urdu teachers admired her writing in either script and had hopes for her in the annual composition contest sponsored by Sir Syed Atallulah Khan. 'My house is new,' she wrote in flowing green letters, with not a mistake or a blotting because she would discard an entire page for one straggly aleph. She had the universal reputation of being a good girl, serious and obedient, and in her new house she liked to help in the kitchen.

'Are you finished, Nikki?' Mata-ji sang from inside the kitchen.

'Coming, Mata-ji,' Prabhjot Kaur called, and jumped up to pump water, leaning on the handle with all her weight. The water fell in happy gushes, sparking and bouncing in the sunlight. In the kitchen, Mata-ji slapped the paraunthas back and forth between her hands with a sprightliness that made a quick music, tossed them down on the hot tava, each with a final wristy flick. Prabhjot Kaur laid the karhai down carefully. Mata-ji patted at the beaded moisture on her cheeks with the corner of her dupatta, and Prabhjot Kaur watched intently her round red face, with the upturned nose they all teased her about.

'Take these in,' Mata-ji said, putting a perfect, glistening parauntha on a pile of four. 'Then you also sit down.' Prabhjot Kaur always ate second to last. Her two brothers ate mightily, putting away whole dozens of paraunthas, canisters of ghee. Mani was sitting next to them, one knee up under her chin, picking at a pile of bhindi, arranging it in a circle. She paid Prabhjot Kaur no attention, not even a beady stare, she was listening intently to Iqbal-veerji and Alok-veerji, who were talking cricket. Prabhjot Kaur squatted and served herself from the plates scattered on the chatai, and ate, quiet and intent on her food. It was a holiday morning, Sunday, and her father was away, gone to buy a last cartload of bricks. They had been living in the new house for almost a year, but the back was still unfinished. There was to be a store-room and a little separate house of one room and patio, for servants. It seemed like the house had been building for ever. For as long as Prabhjot Kaur could remember, it had been always the Adampur house, for which her father had disappeared on evenings after work, for which her brothers had spent weekends supervising construction, it was a home that had seemed always eternally distant. It had taken them three days to move in, and when they had finally spent their first night, all together in the courtyard on new charpais, none of them had slept until it was almost light. The next morning, through a warm white sheet and puffy, delicious dreams, Prabhjot Kaur had heard the laughter of her mother from the roof. There was a comfortable freedom in the sound, a lack of care so unusual that Prabhjot Kaur still remembered it. This laughter had lingered in their new house, brightened the corridors and mingled with the smell of fresh plaster. Mata-ji now sat down next to Prabhjot Kaur, with the little grunt she always made when she bent her knees, and she was tired from the morning's work, but still there was something different about her, a rotund contentment that had never been there when they had lived for years in the two rooms at the back of Narinder Dhanoa's house. She ate with concentration, bending low over the food, smacking her lips with every bite, and Mani stood up abruptly to her full towering length and went stalking away to the kitchen.

'So, Sethani-ji,' Alok-veerji said, with a hand on his mother's shoulder. 'When is your maid starting work?'

'I was thinking I can manage alone,' Mata-ji said. 'What will I do with my time?'

Alok-veerji collapsed on to Mata-ji's shoulder, laughing.

'We'll just tell her to start coming from tomorrow,' Iqbal-veerji said. 'Otherwise you'll keep doing this for another ten years.' As the oldest son he practised an indulgent authority with her, a smiling patience.

'Right, right,' Alok-veerji said. 'Otherwise our biggest-kanjoos-in-the-world won't let the maid near the house.'

'When you start earning,' Mata-ji said, shrugging his chin off her shoulder, 'then you'll know the price of your paraunthas.'

'When I start earning,' Alok-veerji said, 'I'll get you a motor car, with two flags on front.'

'A laat-saab you'll be straight away,' Mata-ji said. 'It took *him* twenty-one years to build this house.'

Twenty-one years and some bricks which are still coming, Prabhjot Kaur thought, but she could see that despite the toss of her head, Mata-ji was pleased by Alok-veerji as laat-saab in motor car. It made her smile that downward-looking quick quiver of a smile. That afternoon, when Prabhjot Kaur was settled on a corner of the chatai, her arm under her favourite gadda and head on it, falling densely into sleep, she heard the two veerjis still talking as they lay next to each other, going on about the mysterious maid, who must be found and made to come, who must work, who must sweep the house inside all its many many rooms and outside also, who must push the pocha until the tiled floors are glistering gleaming, who must thrash the laundry and hang it dewy and flapping on the lines in the back, who must winnow wheat, light lamps, clean shoes, gather books, get milk, buy vegetables, who must, who must, who must. Prabhjot Kaur thought that it would be a very strong woman who could do all that.

But three days later, when the maid came, she was a tiny woman named Ram Pari who wore a funny red salwar-kameez with a ragged dupatta and spoke a rough, blaring dialect that Prabhjot Kaur understood but found hilarious. Ram Pari called Mata-ji 'Bibi-ji' and squatted in the courtyard to haggle over wages. When she stood up, after agreeing to five rupees a week, Prabhjot Kaur went and stretched herself up next to her, and it was true, Ram Pari was barely a head taller than her, but standing that close, Prabhjot Kaur discovered a smell. She backed away quickly. It wasn't exactly a bad smell, but strong, it was like damp earth, or the back of a halwai's shop, where you got a little dizzy from all the old milky odours. Prabhjot Kaur reeled away from the richness and went and sat next to Navneet-bhenji in the baithak, where as usual Navneet-bhenji had her nose in a big book. Prabhjot Kaur leaned her head on the cottony comfort of Navneet-bhenji's shoulder, and spelt out the title on top of the page: 'Wordsworth'. Under the washed briskness of the soft salwar there was the sweet tinge of soap and warm skin. It was a flavour that Prabhjot Kaur had known all her life, and now she breathed it in, scrunching her nose into the cloth and making little snorting noises. 'What're you doing, jhalli?' Navneet-bhenji asked, and reached around with her other hand to pinch the burrowing nose. Prabhjot Kaur didn't feel crazy, not even close, but it was too difficult to explain why she needed it so, just then. She settled her face into the crook of Navneet-bhenji's arm and was still. Ram Pari was gone from the courtyard, and Mata-ji came across it, with a plate full of peas. She sat near and began to split the pods and rattle the peas into the plate with her thumb, shuck-shuck-shuck, so quickly that the sound was one long hum. Mata-ji was intent on the peas, and Navneet-bhenji kept the book high on her knees. They were quietly cordial with each other nowadays, but Prabhjot Kaur remembered a year ago when they had quarrelled mightily, after Navneet-bhenji had finished her FA and wanted to go to college for a BA. Mata-ji had told her to think of her brothers and sisters, who were being kept back from marriage and happiness by her selfishness, and when Navneet-bhenji had pointed out reasonably that her brothers and sisters were years and years away from any marriage, Mata-ji had screamed at her, something entirely strange about disgracing the family, and then had refused to eat for two days. Finally Papa-ji had put his large fatherly foot down. If Navneet wants to do her BA, he said, she will, and that is that. But Mata-ji had powers that moved in mysterious ways. She had retreated to her room, and Papa-ji had rolled his eyes and followed her in, and when he emerged the next morning, it had been settled that marriage could be delayed but not put off altogether. So now Navneet-bhenji was engaged, to Pritam Singh Hansra, who was a junior engineer in the PWD and stationed at Gujranwalla. After the engagement Papa-ji had gently stroked his beard, which had just some white in it, under his lower lip, and said, happiness follows from reasonable thinking. Mata-ji had kept quiet. And Prabhjot Kaur, awed by Papa-ji's way of commanding things out of the air – a boy for Navneet-bhenji, a house for them all – had nevertheless understood that that was never quite that.

Ram Pari came every day to the house, and Mata-ji engaged in epic struggles with her. Teaching her to wash dishes properly, to a sufficient degree of cleanliness, was a lesson that lasted three days, with many practical demonstrations and stinging criticisms. Ram Pari didn't talk back, shrugged off Mata-ji's homilies, performed at high standards for two bowls and maybe a plate, and then went back to her usual cheerful sloppiness. Her quick sweeping technique, which was efficient and fast but which left snaggles of dust in corners and ignored the spaces underneath almirahs, altogether drove Mata-ji into crescendos of outrage. Meanwhile the two brothers of Prabhjot Kaur fell over laughing and sniggered, not too quietly, about 'Badboo Pari'. Prabhjot Kaur laughed along with them, to show solidarity, but privately she thought the smell wasn't a badboo at all, more like a fierce-boo. Ram Pari was small, with a wiry threadwork of muscles across her stomach, which Prabhjot Kaur saw when Ram Pari lifted her kameez to wipe her mouth, her old woman's wrinkled face. She did that sometimes, in the late afternoon, instead of using the dupatta from over her head, and Prabhjot Kaur thought it was mainly to get cool, get a little bit of breeze on her skin, but it released a huffing breath of smell, round there in the air, as real and inescapable as a cloud of heated sparks from the fire in the chaunka. Prabhjot Kaur flinched from it, but tried also to keep herself still, to experience the sting of it against her skin. She looked forward to it, and was shamed by this, and kept it a secret. It was her most secret secret, more hidden than the one-rupee coin she had found under the cushion of the sofa in the front room, which she had known to be Papa-ji's, but which had gone to school the next day in her pencil box, which had been good for a week's worth of kesar kulfis, not only for herself but also her two best friends, Manjeet and Asha. She told nobody of her hesitating hunger for Ram Pari's smell, the thick tang and savour of it, not even the others of the Terrific Trio, who wore their double plaits in exactly the same neat style, who had sat together in the second row since Class I.

That day in April the Trio were swaying in the back of Daraq Ali's tanga, with Manjeet in the middle as usual. She was the unquestioned leader, in spite of the other two's better marks and fathers with better jobs. Manjeet's father was only a hotel manager, but she had a tall, lean body and a muscular force of personality and a directness that Prabhjot Kaur and Asha admired but couldn't imagine emulating. They were content to shelter under its somewhat risky shade.

'Chacha, go faster,' Manjeet said now to Daraq Ali, with her arm over the back of the seat. 'Go faster, please, or we'll become blackened cinders here on Larkin Road itself. We'll get seared and disappear in a flash of smelly smoke. Go faster, faster.'

It was after three-thirty and hotter than Prabhjot Kaur could ever remember, and the sun caught them all directly in the back of the tanga, and the road was endless ahead, and Daraq Ali was the oldest and slowest tanga driver in the entire city. He picked them up individually in the morning and trotted, no, ambled them over to school, and then waited for them at three in the afternoon for the endless, draggy, creaking trek back. He thrust his bushy hennaed beard over his sweaty shoulder and said what he always said, 'Bibi, she's been working hard all day in this sun. See how tired she is. I'll ask her to go faster and she'll try, but it'll break her heart.' And then, to the bony brown haunches that rose and dipped under the reins, 'Oh, Shagufta, faster, faster. Faster, Shagufta, for the great Mems who wilt in the hot hot sun.'

'That nag of yours is older than you, Chacha,' Manjeet said. 'Sell her to the knackers and get a strong new mare.'

'But see how hard she's trying,' Daraq Ali said. 'See how she goes. How can you say such things, bibi? You'll break her heart.'

Manjeet snorted and held her basta in front of her face to keep off the sun. 'Oh, yes, we're speeding along now. Just risking our lives in a fantastic chase. I'm really really scared.'

Prabhjot Kaur giggled and then instantly wanted a long glass of water from the surahi which Mata-ji kept wet through the whole day.

She thought of it, of tilting the surahi, its clay neck round in her palm, and the water in a smooth stream dropping into the glass with a deepening circular gurgle, and the black road slipped away between the dusty tips of her shoes, and the dreary plonk-plunk plonk-plunk of Shagufta's hooves beat slowly at her temples. She shut her eyes, but she knew they were passing Kalra Shoe Emporium on the right, with its sharp-tipped tree of Lady's Pumps, then Manohar Lal Madan Lal Halwai, where at the back there were Family Booths and a huge mirror etched with a turbaned man and a woman sitting by a stream, and then Kiani Fine Furniture, which had a long red sofa in the front window and had been At Your Service for Fifty Years, not the sofa but old Mr Kiani and his three sons. Prabhjot Kaur made a bet with herself and opened her eyes and yes indeed they were directly opposite the Tarapore Bakery, which was a heaven of cakes and fizzy drinks, visited by Prabhjot Kaur only once in her entire life, on her ninth birthday, and she remembered the loud pop of the glass ball-stopper falling into the strawberry-soda bottle under the weight of Papa-ji's palm. The sides of Prabhjot Kaur's mouth ached, actually hurt her as the memory came fully back, the flood of pink eruptions into her mouth, the tingling on the inside of her lips, and Shagufta pulled ahead, drew them beyond the Tarapore Bakery, and right then Prabhjot Kaur saw Ram Pari. She was walking along the side of the road, with her dupatta flapping behind her and her arms straight by her sides. Prabhjot Kaur squiggled back into the seat, unaccountably ashamed. Something about seeing Ram Pari on this wide road, next to the two white ladies with their hats like lacy gardens and gleaming white strappy shoes and astonishing gauzy dresses from deep in the mysterious foreign regions of Perreira's Ladies Wear, something about Ram Pari's wide-legged walk made Prabhjot Kaur not want to know her right now. And so she turned her head, as if she was looking at something on the far side of the street, but the side of her neck burned, not from the sun but from what she thought was Ram Pari's gaze, and she was unable to resist a quick glance backwards. Shagufta was slowly drawing away from Ram Pari, whose face was taut as a sheet billowing under a hot summer wind, whose eyes were hard and unseeing, even though she was looking straight at Prabhjot Kaur. The angry hunch of her shoulders receded slowly into the glare on Larkin Road, and finally Prabhjot Kaur lost sight of her altogether, just before they took the left turn on to Fulbag Gali and into Chaube Mohalla, where

Manjeet jumped off and ran ahead to her house, her two thick plaits jiggling and jogging behind her.

When Prabhjot Kaur got home, her father was sitting in his baithak with his friend Khudabaksh Shafi, who was drinking tea out of a cup that was kept especially for him. Prabhjot Kaur always thought of it as the Muslim teacup, and there was always trouble with Mata-ji when Papa-ji carried it inside and washed it himself under the hand-pump. Mata-ji always made a face and Navneet-bhenji and Mani always rolled their eyes and said she was being horribly silly. Prabhjot Kaur liked Khudabaksh Shafi, who had a great straight moustache across his face and who never came without gifts. Today he had brought a basket of leechies. 'Especially for you, beta,' he said, and laughed. 'Eat them after dinner. And don't let those two mustandas inside cheat you.' Her two brothers were sprawled on charpais in the courtyard, in cricket whites, drinking enormous brass tumblers of khari lassi. Iqbal-veerji jumped up and picked up his bat – which he seasoned every other day with special oil – and showed her how he had hit three sixes in a single over, off that Shahidul Almansoor, who thought he was the best bowler in the entire province. Prabhjot Kaur rocked forward and back on her toes, trying to be interested, but as soon as she could she shifted sideways away to her mother's room, leaned against the door until a triangle of light opened on the floor. She slid herself through and sat on the end of the bed, on Papa-ji's side. The bed was high enough that she had to use both her hands to climb up, and then the shape of her mother's side was a ridge in the close darkness. A table-fan swept the air to and fro.

'What is it?' Mata-ji said finally, still facing away.

'Is there some trouble with Ram Pari?'

Mata-ji took a long breath. 'These people.'

'Did she do something, Mata-ji?'

'No, no. Her husband.'

'She has a husband?'

'Beta, nine children she has. He's not been home in a year and a half. She was sure he had another wife somewhere. Then yesterday he came back. Like a laat-saab he spread his legs and shouted for his dinner. It's my house, he said.'

'Is it his house?'

'He hasn't earned ten rupees in his life.'

That was very conclusive, somehow. Mata-ji's shoulder shifted and settled and her breathing changed, and Prabhjot Kaur let herself down slowly to the floor, her cheeks stinging. Ram Pari was still trudging away somewhere, in a line as straight as fate, but all Prabhjot Kaur could think about was that she herself had never earned a rupee in her life, only stolen one. She stood in the shadow of the fluted pillars at the edge of the courtyard, watching her brothers and the red stains on their pants from the cricket ball, their pleasant exhaustion, and wondered if this house was hers. It slid away from her all evening, the feeling of home that she'd had from the first day she had seen the rising beams and the hole in the ground half-lined with bricks. Even as the sun walked up the pillars and she sprinkled water in the courtyard and the smell rose of fresh evening, she was not able to plant herself in the place. She slept fluttering and light, wafting and skipping and windblown in her dreams over the white rooftops of Sabhwal city, where she had been born.

She awoke to quarrelling. Mani was arguing that Ram Pari must be allowed to stay. 'She has nowhere to go,' she said, and Prabhjot Kaur could hear the effort it cost her to keep her voice low and reasonable, how it thickened her throat.

'That's all very sad,' Mata-ji said. 'But since when has she become my mausi that I should take care of her? Let her go to her relatives.'

'Mata-ji, I *told* you already, she *has* nobody here. Her husband brought her here from her village. Do you want her to sleep on the streets, with all of those children?'

'When did I say I want her to do anything?' Mata-ji was sitting cross-legged near the kitchen, with a big thal in her lap piled high on one side with wheat. The grains skittered across the metal to the other side under her rapid fingers, without cease, and on the floor next to her there was a small pile of black pebbles and husks and stubble. 'I don't want her to do anything at all.'

Prabhjot Kaur ran through the courtyard, out to the front gate. Ram Pari was squatting just inside the gate, her wrists resting on a rolled-up blue mattress. She was surrounded by children, an incredible sprawl of them. A toddler naked but for a black thread tied around its waist clambered over ankles and shins, its fat legs pedalling rapidly. When he had almost escaped the circle of bodies, a girl of Prabhjot Kaur's age bent and reached for his arm and dragged him back.

'Ram Pari,' Prabhjot Kaur said. 'What happened?'

'What to say, Nikki?' Ram Pari said. 'What to say? My man, he came back.' She spread her hands wide, taking in not only the children and Prabhjot Kaur but the world itself.

'But he can't just drive you out. That's not right.' Now Ram Pari was quiet, and Prabhjot Kaur had the uncomfortable feeling that they were all looking at her, even the baby, all these hot black eyes, quite expressionless but still making her shift about and look for some-where else to go. She made herself back away, and then turned and ran into the house. In her chest there was a panic, a biting dread that was coloured black and crimson, that tasted like a rotten apple she had bit into once, all spongy and brown under the crisp skin. She flung herself at Mata-ji's shoulder. With her face in Mata-ji's hair, she panted, 'Oh Mata-ji, let her stay.'

'You also?' Mata-ji rolled her eyes. 'Saints and social workers my daughters have become.'

Navneet-bhenji laughed. She was sitting at the hall table, a little cup of oil in front of her, and she was combing it through her hair with long, slow strokes that lifted up the black lengths and let them fall like undulating waves. In the new light the heart-shape of her face was glowing, and her lips curled red, and Prabhjot Kaur had never seen her so beautiful.

'Navneet-bhenji,' Prabhjot Kaur cried, close to tears. 'Tell Mata-ji to let her stay.'

'Mixing up in these people's quarrels will only lead to trouble,' Mata-ji said. 'Do you want that man walking about in the lane out-side, and in and out of this house? And that dirty brood of hers . . .'

'Mata-ji,' Navneet-bhenji said, 'you can wash them all, three times.'

'Don't you start, Navneet,' Mata-ji said. 'And you two, get dressed for school.'

When she got that swollen look about her face, Mata-ji was as unmovable as a full canister of desi ghee. Prabhjot Kaur buttoned her uniform with trembling fingers, and all day at school was completely distracted by visions of Ram Pari walking through an endless thorny wasteland, her children whimpering from thirst and dropping one by one. Manjeet and Asha watched Prabhjot Kaur quizzically as she struggled to take notes. At recess she told them about Ram Pari's plight, but they were unmoved, or at least only half as, or quarter as, moved as she was. If that. 'These people keep fighting like that only,' Asha said. Prabhjot Kaur heard the words, and saw the prim little twist to Asha's mouth, and fought down a surge of tears. Manjeet just shrugged. Then they both turned to more urgent matters, to the question of whether it would be possible to persuade Manjeet's father to sponsor an outing over the next weekend. Their heads were close together, and Prabhjot Kaur saw their bright plaits and the clean white of their dupattas, and she wanted to speak, but her feeling for Ram Pari belonged in some dim interior fold, in a turn in a cave, and it was impossible to drag it out squirming and scared into the hard summery light. So Prabhjot Kaur took a deep breath, and was quiet. She was quiet all day, and quiet on Daraq Ali's tanga, all the way home.

The children were still outside, still scrambling in the patch of shade, which had moved across the courtyard and narrowed. Ram Pari was inside the house, scrubbing the last of the pots. Navneet-bhenji was dozing with a book spread over her belly, flapping a fan lazily. Without opening her eyes, she told Prabhjot Kaur the tale of the day's struggle: Ram Pari had come in, without asking, and had started sweeping the courtyard, just as usual; she had gone about her tasks, and Mata-ji watched her, and the two women passed each other in silence. They had not said a word to each other the whole day. Even now, as Prabhjot Kaur watched, Mata-ji came diagonally across the baking bricks, holding a wet knot of clothes in her hand, and she passed within a foot of Ram Pari as she went to the staircase leading to the roof, but both of them swept their eyes away from each other, as if clothes and pots left no attention available for anything else.

'She didn't look at her, yes?' Navneet-bhenji said, still with her eyes closed.

'Who?'

'Mata-ji. She didn't even look at Ram Pari?'

'No, she didn't.'

'That's what she's been doing all day. Oof, Nikki, she drives me crazy. All these silences full of meaning, and everyone else is supposed to understand them and do what she wants. And she's very good at it. Everyone does do what she wants.'

Prabhjot Kaur was silent herself now. She had felt, herself, little stabs of resentment at her mother, when she wasn't allowed to go on a school picnic, when she was served last from the bowl of kheer and less than her brothers, but all of these small angers vanished daily under the vast presence of her mother's warm influence, under the damp, all-enfolding embrace of her motherly arms, which you could feel as soon as you entered the main gate, in the half-bricks painted white with which she had lined the walkway, in the lacy trimmings on the table cloths on the tables in the baithak. But to hear this strange, tinny edge of contempt in Navneet-bhenji's voice was to suddenly know a separation between mother and daughter, between Mata-ji and herself, that Prabhjot Kaur had never imagined before. It made her feel queasy and very alone.

Navneet-bhenji opened her eyes. She looked full into Prabhjot Kaur's face, her eyes still hazy and abstracted. Then she blinked twice. 'Arre, why're you looking like that, bachcha?' she said. 'Don't worry. She can be infuriating, but you'll go away from this house also.'

Prabhjot Kaur had to swallow twice before she could speak. 'Away?'

'Yes,' Navneet-bhenji said, and drew her close. She nestled her in the bend of an elbow and whispered into her hair. 'Haven't you heard? A girl is born into a house, but her home is somewhere else. This house doesn't belong to you. Your home is elsewhere.'

Saying this, Navneet-bhenji stretched and sighed luxuriously, and Prabhjot Kaur felt, through her own head and into her toes, her sister's pleasure in life, her eagerness for the future, her happiness at leaving, at being gone, and yet Prabhjot Kaur felt only an inexplicable loss, and foreboding. And the rough, ashy sound of the pot being scrubbed mingled with her sister's pulse, which throbbed under her ear.

She covered her head with Navneet-bhenji's dupatta and tried to sleep. When Mani came in an hour and a half later, and flung her bag full of books on the floor, Prabhjot Kaur understood that she had seen Ram Pari and the children, who were still camped by the gate, and that she was incensed and ready for battle. But Mata-ji gave Mani such a look, all twisted brow and bulging eyes, that even she quailed, and quietly came and sat down next to Prabhjot Kaur. She picked furiously at a toenail. Then she said, 'We'll have to wait for Papa-ji.'

But Papa-ji was in no mood for struggles. He was exhausted, and he lay back against a masnad and combed his fingers through his beard, and Prabhjot Kaur could see that even though Mani had put her case squarely before him, and had done it well, in a few short, precise sentences, he was thinking of something else. 'That's difficult,' he said. And then he cupped his eyes. Mani was leaning forward, her fingers twisted and twisting in a kind of net. 'That's difficult,' he said, and then got up. He walked towards his room, and had already forgotten about Ram Pari and her difficulties, this was clear. Mani threw back her shoulders and raised her hands in defeat. Prabhjot Kaur drummed her heels on the floor. What to do, what to do? The silence continued, widened. Ram Pari came in at dinner time to make the phulkas, and the only thing that Prabhjot Kaur could hear were the slap-slaps of her hands on the atta. Her brothers were home, but even they ate quietly. Everyone looked worried, except for Navneet-bhenji. Finally, when the dishes had been cleared away, Mata-ji was nibbling on a little thimble of gur, which she held in two fingers above a cupped left hand. Ram Pari came and stood by the wall, leaning against it. She had a hand cocked on a hip, and one ankle crossed behind the other. 'Bibi-ji,' she said. 'I'm going.'

'Go,' Mata-ji said, and Prabhjot Kaur felt something twist and give in the exact middle of her chest.

Ram Pari was half-way across the courtyard when Mata-ji spoke again. 'Where will you go?'

Prabhjot Kaur could see how still Ram Pari was. Her shoulders were thin, dark rectangles, pinned against the moonlit white of the wall behind, against the sharp edge of the roof. She said nothing.

Mata-ji was looking at the tiny piece of gur left on her finger, as if she were weighing it, considering its possibilities. 'All right,' she said. 'You can stay for one night, behind the house.'

'Yes, Bibi-ji.'

'But only one night. Hear me?'

'Yes, Bibi-ji. One night.'

Ram Pari left quickly. Prabhjot Kaur knew that she was hurrying to get out of earshot before anything more could be said, and she herself couldn't bear the thought of any more talk. She felt suddenly limp, tired, as if she had walked all the way to school and back with a great bag hanging on her shoulders. She settled forward, slumped for a moment against Mata-ji's knees, then got up herself without being told to and got ready for bed. But in spite of wobbly knees and dragging eyes, she clambered up on a stool in the corner of the room where she slept with Mani, and craned her neck out of the window at an angle, so that she could see the busy crowd of dark figures bustling about at the back of the house. There was broken light from two windows, that was all, but Prabhjot Kaur saw how Ram Pari and her children were making their home. They had bundles, none of which Prabhjot Kaur could remember seeing during the long day, but from these bundles they now pulled sheets and rags, strips and tatters, which, arranged on the ground close to the house in a rough, jagged circle, became a habitation. Prabhjot Kaur saw how the shadow of a wall alone could be a shelter. She went to sleep filled to the brim with this new knowledge. She remembered all the drawings she had made of 'My Home' in her long life, and now she knew that all those simple boxy houses she had drawn were somehow a lie, and there was some satisfaction in looking back and thinking what a silly-silly child she had been.

The next afternoon, when Prabhjot Kaur got back from school, she went straight around to the back of the house, and there were two thick sheets nailed to the back wall at the upper end and weighted with broken bricks at the other, forming a kind of half-tent, under which the baby dozed. The other children were scattered in disarray around the garden, which wasn't quite a garden yet but mostly dusty earth, two forlorn trees and a wall at the far end. Prabhjot Kaur stepped close to the mouth of the tent and leaned in. Two poking-out bricks had been made into a little shelf, on which sat a bright picture of Sheran-walli-Ma resplendent on her tiger. From a nail hung a cloth bag which contained clothes. Another two nails held a gunny sack with grain in it. In the furthest recess, in the shadiest part of the tent, there was a small mountain of little bags, and against it the baby slept. Prabhjot Kaur thrilled violently, in the little green world behind the sheet, feeling newness jump up her arms in ecstatic little leaps. She was filled with admiration. How competently so little had been made into so much! How brave it was, all of it! She looked down at the baby. He had a thin bracelet on his right wrist, and a black string around his left arm with a taveez hanging from it, and a penis exactly like a little downturned water-tap. Prabhjot Kaur resisted the urge to pick him up and cradle him, and turned around instead. From a foot away the oldest of the girls was watching her, her hands behind her back. She had a dirty and very long plait that came down over her shoulder and hung in front of her, and alert black eyes, and one protruding tooth on the left side of her mouth. Prabhjot Kaur thought she must be about fourteen, but felt – instantly and without question – older than her. 'What's your name, girl?' she said.

'Nimmo,' the girl said.

'Do you know how to read, Nimmo?'

Nimmo shook her head. In half an hour Prabhjot Kaur had learnt, by heart, all their names – Nimmo, Natwar, Yashpal, Balraj, Ramshri, Meeta, Bimla, Nirmala, Gurnaam, in that order – and that none of them knew how to read, that not one of them, not even one of the boys, had ever seen the inside of a schoolroom. Prabhjot Kaur was horrified, because here was the illiteracy of our country, literally in her back veranda, but she was also secretly pleasured, because here was clear direction, a necessary task. She knew what she had to do. She would set about teaching them. But there was the question of how long they would be allowed to stay, whether or not Mata-ji would stick to her one-night policy and ruthlessly force them out into the wide world. Inside the house, Ram Pari was cutting onions, and Mata-ji had her hands slathered in besan, and there were pakoras sizzling madly in the karhai. They were gossiping about the widowed neighbour four plots down, who had a son given to bad ways and alcohol. They seemed quite content together. Prabhjot Kaur tiptoed around all evening, terrified, unable to bring up the one-night question for fear of reminding Mata-ji of it, and unable to forget it. But when bedtime came, and she stuck her head out of the window, the other family was still there, that round cluster of shiny heads in the dark. It was all quite baffling, Prabhjot Kaur thought as she waited for sleep, her head full of plans. People had stances, they threw out opinions, they made ferocious noises, but decisions were often made in a flurry of competing silences, and what was not said mattered more than what was. The world grew more complicated every day, she thought.

The next afternoon, which was Friday, Prabhjot Kaur lined the children in three columns of three, smallest to largest at the back, and started on the Punjabi alphabet. 'Ooda, aida,' she had them chant. For a blackboard she used the bottom half of a broken old carrom board. She drew the letters across the faded lines of the old game, precise as always, looking not just for correctness but also beauty. She immediately discovered that the younger ones were easier to teach. Meeta and Bimla eagerly took to the letters, and bent low over their pieces of paper, tongues curled between lips, and drew clumsy but correct shapes. Nimmo, on the other hand, mooned about, stared into the distance, lay down on her side and put her head down on her arm and drew letters that looked more like smashed kites or tangles of grass than the elegant, swooping, swan-like constructions Prabhjot Kaur wanted. As soon as Nimmo learnt the third letter, she forgot the first one, and when Prabhjot Kaur urged her to try again – 'Ooda, aida, Nimmo, ooda, aida' – she stuck out her tooth and twisted her face into a grin of such happy stupidity that Prabhjot Kaur felt her patience leaving her and wished she had the authority to give her one tight, biting slap on the ear, like the cracky ones the drawing mistress at school flung out with bloodcurdling suddenness. But Nimmo remained as thick as ever, as stubbornly gooey as old cartwheel grease. And Natwar disappeared altogether. On that very first Friday, Prabhjot Kaur turned from her carrom board, and her middle column was missing one student at the very rear. She stamped her foot, and ran to the corner of the building, but he was already outside the gate, running fast, and he didn't turn his head at her call. He never came back for lessons, but appeared regularly just when they finished.

'Never mind about Natwar. He's another one like his father,' Ram Pari said. 'You put something in their heads.' She appeared every afternoon, late, after she had finished the afternoon dishes and there was still time before chai, and she sat cross-legged with her back against the wall to watch the children being drilled. Prabhjot Kaur watched her watching, and after a week decided that she wasn't nearly grateful enough. Yes, Ram Pari rattled at the kids – 'Learn something, you ganwars!' – but she seemed to think it was a kind of game, and when she needed help with some task that Mata-ji had set her, she would march everyone away except the baby, as if hanging a set of dhurries and beating them free of dust was vastly more important than the three-times-table. Prabhjot Kaur's two brothers pretended serious admiration, but when they started calling her 'Adhyapika-ji', she understood that they were mainly amused and gave them a pert shoulder. Navneet-bhenji was too dreamy to care, and Mani didn't have time to discuss it, the exams were coming on. Only Papa-ji understood how important it was. By the time Prabhjot Kaur had got her class, or at least a part of it, to the nine-times-table, he was regularly drinking his evening chai while sitting on a high-backed chair set at an angle to her classroom, so that it squarely faced the garden, where there would be trees some time soon.

'You're doing a good thing, beta,' he told her one day. She was leaning against his arm, watching him pour the chai cleanly from the cup into the saucer. Like all things he did, the motion was parsimonious, without the slightest possibility of waste. His moustache, and the hair on his chin, was a silvery white, but his cheeks were covered with the softest black, and Prabhjot Kaur loved the way the white curved into the black. He drank, tilting the saucer and somehow not getting his moustache the slightest bit moist. He worked for a British company, and Prabhjot Kaur knew the English for what he did, 'Assistant-Regional-Manager' for a medical supply company, and that he had worked his way up from 'Salesman', but what 'Manager' really meant she had no idea. She knew that they also had dada-pardada land in the absolutely fast-asleep village of Khenchi, which despite its deliciously ridiculous name produced eleven quintals per acre of good wheat every year, and this grandfatherly bounty was a great help to them. She did know what a quintal looked like, because she had been to Khenchi once every winter ever since she could remember, to the broken-down yellow house squatting lonely in the middle of green fields. She knew that from the yellow house to this new one was progress, and that all of it had happened because of education, because Papa-ji had been the first boy in the village to pass his Inter and go to college.

'In another six months I'll have them all to class one level,' she said. 'In one year, to class two.'

He looked at her then, from under white eyebrows. 'One year?'

'Yes.'

He put the cup back into the saucer, even though it was still a third full, and handed it to her. She watched while he walked round and round the edges of their plot, brushing the wall with his sleeve. When Mata-ji called Prabhjot Kaur in, he was still out there, trudging in circles with his head low.

Why were old people sad? Mostly Prabhjot Kaur had no idea. Mata-ji had running feuds with aunts and cousins and neighbours, and sometimes she muttered about them and went on the whole day about some ancient betrayal or slight, but there were other days when, for no visible reason, she was just beset by sighs and a powdery sadness that paled her face. Even Navneet-bhenji had days when she seemed silenced by a shapeless melancholy, even after the engagement and the letters had made her languorous and lovely. So Prabhjot Kaur didn't think much of Papa-ji's mood. The next morning he seemed back to his normal sprightly self. There were workmen at the back of the house, and as she was leaving, Prabhjot Kaur gathered that they were to put grilles over the wooden shutters on the windows. What she found when she got home were more like bars, thick rectangular lengths of iron that sat squarely across the windows, and up and down. 'They'll be painted green when they finish,' Papa-ji said. 'Like the shutters.' But now Prabhjot Kaur's window didn't even open all the way, so that Ram Pari's family was hidden from her. She pointed this out to Papa-ji, this inefficiency in the construction, and incredibly enough all he said was, 'There's no time to fix it now, beta. And the window opens all the way, almost.' This was the same man who had had four cartloads of bricks taken back to the supplier because they weren't exactly what he had paid for. Prabhjot Kaur was going to talk about all this the next morning with Manjeet and Asha, but when she got into the tanga, she was amazed to find herself followed by Iqbal-veerji, who swung himself into the front seat and sat next to Daraq Ali, with his cricket bat between his knees and the handle held between two large-fisted hands. He didn't say a word all the way to school. And the three girls sat with their heads half-turned, and nobody in the tanga spoke. Only after they were inside the school gates did Manjeet snap her head and signal a conclave, and they found a corner to stand in, with their shoulders hunched and foreheads almost leaning against each other, and she whispered, 'In Minapur there were three murders last night. Three Hindus were killed.' She was trembling, Prabhjot Kaur could feel Manjeet's elbow twitching against her arm. 'One was a girl.'

Prabhjot Kaur couldn't learn even part of a lesson the whole day. She didn't write a word in her notebooks, and during recess the girls in the whole school stood around in huddles, and not one game of kidi kada was started. When the final bell rang and they all came to the gate, Prabhjot Kaur saw Iqbal-veerji standing by the tanga and felt a relief so gigantic that she ran forward to him, and stood a step away from him almost in tears until he put a hand on her head and walked her back around to the seat. Now there was that silence again, thick and uncomfortable as woollen blankets in the summer, and Daraq Ali didn't say one word to Shagufta, which frightened Prabhjot Kaur more than anything else. The streets seemed less crowded than usual, and Prabhjot Kaur could see that people weren't saying a thing to each other, nobody lingered on street corners or in front of shops to talk. When the tanga finally turned the corner, and she saw the famil-iar tall rectangle of the gate, Prabhjot Kaur exulted in a huge warm gush of safety which felt like a rising bath of honey, all cushiony and caressing against her skin. She ran inside, and hugged Navneet-bhenji, and sat close to her, and drank down an enormous tumbler of milk without even a squeak of ritual protest, gurgling it down in one long run of gulps. Only when the last drop was gone did she notice that Iqbal-veerji had gone on in the tanga, to escort Asha home. That night, she was glad of the bars, for the metal which at least held away dread, even though it couldn't make the fear vanish. She felt lucky she didn't have to sleep outside.

The light pressed on her face and she was awake. The courtyard was bright outside, and she knew it was late in the morning, very late. When she saw the time in the clock on the mantelpiece her heart thumped. The first assembly bell would ring in less than ten minutes. She threw herself out of bed and ran through the door. 'Why didn't you wake me?' she gasped at Mata-ji. 'It's so late.'

Mata-ji reached out a hand. 'It's all right, beta,' she said, her voice soft. 'There's no school today. Or college. Everything is shut.'

'Why?'

'There's some trouble in town. Go and wash your face and then eat.' She reached out further and touched Prabhjot Kaur's hand, held her by the wrist a little. 'Go.'

It was the quietest holiday Prabhjot Kaur had ever had. She stayed inside her room, arranging her books and cleaning out her school-bag, but at eleven she couldn't stand it any more and tiptoed through the house and slipped out of the front door. Standing by the gate, she could feel an absolute lack of motion in the streets, as if everyone had made an agreement and left town simultaneously. And yet she knew they were all there. She went back through the gate and walked around the house, and at the rear all of Ram Pari's brood were huddled together, even Natwar, who was usually bouncing about the lanes on filthy bare feet, rapt in some mysterious secret life Prabhjot Kaur knew absolutely nothing about.

'Go inside, Nikki,' Ram Pari said. 'You shouldn't be out here. Stay inside the house.'

'Why?'

'Bad things are happening, Nikki.' Ram Pari was looking straight at the rear garden wall, and Prabhjot Kaur saw that what had just been an untidy lane beyond, an insignificant ribbon of parched mud covered by a perpetual shifting mist of scraps of paper, was now even in bright daylight a darkness from which danger came. Prabhjot Kaur studied the top of the wall, and wondered if it was high enough. She wanted to go and stand at its foot, to measure its height and so its protection. But now the garden seemed a foreign wilderness, and she couldn't make herself step off the brick on to the earth. She nodded and went back inside, and sat herself on her bed, cross-legged. She was waiting now, and didn't know for what.

Lunch was also a hushed affair, with everyone speaking in low tones, and Navneet-bhenji not saying a word at all. Papa-ji and the two brothers sat in a tight little circle and spoke with their heads lowered. Afterwards, it was back to the bed for Prabhjot Kaur, and more sitting, and then lying down with her heels drumming against the bed-cover. 'Will you stop that?' Mani burst out. 'You're driving me mad.' Madness was what Prabhjot Kaur felt pooling behind her shoulder-blades, in that afternoon that passed like a slow procession of ants crawling up her leg. So when the chain at the front gate rattled, the metal sound of it echoed through the house and into Prabhjot Kaur's head and she felt a violent spasm of fear, but it was also a relief. Mani was twisted up on to her elbows, her mouth wide open and her neck a bunched bundle of thin ropes just under the skin. Prabhjot Kaur leapt from the bed and ran. She reached the door and swung out with a hand on a wall and saw Iqbal-veerji and Alok-veerji going through the gate and Papa-ji stepping out. She ran forward and saw Papa-ji standing at the other side of the lane, craning his neck, and there were running feet and the hubbub of voices. Now there was a quick panting next to her, and she saw that it was Natwar. They leaned together against the gate. He had eyes as bright as black agates. He slipped past her, and was out into the lane. Without a moment's hesitation she went after him, and was instantly in the shelter of a group of running men. She kept her eye on Natwar, and followed his dodges through the crowd, his sudden swerves and cuts amongst the huffing bodies. Now they came to a gathering halt, in a dense crowd. Natwar reached, without looking back, and pulled her through, bumping her head on hips and buttocks. She fell out of the jostle, and forward, stubbing her nose on Natwar's shoulder, and the way was clear before them. A tanga stood, tilted forward at an angle she had never seen. Tangled in the harness and traces lay a horse, its neck craning forward in a taut curve, as if it were trying desperately to inch along the ground, pull itself along. It was Shagufta. Prabhjot Kaur saw this straight away. Shagufta's lips were curled back, exposing the huge teeth in a rictus of effort. The front legs were curled together. The back ones were splayed out open, and between them and over them spilled fat blue coils from her belly. Prabhjot Kaur could see straight into Shagufta, into the cavity which was the colour of a very ripe winter jamun. The stuff from inside had come out as if with force, and even though it was not moving, Prabhjot Kaur felt it was still forcing itself out from the body, boiling over in oily billows. The road under the tanga was black and wet. On the other side of the tanga, as far away from it as Prabhjot Kaur, was a heaving crowd of men, Muslim men all of them, she knew this somehow, it wasn't the clothes alone, and at their front she could see Daraq Ali. He was shouting something and Prabhjot Kaur could see his teeth. All their mouths were open and she could see the white shine of teeth. That crowd was coming forward in small jerks and then going back. A shove in Prabhjot Kaur's back moved her forward, and she saw that Shagufta's eyes were wide open and moist. She thought now that Shagufta was still alive and was stepping up to her when she was lifted by her arm, twisted and lifted by it, and she cried out in pain. It was Papa-ji. He ran her back through the crowd, held against his side. He ran and ran. All through the lane she felt his fingers hard on her arm. Inside the gate, inside the courtyard, at home again, he took her by the shoulder and shook her, and his own head was moving back and forth and his face was sweaty, and pulled and pushed by his anger, Prabhjot Kaur saw only a blur. 'Why did you go out?' he said, and slapped her. 'Why did you go out? Haan? Why?' He slapped her again.

'Let her be,' Navneet-bhenji said, and took Prabhjot Kaur to her bed. She laid her down and then climbed on to the bed and held Prabhjot Kaur's head in her lap. She was stroking Prabhjot Kaur's face and shoulders, and Prabhjot Kaur could feel her fluttering heart. Mani was sitting on the floor, her knees up and her back against the wall. Mata-ji came in and shut the door quickly and put up the chain. She sat on the bed, her head covered with her dupatta. In the distance they could hear a confused and continuous shouting, like the steady crackle of a dim fire. 'Vaheguru, vaheguru,' Mata-ji said. They sat together until dark. And then it was quiet.

After that night none of the women went out. Prabhjot Kaur hardly even left her bed. She came out to eat and ran back to it, went out when called by Mata-ji, but then sidled away as soon as possible.

Papa-ji came and sat cross-legged with a pillow over his lap and teased her and made her laugh and tickled the soles of her feet, and she understood that he was apologizing for his moment of panic, and she was able to go out into the courtyard with her hand in his, but despite herself she grew anxious out in the open, she got a feeling in the middle of her chest as if a hard bubble was expanding to the size of an onion, making it hard to breathe. She came back fast, into her room. The white walls made her feel better, and the bars. She looked out of the window sometimes, to find Ram Pari and Natwar and all the rest huddled below, but she avoided raising her eyes to the garden, and what lay beyond. When she turned around, and she was securely in the room, on her bed, she was all right.

Outside, men and women were killed every night, and every day. Prabhjot Kaur knew what this was called: khoon. Prabhhjot Kaur held the word on her tongue, and to her it felt like a square metal apparatus with a gaping hole in the centre. Dripping with viscous fluids and sharp edges glinting. Manjeet had shown her this thing in a senior class history book once, this engine of death, and now it came back to Prabhjot Kaur. Khoon. Papa-ji and the brothers came into the house laden with the names of those who were already gone. A sardar named Jasjit Singh Ahluwalia on the corner where Pakmara Street ran into Campbell Road, near Tarapore Bakery, slashed to hanging bits by men with swords. Ramesh Kripalani, aged sixteen, found with his throat expertly cut around, head hanging into the gutter so that Ali Jafar Road was not sullied by a drop of blood. 'They say a butcher from Karsanganj did it,' Alok-veerji said. 'Caught him on the way home from his Chacha's house.' *Khoon.* There were more, many more. Mata-ji and her daughters listened to the lengthening list. On the day that final exams would have started, Ram Pari's husband was killed. He was one of three looters shot by the police on Larkin Road at six a.m. – Prabhjot Kaur heard about this the next day, first as a rumour, then as a certainty. A wailing rose behind the house, a blurred chorus that rose and fell, and there was nowhere to escape it, and Prabhjot Kaur learnt for the first time his name, Kuldish. All through the day they mourned Kuldish, the bad man who had never come to threaten Ram Pari, and the wails slid under Prabhjot Kaur's skin and made her shiver.

That evening Mata-ji told the brothers to stay at home, not to go out on to the street, and Iqbal-veerji laughed, and the sound fell into the room with a clank like iron. The brothers left anyway, and Alok-veerji glanced back as he shut the door, and Prabhjot-Kaur saw that he looked at her, all of them, his sisters and mother, with anger and something very much like contempt. Mata-ji began to curse Muslims. 'No one can ever live with these people,' she said. 'They are incapable of living peacefully with anyone.' Her face was suffused with blood, flushed and thickened by it. 'Dirty lying people,' she said. Prabhjot Kaur made lists in her mind, of the Muslims she knew. Daraq Ali, of course; Papa-ji's friend Khudabaksh Shafi, who came to visit always with baskets of strawberries or apples or mangoes, and all his sons and daughters and grandchildren; Parveena and Shaukat Shah, who owned the Excellent Store, from which Prabhjot Kaur and all her brothers and sisters had bought school uniforms and shoes all their lives; all the Muslim girls at school, especially Nikhat Azmi, who was a round-faced girl that the Trio played with whenever they went to Manjeet's house. The list went on and on, and once Prabhjot Kaur started, it seemed to her there was always one more person, one more face that she remembered late at night, before drifting into sleep. But Mata-ji cursed. And Pritam Singh Hansra wrote letters to Papa-ji. He had stopped writing to Navneet-bhenji, and instead wrote letters to Papa-ji begging him to come to Amritsar, to bring the family, all of it, but especially Navneet-bhenji. He had been in Amritsar for a month and a half already. 'You know yourself what is happening,' he wrote. 'And things can only get worse.'

But Papa-ji was paralysed. He shook his head in the morning at the newspapers' reports of flames and murder and ambushed trains full of refugees, and in the afternoon he was completely still. He sat cross-legged on an armchair in the courtyard, not even shifting in his seat, as if he were bound with tight chains that slowed even his breathing. He stopped changing his clothes then, and sat through the whole day in a banian and pyjamas, his hair loose under a patka and bare feet resting on the brick. Prabhjot Kaur knew he was waiting for something, and saw that he had been emptied of vigour, suddenly drained of volition like an upended bucket. She remembered how he had bounded from one side of the excavation to the other when the foundation was being dug, how he had not minded that his arms were muddied from grasping at the earth, how he had held up handfuls of mud from the bottom of the pit for her to test for moistness, how he had dusted his hands with great slappings of them, with wide sweeps to the sides and sharp cracks that she had jumped at. There was no more motion in him, and even the blinks of his eyes were slow, mournful sweeps, which Prabhjot Kaur could follow down and up. One day, she thought, I'll come out and even that will be stopped, finished, unmoving. She tried not to think this, but it came back as slyly as a persistent fly, this thought, and then its buzzing grew louder and louder until she hit at her forehead with the heels of her hands. I'll go mad, she thought. I will.

Finally Mata-ji took charge. It was now past summer and everyone they knew had gone, Manjeet and Asha and their families also. One evening a Pathan policeman rattled the gate. When Iqbal-veerji cracked the door an inch, the chain still firmly in place, the policeman flicked in an envelope that landed at Alok-veerji's feet. 'I'll be back in half an hour for an answer,' the policeman whispered, and went down the lane. Inside the envelope was an unsigned letter.

Sardar Saab, I will not sign my name, for this letter may be read. But you know who I am. I am your friend who brings fruits from the mountains. Now listen to me as your friend. You must go. You are being talked about, and today or tomorrow your house will be attacked. Understand what I am saying. Specifically your house. Your sons are known and there is talk about what they have done and they are in danger, much much danger. You must go. I will make arrangements. We have known each other for thirty years and I have sat in your house and you have come to mine. You must go, my friend. I will look after your house.

Papa-ji listened to Iqbal-veerji reading this out, and his face sat still as a lump of slack clay, blurry and softened. Mata-ji took the letter from her son's hand, and she put her dupatta over her head and wrapped it around her face. She waited by the gate, and when the small hollow knock came she put her mouth to the wood. 'Tell him we'll go,' she said.

'Be ready tomorrow night at nine,' the policeman said. 'A tempo will come. It will be a thousand rupees per person. No more, but no less. Understand?'

'Yes,' Mata-ji said. 'I understand.'

They packed all night and all day. Prabhjot Kaur was amazed at how many things were in a house. Papers, clothes, books, silver jars, photographs, chairs, more clothes, mattresses, expensive combs, shoes, each person had an array of things that were attached to them with tight knots of many-threaded time, each person had a heavy load of things that couldn't be left behind. Prabhjot Kaur looked at several ranks of dolls she no longer played with, threadbare heads that she hadn't petted in years, but then she tugged and strained at a paper sack trying to fit them all in, filled it with these long-ago companions until the paper gave way and tore with a single sharp rip. By late afternoon the courtyard and the baithak were full of tottering bundles tied in sheets, and staggeringly heavy suitcases, and iron trunks which took four people to lift. Prabhjot Kaur was trying to decide which books to take when Mata-ji came rushing in. 'Here, put this on.' It was a blue salwar-kameez with a square geometric print on rather thick cotton, which Prabhjot Kaur had decided three months ago was fit only for everyday house wear. But here was Mata-ji quite impatient. 'Take, take.' Prabhjot Kaur took it and wondered at the heavy tug of its weight. Mata-ji was gone already, out of the door. The salwar was what was heavy. Prabhjot Kaur turned it over and saw that there were little packets of cloth that had been stitched to the waistline, on the inside, just under the nada. There was metal in these little secret pockets, gold, she could feel the smooth, slippery density of necklaces and bracelets. When she walked out into the courtyard after changing, she saw that Mata-ji and all the sisters were wearing the same loose, rough clothing, ready for a strange kind of travel, and that they were all moving with a care-laden awkwardness, as if they didn't know the edges of their bodies any more. Mani clinked as she walked past Prabhjot Kaur, and yet Prabhjot Kaur was unable to be amused by her attempts to silence herself, her rolling heel-toe walk. Now nobody was saying a word. The sun was gone, sunk, and Prabhjot Kaur sat on a trunk and saw the surfaces of her home recede into dimness. Iqbal-veerji came in, his arms muddy, and washed his hands under the hand-pump. When the water fell on the brick it was very loud, the splatter like an explosion, and Prabhjot Kaur flinched. Then, again, silence.

'Bibi-ji.' It was Ram Pari. 'Bibi-ji.' She was whispering. Mata-ji said nothing. Ram Pari came in and squatted on the ground next to her, next to the charpai. 'What will we do?' she said. 'What will we do?'

'Here,' Mata-ji said. 'I'll give you some money.'

Prabhjot Kaur was glad of the darkness, because it hid her face. She had both hands to her mouth. For days now, or maybe it had even been weeks, she hadn't thought of them. She hadn't thought of Ram Pari, or Natwar, or Nimmo, or any of the others, the family just outside her window. They had been her students, and she had forgotten them completely. She had retreated to her bed and had given them up.

'Bibi-ji, where will we go? How?'

'I don't know, Ram Pari. Just take this.'

Prabhjot Kaur could see the long shape of Mata-ji's arm, held out. Ram Pari was the dark lump at the end of the charpai.

'Take,' Mata-ji said.

The shapes stayed the same, tilted slightly away from each other, the same distance with the same reaching between them, and a breath forced itself down Prabhjot Kaur's chest, pierced it, and in that sudden rough pain she had the certain knowledge that the world would never be the same again. She wanted to say something but there was nothing to say.

'You will leave us, Bibi-ji,' Ram Pari said. 'We will die.'

'Vaheguru will look after all of us.' Mata-ji held the hand out further, and shook it assertively. Ram Pari sank further into the tight huddle she had made of herself. Prabhjot Kaur thought they might all sit there for ever, under that huge, still sky. Then Alok-veerji came out of his room, loomed out tall above them all.

'Take it,' he said, and he took the money from Mata-ji's hand and lifted Ram Pari by the shoulder and walked her past Prabhjot Kaur. 'There is a kafila leaving two days from now. There will be thousands of people walking. You can go with them.' Prabhjot Kaur slipped off the trunk and walked close behind Alok-veerji, and though she couldn't see him doing it, she knew that he had thrust the money into Ram Pari's hand. 'We can't do anything now. Go.' He pushed her through the door and turned and went back to his preparations. Ram Pari stood in the passageway between the courtyard and the outside, stood very close to the wall. Prabhjot Kaur took a step forward and put both her hands against Ram Pari's side, clutched at her, leaned on her, she could feel the cloth against her face, against her eyes, and there was the living exhalation of another person, sweaty and sharp, bitter, Prabhjot Kaur breathed it in. Then Ram Pari forced her hands open. Down the passage she went, a shadow close to the wall, and Prabhjot Kaur watched her go.

The tempo, when it came, an hour late, was not the truck they were expecting but a creaky black car. The driver was a tiny bald man, and he was accompanied by the policeman of the afternoon. 'Hurry,' the policeman said. 'Hurry.' Iqbal-veerji and Alok-veerji loaded up the boot of the car and tied it down with rope. Two trunks and various bundles went on the roof, and inside the car, on the floor around the seats, they had bundles. But then the car was full.

'Come,' Iqbal-veerji said. As they slipped past the baithak, Prabhjot Kaur saw the figures clustered by the corner to the left, she couldn't see any faces but knew it was Ram Pari and Nimmo and Natwar and the rest. All the way to the gate she stumbled against packages that were being left behind. The engine of the car was already thumping. Papa-ji sat on the right in the back seat, then Mata-ji, then Navneet-bhenji and Mani and then Iqbal-veerji. Prabhjot Kaur sat in the front between Alok-veerji and the bald driver. The policeman patted the bonnet of the car.

'Go,' he said. 'Go quickly.'

As they went, Prabhjot Kaur twisted on the seat, came up on her knees to look back. But all she saw was the policeman, standing quite erect in front of the gate, and Mata-ji and Navneet-bhenji and Mani curled up in the back seat, heads low, like little children settled in to sleep on a long journey. 'Get down,' Alok-veerji said, and caught Prabhjot Kaur by the neck and yanked her low. His voice shook and now Prabhjot Kaur was very afraid. Her face was against his side and against the seat, but her eyes were strained open and she could see past the driver's elbow and through the steering wheel and through the glass, she could see the shape of homes and shops, the white of signs and the sudden deeper black when a street opened out, they turned and turned again and the engine grunted and choked and Prabhjot Kaur was completely unable to tell where they were. Then a series of pops sounded into the sky that Prabhjot Kaur could see through the dirty glass, pops like phap, phap-phap-phap as if a child had burst a balloon, and then a series of others very quickly. It was a happy sound. But the car jogged and twisted and came to a halt, sliding Prabhjot Kaur forward. And now it went backwards. Backwards and backwards so fast that Prabhjot Kaur twisted her hands around Alok-veerji's shirt and was now crying. She could hear men's voices, shouting and echoing. And Iqbal-veerji: 'Take this left here and then the Ravi Road.' The car moved forward now, turning to the left and throwing Prabhjot Kaur again. They were moving fast now, she felt it in the vibrations jolting her body. Orange light filled the inside of the car, spiralling through the glass and brightening every corner, and she could see the round silver rupee dangling from the key-chain, every detail of the King-Emperor's face. With a sound like a huge threshing watermill the flames towered up, for a moment filling the windscreen and the window and she shut her eyes. Another turn, this time to the left, and glass broke somewhere and then a sound so loud and so close and so ugly that Prabhjot Kaur knew instantly that it was a gunshot. The car lurched violently from side to side, a screech filled Prabhjot Kaur's head, she flew forward, and felt the impact of metal against her forehead, and a flowering, tinny echo inside which swallowed her up. Then she was lying on her side listening to a babble of voices, a continuous scream not very far away, and she could not tell where she was until the dark bar above twisted and receded and became one of the spokes of the steering wheel, and again that barking explosion, right above her head, this time she saw a flash, and she twisted herself and thrust herself further into the shadowed space under the wheel, and then again a shot and she shut her eyes.

She could hear Mata-ji weeping. Other than that hoarse gargling noise, it was very quiet. Prabhjot Kaur tried to still the movement of her knees, a shaking which grew from the convulsing of her stomach. She was convinced that this would give her away. She held her right hand against her right thigh and pressed it down hard. Metal scraped, and she knew it was the door of the car, and there was nowhere to go, and she wanted to scream but she held it in, fought against it with her muscles. 'Nikki, Nikki.' It was Iqbal-veerji. He drew at her softly and she came out of her coil and held on to his arms and cried. He got her out of the car and she wrapped herself around him. 'It's all right,' he said. But Mata-ji was sitting on the road, and Mani was trying to comfort her. And Papa-ji leaning against the back of the car, his head low and his hands on his knees, and spittle hanging from his mouth. Alok-veerji a little down the road, his body twisted to one side as he tried to see around a corner. Just beyond him there was a shape on the ground, like a bundle of clothes had come apart and scattered its contents haphazardly. It was a man's body. There was the head, and there was a hand. It was the driver.

Alok-veerji turned. 'We have to get out of here.'

'I don't know how to drive,' Iqbal-veerji said mildly.

They both looked stunned, as if this one skill they had forgotten to add to their sporting repertoire had suddenly revealed its hidden importance, its secret meaning.

And then Mata-ji stopped crying and said, 'Kill them.'

Her weeping had been so constant and so loud that when it stopped Prabhjot Kaur felt keenly how quiet it had become all over again, after all the bedlam. It was rather nice. But who did she mean? Mata-ji looked at her husband, and at one son and then at another.

'Kill them,' she said. 'Before they take them too.'

Prabhjot Kaur turned her head towards the car, and then to the street. Navneet-bhenji was gone. Prabhjot Kaur had not noticed until now, but now it was impossible to escape this fact. Navneet-bhenji had been taken.

Alok-veerji came towards Mata-ji, and Prabhjot Kaur saw that in his right hand he had a pistol, and in his left something long and curving. The front of his shirt hung down on the left side like a flap, revealing the inverted arc of his chest. There was blood on his neck, black and flowing, she could see it. And dangling not very far from her face, from Iqbal-veerji's hand, was a kirpan, no, a sword.

'Kill them,' Mata-ji said again. Mani's face was hidden from Prabhjot Kaur, darkened. Prabhjot Kaur could see only her unmistakable thin shoulders, her forearms as she held Mata-ji. Prabhjot Kaur stepped away from Iqbal-veerji, and raised her head, and saw that his pagdi had come off, his hair hung in a loose coil over his forehead. His mouth was shaking. He was looking at her and she saw him fight for control, bite down on his lower lip to stop it from trembling. Her fear now felt different, like a long, continuous fall from a great height, but in spite of this hurtling drop she felt embarrassment for her brother. She lowered her head and waited. She was waiting for death, a khoon ordered by her mother.

'I'll drive,' she heard Papa-ji say. 'I can drive.'

Of course, Prabhjot Kaur thought. He used to be a salesman. The car started on the first try, but then they had to push it back and up from the gutter it had dropped its front left wheel into. Prabhjot Kaur turned round and round on the dark street, unable to stay still, trying to face everywhere and afraid of what was behind her back. Then they were all in, and Prabhjot Kaur this time crouched down as far as she could get in the front seat. She pushed at the bundle in front of her with her legs, and when it gave way a little she forced her legs and hips into the little space she had made. She wished she could get under the bundle. She wished there was a little secret space under the seat that she could tuck herself into. She wished for a dark little metal hole which nothing would ever be able to get into, where she could get away from Mata-ji's horrible croaking sobs, her 'Vaheguru, Vaheguru' and her Japji Sahib which pierced all the clatter of the car and Prabhjot Kaur's own clamorous breathing, and Prabhjot Kaur clapped her hands hard and desperate over the ears.

She saw nothing. She kept her eyes closed. But there was a change in the sound of the road, a difference in the texture of the black under her eyelids, and she knew that they had left the city behind. Near dawn they came upon two trucks of soldiers, stopped by a well. Alok-veerji was afraid, but Papa-ji said there was no choice. They approached them slowly, and just before the car stopped Prabhjot Kaur opened her eyes. The sky was a neutral grey, the colour half-way between black and white. She had never stayed up all night before.

'These are Muslims,' she heard Mata-ji say. They were, and their leader was a major by the name of Sajid Farooq. Prabhjot Kaur read it on his breast pocket as she sat on a villager's charpai, shivering. Sajid Farooq put their car between the soldiers' trucks that morning, and by the afternoon they had a caravan thirty-one vehicles long. The next morning Prabhjot Kaur saw a line, a stream, a river of walking people that stretched to the horizon. The men and women and children walked behind each other in silence, trudging in the same direction as Sajid Farooq's trucks, and all the cars. They were moving very slowly, and the trucks and cars moved past each one of them with ease, but it took three hours to leave behind that whole lot. That evening they were met by other soldiers, in the same uniforms and the same trucks, but these were Hindus escorting a convoy of Muslims. Alok-veerji said the soldiers were Madrasis. This was the first thing Prabhjot Kaur had heard him say in two days. His eyes were red and sometimes tears ran down his face and he seemed not to notice them. Sajid Farooq took the convoy of cars and trucks that had come with the Madrasis, put his soldiers in front of them and behind them and drove away. Prabhjot Kaur watched the Muslims drive past, going to Pakistan. Then the Madrasis took the Sikhs and Hindus to India. The trip was uneventful. In two days they were in Amritsar.

Here they lived in a city of three thousand tents. People came from the city with clothes and food, to give to the refugees, and a politician came to walk through the filthy lanes that had been ploughed out by hundreds of feet between the walls of canvas. Prabhjot Kaur hid in their tent when she saw the photographers that came with the Congressman. She felt shame, a powdery burning that sizzled across her arms and shoulders. She saw it in Papa-ji's face when he took a half-sack of wheat from a bania who had brought a cartload of food-stuff from the city. She saw it in Mata-ji's crouch, how she sat with her dupatta pulled over half her face, and she saw it in Mani's long bouts of sleep, in the determined way that she lay herself down and turned away to one side, even when the sun burned on the canvas and the ground felt as if it were heated from underneath. They were all ashamed. Prabhjot Kaur felt it most when she looked at Mata-ji's face, her nose, her mouth, her lined forehead, and so she never looked at her. She cast her eyes up, or to the side, or examined her own hands, or sometimes, while walking by, just shut one eye or the other so that there was no chance of seeing. In Mata-ji it was unbearable, this shame, but it was in all of them, it hung around them like a bad, unwashed smell. It was shame that constricted Alok-veerji's throat, so that each word cost an effort of the muscles and emerged compacted and slow.

'It was an ambush,' Alok-veerji was saying. 'It was that Khudabaksh Shafi. He had it all planned.'

Prabhjot Kaur was standing outside the tent, holding a pile of damp clothes higher than her head.

'You mean for the house? He wanted the house so he scared us out?' This was Iqbal-veerji.

'Yes,' Alok-veerji said. 'The house. And everything else.'

Prabhjot Kaur's head hummed with an onrush of blood. This 'everything else' was something they never spoke about. Nothing was ever said, not one word. One name had disappeared from the world, taking with it a whole life.

'I can't believe that,' Iqbal-veerji said. 'I can't.'

'Believe it,' Alok-veerji said. 'They took the house, they took our land, but they weren't satisfied with that much. It was all planned. The driver drove us straight into an ambush, they were waiting. There were enough of them to – to take what they wanted. But they didn't expect us to be well-armed. So they got what they wanted, but they couldn't kill us all. So they ran. That is the truth about those people. I only wish I had done more. Instead of burning three houses I wish we had burnt a thousand. And killed a lakh of them.'

'Alok. Be quiet.'

'Why? Why be quiet? I'll shout it out loud. These Muslims are bhenchods and maderchods. If all their women were standing in front of me, I would hang them up and cut them open like goats. I would pull out their intestines with my own hands. With pleasure I would do it. Bhenchods. Maderchods.'

Prabhjot Kaur ran. She dropped the clothes and ran away. Her mother's words followed her: 'Kill them.' She tripped over tent-ropes and skinned her palms on the black gravel, and she ran past children kicking a piece of wood from one side of the pathway to the other, past women squatting in the doorways of tents repairing torn shirts, past bubbling pots on makeshift choolas of six bricks, past everything until she was finally at the edge, beyond all habitation. Ahead there was a brown path, and on the other side of that a bare maidan strewn with rocks, and then endless fields, green and thick. She stopped and held her sides, bent over until the sweat fell straight from her forehead to the ground, making dark circles on the earth. She straightened up. She wanted to go away. She wanted a place to go to, somewhere very far away, hundreds of miles from her family, thousands of miles from everyone. *Haven't you heard? A girl is born into a house, but her home is somewhere else. This house doesn't belong to you. Your home is elsewhere.* If I could keep walking, she thought. But she knew her geography too well, those lessons she had learned with the Trio, the ones she had written down in fair handwriting in books covered with brown paper. And now, now she knew more. There were seas to one side, mountains to another, nowhere to go, and fear everywhere. You would have to cross fear to get nowhere. The maidan was still, and the fields waited, silent. Prabhjot Kaur stood alone, at the edge of the city of refugees. Then she turned and went back to her father and mother and brothers and sister.

Finally they managed to go to Delhi. Mata-ji took out from underneath her clothes some of the jewellery she had carried, and this time they went by train. The two brothers deposited the rest of the family in the house of Gunjan Singh Parvana, who was not really a relative, but the son of a man from the village Khenchi. There was an ancient story about how Papa-ji's father had saved Gunjan Singh Parvana's policeman father from summary dismissal and unemployment, and so now he took them in. They had two tiny rooms and a veranda at the back of the house. Then the two brothers went to what was now the border, and beyond, to a foreign country. They had not wanted to go, but Mata-ji now said, for the first time, 'Go and find my daughter.' Prabhjot Kaur heard this while she pretended to sleep. Nowadays there were many discussions among the elders of the family that she and Mani were kept out of. Mani was really asleep, and even whimpering a little, but Prabhjot Kaur kept herself awake every night. She wanted to know, had to know. Staying awake got easier and easier. There were certain practices that kept you from an unknowing slide into yourself, from a feathery fall into the vacuum of rest: you paid attention to details, you kept the mind working and turning and racing, you listened. And Prabhjot Kaur heard Mata-ji's voice, low and full of phlegm and fierce: 'Go and find my daughter.' The other murmurs were all run together and powdery and hard to catch, but Prabhjot Kaur heard the command: 'Go and find my daughter.' It brooked no resistance. So they went. What Prabhjot Kaur couldn't understand was why they were reluctant to go. Of course they should go, she thought, why don't they want to go? and felt instantly a hurt in her stomach, a fist that grew upwards and twisted her heart so that she thought she would cry out loud. But she was silent, silent and awake, night after night, and she waited.

They returned a month and a half later, forty days and forty-one nights later, to be exact. Prabhjot Kaur, who now kept strict track of time, jerked out of a sleep that she was sure was only a few minutes old, and knew they had come back. The door to Mata-ji's room was shut, and the tones were very soft, but she heard them nevertheless, and she was certain. She got up and stood next to the door for a minute, and rested her head on the rough grey wood, and the voices passed into her forehead. She had no hope. Night after night she had imagined it, the happy moment, that sliding swish of salwar-bottoms over ground, that sound she knew so well, how she would cling to Navneet-bhenji, with her head buried in the soft comfort of home, and the beloved blood singing in the arms that held her. Now she knew this would not happen. She turned away, walked out on to the veranda. There was a wire fence, and beyond that a line of gulmohar trees, and in the distance a rising ridge. This was all the Delhi she knew. Next to the fence there was a woman crouching, and Prabhjot Kaur knew right away who it was: Ram Pari. She knew that squat, that comfortable ease so close to the ground, that position she could hold for hours.

'Is that Ram Pari?' Mani came out on to the veranda and ran down to the fence. She bent down to Ram Pari, and then Prabhjot Kaur saw Ram Pari's upturned face. She was an old woman. The skin hung off her cheekbones in limp whorls. She had a dupatta wrapped over her shoulders, a red one, and Prabhjot Kaur remembered it well from before. Now it was tattered and faded to a rusty brown. 'Where did you come from?' Mani said to Ram Pari.

'Iqbal-veerji, I saw him at the bus station,' Ram Pari said, and it was a shock to hear her husky voice, with the familiar village rhythms. 'We had come across the border. Walking.'

'And . . . and where is everyone?'

Prabhjot Kaur wanted to shout something at Mani. It seemed an unbearable question to ask, and she had no wish to hear it, or wait for an answer. But she stood absolutely still, unable to move.

Ram Pari shook her head. Slowly, she shook her head. To one side and then another.

There was the creak of the door, and Papa-ji came past Prabhjot Kaur, and then the brothers. The three men stood in the veranda, uncertain, it seemed, of what to do or where to go next. Mani had a hand on Ram Pari's shoulder. Prabhjot Kaur willed movement into herself, she turned and went into the house. In the small airless room to the right, her mother was weeping. She was sitting on the ground, next to a charpai, with her arms thrown over the sheets, and her head was down and she was sobbing. The sound was small and infant-like. Not angry, or outraged, just surprised. Prabhjot Kaur went in and stood next to Mata-ji, her knees feeling a small rattling from the bed, and sensed in herself a large anger, felt herself swell with it, become as hard as a rock, and also a sharp, cutting river of pity, a helpless over-flowing of it. Her mother's head had grey hair, very dry and broken and ugly, and a balding patch at the back, and underneath, scalp as young and smooth as a baby's. Prabhjot Kaur shut her eyes for a moment, and then reached forward and put her hand on her mother's head. Mata-ji's body arced, and she came towards Prabhjot Kaur like a blind, nuzzling animal and held her around the waist with both arms, and leaned on her, and Prabhjot Kaur steadied herself, and pat-ted her gently on the shoulders and neck, and tried to comfort the woman in her grief.

Burying the Dead

❦

Sartaj woke at seven. Ma was already sitting at the dining table, reading a newspaper through thick bifocals. She was bathed, dressed in a crisp white salwar-kameez, her hair neatly combed. He never in his life had managed to wake up before her, and sometimes he wondered if she ever slept.

'Sit,' she said. She brought out a plate, a cup. He read the paper: the cross-border peace process was picking up momentum. But twenty-two men had been killed in Rajouri by Kashmiri militants, maybe foreign mercenaries. The militants had stopped a State Transport bus on a main road, lined up the Hindu men on one side, and fired at them with AK-47s. One traveller had survived, under the bodies, with a bullet in his groin. There was a photograph of the corpses, lined up in a lumpy row. Sartaj smelt cooking eggs. He thought, why do we always line them up? Why not put them in a circle? Or a V? Or just anyhow, this way and that? It was one of the things you did when you had lots of victims, line them up, as if this controlled and contained the chaos of the event, metal exploding through living flesh. Sartaj had himself dragged limp bodies into ordered ranks, and felt better for it.

'These Muslims will never let us live in peace,' Ma said as she put down an omelette in front of him. It was the way he liked it, very fluffy with lots of chillies but no onions.

'Ma,' Sartaj said, 'this is a war. It's not like all Muslims are monsters or something.'

'I didn't say that. But you don't know.' She had taken off her glasses, and was polishing them now with her dupatta. When she looked at him, her face was absolutely expressionless, closed up like a steel-shuttered window. 'You don't know these people. They are just different from us. We will never let them live in peace either.'

Sartaj turned to his omelette. There was no arguing with her, she was set in her ways, and finally she would bring out heavy, simple assertions that she treated as unquestionable, and would hold to them like anchors. It was annoying and useless, any attempt to have this discussion, and it would just raise her blood pressure. Sartaj turned the page, and read a long human-interest story about a paan-wallah and his luxuriant moustaches.

In the crowded calm of the gurudwara, later, he watched his mother. She was sitting with her knees up, holding her arms around them in a way that he always thought of as girlish. As the massed voices rose and soared in a kirtan, she was lost in memory. He knew that look, soft, with half-drooped eyes gazing into the middle distance, that inwardness. She was very small, very fragile, and looking at her thin wrists he was full of fear and thought again that he should take her to live with him. How long do we have them, he thought, our parents? How long? But she was very stubborn, and clung to her house like a soldier fighting a war. The last time they had argued about this, she had said, this is my home. I will only leave it one way, when the time comes. And he had seen suddenly how alone one could be in this gigantic world, when time took your father and mother from you, and he had said, spluttering, don't talk like that.

'Tarai gun maya mohi aayi kahan baydan kaahii,' the singers sang. We are walkers on this journey, Sartaj thought, and we drop one by one. On the other side of Ma there was her oldest brother, Iqbal-mama, swaying from the shoulders to the hip. He was a very religious man, a trustee of the gurudwara, occupied always in good works and charity. Sartaj liked him, but found his constant piety stifling. There had been another mama, Alok-mama, who all the children had liked a lot more. Sartaj still remembered with awe how much that elephantine sardar used to eat, roasted chickens for breakfast, rogan josh for lunch with fresh jalebis afterwards, dinner was an epic struggle, with Scotch whisky added and Alok-mama's face glowing red. The children, all the cousins, used to joke that there was a trapdoor inside Alok-mama which led to an enormous cave where all the food disappeared, it was incredible that one man should eat so much. He used to wheeze going from one room to another. His wife found him dead one morning in the bathroom, with water from the tap falling on his face. This was when Sartaj was fourteen.

Iqbal-mama was very religious, and Mani-mausi was not at all so. There had been fights, shouted quarrels, when she had been sarcastic about Iqbal-mama's eternal worshipping. Ma always offered sisterly counsel to Mani-mausi, tried to keep her from baiting their brother. But nobody could rein in Mani-mausi when she was in one of her moods. She was quite the scandal of her family, with her divorce and her fiercely communist political beliefs and her vocal atheism. Sartaj didn't know how much he himself believed any more. He of course kept his beard, the hair, the kara, but he hadn't prayed of his own accord for years. There were pictures of the gurus in his house, but he no longer asked them for advice, or expected miracles from them, or even an easier day. The colours in the pictures seemed too bright to him now, the absolutely pristine whites of Guru Nanak's turban too far from dirty life. Still, Sartaj thought, it was good to come with his mother to this place. There was good light, and companionship in the aligned shoulders of the worshippers, and comfort.

Ma adjusted her salwar over her feet, and Sartaj thought then of the woman in Gaitonde's bunker, the long sprawl of her legs in her stylish pants. They had found no evidence of religion in her apartment, no cross or bible or rosary. So perhaps she was irreligious, or maybe just indifferent. But she had consorted with Gaitonde, whose long prayers and donations to religious causes were legendary. For a while during the late nineties, he had projected himself in the media as the Hindu Don, brave defender against the anti-national activities of Suleiman Isa. Sartaj remembered a *Mid-Day* interview in which Gaitonde had predicted the early demise of Suleiman Isa. 'We have teams active in Pakistan, looking for him,' Gaitonde had said. There had been an old file photograph at the top of the story, a very young Ganesh Gaitonde wearing a red sweatshirt and dark glasses. Sartaj had been impressed by the look. He had his own style, Ganesh Gaitonde did, but finally he had been the one who died, without any intervention – it seemed – by his old enemy. Why? It was an interesting mystery, somewhat pleasurable to contemplate, and Sartaj gave himself to theorizing about it for the rest of the morning.

He was still speculating when he and Ma finally got home, late in the afternoon. After leaving the gurudwara, they had spent two hours at Iqbal-mama's house, amongst a swirling welter of nieces and nephews. Sartaj had grown up an only child, and he rather liked – in small doses – the comfortable chaos of large families. Now Sartaj was pleasantly tired, but his mind was lazily ticking along, building stories about Ganesh Gaitonde. He was lying in bed, in a curtained darkness, wondering whether there had been a failed love affair between Gaitonde and Jojo Mascarenas, some tangled tale of fleshly desire and betrayal which had led to a murder-suicide. That was likely, he decided. Men and women did that kind of thing to each other.

'Sartaj, I want to go to Amritsar.'

Sartaj jerked up. Ma was standing in the doorway. 'What?'

'I want to go to Amritsar.'

'Now?' Sartaj rubbed his eyes, swung his feet to the floor.

'Arre, no, beta. But soon.'

Sartaj pulled back a curtain, letting in a spill of light. 'Why suddenly?'

Ma straightened the sheet. 'Not suddenly. I have been thinking about it for a while.'

'You want to see Chacha and all those people?'

'I want to go to Harmandir Sahib once more before I die.'

Sartaj stopped, his hand on the wall. 'Ma, don't talk like that. You'll go many times.'

'You just take me once.'

A heaviness had settled in Sartaj's chest, squeezing away his voice. He came around Ma, picked up his empty suitcase and touched her awkwardly on the shoulder. 'I'll see when I can get leave.' He coughed. 'Then we can go.'

While Sartaj packed, Ma brought in a pile of freshly ironed clothes. She sat on the bed and watched him. She had never done this, in all the hundreds of times he had prepared to leave home, and he felt her gaze slowing him. He had always been a neat packer, but now he tucked his socks into the rectangular slot between his shirts and pants with fanatical care. Ma told stories about Amritsar relatives, and by the time Sartaj had the suitcase closed, he knew he was late starting out for the station. Still, he lingered by the front door, and repeated his peri paunas, and tried not to think of the last time he had said goodbye to Papa-ji, at this same door.

Sartaj made it on to the train, but barely, and he was unable to sleep through to Dadar station as he usually did. Through dirtied glass, he watched the familiar darkening ridges slide by, outlined against the shape of his own face. He had made this journey many times, and loved it well, the long tunnel from Monkey Hill to Nagnath which had so excited him as a child, the steep inclines and the sudden turns that swept back hillsides like stage curtains to reveal the astonishment of plummeting green valleys, and you felt an exhalation and wonder in your chest, and were glad you were going somewhere. He got it still, that little puff of excitement, but now it had inside itself a little twinge of loss and nostalgia. Maybe this was why people had kids, so that when you could no longer travel with your parents, your children made all train trips new again. Then you could watch the lights of Mumbai appear, and be fully happy that you were home.

'Yes, bring in Bunty,' Parulkar said. 'By all means, bring him in, indeed.'

'I should do it, sir? Not one of your people?' Sartaj meant one of Parulkar's picked men who dealt with gangs.

'No, Bunty probably trusts you best. If I send one of my inspectors, he'll get frightened.'

'Right, sir.' They were sitting in Parulkar's car at Haji Ali. Parulkar was on his way to headquarters and had asked Sartaj to meet him on the way. Sartaj thought he was joyless, that he looked worn down. 'You have another meeting, sir?'

'Yes. I have nothing but meetings nowadays.'

'With DIG Saab?'

'Not only him. Everyone I can. The government is bent on pushing me out, Sartaj. So I have to see who can help me stay in. So I run from here to there.'

'Sir, you will take care of it. You always have.'

'I am not so sure. This time, even the money I am prepared to spend is making no difference. There is too much old history. They hate me personally, they think I am too pro-Muslim.'

'Because of Suleiman Isa?'

Parulkar shrugged. 'That, and other things. But mainly they suspect me of helping Suleiman Isa. They are fools. They don't seem to understand that to operate successfully against this gang, you have to exchange information with that one. They just know who they hate. They are politicians and gangsters themselves, but they see the world like this. Stupid.'

'That's why you will outsmart them, sir.'

'Don't be so sure, Sartaj,' Parulkar said, jabbing a hand towards the rising arc of buildings, 'nowadays, stupidity is what wins here.'

Behind him, the sea lay flat and quiet. His driver and bodyguards were standing close by, shading their eyes from the glare. 'The times have changed.'

There was no arguing with this simple truth, the times had indeed changed. 'If there's anything I can do, sir,' Sartaj said, 'please tell me.'

That was all the comfort Sartaj could offer to the old man. Sartaj watched Parulkar's three-car convoy edge away from the promenade, and thought that this was the first time he had ever thought of Parulkar as old. He had always seemed ageless because of his appetite for the job, his unflagging cheer and amusement at the absurdities of the policeman's life, his energy, and his steady and amazing progress. Maybe he had risen too far, maybe it was inevitable that at these high professional altitudes his sharp ambition would betray him, yes, it had twisted and cut him and emptied out his confidence and his joy. Perhaps it was better to stay at a respectable middling level, like Papa-ji had, to do one's job well and go home and sleep soundly.

But no, it was impossible to believe such a thing in these changed times, when a lack of passionate careerism was considered a fatal character flaw. Sartaj slung a leg over the motorcycle and kicked it into grinding life. He turned back along the causeway, coasted along and went past the entrance to Shiv Sagar Estates, where Harshad Mehta had once owned seven – or was it eight? – apartments. Sartaj had come there long ago, to support a huge CBI team which had searched Mehta's apartments for evidence of his multi-crore perfidy. Sartaj's contribution to the stockbroker's arrest had been crowd control, he had held back the rapidly growing crowd of onlookers and Mehta-supporters, and kept the building gate clear. That night and the next day, everyone he had met – policemen, friends, Megha – had asked eagerly, 'Did you see Harshad Mehta's house from inside? What was it like? It must have been great, no?' Sartaj didn't mind, at first, telling them that he hadn't seen anything except the outside of the building, but each enquirer had been so disappointed that finally Sartaj had felt obliged to make up a story about Harshad Mehta's extravagant living. There were indeed some fragments of fact in the mosaic he had built, little shiny nuggets harvested from constables who had been inside the building, but mostly Sartaj had thrown together pictures taken from television and films, he had talked about duplex drawing rooms with staircases that went coasting up to family quarters, doors that slid into walls, bedrooms as big as entire ordinary apartments, all floored with exquisite Italian marbles, and with an intercom tying it all together. 'Thirty thousand feet,' Sartaj had said. 'Can you imagine, he lives in thirty thousand feet?' And all those who could barely afford five hundred feet, or a thousand, had become a little wet-eyed and dreamed of a perfect life. Sartaj knew the admiration they were feeling, because he had felt it himself: Harshad Mehta was a thief, but he had dreamt big and lived large. He had been arrested, and then arrested again, and he had died of a heart attack, but in his own time, he had been a hero.

Sartaj gunned the engine, and liked the howl it made. Ambition had spread like an inescapable virus in those Harshad Mehta days, and there had been stock-market crashes and burst bubbles since, but the contagion had taken firm hold. Now these outsize aspirations were something like a universal condition. Maybe it was a form of health – after all, it gave you vim, zip, velocity. He had read an editorial in the papers not long ago, which had noted gratefully that the Indian cricket team had finally acquired some killer instinct. Yes, they had acquired cash and killer instinct. Very correct. Sartaj speeded up. It was time to go and hunt eve-teasers.

Wasim Zafar Ali Ahmad, of the lengthy name and the long political aspirations, had given Sartaj the names and address of the tapori brothers he wanted disciplined, and so Sartaj and Katekar went visiting. They had no hope of finding the two at home, but their intention was to cause terror and discomfort to the family, and thereby impel the brothers to give themselves up. So they went into the kholi with extravagant amounts of shoving and shouting. Sartaj kicked open the door and roared, 'Where are those two gaandus? Where are they?'

Katekar gathered up the family from the three cramped rooms. There was a tottering old man, a woman and a girl of eleven or twelve. The girl began to curse Sartaj in a steady monotone, and the woman clapped a hand over her mouth.

'What have they done?' said the trembling grandfather. 'What?'

Sartaj spoke to the woman. 'Are you the mother of Kushal and Sanjeev?'

'Yes.'

'Where are they?'

'I don't know.'

'You're their mother but you don't know where they are?'

'No, I don't know.'

She was a sturdy woman, short but big in the shoulders and bigger in the hips. She was wearing a bright red sari, the pallu of which she now wrapped tightly around her shoulders with one hand as she held her daughter with the other.

'What's your name?' Sartaj said.

'Kaushalya.'

'This is your father?'

'No, his.' Meaning her husband's.

'And where is he?'

'At his factory.'

'What factory?'

'They make mithai.'

'Is it near by?'

She jerked her chin towards her left shoulder. 'Next to the bus depot.'

Sartaj pointed at the girl, who had stopped muttering under her mother's hand. She was looking at him with an unblinking concentration. 'What's her name?' he said.

'Sushma.'

'Sushma, go and get your father.' Kaushalya removed her hand, but her daughter didn't move. Sartaj was used to being disliked by the public, but the little girl's hatred stung him. 'Go,' he growled.

'Listen to Saab,' Kaushalya said, and the girl ran out of the door.

Sartaj settled himself on the chair next to the door. He spread his knees wide and planted his feet firmly. Katekar turned to the small kitchen area on the left, and began to search, rattling pots and plates. He picked up a bottle from a shelf and sniffed at it loudly. Kaushalya and her father-in-law retreated to the other room. Sartaj could hear their urgent whispering.

Hunting apradhis should've meant car chases, sprints through crowded streets, motion and movement and pounding background music. That's what Sartaj wanted, but what hunting actually meant was intimidating a woman and an old man in their own home. This was a tried and tested policing technique, to disrupt family life and business until the informant sang, the criminal caved, the innocent confessed. Katekar spread himself over a couch covered with a bright blue sheet, and Sartaj called to Kaushalya and asked for chai and biscuits. She twittered angrily behind the wall, but went outside and asked a neighbour to walk down to the dhaba at the corner. She came back in, her head ducked down low, her jaw working, and stalked past them to her back-room refuge.

The walls were bare white, but on a single shelf there was a row of photographs, the record of Kaushalya's marriage and three children. Sushma laughed happily from a pink heart-shaped frame. Sartaj leaned his head on the wall and shut his eyes. But he was restless, too tense for a doze. He sat up, and Katekar was studying, intently, an old copy of *Filmi Kaliyan*. On the left corner of the cover, Bipasha Basu had her arms folded under the rolling expanses of her chest. Sartaj instantly resented her for the keen cut of desire that came up from his groin. He straightened up, rearranged discreetly and then had to lean forward to hide himself. The hell with you, Bipasha. The last time he had had sex was eight months ago, with a stringer for one of the Marathi afternoon papers. She had first come to him with tough questions about dance bars and bar girls, for a big lead story, and he had been impressed by her big shoulders, her loose green jeans, her cynicism and her rangy competence. They'd met three times, in three different restaurants, and she had each time carefully mentioned her husband, who was also a journalist, for another Marathi daily. But by the third afternoon, by the third cup of tea, she had run out of questions about bar-balas, and it was obvious that something else had to happen. They'd said goodbye awkwardly, and this time she'd not offered her hand for a hearty from-the-shoulder handshake. She called ten days later, and this time they'd walked on Chowpatty beach, brushing knuckles. He didn't think she was pretty, exactly, but he couldn't pause himself, cease short the impulse to rest his hand on the small of her back, under her loose, full-sleeved white shirt. They'd had weekly sex for four months, always in PSI Kamble's room in Andheri East, in the afternoons. Ghochi karo, boss, Kamble used to say. Had sex, made love, ghochi, whatever it was, it made Sartaj precariously alone, put an insoluble knot in his throat. To feel her skin against his was good, her crises tripped easily through her long body, and she was comfortably undemanding, relaxed and relaxing in her distrust of drama. And yet Sartaj felt no yearning for her, suffered none of the agonized need he had once endured for Megha, and this absence made unbearable those moments when he lay panting on Kamble's flowered sheets. He felt small and lost inside his own body, submerged far under the skin and drowning. Finally he had to stop, had to end it.

Now she was hurt, but she hid it under a journalist's shrug: *marad saala aisaich hota hai.*

Yes, men were like that. Before her, there had been other women. A call-girl, Kamble's gift on Sartaj's first post-divorce birthday: 'Fine high-class item, boss, total actress material.' Sartaj had been unable to perform, and the actress-item had patted his shoulder comfortingly. And there was a married friend of Megha's, who had waited to call until his divorce decree was final, so that it was all above board and incontestably moral. After sex, she loved to hear stories about murder, about gunshots on dark streets, about desperate and violent men, she lay next to Sartaj, plump and golden, a shine like metal hooks in her eyes, eddying little gusts of Obsession. And there had been a firangi even, an Austrian woman who had been pickpocketed on a local train and had come into the station to file a complaint. He had liked her blunt accent, all clangs and sudden stops, and the unreadable blue of her eyes, but she was so beyond his ken that he had no idea what to do, even when she stopped in two days later. He confessed to her that they had made no progress, that progress was unlikely, and then felt ashamed of Indian inefficiency. In Austria the thief would already have been convicted and sentenced. In that pause she asked if he would like to have some coffee. After three days of coffee he asked if she would like to see his house. At the apartment, she made him take off his turban. 'I want to see your hair open,' she said. 'You Amitabh Bachchan,' PSI Kamble had chortled when he had heard about this, squeezing Sartaj's hand, 'you bloody Rajesh Khanna, you're the King of all Sardar Studs.' Sartaj had recognized much of his own heady triumph in Kamble's exuberant thrill, that glad rush he had himself felt from the pornographic paleness of the Austrian's breasts, from the discovery of the light blonde hair under the white of her panties. As he had moved inside her, he was inside a thousand blue movies, and inside him were the impossibly unblemished glossy-paper phantoms of his adolescence, beckoning and very far. After they had finished she was quiet, and he had no idea what her silence meant. And the King of all Studs lay with his mouth open, terrified by the white vacuum of disappointment he was discovering inside his bones.

Sartaj shook his head and got up. Kaushalya's husband liked to be photographed. He sat squarely in the middle of every photograph, surrounded by women and children. Sartaj stood near the wall, his back to Katekar, and investigated the pictures. Here was the father of the two harassers. Did he have mistresses in addition to the wife? Looking at the belligerent thrust of his belly against his shiny white kurta, in the largest of the photographs, Sartaj was sure he did. He was a man, and so he had women. Sartaj had a long reputation as a policeman for the ladies, and he had told nobody that he had given up on sex. Kamble and Katekar and the others at the station crowed about ghochi, there were long stories that rose and fell and rollicked on about chut and khadda and tope and daana and hathiyar and mausambis, yes, she had mausambis so round and sweet you wept to look at them. Mausambis, grenades, dudh-ki-tanki, coconuts. And yes, maal, chabbis, chaavvi. Maybe I'm the only one, Sartaj thought, with stories about silent sex, far sex, aching sex, dull sex, doomy sex, stopped sex, needless sex, painful gloom-ridden bitter lonely sex. Sex. What a word. What a thing.

The chai and the father arrived together. Kaushalya's husband came in hard on the heels of the barefoot little boy who swung in with the cups of chai, which he carried in a special wire basket. The boy cocked an eyebrow at Sartaj, and getting the nod, he handed over the chai, very wristy and professional. 'Biskoot?' he said, and held up a pack of Parle Glucose. Sartaj paid, and fumbled in giving him a five-rupee coin. The boy picked it up from the floor with his toes, with his right foot, and then moved the coin to his left hand with a smooth dance move that lifted his shin parallel to the floor. For that Sartaj gave him a five-rupee tip, and the boy grinned and was gone.

Kaushalya had emerged, followed by the old man. Sartaj moved between her and her husband, took a sip of chai and said, 'What's your name?'

'Birendra Prasad.'

'You make mithai?'

'Yes, saab. Cham-cham, burfi and pedas. We supply to restaurants and shops.'

'You own the factory?'

'Yes, saab.'

'And your sons work with you?'

'Sometimes, saab. They are studying still.'

'That is good.'

'Yes, saab. I want them to move ahead. In today's world, you can't get anywhere without education.'

Birendra Prasad had seen the world, no doubt of it. Today he wasn't wearing a silvery kurta, he had on a green shirt and black pants, and his stockiness made him a good match for his wife. He was sturdy and determined and didn't like having policemen in his home, but he was making an effort to be calm and polite. His daughter was holding on to the back of his shirt and glowering at Sartaj. There were a lot of people now in a small room, and Sartaj could see the sweat pooling down Birendra Prasad's neck. Sartaj grinned, showing his teeth, and took a sip of chai.

'Saab,' Birendra Prasad said.

Katekar was moving around Prasad, to his left and behind him. Sartaj saw that it made the mithai-man very uneasy, his eyes twitched left and back and left again. 'Have you been in jail, Birendra Prasad?' he said.

'Yes, a long time ago.'

'What was the charge?'

'Nothing, saab. It was a misunderstanding . . .'

'You went to jail for nothing?'

Katekar moved in close. 'Saab asked you something,' he said, very softly.

The girl was crying now.

'It was for one year,' her father said. 'For theft.'

Sartaj put his glass down on the chair, and stepped close to Birendra Prasad. 'Your sons are going to jail also.'

'No, saab. For what?'

'You know what they are doing around here? You know how they behave with women?'

'Saab, that is not true.'

Katekar shoved the man gently, just a hand on a shoulder and a short push. 'Are you saying Saab is not telling the truth?'

'People spread all these rumours, and they are just boys. But . . .'

'You send your boys to see me tomorrow at the station,' Sartaj said. 'At four o'clock. Or I'll come and visit your family here again, and you at your factory. And I'll put your sons in jail.'

'Saab, I know who is doing this.'

Sartaj leaned in close and whispered in his ear, 'Don't argue with me, gaandu. You want me to take your izzat in front of your family? In front of your daughter?'

To this Birendra Prasad had no reply.

216

Katekar nudged at his shoulder, and he moved aside. Sartaj stepped around Sushma and over the sill. He and Katekar walked through the sunny lane, scattering a group of boys coming in the opposite direction.

'That Wasim Zafar is a deep one, saab,' Katekar said. 'The move is against the father as much as against the boys.'

'Yes,' Sartaj said. 'This Birendra Prasad must be a problem for him. He should have told us, the bastard.' Because it was quite possible that Birendra Prasad had his own connections. But Sartaj wasn't overly worried. Every man or woman you arrested or even touched was part of some web, and you couldn't spend your professional life worrying about who knew whom. You were a little careful, and if some problem came up, you dealt with it. Still, Wasim Zafar Ali Ahmad should have told them. 'Here,' he said, and gave Katekar the biscuits. He dialled on his mobile phone, and Wasim Zafar picked up on the second ring.

'Hello, who is it?' he said, very fast.

'Your baap,' Sartaj said.

'Saab? What is wrong?'

'Where are you?'

'I am near the station, saab. I came here for some work. What can I do for you?'

'You can tell us the truth. Why didn't you tell us you were moving against this Birendra Prasad?'

'The father? Saab, really, he's not such a problem. But he spoils his sons, and starts puffing up if anyone says anything to them. They are the ones who instigate him. He is a simple man, a dehati really, they are the haramzadas who think they are too smart. Once the boys are squeezed a little and become quiet, he will also sit down.'

'You have everything calculated out, don't you?'

'Saab, I was not trying to hide anything.'

'But you didn't give us all the information.'

'My mistake, saab. Saab, where are you?'

'In your raj.'

'Saab, where in Navnagar? I'll be there in five minutes.'

'Make it ten minutes. I'll see you in Bengali Bura, at Shamsul Shah's house.'

'Yes, saab. At their new kholi?'

'Yes, at the new kholi.'

'Okay, saab. I'm putting down, saab.'

Katekar was eating a biscuit. 'He's running to meet us?'

'Yes. He's very dedicated to justice.'

Katekar snorted. Sartaj took a biscuit, and they walked through the basti, towards Bengali Bura. Wasim Zafar Ali Ahmad was eager to be seen with the police. It would give him a chance to demonstrate his affinity with power, his ability to get things done. He would probably let it be known that he had summoned them himself, asked them not to forget the investigation into the murder of Shamsul Shah, urged them to keep working hard. In his telling, he would be the concerned community leader who was getting action from the police. Sartaj didn't begrudge him his spin. The man was revealing himself to be an adept politician, in spite of his error in not telling all about Birendra Prasad, the inconvenient father.

Sartaj paused at an intersection. The narrow lane directly ahead led to Bengali Bura, and the wider one to the right towards the main road. He brushed the crumbs from his fingertips, and said to Katekar, 'Let's go and see Deva first.'

Sartaj had an old contact in Navnagar, a Tamil named Deva. Sartaj had met him nine years ago, when he had arrested a gang of four tyre-thieves in Antop Hill. Deva had lived with the thieves, in the little closed porch at the entrance to their kholi. He had protested his innocence, said that he was just a tenant, he had nothing to do with the burglaries, he was just in from his village and new to the city, he had thought that having tyres stacked in the house was normal urban practice. Sartaj had liked Deva's cheerfulness, his humming of weird-sounding Tamil songs, his resolute nineteen-year-old attempt to muster up courage, despite the twitching in his skinny, pole-like legs. So Sartaj had decided to believe him, and looked after him, he had not put his name in the FIR and had spoken to a couple of people about a job for him, and now Deva was very respectable, settled, married, he had a son and another one on the way, and he had grown a small moustache and a paunch. He ran an ironworks in Navnagar, where a sweaty cadre of Tamils made enormous iron wheels for use in hand-loom mills, and fences and fittings, and all kinds of special-order items.

So Sartaj took the right-hand turn, and called Wasim Zafar Ali Ahmad as they walked, to tell him they would be delayed. The road had been recently tarred and maintained, and there was a constant traffic of cycles and scooters. The houses in this part of Navnagar were old and well-established, all of them had good water connections and electricity. Many of them were two and three stories tall, with shops and workshops on the ground floor fronting the street. A face floated above the staggered roofs, huge, luminous brown eyes that went and came from behind the parapets, larger than any of the windows, and there was a gleaming brow touched by blue light, half-open lips and swirling hair, all of it somehow completely weightless and paradisiacal. Sartaj knew that she was only a cunningly lit model on a vast billboard across the main road, but it was distracting to be watched so intently by her. He turned his eyes down and went on.

Deva called for refreshments as soon as he saw them, and wouldn't accept a refusal. A boy came around the corner with two Limcas, which Sartaj and Katekar drank standing near the door of the workshop, just outside it. There were no lights inside the workshop, just two livid streams of sunlight pouring through the roof, heating the glow of the molten iron as it slushed into the moulds and the faces of the nearly naked men who worked the bellows with their feet, stepping up high and then down in a slow and endless climb.

'Haven't remembered me for a long time, saab,' said Deva.

'The Tamils have been behaving themselves, Deva.'

Deva roared. He leaned in through the doorway and shouted a translation to his workers. There was a quick winking of gleaming smiles among the sparks. It was possible to live in Navnagar and never speak anything but Tamil. A shouted answer came back over the blaring rush and banging of work. 'He says,' Deva said, 'that we're so well-behaved now that even the Rakshaks love us.'

There had been a time when the Rakshaks had demonstrated son-of-the-soil Mumbai patriotism by hounding Tamil immigrants. Sartaj put his empty Limca bottle down, next to the door. 'Sure. They're chasing other people now.' Muscular chauvinism still won votes, but you had to be canny in your selection of enemies. So now the Rakshaks protested about the Bangladeshi menace, and told 'unpatriotic' Indian Muslims to leave the country. Same game, different targets. Sartaj motioned Deva away from the door and its exhalations of heat, and they walked down the lane a little, stepping over a gutter. Katekar followed close behind.

'You're investigating that murder,' Deva said. 'The boy who was killed by his friends.'

'Yes. Know anything about it?'

'No. I didn't know any of them.'

'Ever heard of a social worker named Wasim Zafar Ali Ahmad?'

'Yes, yes. That bastard. He's a sharp one.'

'How sharp? What are his dhandas?'

'His father is a local butcher. The son does mostly social work, I think. But he has a lot of cousins, these cousins have garages. Two around here, one somewhere in Bhandup. They are a well-settled family.'

'And these garages, are they crooked or straight?'

'Medium, saab. I hear they do business in second-hand parts.' Deva had an extraordinary smile, he thrust his jaw forward and his eyes narrowed and a bank of sparkling teeth split his face in half. Second-hand parts could come from anywhere, from legitimate sources or some poor fool's car. 'One or two of these cousins have been in trouble. Never arrested, saab, but little things here and there.'

'You know the names of these cousins?'

'No. But let's see.' Deva led Sartaj and Katekar around the corner, to a bakery, a large tin-roofed hall with towering ovens at one end and ranks of men kneading dough. At the very far end, there was a small cubicle, almost filled by a portly owner. He gathered up his lungi and his bulging stomach and walked amongst his workers while Deva used his phone. Sartaj listened to the nasal southern rhythms, which reminded him as always of Mehmood and childhood laughter, and tried not to breathe too deeply. The smell of the fresh loaves of bread was good but overpowering, too rich, too dense in the stifling heat. Deva made two phone calls, and Sartaj knew he was tugging at his Tamil connections across Navnagar, strumming them and listening to what came back. The Tamils had once been the feared newcomers into the city, the ones denounced and hated by the Rakshaks as the threatening outsiders who supposedly stole jobs and land. Now they were old Mumbaikars.

Deva sat back and settled into his chair. He held up his fingers in a little cone, and said, 'Ready, saab? Write down.'

He gave Sartaj five names, and their exact genealogies, how they were related to Wasim Zafar Ali Ahmad, and estimations of his involvement in their work, both legitimate and otherwise. It was solid intelligence.

'Good work, Deva,' Sartaj said. Katekar nodded benevolently. Sartaj put two five-hundred-rupee notes on the desk next to Deva.

They were old friends, but it was better in the long run that they conduct their business professionally. You could only do favours for each other for so long before resentment set in on both sides. Cash for information assured a future flow.

Sartaj and Katekar left Deva and walked over towards the Bengali Bura. Sartaj looked over his shoulder as they came up the slope, and the endless mud-brown and white roofs of Navnagar made a vast serried crescent, horizon to horizon, under the falling sun. The tableau impressed Sartaj as always with its gory reddish gigantism and melo-drama, with the pressing energy of its very being, it was incomprehensible that such a thing should exist, this Navnagar. And yet here it was, astride Sartaj and towering, crimson-mouthed and real. He turned away. He noticed now that Katekar was carrying a large paper bag full of fresh pavs, to eat with his family over the next few days. Much of what Katekar and everyone else ate came from or through Navnagar, and other nagars like it. Navnagar made clothes and plastic and paper and shoes, it was the engine that pumped the city into life.

Wasim Zafar Ali Ahmad was waiting near Shamsul Shah's kholi, surrounded by a thick cluster of supplicants. His mobile phone glinted in his hand as he waved to Sartaj and Katekar. A woman tugged at his elbow, and he spoke to her in rapid Bengali, and extracted himself with many gestures of assurance.

'Saab,' he said. 'Sorry, these people, once they get hold of me, they don't let me go.'

'You speak Bengali?'

'A little, a little. Their Bengali has quite a lot of Urdu in it, you know.'

'And what other languages do you speak?'

'Gujarati, saab. Marathi, some Sindhi. You grow up in this Mumbai, you pick up a little of everything. I am trying to improve my English.' He held up a copy of *Filmfare*. 'I try to read one English magazine every day.'

'Very impressive, Ahmad Saab.'

'Arre, sir, I am younger than you. Please call me Wasim. Please.'

'All right, Wasim. Have you talked to Shamsul Shah's family already?'

'No, no, sir. I thought you would want to do that yourself. But one of these people said the father is not at home, he is working. The mother is here.'

'Inside?'

'Yes.'

'Keep these people away while I talk to her.'

The dead boy had purchased a better home for his family, you could tell that just from the substantial frontage of the property on the lane. Sartaj knocked. Standing at the door, he could see four rooms, a separate kitchen and cupboards finished with Formica. The dead boy's mother sent his sisters into the back rooms, and stood very straight and waited.

'You are Moina Khatun?' Sartaj said. 'Shamsul Shah's mother?'

'Yes.'

Moina Khatun's daughters were kept in strict purdah, but her own regime had been relaxed a little by old age, at least while she stood in the doorway of her own house. Sartaj thought she looked to be about sixty, although her real age could have been at least a decade less. She wore a blue salwar-kameez and a white dupatta over her head.

'This is a good kholi that your son got for you.' Sartaj couldn't tell if Moina Khatun's inscrutability was a tactic or a trait. He couldn't read her at all. 'He was a good boy. How did he get mixed up with those other two?'

She tipped her head to one side. She didn't know.

'Did you know this Bihari friend of theirs, this Reyaz Bhai?'

Moina Khatun slowly moved her head again.

There was a hush in the lane, and under that silence a vast chasm of loss. Sartaj felt like he had stumbled over an edge, and he didn't quite know what to do next, where to press, or whether pressing was a good idea. Into this quiet, Katekar spoke.

'It is against nature, that a son should die before his parents. It is impossible to accept. But He' – and here Katekar pointed upwards – 'gives and takes for his own reasons, he writes our destinies.'

Moina Khatun began to weep. She dabbed at her eyes, and her shoulders rounded. 'We must accept,' she said hoarsely. 'We must accept.'

Katekar had his hands clasped in front of him, and he tilted forward slightly from the waist, completely solicitous and not in the least bit threatening. 'Yes. How old was Shamsul?'

'Only eighteen. Next month he would have been nineteen.'

'He was a fine-looking boy. Did he want to get married soon?'

'There were already proposals for him.' Moina Khatun was animated now, brightened under her tears by the memory of past arguments. 'But he said he wanted to get all his sisters married first. I told him, the youngest is nine, you will be an old man by the time she has her mala badol. But Shammu, he said, getting married too young is a stupid thing we do. Let me get settled first, have a nice house. What is the use of getting married and lying at your parents' house, having fights between the wife and the mother-in-law? He wouldn't listen to us. First them, then me, he always said.'

'He was a good boy. He set up a good kholi for you.'

'Yes. He worked very hard.'

'Did you know what work your son was doing?'

'He worked for that company, taking parcels.'

'Yes. But he was doing some work with Bazil and Faraj also, no?'

'I don't know anything about that.'

Sartaj could see that Moina Khatun wasn't trying to hide anything, she really didn't know anything about her son's dealings with the murderers. This made sense, there was no reason for the boy to talk to his mother about his criminal activities. But Katekar didn't want to give up yet.

'They were good friends, the three of them. They grew up together, in this basti?'

'Yes.'

'Why did they fight?'

'That Faraj was always jealous of my son. He didn't have a job, he did no work. Even when they were young he was always fighting with Shammu.' Her face flushed dark, and she shook her fist, and spoke Bengali. The angry stabbing gestures she was making slipped the dupatta from her head, her voice cracked and rose, and now she was shouting. Her grief cut across Sartaj's throat, and he stepped back and looked for Wasim.

'She is cursing Faraj and his family, saab,' Wasim said. 'She is saying they are devils. Just everything like that.'

Moina Khatun's face had dissolved from its angular rigidity into something that Sartaj found difficult to look at directly. He cleared his throat. 'Nothing useful?'

'Nothing,' Wasim said.

'All right. Let's go.'

He walked away. Katekar raised a hand at the woman, and followed. They were almost around a corner when she called after them
in Hindi. 'Don't let them escape,' she said. 'Get them. Don't leave
them.'

Sartaj looked back at her, and went on. The lane widened as they
came near the main road, and he could feel Katekar behind him.
Sartaj slowed, let Katekar catch up and gave him a nod. They came
down to the main road, towards the Gypsy.

'Wasim,' Sartaj said.

'Yes, saab.' Wasim scudded up beside them, unruffled and slick and
brimming with sincerity.

'Okay, listen to me, bastard,' Sartaj said. 'About this Birendra
Prasad . . .'

'Saab, truly, he will be no problem. Like I told you, the two sons
make him the problem.'

On their left there was a wall covered with painted advertisements
for cement and face powder. Sartaj stepped up to it and unzipped his
pants. 'Listen, you said I was older than you. So let me give you a bit
of advice. Don't think you are smarter than the people you want to
work with. Don't hide things that they need to know.' Sartaj's stream
spattered loudly against the bottom of the wall, and he only now realized how pent-up he had been. 'Don't surprise me. I don't like
surprises. I like information. If you know anything, tell me. Tell me
even if you don't think it's important. More information is better than
less information. Understood?'

'Saab, really, I wasn't trying to fool you.'

'If you think I am a fool, then maybe I am the kind of fool who will
have to look into certain businesses in this area, investigate certain
people. Let me see, what were their names, your cousins? Salim
Ahmad, Shakil Ahmad, Naseer Ali, Amir . . .'

'Saab, I understand. It will not happen again.'

'Good. Then maybe we can have a long relationship.'

'Saab, this is exactly what I want. A lasting association.'

Sartaj squeezed and shook, jogged his hips back, tucked and
zipped. 'You can play the politician elsewhere. Not with us.'

'Of course, saab.'

Sartaj reached into his pocket for his handkerchief, and turned, and
Wasim was holding up his copy of *Filmfare*.

'Please take, saab.'

224

'What?'

'There is good information inside this magazine, saab.'

Wasim's smile was very sly and small. Sartaj took the *Filmfare* and thumbed it open, and the pages fell apart naturally to a black-and-white picture of Dev Anand, partly hidden by a thin, paper-clipped stack of thousand-rupee notes, neatly staggered from right to left.

'It's just a small nazrana, saab. With hope for our future friendship.'

'We'll see about that,' Sartaj said. He rolled up the magazine and tucked it under his arm. 'I've told Birendra Prasad to bring his sons to the station tomorrow. In case he doesn't, keep track of the boys tomorrow, so we can get them if we need to.'

'No problem, saab. And saab, if you could also mention my name to Majid Khan Saab, and give him my salaam . . .'

'I will,' Sartaj said. 'But for four thousand rupees, don't expect to become the honoured guest of the station. This is only chillar.'

'No, no, saab. As I said, this is only a nazrana.'

They left Wasim there, and Sartaj was satisfied now that the man truly understood the nature of their mutual dependence. In the Gypsy, he unrolled the *Filmfare* and peeled off one note and handed it to Katekar, who tucked it into his breast pocket. Sartaj would also give some to Majid. He was under no obligation to pass any money upward, small amounts like this – under a lakh – were the field officer's prerequisite, and the senior inspectors and DCPs only shared if there was a respectable cake to cut. Still, he would give Majid the greetings from Wasim Zafar Ali Ahmad and offer a thousand, which Majid would laugh off. They had known each other for a long time, and a thousand – or even four thousand – was really only pocket change.

'Saab,' Katekar said. 'About this evening?'

'I hadn't forgotten.' Katekar had asked for an evening off, to take his family for an outing. 'Drive to Juhu now, I'll drop you and go.'

'Sir, there's no need . . .'

'It's all right. Drive.'

Sartaj felt a warm uprush of affection for stolid, dependable Katekar. Megha used to say that Katekar and he were like an old married couple, and maybe they were, but Katekar was still capable of springing surprises. Sartaj said, 'I thought you didn't like these Bangladeshis.'

'I like Bangladeshis in Bangladesh.'

'But that woman? Moina Khatun?'

'She lost a son. It is very hard to lose a child. Even if he was a thief. What was that dialogue from *Sholay*? Hangal's line? "The heaviest burden a man can carry on his shoulders is the arthi of his son."'

'Very true.' And true to filmi logic, this particular Bengali son had committed robbery to marry off his poor sisters. They went over a fly-over, over a clattering train with its late-afternoon crowds already swelling from the doorways. The dead boy had wanted more than marriage for his sisters, he had wanted a television set and a gas range and a pressure cooker and a larger house. No doubt he had dreamed of a brand-new car, one exactly like the brilliant silver Toyota Camry that was overtaking them now. What he had dreamed was not impossible, there were men like Ganesh Gaitonde and Suleiman Isa, who had begun with petty thefts and had gone on to own fleets of Opel Vectras and Honda Accords. And there were boys and girls who had come from dusty villages and now looked down at you from the hoardings, beautiful and unreal. It could happen. It did happen, and that's why people kept trying. It did happen. That was the dream, the big dream of Bombay. 'What was that song?' Sartaj said. 'You know, the one that Shah Rukh sings, I can't remember the film. *Bas khwab itna sa hai . . .*' Katekar nodded, and Sartaj knew that Katekar understood why he was asking, they had spent so much time together, on these drives across the city, that they followed each other's leaps and conceits.

'Yes, yes,' Katekar said. He hummed the tune, marking time with a forefinger across the steering wheel. '*Bas itna sa khwab hai . . . shaan se rahoon sada . . .* Mmmmm, mmmmm, then?'

'Yes, yes. *Bas itna sa khwab hai . . . Haseenayein bhi dil hon khotin, dil ka ye kamal khile . . .*'

And they sang together: '*Sone ka mahal mile, barasne lagein heere moti . . . Bas itna sa khwab hai.*'

Sartaj stretched, and said, 'This Shamsul Shah, yes, he had a big khwab.'

Katekar snorted and said, 'Correct, saab, but the big khwab took his gaand finally.'

They both burst out laughing. In the auto-rickshaw to Sartaj's right, two women turned their startled faces away and leaned back under the cover of the canopy. This made Sartaj laugh even louder. He knew it was frightening to other people, this furious, rasping mirth coming from policemen in a Gypsy, but that made it all even funnier. Megha used to say, 'You tell these horrible police stories and then you cackle like some bhoot, it's very scary.' He had tried, for her sake, to stop, but had never been completely able to. It felt good now, anyway, to be rolling across the city with Katekar, laughing wildly, and there was no need to restrain himself, and so he laughed some more.

They were quiet when they pulled up into the curve of Juhu Chowpatty, through the compacted clog of rush-hour traffic. Sartaj walked around the front of the Gypsy, feeling a faint brush of air from the ocean. The chaat stands were neon-lit already, and the customers were streaming in from the road. 'Tell the boys I said Salaam,' Sartaj said.

Katekar grinned. 'Yes, saab.' He put his hand on his chest for a moment, and then walked towards the beach.

Sartaj watched him go, the confident rolling walk, the heavy-shoul-dered sway, the clipped hair. An experienced eye would pick him out for a policeman in a moment, but he had a talent for shadowing, and they had made some good arrests together. As he rode through Ville Parle, Sartaj hummed *Man ja ay khuda, itni si hai dua*, but he could-n't remember the end of the song. He knew the tune would spin in his head all day, and the last antra would come to him very late, some-where between night and sleep. *Man ja ay khuda*, he sang.

Katekar found the boys and Shalini waiting, as appointed, near the stall called Great International Chaat House. He rubbed Mohit's head, poked him gently in the stomach. Mohit gurgled out a titter that made Rohit and Shalini smile.

'They're late again?' Katekar said.

Shalini twisted her mouth to the side. Katekar knew that look: what could not be changed had to be endured. And Bharti and her husband were always late.

'Let's go and sit,' Rohit said. 'They know where we sit.'

Katekar looked up and down the row of stalls, and across the road. There were two buses staggered behind each other, and it was hard to see. 'Rohit, go and see, maybe they're trying to cross.'

Rohit didn't like it, but he went, flapping his chappals angrily on the concrete. He had been stretched thin by his recent growth, but Katekar was certain that he would fill out once he hit his twenties, once he was married and settled. All the men in the family had attained an impressive thickness, shoulders and arms capable of intimidation, a respectable stomach. Rohit turned back, shaking his head.

'Papa, I want sev-puri,' Mohit said, tugging at Katekar's shirt.

'Let's go and sit,' Shalini said. 'They can find us.'

Rohit hadn't really gone far enough, but Katekar didn't need any more urging from Shalini. Bharti was her sister, and if Shalini thought they could go and sit, Katekar would sit.

They found two mats, as far right as possible, and arranged themselves. Katekar took off his shoes, sat cross-legged, sighed. The sun was still high enough to heat his knees, but there were the beginnings of a breeze against his chest. He opened his shirt, and mopped at the back of his neck with his handkerchief, and listened to Shalini and Rohit and Mohit place their orders with the boy who had shown them to their places. Katekar didn't want to eat yet. He was savouring the feeling of being at rest, of not having to shift from foot to foot like the waiter, who now sped off to his stall.

The boy hurried back, expertly balancing the food as he manoeuvred around and through the walkers. 'Eh, tambi,' Katekar said, 'get me narial-pani.'

'Yes, seth,' the boy said, and he was away.

'Narial-pani?' Shalini said, looking arch.

He had told her the previous month about an article he had read in an afternoon paper which asserted that coconuts were full of harmful fat. She had waved her hand at him and said that she didn't believe all these new-fangled things he read in papers, who had ever got ill from eating coconuts or drinking narial-pani? But she never forgot anything, and she wasn't going to let him get away with his backsliding from science. He tilted his head to one side, and smiled. 'Only today.'

She smiled back, and let him be. So Katekar sat and drank his narial-pani, and watched Mohit devote himself to his sev-puri, and Rohit watch the passing girls. A ship balanced on the gleaming horizon. Katekar watched it, and he knew it was moving but could not see it move.

'Dada!'

Katekar turned, and there was Vishnu Ghodke, waving frantically. He made his way over, followed by Bharti and the children. There was the usual flurry of greetings, and a lot of shifting about, and then the family was finally established on two mats. Shalini had Bharti close to her, and Vishnu was near Katekar. The children were hemmed in between Bharti and Vishnu. The two girls were typically beribboned and fancy-frocked, but the boy, who had been born last after much prayer and ritual, was dressed as if he were going to a wedding. He had on a little blue bow-tie, and a big red plastic wristwatch which he was winding and rewinding. Mohit and Rohit leaned over to push him about, and Katekar felt a surge of affection for the two, for wanting to mess up the prissy little brat's careful coif. He squeezed the cheeks of his two nieces as Shalini and Bharti launched instantly into an animated conversation about some ongoing family intrigue involving relatives of relatives. Katekar liked his older niece best, the girl who had quietly watched the boy become the centre of her parents' world with an increasing understanding and resignation.

'You've grown taller, Sudha,' he said. 'Already, so soon.'

'She eats like a horse,' said her father, with a guffaw and a hand on her head.

Katekar saw the angry squeeze of Sudha's jaw as she ducked away to whisper something in her sister's ear. Vishnu had a voice that didn't need any loudspeakers. Katekar said, 'She wants to grow up to be tall, like me. Sudha, you come here and sit next to me. I'm also very hungry. Arre, tambi.'

So Sudha sat next to Katekar, and they went over the menu together, and from that much-stained paper, chose a feast of bhelpuri, papri chaat and Sudha's favourite, pav-bhaji. They ate together, and now Katekar relished the break of sour into sweet on his tongue. Food was the greatest and most reliable of pleasures, and to sit on Chowpatty and eat it with wife and family, with the sea heaving gently, was as close to contentment as Katekar had ever been. So he sat and listened to Bharti go on. She was wearing a shiny green sari. A new one, Katekar thought. She had been a stocky little girl when he had first seen her, too shy to speak to him. A very few years later, Vishnu had given her a heavier mangalsutra than Katekar could remember from any wedding in the family, and she had never stopped talking since. She was wearing the mangalsutra now, along with a gold chain that went around her neck twice.

'That Bipin Bhonsle is such a haraamkhor,' she said. 'Before elections he told us that he would get a new extra water pipe to the colony. Now there is no new water pipe, but even the old one gets leaks every second week. Three children and no water, it is impossible.'

'Vote him out in the next election,' Katekar said.

'That is impossible, Dada,' Vishnu said. 'He has too many resources, too many connections. And the other parties have all gadhav candidates in that constituency. None of them can win. Putting a vote in for someone else is a waste of a vote.'

'Then find a good candidate.'

'Arre, Dada, who will stand against that Bhonsle? And where does one find good candidates nowadays? You need someone who is tough, who can give a jhakaas speech, who is attractive to the people. That type doesn't exist any more. You need one giant, all you get nowadays are crowds of small men.'

Shalini leaned to the side and brushed her hands off, then neatened her sari over her knees. 'You're looking everywhere but the right place,' she said.

Vishnu was very surprised. 'You know someone?'

Shalini pointed with both hands at Bharti. 'Here, here.'

'What?' Vishnu said.

Katekar pitched forward and back, shaken by laughter. It came more from the dismay on Vishnu's face, from his abject horror at his wife somehow becoming a giantess, than from Shalini's joke, but the children took it up and instantly they were all guffawing.

'See,' Shalini said, 'my sister Bharti is brave, she can impress anyone with her style, and nobody gives a speech like her. You should make her a mantri.'

Vishnu had understood by now that this was all humour, and he was grinning tightly, stretching his lip over his lower teeth. 'Yes, yes, Tai, she would make a good chief minister actually. She will keep everyone in control.'

Bharti had both hands in front of her mouth. 'Arre, devaa, I don't want any such thing. Tai, what are you saying? I have my hands full with these children, I don't want to sit on top of fifty thousand people.'

Katekar wanted to say something about her weight crushing fifty thousand, but then thought better of it and contented himself with a snort at the image of Vishnu's face compressed by her ample haunches. Vishnu looked uncertain, and then laughed along with him.

After Katekar finished eating, he and Vishnu walked along the water. Katekar had his pants rolled up, and he had left his shoes behind with Shalini. He liked to walk on the wet sand where it had been smoothed by the sea, feel it under his soles. Vishnu was walking a good five feet away, protecting his sandals. He hopped away now to save himself from an oncoming surge. 'Dada,' he said, 'one of these times you must let me pay. Otherwise we will feel embarrassed to come again.'

'Vishnu, don't start that whole argument again. I am elder, so I pay.' A bitter wash of irritation gushed up from Katekar's stomach. It was stupid, this pride of his that refused to eat meals paid for by Vishnu, but he could not stomach Vishnu's smugness, his satisfaction at his own success.

'Yes, yes, Dada,' Vishnu said, raising both hands. 'Sorry. You are doing well nowadays?'

'I am getting along,' Katekar said. Vishnu had of course noticed the thousand-rupee note that Katekar had used to pay the waiter. He never missed anything, the watchful Vishnu.

Vishnu stepped thoughtfully over a ragged branch from a palm tree. 'Dada, at this age, you should be doing much better.'

'At what age?'

'Your sons are growing up. They will need education, good clothes, everything.'

'And you think I can't give them all that?'

'Dada, you are getting angry again. I will stop talking.'

'No, say what you mean.'

'I'm saying only a little thing, Dada – this chutiya sardar inspector of yours will never make a decent income.'

'I have what I need, Vishnu.'

Vishnu lowered his head and became very meek. 'All right, Dada. But I don't understand why you stay with him. There are other postings you could have very easily.'

Katekar didn't answer. He turned and went back to the families. But later that night, lying in bed with Shalini next to him, he thought about Sartaj Singh. They had worked together for many long years. They were not friends exactly, they did not visit each other or go on vacations together. But they knew each other's families and they knew each other. Katekar could tell what Sartaj Singh was feeling from moment to moment, he could read his melancholy and his delight. He trusted the sardar's instincts. They had done some good detection, and when they had failed, Katekar always had the knowledge that they had tried hard. Yes, there wasn't as much money as could be made elsewhere, but there was job satisfaction. That was something that Vishnu would never understand. People like him wouldn't believe that a man could want to be a policeman for reasons other than money. The money was welcome, of course, but there was also the desire to serve the public. Yes, really, *Sadrakshanaaya Khalanighranaaya.* Katekar knew he could never confess this urge to anyone, much less Vishnu, because fancy talk of protecting the good and destroying evil and seva and service would elicit only laughter. Even among colleagues, this was never to be spoken about. But it was there, however buried it may be under grimy layers of cynicism. Katekar had seen it occasionally in Sartaj Singh, this senseless, embarrassing idealism. Of course neither of them would ever so much as hint at the other's romanticism, but perhaps this was why their partnership was so enduring. Only once, when they had rescued a trembling ten-year-old girl from a shed in Vikhroli, from her kidnappers, Sartaj Singh had scratched at his beard and muttered, 'Today we did good work.' That had been enough.

It was still enough. Katekar sighed, turned his head and stretched his neck, and went to sleep.

Sartaj saw the crowd first, a thick clutch of people pressed up to the front of a double-height glass window. The building was a new commercial complex, very beautiful with its expanses of grey stone and accents of polished steel. Sartaj had gone to the new office of his bank, to deposit some dividend cheques into his mother's account, and had come out dazzled by the sweep of the counters and the unprecedented cheer of the bank clerks. Now he peered over the collection of dark heads and saw a flash of deep red.

'Saab, come inside and see.' A blue-suited security guard was beckoning to Sartaj from the left.

'Ganga,' Sartaj said, and went through the door Ganga was guarding. Sartaj knew Ganga from the old bank building, where he had kept watch over a jewellery store with a long-barrelled shotgun and a baleful stare. 'Did your seth move here as well?'

'No, saab, I am working for a new company now,' Ganga said, pointing to his braided shoulder, where a blue-and-white patch announced his new allegiance: Eagle Security Systems.

'Better company?'

'Better pay, saab.' There were a lot of new security companies, and demand for ex-servicemen like Ganga was high. He shut the door behind Sartaj, and turned towards the window. 'Tibetan sadhus, saab,' he said, with proprietary pride.

There were five of them, five self-contained, serene men with very short haircuts and flowing scarlet robes. They were working around a large wooden platform, on which there was the colourful outline of a circle within a square within a circle.

'What are they doing?'

'They are making a mandala, saab. There were reports about it on yesterday's TV, you didn't see?'

Sartaj hadn't seen, but now he could see the apertures let into each side of the square, and the deep green that one of the sadhus was using to fill in the area just inside the innermost circle. Another sadhu was filling in the small figure of what looked like a goddess against the green background. 'What are they using, powder?'

'No, saab, sand, coloured sand.'

It was restful to watch the fall of the sand from the sadhus' hands, their sure and graceful movements. After a while, the general structure of the mandala emerged for Sartaj in dim white outline. Inside the final circle there were going to be several independent regions, ovals, each with its own scene of figures, human and animal and godly. Between these ovals, at the very centre of the entire wheel, there was a shape, Sartaj couldn't make out what it was. Outside these ovals there was the inner wall of the square, and outside the square there was another wheel, and more figures, and then a rim with its own patterns, all of it hypnotically complex and somehow pleasing. Sartaj was content to be lost in it.

'When they are finished, saab, they wipe it all up.'

'After all this work?' Sartaj said. 'Why?'

Ganga shrugged. 'I suppose it's like our women's rangoli. If it's made of sand, it won't last long anyway.'

Still, Sartaj thought, it was cruel to create this entire whirling world, and then destroy it abruptly. But the sadhus looked quite happy. One of them, an older man with greying hair, caught Sartaj's eye and smiled. Sartaj didn't quite know what to do, so he bowed his head, touched his hand to his chest and smiled back. He watched them work for a few more minutes, and then walked away.

'Come back tomorrow evening,' Ganga called. 'The mandala will be finished by then.'

Sartaj spent the day in the courts, waiting to give evidence in an old murder case. He had missed the last two dates, and the defence counsel had made a mighty noise, but today the judge himself was late, so the various parties to the case waited quietly. Sartaj read about the Tibetans in *Afternoon*, which described them as 'monks' and said they were making their mandala for the peace of the world. The judge finally arrived after lunch, and Sartaj gave evidence, and went back to the station. Birendra Prasad and his two sons were waiting under the portico.

'You wait here,' Sartaj said to Birendra Prasad. 'You two come with me.'

'Saab?' Birendra Prasad said.

'Quiet. Come on.'

The boys followed him inside. Sartaj took them through the front rooms, to his desk. He was tired, and he wanted a cup of chai very badly, but here were these two bastards. They were good-looking, strapping young men, both in bright T-shirts. 'Who is Kushal, who is Sanjeev?'

Kushal was the older one. He was chewing on his lip. He was only tense, though, not scared. He still had some confidence in his father and in himself.

'So you have eaten a lot of mithai in this life, Kushal?'

'No, saab.'

'That's why you have become such a hero with big muscles?'

'Saab . . .'

Sartaj slapped him across the face. 'Bastard, shut up and listen to me.' Kushal's eyes were wide. 'I know you have been bothering the girls in your area. I know you stand around the gallis and think you are the rajas of everything you see. But you aren't bhais, you aren't even taporis, you are little insects. What are you looking at, bhenchod? Come here.' Sanjeev cringed, and shuffled forward. Sartaj fisted him in the belly, not too hard, but Sanjeev doubled over and turned away. Sartaj thumped him on the back.

It was an old routine of violence and intimidation, and Sartaj performed it automatically. If Katekar had been there, they would have enacted the ritual with a practised co-ordination that approached a kind of beauty. But Sartaj was hot, and tired, and so he hurried up the sequence. He wanted to get it over with. The boys were amateurs, and required no great subtlety or skill. In ten minutes they were panting and stammering and terrified. Sanjeev had a stain down the front of his pants.

'If I hear about any trouble from you two again, I'll come and get you and give you some real dum. You understand? Maybe I'll bring in your father also. Maybe I'll string him up too.'

Kushal and Sanjeev shuddered, and had nothing to say.

'Get out of here,' Sartaj shouted. 'Go!'

They went, and Sartaj sat and leaned back and took out his handkerchief and found it already damp. It was disgusting, but he wiped his neck and shut his eyes.

His mobile phone rang.

'Sartaj Saab?'

'Who is this?' Sartaj said, although he knew the rough rumble of the voice. It was Parulkar Saab's old woman, the high-up contact in the S-Company he had spoken to a few days ago.

'It is your well-wisher, Iffat-bibi. Salaam.'

'Salaam, Bibi. Tell me.'

'I heard you are interested in a chutiya named Bunty?'

'I may be.'

'If you haven't decided yet, beta, it's too late. Bunty is dead, lurkaoed, finished.'

'Did your people arrange it?'

'My people had nothing to do with it.' She sounded completely convincing. 'The man was useless anyway, saala langda-lulla.'

'Where?'

'It will be on your police wireless in a few minutes. Goregaon. There is a building complex called Evergreen Valley, in the compound of that.'

'I know the place. All right, Iffat-bibi, I'm going.'

'Yes. And see, next time you want something, somebody, anybody, talk to me first.'

'Yes, yes, I'll come running to you.'

She guffawed at his sarcasm, said, 'I'm putting down now,' and hung up. Sartaj drove fast, accelerating through intersections and weaving across the lanes of traffic. There was already a police van in front of Evergreen Valley, and a crowd of plain-clothes officers in the car park to the rear. Sartaj saw several men he knew to be in the Flying Squad. As he walked up to the body, he saw their boss, Senior Inspector Samant, and then he was sure Bunty had been hit.

'Arre, Sartaj,' Samant said, 'what news?'

'Bas, sir, just work.' Sartaj pointed at the corpse, which lay face-down and twisted to the left. The wheelchair was on its side, three feet away.

'You know this maderchod?' Samant said, arching an eyebrow. 'What, Parulkar Saab has an interest in him?'

'Is it Bunty?'

'Yes.'

'I had an interest in him.' Sartaj squatted. Bunty had an interesting profile, very craggy and distinct, with a finely shaped nose. The back of his head was gone, and brain matter and blood spread in a fan-shape from him. His checked shirt was soggy too, in the back. 'One in the head, two in the back?'

'Yes. I think the back first, then the head. I didn't know you were working organized crime.'

'No, not generally. But I had contact with Bunty.' Sartaj stood up.

'After you got Ganesh Gaitonde I thought you might be on some special detail for Parulkar Saab.'

Samant was bald, pudgy and prosperous, and he was looking very hard at Sartaj. He was said to have killed at least a hundred men him-self in encounters, and Sartaj had no trouble believing it. 'No, nothing like that,' Sartaj said. 'This Bunty business was just part of another case.'

'Bunty's business is finished,' Samant guffawed. 'Maderchod tried his best to get away. That wheelchair must have moved faster than a car.' He pointed at black skid marks that went across the car park, almost to Bunty's body.

'You thokoed him?'

'No, no. That would have been good, I've been after the bastard for a long time. But his own boys finished him. That's our theory at this time. Nobody saw it happen, of course.'

'Why would his own boys do it?'

'Arre, yaar, Gaitonde is dead, so poor lame Bunty's reach is lame also. On his own, he was not so much. Maybe his boys switched to the other side, maybe the other side paid them.'

'Suleiman Isa?'

'Yes. Or someone else.'

So Bunty hadn't managed to come in safe, after all. Sartaj walked over to the wheelchair. It was indeed impressive, with thick wheels that looked as if they belonged on a racing car. The machining of the body was solid, all in some sort of very modern, sturdy and precisely engineered steel. An engine pack and battery sat under the seat, which was thickly cushioned in black. A joystick and some controls on the right-hand armrest must have allowed for steering, and for raising the chassis on its hydraulic suspension and going up and down stairs and whatever else this sleek chariot did. All those foreign tricks hadn't managed to get Bunty away from his murderous friends, and so maybe now Miss Anjali Mathur's investigation had run into a dead end. Sartaj stood up. It wasn't really his case anyway. 'The wheelchair looks undamaged,' he said.

'Yes. The wheels were still running when we got here. There's one button there that switches it off. We'll keep it. Soon one of these gaan-dus will get shot and become a langda-lulla' – here Samant made a lolling face and let his arms go limp – 'and we'll use it to take him to court.'

'Very smart,' Sartaj said, touching his forehead. 'What was Bunty doing here?' Evergreen Valley was three massive buildings in a rectangular compound edged by small two-storey houses. The only green Sartaj could see were a few patchy hedges scattered at odd angles between the buildings.

'We don't know yet. Maybe they were visiting. Maybe they had an apartment here.'

'Please let me know if you find out anything, sir.'

'Yes, yes.' Samant walked with Sartaj towards the gate. 'If you are interested now in all this company business, Sartaj, we can work together. It is very good, you know, professionally and otherwise. We can exchange information.' Samant handed Sartaj a card.

'Of course.' What Samant wanted was that the next time Sartaj got a tip about a big catch like Ganesh Gaitonde, he should call Samant, the encounter specialist. Apart from professional praise and stories in the newspapers, putting a bullet in a big company bhai could make you a lot of money. Other companies would pay for a job well done. Samant was said to have single-handedly built a grand and very modern hospital in his village in Ratnagiri. 'I will call you if I learn anything.'

'My personal mobile number is there. Call any time, day or night.'

Sartaj left Evergreen Valley and Samant and Bunty and the wheel-chair, and went back to the station. Sitting at his desk, he examined Samant's card. Samant was actually 'Dr Prakash V. Samant', according to the elaborate gold lettering. He was also a 'Certified Homeopath', in addition to his achievements in the force, which included the Police Medal for Meritorious Service. Sartaj sighed at how undistinguished his own career had been, and then called Anjali Mathur and told her about the unfortunate demise of his source.

'So all we know is that Gaitonde was looking for a sadhu?'

'Yes, madam.'

'That is interesting, but not enough.'

'Yes, madam.'

'These things happen. Keep following up with the sister. You will get background, at least.'

'Yes, madam.'

'Shabash,' she said, and hung up.

Sartaj was glad that she understood that such things happened. You could never depend on a source, and even when they were talking, the information was always incomplete. You could only piece together a supposition about what had happened. And if your source was a bhai constantly dodging his occupational hazards, it was inevitable that he would one day end up with a bullet in his head. There was nothing that you, or he, could do about it. A policeman would fire the bullet, or an enemy, or a friend. If he hadn't spilled the information you needed by the time his skull compressed under the impact of flying metal and exploded, that was your very bad kismet. Bas. Bunty finished and your case finished.

But Sartaj knew he was only trying to console himself with this things-happen line. The truth was that he had never got used to violent death. He didn't know Bunty at all, he had only spoken to him for a few minutes, but now that Bunty had been shot he would stay with Sartaj for a few days. For a few nights he would show up, wagging his aquiline nose at Sartaj and waking him at odd hours. Sartaj had struggled with this weakness throughout his life, and it had kept him from making the professional choices that men like Samant grabbed eagerly. Sartaj had killed only two men during his career, and he knew he couldn't kill a hundred, or even fifty. He just didn't have the forti-tude for it, or the courage. He knew this about himself.

Sartaj sat back in the chair, put his feet up on the table and dialled Iffat-bibi's number.

'So you have had Bunty's darshan,' she said.

Sartaj grinned. He was beginning to rather enjoy her abrupt pronouncements. 'Yes, I saw him. He didn't look too happy.'

'May he rot, and all his lineage too. He was a cowardly bastard all his life, and that's how he ended: running away.'

'So you know even that, Bibi? Are you sure your people didn't do it?'

'Arre, I said so, didn't I?'

'There is a theory that Bunty's own boys did it.'

'Did that fool Samant tell you that?'

'Samant is very successful, Bibi.'

'Samant is a dog who feeds on other people's leavings. You watch, he'll claim this as his own encounter. And the chutiya doesn't even know that Bunty's boys left him two days ago. He wasn't making enough income, so they went to other jobs.'

'You know everything, Bibi?'

'I've lived a long time. Don't worry, we'll know soon who took Bunty's wicket.'

'I would like to know.'

'Very good, beta – when you want to know, ask.'

Sartaj burst out laughing. 'All right, Bibi. I will remember that.'

Sartaj hung up, and thought about Bunty speeding around the city in his wheelchair, from hideout to hideout. He must have been very alone and terrified without his bodyguards, and sure enough, someone had found him and overtaken him. A small shudder of sympathy extended itself across the small of Sartaj's back, and he twisted angrily and stood up, bringing his feet down hard. Bunty had caused enough misery in his time, and the gaandu deserved whatever he got. Whoever had stamped him out deserved some money, or at least a medal. He hoped they had been well taken care of.

On his way home that evening, Sartaj took a detour to see how far the sadhus had come on their mandala. The crowds of the morning had thinned, but the sadhus were still working in the dusk, under a bright pool of lamplight. Sartaj stood by the window, and the older sadhu from the morning saw him, ducked his head and smiled at Sartaj's namaste. He was doing some fine work on one of the inset panels, colouring in the blond flank of a deer. The deer had impenetrable dark eyes, and sat against the deep greens of a forest glade. Sartaj gazed at the falling golden sand. The sphere was about half-done. It was inhabited now by a host of creatures, large and small, and a swirl of divine beings enveloped the entirety of this new world. Sartaj did not understand any of it, but it was beautiful to see it come into life, so he watched for a long time.

Ganesh Gaitonde Wins an Election

❧

Kanta Bai died on a Friday in February. Just four days earlier, on Tuesday morning, she had woken up with a fever. She prided herself on her resilience, and cultivated a fine contempt for doctors. She had told me that more people died from going to hospitals than from their diseases. So she drank glass after glass of mausambi juice, and went out to her tharra-still as usual. She met her employees and sent out her consignments. By late afternoon she was very tired, and came back home and slept. She woke at eleven at night, shivering, with pain in her arms and legs, and loose motions. But still she – the fool who believed that she would survive anything, bacterial or human – she didn't call a doctor. She ate a plate of rice with curd, took two Lopamide tablets and sent her people away. At eight that morning her sister found her, eyes rolled up, torso twisted in soiled sheets. I learnt of this at nine, after they had already taken her to a private hospital in Andheri. She had malaria, the doctors said. I had her moved to Jaslok, and told the doctors that they should give her any foreign medicine, any treatment she needed. But she was dead on Friday afternoon.

We took her to the electric crematorium in Marine Lines. When she was laid out on the track that led into the fire, her cheeks were fallen, and her body under the sheet looked flattened, as if the quick sickness had shrunk her. Her skin no longer had that dark, reddish bloom, it was pale mud. I forced myself to look as the metal doors closed her off from us for ever. And then I stayed until they gave her sister the ashes. I could do nothing but sit quietly next to this sister as we waited, and then give her a ride home.

I had done nothing to save Kanta Bai – this thought tormented me that day, and over the nights that followed. I told the boys to pay attention to their health, and to seek medical advice as soon as they felt an illness coming on. I gave free physical check-ups to all my controllers, and started an anti-malarial campaign in the basti. I had the gutters cleaned, and took measures to remove pools of stagnant water. But I was only putting on a show. I knew I had been defeated.

It was at this time that they came to me. I want you to know that, Sartaj Singh. I never went to politicians, they came to me. I had Gopalmath, I had all the area that had belonged to the Cobra Gang, I had my hand in many businesses, money came in, and apart from the matter of Kanta Bai I was happy. I had dealings with corporators often, especially when we were arranging regular water supply to Gopalmath, but I had no liking for the breed, they were born lying. I had no love for politicians, and so I never tried to cultivate MLAs and MPs. But Paritosh Shah brought one of them to me. He said, 'Bhai, this is Bipin Bhonsle. He's standing for assembly elections next month and needs your help.' Now this Bipin Bhonsle, he was smartly dressed, good blue pants, printed shirt, dark glasses, he didn't look at all like those khadi-kurta bastards with their Nehru-topis who you see on television all the time. Bipin Bhonsle was young, my age and respectful.

'Namaskar, Ganesh Bhai,' he said. 'I have heard a lot about you.'

'This fat man has been telling you?' I said, waving Bhonsle to a chair. I took Paritosh Shah by the hand and made him sit next to me on the divan. He had grown and grown in the several years I had known him, so that the Paritosh Shah I first knew was disappearing slowly inside this cushioned mass. 'Look at him wheeze. I worry about his heart.' He was breathing hard from his climb up the two flights of stairs.

Paritosh Shah patted my arm. 'I am taking Ayurvedic medicine, bhai. No need to worry.'

He had told me about his new Ayurvedic doctor, who had five computers in his air-conditioned clinic. 'Better that you run a few miles every day,' I said. He made a running motion with his arms, pumping them up and down, and he looked so funny, with his jiggling breasts and his belly swaying from side to side, that I burst out laughing, and then he did. But Bipin Bhonsle only smiled, and not too much. I liked that. He had good manners. Meanwhile a boy brought out tea and biscuits. We drank and talked. The job was simple enough, I thought. Bipin Bhonsle was the Rakshak candidate for the constituency of Morwada, which bordered Gopalmath to the north. The voting population in his area was less than half white-collar Marathas, people who had lived there long before the building boom, before the developers had started building the posh colonies in the suburbs. Bipin Bhonsle was sure of these Marathas, of the office workers and Class II government officers and clerks, as he was of the pockets of Gujarati and Marwari shopkeepers and traders scattered here and there. The problem was the other half, the Congress voters and the RPI diehards who lived in the Narayan Housing Colony and around Satyasagara Estates and in the bastis of Gandhinagar and Lalghar. The Rakshaks had never been able to win an election in Morwada, mainly because of these bastards, who were all sorts, seths and professionals and airline crew and retirees, but Bipin Bhonsle was most resentful of the poor chutiyas who lived in the shacks of Lalghar. 'Bhenchod landyas,' he said. 'Of course not one vote for us from there. You put out a hand of friendship to them, they turn away.' Lalghar was a Muslim basti, so of course there were no votes for the Rakshaks from there. To expect votes from people you made a policy of hating was stupid, and typical of the Rakshaks, but I smiled politely at Bipin Bhonsle.

'So, Bhonsle Saab,' I said. 'What can I do for you?'

He put his teacup down and sat forward on his chair, very eager. 'Bhai, first we need help with the campaigning. They intimidate our workers when they go out to canvass, only yesterday they pushed around some of our people and grabbed our posters from them. They took two hundred and fifty posters. Later we heard they made a bonfire out of them.'

'And you Rakshaks are so helpless? I've never heard of you people needing to hire anyone. You have your own boys and your own weapons.'

He heard my sneer, and didn't like it. But he was still soft and polite. 'Bhai, we aren't scared of anyone. But I am very junior in our organization, this is my first election, and anyway this constituency is not considered that important. All the resources will go elsewhere. And I know those Congress and RPI bastards have brought in a lot of muscle. Even those Samajwadi fellows, I hear, are planning to strengthen up.'

'All right. So?'

'Once the campaigning stops, on the voting day, those are the crucial hours. We want to make sure that certain people don't vote.'

I laughed. 'Okay. You want the election given to you.'

He wasn't embarrassed. He smiled, and said, 'Yes, bhai.'

'I thought you Rakshaks wanted to clean out corruption in the country.'

'When the whole world is dirty, bhai, you have to get dirty to do any cleaning. We can't fight their money without tricks. Once we are in power, it will all be different. We will change everything.'

'Don't forget me then. Don't forget and clean me out with the general cleaning.'

He held out both his hands towards me. 'You, bhai? No, no, you're our friend, one of us.'

He meant that I was a Hindu, and a Maharashtrian. I didn't care for any of those things, not where business was concerned, but he was reassured that I was Ganesh Gaitonde. I shook his hand, and said, 'We'll meet in a day or two. We'll talk then about how much money will be needed.'

'Bhai, money can be managed. Please take your time to think about it, and just tell us what your requirements are. I think we will need fifty, sixty boys.' He stood up and folded his hands. 'Let me know when to come.'

After he was gone, I said to Paritosh Shah, 'Level-headed chutiya.'

'He's a little mad, like all those Rakshaks.'

Paritosh Shah believed fiercely in profit, and gain was his god, so anyone who let religion interfere in money-making was quite obviously crazy to him. The Rakshaks believed in a golden past, and blood and soil, and all such things, which made no sense to Paritosh Shah. I said, 'Not so mad. He's hiring us as much because he doesn't want us to work for one of his opponents as he is hiring us for our help.'

'That is true. I didn't say he was stupid. These Marathas are mad but cunning. You know that.'

'Where are you from?' I said. 'From Bombay?'

'I was born here. My great-grandfather came here from Ahmedabad, we still have relatives there.' He was puzzled. We had known each other for many years but I had never asked these questions. But now since I had asked, he did also. 'And you?' he said. 'Where are you from?'

I waved my arm over my shoulder. 'Somewhere.' I stood up. 'How much do we charge them for an election?' And so we talked about money. It seemed to me that to give somebody an election was to make them a raja, or at least a minor nawab, and so our help was worth a lot. But it seemed that this business of giving and taking elections was an old-established one, and there were already set rates, not princely ones. Twenty-five thousand to each boy, maybe fifty for the controllers. So for only twenty-five, thirty lakhs to us, Bipin Bhonsle would become a member of the Assembly. 'You can buy democracy for that much?' I said to Paritosh Shah.

'Now you want to become a politician yourself.'

'Not even if they were giving away seats.'

'Why?' He was smiling indulgently.

I shrugged. I had a congestion in my throat, a swelling of memory and anger, and I didn't trust myself to speak. So I spat out of the window, dismissed the whole filthy business of it, the lying posters and the whorish speeches and the pretended humility, and he knew me well enough not to ask more. Anyway, he was happy to talk about business.

After he left I turned to my English books. I was teaching myself, with children's books and the newspapers and a dictionary. Only Chotta Badriya knew, because he had bought me the books and the dictionary. I closed my door when I studied English because I didn't want anyone seeing me squatting on the floor, one uncertain and slow finger on the letters, which I had to laboriously knock together with moving lips until they adhered into a word: 'p-a-r-l-i-a-m-e-n-t . . . parliament'. It was humiliating, but necessary. I knew that much of the real business of the country was done in English. People like me, my boys, we used English, there were certain words we used with fluency in our sentences, without hesitation. 'Bole to voh edkum danger aadmi hai!' and 'Yaar, abhi ek matter ko settle karna hai,' and 'Us side se wire de, chutiya'. But unless you could rattle off whole sentences without having to stop and struggle and go back and build them bit by bitter bit, unless you could make jokes, there were whole parts of your own life that were invisible to you yourself, gone from you. You could live in a Marathi world, or a Hindi colony, or a Tamil lane, but what were those hoardings speaking, those towering messages that threw their sharp-edged shadows over your home? When you bought an expensive new shampoo 'Made with American Know-how', what was that it said in red on the label? What were they laughing about, the people who skimmed by smoothly in their cushiony Pajeros? There were many like me, born far from English, who were content to live in ignorance. Most were too lazy, too afraid to ask how, why, what. But I had to know. So I took English, I wrestled with it and made it give itself to me, piece by piece. It was difficult, but I was persistent.

At four in the afternoon I closed my books and lay myself down on the floor and took a nap. I had a good bed, soft pillows, but of late I had been sleeping badly at night. An uncontrollable twitching in my limbs woke me as soon as I settled into slumber. I sometimes managed an hour in the afternoon, but today I thrashed about, full of plans, angles for the future, thoughts of expansion, suspicions about this man and sudden insights into that one. I ruled my corner of the island but couldn't still my mind. The cool pressure of the floor seemed to help, its rigid discomfort drew me to the surface of my skin and kept me there, in a hazy doze. When a boy knocked on the door at five, I jerked up with my heart squeezing hard. I washed my face, took deep breaths and then we went out. Once a day, at different times but always once a day, I took my boys and walked through my area. We took different routes, I wasn't stupid, but I wanted to show myself, to be seen. I won't tell you that there was no fear in me, but I had learnt to bury it, to layer it over with thick sheets of indifference. Ever since that bullet had hurled into me, I knew how real death was. I had no illusions. I had seen that a woman can be alive one day, eating mutton and sneering and joking and thrusting out her chest, her eyes humming with laughter and hunger, and then the next day can find her unconscious in a hospital bed, her mouth open and gasping. I knew I was going to die, I was going to be killed. There was no escape for me. I had no future, no life, no retirement, no easy old age. To imagine any of that was cowardice. A bullet would find me first. But I would live like a king. I would fight this life, this bitch that sentences us to death, and I would eat her up, consume her every minute of every day. So I walked my streets like a lord of mankind, flanked by my boys.

And so I maintained my grip, my reign. Fear was part of it, the fear the shopkeepers felt when they looked at me, the fear in the eyes of women who stepped back into doorways to let us pass. But that was not all, not at all. There is of course an excitement in the exercise of power, but there is also a safety in the bending to it. I tell you this is true. I felt it when they gave me chicken tika and bhakri, and asked me if I wanted a cold drink or tea, I knew it in the widening pools of their pupils when they dragged out their best chair for me and dusted it with their pallus. The truth is that human beings like to be ruled. They will talk and talk about freedom, but they are afraid of it.

Overpowered by me, they were safe, and happy. Fear of me taught them where they could live, it made them a fence, inside which was home. And I was good to them. I was fair, and didn't ask for so much money that it would hurt, and I taught my boys restraint, and above all I was generous. A factory worker had his leg broken under a tipping loader, and I supported his family for six months; a grandmother needed an operation to widen her veins and save her heart, and I gave her life, a chance to play with her children's children. 'Ganesh Bhai,' said a printer to me one afternoon, 'let me make a first-class business card for you.' But I didn't need any card. My name was known in my raj, and there were many who blessed it.

That evening, after my conversation with Bipin Bhonsle and my walk, I went to Paritosh Shah's house. His eldest daughter, first of four, was to be married in seven days. The house was sparkling already, three storeys of cascading lights, red and green and blue, blinking happily. It was a big house, finished only a year ago by him and his two brothers, and they lived in it all together, wives and cousins and countless visiting mamas and kakas, a whirling Gujarati chakkar. Dandia raas before weddings was definitely out of style, but for all his business innovation, Paritosh Shah was a firm traditionalist. So there were excited eddies of young girls in the courtyard, swirls of heady silk. They were waiting for me to start the dancing, and once I was seated in an armchair, all the men and women fell into four circles, the children in the inner two, and the singer raised a declamatory hand and began, 'Radha game ke game Mira', and the circles whirled slowly, and then faster, and the steady clap-clap of hands echoed out the happy beat. When they brought out the sticks for dandia I stood up and asked for a pair. They laughed to see me tripping clumsily, unable to keep time inside the circles moving against each other, unable to find the clicking rhythm. I think at first this was equally the fault of the other dancers, especially the men, who were afraid to be dancing with me, stripped of their grace by my presence. They hesitated to knock their dandias against mine, they were scared of putting in too much force, they shrank from my strokes. But when they saw how I laughed at myself, and when my boys, who were leaning against the pillars, shook their heads and smiled, everyone relaxed, and the disco-dandia song tumbled on gleefully, and I found my hips loosening, and my shoulders were easy, and I was flowing, falling into step without effort, and the dandia rose and fell, a flourish here and click, another swing and click, a round face spinning to me and click, and I was dancing.

At home Chotta Badriya had a woman waiting for me. I was happy from the dancing, humming away and doing a step here, another one there. But she brought me down. There's nothing more depressing than a depressed randi. She was nicely plump and with a little round nose, and nineteen, but she lay there with a swollen batata-wada face, and I tried to liven her up with a few nips and pinches and squeezes, but she winced and set her jaw, so I took her by the hair and threw her out. Then I drank some milk, lay on my side wrapped around a pillow and tried for sleep, but it larked away from me and my head was full of the dandia and Paritosh Shah and the lights skidding down the side of his house and up again, and I turned to the other side, and now I thought of the men I had killed. I stood them in a row and compared them for character and strength and I decided I was better than any of them, and then I made plans to have the approaches to my house checked and tested, and to put more boys in place at the head of the lanes, just in case. It was late now, very late, and for the first time in many months, I used my hand on myself, and all the women I had known came and slid over me and also Rati Agnihotri with her malai skin. After I was finished I turned again, back to the other side, settled down into comfort and took regular, deep breaths. But finally I threw off the covers and cursed and reached for the clock. Three forty-five. I would have drunk then, anything, a bottleful of whisky or rum, but there was nothing in the house, and I would have got the boys to bring some, but the thought of what they would think and not say made me ashamed, and I lay on my back and decided to see it through. I would get up from bed at six and have an early day. I watched the fan gleam in its flight and then suddenly I was waking up and it was bright day, and I could hear the street fully alive outside. Noon. I had slept for six hours, maybe seven, but I was tired.

My exhaustion deepened as the days passed, as we fought the elections. My boys went out with the Rakshaks, and we pushed their campaign into every nook, their posters harangued the voters from every surface for miles. Two of my boys, armed with pistols, with a group of Rakshaks was enough to keep the peace and let them do their work calmly, no bhangad. A reputation for ruthlessness can do wonders for peace. For us, it was easy money. Meanwhile, it was almost time for the wedding. Even before the ceremony I went to Paritosh Shah's house for the mehndi party, and I could see that he appreciated it, that I was so much a part of his joys and sorrows. Even in the midst of the thousand things he had to do, food and gifts and hotel arrangements for the groom's relatives, he noticed my wobbliness, how I was holding on to wakefulness with effort. 'Your doshas are out of balance,' he said. 'I'll set up an appointment for you with my Ayurvedic man.'

'I won't put myself in that bastard's clutches,' I said. 'It's just insomnia. It'll pass.'

'Nothing is *just* anything. The body is speaking to you. But you won't listen.'

Then he had to go and sit with the women, and the jewellers. There was some question of how many tolas of gold were to be used in the wide necklaces and bracelets and earrings for the dowry, how much payment for the making. I watched him step delicately down the steps to the courtyard and wondered what his body was speaking. How did one read those sheets of fat that surged and billowed on his frame? I rubbed my eyes. He had been good to me. He had never lied to me about money, he had never pretended to lay aside his self-interest, he had backed me as far as possible, to the risk of his life and then a little further, and he had shown me how in this world one thing connects to the next, where business comes together with politics and bhaigiri, how one must live. In this way we had been friends. He was a good man as far as he could be, he had grown fat with hard work, and so his bulk was his virtue. That was why his fat was light on him.

The whole house was fragrant from the cooking. I was hungry, but very tired, and eating would tire me more, I knew this. But to leave without eating would be an insult, so I took a thali and touched some food, and then pushed myself to my feet, and waved up the boys, and told Paritosh Shah to take care of his guests while he tried to see me to the door, and after a little argument, finally off we went. I was looking for my shoes in the great sprawl of footwear near the front door when Dipika came to me. Dipika was Paritosh Shah's second-oldest daughter, a serious-faced, quiet one with big-big eyes. She held out a thali piled with puris, and a glass, and said, 'But you haven't had any ras, Ganesh Bhai.' I had, but I was willing to take another puri from her, polite as she was. As I reached out she whispered, with her head still down, 'Can I please talk to you, Ganesh Bhai?' On the edge of the thali her thumbs were white.

So I took her, thali and glass and all, outside to the car and we talked. 'They're already talking about my marriage,' she said bitterly. 'And my sister's not married yet.'

'They're your parents,' I said. 'Of course they will. And you'll be happy, it's a good thing.' I knew that she was going to college, and I thought that she must have some modern-girl fashionable objection to marriage, some idea of job and career, all got from some silly magazine, so I started lecturing her on her duty, what real life was. She shifted about restlessly, rustling her red and green ghagra and gold chunni.

'But, Ganesh Bhai,' she said.

'Don't do but-this-and-that,' I said. 'Your parents are right.'

'But, Ganesh Bhai,' she said, with a little wail to her voice, 'I *want* to get married.'

And right then, from the small, painful furrowings on her smooth forehead, I knew this was going to be a lot more trouble than just girlish fantasies about a career. 'What?' I said. 'You have someone in mind?'

'Yes.'

'Where did you meet him? In college?'

She shook her head. 'NN College is all girls. His sister is my friend. She goes to NN.'

'What's his name?'

At least she still had the grace to be shy. Two tries, and a lot of blushing, and she got it out. 'Prashant.'

'What's the trouble? He's not Gujarati?'

'No, Ganesh Bhai.'

'What then? Maratha?'

A rapid shake of the head, and now she had her frantic grip on the thali again.

'Then what?'

She had her face almost in the thali now. 'Dalit,' she said. 'And he's poor.'

Her problem was gigantic, as elephantine as her father. I had always found the Gujaratis to be more advanced, more tolerant than other communities, but this would strain her father's understanding. He would do business with anyone, but marriage was another matter.

He had sent her to college, but not for this, not to marry some gaandu who was not only a Dalit but a poor Dalit. Maybe a very rich Dalit could have been approved, but I could hear Paritosh Shah saying it already, 'This is the family you want to marry us into?' Her mother and aunts would be harsher, more violent in their disapproval. Young Dipika had set herself to a hard battle. 'Why do you want to do this to your family?' I said. 'This is not some film. Your father will have this Prashant of yours torn to pieces.'

She looked directly at me then, and her back straightened, and her neck was graceful in its anger. 'I know it's not a film,' she said. 'I'll die, Ganesh Bhai. If anything happens to him, I'll kill myself.'

How little the young value life, they who are so full of it. How little they have seen of death. They think it's a mere pause in a drama, and they imagine the oppressing parents beating their breasts and wailing, and lost in that pleasure they never see the fall, the finality of one's own vanishing. I said as much to Dipika, and she laughed. 'I'm not a child,' she said, and I saw then how far she had gone with this Prashant, her young woman's splendid pride in the pleasures she had taken and given.

'What do you want me to do, Dipika?' I said.

'Talk to Papa. He will listen to you.' She took my hand and placed it on top of her head. 'Since I was a girl you have been kind to me. And I know you do not think in any old-fashioned way.'

What she meant was that in my company there were Brahmins and Marathas and Muslims and Dalits and OBCs, all working together, without difference or suspicion. We had OBCs who were controllers, and Brahmins who were foot-soldiers, and nobody gave it a thought. Muslims and Hindus were yaars who put their lives in each other's palms every day, every night. But this was not special to my company, it was true of many others. We who were bhais were truly brothers, we lived outside the law and were bound to each other. We were desperate men, and therefore free. But a company was a company, and marriage – especially in a joint family like hers – was something else. But how to tell this child, who now held my hand in both of hers, how?

'Go inside,' I said. 'Do nothing. Say nothing to anyone, not one person. Let me think about this.'

She was now dripping tears down her chin. I wiped her face with her pallu, and set her on her way with her wobbly thali. And I told Chotta Badriya that we were going to drive out to Film City.

'Now, bhai?' he said.

'No, next week, chutiya,' I said. 'Get in the car.' He was a funny boy, that one, built like a truck, not scared of swords, willing to play with flying bullets, but scared of Film City in the dark because someone had told him that leopards came down from the wooded hills at night. He sat next to the driver with his arm draped over the back of the seat and his fingers drumming nervously. Finally I clamped down his hand gently, and said, 'Okay, okay, stop shaking so much. You can stay in the car.'

He waggled his head delightedly. 'Yes, bhai. I'll watch the car.'

Every man in the car burst out laughing. I slapped the back of his head. 'Bhadwe, you guard it fiercely, okay? Make sure the mosquitoes don't steal it, okay? And if a big cockroach comes, you blow him to pieces with your gullel, okay?'

We laughed all the way to Film City. We slowed a bit for the guards at the gate, and then swept up the rising road, through the sudden darkness and quiet of the bushy slopes. It was already dusk, so the road was clear. There were the clustering shadows under the leaves, the flashing jigsaw of branches, and then suddenly in the clear there was a looming castle, high-turreted and fluttering with flags in the coming moonlight. It was made of wood and canvas, of course, but in this light it was absolutely real. We went past an entire Goan town square, capped by a high church holding up its crucifix, and also a fishing dock with boats asleep against each other in a leaning row. Here, in Film City, they made dreams of perfect love, they choreographed the songs that Dipika and her boyfriend no doubt sang to each other. The road curved sharply, and the engine whined, and we went up and up, to the helipad. The moon was low and close, hanging just above the lip of the high hills, and the valleys were cut sharply into silver and black, and a breeze slid up my neck. This was the deep quiet I craved, away from the city, that I came for again and again. I stepped to the edge of the helipad and the boys let me go, they stood in a distant arc and left me alone. I sat at the edge of the plateau, and looked for a leopard in the dappled patterning below. Come on, leopard, I said. Save me from this problem. I had promised the girl I would help, but how? She was a clever one, asking first and drawing me to her side. Otherwise, if her father had found out first, and asked me, without a thought I would have had her tattered Dalit boyfriend picked up and dropped off a cliff. Just like that. But now what? The daughter had asked for mercy, and I was Ganesh Gaitonde. But the father was my friend.

I sat until the moon had receded into the heights of the sky, and the leopard didn't come, and no easy answers. There was no solving this problem by killing anyone, and no amount of money would buy peace. There was love between the father and daughter, and so they would hate each other all the more, and wound each other, cutting nerves no assassin could ever reach. I got up and walked back through the boys, who sat in a dozing line. They staggered up and came after me, to the car. Chotta Badriya was fast asleep, his face against the window glass, lips plumped up and cheek flattened. I tapped the glass at his nose, and he came awake, groping under his shirt until he saw me. In that first waking clutch at the world, he had been afraid. I recognized the panic. We were all afraid. To walk out of the house, into a city street, into the air which hummed with the bullets of the next moment, to do this we cast aside fear, dropped it and pushed it into the deepest valley where the moon never shone. But the fear still moved, lived and fed, like an animal in the night. Chotta Badriya liked girls, very young ones. He even liked smallish women of older years who had no mausambis, who were flat before and behind and wore pigtails for him and sat on his lap and talked of dolls and held their heads to the side and giggled. He chodoed them sometimes, but I think only because the other boys would have laughed at him otherwise. For himself, he would have been happy just to hold them, to play at a dream of play, and so live a childhood which was free of the future. Now he was clearing his throat mightily and rolling down the window to spit.

'Bastard,' I said. 'What a fine guard you are.'

'Sorry, bhai,' he said. 'I was seeing leopards all over the place. So I thought I would never sleep. But then suddenly I must have fallen asleep.'

'You were, chutiya. Like a baby.' But I was rubbing the top of his head. He was a good boy. Brave and watchful, watchful for me, and intelligent. He noticed things, the look on people's faces, cars parked where they shouldn't be, and felt rumours on his nerve-endings. But he couldn't help me now, with my quandary, my delicate puzzle which could break hearts and heads. None of them could. It made me angry, this sudden slide down and back into the slithering mess of family. I had lifted away, I had left everything behind. I had been alone. But there was no escape. The wheels slapped at the road and we went back to the city.

The next day we waged the final battles of the elections. Bipin Bhonsle called again and again, polite as he had been during our first meeting, but nerve-racked and needing reassurance that we would give him his precious seat yet. The Congress incumbent had been going around the bastis, handing out hundred-rupee notes and rum and whole sheep to the citizens. Good fresh mutton is the basis of many a political career, I came to know. It made sense. A poor man fills his stomach, he takes pleasure in his dinner, he lubricates himself with two free pegs, maybe three, not too many because he has other plans, he rides his wife, in the morning they both go to the voting booth happy, in that uplifted haze their bodies feel light, and they forget all about how the khadi-wearing bhenchod politician has done nothing for them for years, how he has robbed and stolen and maybe murdered. All of that is gone, vanished, and the happy couple cast their votes, and the servant of the people is in once again, ready to serve them out of roti, kapda and makaan. Hungry, naked and without shelter, they have no memory after meat. So you feed sheep to sheep to herd them in the right direction, towards the slaughterhouse gate. Quite simple.

But I had my own schemes ready. For two days I had sent out rumours. My boys went into the markets and bazaars and restaurants of the Congress and RPI areas and whispered, 'The goondas are coming on election day, thugs have been hired.' A rumour is the most cost-effective weapon ever, anywhere, you start it for nothing and then it grows, mutates, has offspring. In the morning you plant a little red squirming worm in some shopkeeper's ears and by night there are a hundred skyscraper-sized gory Ghatotkachas stalking the land. So I had the enemy voters nicely primed, covered in a sticky marinade of fear. Now it was time to stoke the fire. I had thirty motorcycles ready, with licence plates removed. We put two boys on each, faces covered with dakoo scarves, with bags full of soda bottles for the pillion riders, a crate's worth for every bike. They went roaring out into the lanes. Through the enemy area they went, roaring and hooting. They cleared the streets with the bottles, gave each bottle a few shakes and lobbed it end over end at the few citizens brave enough to be still walking around. The glass flies like shrapnel, but really with soda bottles it's the shattering burst that does the trick, sends the trembling civilians scuttling back to their homes with their pants heavy with piss. The boys had a good time, riding around in the cool of the morning, exercising their bowling arms. Chotta Badriya came back home flushed red and singing. 'Any more, bhai?' he yelled up to me from the road. I was sitting on the water tank on the roof. 'Any more to do?'

'Bas, Badriya, bas,' I said. 'Calm down. That was enough. Now the police will come.'

'Phatak, phachak, the bottles burst, bhai.'

'I know.'

'Great fun, bhai.'

'I know. Now sit quietly, and maybe we'll do it again next year.'

Sure the police came, they came running to the affected areas. They came with their rifles and lathis all ready. Inspector Samant slipped around a corner and found a phone and called me. 'DCP Saab and ACP Saab are here, bhai,' he said. 'You got everybody moving. We are patrolling the streets. Preventing any disturbances, you see.'

'Good, good,' I said. Bipin Bhonsle had paid the policemen too, all the way to the top. They would organize the right kind of peace. 'No more disturbances must happen. But you see anyone on the roads?'

'Not one man, not one woman. I see only three dogs.'

'Good,' I said. 'Typical Congress voters. We'll let them go.'

So I laughed and put down the phone. Just this much was enough to keep the enemy at home, to make the battlefield ours. No booth-capturing, no ballot-stuffing, just this. Meanwhile the boys had fanned out in our areas, and were taking the voters to the booths. 'We are from the Fair Election Committee,' they said, and they took our voters, in tens and twenties, to the voting centres. 'All is peaceful,' they said. 'Come, come.' And the voters came, safe and escorted, and Bipin Bhonsle's men, wearing nice yellow party badges, smiled at them outside the booths. And the voters filed in, and were left all alone, and they made their little black marks on the ballot, and the folded pieces of paper fell into the slotted wooden boxes, making small rustles, and the lines moved efficiently along, and the day passed, and so the machinery of democracy moved and spun, with a little help from us.

In Gopalmath, I sat on my roof and did my daily business. In the courtyard below, and out on the street, the usual clusters of suppli-cants gathered. Money was brought in, and I gave it out. Lives were brought to me, and I mended them. I gave justice. I ruled. The sun puddled, hovered and died its daily death. I ate, and retired to my bedroom. It was another quiet, ordinary day.

Bipin Bhonsle won by six thousand three hundred and forty three votes.

I was dreading the wedding. Of course I had to go, but I didn't know how I would face Dipika, show her my face with no magic solution to grant her eternal happiness. I was angered by this feeling of helplessness, this paralysis of will. The problem stayed with me, gnawing with a thousand tiny teeth at the edges of my mind, like a flood of relentless ants. I was furious with Dipika. Who was she? What did she mean to me, that I owed her this? A little nothing of a girl, to come between me and my friend, to haunt and bother me with her huge staring eyes, she wasn't even pretty, why couldn't I just tell her to take her dirty mashooq and go to hell? Why? But I couldn't. She had begged me, and I had made a promise. There was no logic in it, but it was the truth, it had happened. So I had to act. But I still didn't know what I was going to do.

I took my gifts – gold bracelets, gold earrings and a gold necklace – and went to Paritosh Shah's house on the wedding day. I hardly had my shoes off when Dipika came running to the door, stopped herself from falling by clutching at the jamb. She swayed there, in her sari of gold, and I could sense my boys averting their eyes. I knew they were thinking: what is Bhai doing now? This much was all it took to start a story that would get longer and fuller as it went out across the city. 'Beti,' I said. I patted her head paternally. Then I took her by the shoulder and led her inside. In a corridor, while her aunts and cousins brushed past, all shiny and magnificent in their very best, I leaned close to her and pretended to give her something out of my wallet. 'Be calm, you fool,' I told her. 'If you act mad I can't do anything for you. Behave yourself now. When I want to tell you something, I'll tell you.'

'But,' she said. 'But.'

'Be quiet,' I said. 'If you want to do this big thing, be brave. Control yourself. Learn control. Leave fear behind. Look at me. Learn from me. You told me you were not a child, but you behave like one. Can you be a woman?'

She blinked away her tears, and wiped her nose with the edge of her pallu. Then she nodded.

'Good,' I said. 'Go and be a part of your sister's happiness. Be happy, or people will notice.' She was still tremulous, aflicker with thin bolts of emotion up her neck and into her cheeks. 'Listen to me,' I said. 'I am Ganesh Gaitonde, and I am telling you that everything will be all right. Ganesh Gaitonde is telling you this. Do you believe him?'

'Yes,' she said, and as she said it she started to believe it. 'Yes.'

'Go.'

She skipped off, and at the edge of the courtyard she took two little girls by the hand and whirled with them, and in their pealing laughter there was her happiness, as palpable as the breath of the hundreds of flowers hanging in the doorways, on the walls. She was happy. I had given this to her, and I didn't have it to give. I had no idea where to find it, how. And so in the mandap, sitting next to Paritosh Shah, as the priests sang and thick sacrificial smoke gusted from the fire and an elder sister's happiness was chanted into being, I was helpless before the younger sister's life. Yes, Dipika was happy now, sitting behind her sister, leaning on her mother's shoulder, her face flushed and perspiring a little from the heat of the fire, eyes gleaming wet from the sting of the smoke. Looking at her, I thought: what makes a woman so much a prisoner, why? Why is one man a Dalit and poor, and another not? Why does this happen, and not that? Why did this woman die, and not that one? Why are we not free? And the Sanskrit choruses moved under my skin and I felt them shiver my soul, and the question came to me: what is Ganesh Gaitonde?

After all the functions were over, after the eating and drinking and rituals of farewell, I said goodbye to Paritosh Shah and his wife and his parents and his entire battalions of Gujaratis, and he walked with me to the car, and even in the midst of all this, he noticed my distraction, and asked, 'What's the matter, bhai? You look tired. Still not sleeping?'

'Yes, I'm very tired,' I said.

'Listen to me, then. You can't go on like this. Take a Calmpose tonight, and tomorrow we will see to your health.'

'Tomorrow I need to ask you a favour.'

'Favour? What? Tell me now.' He bent towards me, and had his arm over my shoulder. There was the big red smear of the tika on his forehead, and I could see the tiny white grains of rice in it. 'Tell me.'

'No, tomorrow, Paritosh Shah. Not today.'

'All right, tomorrow then.' He came close to me, drew me into his soft, cushiony hug and thumped me on the back. 'I'll come to your place in the morning.'

'No, I'll come to you.' I squeezed his shoulder and drew away. 'Let me.'

'Fine, whatever you say, boss. Whenever you're ready. I'm here all day tomorrow.' But he was puzzled. He was not used to this Ganesh Gaitonde. In truth, it was a Ganesh Gaitonde I didn't know well, either. I had been struggling to get some sleep lately, but now I had been cut adrift, cast into some unknown, tossing waters by a mere slip, a sliver of a girl whom I hardly knew, owed nothing to.

'Tomorrow,' I said, raised a hand and went home. That night I didn't care about seeming weak, and felt my own shame like a distant irritation. I took a Calmpose, and slept, but I dreamt of a black sea, heaving its endless swells at me, and nothing else was alive, nothing lived under that flat white sky, and I was alone.

Bipin Bhonsle came to me the next morning, with gifts. He brought the cash he owed me, in four plastic bags, but he also brought a brand-new Sony video player, and four tapes, all of American films, and four big boxes of mithai. He said, 'My father told me, "Take him some good Scotch," but I told him, "Ganesh Bhai doesn't touch the stuff, and I can see why. That's why he's so efficient."' He was sitting at the edge of the chair, all serious and enthusiastic. 'You know what, Ganesh Bhai? I've made up my mind. From today, no more liquor for me also. I will learn from you. Now that we've won, there is a lot to do. No time now for drinking-shinking. We have to keep on winning.'

'Yes,' I said. I had woken up more tired than before, and my legs were heavy, unwieldy, as if the blood had become congealed and dense. But I roused myself to Bipin Bhonsle's eagerness. 'Good, Bipin, good. A sober man is focused, he is awake, he is watchful. No need for all this whisky and rum. Life is enough.'

It was a speech I had given many times before. For him it was all new. 'Right, Ganesh Bhai, of course: life is enough. But please, enjoy.' He held out the tapes. 'Each is an international hit, Ganesh Bhai. Action-packed. You will enjoy.' He was so grateful it took an hour to get him out, and that only when I told him I was already late for a meeting at Paritosh Shah's house. He left, but loudly protesting eternal loyalty, and anything I needed I should remember him, and of course he was only a small man but if there were anything I wanted I only had to call him, and on international pleasures he was an expert. 'Hot tapes, electronics, cigars, anything, Ganesh Bhai, anything,' he was saying even as he went down the stairs. He was wearing an orange shirt with a flower print, and brown gabardine trousers, and shoes of a deep reddish-brown hue, gold-buckled and glowing. When he turned to wave from the gate, the chain at his neck flashed fiercely in the sun. He was altogether a shiny man.

We sped over to Paritosh Shah's. I would rather have gone slowly, I still had no plan, no tactics of persuasion worked out. But I couldn't say it to Chotta Badriya, go slow, don't go, never go, because I am helpless. I was, after all, Ganesh Gaitonde. I had taken the role, now I had to play the part. So hero-like I got out of the car, walked to Paritosh Shah's door, which was auspicious still with flowers and vines, and into the house. By the time I was barefoot in the courtyard I had lost all my swagger and style. I entered Paritosh Shah's office quite humbly.

He was on the phone, in one of his interminable dealings, arranging for money to go from here to there, breeding the currency notes with each other as they swept past him, and keeping one subtle, careful hand in the stream. Money leapt to him, and he delighted in its antics. He started to put a hand over the mouthpiece, and I waved him on. Talk, talk, I signed at him, my hands at my mouth, and I sat down and watched him. Behind him there was a gold-framed painting of Krishna with his flute. The top of Paritosh Shah's desk was gold, and he had five phones on it. The walls were a darker gold. I looked at Krishna, at his easy, turning stance and his slanty smile, and I hated him. You are arrogant, god. I changed seats, but Krishna's eyes followed me. I couldn't get away from him.

Paritosh Shah put his phone down, all bright from the thrill of money. 'Namaskar, my friend,' he said. He rubbed his hands together and rocked back in his chair and looked happy with the world. And Krishna smiled at me from above his shoulder.

Paritosh Shah had remembered by now our conversation from the day before. 'So, bhai,' he said. 'What's the matter? What can I do for you?'

In that moment I realized what Krishna was smiling at. I realized the limits of my power. And I told Paritosh Shah everything I knew and had found out about Dipika and her lover, that his name was Prashant Haralkar, that his father used to work for the sanitation department, that the mother had taken the children and left this alcoholic father twenty years ago. And also that Prashant Haralkar had been a dedicated student, that he had studied by the light of street-lamps and had gone to night college, that he now had a permanent job with the BMC, and that he now lived in a small but good-enough house in Chembur and supported his mother and younger sisters.

Paritosh Shah covered his face with both of his hands.

I walked around the corner of the desk, and sat on the couch close to him. I put my hand on his knee, patted clumsily. He flinched away from my touch. 'Who will marry my children?' he sobbed through his fingers.

I had no answer. I had promised Dipika happiness, but what about Paritosh Shah's two other daughters and two sons, what were they to do? I could win elections, I could move men up the steep ladders of success and kill them in the next moment, I could burn down houses, seize land, bring half the city to a standstill with an arbitrary procla-mation of a bandh, if that was my pleasure. But who would fight the rows of meek matrons who had sat primly, heads covered, at the wed-ding of Paritosh Shah's daughter? Who would push their portly husbands into enlightenment? Paritosh Shah's natevaik would declare themselves busy in response to his invitations, they would forget to ask him to their functions, and their sons and daughters would be engaged and married elsewhere, no matter how much money he had or how close he was to me. And he would feel shame every time he saw some acquaintance, each time he walked in the street. Sitting next to Paritosh Shah, abased by his tears and unable to look at him, I knew how helpless I was. I would have beaten all his relatives, thrashed each of them with my shoes, broken all their smug, snug heads open to the modern air, if only that would have made any dif-ference. But custom floats between men and women, it hides in the stomachs of children and escapes and expands and vanishes in every breath, you cannot kill it, you cannot hold it, you can only suffer it.

'Have you met that bastard maderchod?' Paritosh Shah asked. He was angry now.

'No, I haven't. Listen, I didn't come to you for him. He matters less than an ant to me. But Dipika asked me.'

'Kill him,' he said. 'Just kill him.'

'Easily done,' I said. 'I'll give the order now. In an hour he'll be gone, no part of his body will ever be found, not one fingernail. But then what? He'll be gone and so she will be able to love him the rest of her life. And also hate you for the rest of her life.'

'She is young. This is foolishness. She will cry for a week and then she will forget him.'

'Is that how much you know your daughter?' His cheeks were burnished wet, and his jaw clenched and opened and shut, sending little rushes of torment up into his eyes and forehead. 'She told me she would kill herself, and I believed her. Do you understand? I believed her. You'll find her dead.'

'Then what?'

He was walking in small circles now. 'Let her marry him,' I said. 'Marry them quietly and send them away. Settle them in Madras, in Calcutta. Amsterdam, if you want.'

'That won't change anything,' he said. 'Everybody will still know. If she suddenly goes, disappears, they'll ask questions, they'll make up stories. Everybody always knows. You can't keep something like that a secret for ever. I am a well-known man.' That he was. 'Bhai,' he said, 'what do we do, bhai?'

'You won't marry her to this fellow?'

'No. I can't. You know that.'

So here we were. He was trapped, and I could do nothing. 'Marry her today to someone else,' I said. 'Marry her this hour. Find a boy and get a pandit and marry her off now. Then send them away. Somewhere. Maybe she won't kill herself. Maybe she will, but maybe she won't.'

He was panting. 'Yes,' he said, and picked up the phone.

I left by the back door to the house. I had betrayed Dipika, and I could not face her. They married her that afternoon, to a boy who was flown down from Ahmedabad. Dipika and her husband went by the next morning's flight back to Ahmedabad. The in-laws told Paritosh Shah that after a few days of gloom, she seemed to have adjusted, she began to smile and laugh. Paritosh Shah was satisfied that the reality of the marriage had already erased the silly illusion of romance. The boy's parents told him, over the phone, that Dipika was talking a lot to the younger girls in the family, and had been to the cinema twice with her husband and her devars and their wives. So, two months later, Dipika and her husband were sent on their honeymoon to Switzerland. On the fifth night of the honeymoon, in Bern, she left the hotel suite while the husband was sleeping. She walked out of the lobby, and out of the gates and on to the road beyond. She was hit by a car that came fast around a curve. The driver said later that she was walking in the exact middle of the road, on the painted dividing lines, and he never had a chance to swerve, he didn't even know what he had hit until he came to a halt and reversed. Dipika was killed instantly. The husband said she had seemed happy, that their relations were joyous, as between any new husband and wife. In the Swiss records they put it down as an accident.

Three months after Dipika's death, I was watching one of Bipin Bhonsle's American movies when Paritosh Shah came to me. I had been awake all night, so excruciatingly awake that I could hear the creaking of the settling joists, the click of a passing dog's toes on the concrete outside. I watched the red second-hand of my bedside clock scything smoothly around its eternal circle, and I felt it tearing at something inside my head. So I popped in one of Bipin Bhonsle's tapes, switched on the television and pressed buttons on the control, and where there had been black fuzz a lion appeared, stretching its mouth in a yellow-toothed yawn. I watched, and the first time I understood very little. But I used the rewind button, and by morning I understood the story, who wanted what, what was standing in the way, and who must be killed. It was a good story, but it was the words that were the pleasure for me. I ran one scene back and forth, and the hero raced backwards under fine white lines, jerky and clown-quick, and his mouth twisted, and sounds came out glistening with his anger, and I ran it back, and forward, and back, and the syllables fell on my ears like pattering drops, and suddenly they fell together and the sense came to me, he was asking, 'Where did he go?' He had his pistol ready and was asking, 'Where did he go?' And in that moment there was a humming joy in every part of me. 'There,' I shouted in English at the hero. 'He went there.'

When that film was over, I put in another one, and learned. Paritosh Shah came at nine o'clock, and sat on the bed and watched with me, watched another hero and his men move down a jungle river with water to their chests, their faces blackened. 'These are commandos,' I said. 'Their country's secret missile has been stolen by one bastard. So they are going to get it back from his jungle den.'

Paritosh Shah smiled. 'A jungle den? It would be expensive to supply and maintain. That's what I always wonder about. How do they get the oil and atta and onions to it, for so many henchmen?'

I switched off the tape. 'You're just too much of a bania,' I said, 'to appreciate a good story.'

'I just don't understand these foreign films.'

'I can see that. Everything all right at home?'

After Dipika's death, his wife had taken to bed with palpitations of the heart. She was still weak, and given to fits of crying. 'We are going along,' he said. 'And you? Did you sleep?'

He knew that I lay awake at night, that I watched television in the grey hours of the morning, that I fell fitfully asleep in the car on journeys. I shook my head. 'I'll take a pill tonight.'

He made a sweeping motion in the air between us, like a man wiping a window clean. 'That's what I wanted to talk to you about.'

'About sleeping pills? Your ved-maharaj has some new recipes?' I had tried his Dhanwantri's pills, had got indigestion and gas and no sleep, and had gone back to the allopathic doctor for his strongest medicines.

'No. Not that,' he said, very serious. 'Listen, bhai, I think you should get married.'

'Me?'

'Look at you. You're not happy. You can't sleep. You're distracted, you do this and that, nothing works. You're restless. A man needs to settle down. You have everything now, you need to become a grahastha, start a family, everything has a place and time.'

'Marriage doesn't bring happiness to all of us.'

'You mean Dipika. Bhai, she was my daughter. It wasn't the marriage that was wrong, it was the other thing. Once she had gone past all boundaries, where was the chance for happiness? But you need to get married. All the scriptures say a life has its stages. First you are a student, then you are a householder. But you, you live like you've given up the world already. Look at this.' He meant the room, the bare walls, the white sheets, the crusted thali from dinner on the floor. 'Chotta Badriya and the boys are all very well, but they can't be your life. You need a woman, she will make a home for you.'

'Who will marry me, Paritosh Bhai? Which respectable girl?'

'You worry too much, bhai,' he said. 'We have money. Everything is possible.'

Everything is possible. Yes, he and I had created possibilities, we had snatched dreams out of the air and snapped them into solidity. Everything was possible. And yet Kanta Bai and Dipika had died. Looking at Paritosh Shah, I was reminded of the smile of the god above his shoulder, the blue conjuror who had regarded me with his

sleepy eyes. He had had a family too, many families. Now he was trying to trap me into one. Yes, I now knew that certain things were
impossible, even for me, and it was true that money made marriages
possible. Most of our boys had chavvis, and some of these chavvis
became wives. Sometimes the parents objected, made a fuss about the
boy's profession, but always finally agreed. After all, the boy was
earning, and earning good money. 'Yes,' I said sourly. 'Money can
bring a bride. At least it can do that.'

'Do you have somebody to love-marry?' Paritosh Shah said with
the satisfaction of a player moving rapidly towards checkmate.

'No.' I had women aplenty, bar-girls, whores, would-be actresses.
Certainly no one to marry.

'Then don't refuse me, bhai,' he said. 'You came to me that day and
asked me for something. And I couldn't give you what you wanted.
But don't say no to me today. I am asking you for something. Say yes,
bhai.'

I knew in that moment that we are trapped for ever in the connections that wrap us from head to foot and bind us to each other, as
invisible as gravity but as powerful. From this net there is no escape. I
had come to this city alone, to be alone, but my solitude was illusion,
a story I had told myself to convince myself of my strength. I had
found a family, a family had found me. This Paritosh Shah was my
friend, and he was my family. All the rest of them, Chotta Badriya and
Kanta Bai and my boys, they were my family. I was a part of this family, and they wanted me married. I couldn't fight them. I was defeated.
I nodded. I said, 'All right, I'll do what you want.'

While we looked for a girl we fell into a war. Paritosh Shah wanted
my janampatri, he wanted to know about my parents and my gotra
and my village. 'Only by knowing a man's past,' he said, 'can you
settle his future.' And I said, 'Forget all that. I have none of that, I
have money. Past is passed. Future is future, so make it for me.' I
believed then that a man can become anything he wants. I wanted it
to be true: no past, any future. But Paritosh Shah, that fat bastard,
that slippery Gujarati schemer, that faithful friend of mine, he looked
at me as if I was crazy, and then dreamed a past for me. He ordered
up a janampatri, a long roll which unfurled across the room, sprinkled with stars and secret hatchings and vermilion Sanskrit and all
good things. 'But not too perfect,' he said. 'Otherwise no Papa will

believe it.' So, according to Paritosh Shah, there had been bad times in my early youth, poverty and danger and near-death because of a rising Shani, but I had overcome these malign inevitabilities, I had faced down fate itself through the strength of my will and my single-hearted devotion to Krishna-maharaj, I had turned destiny through the energies of my uncountable devotions. This too he invented, all this, my God-fearing daily poojas, my temple-building, my love of Krishna. 'It is good publicity, bhai,' he said. 'So give up your godless ways, nobody likes that stuff. People will think you are a communist, and anyway your children will need a good, God-fearing household.' His special-order janampatri predicted many sons for me, and a daughter or two, and a long life of rising power and stability and eminence. Only one or two periods of illness were foreseen, like beauty-marks on a perfect face, and even these were easily surmounted through wearing of the right stones. Paritosh Shah rolled up the scroll with quick, practised little twirls of forefingers and thumb, his underarms jiggling, and smiled at me. 'You are a very eligible boy. You'll get a queue of candidates, you wait.'

I had my doubts. We might have moved the planets to shine a golden light on my future, but the fact remained that men had died at my hands. The newspapers called me 'Ganglord Gaitonde'. I was hated and feared. I knew this. And yet, the photographs came in. The Papas sent in pictures of their daughters, through intermediaries and marriage-brokers. Paritosh Shah spread a sheaf of them on his golden desk, like a pack of playing cards. 'Choose,' he said.

I picked up the first one. She was sitting in front of a red backdrop, wearing a silky green sari with a gold dupatta, with her sleek hair pulled tightly back from a long forehead. 'This one looks like a schoolteacher,' I said.

'So don't choose that one. Make a shortlist. Then we'll consider family background, education, nature of girl, horoscope, and move on from there.'

'Move on?'

'See the girls, of course.'

'We'll go to her house? And she'll bring in tea while her parents watch?'

'Yes, of course. What else?'

I flicked the picture back on to the table, where it slid smoothly into the rest. 'This is completely mad,' I said.

'What, marriage is mad? Bhai, the world does it. Prime ministers do it. Gods do it. I mean, what else are you going to do with your life? What else is a man born for?'

What is a man born for? I had no answer to this, and so I took the photos back home and laid them out on the floor of my room in rows of ten. They shivered in the draught from the air-conditioner, these faces patted smooth with powder, softly gleaming with hope. It was April, and without the blast of frigid air, even with the fan on 'Full', I sweated into my mattress, left damp stains on chairs. My blood was hot, and needed wintry air, more cold than this city could ever exhale. Outside, under the sun, my trousers stuck to my thighs and drove me into rages of restlessness, my shoes left red rings around my ankles. In these moods I was capable of rash anger and carelessness, so the boys had special power cables laid, and they knocked a new window into my bedroom wall for the machine, and so I was cooled. I was now comfortable and calm, and yet those faces on the floor were all the same to me, each was as good or bad as the next one. They were pretty enough, not phatakdi beautiful –who would want that in a wife? – but pleasant and welcoming and shy. They were sufficiently educated, well-cultured, no doubt each knew cooking and embroidery, they were all qualified, so why pick this one, and not that one? I waited for a sign from one of them, a wink of the eye as they fluttered in the chill blast. And there I was, Ganesh Gaitonde, leader of my own company, master of thousands of lives, death-giver and generous benefactor, completely and wholly unable to make a decision.

'Bhai, there's trouble.' Chotta Badriya was knocking urgently at the door. I called him in and he said it again. 'Very big trouble.'

'What?'

'Tonight's shipment, bhai. The police have it. They were waiting at Golghat. They were above the beach, behind that line of trees. They waited until all the maal was loaded into the trucks, then they came out and arrested everyone and took it all.'

All of it was forty lakhs worth of computer chips, vitamin B-complex tablets and video cameras. The maal was brought to the coast off the fishing village of Golghat on a hundred-foot dhow, then put on neat little fishing boats for the trip to the beach, where three trucks were waiting with plastic sheets on the flatbed, all ready for my precious cargo. But now the police had it.

'They knew,' I said. 'They had information.'

'Yes,' said Chotta Badriya.

'It was only police? No customs?'

'Yes, only police.'

'Who was it?'

'Zone 13 officers. Kamath, Bhatia, Majid Khan, those fellows. Parulkar's boys.'

We both knew what that might mean. It was possible that the police had their own sources who had tipped them off, or it could be that one of our rivals had given them my maal. At the time, there were four other big companies in Bombay, the Pathan company down in Grant Road, the Suleiman Isa outfit in Dongri and Jogeshwari and Dubai, the Prakash brothers and their company in the north-eastern suburbs and the Ahir company in Byculla. Any of those four – no, five, if you counted the Rakshaks – could have thought us tiny fish, easy to feast on. It wouldn't be the Pathans, they were weak from their long war with Suleiman Isa, which they had barely survived. Any of the other companies could have thought of us as a tasty passing snack, we were by far the youngest, the most inexperienced, least connected, with the smallest money and weapons. Which was it?

Parulkar had just come in as Assistant Commissioner in Zone 13, and he was said to be close to Suleiman Isa. And Suleiman Isa and his brothers headed the most politically connected, best-armed, largest gang that Bombay had ever seen. Maybe they saw us as a growing threat, and maybe they were trying to eat us.

'Is that all we know?' I said.

'That's all, bhai.'

I was so angry that I felt it as a pain in my joints, a shifting throb in my stomach. I wanted to kill someone. But slowly, slowly. Suleiman Isa was big. I had to know for sure. 'Call Samant. Find him wherever he is. I need to speak to him.'

Who was hunting us? Samant investigated, inside the department, fielding rumours, giving out a little cash here, a bottle of Black Label there. He had friends everywhere, constables and clerks and peons, and through these hands the secret would finally slip. But it was taking too long. There was a spy in my company, somewhere close to me, some chutiya who had sold the secret of my shipment, and with every passing minute the danger to me loomed and grew, like a leaning hill. I had to pick up the mountain, or it would topple and crush me. I could lift this weight, I knew it. But first I had to find the snake in my house, I had to crush his head. Where was he hiding? How to get him out in the open? In my air-conditioned room I slid the heads of the girls into patterns, formations, and thought. On the last day of May, I went to Paritosh Bhai. 'I want to *do* something,' I shouted at him. 'I'm sitting here like a chutiya while a bunch of bhenchods laugh at me. My own boys are laughing at me.'

'Nobody's laughing at you,' he said. 'Be patient. It's a big matter, and nothing big gets done in a day.'

I was about to let loose at him again, but there was a knock at the door. Bada Badriya peered around the door, then let a timid little tailor into the room. Paritosh Bhai was getting fitted for new safari suits. The tailor stretched his tapes around him as Paritosh Shah kept up a rapid series of calls on his cordless phone. I sat and watched. He had been very busy recently, launching his airline. My fat man wanted to fly. He had dozens of businesses, he gloried in his construction companies, his restaurants, his rental properties, his plastics factories, his garments factory near Ahmedabad, but he dreamt of soaring high above the earth, and so he had been appearing recently in all the newspapers, beauteous and polished from his gleamy hair to his gold chain with Krishna locket and the gold Rolex which set off all the birth stones on his fingers. There was some comfort for me in the thought of him flying high above the stepped cliffs of Bombay's buildings, above the brown lowlands of its bastis, of him hovering like a smooth and rotund balloon over it all, shading the city's long-toothed silhouette in the benevolent umbra of his blue safari suit, more delightfully blue than the sun-bleached sky. Maybe one day his shadow would fall west and north, all the way to Delhi, and beyond. He had the intelligence, the ambition, and a clear cold eye. But for now the airline would extend its service from Bombay to Ahmedabad and Baroda. He was arranging the celebrations and formalities surrounding the maiden flight.

'Listen,' he was saying. 'Just listen. I knew that randi when she would suck a lauda for a whole night for five thousand rupees. Now she's become such a big star that she wants three lakhs to sit on a plane for an hour? To cut one ribbon? Be serious.' He was talking to Sonam Bhandari's secretary, negotiating a personal appearance. He listened, then settled into his no-nonsense negotiating voice. 'I can give one lakh. I'm starting an airline, not a fund for starlets who are already finished. One lakh.' The tailor was measuring from waist to floor now. 'How much? Okay. One-fifty. Done. I'll send over fifty thousand today. Okay.' He put the phone down. 'Done,' he said to me. 'A film star will come for the flight. We shall be on TV.'

'You be on TV,' I said. 'I'm not coming anywhere near your flight.'

'Not even with Sonam Bhandari on it?' he said. 'If you see her jiggle those coconuts, you'll forget all about your shipment.'

'No woman has coconuts good enough to make me forget that.'

He was quiet until the tailor gathered up his scribblings and samples and left. 'You've done everything that can be done,' he said. 'Now we just have to wait.'

And wait and wait and wait. Waiting was grindingly hard for me. 'Listen,' I said. 'I don't want to wait. We have to do something.'

'At times like these, we need help,' he said, looking crafty. 'Let's do a puja.'

'Fine.'

'What, really? You mean that?' That he was amazed was only natural: in all our years I had never said a prayer, never begged for divine favours, had eaten prasad only as a quick snack. But now he wasn't interested in my reasons, just in moving fast through this unexpected opening. He was picking up one of his phones already. 'We'll do a Satyanarayan Katha. I know just the pandit. You'll see, all his kathas bear fruit without fail. Not to worry. Before you blink we'll be on top of the situation.' He was smiling at me most benevolently. I could see the story he had in his head, hear the katha he was going to tell as resoundingly as if he was loud-speakering it into my ear: Bhai has come home, he was going to tell the boys, he has come home to the Lord, by the grace of God he has been woken up, in his heart devotion has come alive like a flame. The truth was that I didn't feel very lit-up, just inert. I had the sensation of drowning slowly, and as the water eased over my cheeks I had flung up a hand and clutched at whatever was floating by. This puja was a twig, and I grasped it.

I could see the heavy boat motionless on the shifting silver surfaces of the enormous waters. Paritosh Shah had picked a bhaiyya pandit for his puja, so I could understand the katha in Hindi without effort. This pandit was a very dramatic story-teller, and he was doing the Satyanarayan Katha with vivid expression, with different voices for the characters and full Dilip Kumar expressions, and now we were at the part where the trader and his son-in-law were on their way home with a boat laden with gold and pearls and perfumes and ivory, all the weighty profits of a long, windy voyage away from home. Then a dandi-swami appeared on the bank, crafty old Satyanarayan himself in disguise, to ask the simple question, 'Bachcha, what's in the boat?' And the businessman, afraid of having to give alms, greedy short-sighted bastard, said, 'Oh, nothing, Swami-ji, just some lata-pata,' and the dandi-swami nodded and said 'Tathastu' and the boat was indeed suddenly bobbing up like a cork, filled now only with fluffy grass and dry hay. The dandi-swami now went into a deep meditative trance, and exactly at that moment, before we could get to the busi-nessman's final comeuppance and regret, Chotta Badriya tapped me on the shoulder, and whispered, 'Come, bhai.'

Outside the room, he gave me a phone. I took the call with Paritosh Shah and Chotta Badriya and his brother Bada Badriya watching. It was our breakthrough. The night before, one of our landing agents from Golghat had spent the night with a girl named Simky in Colaba. This landing agent, one Konkani named Ashok Khot, had been on our payroll for four years. Last evening, he had come to Bombay to put his wife on a train to Delhi, where she was going for her brother's daugh-ter's wedding. She had gone off on the Rajdhani, well-settled with her two sons in the chair car, and then Khot had decided to partake of the delights of the city. He had called this Simky from the station itself, then picked her up an hour later in front of the Lido Bar, near Regal. Khot was flush with money. He had arranged for a private air-condi-tioned taxi with darkened windows, and he took her for dinner to Khyber, and then for a drive down Marine Drive. All during dinner he drank Johnny Walker Black and told her stories about men he had fooled and money he had made and high officers he had ruined, and in the car, between massaging her mausambis and laughing at jokes he never finished, he took sips from a silver glass attached to a flask by a silver chain. She lay back in the seat and listened, humming along with the songs on the cassette player. They ate kulfi at Chowpatty, and he staggered to the water and tried to sing a song, and then threw up into the sea, and then drank another peg just to show how much of a man he was. On the way back, he had the driver turn up *Makhmali and-hera* and opened fully Simky's choli and was nuzzling into her with small slobbering sounds and babbling softly, and under the music she heard it, 'Saali, you better be good to me, do you know who I am?

Nobody can look cross-eyed at me in this city. Masood Meetha himself comes to my house.' In the hotel room in Colaba, Khot looked dully at her while he pawed at her skirt, and then he slid slowly to the side and fell fast asleep. Simky took his shoes off, and his socks, then tugged off his pants and Jockey underwear. She found twenty-four thousand rupees in five-hundred-rupee notes in his various pockets, of which she counted off five thousand, which she hid deep in her red purse. From this purse she carefully extracted a small paper pudi, and from it pinched a judicious nip of brown sugar and breathed it up her nostrils, sending a voluptuous shudder through her breasts. Then she lay back and slept. In the morning, Khot turned over and stretched, and she kept herself still despite the gutter-reek of his breath. When he tried to climb on to her, she turned her head and winced and in a little-Simky voice said, 'Raja, you made me so sore last night, I can't take any more, really I can't.' He laughed proudly, and magnanimously let her off. The next day she had lunch with one of our boys, Bunty Arora, from GTB Nagar. When Simky had first come from Chandigarh, Bunty had taken care of her, she had been his chavvi. Now he wouldn't touch her, she had a nasty brown-sugar habit, but still there was the feeling for an old mashooq, and occasionally when he was on that side of town, he looked her up. She told him about her night with Khot. Now, our Bunty had been the one who had introduced Khot to Simky. So he said, 'That bevda bastard, he's unbearable when he starts drinking.' And she said, 'Yes, he talks and talks, he won't stop! I'm this, I'm that, nobody had better look at me, Masood Meetha comes to my house. I wanted to hit him on the head with a cricket bat.' She tossed her hair, and for a moment she had that old Simky fire. Then she went back to her golden falooda and foggy humming. Our Bunty, he kept his face calm, and moved the conversation on, talked about films and stars and this and that, and when they had finished lunch, he saw her off and then walked to the nearest shop and made a phone call. Just as the dandi-swami was saying, 'Tathastu.'

So there it was. Masood Meetha was Suleiman Isa's number one man in the city, had been ever since Suleiman himself had taken off for Dubai. The enemy who had stolen our goods was Suleiman Isa, he and his bastard brothers. I put the phone down and said this to Paritosh Shah and Bada Badriya and Chotta Badriya. 'It's Suleiman,' I said.

'Are you sure?' Chotta Badriya said.

'Of course I'm sure. I was sure of it before, now we have proof. That bhenchod Parulkar and Suleiman have been close for years and years.' This was common knowledge, and Chotta Badriya's face showed it, he looked down and was quiet. Parulkar and Suleiman had risen together, or at least in parallel. Many of Parulkar's most famous arrests and encounters had been based on intelligence passed to him by Suleiman, and those who had gone to prison or bled out their lives in some lane had been the enemies of Suleiman, his rivals, or just those who had grown big enough to be seen by him as competitors. He and his clan had eaten up many in this city, they had grown fat on this daily diet, and they swaggered through the streets. Suleiman Isa and his many brothers, the Nawabs of Bombay. 'I am going to kill them all,' I said.

The fan was skipping above us, aslant in its fast circle and letting out a periodic creak. This was the only sound. This was very serious. The Pathans had fought a war against Suleiman, had killed one of his brothers and many of his boys, but he had struck back and bled them weak. Finally a truce had been called, and the firing had halted, no more pistols snapping away in restaurants and AK-47s at petrol pumps, but the Pathans were left crippled. It was madness to doubt Suleiman's will, or his brain, or his wealth, or his contacts in the police and in the ministries. So my friends were quiet. Finally Paritosh Shah said, 'There's no other choice.'

War comes upon us. We are led in leaning curves towards the battlefield. You may try to avoid it, but find that last flower-lined turn you chose was really an entrance into a blood-soaked arena. So we were here. 'Good,' I said. 'Let's start.'

We were victorious at first. We had the advantage of surprise. On that very first day, I had Khot picked up. His wife was still in Delhi, so some of the boys just went over to his house that night and picked him up from his bed, lifted him and brought him to me. I didn't want him in my home, so we dealt with him outside, behind the house. At first he tried to tell me that he didn't know anything about any Suleiman Isa, why would I think that he would even try anything as low and crazy as that, everyone knew he had been faithful to Ganesh Bhai for years and years, he swore on the heads of his children. Finally, the shameless bhenchod, he tried a religion angle. 'Why would I go with that kattu bastard?' he said. 'Ganesh Bhai, think about it. Like you

I'm a God-fearing man. Every week I give to the temple. This is only some Muslim plot to break our friendship.'

I hit him so hard I skinned a knuckle. 'Listen, you bastard,' I said, and then was too angry, I felt my blood swell up behind my eyes. 'Beat him' was all I could say. 'Beat him,' I said, and walked away.

He made coughing, gasping noises, and called on his father. 'Papa, Papa,' he wept. That was interesting. Pain makes babies of most men, and their mothers are usually who they cry out for. Maybe Khot didn't have a mother. I went back and watched, rubbing my hand. When I pressed at the second knuckle on my right hand a hot fan of pain bloomed into my hand. I pressed harder. Now it was a cold movement, quick and edged and stabbing into my wrist. It was a slippery tooth just under the skin, biting. Under the quick rain of kicks, Khot was convulsing on the ground. I pressed harder. He broke first.

He told us everything. There wasn't that much to tell. He and Masood Meetha had known each other since they were young men. The families were from adjoining villages originally, somewhere near the coast. Masood had approached him a year and a half earlier, in Bombay, had called and invited him for tea and biscuits in his Dongri office. Khot had refused to meet in Dongri, so they had chai at a cheap restaurant in Ghatkopar. All they had done that first time was talk about Konkani villages and the food and whatever happened to old so-and-so whose father was a postman. Then, a month later, late at night, Masood had casually stopped by Khot's house near Golghat, on the spur of the moment, he just happened to be near by, and he had asked for dinner, for all the traditional Konkani dishes that Khot's wife could make, and so then he had Bhabhi's cooking which was just like his mother's. After this dinner, there had been phone calls and gifts of watches and bottles of whisky, but never any face-to-face contact. Khot was no innocent, he knew from the very first sip of Meetha's tea during that first meeting what this whole game was about, why after all these years Masood Meetha had remembered him. And when it came time to make arrangements for my shipment, my forty-lakh shipment, it was Khot who picked up the phone and called Masood, 'Bhai, shall we have dinner?' He cried and told us all of this.

'Kill him,' I said. I turned and walked away, and before I was at the steps leading to the back door, it was done. Two flat thumps and Khot was done. Chotta Badriya followed me inside, and I heard the snick of the safety before he put his pistol back under his shirt. 'Don't dispose of the body yet,' I said. 'We'll send it back to Suleiman tomorrow. Afterwards.'

'Afterwards,' he said, and grinned. So we set to work. We had been preparing. We had our lists, our hand-drawn maps, our information. So we set up our fielding. The next day, between eight in the morning and four in the afternoon, we killed Vinay Shukla, Salim Sheikh, Syed Munir, Munna, Zahed Mechanic and Praful Bidaye. That same night Samant encountered Azam Lamboo and Pankaj Kamath, for which action he got big stories in the papers, 'Encounter King Guns Down Top Suleiman Shooters', and three lakhs from me. And that same night, actually at four-thirty in the morning, a car pulled up to the corner near the Imperial Hotel in Dongri and Khot slid out on to the pavement, his head wrapped in a crusted towel. So, we told them who we were. We wrote our answers in blood.

What I wanted was Suleiman's head, to kick around like a football. But he was safe in Dubai, where he had gone after the Pathans had killed his brother, after he had killed many of them. Bombay had become too dangerous for him, and so he had fled, the bhadwa, but still he ran his operations in the city, through Masood Meetha and others. We were braced for their assault, and for a day we waited, and then sure enough it came. They ambushed three of our boys as they left a relative's house in Malad. All three of ours died, all three before they could draw their pistols. Ajay Kumble, Noble Lobo, Amir Kenkda. The next day Parulkar's inspectors were waiting in ambush for our weekly collection run to Darya Mahal Bazaar, where the shop-keepers had their contributions ready. The police party, led by Majid Khan the muchchad, were dressed as labourers. They gave no warning, and fired thirty-four bullets. Vinay Karmarkar, Shailendra Pawar, Ziauddin Qazalbash.

So we fought Suleiman Isa through the summer, and into the monsoon floods. When we collected our bodies from the morgue, carried them through the white waterfalls of water, it seemed as if we had been fighting them for ever, that the war had always existed. They hurt us, but they couldn't kill us. And we ate away at them, we bled them a little every day. Meanwhile Paritosh Shah's Rajhans Airline flew, and he got hair implants because he decided he looked too old on television, and he gave me lectures every day on the power of his dandi-swami. 'You saw how he answered your need. You asked and he gave. Now how can you not believe?' I was tempted to believe. But early in my life, I had seen how belief was an inner rot that hollowed out a man and made him a eunuch. I knew faith was a convenient crutch for cowards and weaklings. No, I wanted no such disease inside me.

So I resisted, I argued coincidence to myself, that the fact that our information had come to us during the puja was clearly a trick of unconnected movements shifting past each other in a way that made sense only to me, random particles bumping themselves into an illusion that seemed like a shape. And what about the thousands of moments in every minute where there were no connections, no sparkling threads of meaning from one event to the next? Paritosh Shah saw Dandi-swami behind the flashing face of every second, he entreated him with gifts and bhajans, and pressured him with stones and charms and secret mantras, and quarrelled with him on occasion. And always he then apologized to Dandi-swami and flew on the wings of his bless-ings. He was convinced that if only I would let go of my resistance and fall into marriage, I would automatically slide into belief. 'Once you are well-settled,' he said, 'all this nonsense will settle itself also. One-two, like that it'll happen.' And he snapped his fingers, one-two. Every day he asked me for my shortlist of girls.

So the year wore on. September, October. In early November Samant called. We had been doing business all during this struggle and had profited mutually, him in cash, me in dead bodies. But it had become harder for us to meet face to face since we had both been writ-ten about in the newspapers. We were trapped by fame. Only Bombay-fame so far, not all-India, but it was enough to make us very careful. So we spoke on the phone, on numbers we changed every week.

What Samant had to say was simple enough. A month after the seizure of my shipment, the government had distributed monies worth almost a fourth of its value to various officers and a certain anonymous informant. We knew that this unnamed bastard was not Khot or his survivors – we had kept a careful watch on them. So who was it, this gaandu who had taken what was mine? Now Samant had a name: 'Kishorilal Ganpat'. I knew the name. All of Bombay did. He was a builder, for ten years now he had spread his constructions across the east of the city. From the highway you could see his build-ings rearing their heads out of the green fields, above the villages and the old colonies. He was big. There had been talk of his dealings with Suleiman, but their interaction had been just ordinary, of the necessary sort, what any builder would have with Suleiman Isa in the normal course of events. Nothing close, nothing special. We ourselves had talked to Kishorilal Ganpat when he needed some help with clearing slums from four residential plots in Andheri. But if he had taken my money, if he had stolen from me, he was closer to Suleiman than anyone had known. This meant he was a banker for Suleiman, that he ate from the same plate as that maderchod.

I thanked Samant, and hung up. His reward would follow later, and we had nothing else to talk about. I had the option to swallow this news quietly, to forget that I had heard it, and I also had the option to act. I kept the information to myself, locked it away in my stomach. I wanted to think it over carefully.

Just before dawn the phone rang again. Another one of ours was dead. This was a boy from Gopalmath itself, a boy I had seen growing up in the lanes I had built. His name was Ravi Rathore, and he had come back on the bus from Aurangabad, where he had relatives. Suleiman Isa's dogs had picked him up in Dadar at the bus station. An ice-cream-wallah had noticed some pushing and shoving. There had been a black van parked near by. At one in the morning someone had noticed a body in a reeking pile of garbage near the highway in Goregaon East and had made an anonymous call to the police. There was a bullet hole in each of Ravi Rathore's thighs, and one in his forehead. We brought back the body, to his kholi, in the late afternoon. He had no relatives in Bombay, so I gave the fire to his pyre. The body in its white shroud was tiny under the wood, under the spray of flame. He had been very skinny, Ravi Rathore, with a chest bent inwards, and his favourite belt with heavy silver buckles used to wrap nearly twice around him. When the boys played cricket on Sundays on the sloping pitch close to the hill, running between the wickets made Ravi Rathore heave and pant. Now he was dead. We burnt him and came home. I sat on my chair, on the terrace, and watched the night come again. This valley we live and die in is a valley of light and shade. We flicker in and out of it. How easily Ravi Rathore gave up his small space in it. I turned away tea, and dinner, and remembered a monsoon long ago, and Ravi Rathore's skinny legs in shorts, paddling in a flooded corner between two twisting lanes. That was what I knew of him, that and his belt and his wheezing enthusiasm for cricket.

'What are you thinking of, bhai?' said Chotta Badriya. He was sitting on the floor, at the end of the terrace.

'Bachcha, what's in the boat?'

'What?'

'I'm thinking of Dandi-swami.'

Chotta Badriya ducked his head down low, rubbed at his ankles. He was trying to decide where my temper was, if he could risk another question. He picked at the roof, took up a flake with his fingernail.

'Leave my house alone,' I said. 'Here's what we're going to do. We're going to sink a boat.'

Kishorilal Ganpat was a great Shiva-bhakta. He thanked Bholenath every morning for all the crores he had swindled, for the bribes he had given, for sand-mixed cement, for shoddy wiring that spilt out of rough-finished walls, for illegal and unlicensed buildings, for encroachments, for extra floors towering far beyond FSI limits, for middle-class money desperate for homes, for starving labour, for slums, for tough, sword-swinging boys, for Suleiman Isa. Kishorilal Ganpat was properly careful in these bad times, so he had two sinewy bodyguards who were so tight-muscled that they walked wide-legged, like somebody had tweaked a rubber band around each of their golis. Kishorilal Ganpat also liked appearances to be just so, so he dressed the driver of his Mercedes in a white suit and a cap, and the two bodyguards in grey safari suits. Kishorilal Ganpat was also a hoarder of time. He collected short-cuts that saved two minutes or three in this jangling maderchod jam of a city, he gave speeches to his employees about Japanese punctuality, he came to the Shiva temple on Satyagrahi Jamunanath Lane every Tuesday morning at eight-thirty precisely, on the 'dot of the dot of eight-thirty', as he liked to point out to anyone listening. All of which made the game childishly easy for us. We set up our fielding. Six boys, six Star pistols. We knew where Shiva sat, on his pedestal, we knew the steps that led down to the lane lined with houses and hawkers, we knew where the Mercedes would wait for its master, we knew where the bodyguards would be. It went smooth, like an oiled lauda into a wet chut. Kishorilal Ganpat came down the steps, holding his prasad aloft on a special silver thali. He had positioned his shoes pointing outwards at the bottom of the steps, and he stepped into them efficiently, saving a good three seconds. The bodyguards were bent over still, their backs to their boss as they pulled on their sandals, and Kishorilal Ganpat was stepping high, skipping over a puddle of water, when my boy Bunty moved sideways and into his path, and Kishorilal Ganpat turned his head to look, and Bunty raised his right arm and blew out Kishorilal Ganpat's left eye. One of the bodyguards reached under his shirt and was cut down. The other sat down on the temple steps and never raised his hands from the stone, which he grasped with whitened fingernails. Meanwhile Kishorilal Ganpat staggered and stumbled at the corners of the lane, from door to door, looking for a way out, any way out. Bunty walked after him, squeezing rounds tenderly into his back and buttocks. Finally Kishorilal Ganpat knelt in front of a vermilion door, under an elegantly painted Om in white, his head down and gaand high in the air, his clothes soaked through with blood, quite dead.

Bunty and the boys walked away, not too fast, not too slow. The exit was as uncomplicated as the job, they got into two cars and left. They then left the two cars on a corner in Malad and got into a van. In three hours they were all out of the city. And those of us who stayed behind grew careful. We knew we had escalated, and so we were prepared. I lived now in three different houses, and went between them at unequal intervals. Paritosh Shah dreamed of flight in a lumbering Mercedes fitted out with armour plate and hardened windows. Chotta Badriya had boys taking strolls through far lanes, watching over our interests. The death of Kishorilal Ganpat moved from the front pages to smaller squares at the back of the newspapers, and then finally disappeared altogether. Apart from two encounters executed by Parulkar's people, which lost us three boys, life went on as ever before. Don't get complacent, I told my boys every day. Don't go to sleep. They aren't sleeping for sure, they're preparing something. It'll come: the axe, the bullet, the fall. It must. We are making war with Suleiman Isa. Suleiman Isa.

Ganesh Gaitonde: the name had a heft, a certain sturdiness. It stood up straight, it didn't back down, it was a strong name. In print it had a certain symmetrical solidity, and it rang on the ear like the double clash of a nagada. People trusted it, and people were afraid of it. And yet: Suleiman Isa. All those hissing 's' sounds, they spoke of cunning. Mean, twisty, rat-skinned cunning. Which caught up with us one morning in late November. I was phoned minutes after it happened. Paritosh Shah left the offices of Rajhans Airlines in his impregnable Mercedes. Security guards swung shut the double gates behind the car as it accelerated tank-like down the lane. In the front seat there was a driver, an old trusted employee, and a bodyguard, not Bada Badriya, who was on a week-long holiday in his village in UP, but a stand-in named Patkar. Paritosh Shah sat in the back, entering names into an electronic diary he had received that morning on special order from Singapore. He wanted to do business from the car, make even more money. The lane from Rajhans swung left on to Ambedkar Road. Just as the Mercedes approached the intersection, a van pulled out behind it, and pressed close. And a truck slammed across the lane, blocking the turn, trapping the Mercedes between its side and the van: no way forward, no way back. The van crashed against the back bumper, shoved the Mercedes forward into the truck. Bullets exploded the rear tires. Then there were two men swinging sledgehammers against the Mercedes' left rear window, which, for all its bullet-proof hardening, starred and curved concave under the blows. The bodyguard had his pistol out, but there was a man pointing an AK-47 at him through the window. To protect Paritosh Shah, Patkar had to lower the window, which would let in the AK-47. The bodyguard pointed his pistol, but the front window stayed up. Meanwhile the sledgehammers crunched on the back window. Paritosh Shah flopped about on the back seat and stabbed his car phone with scrabbling fingers. Then, at the top of a large inward bulge in the rear window, a small hole crumbled open under the sledgehammers, a hole about the size of a rupee coin. Enough for a muzzle to press in, a second AK-47. An entire magazine was fired into the car. The bodyguard tried to fire, to shoot at the braying blaze that sprayed into the inside of the Mercedes, but his bullets stopped nothing, and may themselves have bounced around on the inside of the car.

My boys tried to stop me from going there, from going to my friend. I shoved them aside and drove myself. I was there minutes after the police arrived, and they at least didn't try to stop me. The rear and side windows of the Mercedes were webbed crystalline, smeared on the inside with a dark jelly. The front left door was open. The driver had survived, and had crawled over the dead bodyguard to get out after the booming fire had stopped. I leaned into the car, rested a hand on the satiny leather of the front headrest, and looked into the leg-space at the back. There was no Paritosh Shah there. There was a mass of deflated flesh, punctured and holed and ripped. There was no face there. Under a broad forehead, a splintered bowl of uncooked meat, shards of sharp white bone. No Paritosh Shah. He could never have fitted into that small flume behind the seat, not Paritosh Shah, not my fat man. But there was a hand with rings, with shiny protective stones. Here was a foot, still in its new tasselled burgundy loafer. He had said that word to me, with much indulgent patience: 'Not red, bhai, that's called *burgundy*. Burr-gandy.' Here was a styled thatch of dark hair. But where was Paritosh Shah? Not here.

I went to his house, where the women said nothing to me. Yet I felt their hate. He had died because of me. He had died for me. I had killed him. Nobody dared say it, but it needed no saying. When his body lay in the courtyard, wrapped in white sheets, covered everywhere, while his daughters wailed, nobody said it. Near the heat of the pyre nobody said it. I went back to Gopalmath without hearing it said, and yet it echoed along each whistle of my breath, each squeeze of my pulse. I drank whisky. I told the boys to bring me something, anything, as long as it was here, right now. Now. My throat burnt from the whisky and I saw myself dying. I was knifed, sabred, shot, hanged. My body fell. And then fell again. Bullets separated my elbows, cut my torso in half. I welcomed each fall. Where was death? This life squeezed my head in its iron hoop. Paritosh Shah's plump flesh emptied of blood, of air. How life lets out. How it goes. Does the spillage make a sound? Or was there only the breaking crack of the bullets? I raised my hand, brought it close to my eyes, pressed my face into the springy growth of hair on the forearm, felt the life in it. Each follicle was alive. A turn of my other wrist broke the whisky glass on a bedpost. With a splinter shaped like a half-moon I cut at the ridge of muscle under my clenched fist. Through the serried stalks of the hair I went, and the blood seeped noiselessly. I turned the arm, and there was the bumping of the pulse on the wrist. Easy to cut, to cease. How easy.

And then I was disgusted with myself. Paritosh Shah had lived. He had lived fully, he had fed his women, his children, his hundreds of employees. He had fed the world, and even as he had died, he had fought to dial his phone, to say something. He had tried to call me. I knew this. Not his wife, not his children, it was me. What would he have said, through that miraculous leap of electricity, over the distance? Death was already on him, and I could not have saved him. He must have known that. What would he have said, at the end? To me, his friend? I looked into the broken curve of glass, speckled with my blood, and I knew. I crawled to the other end of the bed, found the pile of photographs. From the middle of the stack, without looking, by feel alone, I pulled one. And I called to the boys.

'That's the one I want,' I said to Chotta Badriya, who was sitting with half a dozen others, cleaning his pistol. They were all puzzled. They had been expecting a war meeting. Whenever we had lost someone in this fight, after the funeral we always gathered to pick our hits for the next day, the next week. Who to kill, and how, that's what we talked about. But now I wanted a woman.

Chotta Badriya picked up the photograph from the table, where I had dropped it. 'Now, bhai?'

'No, no, not like that.' I could see he thought I wanted a midnight ride, a quick relieving of my tensions, but this was a respectable-looking girl, and he was puzzled. I thumped him gently on the shoulder. 'Not that, dhakkan. Paritosh Bhai wanted this. And Dandi-swami. I want to marry her.'

Her name was Subhadra Devalekar, and I married her four days later. At first, her father thought it callous that I should marry so soon after my friend's death. I know most of my boys felt this also. But I explained, that this was my friend's last wish, and then they remembered all his lectures, his shortlist, his nagging. A rumour appeared out of nowhere, and hardened into a certainty, that he had actually called me from the Mercedes, as the hammer-blows had rung on his life, and managed to say to me, 'You must marry.' So by the time we walked around the fire, Subhadra and I, our marriage had become an act of adherence to a dead friend's last wish. The boys came out, in their dozens and dozens, from all over the city, and watched our austere ceremony at Gopalmath temple with moistening eyes, with ready pistols, with ferocious loyalty.

After the ceremony we sat in front of the house and the people of Gopalmath came to pay their respects. Subhadra's father collected envelopes. He was a bus conductor who had retired from the 523 route, and he had four daughters. He had been hesitant at first when Chotta Badriya had come calling, after all the afternoon tabloids were still publishing pictures of the 'Death Mercedes', but a stack of five-hundred-rupee bricks on his tea tray had persuaded him. Daughters are a care. Now the bus conductor stood to my right and took the gift envelopes from the line of well-wishers. Bada Badriya came forward with a fat red envelope. He had rushed back from his village as soon as we had contacted him, and was still ashamed at letting his boss out of his care, I could see that. But he hadn't been back to his village for five years, and what had happened was no fault of his. I told him that and hugged him.

And then I was sitting on a bed, a bed strewn with rose petals. A song played somewhere, a flute threaded through it. On a corner of the bed there was a huddled red tent of a sari, holding within it a trembling, skinny body. My wife. I was married. My head was floaty, as if I had just woken from a long dream. I asked: how did this happen? There was no answer.

Old Pain

Mary Mascarenas was ready to talk. Sartaj waited for her, alone, across the road from the Pali Hill parlour in which she worked. The road down the slope was alive with expensively dressed teenagers, boys careening through in sleek cars bought by their rich fathers, girls in swirling groups of three and four. Sartaj was waiting next to a cigarette stall, near a row of servants and drivers having their evening smoke and gossip. He had called Mary that morning, told her gently that he would like to speak to her. After work, she had said, and there had been no more anger in her voice, just resignation. So Sartaj was confident that he would get good information: she would need to explain now, to herself, what had happened, and why. He had come a little early, and now the drivers were talking about stock prices and the fortunes of companies. Drivers knew more than anybody else, they listened in on Saab and Memsaab's conversations in the car, they knew their movements, they carried documents and cash. Sartaj watched the flirtations between the boys and girls, and tried to keep an ear on the stock conversation, for Katekar's sake. Katekar didn't gamble, but he insisted that the market was logical, you only had to know the rules. If you could feel the rhythms, you could be king. All you needed was information and education. So Sartaj listened, but the drivers knew more than him, and he could make no sense of their lively arguments. Their very glossy memsaabs came out from the salon, and the little flock of drivers contracted and expanded, but their banter never flagged. They smoked cigarettes and ate from little packets of channa. They were well-paid, these drivers, and smartly turned-out, in keeping with the status of their employers.

It was past seven when Mary came through the blue glass door of the salon. She was wearing a black T-shirt, a slim black skirt to the knee and black flats. Her hair was pulled back into a ponytail, and

Sartaj was suddenly struck by her elegance. She was all quietness, and if you stood her in a row next to these teenage queens strutting past her, you wouldn't notice her. Not unless you were looking for that straight back, that symmetry of the shoulders with both hands on a black purse. She saw him, and he raised a hand.

He walked over to her side of the road, to the gleam of expensive shops, Gurlz, Expressions, Emotions. 'I'm late, sorry,' Mary said. 'There is some big party at the Taj tonight. I had three extra appointments.'

'Taj party definitely needs extra-fancy hair.'

'I have never been, so I don't know. But I can do the hair.'

Her Hindi was accented, functional and fluid, but improvised, it stumbled confidently past feminine possessives and tenses. Sartaj was sure her English was better, but his own English had rusted into awkwardness. They would get by in some knocked-together mixture, some Bombay blend. We're all right in these khichdi tongues, he thought. 'My car is over there,' he said. On the phone she hadn't wanted him coming to her place of work, and he had reassured her that he wouldn't be in uniform, he wouldn't be driving a police jeep, that he would be alone. He reversed out into the road as the drivers watched, and then waited for Mary to get in. 'We'll go down to Carter Road,' he said, and she nodded. She wouldn't want her neighbours wondering either, about visits from policemen, or strange Sikhs.

He found a curve far down on the sea-wall, a gravelly shoulder a little less occupied by hawkers and strolling lovers and beggars. 'That ship's gone completely,' he said. 'Not even a little bit left. What was it called?'

There had been a foreign freighter that had been forced aground with a dead engine by a monsoon storm. It had become something of a tourist attraction for a while, its hull far up out of the water. Very late one night, Sartaj had sat on a bench facing the ship and kissed Megha. They had separated not long after.

'It was the *Zhen Don*,' Mary said. 'They cut it up for scrap. It's been gone for years.'

'I thought they were going to turn it into an offshore hotel.'

'It was worth more as scrap.' The sky was the same indeterminate grey it had been for two days, and under it were the vague shapes of foreign ships, skimming the horizon. Mary turned her head towards Sartaj. 'I read in the papers you were supposed to have a policewoman present when you interrogated a woman.'

'I'm not interrogating,' Sartaj said. 'You're not a suspect. Nobody is a suspect. I'm just trying to understand what happened, why your sister was there. And I didn't think you would want to talk in front of more people. This is just a sort of private conversation. What you tell me remains with me.'

'I don't have anything to tell you.'

'You don't have anything to say about your sister?'

'I haven't seen her for a long time. Not talked to her for, for years.'

'Why? You had a fight?'

'We had a fight.'

'About what?'

'Why do you need to know?'

'It might show me what sort of woman she was.'

'Which will show you how she got to that place?'

'Maybe.'

'She was not a bad woman.'

She was anxious, squeezed up as far from him as she could get on the grimy blue seat. Looking at her little black bag, which she had placed between them, Sartaj realized that she was afraid of him, of the parking on the sea-wall, of what she thought he might demand of her. That's why she had asked about the policewoman. He was used to people being afraid of his uniform, but the idea that this woman thought that he might assault her sickened him. He fumbled for the ignition, and changed gears with a metallic scraping. He drove fast down the road and stopped near the thick of the evening walkers, right next to a boisterous group of teenagers eating ice-cream. Mary was watching him wide-eyed.

'I need some narial-pani,' he said. 'And understand, I'm not going to harm you. I just want to talk to you. Clear?'

She nodded, and watched him intently as he beckoned to a hawker and paid for two coconuts. She held hers in both hands and drank from it in great thirsty gulps until it was finished. Sartaj held out his. 'Want more?'

'No,' she said, and she was relieved, not quite easy yet but not cringing away from him any more.

Sartaj sipped at his narial, and watched her, and waited.

'My sister was fifteen when she first came to Bombay,' Mary said. She was looking out of her window, towards the slow rumbling of the sea. 'I lived in Colaba with my husband. She came to stay with us. We grew up on my mother's farm outside Mangalore. Our father died when I was eleven. I got married, moved to Bombay. So Jojo came to stay with John and me. She was young, but she said she wanted to be a nurse, and the school in our village was just a village school. She had passed her tenth exams, first class. She wanted to learn English and be a nurse. We had only a tiny place, but she slept on the sofa, and after all, she was my little sister. She was so small and thin, in those days. She used to wear three little ponytails. I thought she was watching too much television, I told John that. She used to sit in front of it, cross-legged, all day and night. But he said it was good for her, she needed to learn English and Hindi. He used to tease her and make her laugh, telling her that she knew only the jingles, Vico-Vajradanti! He said she could only talk about teeth and hair. But she was very intelligent, you know. Day by day she picked it all up. After a while she wasn't scared to do all the shopping. I had a full-time sales job at a leather-goods store, so having her there at home helped a lot. She was suddenly so confident. And she stopped wearing those print skirts, her hair changed, her walk became different. In six months she became somebody else. A Bombay girl. Then one day she started talking about acting. She used to imitate the heroines of the movies and serials, and the VJs. I can do that, she said. At first I just laughed and forgot about it. Then she said it again and again. John paid attention. He said, she's right, you know. Look at her. She's as good as any of them, better. Why shouldn't she be able to do it? He was right. She sparkled. I hadn't seen it, she was my little sister, but without her ponytails she was a star. She stood in front of the mirror on the cupboard, and she watched herself in the apartment windows. Now I saw how the neighbours watched her, when she ran down the stairs to get bread in the mornings. The boys from down the street waited for her in the evenings, just for her to walk by. I started to believe it too, that summer. Every heroine came from somewhere, after all. Nobody was born with the lights on their faces. This one was from Bangalore, that one from Lucknow. Some of them had come from very ordinary families. Now they had money, they had fame. So why not Jojo? Why not my sister? We were all caught up in it, in that fantasy. We had seen it come true for other girls. So why not Jojo? John had a friend who worked for MTV, as an accountant only. But this accountant knew people at the channel. So John took an afternoon off work and took Jojo to Andheri East, to meet some people at MTV. They caught the train, and then an auto-rickshaw. They came back all excited. The MTV executive, an Englishman, said that she was charming and beautiful. Imagine. She didn't get a job out of that, but just getting a meeting with somebody so important was thrilling. Such a huge distance, from our little flat to MTV, and they had crossed it all in one afternoon. The impossible was possible. So then the summer was over, and Jojo was enrolled in school, but school didn't seem that important. She was taking dance classes, and acting classes. She was talking to producers, directors. John took her sometimes, often, to these meetings in Bandra, in Juhu, in Film City. At his work they were concerned, then they were upset. I worried. But he said, big rewards need big risks. We need to see far ahead, and not be afraid. Don't be afraid. And I tried not to be afraid. But I was. I was afraid for Jojo. I saw how much she believed in her future. Everyone struggles, she said. You have to struggle. Aishwarya struggled, even Madhubala struggled. So I have to struggle, Jojo said. But finally I will win, she said. I will.'

A luxurious breeze came in from the sea, fluttered the sari of a walking woman in a swell of purple, stirred Mary's hair across her eyes. But she was far away, speaking not to him but to herself.

'We were all caught up in the struggle. I saved money for Jojo's lessons. John was always phoning his new MTV-type friends, keeping in touch. He was a new John also. I hadn't seen such excitement in him for a long time. I went with them, John and Jojo, to one or two of these filmi and television parties. Parties with the famous faces of television. Archana Puran Singh here, Vijayendra Ghatge there. I saw how John shook hands and laughed, how he hugged and thumped backs. That night in bed he held me and explained to me. This is how it works in this business. This is how you get jobs. It's all about contacts, it's all about goodwill. That's how it goes. That's how we spent that year, on the edge of something big. That's what it felt like. Jojo got one modelling job, and then a second. The first one was a small television ad for Dabur shoes, she was dancing with two other girls on a divider in the middle of a highway. We had the television on, waiting on a Tuesday night to see it. How we screamed when suddenly she was there. Jojo on television, dancing. We danced, and John had got a small airline bottle of champagne from his accountant friend, he opened it and we all drank straight from the bottle. After that dance on the highway, we were so sure. Nothing can stop us now. Only a matter of time. John said that all the time, only a matter of time. But nothing came. Jojo was tantalized by endless meetings, "Come back and see us again, we are still thinking," but then somehow it was always the other girl. She used to think and talk about it endlessly, why not me? She and John talked about clothes, make-up, attitude. Next time we'll do this. Next time it'll be like this. They planned and planned. Next time. And then I caught them.'

She stopped short, and wiped the hair away from her face. She was looking away from him, but she was with him now, no longer in memory.

'Caught?' Sartaj said very quietly.

She cleared her throat. 'I was at work. I started feeling very sick, weak. There was a viral fever going around at that time. Everyone had it. You could feel the temperature on my skin. The shop-owner said, go home. So I went home. They were in my bed.'

There was danger always in this moment, when the subject first revealed her or his humiliation. Too heavy a touch, even of sympathy, and you would lose them as they curled up around their exposed pain, closed up and hid all the essential detail. 'I understand,' Sartaj said. 'He must have tried to say it was all right, that nothing had changed.'

At this she was faintly startled, surprised by him, and now he could see the glisten of her pupils. 'Yes,' she said. 'I think he had some idea that we could all live happily together. That I would keep working for them, making the money to dress both of them and send them to their meetings.'

'And she?'

'She . . . she was angry at me. As if I had done something wrong. "I love him," she said. She kept saying that. I love him. As if I didn't. I finally said that. He's my husband, I said. And she said, no, you don't love him. You can't. She was screaming. And I was so angry. To hear my sister say that. To know what my sister and my husband had done. Get out, I said to her. Go away.'

'Then?'

'He left with her. He came back two days later to get their clothes.'

'Yes.'

'Then we divorced. It was very difficult. I couldn't pay the rent. I tried to get into the women's hostel, but they had no space. For a while I stayed at the YWCA. Then I had to live in a jhopadpatti, in Bandra East. All kinds of places I've seen.'

'You didn't want to go home?'

288

'To my mother? To that house I grew up in, with Jojo? No, I couldn't live there. I couldn't go back.'

So even a slum was better, better than that home left far behind. 'You have a good place now,' Sartaj said.

'It took a long time. I started in this salon cleaning the hair from the floor, washing the scissors and combs.'

'Did you see her again?'

'Two, three times. The judge makes you go to counselling before they let you get a divorce. She was there to meet him afterwards. I didn't speak to her. Then I saw her when the judge granted the divorce.'

'And after that?'

'I heard about them once or twice, from relatives and friends. They were living in Goregaon. Still trying to get her into films, anything. I saw her on television once, some advertisement for saris. Bas, that was it.'

'You never spoke to her again?'

'No. My mother was very angry at her also. Ma was sick, and Jojo tried to get in touch, but Ma said no, she didn't want to speak to her, to that sinful, shameless girl. She died without ever speaking to Jojo. And I didn't really want to know anything about Jojo.'

'So, not even a little news from somewhere?'

She shook her head. 'Once. Maybe two, three years ago. I have an aunt in Bangalore. My mother's sister. She said she saw Jojo at the airport.'

'Your aunty spoke to her?'

'No. She knew what she had done.'

'Jojo was getting on a plane?'

'Yes. She must have made money. I don't know how. I don't know anything about her. About what happened to her.'

What happened to her. How an ambitious, lovelorn teenager became a trader in bodies, how she ended up dead, murdered by a suicidal bhai. He didn't know how, but he could imagine it, the descent from filmi parties into many kinds of underworld. 'We also have very little information about her,' he said. 'She worked in television, produced some shows. There were some other activities.'

'Activities?'

'We are investigating. When we know more, I will tell you. If you hear anything, anything at all, please call me.' She would, Sartaj thought. She had a certain hope in him now. From these little scraps, these fragments, maybe she could reconstruct her sister, and forgive her, and herself. 'I'm glad you spoke to me,' he said.

'She was a sweet girl,' Mary said. 'When we were small, she was scared of thunder. She used to crawl into my side of the bed late at night and push her head into my stomach and sleep.'

Sartaj nodded. Yes, Jojo was also that scared little girl, holding on to her sister. It was a good thing to know. He drove Mary home. From the car, he watched her climb the stairs to her room. The light went on inside, and he reversed out into the main road. On the way home, as he veered left into the curve at Juhu Chowpatty, it began to rain.

Iffat-bibi called Sartaj just as he was finishing his dinner of Afghan chicken and tandoori roti from the Sardar's Grill down the road. 'Saab, I have an answer.'

'To my question?'

'Yes. Bunty was thokoed by two freelance shooters.'

'Working for whom?'

'Nobody. It was personal. Bunty took a girl from one of them some three, four years ago.'

'Took?'

'She liked Bunty's money better than the freelancer. This idiot free-lancer was in love with her.'

So Bunty had died for a woman, not land or gold. Or for anything to do with Ganesh Gaitonde. 'Okay,' Sartaj said. Bunty had wounded a lover, and the lover had waited and nursed his anger and been patient until Bunty's fortunes fell into steep decline. 'Okay.'

'You want them?'

'Who?'

'The freelancers. We know where they are right now, where they will spend the night. Where they will be tomorrow.'

'You want to give them to me?'

'Yes.'

'Why?'

'Think of it as just a gift between new friends.' Her Urdu was impeccable, and her voice could go cushiony and soft.

Sartaj got up, stretched and walked to the balcony. He leaned over the railing, and watched the treetops swaying in the damp breeze. The lamps threw the shadows of their leaves across the smooth surfaces of the cars.

'Saab?'

'Iffat-bibi, I am not worthy of such a gift. You have an old relationship with Parulkar Saab. Why don't you give it to him? I don't handle these bhai and company and shooter matters.'

'Is this true? Or do you think I am not worthy of giving you something?'

'Arre, no, Bibi. I am just afraid that when the time comes, I will have nothing equal to give you in return. I am a small man.'

She made a smacking sound full of exasperation. 'The son is just like the father. All right, all right.'

'Bibi, I meant no offence.'

'I know. But really, I used to tell this to Sardar Saab also, how will you get ahead if you don't make the big deals? And he always said, "Iffat-bibi, I have flown as high as I can. Let my son go further."'

'He said that?'

'Yes, he spoke about you often. I remember when you passed your twelfth, he distributed sweets. Pedas and burfis.'

Sartaj remembered the pedas, the saffrony taste of them that contained all the future. 'Maybe I am like him also, yes. Parulkar Saab moved ahead.'

'Yes, with Sardar Saab's help all the time. Parulkar was a sharp one from the beginning, see. Always thinking, thinking. There was this case, a robbery gang on the docks.'

She told him then about this gang, which had people on the inside and outside of the docks. They pilfered goods, of course, but they also took equipment and fuel, anything worth a little money. Parulkar had broken the case, with lots of Sardar Saab's help, his contacts and sources, all of which Sardar Saab was glad to give him. But when the time came for arrests, Parulkar let a senior inspector take the apradhis in and enjoy all the credit. 'It would have been a big case for Parulkar, but he saw ahead, see? Lose some heavy arrests now, but profit later.'

'He's fast like that.'

'How fast, you don't even know. But you haven't learnt much from him.' He knew she was smiling, and couldn't help smiling back.

'What to do, Bibi? We are who we are.'

'Yes, we are as Allah makes us.'

They said their farewells, and Sartaj went back to picking at his chicken. He was craving a peda, but it was late and he was tired. He comforted himself with another shot of whisky, and promised himself two pedas at lunch. He was sure it was going to be a good day.

By the next morning the rain had turned into one of those endless monsoon drenchings that felt as if the sky had collapsed under the weight of water. Sartaj ran from the car to the station, and by the time he was under cover his shoulders were drenched. He could feel the water inside his shoes.

'Your girlfriend's waiting for you, Sartaj Saab,' Kamble said from his perch on the first-floor balustrade above. He was leaning out, head close to the smooth fall of water from the roof, a cigarette in one hand.

'Kamble, my friend,' Sartaj said, 'you are full of bad habits and bad beliefs.' He had to raise his voice to be heard above the drumming of the water on the bricks. Kamble grinned back at him, very comfortable with his badness. By the time Sartaj got up the stairs, he was lighting another cigarette and he had his answer ready.

'Sometimes you need a bad one like me, Sartaj Saab,' he said, 'for all the bad work that has to be done in this world.'

'Since when have you become a philosopher, chutiya? You never needed any excuses before, so don't start blaming the world now. Who is waiting?'

'Arre, your CBI girlfriend, boss. You have so many you don't know which one is coming to visit?'

Anjali Mathur was at the station. 'Where?' Sartaj said.

'Parulkar Saab's office.'

'And is Parulkar Saab there?'

'No, he got a call, he had to rush to a meeting with the CM at the Juhu Centaur.'

'With the CM. Very impressive.'

'Our Parulkar Saab is a very impressive man. But I don't think he likes your chavvi very much, Sartaj Saab. I just see something in his look. Maybe he wants her also.'

Sartaj thumped Kamble on the shoulder. 'You have a very dirty mind. Let me see what this is about.' He walked down the corridor. Kamble was indeed dirty, but maybe it was just that he took more pleasure in the same dirt that everyone was swimming in. He certainly understood the politics of the station, and knew everything that went on in it. Sartaj nodded at Sardesai, Parulkar's PA, who waved him towards Parulkar's door. Sartaj knocked and went in. Anjali Mathur was sitting alone on the sofa at the rear of the room, at the end furthest from Parulkar's desk.

'Namaste, madam,' Sartaj said.

'Namaste,' she said. 'Please sit.'

Sartaj sat and told her what he had learned from Mary, which was very little. As usual, she took in the news, such as it was, and then stayed perfectly still. She was deliberating. Today she was in a dark red salwar-kameez. Wine-coloured, Sartaj thought. An interesting hue on her dark-brown skin, but it was loose, and covered her quite impersonally. There was no cut there, no personality. She carried her face the same way, shut off. Not hostile, just guarded, closed.

'Shabash,' she said. 'Every little thing is important. You know that. You never know what will open up a case. Now, I have two things to tell you. One, that Delhi has decided to halt this investigation. We were interested in Ganesh Gaitonde's return to Mumbai, the reasons for it, what he wanted here. But from what we have found out so far, Delhi doesn't think there's enough there to justify further enquiries. Frankly, nobody cares. They say, Gaitonde is dead, he's finished.'

'But you don't think he's finished.'

'I don't understand why he was here, why he killed himself, what he was looking for. Who he was looking for. But I have been called back to Delhi. There are more important things to work on, it is felt.'

'At the national level.'

'Yes. At the national level. But I would appreciate it very much if you would continue looking into the matter a little. I appreciate very much your hard work. If you could continue, maybe we would have some answers to our questions.'

'Why are you so interested in Ganesh Gaitonde? He was a common gangster. He's dead.'

She thought for a moment, considered her options. 'There is not much I am allowed to tell you. But I am interested in him because he was connected to certain very important people, to events at a national level. Whatever brought him back here, that could have an effect on future events.'

And you want me to risk my head under these huge juggernauts, Sartaj thought. You want me to put my golis in the path of those oncoming, grinding wheels. You want to involve me in Research and Analysis Wing matters. International intrigue, derring-do in foreign

lands, desi James Bonds. He knew the agency existed somewhere, he
had been told it did exist, but it was all very fantastic and very far
from his very ordinary life. He had never really felt it was real, all that
sinister spy stuff. And yet here was serious, small Anjali Mathur, in
her dark red salwar-kameez, sitting on the sofa a few feet from him.
And she was interested in the death and life of Ganesh Gaitonde.

The next question was obvious, but Sartaj kept himself from asking
it: why does RAW have an interest in our friend Ganesh Gaitonde at
all? Maybe some of the important people that Gaitonde had connections with were in RAW, maybe some mutual dealings had existed
between the agency and Gaitonde, but Sartaj didn't want to know. He
didn't want to be in this room any more, with quiet Anjali Mathur. He
wanted to be back in his own life. 'Yes,' he said. 'Very true.' He was
quiet. These RAW things happened far away from him, as they
should. He didn't have any questions, he didn't want answers. He was
done.

'I have to go back,' Anjali Mathur said finally. 'To Delhi. But I
would be grateful if you would continue to investigate this issue. For
you to do so would be completely logical, expected. If you learn anything, here is my number in Delhi. Please call me.'

He took the card, and stood up. 'I will,' he said.

She nodded, but he knew she saw his nerviness, his desire to be out
of the room, away. Outside, Kamble was sitting on the visitor's bench,
one leg crossed comfortably over the other. 'So what happened, boss?'
he said with his customary leer.

'Nothing,' Sartaj said. 'Absolutely nothing. Nothing happened.
Nothing will.'

Ordinary life had its own savoury pleasures. Sartaj was eating a very
hot chicken Hyderabadi with Kamble when his mobile rang and
began to skid slowly across the table. Sartaj nudged it back with a
knuckle, and saw that Wasim Zafar Ali Ahmad was calling. 'Arre, tissue, tissue!' he called to the waiter and thumbed the phone. 'Hold,' he
managed to get out before a cough caught at his throat.

'Saab, take a sip of water,' Wasim Zafar Ali Ahmad said paternally
when Sartaj finally got the phone up to his ear.

'What do you want?'

'You are eating lunch, saab. I have your dessert.'

'The Bihari and the boys?'

'Yes.'

'Where? When?'

'They are coming tonight after midnight to collect money from a receiver.'

'After midnight, when?'

'I only know that the meeting is after midnight, saab. Maybe they are being careful. But I have an exact address.'

Sartaj wrote down the street and the landmarks and the name of the receiver. Wasim was very exact indeed. 'Saab, there are many kholis on the track side of the road, and there are always people moving around there, even late at night. So you must go in carefully, otherwise there will be trouble.'

'Chutiya, we have done a thousand of these arrests. This one will be nothing special.'

'Yes, yes, saab. Of course you are the master of these matters. I didn't mean . . .'

'All that matters is that the information should be good. Is the information good?'

'Saab, it is solid. You don't even know what I went through to get it.'

'Don't tell me. Keep your mobile on tonight.'

'Yes, saab.'

Sartaj put down the phone. He took up his tandoori roti and ate a large mouthful of chicken. It was delicious. 'What are you doing tonight?' he said to Kamble.

Sartaj and Katekar were waiting. They were in disguise, in tattered banians and dirty pants and old rubber-soled keds. Sartaj had an old patka draped loosely over his hair and tucked behind his ears, and thought that he looked like a rather debonair, dashing thela-wallah. They were sitting, reclining, under a thela pushed up on the pavement, across the road from a barred iron fence that edged the railway tracks. Katekar was complaining about the crowds on the trains. 'This country is hopeless,' he said. 'People push out babies with no more thought than street dogs making puppies. That's why nothing works, all progress is eaten up by new mouths. How can there be development?' This was one of his favourite themes. Any moment now he would start advocating a scientific dictatorship, universal registration and identity cards, and a strict birth-control policy. But now they were both silent as a train clattered by, going up the line, almost empty. During the day pods of men hung from the doors, swelling out over the rushing tracks, suspended by fingertips and toes. 'Almost one hour since the last train,' Katekar said. It was almost two-thirty. 'You watch. One heavy rain and trains will stop. This chutiya central line, if ten schoolboys stand in a row and piss on the tracks, bhenchod service is disrupted.'

Sartaj nodded. All this was true, and it was a restful pleasure to lie under a thela and complain. They had already complained about the municipality, corporators, transfers of honest civil servants and policemen, expensive mangoes, traffic, too much construction, collapsing buildings, clogged drains, unruly and uncivilized Parliament, extortion by Rakshaks, bad movies, nothing worthwhile to watch on television, American interference in subcontinental affairs, the disappearance of Rimzim from soft-drink stands, inter-state quarrelling over river waters, the lack of good English-language schools for children whose parents didn't have truckloads of money, the depiction of police on the movie screen, long unpaid hours on the job, the job, and the job. When you had complained enough about everything else, there was always the job, with its unspeakable hours, its monotony, its political complications, its thanklessness, its exhaustion.

Sartaj yawned. Near the iron fence, there was a rank of kholis with tin roofs. Some of the kholis were two-storeyed, and had leaning ladders, posts with pegs really, to allow access to the upper levels. There was a sturdy-looking pucca house about two-thirds of the way down the row, new and unfinished. A light burned behind a newspapered window in one of these upper storeys, and that room was where the apradhis were expected tonight. Not far from the lighted window, at the far end of the kholis, PSI Kamble and four constables were wrapped in sheets on the pavement, trying to look like tired labourers deep and fast in their sleep. Sartaj was quite sure they were complaining. On that side of the kholis, there was a sloping ridge of rubbish, its top higher than a tall man's head, banked up against a brick wall. Sartaj had passed it many times over the last few years, this noisome mountain, and it had grown and shrunk many times but never disappeared, and now at this far distance, he could see the bright neon blue, green and yellow of plastic bags winking from its archaeological layers. As senior officer on the operation he had the privilege of avoiding the gigantic stink, so Kamble and his fellows lay directly under its influence, and Sartaj knew they were cursing him. The thought of Kamble holding a perfumed handkerchief to his nose gave Sartaj a smile.

Now Katekar stopped in mid-complaint. Two men were coming up the street, leaning against each other's shoulders. 'Drunks,' Katekar said, and he was right. These men were only two, and it was unlikely that the actual apradhis would stagger drunk to a meeting with a receiver to collect money. Still, Sartaj stiffened, watched. The drunks went by, giggling. Down the road and three lanes to the left there was a country bar and a gambling den. Men went from one to the other and then went home. These two were happy, which only meant that they would wake up in the morning to find out what they had lost. Sartaj watched them go, feeling the warm tingle of anticipatory satisfaction moving up his shoulders. He would get the apradhis tonight. He would take the bastards in, and then he would sleep well afterwards. He had done well by Wasim Zafar Ali Ahmad, and now it was his turn to gain.

Katekar had, for the moment, run out of things to complain about, so now he was telling a police story. In the old days, he said, during the very early part of his service, he had known a hoary old inspector named Talpade. This Talpade was wizened and gnarled, stained not only by the paan he chewed incessantly, but also by the four corruption cases he had fought off and survived. It was said – and generally believed – that he had killed more than a dozen innocent men during his career, shot them dead during riots and encounters. He had once beaten an apradhi to death in the lock-up, and had been suspended for eleven months before he managed to extricate himself from the bloodspattered mess, mainly by scattering money up and down the chain of command until even his most ardent admirers and enemies marvelled.

Two years before his retirement, Talpade fell in love with a dancer. There was something admirable about a man that age gripped by a great passion. Of course he was ridiculous: he had new clothes tailored, his mehndi hair now was suddenly jet-black, his teeth gleamed an unearthly white. But you had to recognize and respect the completeness of his devotion. He went every night to worship at the altar of his beloved, he brought her home from the bar where she worked, he gave her messages from her lovers. Yes, she had other men, younger ones and more handsome, but Talpade accepted this pain as the price of his proximity to her, and suffered it with humble gratitude. He was transformed. There was something new moving under the age-old creases on his face, under the bitter valleys – you only had to spend a minute with him to know it was joy.

The force laughed at him. It was not his aged-rooster's walk or the new dark glasses he sported. The problem was that he loved Kukoo ('just like that actress from long ago'), and as Talpade told anyone who would stop and listen, Kukoo was as beautiful as a Kashmiri apple, and nobody could deny the fragile and fatal charm of Kukoo's nakhras. But she was a man. She said she was nineteen, but she had danced at various bars for the last five years, so it was more likely that she was twenty-five, at the very least twenty-two or so. She had luxurious straight hair to the small of her back, lightened to a striking almost-golden, a pert bottom of astonishing roundness, and opulent lips that deserved a poem of their very own. But there was never any doubt that Kukoo was a man. She never attempted to hide this. She had a slim, long chest, and her voice was husky. But she still accumulated a following as she moved from bar to bar, increasing her earnings each time.

So why had Talpade become such a majnoo for Kukoo? Was he, after all – despite his long marriage and three children – a gaandu, literally? Most of the men and women in the force believed so. But his friends, and those close to Kukoo, knew that Talpade never touched her. Not that she would have refused, no, Kukoo had a finely developed sense of how far you could tease a man, and above all she was practical. She knew when to be shy and when to be very forward. But Talpade didn't want to catch her and squeeze her and take her, he was content to sit at his regular table, just to the left of the dance floor, and look at her. On the sparkling silver of the dance floor, she was indeed something to look at, floating on the whirling lotus of her ghagra, her waist turning like a slender fall of water. Under those cunning black and red lights she was more beautiful than any other girl in the bar, more graceful than any woman on the street outside. Talpade sat and drank Old Monk and watched Kukoo. He gave her money just before he left, never called her to his table to take the cash like other men, never expected anything but an occasional glance and smile. He was happy to talk to friends who came into the club, he joked with the waiters, his concentration on Kukoo was not one-pointed or obsessive enough to be frightening, but it was obvious that he cared only about her.

His best friend, David, got sloppy drunk one night, grabbed Talpade's hand and said, 'Bastard, come, touch that thing between her legs. Then you'll know what she is.'

Talpade said, 'I know she's not a woman.'

'So then?'

'I like looking at her.'

'Tell me why.'

'It just feels good.'

And that's all he would say. David cursed Talpade for subjecting himself to open ridicule, for spending money and getting nothing, for plain stupidity. Talpade smiled and went back to watching Kukoo.

Two months later, Kukoo called David. She told him that Talpade was now weeping as he watched her. He had been doing this for the last three nights, watching her for hours as usual, and then, very late, crying without a sound or any indication that he was unhappy. 'Now he has finally gone mad,' Kukoo said. She wanted the friend to get Talpade away from her. He was depressing her with his big watery eyes, and offending the other customers, who came to have fun, not to mourn.

This time, David asked gently, 'Why?' And Talpade said, 'She reminds me of my childhood.'

They took him out of the bar, took him home, put him to sleep. The family brought in doctors, kept a careful watch over Talpade, comforted him and made him take his prescribed rest. He went back to work two Mondays later, and that same night he was at the Golden Palace, where Kukoo was dancing now. This time, when he began his usual tamasha, she had the bouncers take him out, followed them on to the road and screamed at Talpade, 'Don't follow me.' Once she had been afraid of him, but now she couldn't help herself. 'Bastard, making drama out of nothing. I don't want to see your face again.'

Talpade obeyed her. He never tried to see her again. He went about his life, but he was a listless man, emptied of all his ferocious force and energy. He died four months later, peacefully passing in his sleep.

Sartaj sighed. That was the end of the story. Like all the other police stories Katekar liked to tell, this one stopped suddenly and remained enigmatic, refusing to give up a moral or even a purpose. Sartaj had heard it before, from other people, and in its details he believed it was true. No doubt it had been embellished and changed in the telling and in the passing along.

'This is them,' Sartaj said. There were three figures throwing shadows across the pavement now, far up, too far to really make out, but Sartaj knew they were male, and that they were murderers. He felt it in his nostrils, in his teeth. He forced back the upper half of his body, which had risen in anticipation, back into the semblance of sleep. He waited.

'What are their names?' Sartaj whispered.

'Bazil Chaudhary, Faraj Ali and Reyaz Bhai.'

In the distance, there was a Fiat's particular whine as it turned a corner, and very faint, a flat electronic buzz from a light, and a metallic clinking down the tracks, all the silence of the city. The three men walked past Kamble's position, and then past the lit window. Katekar breathed out. And then the three stopped, turned and went back. One reached up, rattled the bottom of the second-floor door. 'Okay,' Sartaj said. Katekar slid out from under the cart, went right. Sartaj went left.

'Police,' Sartaj shouted. 'Put your hands up. Don't move.' Kamble's people were moving at the edges of Sartaj's attention, somewhere to his left. The three apradhis were twisted together, frozen in a clutching cartoon tangle, and then they broke, right and left. One ran up the road, and Sartaj let him go out of vision, out of sight. He was concentrating on the middle one, who had run forward, then back. He was skittering back and forth, holding a sharp, moving glint. 'Let it go, maderchod. Let it go. Hands up or I'll take your head off.' Something clattered on the road, hands went up and Sartaj risked a glance to his right. Katekar was aiming down a narrow gap between the shacks, a crevice that led to the fence.

'Out, bhenchod,' Katekar said. 'Throw it out.'

A square blade spun out into the light. A chopper, Sartaj thought. The stupid bastards are still carrying the choppers. He still had the high pulse of victory in his throat when a dark figure exploded from the shadowed cleft and collided with Katekar. Sartaj heard a snicking zip and then Katekar was sitting down and the apradhi was running. Sartaj took two steps back, steadied his arm, found the light polished smoothness of his sights, front and back, and then the kinescoped, flashing figure of the apradhi and he fired, two three four times. The apradhi slid into the ground. The flash subsided slowly from Sartaj's eyes. And Katekar was still sitting.

Sartaj knelt beside him. Dark fluid gouted from the nape of Katekar's neck in steady beats.

'Artery,' Kamble said from somewhere above Sartaj's head.

'Gypsy,' Sartaj shouted. 'Get the Gypsy.' He fumbled in his pocket, put his handkerchief on Katekar and the blood welled smoothly through Sartaj's fingers, swelled and billowed over his wrist.

'Here,' Katekar said calmly. 'Here.'

Three of them lifted Katekar into the vehicle. Sartaj struggled with his legs, and Kamble was whispering in his ears, so close that Sartaj felt his lips on his beard. 'All three apradhis died in the encounter. Yes?'

Sartaj heard the small sounds through the roaring of his own panic. He shook his head and ran around the car and pulled himself into the seat.

Kamble slammed the far door. The light fell on his face from above, dividing it into triangles of black and gold. 'All three,' he said. 'All three finished.'

There was no time to talk. Then they were careening past the blurring fence, and Sartaj was trying to hold Katekar steady and had a hand on the wound. Now the sense of what Kamble had said came to Sartaj. The jeep took a yawing left, and he heard the shots, mere pops, a rapid series of them.

At the Jivnani Nursing Home, at two forty-six a.m., Ganpatrao Popat Katekar was declared dead on arrival.

Sartaj felt old. From the paperwork he had learnt, remembered again, that Katekar was five years older than him. But he had always thought of Katekar as younger, young. Katekar had a complaint for every hour of the day, he had antic Marathi songs, he had obscure scientific facts, he had endless stories about the short lives of hard men. He took a paunchy pleasure in eating the aged-and-cured wickedness of the city, its piquant scandals, its bitter breakdowns, its ferociously musty unfairness, he made a meal of its resplendent and rotting flesh. Now, Sartaj had to write in a box on a form: 'Cause of death'. He shaped the letters carefully, convinced somehow that good writing on a departmental form was a kind of respect for the departed. He inked in, slowly, all the way to a full stop, and his hands started to shake. It was a vibration that started in the elbows, a pain drawn from the bone that went straight to his palms. Sartaj put his hands under the table, on his thighs, and waited for the shaking to pass. He clenched his fists, relaxed them. The shaking stopped, then came again. Sartaj looked about. Two constables sat just outside the door, he could see their shoes. The inspector on duty, Apte, was in the office across the hall to the left. He had left Sartaj alone out of concern, sympathy, given him his privacy. Sartaj breathed in, edged his chair back. The hands lay on the dirty white cotton, trembling. That was the word: tremble. Not twitch, not shake, but a small quivering that came from within to the skin. How melodramatic, Sartaj thought. He thought the word in English. *Melodramatic.* He remembered it. He made an effort and stopped the trembling. With a delicate, firm grip, he turned the form over. He picked up the pen again and poised the nib and then had to put it down. What strange things are hands. A belly cushioned by bulbous fleshy pads, fine fur patterning the back. Sartaj bent a finger back against the wood of the desk. If he leaned in with the weight of the shoulder, he knew the finger would break. The pain stood sharp against the humming haze of Sartaj's confusion, like a blue light in fog. Sartaj knew the sound a breaking finger makes. He had had Katekar do it once, break an apradhi's finger, a kidnapper's, the man had come to collect the money for a child, a businessman's daughter taken from her nursery school. The finger had been the kidnapper's little one, on his right hand. They had got the girl back, from a hotel in Bhandup. The sound of a finger breaking is not very large, but it is dry, sharper than you expect. It is a quick, creaky sound, a small firecracker bursting. Katekar had done it. Sartaj had made him do it, he had done it for the girl. Katekar had heavy hands. Sartaj remembered them and took the pressure off his own finger and stood up. This was self-indulgence, all of this, the hands, the memories, the form. He was avoiding what he knew he had to do next, what he had put off until morning: the visit to Katekar's family. He had said to Apte, let them sleep. Why wake them up now, in the middle of the night?

But light was inevitable. It was time to put his uniform back on.

Katekar's wife knew as soon as she opened the door. Sartaj saw this in her face. He had rattled softly at the hasp high up on the door, she had opened it still sticky-eyed and stumbling, and the sentence that Sartaj had prepared – 'Bhabhi, please forgive me' – vanished into the sickening knowledge of his own responsibility. She closed the door behind her, and folded her arms across the scalloped white lacy trim on the loose gown she wore. It had a rose pattern, the gown, complete with thorns on the green stalks. Sartaj had only seen her in slightly glittery saris, on very formal occasions. Maybe three, four times in as many years. She shut her eyes for a long moment, then opened them. Suddenly, she had changed. She set her bony face forward, like a prow, and reached out and touched his forearm. He realized then that he had been trembling again.

'What happened?' she said.

They brought the body home at two the next day. They laid Katekar on his bed, and took off the sheet in which he had been wrapped after the post-mortem. Then they sat him on a chair, and bathed him. The wound, low on his neck to the left, had been stitched shut. It looked too small to kill a man with a respectable belly, with heavy shoulders. The long post-mortem cut had been closed with thick black thread. Katekar's skin now had the colour and texture of cardboard that had dried fast after a soaking in monsoon rain, and Sartaj tried not to look at him. Sartaj pressed himself into a corner and averted his eyes from the men and women pushing in through the door, and tried to read the labels on the stacked cassettes next to the player, across the room. He listened to Katekar's wife speak to a relative about how many bottles of kerosene were needed, how many cow-dung patties, how much wood. Now they were putting new clothes on Katekar, his heavy steel watch on his wrist. His wife knelt and slid his chappals on to his feet. She had to struggle to get them on, she held Katekar's heel and pushed and then gently moved his toes apart to get one through the leather hoop. She stroked gulal on to his forehead, dabbed on a red tikka. She tilted her head back, was concentrated, serious. Another woman brought her a steel thali, a match sizzled and made a flaring arc in the air and Sartaj smelt incense, burning oil. She moved the thali in slow circles around Katekar's shoulders, his head. She was weeping.

They walked to the shamshan ghat. A man, another constable, carried a matka full of water. Sartaj could hear the rhythmic gulp of the water as he walked. The thali full of flowers and gulal was carried by another constable, close behind. From the thali, the constable threw grain and gulal as they walked. They entered the shamshan through a tall black metal gate. Standing under the towering open-sided shed, with its corrugated tin roof, Sartaj could hear the traffic over the high walls. He could hear voices, schoolchildren shouting, a vegetable-wallah's high cries. At the top of the wall, through drooping branches, he could see signs on the other side of the road, a tall commercial building. Katekar was laid on to the wood. A man stepped forward, this one Sartaj recognized, Potdukhe, a senior constable who had retired the year before. Potdukhe had a blade in his hand, a razor blade. He held Katekar's white sleeve with one hand, and with a swift motion cut the cloth from shoulder to wrist. Sartaj hunched his shoulders: the hissing pass of the blade came to him over all the sounds of the street. He swallowed and held himself still. Potdukhe slit the other sleeve, then opened the buttons on Katekar's pants: there must be no restrictions on the soul.

There was the distant mechanical growl of vehicles stopping, and a moment later Parulkar came into the shamshan ghat. He walked straight over to Katekar, stood for a moment over him, and then stepped back. He stood next to Sartaj, and put a hand on his wrist and squeezed. Then they waited.

The women stood at a distance, at the other end of the yard, near the wall. A rank of uniformed policemen turned, stamped, raised rifles to their shoulders and aimed high, at something far far above. Katekar's sons, who were still with the women, flinched under the roll of whiplash cracks. Then they were brought forward, through the cluster of men around the bier. Potdukhe put a hand on the older one's shoulders, and led him around his father, in a circle. The son – What was his name? His name? – carried the water-filled matka, and water dropped from a hole in it, spattered on the ground and danced up in quick, stammering splashes. A dhoti-clad priest now had a splintered fragment of wood in his hand, and it was flickering at one end. Sartaj suddenly wanted to see Katekar's face. He stepped to the left, but the wood was piled high, and what he could see was a coil of white cloth, a chin, the bridge of a nose. From this angle, close to the crown of Katekar's head, there was no Katekar, only some fragments. Sartaj shuffled to the right, it was important to see Katekar fully, but it was too late, the priest was holding the son's hand, showing him how to tap his father's head with a stick. It was a small tap, symbolic, but now the real blow, from the priest, would crack the skull. Sartaj swallowed. This was always the moment during funerals when he began to feel sick. It was necessary, he told himself yet again, or the skull would explode under the fire. But he felt the churning in his stomach begin. Somebody, it was Parulkar, took Sartaj's arm, and with the other men he moved back, three, four, five steps. Still, Sartaj heard the round crunch of the skull, when it came open, and Katekar was now open to the sky, completely and fully open. His son leaned forward, holding the burning wood. There was a small shifting inside the pyre, a series of tiny, rapid, racing convulsions. There was this movement and the gentle smell of ghee, that childhood smell from weddings and festivals. Then with an urgent gasp the fire took the wood, the body, Katekar. Now there was all motion, leaping up, up, and heat slid across Sartaj's face. He watched the fire burn, and did not look away.

After the friends and relatives had left, after the ashes had cooled, after the ashes had been collected and taken home and hung in a matka near the door, after everything, Sartaj went home. There was whisky, almost a bottleful, and Sartaj brought it out and put it on the coffee table, and a bottle of water, but after he poured out a drink the smell of it made him gag. So he shut his eyes, lay back on the sofa. Katekar was dead, the murderer was dead, the murderer's friends were dead, it was all over. Nothing to do, nobody to pursue. Katekar's death was a murder, an accident, an act of fate. It was a simple story, the way Kamble and others would tell it: three apradhis cornered, we should've fired first, encountered the bastards, but it was Singh's operation, Katekar got too close and didn't shoot, so he died. Case closed. These things happen. It's the job. But after everything, after all, Sartaj was unable to rest with this story, to be comforted by the neatness of it, by its clean forward velocity and its final rest. He was beset by questions: where was Bangladesh, what was it? Where was Bihar? How do three men travel thousands of miles, to one city, to a particular stretch of road, to a constable waiting under a thela? We are debris, Sartaj thought, randomly tossed about and nudging into each other, splitting each other's lives apart. Sartaj opened his eyes, and the room was still the old one, the shadows outside completely known to him, known a thousand nights over. This was his corner of the world, safe and familiar. And yet here was this question, sitting on his chest: why did Katekar die? How did this happen?

❧ INSET: *The Great Game*

'The purpose, the meaning, the intent and the methodology of intelligence is the discernment of patterns.' The students are waiting, eager for the revelation that will grant them understanding, hone their edges into preparedness, allow them to survive and triumph. 'The ability to sense method, orderliness, design, is the greatest talent an intelligence officer can possess,' K.D. Yadav proclaims, projecting to the back of the room. 'The old saying goes: once is happenstance, twice is coincidence, three times is enemy action. Remember that. If you can see the connections between data points, see the shape they make, read the story the data is telling, you will win. A patrol notices bootprints on a ridge in the Karakoram, a field officer on posting in Brussels writes a report mentioning the sale of miles of toughened communication cables. He who sees meaning in that, wins.' K.D. says 'he,' but there is a woman in the first row, a girl. He has known her for years, he has seen her grow from a child into a serious-faced young person, and one of the great pleasures of his life has been observing that very distinct personality that gazed up at him from the pram growing into the self-possessed, independent woman who sits before him now. He likes to think he had something to do with that growth, with the nurturing of that courage. But what is her name? How can he not know her name? How could he have forgotten, when he has voiced that name for years, decades?

And then he knows. He understands how he has forgotten. He has not forgotten her name in that room in the house in Safdarjung, in the classroom they have hidden away in a nondescript bungalow. He has forgotten it now, in this hospital room he is lying in. I am here, I am Karpuri Dwarkanath Yadav, known always as 'K.D'. I am in a small white room with drawn curtains. I am lying on a white metal bed. I am not teaching, not lecturing. I am ill, which is why I have forgotten her name. In the real classroom, years ago, I knew it. Now I don't.

She is sitting in front of him now, in the hospital room. She is reading a book. He remembers her as a child, always reading. She carried a book from one room to another, took a book to the dinner table and was always told to put it away by her mother. K.D. gave her books, he saw in her his own desperate childhood hunger for books to read, and was drawn to her by her precocity. He gave her Classics Illustrated comics, Enid Blyton and then P.G. Wodehouse. She still reads with that same one-pointed concentration, curved over the book she holds with both hands. He remembers that tense arc, that need, as if she wanted to eat the words. 'What are you reading now?' he says.

She looks up, pleased by the question, pleased that he is talking. 'It's called *A Search in Secret India*.'

'Paul Brunton.'

'Is there anything you haven't read?'

'I read it years ago.' He remembers exactly when he read it, in June of 1970 in an army mess in Siliguri. The book was an old leather-bound copy, with faded gilt lettering and three raised ridges on the spine. He can feel it in his hands now. He found it on a glassed-in shelf, above Ming vases from a long-ago punitive expedition to Peking. Outside the mess, there is a veranda which a lance-naik is sweeping. A barbed-wire fence. A cracking road and fields. But he still can't remember this woman's name, in this yellow hospital room. 'They must have reprinted it. What do you think of it?'

'Orientalist nonsense. White man looking for sadhus and enlightenment in a mysterious dark land. Same old fantasy.'

K.D. laughs. 'Just because it's somebody's fantasy doesn't mean it's not true.' This is an old argument between them. He always tells her she has to be weaned away from her JNU-bred fantasies of world citizenship and anti-imperialism and eternal peace. She always tells him that his realism is a fantasy too. But the argument has become over the years a formal exercise, a ritual which looks like a quarrel but which is really a demonstration of affection. And he is aware that he has the advantage. After all, he has recruited her into the organization. She is one of us now, one of the shadow soldiers. She has no choice but to be a realist. I trained her, I taught her tradecraft, analysis, recognition, action. I drew her into the secret world, into our troubles, into the web of secret causes. He smiles at her. 'Do you mean to say that sadhus don't exist? Or enlightenment?'

She puts her book down, draws her chair closer to the bed. 'I'm sure sadhus exist.'

'They do indeed. Real ones and fake ones. Both are useful.' She nods, and he is sure she understands, that she has not forgotten her lessons. He had insisted on a knowledge of the organization's history, of its antecedents, and so he had taught them about the Pandits, Nain and Mani Singh Rawat, and Sarat Chandra Das, and others, small and unsung men who had a century ago plunged into the forbidden northern lands disguised as pilgrims, who had walked north and west of the Himalayas, who had measured out thousand-mile routes by counting their strides as they walked. Prayer-wheels hid compasses, thermometers were snuggled into walking staffs, and the distances the walkers had measured had resulted in the first survey maps of these wild territories. And a map is a kind of conquest, the precursor to all other conquests. K.D. had told his students: remember those prayer wheels, one kind of knowledge can conceal another. Information nests inside information. Watch everything, listen to everything. Useful hides inside useless, truth in lies. And so this girl, his student, is now reading an Englishman's quest for peace, which she believes is nonsensical. Good. She is a good student. She is a good reader. She is holding his hand now. K.D. says, 'Why are you reading Brunton?'

'Uncle,' she says quietly. 'I need help. I need to know about Gaitonde. I need more. I need to know why he would be interested in sadhus.'

Ganesh Gaitonde is a bad man, but he was once an ally of the good men. K.D. had recruited him too. The organization needed bad men sometimes, for certain tasks, for specific missions. Only bad men had access to positive information in certain areas. So K.D. had found Gaitonde, in a jail, and recruited him. And Gaitonde had been a good source, his data had been cross-checked and corroborated and verified, and it had proved solid, and useful. He had executed commissions as well, performed jobs efficiently and with discretion. At the end he had gone renegade, he had betrayed the service and made up data and used their resources to expand his empire, but early on Ganesh Gaitonde had been a bad man on the right side, and K.D. had been his handler. To play this game well, you had to handle bad men, you had to have them do bad things which were finally good things. It was necessary. Only those who had never been on a real battlefield asked for unstained virtue and unblemished deeds. On the field, all actions were only provisionally moral, and the game was eternal. So was Ganesh Gaitonde a bad man? Was Nehru a bad man?

Hold on, cling tightly to lucidity. Don't think of Nehru, he is a distraction. Your mind is weaving, slipping. You are ill. K.D. clenches his fists, raises his head. The girl is intent, frowning a little. Just like her father. Her father's name was Jagdeep Mathur, and they had met each other early on a winter's day, in a conference room in Lucknow, on the campus of Lucknow University. The conference table has a green felt surface and is overlooked, from all four walls, by paintings of grand Europeans in academic gowns. There are seventeen men seated around the table, all of them in their early twenties, all of them sharp-eyed, intelligent, educated. K.D. has never seen any of them before, each has been told to report to this room at nine a.m. sharp. They are not talking to each other, they are waiting, they are practising discretion because they all know they are being recruited for secret work, in an agency which has not been named to them yet, which most of them have never heard of. K.D. has been interviewed twice already, after a very quiet approach by the vice-chancellor of his university in Patna. He thinks he knows why: he has a BA Honours in History and an LLB, and a National Cadet Corps 'C' certificate, and state-wide fame as a sportsman. He is tight, taut and very ambitiously educated. He has been thinking mainly of a career in law, but now he is vividly interested in this sequestered world, in these secret interviews and this promise of urgent and all-important work. So he waits at this table, with these other men who he recognizes as mirror-images of himself, from their strong forearms and alert glances he knows them to be sportsmen-scholars. The big double doors at the end of the hall swing open, and two men with military haircuts enter. Hard on their heels is an older man in a grey jacket, a professor perhaps, judging by his thick, wire-rimmed glasses. The professor walks towards the table, then turns back to the door, his neck bent forward expectantly. And Nehru enters. K.D. feels himself flush. It is unbelievable but it really is Jawaharlal Nehru. 'Gentlemen,' Nehru says, and his voice is hoarse, almost cracking. All the young men spring to their feet with a tremendous scraping of wood and shoes, and he waves them down impatiently. He sits without ceremony, leans forward and puts his elbows on the table. His hands are white, and K.D. can see how clean the nails are. But he looks tired, this Nehru. His eyes are yellowed, his cheeks are puffy. It is 18 February 1963. 'Gentlemen, you have all experienced the crisis India has struggled through recently. We live in dangerous times, we are struggling through an hour of crisis. Our borders have been invaded, our trust shattered. And that by the Chinese, who we thought were our friends. We must make sure such a thing never happens again. And so the nation must call upon its young men, its best and brightest. As I look at you I see the blessed light of an ancient past in your faces, and so I am confident again. I will ask much of you. In your work, your country will want the impossible from you. But you must endure. On your shoulders is our future. I trust in your strength, and in your unfailing dedication to your duty. Jai Hind.' He rises abruptly, and shakes hands with the man to his left. And then the next interviewee. K.D. has time to watch Nehru as he waits his turn to shake hands. He finds that he is breathing hard, as if he has just sprinted a quick mile. When his turn comes, Nehru reaches out and says something. K.D. is startled: 'Sir?' Nehru is already reaching for the next man's hand, but he says – without looking at K.D. – 'Do your best, son.' There is a trace of impatience in his voice at having to repeat himself, but K.D. treasures the words, and he watches carefully, but Nehru doesn't say a word to anyone else, not even to the professor. Nehru leaves, the doors shut behind him. Nehru has only spoken to K.D., only him.

The professor waves them back to their chairs. 'Gentlemen,' he says, 'as the PM said, you have been picked because you are the best. Welcome to the organization.' It turns out that the professor is not a professor after all, but an additional commissioner in the Intelligence Bureau, which – he informs them – is the oldest intelligence agency in the world. And they, if they choose to sign their recruitment papers, will be members, workers, soldiers for this venerable organization. They all sign eagerly, they are dazzled by Nehru.

Later that morning five of them celebrate at Yusuf in the Chowk Bazaar, where they have been taken by Jagdeep Mathur, a fellow-recruit who has grown up in Lucknow. They eat what he tells them are the best kakori kababs in Lucknow, and they discuss the magical appearance of Nehru in their midst. Mathur blames Nehru for the recent débâcle in the Himalayas, for all the defeats and all the dead, and K.D. cannot help but agree, but finds himself defending the old man's idealism, his belief in a future of peace and rationality. 'K.D., yaar,' Mathur says, 'you're just like my mother, always going on about how bloody good-looking Pandit-ji is, how he means well, how Gandhi-ji loved him like a bloody son, what a good good man Nehru-ji is. I say a good man shouldn't be our bloody prime minister. Good men are usually fools. Good men get people killed. When we live in a world with the bloody Chinese and the bloody Americans and the bloody Pakistanis we don't need good men, we need men who eat kakori kababs and carry big sticks.' K.D. nods, and says, 'Big lathis, actually.' Mathur laughs, he has a face like a perfect cube, with massive and ridged jaws, but he is quite striking with his fair skin and light-brown eyes. K.D. thinks he looks quite the Lucknow Kayastha, and he is aware that Mathur has noted his own surname immediately it was uttered, has perhaps filed him in some slot reserved for Yadavs and other backward castes, as no doubt every other of his new colleagues has already done. K.D. has noticed this, that the organization is old, and like other old organizations it is indisputably Brahmanical, with a light sprinkling of Kayasthas and Rajputs. And yet Mathur's grin is unfeigned, and there is not a moment's hesitation as he reaches across the table and thumps K.D.'s shoulder and chortles. 'Bloody big lathis,' he says. 'Exactly right. Bloody big lathis. Are you a lathait, K.D.?' 'I am,' K.D. says. 'I spent many years in shakhas.' It's true, he has spent many evenings in a starkly lit sandpit, whirling the lathi over his shoulders, learning defences and attacks from khaki-wearing instructors. Mathur approves of this, K.D. can see. He has passed some kind of test. Mathur likes him.

And after that kakori morning Mathur is known affectionately by his colleagues as Bloody Mathur, all the way until his disappearance two decades later. He leaves behind, on a road sixty-three miles north of Amritsar, a white Ambassador with two blown tires, one dead driver and one dead bodyguard and one dead informant named Harbhajan Singh, all killed by close-range AK-47 fire from at least three rifles. On that day, that year, K.D. is very far away, on the other side of the churning world, in London. He learns of Mathur's vanishing, is informed of it by the Europe desk in Delhi, puts down the phone and looks out of the window at the evenly ordered rhythm of staircases in an English square, at the white and grey fronts of the houses under a shadowed autumn sky. There is a six-hundred-year-old hospital on one side of the square, and a museum on the other. K.D. has a meeting in fifteen minutes, in a pub three squares down, with a Sikh militant he has been courting for six months. He has to be alert and careful, because he knows that this militant is also being run by a Pakistani officer, an ISI man named Shahid Khan, but all he can do is think of Anjali, little Anjali.

Anjali. Her name is Anjali. She is Bloody Mathur's daughter. She is sitting in front of me, now, in this hospital which is in Sector V of Rohini, in New Delhi. I am not in Lucknow, I am not in London. I am here. Anjali. Hold on to it. Don't mix up times, dates, places. Hold on to the sequence. There was Lucknow, where you met Mathur, and there was his disappearance in Punjab, but there were decades in between. There was NEFA, Naxalbari, Kerala, Bangladesh, London, Delhi, Bombay. Remember the dispositions, the distances, in the connections between the points is a shape. The shape is the meaning. In the shape of my life there must be a meaning. What is the shape? Apply analysis to the events, look for proximity, conjunction, repetition, similarity, find the impetus behind the momentum, the intent on the other side of the action. This is the business of intelligence. K.D. Yadav remembers teaching this, in a room in a house in Safdarjung. With this girl sitting in the first row. Anjali.

'Anjali,' K.D. says. 'Anjali.' His voice comes free of rust with a painful grinding, and he wonders how long it had been since he has spoken. 'Where have you been?' he says.

'Uncle, I need your help with Gaitonde.'

'Gaitonde is dead.' Gaitonde was dead. K.D. knows that, but doesn't know how he knows it. I am not in my right mind, he thinks. His greatest, his most secret and enduring pride has been in his memory, his precise eye for detail, his razor-edged logic, his capacity for analysis, his huge, humming, incandescent mesh of an intellect. In the corridors of the brahmins, in Nehru's royal gardens, he had walked proudly because of this famous mind. But what was my right mind? Was NEFA right, was London? In the ruin of his faculties, in the drifting, smoking aftermath of his collapse, there is a great lurking emptiness. It is an absolute vacuum, an utter absence, and K.D. flinches from it. And yet there it is, this loss, this suspicion that his whole life has amounted to nothing. He says to his little girl, his Anjali, he says, 'The spider weaves the curtains in the palace of the Caesars; the owl calls the watches in the towers of Afrasiab.'

She frowns. 'What does Sultan Mehmet have to do with Gaitonde?'

He is delighted, he has to laugh. What a mind she has! She has a doctorate in history. She understands his most obscure allusions, she has read the most esoteric and useless of texts, she needs them as much as he does, she is his inheritor, she is his daughter as much as Bloody Mathur's. Only she would have remembered, without a

312

moment's hesitation, that after Sultan Mehmet led his armies over the walls of Byzantium, after he and his men brought to a fiery end an empire which had lasted for 1,123 years and 18 days (Know the details! Remember the specifics!), after a day of killing and capture and rape and plunder, after everything, after Byzantium, the Sultan walked in the Palace of the Emperors, where the Byzantine rulers had endured lives of luxury and intrigue. He had won. And in the moment of his victory – the chroniclers tell us – looking up at the twilight sky, Sultan Mehmet whispered something to himself: 'The spider weaves the curtains in the palace of the Caesars; the owl calls the watches in the towers of Afrasiab.' But, K.D., control yourself, have discipline. Anjali needs you. What does Gaitonde have to do with Mehmet? What, indeed? 'Sorry,' K.D. says. 'I'm sorry. Gaitonde.'

'Yes,' she says. 'Gaitonde.'

'What was the question?'

'My latest information has Gaitonde, before his death, looking for three sadhus in Bombay. Why? Why sadhus? What's the connection?'

'Gaitonde was learning yoga in jail when I recruited him. The teachers were from some yoga school.'

'Abhidhyana Yoga. They're very old, very established, very respectable. I checked it out. As far as we know, Gaitonde had no contact with them after leaving the jail.'

The yoga teachers dressed in white, they taught yoga in the main courtyard of the jail, with discourses from the *Mahabharata* and *Ramayana*. The yoga was supposed to soothe the criminals, to make them better citizens. But K.D. always wondered why they believed this, the teachers. Why wouldn't yoga just produce better criminals, more centred, calmer thugs who were more efficient in their criminality? That master of villains, Duryodhana, was surely a yogi. They all were, those evil warriors. Gaitonde had looked quite calm, sunlit in his prison whites, in the superintendent's room. He was a bad man. Was Duryodhana a bad man? He had been killed through trickery and had risen to a warrior's heaven. Is there a soldier's paradise waiting for K.D. Yadav? I did my best, Nehru-ji, Pandit-ji, sir. No, no, think, think. Gaitonde. Why was he chasing sadhus? Help Anjali, help her. 'Gaitonde was religious,' K.D. said. 'He was always doing pujas, donating money for temples. He gave money to all the muths, we have pictures of him with the holy representatives. He knew some sadhus, surely, plenty of them. What's special about these three?'

'We don't know. All we know is three sadhus. They were important enough for him to break cover and come back to India. He knew we were displeased with him, he must have been afraid that we would sanction him. He must have been afraid of being killed. Still, he came back. Why? Do you know anything? Can you remember anything, Uncle?'

Yes, he can remember. She is looking for detail, for texture, for one or two particulars that will come together to unlock her conundrum, make sense of Gaitonde and his life and his death. That is what K.D. Yadav taught her. K.D. Yadav now has memory, but not sequence. He has elements, but not the distance between them. To him the past is no longer separated from the present by a distinct and comfortable boundary, everything is equally present, all things are connected and are here. Why? What's happened to me? K.D. can't remember. But he can remember. He is in a chopper flying up a valley. K.D. is laughing, grinning, because he can't help it, he hasn't ever been off the ground before, and now they are following the long mercury sliver of a river, they are curving and buffeting above the thick green, the shadows fall a deep black at the bottom of the ridges. There is a brilliant light, an early-morning gold that fills the rattling plexiglass, and the sky beyond is a colour that K.D. has never seen, a vivid, saturated hue that moves across his face, he can feel this blue in his skin. He's smiling, and one of the pilots turns and laughs at him. These are army flyboys, out of the base at Pasighat. The pilot is pointing down, at a patch of brown near the edge of the water, near the sprays K.D. can now see pummelling past the rocks. Then the river is spiralling up, and they are on the ground. The chopper takes off as soon as K.D. is out, and it is gone in a moment, invisible, drawing its thunder with it. Now there is another sound that K.D. can hear, a small but resonant chirping. It's not a bird he has ever heard, he's sure of that. Now there's another one, which sounds like a tin can full of stones being rattled. And one more, but K.D. isn't sure this last one is a bird, it's a whooping call with a click at the end, a snap. The tree-trunks at the other side of the clearing hold between them a blue-green light that is infinitely deep, a whole hazy world that K.D. knows absolutely nothing about: NEFA. He is alone in the North Eastern Frontier Agency, with a green army bag by his side, wearing a yellow bush-shirt and cheap Bata leather street shoes. He is suddenly afraid, completely afraid. Two bloody months of training, he thinks, only two months, and they did not train me for this, not for this jungle and for this unknown sky above.

A platoon of Assam Rifle boys arrive two hours later and explain they were delayed by a landslip three kilometres down the road, they had to detour. K.D. listens intently to the subedar's strange Hindi, and asks, how far are we going? The subedar grins, and says nothing. He has a pair of boots for K.D. The boots are too big, but that's better than too small. K.D. puts on three pairs of socks and walks. He walks for twenty-one days. On the third morning his legs are so tightly cramped that he can't squat to ease himself, and he leans against a tree and weeps. It's an oak tree, he knows this, and in that recognition he feels better. When he found out he was coming to these mountains, he bought a book about the flora and fauna, and studied it in spare moments. So he knows these are magnolias, and scattered poplars, and a chestnut. They have been following the line of the river, walking steadily upwards along a path that twists and backbends through the forest but always moves higher. In those early days of the walk, in that first week, they pass pairs and groups of stilted houses surrounded by patches of cultivation, rice and millet still surrounded by the charred ashes of burnt forest. Women sit in front of these houses, weaving, and the soldier-boys make sneering remarks about the nose-plugs they wear. The local men all wear straight blades at their waists, and the subedar tells him that they used these daos to take heads until not many years ago. These men look athletic enough to swing the daos and lop off limbs, but it's not them he's scared of, not their alien, slanting eyes under conical bamboo helmets. No. It's the breath of the forest that terrifies him, that creaking sigh of the bamboo that threads under the junipers. There is a belling and a booming that stretches through the long blue light under the canopy. The jungle speaks to itself, long calls and answers that surprise K.D., make him jerky, nervy. The soldiers laugh at him when a shrieking directly overhead makes him start, despite himself. 'It's only a monkey,' says the youngest one of them all, hitching his rifle to shoulder. His contempt is clear, and K.D. feels the justice of it. He knows it's only a monkey, and yet each night he huddles inside his blankets, pulling them over his head. He wakes up each morning more exhausted than the day before. In the mornings, the mountains hulk far above, black and engulfed by the thick cover, shoulder upon shoulder into the pinking sky.

They cross a ridge and descend, go down towards another thread-like river that fattens itself into a thrashing torrent. They wade across it, straining, and eat lunch on the far bank, the flank of a deer the subedar had shot two days ago. The mountains on both sides are precipitous, like walls, and the sky is a distant reflection of the river, a narrow twisting ribbon far above. Then they begin to walk again. They climb, and K.D. knows they are going much higher now. They hump through a forest of blue pines, their heads lowered against the weight of their packs, and K.D. is too tired to be amazed by the unearthly orchids that gleam up white and white from the grass, there is sweat in his eyes. In a long, sighing field of green bamboo the birds flutter above his head. Then they are edging through a last stand of poplars, and a meadow swoops out in a narrow crescent above them. Across it they walk, higher and higher, and looking behind him, to the south, K.D. can see the ridge they have crossed already, and ranged behind it, dozens of others, under the huge red sky. They camp that night in the meadow, and K.D. sleeps at an incline, asleep as soon as he pulls the blanket over his head. The next morning they eat a cold breakfast and walk on, and reach a saddle notched like a big V into the ridge. It has taken them two days, the trek up just this last immense slope. They come through the defile single-file, with K.D. exactly in the middle. He steps around a massive fortress of a boulder, watching his ankles against the cracks that run through the rock, and then he looks up and gasps. There are more meadows across the valley, but above those slopes, beyond them, the jagged white runs to the heavens, canopied by white clouds. The great silver peaks are very far away, and yet K.D. can feel their immense inhumanity, their indifference. He tries to steady his breath, and feels the frigid exhalations of the white crests like a claw in his throat. The next man in line nudges him, none too gently. 'What are you looking at, Raja Saab? That's Tibet over there.'

'China,' the subedar calls from below, without turning around. 'China.' The subedar is thirty-nine years old, the veteran of recent battles with the Chinese not far from here. He has skin the colour and toughness of old oil-paper. His name is Lalbiaka Marak, which is a name that K.D. has never known before. Among the jawans, there is a Das and a Gauri Bahadur Rai, but the rest of them have names like Vaiphei, Ao, Lushai and the exotically foreign Thangrikhuma. K.D. has no doubt that they find him oddly alien. They have taken to calling him Raja Saab, he doesn't quite know why. He doesn't feel very royal, with his stubble, his cracking lips, his blistered and oozing feet. Standing at the threshold of this great, deathly landscape, facing it with these men who are supposed to be his compatriots, K.D. Yadav feels completely alone. Ginzanang Dowara is standing very close behind him, and K.D. can smell the milky sweat on him. K. D. shrugs his pack higher, lowers his head and walks on. And after twenty-one days of walking, they reach their base.

A hundred and sixty men live in this little settlement of rough wooden cabins and tents, all of them from the Assam Rifles. There are two lieutenants and a captain on deputation from the army. 'We are a bit under-officered,' the captain tells K.D. 'But these are hard times.' The captain's name is Khandari, and he has grown up amongst other mountains, in Garwahl, but he hates these hills. 'In Garwahl the mountains have a soul,' he says. 'Here even the mountains are jun-glees.' K.D. laughs at him, points out that these are the same mountains, part of the same rippling chain that writhes over the sub-continent from east to west. But although he doesn't admit it, K.D. knows exactly what the captain means: these valleys which fall away from their feet are foreign in some profound way, they are very far away from anything he knows. Captain Khandari has seen combat in the recent war, in the far northern reaches of Ladakh, and he hates Nehru virulently, for all the men he says died fighting without ammu-nition, without support, without hope. Captain Khandari drinks mightily every evening, vast quantities of army-issue rum, and every evening he and the two lieutenants – Rastogi and DaCunha – play flush in the captain's hut. K.D. joins them, declines to join them in their wagering, in their violent throwing down of the cards, but he does share in their tippling. The rum takes away the awful feeling of isolation, that desolation of being cut off by mountains and impene-trable darkness. It feels cosy to be inside the firelit cabin, warm and woozy, telling stories. In four nights K.D. knows his new friends, his cronies, he knows of DaCunha's hopeless love for Sadhana, for her magnificent Technicolor behind, he knows Rastogi's love of obscure mathematical facts and riddles and tricks, and he has listened – very late at night – to Khandari's slurring and barely comprehensible accounts of terror-filled retreats across barren high plateaus. When K.D. leaves to pick and stumble his way back to his own cupboard-like hut, he can see the dying embers of campfires across the parade ground, the shadowy shapes of tents in orderly rows. And beyond them, the absolute black of immense rock walls under a cool, star-pierced sky.

On the fifth afternoon, K.D. feels recovered enough from the exhaustion of the long trek to make his way to the command tent, to face the impossibility of his job. He has been tasked primarily to investigate the Chinese presence in the area, to establish a network of informants and a fund of information, to make sure that the Chinese have in fact withdrawn and are engaging in no further incursions, to determine future Chinese intentions and the intentions of all and sundry in this sensitive border area. K.D. has no knowledge of the Chinese, or their language or history or politics, he has no experience or knowledge of this area or its peoples or geography. He is quite bewildered, but he makes his way to Captain Khandari. The captain, he is sure, will know where he should start. But the captain is very hung-over and surly, and finally K.D. is able to work out that only one patrol is sent out every week, they go four kilometres along the same route to the north-east, to an unoccupied bunker on a knoll. This constitutes the full effort of this unit to establish a presence in this area and collect intelligence. The shock is plain enough on K.D.'s face, but Captain Khandari shrugs and says, 'There's nobody out there, you know. Nobody at all. The Chinese are gone. It's all bhenchod empty.' K.D. is silent. He is trying to work up his courage to say something. Finally Khandari cocks his head and breaks the silence. 'Well,' he says. 'What do you want to do?'

Three days later two patrols leave the base, with routes that K.D. has picked out on one-inch maps. Now K.D. feels the hostility of men who have had their comfort disrupted, and he lives in silence. Even Marak – his friend the subedar – will not speak to him except in grunted monosyllables. K.D. finds a dead rat under his bed. Rastogi and DaCunha bring the patrols back earlier than expected, Rastogi by three full days out of the planned seven. Of course they report seeing nothing, absolutely nothing, and K.D. is sure they have gone around the next ridge and camped for a few days of rest and relaxation. The week after, he puts together another patrol for DaCunha and Marak and a platoon, and walks along himself. His feet twinge for the first mile, but he has a good pair of boots now, and after his muscles ease up, he enjoys the effort. He has lost weight, and he feels strong. There is pleasure in employing his new map-reading skills, and he examines the distant ridges through his binoculars at every halt. The men watch his binocularing with amusement, and DaCunha is barely civil. K.D. bears it quietly, he is doing his job, and he intends to do his job well. On their fourth day out they make camp in the lee of a rock wall that glitters in streaks of metallic silver, and K.D. opens his backpack and pulls out a book, hurrying because these are the last few moments of sunlight. He has been thirsting for books, for anything to read. He has long ago finished *The Riddle of the Sands*, which he brought with him into NEFA, and has been reduced to reading the labels on bottles of medicine, the fine print at the bottom of army requisition forms, and as even these have run out he has started to experience a kind of panic, as if he is slowly drowning. Then, just before they leave for patrol, in the corner of the command tent, behind a stack of food and supply files, he finds two books, left behind by some long-gone officer, who is now quite possibly dead. So he is now reading, within sight of Tibet, *The Benham Book of Palmistry: A Practical Treatise on the Laws of Scientific Hand Reading*. He is reading it very slowly, savouring each sentence, because it must last him. So he is lingering on the absurdities of each page, which find the shape of the future in the lines of the past, which locate meaning in these fleshy hieroglyphics of the palms. It must last, because in his backpack he has the other book, *Palmistry: The Language of the Hand* by Cheiro, and it is less than an inch thick, and to face these mountains with nothing to read would be unbearable.

Marak leans over him suddenly, cutting off the light. Marak is looking down at the open pages of the book, in which Benham is describing the proportions that obtain between the various mounts and the fingers. Marak is transfixed. He squats, with his arms resting on his knees, and faces K.D. squarely. 'You read the future?'

'Yes,' K.D. says quickly. 'Yes.'

Marak shoves his hand towards K.D.'s face. 'Read,' he says.

K.D. holds Marak's craggy hand in both of his own and tells a tale of the future. It's not so hard really. He uses some of Benham's strange prescripts, but mostly he lets Marak talk about his anxiety about his wife's health, his farmland struggles with his brothers, and from these he extrapolates and guesses. 'Your father was a very hard-working man, until the end of his life he worked every day from morning till night,' K.D. tells Marak, who looks at him with a new awe. Which is entirely misplaced, because there is no Benhamite reading involved in this assertion, just simple deduction from the clues that Marak has scattered about in his very questions, in his eagerness to know the shape of his happiness to come, to have a talisman against the depredations that will come surely, by and by. K.D. leads him along gently, then senses that it will not do to give too much, that you must leave the subject wanting, pleasured and reassured but not satiated. 'Enough for today,' he says authoritatively. 'I am tired.'

'Yes, sir,' Marak says. 'I will bring you some tea.'

And he does. Meanwhile, K.D. has been studying the dramatic fall of light on the mountain that faces them, the deep swathes of red and black. He takes the mug of tea and says, idly, 'We will see Chinese.' He is not quite sure why he says it, except that he has been telling the future, and he is rather hoping they will see Chinese. Not that he is eager for confrontation, or fighting. He is not sure of his physical courage, and knows from his three brief training sessions with pistols that he is a very bad shot. But to see Chinese would make his training meaningful, would give substance to his inductions, make the enemy real. And since he hasn't talked to anyone in days, he lets this slip, 'We will see Chinese.' And they do. The next day, just past three o'clock, Thangrikhuma – who is on point – calls back, 'Dushman.' They edge up to the ridge line and peer across the dry valley at a scattering of grey dots on the grey rock. It is, yes, the enemy. Thangrikhuma has very good eyesight, K.D. can hardly see the dushman, but in his binoculars they become recognizably men, a section's worth of Chinese soldiers moving slowly west. The boys move up with K.D., and they lie close to each other, watching. DaCunha is rustling a map, and now he declares, 'They're on their side. I think.' Their side is indistinguishable from our side: in this waste, here there are no markers, no fences. But there they are, and here we are.

For the next two days, K.D. and his men move along the ridge, paralleling the Chinese. They are careful to stay out of sight, and the Chinese lead them to what is clearly a new outpost, three bunkers built on a spur overlooking a pass, and a dugout for a heavy mortar. This is very good intelligence, but the men are more impressed by K.D.'s prediction, which they attribute not to sagacity, or training, or tactical knowledge, but to mystical insight. They each come to him along the route of march, one by one, and so he soon has an intimacy with their lives, and not just their public selves, but with their fears and hauntings, which he breathes in as they huddle in close to him. Even DaCunha succumbs, so that as they head back to base, K.D. knows about his retarded sister, and about Violet who waits for him in Panjim. As they break their last camp before base, Marak helps K.D. roll up his sleeping bag, and smiles confidingly. 'Saab,' he says, 'on the first day out there was a big discussion. The common opinion was that it would be very easy to nudge you over a cliff. New officer fell off, he was inexperienced, what could we do?' Marak laughs as he tugs hard at straps. K.D. grins back, but he is terrified, and he spends the whole day edging away from the drop, brushing his left shoulder on rock and shale. The possibility of his own death has never occurred to him with any force, with any response in his flesh, which hasn't ever been able to imagine its own disintegration. In the stories of success he tells himself, he is always victorious, sometimes wounded but still alive. But here are these real strangers, who have contemplated his real death. Some of them have killed before, and will again, and it would have been of no great account to them, his demise. One quick push and he would have been gone. He lies in bed that night, in his cabin, and shakes. He is afraid to close his eyes.

He awakens in darkness. He raises his hand, but there is no watch, no luminous numbers. He must get up, shave, bathe, write up his report, raise Captain Khandari from his hung-over stupor, get him to radio the report in and up the chain of command. What time is it? There is much to do. K.D. turns the sheet aside and raises himself, and his head plunges with nausea, and he gags. Why is he so weak? He hadn't been tired enough last night for this fluttering of muscles in his chest, this quiver that lowers him to his pillow again. The white ceiling crushes him into the present again, and he knows with a terrified groan that he is not in his youth, in that first ecstasy of a job well done on the barren peaks of the north, he is in a hospital bed in Delhi, losing his mind.

He considers the phrase: to lose your mind. What would be left, if you misplaced your mind? If there is no mind, is there still a self? He remembers the parable, that to know the I there must be another I, an eye that watches the birds of the self feasting on the nectar of the world. But will there still be a watcher if you take these mind-structures away, these façades of language, these foundations of logic, these narratives of cause and effect? What will be left when it all comes crashing down? Bliss, or numbness? A presence, or an absence? 'The spider weaves the curtains in the palace of the Caesars; the owl calls the watches in the towers of Afrasiab.' He throbs suddenly with rage, with anger against the violence being done to him. I *did* my best. I *did* what was asked of me. The incensed tightening of his tendons becomes a spasm, and he thrashes for a moment, with a pulse dinning in his ear like a Mishmi drum. He gropes up through the darkness that is drowning him. I am lucid. I can remember my life, I can trace its histories. I learnt my trade in NEFA, by creating an intelligence network where there was none, by creating sources and cells and routes. I did this better than any of my colleagues anywhere else, I worked harder and riskier and more *sincerely* than any of them because I was a Yadav and they expected me to do otherwise, I knew some of them did. They were Brahmins, and they had their very certain opinions about OBCs. I never spoke of this to anyone, not even to Bloody Mathur. I just worked. After NEFA, there were the rice fields of Naxalbari where I travelled as a trader and drew out the killers of policemen and judges and district collectors, where I pursued the illusion-ridden boys who left behind their comfortable middle-class homes in Calcutta and came up-country to make revolution. I killed one of them, too, this would-be Maoist who was trying to kill me. I remember his name still, Chunder Ghosh, and the blood that pumped from his ears when I shot him in his forehead. I can recall, exactly, the operations in Kerala against the communist parties, against their electioneering and spread and scheming, against their very infrastructure. For Nehru's daughter we did this, quite illegally but gladly, because we knew from where these parties drew their ideology and direction, and we were on the ramparts, pushing back these hordes run by Peking and Moscow. And then I was in East Pakistan, debriefing the Bengali soldiers who had fled their Punjabi masters. The information I put together caused whole airfields to disappear into broken rubble under the precise fall of bombs. After Bangladesh, back to Delhi, to the manoeuvring with foreign diplomats, the lunches with embassy employees, the slow development of relationships that finally yielded sputters of information. Then London, Punjab, Bombay. My life, spent in this struggle. This constant long war, with its hidden and unsung victories. I did the work. I can remember every payment, every source, every attack by the dushman. I defended. And so this India still stands.

K.D. gasps for breath in the darkness. He had never married. 'K.D. is married to the job,' his colleagues said. Most of them had married and had families, children, grandchildren. He was alone, is alone. He has had women, has known respectable women and disreputable ones. He has been in love, and he has paid for sex, he has been introduced to relatives of friends with the clear intention of marriage. He sees that marriage is a good thing, and he cannot argue against its virtues. 'What else are we working for?' Bloody Mathur said once, exasperated, solicitous. 'If not for our children, for their future, what else is all this for?' There was nothing K.D. could say to this, no disagreement he could offer with his friend's paunchy contentment, his wife speaking in a soft murmur to the cook, his five-year-old daughter Anjali bending over a fairy-tale book on the carpet. Yet he is unable to offer a 'yes' to the proposals his friend brings him, or offer a satisfactory explanation, or an illuminating description of what he really wants. 'What do you want?' Mathur asks. 'What, what, what? Who is this heroine you're waiting for?' And K.D. is unable to name this woman, to reduce her to a list of ten qualities, to conjure up into words this inchoate refusal that rises from his bones.

K.D. lies in his hospital bed, and wonders what he had been waiting for. It is too late now, he will die alone. His father had also spoken about the comforts of companionship, but had Ma really been a companion to him? Simple Ma with her shyness, her perpetual ghoonghat, her quietness, her endless housework. She had supported her husband in his bruising climb out of poverty, and proudly talked about her husband's PT-master job to her relatives, and took him his hot lunch every day herself, all the way to his tiny office next to the school's football ground, his favourite dishes packed in a five-tier tiffin. But she had been unable to follow him into the foreign lands of the English language, and to the end of her life had been confused by phones and remote controls and the true distances of foreign countries, by the size of the world. They had married young, the future trainer of athletes Rajinder Prem Yadav and the simple Snehlata, in the barely formed shapes of adolescence, and had grown into the vividly distinct halves of young K.D.'s life: Papa's glossy-chocolate shoulders against the white of his banian, his voice blasting commands over the ranks of sweating boys, his awkward and hesitant English, his strictness, his envious fascination with athletic training in Russia, and Ma with her hands lathered with besan, her innumerable festivals and fasts and ceremonies which followed each other in endless cycles, her impressive laughter which she hid behind her pallu, her illiterate woman's pride in her son's academic achievements. They had been together for decades, Papa and Ma. What had they said to each other, in their companionship, in their bedroom late at night? Had they saved each other from this early hour of the morning, from this ruinous absence of light? K.D. shivers, and remembers running home after a roadside scuffle with two boys from a rival school, with an aching jaw and his St Xavier's shirt torn at the pocket. Ma had clutched him close, and fussed with a haldi poultice until K.D. had held her away, physically made her stop. Papa had stood as straight as a steel pillar, his eyes narrowed, and told K.D. to find the boys and beat them up. 'From next term we will start boxing as a sport in school,' he said. 'You must learn to defend yourself.' That night, Ma had brought K.D. his glass of Ovaltine and had told him to ignore those hooligans, those government-school barbarians. 'They are just jealous that you are in such a good school. Forget them. Beta, work hard and you will advance. Don't get involved in all this nonsense, think about your future.' Ma expected K.D. to stand first or second in class always, despite his peasant ancestry, and she was full of hope, confident of his future.

And here is K.D. in that future, confident of nothing, uncertain even of the pain in his neck and head, pierced by it but unable to know absolutely, without doubt, whether it is in the present or merely relived memory. And now, in the breakdown of his body, K.D. understands that everything he has ever seen had been nothing but phantoms, that a rock held in one's healthy hand is only a ghost put together inside the skull, that illusions are the only reality. The future is an illusion, but the present is the most slippery illusion of all.

K.D. watches the sun crawl up the wall. He thinks about the colour, which is an orange flecked with red, shading into paler yellow as it climbs. There is no such thing as colour. There are photons bouncing around the world, and into and through a thin membrane on the surface of his eyes. There are electrical and chemical events triggering like novae. But there is no such thing as colour. A nurse moves through the room, prods at him and speaks to him, but he pays no attention. It's easy to ignore her, and the tiny bite of the needle she slips into his arm, they are merely discrete data flowing through the networks of his consciousness, as unreal as the hue on the plaster, which is now the exact tinge of the skin of a Kerala papaya around the aureole of the stem. It is a specific papaya that K.D. is seeing, one he ate in June of 1977, in a dak bungalow in Idukki. The papaya is present to him, with its slightly nauseating bouquet of rot, its flesh slipping, springing between his fingers.

It is as real as this wall, which is turning a dirty white. And then he sees that the lower half of the wall is still dark.

This is not the darkness of night, it is an absence of vision. The lower half of the wall is absent, as if somebody has attached blinders to K.D.'s eyes. If he tilts his head back, and then forward, he can move the edge between vision and non-vision up the wall, and then down. This loss of half his visual field persists if he turns towards the window, or the other way, towards the door leading into the corridor: half-window, half-door. It is a latitudinal loss, an equatorial one. The lower half of his world is gone.

When he tells a nurse about this new symptom, the staff spring into action. He is wheeled out of his room, examined, prodded, scanned by machines. Later that day, Dr Kharas is crisply factual. 'Your CT shows another lesion, a small one, here. We think there is damage to the visual cortex.' She is pointing to a cutaway diagram of a human brain, with the segments exploded out and labelled. The colours are brilliant, a primary blue for the cerebral cortex, a deep red for the thalamus. 'The damage from the tumour is causing a scotoma, a blanking out of part of your visual field. That's about all I can tell you. Did you feel anything last night? Nausea? Pain?'

K.D. wants to tell her, I felt icy air slicing at my throat as I struggled up a ridge, doctor. I felt blisters bursting on my feet, inside my boots. 'No,' K.D. said. 'Nothing.'

She nods, and writes on her notepad. She is thirty-eight, this Dr Anaita Kharas, married, two children. Dr Kharas and her husband were both born in Delhi, have grown up here. Anjali has run a little background check on her. They are wary of each other, Anaita and Anjali, a little prickly, but K.D. sees how similar they are, how alike in their efficiency, their sensible clothes, their assertiveness over the space they move in, the daily work they have to do against the scepticism and aggression of men to maintain their dignity and independence as women. 'I'm afraid there is not much we can do about your loss of function,' Dr Kharas says. 'There is no surgery that can reverse it, no treatment. There is much that we don't understand about the mechanics here.'

'I understand,' K.D. says. 'But will it get worse?'

'Again, this is hard to predict. A glioma is the least predictable of all tumours. Episodes of spontaneous remission have been reported. We will do our best. So, try not to worry.'

325

But he is not looking for sympathy, or comfort. He knows where he is going. What he would like are the percentages, the numbers. How long will his mind last, how fast will it fail? She has no answers. She lectures him a bit, sharply, about relaxation, about not getting depressed, not giving up. He smiles for her. He likes her. They had only one Parsi in the organization when he joined, and no Muslims, none, not one. He used to protest against this, pointing to the clumsy irony of protecting a secular state with a non-secular organization, to the rank unfairness of it. But the old men at the top thought it was too big a risk, not justifiable in light of the stakes that were being played for. Think, K.D. was always told, of who we are fighting. Yes. The dushman. They were there, and here we are. Them and us.

Away she goes, the good Dr Anaita, followed by a trail of interns and nurses. K.D. sits up in bed, watches pearls of clear liquid drip into a tube and into his forearm. He remembers Anjali's question now: why three sadhus, why was Gaitonde trying to find them? K.D. traces his association with Gaitonde, the first approach in jail, the conversations, the understanding reached, and then the jobs given, the favours traded. It was necessity. The world is shot through with crime, riddled with it, rotted by it. The Pakistanis and the Afghans run a twenty-billion-dollar trade in heroin, which is partly routed through India, through Delhi and Bombay, to Turkey and Europe and the United States. The ISI and the generals fatten on the trade and buy weapons and mujahideen warriors. The criminals provide logistical support, moving men and money and weapons across the borders. The politicians provide protection to the criminals, the criminals provide muscle and money to the politicians. That's how it goes. The dushman agency recruits a disaffected Indian criminal, Suleiman Isa, to plant bombs in the city of his birth, makes him a major player in the endless war. To fight their criminal, we need our own criminal. Steel cuts steel. Criminals have good intelligence on their rivals. It is necessary to deal with Gaitonde, for the greater good. And so there is Gaitonde, in a white T-shirt and white pyjamas and blue bathroom slippers, in the jail superintendent's office. K.D. tries to imagine himself back, relive the event. Maybe in the details he can find an explanation for the three sadhus. He closes his eyes and tries to slip into that afternoon, back into the room with its shelves of black files, its black-framed picture of Nehru. His breath is coming in short gulps, he doesn't know why. Stop it. Calm down. Calm, or you'll cause yourself more injury. Think. Why three sadhus? K.D. has no use for religion, and has always thought of Gaitonde's religiosity as a crutch for a terrified man incessantly afraid of assassins. Even strong men, hard men, men who are the bosses of companies, cannot face the blankness of death, the irreversible scissor-cut on the frail thread of awareness. One snip, then no more. Finished. This is unbearable, and so even Gaitonde, that blood-stained monster, dreamed fantasies about an after-life. We cannot bear this darkness. K.D. tries to examine his scotoma, to pay attention to it, but it is just nothing, a blank nothing. How dark it is, this loss under my eyelids, just under the red flutter of my pulse.

'Yes, that's Daddy's handwriting,' Anjali's mother tells her. Anjali has found an old university text that once belonged to her father, an ancient Indian history text, and she is pointing excitedly to the blue-penned notes in the margin, the underlinings. Bloody Mathur has been gone nearly a year now, but to his daughter he is a daily presence, a figure who looms larger because he is away, he is the romantically mysterious father who is not here. She has been told that he has 'gone away for a time', that he is 'on tour.' Within the organization, the generally held belief is that he was taken by the very same Sikh militants he was try-ing to recruit, that he was outwitted and ambushed, that he was probably tortured and then killed. A small minority believes that he was turned, that the ambush was a stage-play that he managed himself, that he has gone over the border, to the other side. But nobody expects him back, except Anjali, who has been told that he is 'travelling for work'. K.D. despises this lie because he sees expectation in Anjali's eyes every time the phone rings, a yearning in her knock-kneed sprint to the door when the postman rattles the gate. But she is eleven years old, and her mother thinks that a father who has gone away is what she can understand, or bear. K.D. knows that children face terrors every day, they walk through horrors that their elders deny and flinch away from. And what could be harder to bear than this expectation, this wanting? But he has no authority here. He has to be very careful. Rekha is pour-ing tea for him. She is formally hospitable to her dead husband's friend just returned from London, but K.D. knows there is no warmth here, no affection. She has always been polite, but distant, more than likely there is a hard armour of caste feeling under the good manners. If he says the wrong thing, he could get himself exiled, sent away from Anjali for ever. And he knows that this banishment would be something he could not bear. This would not be supportable. K.D. has no connections in the world. Papa and Ma are dead, and he doesn't have frequent communications with his relatives in Bihar. He has nobody. But Bloody Mathur has always welcomed him into his home, and K.D. has seen Anjali grow from infant to girl. She has always known him, he has been present through her entire life. K.D. understands that this small person sprang from Bloody Mathur and Rekha, but somehow she has become his daughter as well. Somehow he has become a father. He has no authority, but he has love. He understands that this little girl, in her blue school skirt, is his anchor in the world. She binds him together, with that long gaze of hers. He doesn't know how this happened, or when, but he knows it is true. She leans on his knee now, holding up the English doll he has brought her from London.

'She won't talk, Uncle.'

The doll is blue-eyed, flaxen-haired, with a puckered strawberry of a smile and a tinny voice. K.D. now realizes that he hasn't heard her saying 'Mama' for a few minutes. He turns the doll over, and under the pink dress, the panel in the small of her back is loose. He finger-nails the panel up, and the wires inside are twisted around the battery, a green chip hangs loose. 'What did you do?' he says.

'I wanted to see how she worked,' says Anjali.

K.D. laughs, alight with pleasure and love. The feeling inside him is complete, unrestrained, without any of the holding back that he has felt in every other interaction in his life. She giggles. 'Uncle, I'm too old for dolls anyway,' she says, not unkindly. 'I stopped playing with them long ago. You don't know much about girls. I like reading now. You should bring me books.' They laugh together, sending each other into pealing outbreaks that spiral away. Anjali's mother watches, faintly suspicious. At least for that moment, K.D. doesn't care, and he carries Anjali's warmth with him into the next day, into the office where he sits at the Islamic Fundamentalism desk. In this enclosed, windowless cabin he collects reports from all over the world, he collates, connects, sifts, analyses. The beliefs and hatreds of men and women come to him in fragments, and he puts together the pieces. And then he writes his own reports, has them typed on crisp sheets of white rice paper, and through them information rises up, to the Additional Commissioner and then the Commissioner and then perhaps all the way to the prime minister. Information rises, and orders descend. Action is taken, and that produces results and new cascades of information. K.D. feels always that he is sitting at a node in a web, at the intersection of globe-spanning lines of energy that hum and spin and change shape. He can strum a thread here, and ten thousand miles away a man will slump in a doorway. He can write a paragraph, and two weeks later hear it paraphrased in a speech by the home minister. In this dusty room he sets strings of events in motion, he changes the lives of millions of people.

But he cannot find the men who took Bloody Mathur. He has a file, a thick one full of police reports and on-the-spot evaluations by teams of organization investigators, who evaluate the incident and also its investigation by the Punjab authorities. The facts are few and clear: Bloody Mathur had been cultivating a certain Harbhajan Singh, who had two years of college and no job, who was the son of a small farmer, who had been arrested twice for petty theft. This Harbhajan Singh had contacts in a certain militant group called the Punjab Liberation Army, and for months Bloody Mathur had fed money to Harbhajan Singh, who in turn had passed money to a close friend who had gone over to the militants. Good information had come back, verifiable material but none of it very useful. The source within the PLA asked for a face-to-face meeting, said he would bring another dis-affected friend. Bloody Mathur had a hunch, he went, and then was gone. Leaving a tilted, shattered Ambassador and three dead men. And there the trail stops, ceases. Bloody Mathur has disappeared, and that is all.

But K.D. won't let that be all, he refuses to allow matters to rest. He follows Harbhajan Singh's family, he follows his friends, he makes deals. Bloody Mathur used to say, 'If it's not money, it's lust. If it's not that, it's safety, his fear for his family. Any and every man can be bought. You just have to find out what the price is.' So Bloody Mathur ate tandoori chicken in roadside dhabhas with Harbhajan Singh, because the dushman had widespread operations in Punjab, it was their staging area, their haven, their easy entry into India. And so he vanished. Now K.D. pushes his field officers, he has Harbhajan Singh's brother followed and watched, he asks for backgrounders on known associates, listings of bank accounts. He manoeuvres men and resources and money, because they are in a battle, a war. K.D. fights back. He will not forget. So the great game is played in the streets and farmlands of Punjab.

The game lasts, the game is eternal, the game cannot be stopped, the game gives birth to itself. K.D. plays it, and plays it well. He has a vast memory, and a sensual feel for details: a pair of dark-lensed reading glasses glimpsed in a blurry photograph of preachers in Frankfurt stay with him for six years, so that he is able to spot the same man in another photograph taken on the other side of the world, in Peshawar, when Taliban commanders emerge from a meeting with an ISI major. These prodigious feats of connection and naming, this creation of meaning, give K.D. his reputation, his fame, his place in the organization. He advances. He is now an Assistant Commissioner, a junior one but a man with a future nevertheless. He is moving. Four years, and he moves on, this time to Berlin. In this divided city, he gives study visas to Iranian students, arranges scholarships for them, he gives sympathetic hugs to Afghan doctors and invites them to dinner. He sends parcels to Anjali, who is speeding through school, leapfrogging whole ranks of students with double promotions and impossibly high marks in final examinations. She reads up on Berlin, and asks for biographies of Hitler which she cannot find in Delhi, and books about generals with names as round and full as pink breakfast sausages.

'There are space-occupying lesions in the patient's frontal lobe.' Dr Kharas stands over K.D., surrounded by an attentive rank of interns. 'The effects of the glioma are interesting. The patient presents with reduplicative amnesia, during which he is quite literally somewhere else. Usually patients with this kind of amnesia imagine themselves to be at home, or in some place they like. This patient seems to range in his imagination to places where he has been in his life, all kinds of places all over the world.'

That's because I never had a home, fair Doctor Anaita. My home was a place in my imagination, a beautiful, prosperous land that doesn't exist yet. In all my journeys, that is where I was going, to this peaceful country of the future.

'Patients with this kind of impaired memory also usually present with confabulation. That is, they give incorrect answers in response to questions about remembered experience. Even questions about trivial matters, like details of past employment, dates, locations, elicit answers that seem coherent but are fantastic. The patients describe impossible, adventurous and gruesome experiences. Mr Yadav? Mr Yadav?'

Dr Anaita wants to demonstrate symptoms to her students. K.D. nods. He will give her that, he will give her whatever she wants. He owes her, he owes her because of her ardent curiosity, her skill, her passion for her job, he owes her because she gives him hope. Not hope for his own survival, but hope that he has lived a good life, that all the ugly things he has done might finally amount to something good. She is his hope.

'Mr Yadav, can you tell me your date of birth?'

He cannot remember. No matter, he mustn't disappoint her. He picks a number out of the air. '9 July 1968,' he says. There is a quick fizz of excitement among the interns, a tingle in their eyes. They like symptoms, symptoms demonstrate the inner workings of the defective machine. An abnormality in the organism, by inverse but impeccable logic, demonstrates some truth about its normal functioning. K.D. realizes that his 1968 date is many years too late, he is much older than that. But what happened on 9 July? The date is rough, it sticks and scrapes across his mind like a burr. Then he remembers. He sees it. In the lower half of his world, in the new half-darkness of his vision, K.D. sees a burning village. It is not fuzzy and indistinct like a remembered village, it is not a hallucination. It is a real village, and he can see it. He can see the flames moving under the wooden floors of the huts, a red-eyed sow grunting in panic through the orderly green rows of a turnip garden, he can hear the sharp pop of exploding bamboo. The colours are deep, incandescent, just like reality but more so, he can see the sparkle of saliva on the teeth of a black dog shot through the head, the hair on its splayed rear legs. It is more real than real, this dying village. He has never been to this village, but knows exactly what it is. This is the village of Chezumi Song, in Mon district of Nagaland, which on 9 July 1968 was visited by a unit of the Assam Rifles under the command of a Captain Rastogi, a Dakshesh Rastogi who was the very same mathematically-inclined friend of K.D.'s first field posting. Rastogi has grown, from lieutenant to captain, and he has grown thicker, he has grown into a fine man. He doesn't know it, but he is acting on intelligence that K.D. has collected and collated and passed down the chain of command, and he is after two Naga insurgent leaders, L.K. Luithui and M. Essau. They are known to be in the area, and they have relatives in this village. Rastogi's unit has lost six men to sniping and mines in the last month, and these two Nagas are the tacticians behind the attacks. The village is subjected to a search, and the villagers are interrogated. Captain Rastogi applies pressure. The village chief is beaten with rifle butts, along with the village notables. They all say they know nothing of the two insurgents. More pressure is applied. The chief's daughters, three of them, are dragged out of the square by the hair. Their names are Rose, Grace and Lily. They are raped. Twenty-two women are raped, and the village is burnt. Three of the village men are shot, and Captain Rastogi's report states that these three terrorists were cornered and killed in a running gunfight that resulted in the destruction of the village of Chezumi Song. L.K. Luithui and M. Essau, the two insurgents, are cornered three days later in a forest hideout eight miles to the north, and are killed. Captain Rastogi receives a commendation, and is thereafter a man on the rise. K.D. knows what was in the official reports, and he knows what really happened. He is, after all, an intelligence man. He knows that the tip-off about the hideout was given by a girl named Luingamla, who stuttered out the location because Captain Rastogi had a pistol pointed at her father's head. K.D. knows this. It is his business to know. He wasn't there, but he knows. He can see the village of Chezumi Song now, quite clearly. He can see it blazing. But where are the people? He can see none of the Nagas, and none of the soldiers. He hears screams. The birds are shrilling through his head. Now, a gunshot, and he knows it is a Webley-Scott .38, that is what Captain Rastogi carried that day. But there are no people in this real village.

'The village is burning,' K.D. whispers.

The interns lean close. Dr Kharas is listening intently. 'What village?' she asks. 'What village?'

K.D. says nothing. What can he say? That it was a village that you never knew of, that ceased to exist before most of you were born? It is gone, but it continues to burn. 'The village is burning,' he says again. Dr Kharas whispers to the interns, and finally they leave. The village continues to burn, but still without its inhabitants, or its invaders. K.D. listens to the crackling of the conflagration, the screams, the gunshots. By afternoon he is able to fall asleep, or into a dream of sleep. He wakes feeling exhausted, his joints ache. He slumps to the bathroom, one hand out to keep fingertips on the wall, all the way. Chezumi Song is no longer in his blind spot, in his half-band of darkness, but as he pisses, he sees a chess set. He tilts his head far forward to be able to see what he is doing in the pot, but where he is not able to see, where the square-tiled bathroom floor cuts off, there is now a chess set. He recognizes it, it is actually the top of a stone table, in a park in Berlin. He meets here, on scattered Friday afternoons, an Afghan engineering student named Abdul Khattak. This Khattak is very poor, with four brothers and three sisters, all of whom live in a tiny apartment in Neukoelln, so the lunches that K.D. provides him are especially welcome, as are the small amounts of money that he is given when he performs. For the names of fundamentalist preachers and information on their movements and plans, K.D. hands him slim envelopes, and more envelopes for the names of anti-fundamentalist Afghans in Europe and at home, and perhaps introductions. K.D. and Khattak have talked about Indian visas for Khattak's younger brothers, and the possibility of scholarships at Indian universities and technological institutes. All this, naturally, for more information for K.D. But where is Abdul Khattak? He is not at the bench in the park, under the green canopy of oaks. K.D. can see the squares in the chess board, which are green and white tiles let into the cement. Khattak likes this rendezvous point because he loves chess. Following the international competitions is the one luxury he allows himself, this Khattak who runs between his classes and his laundry job and his siblings. Khattak doesn't like dead drops, although leaving notes under a park bench in a shopping bag, or taped to the back of a lamppost, would be much safer. Khattak likes to talk, after every two or three dead drops he insists on a meeting. Where is this Khattak, why is he not under this lightening March sky with its hint of spring? K.D. shuffles back to his bed, his arms held out, and he knows exactly why: Khattak is dead, lying in an alley between empty crates, behind a furniture store. His wrists are tied behind his back, his cheeks and chest are bruised from a beating, and his throat has been cut. His killers are never found, the police never have any clues and K.D. is not going to give them any. Khattak is dead, but much of his information is good, it is alive. K.D. uses it, he gains access to student networks that lead back to Kabul, and he gains a source in Jallalabad, a secretary to a mullah who is gaining political prominence. And now, in this Delhi hospital room, in his own half-blindness he can see the chess set, sunlit and waiting for the pieces, for the play. K.D. gets into bed, and wonders what happened to Khattak's brothers and sisters. They survived, of course. The survivors survive, that is what they do. And here is this chess set, green and white and glowing in his darkness.

'Who is the prime minister?' It's Dr Kharas, leaning in close to him, holding a bright light close to his eyes. 'Mr Yadav, who is the current prime minister?' It is night outside, and K.D. doesn't know how he got from morning to night. Anjali is standing at the foot of the bed, her hands clenched around the white metal rail.

K.D. smiles at her. 'My short-term memory is failing,' he says. He is trying to comfort Anjali: to have the apparatus to know you are failing is to have something, after all. But she is not comforted, he can see that. She knows that he has no idea who the prime minister is. He can remember the watch that Nehru was wearing, a commemorative HMT with small black numerals, and the fine hair on Nehru's wrist, but he doesn't know who the current prime minister is. It is gone, simply gone. Not here.

'Are you seeing any hallucinations now?' Dr Kharas wants to know.

He must have told her, during his lost day. He hadn't wanted to tell her, to not tell Anjali. He feels ashamed now. It is a shameful thing, to see things that are not there, to lose one's grip on what is, what is not. He could not stand Anjali pitying him, thinking of him as less than efficient. He has never suffered incompetence lightly. But no, she is pained but not commiserating, she will not condescend to him, he can see that. She can still see that he is present, within these ruins. He, K.D. Yadav, is still here, thinking, calculating, *understanding*. He looks at Anjali but addresses himself to Dr Kharas: 'No hallucinations now. Why am I seeing them?'

'It is the human brain,' Dr Kharas says, sitting back. She puts her hands together in her lap, rather like a priest imparting a moral lesson. 'The human brain does not like blanks. It does not tolerate empty spaces. Because of your structural damage, in the visual pathways, there is a gap in your visual field. So then the brain fills in this scotoma, this breach. The material it is finding is from your memories, from your stored sensations and concepts. It throws that material into the blank space. This happens all the time, actually, even in normal functioning. What data comes in is put together with what is already there, it all mixes together and changes and transforms and becomes a perception. This is how we experience everything.' She pauses to see if he is following, if he is absorbing all this information. She wants to be lucid, the knowledgeable Dr Kharas. He nods, and she continues. 'From the data from the outside, and from the material of memory, the brain makes up a story, and that story is what we think is reality. What makes it noticeable now is that you are completely losing half of your external data from the visual stream, and the brain is compensating for that loss. Otherwise what your brain is doing is completely normal. We are built like this only.'

334

'We are built like this only,' K.D. says, and bursts out laughing. It is funny, even though his Anjali and the good doctor are not laughing, no, they don't have even a smile, a twitch of amusement. We are built like this only, to see apparitions, to construct a vision of the world inside this lonely palace of bones, to live in this dream and be terrified of dying out of it, to suffer this nightmare made from impressions as if it were real. A rat's vision of reality is as real as mine, as yours, as ours. But we live and die and kill in this ghostly phantasmagoria of mirroring narratives. This is all dreadfully pathetic, or perfectly hilarious. K.D. cannot tell which, and he cannot stop laughing. He wheezes on. Finally he beckons Anjali to him, and makes her sit on the bed, close to him so he can hold her hand. 'Don't be gloomy,' he says. 'It's an interesting condition, at least. It is very educational.'

'There is a name for the syndrome,' Dr Kharas says, glad to provide structure. She is a great believer in empowering the patient through knowledge. 'It is called the Charles Bonnet syndrome, after the man who first observed it. It is common among people whose eyesight is failing. Often old people who are suffering from cataracts, for example, report seeing things: people, objects, ghosts.'

People, objects, ghosts. K.D. can see people and objects, but he is himself starting to feel rather like a ghost, a flickering network of electrical impulses encased in a leaky, creaky machinery of flesh. He feels himself dying and coming alive, his self fading in and out with every breath. Does Dr Kharas see this, that this self too is an illusion, thrown up by the pattern-seeking brain to fill in the void? He is filled with pity, for himself, for Dr Kharas, for his Anjali. What an agony of seeking and suffering is the unavoidable destiny of this drifting wraith. What convolutions of pain it must know and survive, from birth to death, this piece of nothing. Anjali is sad even now, and he pats her wrist. 'Don't worry,' he says. 'It's nothing.' But she is puzzled, and he knows he cannot make her understand that it is useless to mourn him, to grieve for something which was always a nothing. She is young, full in her flesh, engaged in her battles and hungrily alive. He cannot make her see, he should not. Perhaps only those at the edge of disintegration can understand this. 'The spider weaves the curtains in the palace of the Caesars; the owl calls the watches in the towers of Afrasiab.' But she is waiting to tell him something. Anjali waits for Dr Kharas to finish her instructions and her goodbyes, and gets up to shut the door. She returns to the bed, and sits close to K.D.

'Did you remember anything about Gaitonde, Uncle?'

'No. Nothing new. Only the things you already know.' Gaitonde was his recruit, his client. After K.D. had retired, Anjali had wanted to be his handler. There had been objections within the organization: she was too young, too inexperienced, and finally and most importantly, she was a woman. What kind of gangster would be handled by a female officer, what woman could handle the fearsome Gaitonde, that ruthless monster, that womanizer with no respect for women? This was old and accepted reasoning within the organization, that women couldn't be given field postings because they couldn't handle the kind of criminal elements that were the everyday providers and producers of intelligence, that women couldn't make deals and give instructions to sweaty smugglers, border-crossing petty criminals, drug-carrying mules, the illiterate and the vulgar and the desperate. So women were good at a desk, the reasoning went, they were fine analysts. Keep them there. But Anjali had chafed at her various desks, and struggled against this old-fashioned reasoning, and proven herself as a field operative in her foreign postings in London and Frankfurt. She was a fine analyst and also a good handler of women and men, a certain Pakistani immigrant-smuggler in Marseilles, a moustachioed and particularly brutal Pathan, had called her Bhen-ji and provided vital connections to carriers of Afghan heroin, with implications in Peshawar and Islamabad. So there were particular ways in which women could indeed handle men, but the organization had refused Anjali's request. They had given Gaitonde to one Anand Kulkarni, who was very masculine and very tough. Gaitonde proved finally to be unreliable, and Kulkarni had been criticized within the organization for his handling of him, but he – K.D. – was the one who recruited the bastard. It's his fault that Gaitonde went bad, if it is anybody's. K.D. asks, 'Why is it so important? Gaitonde is dead.'

'Yes, he is dead.'

'So, then? There will be a struggle to occupy his territories. Maybe his company will fall apart. Maybe they will kill each other. So what?'

She is evaluating him. She is trying to decide whether to tell him something, or not. He understands he is a risk now, that he cannot be trusted with information. He is not himself, he may tell Dr Kharas, the nurse, people passing in the corridor. And yet he wants to know. 'Tell me,' he says. 'If you tell me, maybe I can help. Maybe if you tell me, it'll help me to remember.' He is not sure whether this is true, whether the tatters of his once-vaunted memory hold together enough that results can be produced from small cues, from careful direction and prodding. But she has to gamble. Calculated risks are the everyday work of the game, and K.D. has trained Anjali in these small steps through danger: at that very last moment when you are walking towards a drop point, unsure whether you are under surveillance, do you keep walking or reach for the bag? You have come to know that one of your officers has been selling information to the other side, to many other sides, so a number of your sources may have been compromised, and you have a man in a defence research establishment near Islamabad, a physicist, do you call him in or not? Calculate the payoff, and the punishment that failure will inflict, and decide.

She has decided. She speaks fast and low. 'We found Gaitonde in a house in Bombay. The house was built like a very deep bunker, with hardened walls. We found the builder and the architect who built it for Gaitonde. They told us that it was done in ten days, from plans faxed in by Gaitonde. He told them not to worry about money, just finish it. They did. We have a copy of the plans. The title page and some other identifying labels had been removed or erased, but there was enough text to allow us to trace the plans to the source. They were downloaded from the internet, from a North American survivalist website entitled "How You Can Survive Doomsday". We examined the structure in Bombay. Gaitonde built a nuclear fallout shelter.'

Her eyes are silvery black and sparkling and frightened. Outside, night settles with the sigh of thousands of beating wings. The groaning rush of the city's traffic is still alive, far below. There is a certain formless vacuity to this nuclear threat, K.D. thinks, an ultimate white blankness which stops all thought, all motion. Anjali cannot think past it, he can see this. He prompts her. 'So Gaitonde broke cover, he ran?'

'Yes, he came back to Bombay. He was looking for three sadhus. He was found dead from a self-inflicted wound. In this shelter.'

'What was in the shelter? Did you find anything?'

'There was another body, of a woman. A woman named Jojo Mascarenas, a madam who had supplied women to him. Gaitonde killed her with the same pistol he shot himself.'

K.D. had known about the women, the girls that Gaitonde had consumed in a steady flow. He had never bothered to ask where the supply came from. Now he knew. 'And what else?'

'There was an album of photographs, of these girls. And money. One crore twenty-one lakhs, in new notes from the Central Bank.'

'You followed up on this woman?'

'Yes. We found her apartment, searched it. Found nothing interesting. There was some cash. Some of it must have been from Gaitonde, it was the same series of new notes, in plastic wraps. She operated on the fringes of the television and film industry, there is a lot of black money in that business. There were tapes, photographs of actors. Nothing else.'

She waits. She is allowing herself a little bit of hope, but K.D. has nothing to tell her. No explanations have become dislodged from the whirl of his confusion, no clues have come floating up from the drifting masses of his past. 'Let me think about it,' he says. 'I'll have to think about this one.'

She eats dinner with him, from a partitioned steel tray. He spoons up his khichdi and tries to think. The nuclear threat has been present on the subcontinent for decades, and they have dealt with it. The organization has run many ops to extract information about technologies, doctrines, tactics, locations, some of them very successfully. They have data, and they know the capabilities and intentions of the Pakistanis and the Chinese and the Americans. K.D. has seen some of these analytical reports and papers, and the reddish-brown satellite photos which show missile complexes and air bases, and knows there are real weapons at the ready, aimed at his cities, at him. And yet the reality of a nuclear explosion has always seemed unreal to him, very far away from the dirty night-time business of waiting in a freezing hut for a Pakistani informer, sitting on a broken crate with feet up to avoid snakes and scorpions. To put a man under a double barbed-wire fence, through shifting fields of wheat, under the night-scoped guns of Pakistani Rangers and past sleeping cattle, that was craft and labour and vocation, well-known and well-practised. But nuclear destruction, that belonged in the thrillers that K.D. read on long journeys and at bedtime, that he still reads. In the stack of books at his bedside, among the Roman histories and CIA autobiographies, there are these fictions that he reads for pleasure, often to laugh at the wild extremities of the scenarios that they create, the millions of dead and the dastardly plots and the brave, selfless heroes. In these books, and only in these books, bombs sometimes explode, taking whole cities. Only in these books is there the smoking aftermath, that silence without birds. But you always shut the book, you put it back on the night-stand, you drink your little sip of water, you turn over and go to sleep. No need to build grim little bunkers in the middle of Bombay, no need for gangsters to run from their safe foreign refuges and into danger, no need to look for three sadhus. No need at all. But Gaitonde is dead. Why?

K.D. doesn't know. But he is thinking. Anjali is clearing up the trays and glasses and spoons. She looks exhausted. 'Go home,' he says. 'The ward-boy will do that.'

'I don't mind. Actually I asked them if I could stay here. They said they could bring in a cot.'

'Anjali, you don't have to. Really. You need your rest.'

'I can rest here. I just need to sleep, and I'll be very comfortable in their cot.'

He understands that she is concerned for him, but also concerned for her operation, her world which she believes is threatened some-how. She wants to stay close to him, to his fading memory and mind, in case he rants out a name, a place, a word, that will lead her into Gaitonde's bygone life. She loves her uncle, yes, but she is doing her job. She is following her training and her instinct, she is a good stu-dent. K.D. is dying, he knows it, she knows it. Most likely, the dying will lead her only to the country of the dead, but she is being careful – perhaps K.D. will give her something useful before he slips into silence. He smiles at her. 'All right, beta. As long as you are comfort-able.'

'I even brought my toothbrush,' she says, holding it up. She is again the little girl he knew once, and they grin at each other. It is cosy to have someone in the room, splashing in the bathroom. Anjali settles into the cot. They say 'Goodnight' to each other, and K.D. switches off the lamp above his bed. She sleeps, falls into long, even breathing almost immediately. He watches her, the shape of her shoulder. She doesn't have anyone to call, to tell that she will not be coming home tonight. She once had a husband, a Kannadiga boy she married against the wishes of the concerned parents, in the idealistic throes of a metropolitan Delhi love affair. The husband had studied economics at Zakir Hussain College, had gone on to a career in the IAS and had left her four years after the wedding, complaining of her incessant travel and obsession with her career. K.D. doesn't know if she has found anyone else, she certainly never speaks of it, even of the desire,

339

of the longing. Has she come to prefer solitude, like K.D. himself? He
has asked himself sometimes if solitude is preferable to boredom or
betrayal, which seemed to be the inevitable end of all happy love
affairs, of all happy marriages. People clung to one another out of
fear. K.D. has preferred the integrity of being alone. He was a realist,
he is. He has the strength to face death alone.

In the upper half of his visual field, his sight is sensitive and keen, he
can see the fine shadow of Anjali's hair on the far wall, the slender,
upstanding stalks thrown up on the grey. In the lower half, a man
named Palash is walking on a bund between fields of rice. He is wearing a torn banian and a dhoti, and the skin on his neck is creased and
dark. K.D. has watched the sweat sweep across it for ten miles. The
man's neck is more real in this present, in this hospital, in this darkness,
than it was on that afternoon long ago. It is a sheeny chocolate, and the
grey hair that straggles over it is distinctly stranded, picked out by the
failing sun into bright, glittering filaments. The path rolls down off the
bund, and into the distance, straight as an arrow. The fields are
flooded, and the young green shoots are mirrored in the still surface of
the water. An elegant preying bird is making its slow, taut circles overhead, inflecting only the very last spread feathers at wingtip. K.D. can
see its rich golden-brown belly, the white chest and head, and he knows
it is a Brahminy Kite. He knows this bird, he knows this day. Ahead,
there will be gunshots. By dusk, Palash will lead him to a hut on the
outskirts of the village of Ramtola, where a young man named
Chunder Ghosh is spending the night. Chunder Ghosh will say his
name is Swapan, but K.D. will recognize him from Jadavpur University
photographs, from birthday pictures at Kadell Road. That plump-
cheeked boy is gone, but this gaunt revolutionary sitting cross-legged is
Chunder Ghosh all right. Ghosh will ask K.D. many questions, probe
K.D.'s cover, which is resilient and whole: K.D. is Sanjeev Jha, small-
time jute trader and Naxalite sympathizer and possible provider of
information about bigger, capitalist jute merchants who need to be
eliminated in the class war. K.D. will answer questions about Patna,
about the various qualities of jute, and a lantern will fuzz and flicker
under Palash's pumping. K.D. will massage his right heel, where he has
been bitten by some unknown insect, some slithering attacker. The
flesh is raw, pushed up in a lump. Chunder Ghosh is a veteran of many
bites, many fevers, but even he will spare a glance for this sudden
wound. The questions will continue, go on. The questions will go on

340

too long. K.D. will get up to relieve himself. He will take his hard-bottomed blue shoulder-bag with him, which has been searched and found to contain a thermos, a shirt, a packet of peanuts, two news-papers and one thousand six hundred rupees. Outside, K.D. will actually urinate. He will be able to, despite the constriction coming in steady swells through his belly. He will breathe, and reach into his bag, and find at the very bottom a fold of cloth which he will take up care-fully with a small stripping sound. He will find a hidden compartment, and inside it a Polish .32 automatic, loaded and chambered. He will walk back into the hut, his hand by his side, the briefcase held before him. He will shoot Chunder Ghosh in the right eye, and Palash in the chest and in the back of his head. In his fast search through the hut, the only thing he will find is an ancient Colt .38 revolver, which Chunder Ghosh was holding cocked in his right hand, under his thigh. He will take it and flee. But all that lies ahead. What K.D. can see now is Palash walking ahead of him, the incandescent green of the rice, the kite swooping low overhead.

What lies ahead, in that first purple shimmer of dusk, at the far edge of the world? From different directions, K.D. Yadav and Chunder Ghosh are walking towards the same dismal hut, with its collapsing roof and cracked walls of mud. One is still doing his best for Nehru, the other has left behind his comfortable life of club and convent and theatre group for another vision equally grand and equally crazy. Both believe that somewhere on the other side of the hut, on the other side of the horizon, there is happiness. Just that, sim-ply that: happiness. But K.D. sees clearly now, he sees from the great clarity of his illness that they were both betrayed, that they were betrayed before they ever began their journeys. A great knot of con-tempt uncurls in K.D.'s chest for those young men, so confident in their own health, in the rude heartiness of their dreams. What fools. What egotists. What could either of them have built that would not end in more murder, more loss, more sickness? 'The spider weaves the curtains in the palace of the Caesars; the owl calls the watches in the towers of Afrasiab.' And yet we schemed, and tore at each other, and killed each other. And we continue to do so, and we will never stop. We will lurch from massacre to pogrom, all in the name of some future heaven. K.D. feels a vast irritation, an exasperation at the entire species, at everything it has ever done. This life is a sickness, he thinks. Let it end. Let it all end. Gaitonde had been afraid of falling white

light, an explosion and a blasting wind that would tear away everything that had been built on the surface of the watery marsh. K.D.
Yadav turns himself on to his back and imagines it, the huge climbing
explosion, the sudden death, the silence afterwards. Finally there will
be quiet. A vanishing, like the blowing-out of a candle. He thinks of it
and he feels the peace of it, feels the necessity of such an end. He
smiles, contented, and sleeps.

Anjali is sitting by the bed, dressed, when he awakens. She smiles.
'Did you remember anything.'

'No,' he says. 'Nothing. Nothing at all.'

She nods. Behind her there is a young man, a sharp young fellow
with a foxy face, a clipped moustache. 'This is Amit Sarkar,' she says.
'He has just joined the organization, he is my trainee. He will stay with
you today.'

'Good morning, sir,' Amit Sarkar says, vibrating with the proper
enthusiasm of a recent inductee in the presence of a legend.

Anjali is keeping up the surveillance, going with her intuition on
this long shot. K.D. doesn't mind. He is finished with it all. 'Right,' he
says, settles back into his pillow. He wants to be easy, to float away,
but something is working at him. Gaitonde's money. There is something about Gaitonde's money that is nettling, the image of it sticks
and scrapes through his head, one crore and twenty lakhs of Central
Bank stacks. K.D. shoves the memory of the money away, he wants
none of it. He fixes on the wall, on the slight vibration of light across
it from the fan overhead. He passes into a comfortable drowsiness, a
light-feeling awareness that skips across memory and image and
thought without attachment. His mind feels weightless, freed of gravity. The lower half of K.D.'s vision is still visited by ghosts from the
past, soldiers long dead, informants, agents, victims. He watches it all
with a sublime detachment. And in the upper half, visitors come and
go, old colleagues with their grandchildren. Dr Kharas and her
interns. Nurses and attendants. Finally, in the evening, Anjali comes
back to relieve Sarkar. They whisper to each other, and then she comes
to sit with K.D. in the dusk. K.D. eats because she insists and he wants
no fuss. Or he would turn away from the food, also with no fuss. It's
all the same to him now. A night passes, and then a day. He watches
it all, life and the life inside his eyes, and they are all equally insubstan-
tial, all phantoms, Dr Kharas and her pricking needles and diagnoses,
Anjali, the MIGs yawing and screaming down towards a Pakistani

airfield, two men walking through fields of rice. They are all illusions, these unreal men and unreal women, and they live by illusions and suffer for them and die because of them. Let it all end tomorrow, this meaningless cavalcade of ghosts, in an inescapable white flash of light. Tomorrow it is over. K.D. is content with this thought, and he is comfortable.

He dreams. He knows he is sleeping, and he knows he is dreaming. He is aware of himself as the sleeping watcher, and yet he feels the thumping impact of his feet through the thick bottoms of his keds as he runs. They are playing football on the high plateau they have levelled into the side of the mountain. Everyone is there: Khandari in his green Garhwali sweater with its sprays of rough wool, Rastogi on the far left, DaCunha with his incessant calls of 'Put-tru, put-tru, man!', and Ginzanang Dowara, who keeps trying to put through but always loses the ball. It is Sunday, and they have divided all the off-duty men into two teams, forty men to a side, and they play a hectic, savage football on what they think is the highest football ground on earth. They have hacked it out of the mountain in two months of high-altitude labour, widened a natural, almost level slope. This ball has come up all the way from Calcutta, through a chain of personal requests and favours called in. So now they play. Thangrikhuma has the ball, he is small and compact and very quick, he slips through a chain of half a dozen defenders with a leaning and a side-step that is so fast that it looks like some sort of cinematic flicker. K.D. gives a great shout of admiration and chases him. Thangrikhuma is fast, so fast. He knows K.D. is coming and doesn't care, he is grinning. K.D. runs hard. The valley beyond is green and grey, and the white clouds are puffy overhead. Thangrikhuma is running. Then Marak the subedar is in place, near the goalkeeper and the two rough stakes of wood which are the goal. Marak is old and slow, and he hangs back near the goal always, and then manifests himself at crucial junctures. He is experienced. He waits, he waits. Thangrikhuma is jinking and jiving, tempting him. Marak attacks now, he slides, our wily Marak. He misses Thangrikhuma but reaches back with an unerring hand as he falls and hooks a handful of jersey, and down goes Thangrikhuma. Foul, foul, but this is a man's game, and it's too late to cry foul, K.D. has the ball and is speeding it back into enemy territory. His boys are with him, shouldering aside the defenders, and K.D. has speed, such speed, he grins at the lovely jounce of the ball and it sits perfectly on his instep and comes back to him, he has perfect control of it, he takes it past Rastogi easily, past the gasp of breath and the spray of sweat, and he is running free now, down the field, and he can hear DaCunha on his left, and Ginzanang Dowara is keeping up nicely on the right, and the ball glitters black and white in its bounce, K.D.'s chest pains him and he is happy and the air is cold in his throat, and the goal is ahead.

K.D. wakes, and he is weeping. There is a burning in his heel. Long ago, as he sat on the unfinished mud floor of a hut with Chunder Ghosh, sat cross-legged with his shoes off, he was bitten on the left heel by an insect. He remembers now, remembers how he rubbed the angry red stain with his thumb, and how Chunder Ghosh had for a moment stopped his questions and peered at the bite curiously. K.D. remembers and feels a sob come racking out of him. Anjali stirs, in her bed, and K.D. tries to hold down his convulsions, to make them stop. The men and women he is weeping for are mostly dead now, but he is crying for their lives, for the brevity of their struggles, for their brief agonies and joys. He is sobbing for the burning in their stings, for the momentary flaming of their desires.

'Uncle, what's wrong? Shall I call a nurse? Are you in pain?'

In the flaring of an electric bulb, Anjali is leaning over him. He shakes his head, and reaches for her hand. He is unable to speak, but he tries to smile at her, all the while shaking his head. She holds him. She sits on the bed and holds him in her lap.

'What is it?' she says. 'Don't be afraid,' she says.

K.D. is not afraid. He feels no fear at all, at least not for himself. But he can find no words for the great compassion that heats his body, this illusory carcass of damaged flesh. In his collapsing mind there is a fear for Anjali, for the life that surges through this strong young woman who holds him. She values her life, clings to it, as do her colleagues, her friends, her family. I must help her, K.D. thinks. I must. He casts back through his life, and through all that he knows and remembers, and now that he is thinking and has a purpose, his trembling stops. He lies still in Anjali's arms and thinks. Now there is that old joy of cogitation, and the information flows in an intertwining of streams, bright with colour and image and smell. It moves and he swims in it and changes angle and nudges it together in many and various arrangements: it feels like he is ambling through a kaleidoscope. There is that old pleasure. When the sky begins to grey outside, he stirs. 'The money in Gaitonde's bunker,' he says.

344

Anjali is leaning back against the headboard, and she comes out of her slumber. 'What?' she says.

'There was money in Gaitonde's bunker. You said something about wrapping.'

'The bundles were wrapped in clear, thin plastic. Like the kind that toys are wrapped in sometimes. Or chocolate.'

'Five bundles together? A stack like this?'

She looks at the shape he is making with his hands, the emptiness he holds in the air. Her eyes are sequined with pinpoints of early morning light. 'Yes,' she says.

'I want to see the money,' he says.

She runs across the room to her mobile phone, and he sits up to the fast blip of her dialling. She rattles out orders, and comes back to him. 'It's on the way,' she says.

But they both know it could take a while, to cut through the bureaucracy of the organization, to wake up people and have permissions given and safes opened. K.D. may not have time, he may forget. So he has her sit next to him and tells her, while he still has the facts. He tells her what he knows, what he remembers. 'Much of our Indian currency used to be printed in the Soviet Union. The Pakis ran an op after the Union fell apart, when everything was for sale. They tried to buy the original plates from the Russians. If they had got the plates, they would have been able to run a counterfeit operation that would have produced genuine notes, perfect money. But we got wind of it and got the plates from the factory. We killed their operation. But the Pakis did manage to get hold of very substantial amounts of original currency paper. We were too late to prevent that. With that paper, they've produced large-sum Indian currency, several series of big notes. They have some very talented technicians. The forgeries are brilliant. I've seen some of the notes, from seizures in Jammu and Amritsar. They are very good. They were completely wrapped in plastic, in stacks like this.'

Anjali nods, fast. 'Very good for transportation, in all kinds of conditions.'

'Yes, in any weather. The operation in Russia was run by an ISI man named Shahid Khan, who was a major at the time. He's good. I had known him before, from when he was with their embassy in London.'

'Shahid Khan,' Anjali says.

'Shahid Khan,' K.D. says. 'Very religious fellow. Hard worker. One of their best. Shahid Khan got the paper.'

She writes rapidly, on a white pad. He listens to the scratch of her pen, and when she is finished she waits for him, for more. But this is all he has.

They wait, together, for the money. Just after one, Amit Sarkar arrives, clutching a briefcase. Anjali holds up the stack for K.D. to look at. 'Yes,' he says. 'Yes.' He can feel himself smiling. The game, he thinks. It runs. He takes Anjali's pen from her and notches the point into the plastic and pulls. From this cut he pulls a note, and holds it towards the window, towards the brightness of the day. 'Yes,' he says. 'Yes. I think it's their money.' He has no idea what this means to Anjali, or whether it means anything at all. But they are all happy: it is something.

Anjali takes the money, takes her pad, hugs K.D. and hurries away. She must go, but she leaves Amit Sarkar with K.D., to listen, to watch over him. The organization still wants him to play, but it is too late. K.D. lies back in his bed, his arms spread wide. His pillows are very comfortable, good to feel against his cheeks. He is tired. It's time to rest. He shuts his eyes. He breathes, and sleeps.

Money

Put all together, Katekar's benefits and provident fund and small savings amounted to sixty-seven thousand and seven rupees seventy-four paise. The state government immediately announced a relief amount of two lakhs for his bereaved family, but it took nine and a half months for the cheque to wind its way through the convolutions of Mantralaya and the exacting attentions of many departmental clerks. By the time Shalini had the cheque cleared and the money deposited, it was almost a year to the day after her husband's death. She now spent her days speeding through six households where she washed clothes and dishes, did jhadoo-katka, and for this cleansing of homes was paid a thousand rupees by each. With two growing sons, this was not nearly enough, and it was a very steep drop from the days when her husband had brought home packets of cash. Now, finally, there were these two lakhs sitting in her account, and two lakhs seemed rather a lot to have at once, but Shalini knew well that sudden and fat chunks of money produced only an illusion of well-being. This is what she was now trying to explain to her sister.

'Bharti,' she said. 'Two lakhs seems like a lot. But how many days are there in a lifetime? How long will these two lakhs last, over three lifetimes? I have young boys. I have to pay for their school, all their books. And anything could happen. We could need the money at any time.'

Bharti was sitting cross-legged on a pillow she had taken from the shelf, with the table-fan full upon her. She wiped her face with her pallu, and ducked her head in that way she had when she was annoyed. 'Tai, if you are not going to spend it, what good is it doing sitting in that bank? We need it now, and he says the interest he will give you will be larger than the bank's.' Bharti's husband, Vishnu Ghodke, had two friends who were going to start a travel agency. He was to be the very smallest partner, but even for that he needed five lakhs, and he had less than three. Shalini was suddenly sitting on more than two. And so Bharti was here, on a Thursday evening, looking hot and angry. 'He says it's a sure business. People are travelling more and more. And both his partners have contacts in Bahrain and Saudi, and thousands want to go there. Thousands and thousands.'

Shalini shook her head. 'Bharti, even if crores and crores want to go to Saudi, I can't give this money. I am alone. I am alone and I have to take care of my boys.'

The thrust of Bharti's jaw was very bitter now. 'What about us? You have us. Don't you have any trust in us?'

'It's not a matter of trust or no trust.'

'Then?'

'Bharti, anything can happen. Anything.' It was life that you couldn't place any trust in. It was this life that fell out from under your feet, that left you falling and lost.

'But you are safe, tai. He'll pay you in monthly instalments, so there will be money coming in. In addition to what you are earning already. And you don't have any rent to pay. You will never be that badly off.'

Shalini and he had paid six lakhs for this safety over their heads, seven years ago. They had paid in four painful instalments, all in cash, all of it squeezed from thousands of washed plates and petticoats, from innumerable fifty and hundred-rupee bribes. So now she and her sons had a roof, two rooms, a kitchen, that was their own. That is what he had wanted, to own, to have a patch of earth that was not government property or a landlord's estate, he had wanted the safety of home. He had given them that. And then he was dead. The knowledge of his absence came to Shalini in a muscular twinge through her back and into her stomach, as it did now and again. She took a long breath, and then another. 'I can't do it,' she said. 'Bharti, I can't risk the money. Just think.'

'You are the one always thinking, tai. Thinking and thinking. But we people, we listen to our hearts. And so we thought we would ask you. We thought you would understand.' Bharti was getting up, gathering her purse and the folds of her sari about her.

'Bharti . . .'

'No, no, always you've been the smart one. Always you think three steps ahead. Always you get what you want because you think. But we are not like that.'

348

Shalini knew that to protest would immediately reopen and unreel a long and bitter discussion about a gold necklace that their mother had left to her and not to Bharti, and an incident at a family wedding when there had been an argument about the distribution of gift saris, and then exactly how much money had been spent on Shalini's wedding, and how much on Bharti's. They both knew completely the contours of these debates, and yet Bharti would finally weep and burn in righteous pain, her round face dissolving into soft infancy. So Shalini watched quietly as Bharti bent to pull the straps of her fancy green sandals over her ankles. Then she said, very gently, 'At least wait till the boys get back.'

'I left the children at Maushi's. It's been too long.'

Maushi was Vishnu Ghodke's maushi, who lived three buildings away from them. She was dependable but bad-tempered, and the children could not be left too long under her hard-handed discipline. Shalini thought the boy could use a few more slaps and pinches, but this was no time to criticize Bharti's son. As Bharti went out of the door, Shalini touched her above the elbow, just a little pat, her usual sisterly greeting and goodbye. But Bharti marched down the street, her head held high and rigid, and then Shalini lowered herself down, sat in the doorway. She allowed herself five minutes of slackness, of an exhausted lapse into complete relaxation. She watched the passers-by. It was almost seven-thirty in the evening, and the home-going rush was at its thickest. The shadows were long already, the days were getting shorter. Soon the nights would need an extra sheet, a blanket. The season was turning. The walkers passed in a steady flow, hypnotic in its even rhythm, the constant scissor motion of legs and ankles, the swing of bags laden with onions and potatoes and atta and soap and coconut oil. Some of the younger ones had smart office briefcases and a faster stride, all purpose and direction. They all passed.

Five minutes. Shalini knew when they were up. For as long as she could remember, she had had an unerring instinct for time, she could tell it down to the minute without ever needing a watch. She woke always without an alarm, and every day arrived at the station gate precisely six minutes before her train came in. She knew her rest was over, and so she got up. There was only a moment, a heartbeat or two, when her body was reluctant to leave its repose, its luxurious resting on brick and wood. Then Shalini gathered herself up, and got up. 'Ambabai,' she said gently, with a glance towards the deity on the shelf, 'rise, awaken. We have work to do.'

She had dinner ready when the boys came in. Rohit took half a bucket of water and led his younger brother out. Shalini could hear them murmuring under the splash of water. This was something that their father had insisted on, that when they returned from their games they had to wash their hands and feet before sitting in the house. In his presence they had always muttered against it, treated it as an unbearable fatherly burden, especially Rohit, who refused to do it if his father was not at home. Now that his father was really gone, Rohit performed the evening ablutions with a ritualistic seriousness, and led his brother through it with an unrelenting, police-like discipline. He had become very serious, Rohit had. He spoke to Shalini every morning about what was needed for the house, and went to the bazaar in the afternoon, after school. He brought back exact change, and showed her the lists of accounts he kept in a special notebook. He had a key to the house now, and wore it round his neck on a red string, and took it off only to sleep. As he ate now, he had it slung over his right shoulder, down his bent back.

'All homework is done, Mohit?' Shalini said.

Mohit had fast, stubby fingers. He was eating quickly, with his thali held in his lap and his head low. 'Mmmm,' he said. 'Mmmm.'

'Aai, he's got a maths test on Friday,' Rohit said, 'that he hasn't even started studying for.'

'Friday,' Mohit managed to get out between bites.

He had a smear of dal on his upper lip. He meant that Friday was three days away, Shalini understood this. He had done quite badly in his last exams, but that was only to be expected of a small boy who had gone to his father's funeral. Shalini had assumed, as had everyone who knew him, that he would adjust, cope, forget a little, and get back to his quiet, steady ways. But Mohit was still slipping, leaving his work undone while he sped through life on some secret mission. He hid himself behind his bed, in a nook filled with comics with lurid covers featuring moustachioed, pistol-clutching adventurers. He drew rifles in the margins of his notebooks, and muscular heroes firing enormous, blazing guns. He had a private life now, an inner world that Shalini could no longer reach. This happened with children, with sons, but not so soon. She patted the atta off her hands and reached out and tapped the top of his head with her forearm. 'Start studying tomorrow,' she said. 'Yes?'

'Yes,' he said.

'Want rice?'

'Yes,' he said.

Shalini fed them, washed up, slid the dishes into the rack on the wall, hung the pot and the pans and the spoons on their designated hooks on the roof. She took up her tooth powder and a glass of water and sat in the doorway. The lane held only a scattering of walkers, who stepped through the throw of light from each door. In another lane, long ago, he had said once that this repetition of light looked like a waterfall. That had been early in their marriage. Yes, she had said, like the cascade at Karla. They had been very poor then, and the trip to Karla and its caves had been a special treat a year after their marriage. He had walked inside the caves, marvelling at their roofs carved to look like wooden beams, and had stood before the stupas and become solemn, despite his scepticism, which even then was sharp and unrelenting. Now, in this lane, everyone was watching *Sabse Bada Paisa*, and the colours flickered in unison on the mud, up and down the street. She could hear the host's voice leaping from television to television, offering the chance of very large money. In her house there was a television, and usually there was no watching it this late on a weekday. That had been his rule. Study hard, he said to his sons, and when you have your own house you can watch television whenever you want. He made an exception for *Kaun Banega Crorepati*, though, because it was a knowledge-based show. Answer the right questions and you could win, you could own a crore, just like that. If you knew enough, you could be rich. Learn, learn, he told his sons, and they watched it together, seated cross-legged in a row. They used to shout out the answers. She used to call them the three monkeys, and they made monkey faces at her. Now Rohit was watching *Sabse Bada Paisa* intently, and its blues and greens moved across his face. Mohit was back in his nook, muttering out his secret stories to himself. He had lost interest in the show after the funeral. And Shalini sat in her doorway. On the television, the host asked, what is the name of the largest irrigation project ever built in India?

'Arre, Shalu.'

It was their neighbour, Arpana, with her man, Amritrao Pawar, both walking home in outing clothes. They seemed friendly enough tonight, so they must be going through one of the peace cycles in their lifelong war. Shalini made room for Arpana on the step. 'Out so late?' she said.

351

'My niece's Kelvan. In Malad.'

'Sudhir's daughter?'

'Yes. They are doing the wedding near his kholi itself.'

Arpana had two younger brothers, and she was close to the youngest. With the middle one, there was a feud of obscure origin. Shalini had heard the whole story when she had first moved into the house and met Arpana the feisty neighbour, but she couldn't remember the details. For many years she had known Arpana, and watched her quarrel with Amritrao Pawar, who had another woman and another family not so far away. At first Shalini had advised giving him up, sending him away. Then she had seen how they went from fighting to lifelong promises and opulent gifts, and one monsoon night, when she had herself been pregnant, she had gone late to ask Arpana for two onions. And standing outside their door she had heard how they made up, with what extravagant, moaning ecstasies they forgave each other. She understood then why the women on the street laughed when Arpana complained about her man's indifference and cruelty. He was standing facing them now, this Amritrao Pawar, with his hands in his pockets and a lordly smile of satisfaction teasing his mouth. Shalini didn't like him looking at her like that. Let him feast on his Arpana. She turned her shoulder to him. 'How was the boy?' she said to Arpana.

'Too thin,' Arpana said. 'He looked like that drainpipe, only not so black. But the family is good. He has a job at the airport.' She looked up from massaging her feet, at Amritrao Pawar. 'Why are you standing here like some lamppost?'

Shalini was afraid they would start a fight at her door. Sometimes all it took was a certain look. But Amritrao Pawar was happy tonight, and he only burbled into laughter. 'Waiting for you, rani. But I will wait at home.'

They watched him go, and Arpana snorted. 'They were drinking behind the house. He thinks I can't tell.' They nodded together at the foolishness of men, and then Arpana leaned in. 'Bharti came today?'

'Yes. How do you know?'

'That Chitra was on our bus.' Chitra was another neighbour, two doors down on the right. 'She said she saw Bharti at the bus stop.'

And other neighbours would have seen her at the road turning, and walking down the lane, and in the house, and noted her expression, and made their deductions. 'Yes,' Shalini said. 'She was here.'

'In the middle of the week? Did something happen?'

'Nothing, nothing. Just some money troubles.'

Arpana didn't look very convinced, or satisfied with just that much. But Shalini was not about to give in, and she turned the talk to Amritrao Pawar. That Arpana could never resist. She began her recitation of his recent sins, that he had gone to Mahabaleshwar with that randi and her whole brood – including the randi's Kaku – and therefore spent more money than he earned in two months, that he had fought with Arpana when she had remonstrated, when she told him that he had no ambition and was unwilling to take any risks, that he clung to his peon job like a fool scared of the world.

'Jobs aren't lying on the footpath,' Shalini said. 'Let him keep his job at least.'

'There's no income at all,' Arpana said. She meant apart from his salary. 'And they'll never promote him and never raise his salary. They are Muslims after all.'

'I thought his manager was a Brahmin? Some Bajpai, no?'

'Yes, yes,' Arpana said. 'But the company is owned by Muslims. And you know how they are.'

Shalini nodded. She had no arguments with this, but she doubted that Amritrao had anything in him worth promoting. Arpana settled back into her litany. She had tough, blocky shoulders and a thick neck, and she was nowhere near pretty, and over the last decade her cheeks had begun to droop. But still she and Amritrao Pawar returned to each other time and again, and tore at each other in rage and passion. The tragedy, of course, was that after all this, Arpana had no children. That is why she could never finally prove Amritrao Pawar in the wrong, and that was why he had another woman. All this painful need for each other, all this anger, and no children. Ambabai had her ways, her unknowable ways. 'Time for me to put the boys to sleep,' Shalini said.

'Yes. Are they all right?'

The women on the lane kept an eye on the boys, and Arpana especially took an interest in them, and sat with Mohit in the afternoons after school. 'Yes,' Shalini said. 'They are all right.'

They got up, nodded and went to the last chores of the day. Shalini tidied a little, chivvied the boys into bed, spread out the bedding and lay down. This was the hardest time of the day, when she missed resting her shoulder on his belly, when her bones could recall the curve her body made with his. In this waiting for sleep her mind moved sideways, twinkling-quick and unpredictable, his jokes and his laughter and little humiliations and joys from her own childhood came together and mixed up, bright, bright and painful. There was his filthy poem about Dev Anand and Mumtaz, and Shalini smiled, he had told it to her about a thousand times, all with the same glee. She drew in a deep breath, and then the hurt came. She wiped her face. At least she had his sons. His sons were sleeping close to her. She was drifting now. Muslims were like that. They killed my husband. One of them killed him, and now the murderer was dead. She sometimes wished the killer was still alive, so she could kill him again. But Sartaj Singh had shot the Bihari. Sartaj Singh was a killer too. They were all killers, and they had all killed her husband. The rage felt like iron pushing through her throat, and against every last shred of will, it forced itself out, making a low howl that scraped against the walls and frightened Shalini. She waited, but the boys were already sunk in their dense sleep, and outside the open door there was only the murmur of a distant conversation.

Shalini sat up. She took a glass of water and rinsed her hands, face and feet as quietly as she could. Then she sat cross-legged in front of Ambabai and Bhavani. Are you awake, Ambabai? Bhavani, no more of your ferocity – there is nobody to punish – but give me mercy. Give me peace. You failed him, Bhavani, I begged you every day for his safe return and yet you failed him. I won't call you bad names any more, I won't ask you why. You give me no reasons, and I will accept your silence. But give me a little portion of peace, give me relief from this deafening tumult of pain. I need to be quiet, for my boys. Ambai, are you listening? Give me this boon. I mourn him, but give me strength. Bhavani is blinding blue light, even her mercy comes like cool moonlight, but you, Ambai, are fruitful fields and overflowing water, rich mud and baby's breath and wide-brimmed lotus, you are my mother, bring me back from this exile, let me live under your shadow again. He was a good man. He walked to Pandharpur when I asked him to, even though he didn't believe that piety would cure his back. He lived in pain, I saw how he held himself upright with a hand on his hip at the end of the day, but he took care of us and he did his job. He was strict but never harsh, and Rohit and Mohit never feared him. He put a gold chain on my neck on the day of his first promotion and kept it there through our bad times. He never questioned me about money. When we fought he never hit me, only once he caught my elbow in anger and

354

left a bruise. We were young, Ambai, he rubbed away the pain with phatkari and heated haldi, he gentled me with his sorrow. He smelt of coconut hair oil and Shiva-ji bidis then, but later for us he stopped taking tobacco in any form. Later he took women, I knew that, I fought with him, and he said he stopped, but I knew when he really stopped, when he knew truly what it meant to be a father. He wounded me, Ambai, and I him. I know I battered him sometimes with my cold quietness. But I did my duty as a wife, gave the embraces that men want. I fed him. He sustained me. We were companions, friends, not quite without quarrels but without rancour. Aai, I earn money, I go from day to day, but at night a rough rope pulls at my stomach, I twist to his side of the bed, I see things. I see him coughing in bed, he has a fever and I bring him a newspaper and he takes it, and his hand is hot and I feel a stab of worry. Then he is entering the kholi, and Mohit is crawling, his bottom wet. Him seated cross-legged, counting money. I am cutting onions, and the next day is Shayani Ekadashi. Ambai, where are you? Bhavani, are you here? I can feel you close, Ambai, but I am alone. Give me succour, Ambabai. I am alone.

'Aai?'

Rohit was standing behind her. She let him put her to bed, listened to his attempts to comfort her, let him go back to bed to comfort himself. She was remembering, again, that night when she went to Arpana's, to borrow the two onions, how she had stood outside Arpana's door, close to the wood to get away from the dripping rain, and listened to the sounds Arpana was making, somewhere between bitter and sweet. With a determined effort Shalini turned her mind away, made herself not think of it, of any of it. But still there was a small, dull pain that moved with every breath. She bore it, and whispered Ambabai's name again and again.

Anjali Mathur was following money. She did this in her spare time, what little there was at the end of the day or very early in the morning. She had managed to get to work early this Tuesday, so she was reading old files. She had run a data check for forged money, for the large sums of counterfeit currency the Pakistanis were known to have produced. Even with an arbitrary cut-off date of 1 January 1987, the database had given her a list of incidents, of mentions in reports, running to seventy-four single-spaced pages. So she had, over the last four months, been making her way through the original reports, one by one. It was tedious, and it was probably a waste of time, so she hadn't told anyone about her search. She had no idea of what she was looking for, other than detail, some pattern in the detail. A connection would reveal itself across the breadths of geography and time, a string of causes would unwind backwards and reveal a beginning, no, not a beginning but a node where many stories came together, and somehow the death of Ganesh Gaitonde would fit into the stream of events. Anjali didn't want an explanation, she was suspicious of explanations. Any explanation, any solution, always left out too much. But she trusted associations and correlations and rhythms, and the twistings and contractions of time. That was what K.D. Yadav had tried to teach them, to feel the beat and swing of the enemy's intention, that was what allowed you to predict. And this was why, after all the analysis, the cross-referencing and the computers and the mathematics, it came down to this, to reading old reports one by one. Finally it all depended on instinct. In her instinct, in her bones, Anjali felt a question about Gaitonde's return to the country, his death, about his bunker in the middle of Kailashpada, about the dead woman. None of it fitted together, none of it spoke a language that she could understand.

She had long ago learnt to decipher the particular vernacular of the reports, to imagine the event through the jerky telegraphese. She was reading one now, on plain unadorned paper.

TOP SECRET
Code Number of Source . . . 910-02-75P of . . . Unit Jammu Alpha
S. N. of report . . . 2/97 dated . . . 27.1.97

Particulars of source: Source Rehmat Sani is farmer, smuggler, w/family on both sides of border. Info was gathered from cousin Yasin Hafeez in Pak army.
Mode of communication: Personal meeting.
Reliability: II

Source conducted meeting with cousin in village Bhanni 13.1.97. Cousin is Havaldar in 13th Battalion, Punjab Regiment, at Mandi Chappar. His platoon was detailed to escort private three-tonne truck from known counterfeit printing press at 142 Shah Karnam Road (see report 47/96) to Lashkar-i-Azadi base at Hafizganj. Delivery was four crates, 4' x 4' x 4', received by Lashkar deputy commander Rashid

Khan. Source has no further info on contents. High probability
contents are large amounts of medium denomination currency to be
used in spring offensive in Valley and elsewhere. Source instructed to
maintain observation.

Anjali knew the man who wrote this report. He had been her batch-
mate during training. His name was Gaurav Sharma, he had been
completely bald at twenty-six. In 1997 he had been posted in Jammu,
and there was a little hint of him in that 'high probability'. He had
been full of chaos theory during the training days and had tried to
communicate to his fellow trainees, over chai and samosas during
breaks, the rapture of fractals and strange attractors. In this report, as
they had been trained, he had taken himself out of the language, tried
to make it impersonal and objective. This was how it worked, as
information moved upwards. The source was no doubt a sweaty villain, a border criminal, a smuggler and murderer who had fatalism
bred into him by the artillery shells that armies had fired over his head
for the last fifty years, that fell into his village and fields to kill uncles
and aunts. He was the sort of man who knew how to cross the border
on a moonless night, who would think nothing of traversing the
shrapnel-sharp dangers of no man's land. He knew how to lie motionless for hours in a wheatfield under the probing, random fire of heavy
machine guns, when to creep and when to stop. He had undoubtedly
seduced his Pak army cousin into informing, tempted him first with
easy loans for marriages and tractors, and then paid him outright. He
made money at both ends, from his cousin and his handling officer.
And no doubt the handling officer had given him cases of cheap rum,
which he carried three at a time over the border into the ritually pure
regions of Pakistan. The HO had met him in late January of '97,
perhaps in some shack, some dhaba stinking of country liquor, paid
him, and then reported to his supervisory office in Jammu, where
Gaurav Sharma had prepared a report for the consumer desk in Delhi.
The information would form the basis for reports that would go up
the chain, and perhaps finally a chief secretary had been made aware
that all data indicated that the enemy was planning an early offensive
in the spring. Perhaps the prime minister had released funds, asked
for budgetary changes. At every step up the ladder, the information
was abstracted. Details were leached out. Here, in Delhi at the
consumer desk, there were names and places and trucks and crates

and Rehmat and Yasin. Up high, nobody wanted to know how it was done. Your job, K.D. Yadav had said, is also to shield the people on top from knowing too much. They shouldn't know. They need to be able to act, and shouldn't be bogged down in details. They need to preserve deniability. So keep it clean. Tell them what they need to know. Bas.

Anjali put the report aside, and turned to her everyday work. In the organization, within her professional circle in Delhi, her trip to Bombay had been finally regarded as quite frivolous. That man Gaitonde had bumped himself off, after a long career of bumping off other people, and so what? Thugs like that were unstable by definition, and Gaitonde had had an up-and-down history of alcohol and women and much else. This was known. So he had built a safe house in Bombay. So what? The man was dead by his own hand, that was the only fact of any import. So what was the need for fact-finding, and what additional facts had been found? None. We told you so, the wise old men of the organization said, this is why you can't trust women in the field. This is, after all, why Kulkarni had been assigned to run Gaitonde in the first place. He had learnt his tradecraft in Punjab, he had run operations in Kashmir. He had been adjudged tough enough and Maharashtrian enough to deal with the foul-mouthed gangster, and he had – with a fine crusting of condescension – done Anjali the favour of clearing her to read his reports. 'I know you have an interest in the man,' he said, smiling toothily at her, 'and a good analyst can always help.' So she had followed Gaitonde's subsequent history, his use by the organization and his use of the organization, his escape from assassination attempts and his mounting paranoia, his lies to his handler, his instability and his sudden disappearance. When he had reappeared as a corpse in his old neighbourhood, smiling Kulkarni had been kind enough to allow her to go down and investigate.

She had found nothing useful, and so now she was back at her analysis. Her desk was Islamic Fundamentalism, and her beat was the world. Today she was following a Scotsman. He had been born Malcolm Mourad Bruce in 1964, in Edinburgh, to a Scottish carpenter and an Algerian hotel maid. The father had left when Malcolm was seven, walked out without a backward glance, and the mother had moved to Birmingham to live with her brother and his family. At seventeen, Malcolm Mourad Bruce had become Mourad Chaker, passionate advocate of simple living, and had enjoyed a local celebrity in the mosques as the boy-preacher with red hair. At twenty-two he had appeared in Afghanistan, had fought the Soviets, had been wounded seven times. Four years later there were reports of red-haired Mourad fighting for the GIA in Algeria, killing journalists and bureaucrats and army officers and civilians. He gained renown as the most intransigent of the Salafist leaders, who refused to even speak to the moderate Djazarists in his own group. For fierce Mourad, whose belief burned in his eyes and in the flame of his hair, nothing less than a global Islamic revolution was acceptable. In 1999, Indian military intelligence had reported a new band of militants operating in the valley of Kashmir, led by a red-haired Mourad. It was of course the same man. But did his appearance in the valley mean that the GIA was now institutionally involved in the fighting, that they were going to send money and arms and men? Or was Mourad on his own, looking for another war, another mission? This was the question. And so Anjali read through the morning, through the afternoon, looking for connections, for histories of men and women and their ideas and the associations they formed, the journeys they made across borders. She read internal organization reports from the Valley, think-tank papers from Washington, shared intelligence from the CIA, funnelled through a working group, three chapters of a book on the Algerian troubles by a German academic, Xeroxed copies of articles from Algerian newspapers and magazines, with photographs of the dead turned by the machine into flat black-and-white designs, and two years of field reports from organization operatives in Morocco, Egypt and Algeria. Her concentration submerged her like a diving-bell, and she was insensible to the passing office chatter in the corridor outside, the mounting glare of sunlight on the dusty window, the pigeon that stepped curve-clawed through the bars and glared at her. Occasionally she tipped a plastic bottle to the side of her mouth and drank water without a pause in the velocity of her reading. In graduate school she had acquired a note-taking skill that kept the lines steady and legible without needing more than an infrequent glance at the pad, and now she filled up the pages. The day passed. At one-thirty there was a small knock on the door, and Amit Sarkar tilted his head into the room.

'Come in,' Anjali said. 'You can come in, Amit.'

'Madam, lunch?'

Amit Sarkar was newly married, and every week looked a little more prosperous from his wife's cooking. He no longer had that hungry graduate-student leanness from the early days of his training, and had taken to bringing in a three-decker tiffin, to share. He was unfailingly polite, but she felt his disapproval of her bad eating habits, and his solicitude for her solitary divorcee life. She snapped at him sometimes, irritated despite herself by his presumptions. But today she was glad of the interruption. To live always between threat and counter-threat, from aggression to response, was suffocating. With his dal and bhat, Amit Sarkar brought her a whiff of normal life, of home and kitchen. 'What is it today?'

'Chingri macher curry, ma'am. It's Maithli's speciality.'

Maithli was short and round, with a chin-thrusting smile that made her eyes vanish. Anjali had met her twice and found her quite conventional and devoid of conversation. But her prawns were indeed good. Anjali ate, and Amit talked to her about his current project. She had him following the flow of foreign money, mainly from Saudi and Sudan, to radical Islamic organizations within India. He had unearthed, two days before, a link between a student group based in Trivandrum and a seminary in Nagpur, a thread of connections between a student leader and a middle-man trader and a fiery mullah. This was good work, and now Amit was developing the narrative. The student leader had a brother who worked in Dubai, and this brother was perhaps a conduit for money and information and ideology. Anjali ate, and listened. Maybe Amit had the makings of a good analyst: he was excited by detail, pleasured by conjunctions. He had a habit of assuming too much, of wanting his stories to work so much that he let his imagination produce texture and depth. But he could be worked out of that, that was her job, to wean him away from fancy. But he had the necessary fervour. She let him finish, and then took him down to bedrock, to the foundation of fact: the brother, Dubai, daily phone calls. That was all. 'Interesting, but not enough to suppose so much,' she said. 'We need more.'

'Can we request an operation?'

Anjali had to smile. He had all the enthusiasm of a puppy huffing after his first rat. She said, 'We can request, but we will never get. There are many higher priorities.' He nodded wisely, but despite his attempt at mature indifference, Anjali saw the small swallowing of disappointment. Every trainee had this fantasy, of moving a case from analysis to operations, of finding clues that would lead to a conspiracy so dangerous that it could only be tackled by desperate measures and heroic men and gunfights in the dark. That's what the trainees came in thinking, that's how they were recruited into the job. But the job was this, reading and reading, and finding fragmented stories, and understanding that some dangers might be fatal and yet not worth the allocation of resources. You watched some things, and let them go. So she tried to comfort Amit. 'But you never know. We'll keep them on a watch list. They may get ambitious and try something.'

Amit wasn't very mollified, but he put a good face on it and gathered up his tiffin. Anjali thanked him and gathered herself into her papers again. The pages smelt of haldi now, and adrak, and she wondered if years from now some other analyst would catch the scent, barely palpable, and be struck by a sudden longing for home. She read on. Amit's frown stayed with her. He chafed at the confinements of a Delhi desk, he wanted to get his hands mucky. Well, he would get action soon enough. Somebody, some dushman, always got ambitious and somebody always tried something. To sit in a small room in the bowels of the MEA and read reports all day was to be buffeted by the eternal agitation of humanity, by the ceaseless motion of desire and envy and hate. Nobody, it seemed, not one man or woman ever sat unmoving in the grove of contentment. Always, there was somewhere to go, someone to defeat, something to have. Well, it gave her a job, and a path in life. She read.

At six she gathered up her briefcase and purse, locked her safe and her filing cabinets, put her car keys in the outer pocket of her purse and walked briskly down to the garage. The two grandly moustachioed Delhi police constables on duty at the garage gate gave her an even stare as she drove past, that opaque and blankly belligerent gaze that was the routine burden of a single woman in Delhi. They didn't like the fact that she was a woman, that she was alone, that she had her own car, her own pay cheque. There was a time, when she had been younger, when she had looked back, when she had asked, what are you looking at? She had confronted businessmen, and bus drivers, and students, and labourers, and policemen. Policemen were the worst, protected by their authority and drunk on a daily diet of aggression and violence. But she had faced them too, goaded on by the memory of her father, who had laughed admiringly at her early tomboyishness, her courage, her refusal to back down ever. She still pushed hard, but somehow, one day, she had found herself too tired for confrontations. It wasn't the pace of her work alone. She felt worn down at her core, as if some steely metal spring had lost its early bounce. Let the young take their places at the barricades, these girls who traipsed around the college campuses with their bare midriffs and mobile phones. The pitted and weathered have other battles to fight.

Anjali took a wide turn down the boulevard, narrowing her eyes against the sunset, and grinned at herself. What an easy moderate age had made of her, all the early revolutionary fervour corroded away by – by what? – long hours, bills, this jangling traffic, the poisonous pollution that left films of black on her face and arms. And by professional defeats, a divorce and the abrupt amputation of love, a bone-deep realization that the future was not a limitless meadow, but only a narrow valley bounded by night. Looking at her mother's bow-legged, arthritic walk, her papery-skinned hands, Anjali felt the press of mortality. Her mother would die. K.D. Yadav would die, soon. Only her father was immortal, suspended somewhere in that endless youth of the missing. He was legally dead, but he was still alive. Anjali felt his presence in the very early mornings, when she was washing gently up through the wetlands of sleep. He came to her then, with that briny smell of sweat and Brylcreem, with his shoulder as solid against her cheek as the heating sunlight from the corner window. Then he was gone again, quite gone.

A silver Lexus came in close to Anjali's window, and then they all waited for the traffic to move. Behind the tinted glass of the Lexus, a teenage girl chewed gum steadily. She was flicking through a glossy magazine, fanning the pages fast from right to left. She looked quite bored, and she was beautiful. Her father was a minister, a tycoon, a famous doctor, one of those fixers who put deals together at the intersections of Delhi's many worlds. She lived in a Lexus climate, quite distant from Anjali, in a geography of Vasant Vihar and the Senso and farmhouse parties and teeny dresses. She felt Anjali's gaze and blinked up a glance and then went back to her magazine, quite indifferent. Anjali could see herself in the Lexus glass, sweaty and hot and very middlingly middle-class in her brown-red kameez and red chunni, unable to afford a replacement for her car's dead air-conditioning system. The traffic parted, and the Lexus slid away. Anjali mopped at her chin. How easy it was to be resentful, how easy it was to wish that a couple of angry policemen would stop the Lexus and ask for licence-registration, and make legalistic objections to the tinted glass, and accuse the gliding machine of unacceptable emissions. Anjali shrugged the thought away, sat up straight and brought herself back to facts, to what needed to be done, to work. Resentment was useless, all the more pointless because any hassling, sullen policemen would finally settle for a bribe of two or three hundred rupees.

At the clinic, Anjali dashed water over her face, her arms. When she emerged from the bathroom, K.D. Uncle's head was angled at exactly the same tilt she had left him in, towards the window. His profile stood dark against the brightness, that well-known arc of high fore-head and spare, bald skull, that prow of a nose. It had been five weeks since he had spoken a word. He was pliable and easy, he would walk with you if you held his hand, sit if you pushed him slowly into a chair. He ate slowly, but only if you fed him by hand, and he showed no pleasure in his favourite dishes. He was indifferent. He had gone away. Anjali knew this well, she recognized it when she sat directly in front of him and spoke to him. Behind those slow blinks there was neither happiness nor sadness. He was just absent. He had gone far beyond hate and desire, and so he could no longer love. Still, Anjali came as often as she could and sat with him. The nurses turned him over during the day, walked him to the bathroom and into the garden, but Anjali liked to turn him towards the window and the sunset. She had noticed, long ago in her childhood, how he liked the turning of colours. He liked mountains, and snow. He had told her about Himalayan peaks, about how at sunrise and sunset they turned a bright gold against blue.

The doctors gave him two months to live, maybe three. Anjali had seen how hard he had fought to come back to her, when he had told her about the counterfeit money. And after that momentary return, she had accepted, completely and without hope, the fact of his depar-ture. What was here was not K.D. Yadav. Still, she came and sat with him in the evenings. She would not, in any case, abandon him.

She settled herself down into the chair next to the bed and opened her sheaf of papers to the marked sheet. She was reading a Xeroxed journal article titled 'Warrior Ascetics in Indian History'. The infor-mation that Gaitonde had been looking for sadhus had led nowhere, and even Anjali now thought that it was a misrepresentation, a joke or an allusion to something else, or an outright lie. But her initial reading about sadhus had taken her headlong into one of her obses-sions. She called them her 'projects', but her ex-husband Arun had called them her manias: she would become fascinated by some obscure thing, some murky process that twenty people in the entire world cared about, and then she had to know all about it. Her projects had included the life cycle and social organization of the red ant, the history of terracotta sculptures on the subcontinent, the economy and organization of the Soviet gulags, the early history of the steam locomotive and railways. She had once spent four glorious months reading, in every spare moment, about the campaigns of Julius Caesar. None of this was of any practical use to her. She had tried to explain to Arun that the pleasure was in the little specifics, in finding out how something worked, how its components fitted together. When they had been courting, he had found these projects amusing, charming in their eccentricity. He had admired her curiosity and her memory. But later, after they were married, Arun grew tired of her endless reading and questioning. During one of their quarrels, he told her that he found her boring. Of course they had always known they were different, but once it had seemed that his gregariousness and her quiet calm would balance each other out. Later, afterwards, he liked to exchange visits with his ever-growing circle of friends, drink Scotch and watch Formula One racing, which he never missed, even when he was posted as a probationer in a backwater of Madhya Pradesh. He had taken a lift in a coal truck to get to a big-enough television, and some years later he had decided, also on a racing night, that Anjali was boring. She still thought he might not have thought her so boring if she had been willing to give up her career and move along with him on every new posting, like the other IAS wives did. Anyway, that was long ago, and it was all over. Anjali turned to her article and read about the Sanyasi Rebellion.

She was distracted, though. It was hard to read without being able to discuss the material with K.D. Uncle, without debate and exegesis and questioning. Even when he was travelling somewhere on the other side of the world, she had always talked to him about her reading, and now there was this absence which responded with lofty indifference. This silence made a hole inside her, a gap which threatened to expose that other, vaster chasm her father had left behind, and a shudder of panic started in her stomach. It was hard to be so alone, it was impossible. She stood up, walked away the anxiety, striding to the door and then back to the window. She was not alone. She had Ma to look after, and many friends, and good colleagues and essential, crucial work.

She was needed. And there was a man, perhaps a man, a professor of sociology, a little younger than her but very gentle. She could still hope for love, or at least companionship and compassion, unlike poor K.D. Uncle, who had truly lived like some sort of ascetic. She stopped short, tightened her shoulders and told herself to stop being ridiculous. It was heartbreaking to lose K.D. Uncle, but some part of him was here, she owed him at least the serenity and discipline he had inculcated in her. She sat next to him, squeezed his wrist, held on to it and began to read.

Working with hair had taught Mary Mascarenas the ephemeral nature of happiness. Sometimes, now and then, with a client, she would achieve a blazing moment of perfection in which the reigning style and ambition and physiology came together to produce beauty, pure and breathtakingly obvious. In these moments, when the hair emerged from wrappers and coils and heat, when the client turned towards the arrayed mirrors, there was a gladness, an ecstasy as real as love, or motherhood, or patriotism. But time passed. Styles changed, the client grew older and old, and hair grew, how it grew. It lengthened, and changed, it transformed its texture and curl, it fell, it greyed and grew thin. Happiness always passed. Sooner or later the happy client looked into her mirror and grew restless and wanted a new cut. The cuts came and went, and bangs were down one year and up the next and four years later descended again. What was in this season was sure to be out the next. Blonde came and went, and short efficiency was followed by long femininity. Mary was sure that the morning after the oldest profession was invented, the professional went looking for a stylist. She was popular with clients at the Pali Hill Salon, and so she had good job security, and a very decent income from commissions, and much information. Clients liked to talk.

Comilla Marwah was talking now, as Mary worked on her hair with a Yasaka cutting scissor and a comb. 'You don't know, Mary,' she whispered, 'how that woman went after Rajeev. Such drama about how miserable she was in her marriage to that horrible husband, and all of this delivered to Rajeev in little black dresses at Indigo. So of course something started. She used to go to the Oberoi, tell her driver that she was shopping: "Driver-ji, you go and have lunch, I'll take two-three hours." Then she would go in, through the hotel and to the other entrance, catch a taxi from there straight to

Rajeev's building, enter through the side gate and up to his apartment. So, nice afternoon bonk, then back in another taxi to the Oberoi, and ten minutes of shopping so she had some bags, and off to home looking like some Sati-Savitri. And telling Rajeev that she had made a terrible mistake, that she should have never left him in London, all this shit. Meanwhile she meets Kamal, who's rich, rich as in the industrialist type of rich . . .'

Comilla had to stop then, for a stylist to squeeze by with her client. Space was so expensive in Bombay that even the best salons always had too many chairs squeezed in, too much business. And every day the salons were full. There was a lot of money in the city, and Comilla had a fair bit of it, and she knew exactly who had how much. She went on, 'But then she meets Kamal. This is at the same time she's doing Rajeev on the side, on the side of the horrible husband I mean. Kamal is loaded, and socially he's completely connected, he's right in the centre. And let's face it, she's an attractive woman. So then she starts angling for Kamal. Right under her husband's nose, you understand. They move in the same circles, all of them. But again the same story, unhappiness, haay-haay, I'm so sad, all that. Men can't resist that. So stupid. So then she's doing Kamal and Rajeev at the same time. Can you believe that?'

Mary could believe it easily. She had believed reports about Comilla Marwah's own affairs, which affairs were – one had to admit – not simultaneous but serial. Mary made a properly shocked face, and whispered with exactly the right touch of titillation, 'And then?'

'Then what? That Kamal falls completely for her. She's got that chweet-chweet innocent face, you know. And, according to Rajeev, she gives a mean blow-job. So Kamal leaves his wife and three kids and ends up getting engaged to the bitch. Of course her poor husband is totally stunned, but imagine what poor Rajeev goes through. One minute he's her hero and lover who is going to take her away from her horrible marriage, the next he's one discard.'

'When is the wedding?'

'Next week.'

'Sounds like Rajeev is going to need some comforting.'

'Yes,' Comilla said. She was peering at herself moodily, in the moisture-clouded mirror. 'True.'

Mary patted her shoulder. 'You have lost weight. Going to the gym?'

'Five mornings every week,' Comilla said, but even the compliment didn't pull her out of her self-examination. 'And all for what? Men. And men are stupid. Want to know what the moral of this whole story is, with her and Rajeev and Kamal and all?'

'Tell me.'

'If you give a whore's blow-job with a saint's face, men will leave their wives for you.' And she burst into such grandly boisterous laughter that Mary laughed along with her. Comilla lay back in her chair and roared, and Mary had to put her scissors down and lean on the table. After a while the entire salon was laughing along with them, laughing at Comilla's guffaws. Comilla's mood was greatly improved, and she left Mary a hundred-and-fifty-rupee tip. Mary had given her a good cut, tight to the delicate bones of her head, revealing the long stalk of her neck. She looked wonderful, but not in a hundred years and a thousand haircuts would she look like a saint. She looked like a sleek woman in her late thirties, funny and experienced and brightly curious and wearing well, with that buffed gloss only money could buy. Mary knew too much about her, as she knew too much about many of her clients. Mary knew, for instance, that long ago, when Comilla had been in her early twenties, she herself had been made into the other woman, that her moneyed Marwari boyfriend had left her to marry a nice Marwari girl chosen by his parents. That this boyfriend had continued to meet Comilla in Goa for weekends through two children and many avowals of undying love and declarations that he cared nothing for his fat, boring wife. That he had always promised to leave the wife the next summer, and then the next. And that of course he never had. Comilla had finally managed to tear herself away from that disastrous love, but had found herself alone at thirty, an attractive professional woman with a good pay cheque, but quite disastrously single. There were many in Bombay like her, too many. She had flailed around for a couple of years, and had been lucky to land her husband, a widower nineteen years older than her. He was quite comfortable, had his fingers in real estate and travel and had been charmed by her style. He had married her, and they had had two children, and Comilla had found her stable, safe home and also, inevitably, certain discontents. After the children were born, she had taken two lovers. All this Mary knew.

Twilight was Mary's favourite time, and as she often did after work, she walked down Carter Road to the sea wall. She strolled

367

slowly down the walkway, amidst joggers, crowds of teenagers and brisk, ked-wearing grandparents doing their evening constitutionals. There was a greenish tint in the sky this evening, shading from a foggy turquoise up high to a startling underwater jade at the horizon. This was what Mary loved about the dimming of the day, this mingling of colours and people. In this amiable mixing, to be alone in the city was to find companionship with a thousand strangers. Of course she had friends, and sometimes they walked the sea wall together. But often, to be solitary, and free, was the gift she wanted from Bombay. She had learned how to be alone, through dragging nights of terror and nostalgia, and now she prized her liberty. There was a certain temperate calm in being one's own person.

And yet there were women like Comilla, who, despite all their advantages, made their bargains for another kind of safety, full of lies and drama and half-understood and half-spoken compromises. Did Comilla's husband know of her affairs? Certainly half the world did, or at least the world that came in and out of the salon. Certainly there were enough women talking to each other about Comilla's adventures, and to Mary. Maybe he knew. Maybe he knew and looked away, maybe he understood. Mary thought she understood a little herself, but she never mistook this understanding for friendship. Comilla told her all kinds of things, but Mary knew she talked only because leaning back in a chair and offering her head to Mary's scissors drew them both into a momentary intimacy, a limited closeness that didn't need the darkness of the confessional box. But the thirty-five or forty thousand rupees that Mary brought home every month didn't make her a member of Comilla's social circle, not at all, even if it was more money than some white-collar briefcase-wallahs made. Comilla would sooner call in her driver to sit at her table than invite Mary to one of her dinner parties. Mary was a very good hairdresser, that was all. Mary had no illusions, no fantastic dreams about who she was and what she could become. She had found her place, and made her peace with it.

A trio of ragged girls passed Mary, their bare feet slapping the pavement, and they surrounded a tall, blond foreigner walking some ten feet ahead. Mary went past him, smiling at the patter of the girls as they held up their open palms to his face. 'How are you? Uncle, Uncle. Please, Uncle. How are you? Please. Uncle, hungry, hungry. Uncle, food.' They were jumping up, towards his beaky nose. He looked stricken. All this way he had come, to India, and now he was confronting its fabled poverty, and it had acquired English. The foreigner was shaking his head, no, no, but he had stopped, and Mary was sure that he would reach into his pocket in a moment. A band of little beggar boys streamed past Mary, heading for the foreigner. He'd have them all on his tail now, until he got into a taxi and fled. The privilege of his white skin and money cost him this minor trial, this swirling comet's tail of the needy. The kids on the sea wall were energetic and persistent, but they had long ago learnt to ignore Mary. She talked to them, but she gave no money, and they were professionals. This was work, and they had no time for idle chatter at this prime hour of evening.

Twenty minutes of walking had taken her to the far end of the walkway, almost to the Otter's Club bus stop. Under the deepening black, the low tide had pulled the waves far from shore, leaving a bare scrabble of rock and rubbish. Above it, facing the water, sat Sartaj Singh. Mary averted her face and angled to the left, away. She risked a single glance, quick, and he hadn't seen her. He was fixed on the stain of last light on the horizon. On she went, to the bus stop, where a bus was just drawing in. She ran the last few yards, and looked again only when she was safely on the bus, looked through the rear window. She could still make him out, alone on the edge of the walkway, his feet dangling over the rocks. She found a seat, and held her small grey purse tightly in her lap. Her pulse was racing, and she knew it wasn't just from the running. Why had she wanted so much to avoid a conversation with him? She hadn't done anything wrong. She was guilty of no crime. But he was a policeman, and policemen carried grief with them, like an infection. Better to stay away from them.

She held on to this relief all the way home, this sense of having escaped an encounter with something turbulent and dark. Even in the brief glimpse she had had of him, she had sensed a coiling sadness. He had been watching the sea and the sky with a questioning, pained tension in his shoulders and neck, as if he expected an answer. Better to run from such a man.

Mary shut the door to her room behind her, locked and bolted it. She switched on only one lamp, close and low to the wall, so that the shadows held her with a candle-lit cosiness. There was some fish curry left from last night's dinner, and she made a small bowl of rice with swift efficiency. She ate sitting on the bed, sipping from a large steel tumbler of water that she kept on the bedside table. She liked the animal shows on Discovery channel, the eternal round of birth and migration and breeding. Against the high dome of African sky, even the gory killings of deer and zebras by lions seemed only proper, a necessary link in an enormous cycle of harmony. Mary's friend Jana, who was addicted to the night-time serials about three-tier families and straying husbands, called her morbid and strange and made her change the channel when she came over. But the ceaseless longings and betrayals of the serials were offensive to Mary, she grew restless and upset and angry. Sharks at least were honest in their appetites, and beautiful besides.

She washed her plate, and the pots, and then reached to the back of the fridge for her chocolate. She had half a box of rum balls from Rustam's in Colaba, glorious in their individual gold-foil wrappings. She allowed herself one after dinner, and only she knew what a supreme act of self-control it was not to eat the whole box at once. She took the leftmost ball back to the bed, and turned up the sound on a leopard sliding through brush. The foil came off slowly under the very tips of her fingers, crinkling deliciously, so delicate. Then there was the golden waft of the cocoa, and she inhaled it deeply, and then tilted her head away so that she could come back to it anew. The first bite was always a small one, just a little nip so that her palate pinged from the clarity of the warm taste, and an ache started at the back of her jaws. Only after she had lost that first exhilaration did she allow herself a substantial chunk. And it was heaven. The dark taste of the rum swirled around her tongue, and she let out a little hiss of satisfaction at the leopard.

Then she was ready for sleep. She wore no make-up, ever, so her night-time ritual was short: a fast wash with a neem soap, and a good brush with Meswak toothpaste. She put on a faded pink caftan, softened by years of washes, and lay on her back, with her hands by her sides. When they were children, Jojo used to tease her about this pose of the dead, this corpse's motionless pause, but then Jojo even in sleep was a spiralling wind, and awoke often with her feet pointing at the pillow. She kicked and thrashed but wanted to sleep close, and Mary used to grumble about her lost sleep at breakfast.

Mary sat up, went to the bathroom, came back and lay down again. She tried breathing evenly, deeply. But her mind still turned and moved. Sleep, she whispered. Tomorrow is a long day. And, and. And

Jojo had loved rum balls from Rustam's, but they hadn't been able to afford them more than once a month. And today there was that Sartaj Singh, plonked like a squatting toad on her sea wall. The last time she had spoken to him had been in his car, when she had told him about John and Jojo. She had slept very badly after he had come to her with the news of Jojo's death, for a month she had walked around with a reeling heart, feeling dizzy through the day. Then finally the knowledge had settled in, become part of the structure of the new world: your sister is dead. That's how it was, when you confronted something impossible – your husband is sleeping with your sister – at first there was a nausea, a loss of all landmarks. Your own home became a hostile borderland. And then one day you knew that this raw wasteland, this garish alien light, was your home. You just had to have patience and will enough to survive the first terrors.

Mary sat up, propped a pillow against the wall and switched on the television. She found a documentary about space stations, and turned down the sound, and watched spidery white contraptions spin against stars. They were man-made, but soothing. It was always Jojo who had been the religious one, who at eleven had slept with a cross under her pillow, who had gazed up at the church altar with bright, sunlit eyes. Later, she had the same soaring love for celebrity, she had pursued its grail with the same marvellous faith. The closest Mary had ever come to this big-*big* feeling that Jojo told her about was when she watched wildebeest rumbling across a valley, or when she saw some unmanned spacecraft's pictures of the rings of Jupiter. She had been saving, for three years and five months now, for a safari holiday to Africa.

'Chutiya, you could go to Africa tomorrow if you claimed what is yours,' Jana had said, burning with real-estate lust for Jojo's flat, which she had never seen. 'That's a flat at Yari Road that we're talking about, not some smelly kholi.'

'It's not mine.'

'What, it belongs to me, then? Thank you,' – in English, with a bow – 'thank you.'

'You can have it.'

'Like they'll give it to me. Listen, gaandu, these are the facts: she was your sister. She is dead. There are no other living, immediate relatives. So it comes to you. All of it, flat and bank accounts and whatever.'

Jana had a gaali for every occasion and every other sentence, and she was a very good manicurist, an expert at fancy nails. She had a contemptuous bafflement for Mary's scruples. 'Listen, so your sister was a randi. Okay, so that's where some of the money came from. She also made television programmes, na? So you take the money thinking it's from television. What's the harm? After all she took your husband, na?'

This, to Jana's mind, was justice: good money for a husband. This was fair. There was no way to make her understand that this was exactly what Mary didn't want, to be paid off. She didn't want to take Jojo's dirty money, made from filth done on filthy hotel sheets with filthy men, she didn't want to take money in exchange for a husband, for happiness, for a childhood. Maybe Mary had never been able to believe quite wholeheartedly in heaven, but she had once believed quite naturally and easily that life on earth was good, that her future would be one long, gentle story of husband and children and grand-children, marred just a little by scraped knees and fevers but always buoyant with love. Despite her father's early death, she had believed this, that she would find the contentment that had eluded her mother. Jojo had expelled her for ever and without possibility of return from this garden of innocence. Jojo had changed her world. For this, there could be no forgiveness, and no purchasing of indulgences. This Mary was sure of.

Mary clicked off the spaceships and lay back. She took a breath, let it out slowly, tried to find an easy, even rhythm. But Jojo came back tonight and bothered her, kept her awake as she never had during those nights of thrashing about and fast-asleep kicking. Even after Jojo's death, in that first week of shock, she had never lain awake like this. Of late, with days passing when she didn't think of Jojo once, Mary had started believing that she was rid of her at last. But the flat and the money were unfinished business. Mary didn't like slack ends, she had always been the responsible sister. That's why she would have been such a good mother. Again that upward stab of anger in the chest. Forget it. Breathe, breathe. Let it go. Let it be.

Mary woke the next morning to her alarm with a tired head, she felt the exhaustion even as her feet hit the floor. Four or five hours of sleep were nowhere near enough, not anywhere close to her usual nine, and still there was the day to get through, work to be done. So she went. Jana noticed it straightaway. In a break between her clients, she slid past Mary and whispered, 'So got a boyfriend at last, sleepy-jaan?'

Mary shook her head, but Jana grinned and made back-and-forth humping motions with her hips. Mary looked away quickly, and moved to the other side of her own client, afraid of provoking Jana into some further outrages. It was a small miracle that she hadn't been fired already. Over lunch, which they ate from tiffins outside the salon, Mary tried to convince Jana that she had just had a sleepless night. Jana wasn't having any of it.

'You sleep like a bear, even if someone is knocking down a building next door, okay? So try to make a mamoo of someone else. Something is going on.'

Something was going on, but Mary wasn't going to tell Jana about the annoying night-time return of Jojo. She knew well Jana's opinions on the subject, and didn't want to listen to them again. 'It was just a bad night, Jana,' she said. 'Nothing great. So how are Naresh-Suresh?' Naresh was Jana's two-year-old son, and Suresh was her husband, whom she had married against the loud objections of both sets of parents. She called the son and father 'my bachchas', and loved to tell long stories proving her affectionate patience and womanly wisdom and motherly firmness. Suresh was indeed five years younger than her, but Mary had always thought that his quiet forbearance in the face of Jana's temperament was simply heroic. They worked well together, one placid and one loud.

'Don't be too smart,' Jana said, inadvertently flicking mango pickle on to Mary's skirt with her jabbing finger. 'Tell me.'

'There's nothing to tell, idiot,' Mary said, holding off Jana's attempts to clean off the oil. 'Nothing at all. God promise.'

But the nothing kept Mary awake to the end of the week. Every morning she woke more tired. On Friday she declined a girls' night with movie and dinner, went home and took a Calmpose. At first there was a pleasantly dozy feeling in her arms, and she wiggled her head back into the pillow, anticipating the sleep as keenly as a mouthful of chocolate. But then the sweat gathered clammily under her shoulders, and she had to kneel up to switch the fan to its fastest. She lay under its whirl, and time passed. She tried to think of pleasant things, of Matheran in the rain, of *Kaho Na Pyaar Hai* and the song on the yacht, of happy clients. She turned her head to find the clock. An hour had passed. She groped on the table to find the papery leaf of

Calmpose, and thumbed another one into her mouth. That would knock her out, she never took pills, she took care of herself. Again, she waited. An auto-rickshaw putt-putted up the main road and took the corner into the lane, she could hear its gears grind. Loud, it was so loud. It stopped, very close, and she could hear the rattle of the meter as the driver put it up, and then the engine grunted and turned over again. In the pool of silence it left behind, an air-conditioner hummed and rattled. Mary had never noticed all these night sounds before. She turned on her side and put a pillow over her head. She could feel rage collecting in her stomach like a dead weight. Stop, don't raise your blood pressure. Relax, relax. But there it was, this gravity of accumulated anger.

Mary endured the night. In the morning, at first grey, she came off the bed covered in a cold sweat. She showered it off, but a buzzing remained in her head, a small, tinny drone that persisted past her chai and toast. She waited until nine-thirty, and then called the number that Sartaj Singh had given her months ago.

'Not here,' a constable snapped at her.

'Has his shift started?'

'Shift starts at eight. Bola na, he's not here.'

At ten Singh was still not at the station, and not at eleven either. 'Arre, he's out on some work,' a different constable told her, with exactly the same tincture of aggression and boredom. She had to spell her name for him very slowly, and she was convinced that he had tossed the note immediately into some rubbish pile.

Of course there was no call back, not by noon and not by one. How do the police in this country ever solve anything? Mary grew scathingly bitter by two. She felt perked up, revived. She called Jana, and met her at Santa Cruz station to shop. Jana bought little shorts with blue anchors embroidered on them for her son, and also three tiny T-shirts, and a pair of slippers for herself. Mary was distracted and suddenly very tired. Jana bargained ferociously with the thela-wallahs, beat them down rupee by rupee. Mary slipped an arm through Jana's and dragged along with her through the shifting crowds. Jana gave her that old all-knowing sideways glance. 'You know what you need?' she said.

'Jana, don't start that boyfriend thing again.'

'What, yaar, you think I don't have anything more than boys in my head? I was going to say, you need to get out of the city for a while.

When you used to visit your Mummy, you always came back looking rested and fresh. This place, too long in it and you get ragdoed down.'

Mary held on tight to Jana's arm and nodded. The ragda that you were subjected to came from these streets, these shops, this noise, this air. Going shopping with a friend turned into this tiring trek, this weaving through hurrying throngs, this dodging of cars that darted at you from every side. Every minute you breathed in your dose of poison. But there was no Mummy any more, and no farm to visit. She had known, despite everything, that there was no escape for her from this labyrinth of hovels and homes, this entanglement of roads. She couldn't go back, not to live. So after Mummy had died she had sold the house and the farm, all its machines and instruments and furniture, and with that money had paid for her one room in the city, put some in the bank. The will had left everything to her, Mary, and had by name and specific mention removed the other daughter from the family and its inheritance. 'Where to go?' Mary said. 'You want to go to Matheran? Ooty?'

'Ooty would be good, no?' Jana said, full of longing. 'Blue hills.'

'Chal,' Mary said. 'Let's go.'

But a second was all it took for Jana to acknowledge this inevitable defeat. 'No, yaar. How to go?' Jana had many needs to save for. They both knew this, there was no need to discuss it further. But the blue hills were a good thing to think about.

The hills of the south stayed with Mary on the auto ride home. There had been hills on Mummy's farm too, not quite as high as the blue mountains, but hills nevertheless. Behind their property, to the west, Alwyn Rodriguez had a waterfall on his farm. It wasn't much of a waterfall, just a thin stream of water that fell over four feet of black rock. But it did curve in the sunlight, and there had been a time she and Jojo had been able to dance under it. Even later, as fresh novitiates, sitting on the bank with their feet in the water, they had the crisp fall of the water on the stone, and the comfortable settling of their insteps on its smooth, worn curve. Then, they had thought of the village as an awful place, small and stifling, with Alwyn Rodriguez and his endless feuds, and the murderous length of the afternoons when the radio stopped picking up All-India Radio and there was nothing, absolutely nothing to do. Mary pulled a chunni tighter over her hair, against the flapping wind and the fumes and the rush of the auto, and curved herself into a corner of the seat.

The auto came up the last curve towards Mary's house. Sartaj Singh was sitting on her steps, in that same forward-leaning squat from the sea wall. Mary got out of the auto, paid the driver. Her fingers were shaky, and she dropped a ten-rupee note and had to bend to pick it up. She was very annoyed. All she had done was call him on the phone, how dare he show up at her house like this? Just because these people were policemen they thought they could do anything. She took her change, and turned around determined to be stern with him, to get across to him that she paid his salary and understood her rights quite well. He was on his feet now. He had grown older. In the slanting light from the light-bulb above, Mary could see the flecks of white in his beard. He had been a handsome man, but now he looked like he had crumbled a little at all his edges. Once he had been all bite and confidence, but now all that sharpness had melted into a tempered exhaustion. His blue civilian pants were entirely lacking a crease. He had put on weight.

'Hello, Miss Mary,' he said.

'Since when have you been here?' Mary said, pointing with her chin at her step.

'An hour,' he said.

His voice was different too. He was altogether blurred. 'My neighbours,' Mary said, quite curt. 'You could have just called me.'

'I did. You were not here.'

'Still.'

'Yes. Sorry. But I thought it might be urgent. About your sister. Sorry.'

He was too tentative to fight with. Mary shook her head. 'Come.' In her room he stood by the door until Mary pointed to the chair. She didn't feel scared of him any more, of his authority or intentions, but she left the door ajar. He sat, and she saw that he still had that flat, unembarrassed cop's curiosity, he examined the room methodically, from left to right, and then came back to her. 'Water?' she said.

'Yes.'

'Chilled?'

'Yes.'

She opened the fridge, poured the water and walked across the room to hand him the glass. He watched her walk with that same frankness, and she was aware that although he was different, maybe tired and somehow dented, he was very much still a policeman. When

376

she bent forward to hand him the glass, she got a quick, sour whiff of his all-day sweat, of the trains and the crowds and the steady sun.

'Thank you,' he said in English, and drank. He drained the glass, and then stared abstractedly into it. 'I was very thirsty.'

'I need your help,' Mary said. It came out higher than she intended, shrill. She was not used to asking for help.

'Yes,' he said. 'Tell me.'

'My sister's property, you said you would help me.'

'You want to take possession?'

'Yes.'

'There are no other living immediate relatives?'

'No.'

'It shouldn't be too hard. You have to prove to the court that you are really the sister. That should not be hard, even if you had no recent contact. We will give a no-objection statement from the police, saying that there are no implications for our case. I will ask Parulkar Saab, my big boss, to expedite it. Bas, that's all. It might take a while, it is a legal process after all. You will need a lawyer for the papers.'

'I know one lawyer.'

'From your divorce?'

'Yes.'

'You know they say that in Bombay, you should have among your friends one politician, one lawyer and one policeman.'

'She has become my friend, my lawyer. But I don't know any politicians, or policemen.'

'You know me now.'

He was smiling. Mary knew that she was supposed to protest sweetly, to say that he was not her friend, and in turn he would argue that yes, of course he was. 'I'll ask my lawyer to get my papers ready,' she said. 'When can I come and get that statement from you?'

He lost the smile. 'You don't have to come,' he said. 'I'll bring it. No problem.'

'I don't mind coming.'

'All the way to the station. No need.'

A police station was no place for a woman was also what he was saying. 'Listen,' Mary said, 'I go up and down this city. I can come to your station. Just let me know when.'

'Okay.' He was quiet for a moment, quite serious. 'And . . . any more information about your sister?'

'I told you everything.'

'Yes. But. In all these months, something more may have come up. Something you remembered.'

'No, nothing.'

'Something even very little. It may not seem important, but it may open up the case for us. Please think.'

She had been thinking for these long weeks now, these months. How little could it be? How would telling him about Jojo's inexplicable love for fat Rishi Kapoor and his podgy, twinkle-toed dancing help him open up the case? There was everything to tell, and nothing. 'If I had anything, I would tell you. I don't even know what you want to know.'

He nodded, and seemed to come to a decision. 'The trouble is that we don't know exactly what we are looking for. We are still investigating the death of Ganesh Gaitonde. It is a matter of national security, and we don't know very much about why he came back to India, why he killed himself. So we are looking for any information connected to Gaitonde. We know your sister was close to him. We know she sent girls to him. Many girls, over a long period, to Bangkok, Singapore, places like that. So if we knew anything about your sister, what her movements were, who she was connected with, maybe it could lead to information about Gaitonde. That is why I keep asking.'

'Yes,' Mary said. 'Okay.'

He pushed himself to his feet. She could see the effort it took. 'All right,' he said. 'I will call you.' He nodded.

Mary was suddenly aware of how curt she had been. 'Thank you,' she got out. 'Thanks.'

'Don't mention.' He shut the door very gently behind himself, and Mary heard his progress down the stairs.

Don't mention. When Mary had first learnt English, she had said, 'Mention not.' She had said 'mention not' for years, until Jojo had corrected her. Jojo had learnt English very fast, and her English was faster and more natural and more correct, and incorrect in the right ways. She had been good at it. Sartaj Singh's English was ambitious but only half-successful, it stumbled now and then. He probably thought it was better than it actually was. There was that much arrogance left in him still.

Mary shrugged it all away. She took a long shower, stood under the flow and let it beat on her back. She liked the cold water, the thrill of it, even in winter. I grew up in a village, she'd told John when he'd marvelled. We didn't have running hot water like you city folks, and if you wanted it you had to carry it.

The memories came, but they didn't burden her, not tonight. She lay in bed and let them fly. Now that she had spoken to Sartaj Singh, she felt relieved. She had made a decision. Whatever she still owed to Jojo, she would do. Yes. She remembered now a show she had once seen about African elephants, and fell asleep thinking of baby elephants stumbling and tumbling after their mothers.

Ganesh Gaitonde is Recruited

I was impotent every day and every night of my honeymoon. As the floor tilted beneath us, I hunched over my wife, working at myself, cursing her, cursing the sea for a putrid whore, but in spite of all my efforts I was inevitably, astonishingly soft. We were on a boat, a ship called the *Peshwa*, pressing on to Goa. My boys had forced me to go on a honeymoon. After the death of Paritosh Shah, we had killed seven of Suleiman Isa's men in immediate retaliation, including Phul Singh, one of their top shooters imported all the way from UP. They had then got two of our boys, but their response had seemed less than full force, and I was sure more was coming. Meanwhile, as the days passed after my wedding, Chotta Badriya was increasingly horrified by my lack of interest in honeymooning. 'How can you stay here in this dirty hole on your suhaag-raat and most beautiful morning? You have to go some-where beautiful. Everything has to start in beauty. Switzerland!' He kept up his Switzerland song until I threatened to send his golis to Switzerland ahead of me. It was madness for me to leave in the middle of a war. And yet Chotta Badriya's daily campaigning for rose-strewn nights and beautiful days had its gradual effect. This is the modern age, he said, you'll be in constant touch by phone. After all, even Suleiman Isa ran his operations by remote control from Dubai, he said, and you'll be gone for only a few days. Besides, Paritosh Shah had been a man of ritual and custom, who believed everything should be done the way it had been done yesterday and the day before, he knew every rite that marked a man's progress from conception to the feasts after his death. After Paritosh Shah's death, we had followed the accepted prescriptions in the tiniest details, fed a hundred Brahmins when a dozen would have done, and now Chotta Badriya pointed out that if I was marrying for Paritosh Shah, I had better honeymoon for Paritosh Shah. He tried to send me to Singapore on a plane, and I settled for Goa on a ship. Very romantic, he said, on a ship and all instead of some boring hotel. Yes, yes, I said. I disliked this plan the least because the trip was short, and I could always come ashore and speed back, if I was needed. Three days there, two days in Fort Aguada, three days back, honeymoon done. Except that I wasn't doing.

I couldn't talk to the boys, who were in the next cabin, of course I couldn't talk to them. On the second night it again became clear that nothing was happening, that all my pulling and stroking at myself, all my calling back to the swaying cabin of every woman, every girl, every whore I had ever bajaoed, and all my frantic imagining of every filmi star I had ever unbuttoned in my dreams, none of this was going to move the slightest flicker in my dead lauda. It curled up ashamedly against my thigh, raw from my rubbing. I curled up against the wall of the cabin. Finally I managed to get out, 'This has never happened before. It must be the boat, all this up-and-down-and-around like a mela-ride, it makes me sick.'

She was quiet. She lay with her back to me, her shoulder hunched up against the starlit round of the window. Her name was Subhadra. That much I knew about her. I looked at her arm, the bony narrowness of her shoulder, and in her turning away I was sure there was contempt, amusement. I sat up, and my ribs hurt from the deep breath I took then, such a furious gulp of rage I swallowed. When I turned my head more squarely to her, I had to force the muscles, they were so tight from anger. I wanted to say, it's you, you skinny chut, with your starving kutti's lean ribs. I wanted to grab her by the neck and shake her until her head snapped back and forth and shout, who could get it up for you? I would've killed her, thrown her into the water far from anywhere, and forgotten about marriage for ever, no matter what friends had said or wanted. My body wanted murder, there was a pressure down my spine that flexed and pulsed and wanted to cleave her in half. I would've killed her. But then she spoke.

'Have you ever been on a ship before?'

Yes, I had been on a ship. I had plunged down slatey valleys of water in a rattling boat, I had killed a man, a friend, I had taken his gold. I wanted, all at once, to tell her about my journey over the seas. 'Yes, I've been,' I said. 'Long time ago, when I was a boy, when I first came to Bombay. I went on a trip.' She turned over to face me now. She was surprised, I think, by the eagerness with which I spoke, I who hadn't said more than a dozen sentences to her in three days. 'That was my first time on ship, and first time out of the country,' I said. I told her about Salim Kaka, Mathu, but now that she was listening, her cheek resting on her two folded hands, I found that I couldn't tell her the end of the story, I couldn't tell her about the shots in the dark, about Salim Kaka's feet threshing the water, that true ending which was the beginning of everything for me. I had never told anyone, and I could hardly tell her, little Subhadra who was awestruck at my daring. I told her the alternative ending, the public ending: we set off for home, longing for safety and the smell of our own earth, and on the way we were ambushed by the police of that foreign country, who had been tipped off by Suleiman Isa, of course, and Salim Kaka fell in a running battle, he fell with his chest torn open by machine-gun bullets, but we left the ambushers far behind, and we made it home. With the gold. She sighed when I finished, let out the first small sound of satisfaction that I had heard from her. I touched her shoulder, and felt her stiffen. She thought I was about to start again with my pulling and pressing at her, but I hadn't the heart for it. I hadn't the courage to make another attempt. I kept my hand on her shoulder, and we rose and dropped together, and the long swirl of the water came to us, and slowly she grew safe under my palm, and relaxed. 'What about you?' I said. 'Have you been on the sea before?'

She told me about a childhood trip to Elephanta, about getting sick on the boat and trying to reach the edge but ruining her new yellow frock, about how unmercifully hot it was on the water, which lay still like a glittering mirror and hurt the eyes, about how her father's pocket was picked on the return trip. But I had profited from the sea. The sea could be both luck and disaster, maybe. I said that to her and heard her whisper a faint 'yes', and then we slept.

Once she got started talking, on and on she went. She woke up talking and never ceased. What she talked about was hard to know, because she talked about everything, her sister's stomach-aches, Indira Gandhi, going to the airport to watch planes take off and land, *Kati Patang*, a creaky table-fan her father refused to get rid of, the danger of malaria in the rainy season, the best bhelpuri-seller on Juhu Chowpatty, shipwrecks in swollen rivers. She went from one subject to another in a way that made perfect sense when you heard it, but which became madly incoherent and impossible to recount five minutes later. Hours would pass in this, the skipping flutter of her talk. I found it restful. We sat on the deck, under a blue-and-white striped awning, both wearing dark glasses and she still resplendent in her shining bride's jewellery, and I listened to the water singing against the side of the boat, and she talked. It was a pleasant hum that emptied my mind, that kept my nightly humiliation at safe distance. The boys kept at a respectful distance, within call but out of sight. I told myself that I was thinking, planning, analysing, that the hours which were passing were devoted to consideration of the problem of Suleiman Isa, the problem of further expansion of the company, the problem of future direction, but really I was lulling myself into a waking sleep. I was at complete rest. I was still.

Half a day out of Goa, my numb meditation was interrupted by Chotta Badriya. He came clattering up the metal stairs, and in his rapid clanking there was fear, I could feel it. I met him on the stairs, a third of the way down.

'What?' I said.

'The captain says they just heard the news. It's bad, bhai.'

'What is?'

'The masjid was torn down yesterday afternoon.'

He didn't need to say which masjid, for months there had been talk of only one masjid, one old faraway ruin of a building which was now the pivot for leaping political parties, the target for processions of thousands, the standing sign for ancient wrongs. I had thought it all quite silly, the whole question and the quarrelling nothing but politicians' tricks. But if it was destroyed, its falling would shake us all. That much was clear. 'And?' I said.

'In Bombay, bhai, things are bad,' Chotta Badriya said. 'Riots.'

In Goa, we drove from the dock to the airport, and flew back to Bombay the same afternoon. From the Goa airport, I tried to reach our controllers in Bombay, but all the dozen numbers I dialled were dead. 'The police must have switched off the phones,' Chotta Badriya said. That was likely, they did that sometimes when trouble started. The rumours at the airport were of burning buses, snipers shooting from rooftops into crowds below, men and women hunted down in lanes and killed. I wanted to get back to Bombay before Suleiman Isa took advantage, before those bastards came against us with everything they had under the cover of the chaos. During a riot, a war can come out into the open, and when a body falls or when a house burns, nobody is responsible. A riot is a free time for free murder. It was not a time to leave my company rudderless, headless, so we flew back. When we stepped on the plane I felt my golis sweat. The rows of seats were all empty, the passengers had all cancelled, only we wanted to fly into rioting Bombay. I sat shaking in my seat, and my crotch was damp – this creaky contraption would fly, this maderchod bus with wings? But I flew. I hurtled into the air, towards Bombay and my responsibilities. We rushed down the black asphalt, rattling and banging, and I said to Subhadra, 'Talk, talk.' With a grimace of panic she began, and her dread was not from the sudden upward arc of the plane, but from seeing me drenched through with a fear-sweat, her Ravana-husband become a vomit-spewing, snot-dripping hijra. I retched into a paper bag, and she sat up erect in her seat and put a hand on my shoulder. I knew she found it distasteful, the clammy, cold wet of her husband's fright. And what a husband, not the awesome rakshasa she had imagined entering her marriage bed, from whose reputation her mind had turned, overwhelmed, not that king but an impotent clown. But she was dutiful. She talked.

When the plane tilted over Bombay she stopped. I leaned over her and we both pressed our faces against the plastic, and from the muddy coastline emerged a scattering of islands, and then I could see clearly roads, buildings, the shape of colonies and the spreading brown patches of bastis. From behind us I could hear the boys arguing, 'That's Andheri there.' 'Maderpat, where Andheri? That's Madh island, can't you see?' Then they were all quiet. A thick black snake of smoke grew from a coastline settlement and twisted in towards the centre, towards another dark, curving fume – the city was burning.

All the way down not a word was said. The buildings fell towards us at a great velocity, but I was not afraid, I was trying to see what had been destroyed, what was on fire. All of us were quiet. The airport buildings were crowded with passengers huddled on the ground, sleeping with their heads resting on bags and suitcases. No taxis were moving, no autos. The phones were still dead, so there was not a way to call anyone in Gopalmath. For a while it seemed there was no getting out to Gopalmath, but Chotta Badriya went out on the road and wandered among the rows of taxis until he found the drivers huddled together near the police chowki. After half an hour of persuasion and much brandishing of thousands of rupees, one of them seemed tempted, and so Chotta Badriya drew him aside and told him not to be afraid, he was transporting Ganesh Gaitonde. This of course re-assured the driver, and so we jammed ourselves into the taxi, the six of us, and we drove out into the huge quiet. The straining engine seemed too loud, and as I told the driver to go faster, faster, I realized I was whispering. On all the roads that day there was no one, not one person, the bastis near the airport road were quiet, the hotels on the highway were silent, the windows of the apartment buildings were shuttered. I was afraid, we all were except the taxi driver, who gained confidence with each turn under my protection. But I knew we had no weapons, and if a crowd of hundreds had come howling over us, engulfed us with knives and stakes and bars and swords, we would all have died. In that silence trembling from murder, I could have shouted my name and the mob would still have torn out my throat. Against that blood-fed anger there was no name that was protection. Near Gopalmath we saw bodies, two bodies. They lay crabwise on the edge of the road, near a shoe shop. Blood had spattered on the corrugated iron of the shutter, over the raised lintel.

'Brain shots,' Chotta Badriya said.

He was right. Both of them were head shots. I was wondering if they were both Muslim. The board on the lintel said the shop was the Zuleikha Shoe Emporium. We crunched down the street, over splinters of glass, shoes, sticks, I saw a child's ruled notebook fluttering its pages. Subhadra had her eyes shut. Now we took the familiar turn to the left, down to the basti. This road had been smooth, I had had it rebuilt and resurfaced just two months ago. Now it was covered with loose stones, rocks, bricks. Somebody had fought a battle here. A burnt box of a car leaned its charred metal against a lamppost. There was a shout to our left, and from the first row of Gopalmath houses a man appeared, pointing an accusing finger at us. In his other hand he held a sword, a dancing curve of silver.

'Ey, Bunty,' Chotta Badriya called, and Bunty ducked his head in amazement, and ran up to the taxi, followed by the boys of Gopalmath. Bhai, bhai, they shouted. They were all armed, festooned with swords and lathis and spikes and rods and knives and pistols. I asked, what happened here? The landyas came, bhai, from the basti of Janpura over there, they said that one of our boys had stabbed one of theirs, so we showed them, bhai, we ran them back into that smelly dump of theirs. And those two on the turn at Naik Road, bhai, the policiyas did those, dhad-dhad two straight in the head, even the police know what is right and what is wrong this time. And they were thumping each other on the shoulder, all of them, shoving and falling and laughing like they had won a match, all their faces alive with sweat and youth and victory. And I asked, what about the Muslims in Gopalmath, what happened to them, are they all right? On the eastern side of the basti we had maybe sixty Muslim families, mostly tailors and factory workers, some of their sons worked for me. But when I asked about them my boys shrugged. What, I asked again, are they all right? They're gone, bhai, they said.

'Where?' I said. 'Where have they gone?'

Nobody knows, bhai. They're gone. They ran away. They fled.

'Did anybody do anything to them? What happened?'

They just went away, bhai.

'And their houses?'

Taken up, bhai. Other people are living in them now.

'Who? Some of you?'

Yes, some of us, bhai.

Chotta Badriya's face was rigid. He was immensely respected in our company, and until now his religion had never mattered. I took him by the arm, walked him away. 'Don't listen to these fools,' I said. 'Don't take it to heart. They're young and their heads have been turned by all this. They don't know what they're saying.'

But his eyes were full. 'I would have given my life for any of them,' he said. 'But now I'm only a landya for them? Bastards. Will they want my house also?'

'Badriya,' I said, 'this is a bad time. Don't get angry. Keep your wits, keep cold. Listen to me. Just listen to me, only me.'

I had my hands on his shoulder, and finally he let me hug him. I sent him to his home and family with four of my best boys, all armed, and told them if anything happened to Chotta Badriya or any of his family, I would shoot them myself.

Then I looked about, at the homes of Gopalmath. During a lull in my own war I had left my home, and came back to find my home the battleground for a larger conflict. They, somebody, had drawn borders through my vatan. My neighbours were now refugees, they had fled from unsheathed swords, from brain-shot bodies. Here was my Gopalmath, the habitation of my heart, the town that I had caused to be built, brick and brick, where I had walked with my friends, arms on shoulders, with the smell of gajras and falling water in the air, where I had found my manhood, my life. Here was the bright quilt of its roofs, stretching from the bowl of the valley up the hill, this vibrant spread of brown and blue and red knit together by the arcing, thread-like lanes, here were the numerous angular reachings of the television antennae, catching their fierce glints from the hovering sun. All of it lay desolate. And at the very edge of the horizon, to the south, a smudge of smoke. Under that unbearably bright sky I took my bride home.

The riots ended three days later. My impotence continued. We cleaned the streets, gathered up the wounded, I gave money to the families of those who were in hospital, and meanwhile Subhadra settled into my house and became 'Mummy' to my boys. Within days she was their confidante and sympathizer and whisperer and bringer to me of their problems, and mediator if I was angry. The house was suddenly clean, and gods and goddesses appeared in every room, and my stomach was suddenly lighter and happier from the food I ate, and all my shirts were in a neat ironed row in the cupboard, and still I was afraid all the time. When I heard her voice in the next room, kind and flowing and with a rhythm like bells, I feared that she was telling someone how useless I was, how I didn't even go near her, how I lay on my side of the bed with my arms over my head, how I told her to keep talking until I dropped into sleep. No, she wouldn't tell. But maybe it would slip out, some woman from the basti would make a remark, a teasing joke about Subhadra's happiness, some little pun with a little naugh-tiness in it, about marriage beds and nights and cruel men and aching limbs, and Subhadra would laugh, complete innocent that she was, and she would burble, but oh we don't do that. He won't, he can't. He can't, can't, can't. I fled from her voice, from can't, from danger, and spent the day being driven from meeting to meeting. I ate lunch in high and low restaurants, I sat in dance-bars and dully watched the girls pirouette. But I wasn't moved by any of them.

Chotta Badriya noticed this. He had been quiet, he had been upset by what had happened, by the masjid and the days that followed, I could see that. So I kept him close, I took him everywhere. And I could see that he was trying, that for my sake he was fighting himself. He tried to take care of me. 'Bhai, these dance-girls are second-rate finally. I have much better for you.'

'Much better? Where?'

'Actresses, bhai. Stars.'

'Every one of these wants to be a star, chutiya.'

'No, no, bhai. Really, actresses. Promise.' Those days, everyone was becoming a television producer. Oil traders and taxi-owners were suddenly making television serials. One of these was Chotta Badriya's cousin, and he had told Chotta Badriya about a woman who was a model and actor co-ordinator, and also trying to be a television producer. Naturally this woman came into contact with many young girls, all lovely and fresh and young and new in the city, struggling to make their fortunes.

'So she helps them to struggle a little with men, and make themselves and her some money?' I said.

'Exactly, bhai. Otherwise, you know how hard it is in this city. How can a young actress survive, alone in this city? She helps them, bhai, she helps them.'

'Well, we must help them too. And what is the name of this saint?'

'Jojo.'

Jojo. A strange name, but the girls she sent were indeed a cut above the common randi. They were educated, and some of them English-speaking. With them I was successful. With them I was easily hard, and profoundly able. With them I acrobated and strong-manned and warriored until they collapsed on the field. But at home I was nothing. I examined my wife closely, took in her slightly crooked smile, the straight slash of her eyebrows, the small powder-and-toothpaste smell of her, and found her to my liking. I wanted her. But there was no having her. My strength vanished when I was in the safety of my own bed, and I had no recourse. I read the advertisements for clinics on billboards and at the back of magazines, the promises of vigour from tablets and potions, but I was unable to tell anyone, not even Chotta Badriya. I was shamed. I picked up the phone and called one of the clinics, asked to speak to the Vaid, but they wanted money and they wanted to know my name, and the woman on the line was quick and brusque, and I called her a gaandu and slammed the phone down. Subhadra came in then with a glass of milk, and I drank it, and I thought bitterly, yes, that randi on the phone I could have ploughed, but drink my wife's milk is all I can do. So I went through Jojo's girls, one after the other.

But I found that when I was far away from Subhadra, unable to hear her talking, I was even more afraid. Perhaps being at home was the better thing, perhaps my near presence would constrain her a bit, keep her from telling somebody about my failures. So back I went. And I found her happy in her house. That was the truth, she seemed happy, she was happy. Her marriage was a joke, at its centre it had a limp nothing, but she bustled about with her keys in her pallu and rattled pots in the kitchen and ordered servants about and nagged me about eating, and seemed content. She bloomed as we worried about the ruins of the mosque, as the newspapers unfurled ancient histories of bitterness and the convulsing speeches of politicians. The magazines published maps of the country festooned with spiky outgrowths of little cartoon explosions, each tiny detonation representing a riot, bodies, bricks, swords, and meanwhile I was unhappy, and she was happy. One night, she bustled into our bedroom and sat next to me.

'I've been hearing about your friend,' Subhadra said.

'Who?'

'Your friend Paritosh Shah.' She sat next to me, held on to the sleeve of my kurta. 'All the boys keep telling me how he made you marry, what a good influence he was on you. Tell me about him.'

So I told her about carrying gold to him, about his enormous paunch, his feeling for money, his love for the game of gain, our adventures together, his pleasure in festivals and rituals and celebrations, his need for high flight. She listened to me, her hand on my sleeve, head down but eyes shining and blinking up at me, with stray strands of her hair lit up by the lamp behind, each filament aglow, making a small wheel of light above her head. 'And that motu friend of mine,' I said, 'he wouldn't do a thing without praying, if he had to go from Colaba to Worli he would pray, if he had to steal a crore he would pray. And then they killed him.'

'Did you kill them?'

'Kill who?'

'The ones who killed him!'

She spoke of killing men, this little virgin, as if she was speaking of cutting chickens. 'We killed some of them.'

'No, but the ones who actually did it?'

How to explain to her that finding out exactly who pulled the triggers and who swung the hammers was not exactly easy? What would she understand of intelligence-gathering, safe houses, double and triple bluffs, setting fielding and lurkaoing men? She had asked the simple question, did you punish the men who actually did it? There was no simple answer. And then it came to me, looking at the sindoor in her hair and the full trust in her eyes, that she had asked the only question that was worth answering. I had failed Paritosh Shah. I had killed some of Suleiman Isa's men, and considered that revenge. But to take random men and destroy them, that was no revenge. Paritosh Shah had worried about me, he had loved me, he had married and settled me down, and I had abandoned his memory, made excuses to his soul about the punishments I had exercised on his enemies, while his actual murderers ran free. This is why I was cursed within the marriage he had made for me. I could not consummate while his soul was unconsummated, while it searched for its rest. My incompleteness was a direct reflection of his. I laughed. It had taken Subhadra to show me this, Subhadra was also the name of the sister of the god Paritosh Shah had worshipped. It made a kind of sense, really it did. I jumped up. I bent over and kissed my wife. I was rejuvenated, reborn. I ran out to the meeting rooms, and called up my boys, woke up Chotta Badriya.

'What have we done lately to find out which shooters came after Paritosh Shah? Have we offered money? How much? Who have we asked? Who have we captured?'

In an hour I had made new plans, set new schemes into motion, doubled and tripled the flow of money that would ease men's tongues, talked to policemen and company-men and shooters and khabaris, collected names and half-names and the shadows of names, addresses, rumours of dissatisfactions and intrigues. The house hummed and sang and I felt my force extending across Bombay like electricity, because of me women and men were talking, running, moving in patterns that I had set in motion, I had thrown the net of my self wide, and in it I would gather the assassins, I would take them in. They could not escape. Watch me, Paritosh Shah, bhai, fat man. You will have to restore me to myself. I will give you your murderers, and you will give me Subhadra, my marriage, you will give me back to me.

And then the riots were upon us again. News of new murders came to us from the anguished lanes, from the roads still mourning old injuries: Muslim stabbed here, Hindu killed there, and then mathadi workers stabbed and killed, a family burnt to death, and the whirlwind took us again. Again the empty roads and the long silent afternoon and the rushing slap of many running feet on the ground and the sun rolling overhead, and screams, screams moving with tiny rattles up our windows, and news of men and women and children doused with petrol and burnt alive, and Subhadra huddled into a corner, and the abrupt tapping of gunfire lasting into the night. I put my boys on the peripheries of Gopalmath, in relays, and told them to sit tight, to watch, to guard. After three days Bunty came to me, bringing complaints. 'I can't control the boys, bhai,' he said. 'They want to *do* something.'

'Do *what*?' I snapped. 'Go out there and kill old women? For what? For an empty old building?'

He ducked his head. 'They are killing us.'

'And?'

'Bhai?'

'You look like you have something more to say.'

'The boys are saying . . . some of them are asking whether Bhai is with us, or with the Muslims.'

So, inevitably, here it was: us or them. Was I us or them? 'I'm with the money,' I said. 'And there's no profit in this. Tell them that.'

And yet the question stayed with me, through those nights of killing. Us or them? Who was I, who had always regarded the would-be attackers of the mosque and its defenders as equal fools? Now the mosque had come down, and everyone had become an attacker of that and a defender of this, you had to choose whether you were us or them. But what was I? I thought about it, waited for Paritosh Shah to tell me something, and held back from the bloodletting. Meanwhile some of my boys abandoned me. They were frustrated by my standing still, my doing nothing. Caught up in the frothy haze of rage that rose from the burning shops, from the bodies in the gutters, they went out armed with swords, and pistols. They took men from cars and slashed them to death, they raped women they found huddled inside hovels and then cut their throats, they used kerosene and kitchen matches and burnt stragglers alive, they shot children. So in those days of winter I lost my loyal soldiers to this massacre of us and them, this butchery that was not a battle. They left me and felt contempt for me, because I stood apart. I didn't need Bunty to tell me this. I was losing izzat, I was losing power, I was losing the company I had built and defended against so many predators.

Bipin Bhonsle offered me a way out. He drove up on a Sunday morning in a jeep festooned with saffron flags. He was followed by two Ambassadors, also packed with his Rakshaks, each variously armed. Bipin Bhonsle himself openly carried a sword, which he propped up on the side of his chair in my baithak.

'An armed MLA on the open road,' I said. 'How the world has changed.'

'Today we are going to change it back, bhai,' he said, rubbing at his face. He was puffy, exhausted, and he stank. His purple shirt was stained and crumpled, hanging out at the front, and I could see the sweaty folds of his belly. 'Enough is enough. We're going to show these landya bastards.'

I waited. But he seemed to have dropped off into an open-eyed sleep, with his chin on his chest. Lank strips of hair were plastered to his forehead, his usual puffy hairdo had been completely destroyed. What he wanted to show Muslims remained untold. Finally I said, 'Bipin Saab?'

He spoke without blinking, without moving from his statue-like sprawl. 'The word came from the top: show the maderchods. So we showed them.'

'The order came from the top?'

'From the very top top.' He yawned. 'I cut a head off. I mean clean off, sattack! like that. I had to use both hands on the sword. It bounced twice, the head. The funny thing is the blood. It goes far. Like from a pichkari, all over the place. The boys were all running, ducking away from the blood. The head didn't look surprised or anything. The head had no expression.'

'You showed him.'

'Yes. But you're sitting here, safe in your house, Ganesh Bhai.'

'The word didn't come from my top, Bipin Saab.'

'The landyas killed Paritosh Shah. And still you don't want to do anything.'

I could've pointed out that although Suleiman Isa was Muslim enough, he had plenty of Hindus working for him. And also that Suleiman Isa had nothing to do with the Muslim families who lived down the highway, and that cutting their heads off wouldn't make him bleed. But I said simply, 'There's no gain for me in doing this.'

He looked at me, flicked his reddened eyes at me. 'I'll bring you profit. I have much to do, so I'll make you a quick deal. There's a Muslim basti in Abarva. Know it?'

'Behind the white life-insurance building. Yes.'

'The land it's on belongs to an associate of mine. He bought it three years ago, good price, good area for development, but he can't get those slum maderchods off the land. Water connections, electrical, they have it all. They say they've been there for years, all that usual bhenchod nonsense. So, get them off. Burn it down. We'll pay twenty lakhs.'

'Bipin Saab, Bipin Saab. That land is worth four crores, easy.'

'Twenty-five, then.'

'I'll need a lot of boys.'

'Your boys can keep what they find.'

'Find in some miserable hut, while a fire is roaring over their heads?'

'Thirty.'

'One crore.'

He laughed. 'I'll give you sixty lakhs.'

'Done.'

'When?'

'Tomorrow.'

'All right. Do it fast. We'll keep this open season going as long as we can, but at some point they'll tell the army to start firing, not just do flag marches, and then things will become difficult.' He put his hands on his knees and pushed himself up, remained bent over for a moment, wriggling his back. 'Aren't you going to offer me a drink?'

'Bipin Saab, I should've asked.' I called out to the corridor, 'Arre, bring water, tea, something cold.'

Bipin Bhonsle grinned. 'I was thinking of whisky. Or rum. But you are the same, bhai. Water-water all the time.'

'Keeps me alert.'

'Whisky keeps me strong,' Bipin Bhonsle said, and picked up his sword. 'Water is bad for my heart.' He hefted the sword, pointed it at me. 'Good you are with us,' he said. And with that he went flouncing down the stairs, his heels clacking sharply on each step. The jeep spun in tight growling turns, and then they were gone. And I was now with us, I was against them.

This is the elegant way to burn a basti: you do it at night, you move a dozen cars full of boys to the east, to the life-insurance end of the basti, and there you launch a loud frontal assault. Your boys fire pistols and swing swords at the men of the basti, who emerge from their hovels to put up a despairing fight, their faces are maddened caricatures under the ranked headlights. Meanwhile at the far southwestern end of the basti another group of your boys is near the clustered shacks and houses. They are crafty and stealthy, your boys, they get in close and they can hear the screams and curses from the life-insurance end, and now they heave bottles filled with petrol, bottles primed with petrol-soaked rags. There is the crisp tinkle of glass and the small sparking flares now bloom into flowing rivers that run smoothly across rooftops, down walls, into windows. The fire speaks now, it makes a joyous, throaty grumbling as it eats, there is no stopping it. There are no phones, there is no fire brigade to come, no police. The defenders are no longer defending, they run, they dodge back into the corners, now illuminated by the bright glow above the roofs. Your boys chase them, kill some of them, the others flee to their women, their screaming children, and bolt away from the fire, they stagger and drop and get up and go, they disappear. They are gone. The flames swing easily from house to house, and our work is complete.

In the morning, the western façade of the life-insurance building was stained sooty grey, and where there had been a basti there was an empty field of cinders, spiked here and there by a blackened doorpost, a twisted pipe.

Two days later my payment was delivered in full. It came in stacks of crisp new plastic-wrapped notes, which I broke apart to distribute to the boys. By now almost all of them were back with me. Over the next four days we cleared two more plots of land. And we were all satisfied, me, the boys, Bipin Bhonsle. Riots are useful in all kinds of ways, to all kinds of people.

Finally, in the third week of January, the burning and killing stopped, under the bullets of the police and the army, and under orders from Bipin Bhonsle's bosses, and their boss. Finally there were too many dead bodies even for the very supreme top, and the reeling roar of the approaching chaos too deafening, and so it stopped. The city cringed and shook itself and began to clean up the debris, bulldozers swept up the emptied grounds and dug foundations, bodies were lifted from the gutters, from the rubbish heaps, and traffic churned through the lanes again. Here we were, slowly back to normal. And I was restored. Yes, I was able. I came home late one night from a meeting with Bipin

Bhonsle, to collect more monies he owed us from the riot-time work, to discuss new projects, and I took off my shoes and sat back on the bed, my head resting on Subhadra's new embroidered pillows, they were a deep red. She had rearranged the furniture in the room, so that we could look out of a double window as we lay in bed. I could see my darkened basti and the stars overhead. Subhadra brought me my milk, then sat cross-legged on the bed to watch me drink it. I sipped, and she rested her chin on her hand and hummed softly.

'What's that song?' I whispered. The night was so quiet, so fragile and cool, so shadowed, that I could only whisper.

Subhadra peeked up at me, and hummed on.

'What, saali? What's the song?'

She smiled, small and mischievous, and stuck out her tongue at me. And kept humming.

I grabbed her arm playfully, but she let out a theatrical little scream and twisted away. 'Let go,' she said. 'It hurts.'

'Don't act too much,' I said, releasing her. 'I hardly even touched you.'

'No,' she said. 'You're strong.' She rubbed her arm hard. 'See, you left a mark.'

'I can't see anything.'

'Even the boys say it.'

'Say what?'

'That you didn't know how strong you were. Yesterday they were saying, now finally he's showing his true strength. Now we know he's a true Hindu leader.'

'Hindu?'

'Yes.' She was looking down at her pale arm, where the skin showed a soft bloom from my fingers. 'They said, now he's showing those bastards what a Hindu bhai can do.'

There was a sloping river in the sky, a sinuous curve of light. There was the sky above, and us underneath. There were Hindus, and there were Muslims. Everything sits in pairs, in opposites, so brutal and so lovely.

'Close the door,' I said.

Now she spoke: 'What?'

'You heard.'

What happened to me then? Until then, all my life, I had felt like a ghost, a thousand ghosts roaming around inside my body, each equally possible and every one of them more lost than the other. I had come from nowhere and made a name for myself, but I had felt always that I was playing a part, many parts, and that I could switch from this name to another easily, that if I was Ganesh Gaitonde today, I could well become Suleiman Isa tomorrow, and then any of the men I had killed. I had felt anger, and pain, and desire, but I had held back always from allowing the fragments inside me to settle into a shape, a form. I had led men to believe in me, in Ganesh Gaitonde, and always secretly despised them for believing in me, because I was nothing. I had believed in nothing. I had committed to nothing. And so I was a phantom of a man, capable of frenzied couplings with whores, in whose sopping chuts I tried to make myself real, but I was not fit for marriage. Marriage is belief. Marriage is faith. Marriage is wholeness. I could see it now, I had been incapable of marriage, incomplete, imperfect and so impotent. But all the roads I had walked, thinking myself alone, all those broken paths had brought me inevitably to belonging, to the certainty of becoming something, one thing. I had burnt bastis, and so I had chosen, I had been forced to choose one side of the battlefield, wily old Paritosh Shah had had his way after all. I stood ready now. I knew who I was. I was a Hindu bhai. And so I hovered lightly above my wife, my wife, feeling the confident beat of my pulse along every length of my body. I went into her. Her scream thrilled over my shoulders. Afterwards there was blood, on the sheets, on my thighs. I was content. I said to Paritosh Shah, I haven't forgotten about you. I will find your killers. I slept deeply, sprawled in the evidence of my victory, late into the evening.

I had woken up, and for wakening to myself I was rewarded. This reward brought with it a curse. It was a videotape, and on it was a momentary glimpse of the man who had betrayed Paritosh Shah, who had delivered him to our enemies. The videotape came to me from one of our sources in Dubai, a man named Shanker who worked in an electronics store called Mina Television and Appliances. Shanker's boss, the owner of this Mina Television, had a side business of videotaping engagements and weddings and parties, and in November he had been called to a party at the revolving restaurant on top of the Embassy Hotel to tape a shaandaar party, to record for posterity a small but fantastically expensive birthday celebration, complete with Govinda flown in from Bombay to dance. The owner of Mina

Television busily taped, he caught the toasts drunk in champagne; the men standing in little semicircles in their glossy suits, their fists around stubby glasses full of Scotch; the women off in a great cluster by themselves around the sofas, their diamonds glinting, stabbing the lens with their quick flashes; and Govinda dancing, his twists and dips, his white shoes reflected in the black marble floor; and the birthday boy, Anwar, third brother to Suleiman Isa. And Suleiman Isa, yes, the bastard himself, swaying to Govinda's beat but with no expression on his face, no life. The Mina Television man brought his video back to the shop, he had been told to make three copies of it. He handed it to Shanker, told him to make the copies. Shanker made four. He kept one, and he brought it to Bombay when he visited in early February. He gave it to Bunty, and Bunty gave him money. And here it was, the tape, now on my television, in my office.

Suleiman Isa had a broad, flat face, with a sparse beard along the edges of his jawline, and a pencil moustache. In the tape he was wearing a white shirt with a round collar, and a dark grey suit with fancy embroidery on the lapels. I couldn't tell what he was drinking, but he ate kebabs from a plate and laid the toothpicks in a tidy row on the edge of the table. Neat, methodical. I watched the tape late into the night, running the Suleiman Isa bits back again and again. Chotta Badriya watched with me, and we counted four of the brothers at the party, we knew their faces from police file photographs. Finally Chotta Badriya started yawning about once every minute, and I sent him home to bed. I watched Suleiman Isa again, how he washed his fingertips in a little brass bowl, and patted them dry on a napkin. It was late now, and late in the party on the tape. Govinda had long gone, and even Suleiman Isa had left. Still the camera wandered, taking in men sprawled on the sofas, their shoes off, their ties twisted loose. One of them saw the camera, pushed himself up, three tries it took him, he raised his arms and attempted a Govinda twirl and fell, his legs kicking up against a table. A glass shattered on the floor. Much laughter. This was footage I hadn't seen before, we had always gone back to Suleiman Isa and the brothers. But now I watched it through, I wanted one look at all of it before sleep. The drunken man was picked up off the floor by two of his friends, and now all three of them stepped, skipped left-right-left, their arms over each other's shoulders. The camera panned left with them, overshot, and a man sitting on a chair ducked away from it, he slid off the chair and out of frame, his left shoulder raised high and face turned sharply away from the lens, from me. And then the camera twitched back to the right, and found the three dancing men.

But I went back. I scrabbled for the remote, pressed at buttons. There had been something about the man's big shoulder, something effortlessly fluid about his body even as he jerked out of sight, something so confident. He wasn't afraid, just easy, just making sure, he just didn't want to be seen by the camera. There it was, barely a second of blur, he was good, but not that good, not good enough – behind him was a sheet of blackish glass, a tall window with darkness outside, in one bottom edge of it I could see streetlights far below, but also in its flowing sheen I saw a face, a sharp blade of a nose, a long chin, strong neck, the quick undulating dangle of a gold chain with a shiny locket at the end: it was Bada Badriya. Our Chotta Badriya's older brother, Paritosh Shah's faithful bodyguard. It was him. It was him. It was so quick, barely a glimpse, but I was certain. And then I was unsure. When I slowed down the tape, pushed it forward frame by halting frame, the face broke up into blocks of light and slivers of dark, and became shapeless under my straining eyes. I pressed close to the screen. Was it a dull haze of shifting light, or was it him? In the still frames, there was only this vague cloud, this nothing. But when I ran it at speed, there he was, it was Bada Badriya, I was sure.

I stayed till morning, ignored Subhadra's sleepy summonings and went back and forth in that moment, from the chair to whatever lay beyond the camera's edge, until I felt his motion in my shoulders and hips, I knew what it was to move smoothly off a chair, to have reflexes that saw clearly a threat swinging close, a camera lens or a gun barrel, and muscles that stretched and sped with such grace, I was him, I knew why he did it. For the money, for advancement, for the anger of being forever a bodyguard, for the contempt he had for the man he was guarding, for his knowledge of his own big muscles, for his sense that he himself deserved something better. And Suleiman Isa had given him money, I knew, and promised him much more. Suleiman Isa had offered Bada Badriya a new version of Bada Badriya, bigger, better. And so Paritosh Shah had died. Looking at the tape, I knew this.

I ejected the tape, switched off the light and walked down the hall towards my bedroom. Half-way down I stopped, stood stunned, clutching the tape to my chest. I knew what I had to do with Bada Badriya, that was simple. It was as good as done already. But what about the young one, the younger brother, Chotta Badriya, my Chotta Badriya? What about him, the one who called me 'bhai' every day? Who was asleep this very moment in his house not fifteen feet from mine, from this house we had built together? I trusted him, I had not a second's doubt about him. What to do with him, the one who was loyal to me? When his brother died, when I killed his brother, he would know. Even if Bada Badriya was found decapitated in a ditch far away, in Thane, in maderchod Delhi, even if I told Chotta Badriya that Suleiman Isa had done it, finally he would wonder, he would look at my face and doubt me – Suleiman Isa would pass word to him, send him videotapes and photographs of Bada Badriya fraternally together with him in Dubai, and Chotta Badriya would remember Paritosh Shah and me, he would look at me and know I had no choice, that I had to do it, and he would loathe me. Maybe he would accept that his brother had done wrong, but for ever after he would stand next to me, behind me, and despise me. It couldn't be otherwise. This is how brothers are, this is what grows in the womb, this inescapable tie, this hate. Would he be loyal if I let his brother go? Would he stay with me if I forgave, forgot?

I closed the door to my bedroom. Subhadra said sleepily, 'Is it you?'

'Who else would it be, you idiot?' I snapped. 'Suleiman Isa?' I lay rigid next to her, unable to suppress the seething of my breath. She gathered herself in, timid, afraid. And I had the videotape under my fingertips, Govinda's dancing feet, and I knew in the pressured humming of my blood that all gifts are betrayals, that to be born is to be deceived, that nothing is given to us without something larger being taken away, that becoming Ganesh Gaitonde the Hindu bhai was itself an act of murder, it was the murder of a thousand and one other selves, and there was water in my ears, the moonlit bellow of churning water, and something came from my throat, a low groan.

'What's wrong?' my wife whispered.

I turned to her, I climbed on top of her, I yanked up her nightgown and I heard buttons pop and cloth tear, I forced into her. Her gasps, her cries were lost in the frantic exultation of my anger, in the growling grunts that came from my bitterness.

I had Bada Badriya brought to me the next day. My boys picked him up from his new petrol station in Thane. He had a reputation, he was known for his shoulders, for a trick he had of picking up a chair with a man in it and holding it over his head. So six of the boys went out. If he makes trouble, I told them, shoot him in the leg, but bring him to me alive. They waited for him in a little dhaba next to the petrol station, and he actually walked by them on the way to his car, with a bodyguard next to him. He had become a businessman, the bodyguard himself with a bodyguard now. Bada Badriya was bending down to get behind the wheel when my boys knocked down his gunman, laid him out with a three-foot pipe. And then they all had their pistols on Bada Badriya, at his legs, and if he had drawn he would have died then, his thighs chopped open by a dozen bullets. They were all trembling nervous. But he froze. The boys were cocky and contemptuous when they brought him in, very full of themselves, loud from the relief of having no bullets pass their way. Bunty, who had led them, clunked down a gun on the table and said to me in his Punjabi accent, 'Bhai, he had a Glock but he went nowhere near it. And the chodu called himself a bodyguard. He came quiet.'

Quiet he still was, Bada Badriya, sitting on a chair in the storage room where the boys had put him. He stood up when I walked in, and I had to look up at him.

'Why did you do it?' I asked.

'Do what?' he said, raising a hand towards me, palm up.

Until that moment I hadn't an exact plan. I had just wanted to look into Bada Badriya's eyes, and now, looking, seeing the shifty innocence he was trying to paste over his fear, this pathetic acting he was attempting, I grew huge with rage. It grew in my belly and my ribs hurt from it, and I shouted, I roared, 'I saw you. I saw you, maderchod. I saw you dancing.'

'Dancing? What, where?'

I couldn't stand him any more, his broad chest, his beefy life, his small boy's face. 'Kill him, Bunty. Kill him.'

And Bunty did.

Chotta Badriya was waiting for me in Alibag. I had sent him there the night before, to pick up four lakhs in cash that one of our controllers was holding for us. Go and get the money, I'd told him, and check on that controller, there's something slippery about him, I don't trust him. I have a feeling about that bastard, I'd told him. And I'd told him to stay in Alibag, I had a property there, a bungalow on the beach, I'd come to meet him there. I'd wanted Chotta Badriya out of the way, out of contact and touch, I didn't want somebody picking up a phone and calling him to tell him that his brother had been picked up. Stay at the bungalow there, relax, have a good time, I'd said. I'll come and join you. And he'd said, yes, bhai, come, you need the relaxation.

So I went out to the bungalow with Bunty, with three boys. We drove for three hours, through an afternoon thick with traffic and dust. I squeezed my eyes shut soon after we left Kailashpada. When I opened them, the fields had opened up, filled with new construction. I watched a hill roll through the powdery haze on my right. We turned to the east, along the highway, and then south again. I slept. And then the sea glittered ahead of us, a vast open plain shining with sharp, metallic points of sunlight.

Chotta Badriya called to us from the balcony of the bungalow. I got out of the car, stretched and grinned at him. He was wearing red swimming trunks, bright against the sloping white wall of the bungalow, and his stomach rolled gently over the red elastic. When had he become fat? When, in the last decade? We had seen each other so often and so closely that I had stopped noticing him. Do you really see the skin on your right hand? But now I saw his short hair, his belly, his marriage, his children, his love for the movies, his passion for good clothes, his loyalty to me.

Upstairs, he spilled the cash out on the bed. 'No problems, bhai,' he said. 'All of it is here. I don't think we have a problem with the fellow.'

'That's good,' I said. 'I need to piss.'

'Over there,' he said. And as I went into the bathroom, 'Do you want some chai?'

'Yes,' I said, and I shut the door. I heard him calling down the corridor, two chais, something to eat, quick, quick. The mirror over the washbasin was broken, one whole half of it gone, leaving only the raw wood underneath. I tried to piss, shook myself, but even after three hours there was nothing, I was dry. Still, I poured mugs of water down the toilet. Keep it normal, I told myself. Don't make him afraid. You owe him that much. I checked my pistol, then put it back under my shirt, in the small of my back. It had been years, literally many years, since I had used a gun. And my experience had been with revolvers, cheap revolvers, not the good Austrian automatic I now owned. Bunty had had to instruct me: this is how the cassette slides in, bhai, and then you pull the slide back. He'd said, with a look of sympathy, you don't have to, bhai, you know I can do it, bhai. And I'd said, no. No.

I opened the door. Chotta Badriya was sitting on the bed, putting away the money, stacking it neatly inside a blue travel bag. 'Everything all right, bhai?'

'All right?'

'You look a little . . . tired. Stomach troubles?'

'Yes. It's upset.'

'In our climate, you have to be very careful. There are too many germs everywhere, food gets spoiled fast. And we eat out too much, you know, all this greasy outside food. If you eat home food, keep a light diet, it's much better for your stomach.'

'All your light diet-shiet and you still have that,' I said, pointing to his stomach.

He threw his head back and laughed, and held the plump folds of his belly in both hands and lifted them up. 'Yes, bhai,' he said, smiling. 'That I have. What to do? We got rich.'

'We got old.'

'We're still young, bhai,' he said, and was about to go on, but then there was a rattle at the door, and Bunty backed in, carrying a tray. He put it down on the bed, handed me a cup of tea, and his pupils were small and spike-like in their questioning. I said nothing, and he shut the door very gently as he left, and there was a low drone of tension in the room now, which Bunty had stirred up with his cautious walk. Or maybe it was in my beating blood. Chotta Badriya was still looking at the door.

'What were you saying?' I asked, and my voice was too loud.

He looked back at me, and his mouth was small and concentrated as he searched for the thought, and then he relaxed into a big grin. 'I've completely forgotten, bhai.'

'Idiot,' I said. 'Drink your chai.'

'Now these are truly fattening, bhai,' he said, slurping from the cup. He held up a glistening brown bhajiya from the pile on the tray. 'There is more oil in one of these things than your body needs in a year.' He put it down carefully on the plate and took a long gulp of chai.

'Eat it.'

'What?'

'Eat it,' I said.

He had a kind of hatred for the pile of bhajiyas, a murderous attraction for them that knew exactly how much power they had over him. He pushed the plate away, sulky. 'They're bad for me, bhai. I have become fat.'

'Eat them, eat them,' I said. 'I'm giving you permission.'

'Yes?'

'Yes.'

He picked one up, held it up to the slabs of sunlight, examined the bhajiya's brown whorls and complicated branchings. He took a slow bite, and his eyes shut for a moment.

'Mmmm,' he said. 'Have one, bhai.'

'No, you eat. Can you eat the whole plate?'

'All of these?'

'All.'

'Easy. They're not that much.'

'Finish them, then.'

'No, all of them?' He really did look chotta then, with his shiny lips and surprised cheeks and boy's open face, all bright.

'It's an order.'

He began to eat, sitting cross-legged on the bed. He thumped shiny crimson sauce from a bottle on to the bhajiyas, and then held the plate up close to his chest and lowered his head to them. Now, I thought. But the pistol was tangled somewhere behind me, I could feel it cutting against my spine. I would have to get up, draw. No, no. Let him finish. When he finishes. Not now.

The pile was half-way gone now. I got up, walked to the window. The white top of my car sent up a glancing blaze of light into my eyes, and I turned and squinted. The sun was coming down, and the black shore stretched to right and left, all rocks and upthrusting edges. The trees were completely still, not a stirring of a leaf. Somewhere over there were other countries, millions of people sleeping. I saw them curled close to each other, naked, faces relaxed. Behind me was Chotta Badriya eating. I needed to turn around. Maybe he wasn't finished yet. But if he was finished he would look up, he would be looking at me. I took hold of myself, a breath, another one, and the faint swirl of the sea was close by, and I turned. He was still eating. He had two bhajiyas left. His cheek was full, plumped out and moving. Now there was one bhajiya left. The pistol came into my hand easily. It swung up. I swung it up, and I was careful, formal and correct. Get the balance right. Aim well. Hear nothing. See only the target, nothing else. That narrow space of brown skin just above and in front of the ear, just before the hair started.

His blood sizzled. The shot must have boomed, but from the long stifling tunnel of my aim I heard nothing, and in the next moment I knew that blood from a freshly broken skull froths, that it makes a small fizzling sound. It is a small, fast, stuttering hiss. It lasts for only a moment.

Bunty pushed the door open slowly, leading with his gun. He lowered it. There was no need for a second shot.

I was happy. I could understand now what Paritosh Shah had meant when he told me I needed to get settled, why he had always extolled the virtues of marriage. I *was* settled, I felt in place, rooted, held down to my soil in a way I had never experienced before. I knew who I was, I no longer felt that I was attempting at every moment to become Ganesh Gaitonde, that I was groping for the contours of Ganesh Gaitonde. With Subhadra next to me, and my acceptance that I was a Hindu bhai, that I was some kind of Hindu, I felt real. I was no bent-backed, harried husband – I still took Jojo's women – and I was no worshipper of gods and goddesses, but the boys understood me now, and came around me and felt comfortable. I was a leader they could identify with. Our rolls were back up to normal strength again. For the first time in my life, I experienced contentment. It puzzled me at first, this puddling of warmth inside my chest. Yes, Subhadra delighted in the everyday acts necessary to being a wife, she arranged and rearranged the utensils in the kitchen in graduated, gleaming rows, she danced about choosing my clothes in the morning and picked them up from the floor gladly in the evening. She walked efficiently about the house, her keys jingling at her waist. She was slim, not exactly pretty but pleasant-looking, and when I looked at her I was not beset by that angry desire that some randis brought forth from me. I wanted to sit with Subhadra, to watch the evening from our balcony, eat some ghavan and drink chai. Outside, our struggles and wars went on as before, but I was not consumed by these battles as before. We won, we lost sometimes, but we were still strong, and we were growing, and so I was happy.

But I was beset by bodily troubles. My stomach was keeping unwell, I had a bulging pain that came upon me often, late in the afternoons, a feeling of congestion in the lower abdomen, and then of expansion, as if something was trying to get out. Gas, the doctors diagnosed, and prescribed tablets and light food. But only Scotch whisky soothed it, made my tissues calm, took away the sudden pressures that threatened to tear. I couldn't let the boys see me drinking, so Bunty arranged another bungalow for me, this one within easy reach in Juhu, just down the lane from the Holiday Inn. I went every other day to this haven by the sea, where Bunty kept a bottle of Johnny Walker in a locked cupboard, and soda in the fridge. I sat alone on the terrace at sunset, and drank. Two small pegs was what I allowed myself. The drink was calming, but it brought on spasms of nostalgia. There were evenings when I cried for the early days with Paritosh Shah, when we were poor and young, when we had faced insurmountable odds and defeated monstrously strong villains. Where had those mornings gone, when we had gathered our weapons for good fighting? Where were our friends of those bright evenings? Where were the songs of our fleeting spring? I drank and listened to old numbers and remembered. 'Chala jaata hoon kisi ki dhun me, dhadakte dil ke tarane liye . . .'

Meanwhile Bunty tried to learn everything he needed to, to manage our complicated affairs. He had started with us as a shooter, had been noticed early on in our war with Suleiman Isa, and now he was my trusted and main controller. He was full of confidence and vigour. 'Everyone knows what you did, bhai. From Matunga to Dubai, they've heard. They know that you found Suleiman Isa's bastards and tumbled them. Your partner is now fully paid for. You won this one too.' He said it to cheer me up when I was silent for long hours in the car. I knew that I had won. And I knew also that there was no victory in this world without another, larger loss hiding inside it, that in our triumph we were already hunted by some disaster. I knew something was coming. Suleiman Isa was coming. I told the boys to be careful, I increased security in Gopalmath, I forbade Subhadra from leaving the house. Not even to the temple, I told her. You are to stay at home. She looked glum but obeyed.

Twenty-one days from the day of Chotta Badriya's death, on a Friday, in the early afternoon, the bombs exploded. I heard about the first one minutes after it had happened, a phone call came in from one of our boys, he called from the city sobbing, bhai, there was a foot on the pavement, there was a sound, a huge boom, and I didn't know what it was and people were running and nobody knew what was happening and I ran around a corner with them and there was this foot on the pavement, bhai, it just lay there, sliced off at the shin, there was no blood, and then someone pointed around the corner, I looked, the stock exchange is gone, the stock exchange, it's blasted, burst. There was an exposion, bhai, a bomb, a bomb.

I calmed him down, told him to go home. Then more detonations came, at the Masjid Bunder grain market, at Nariman Point, and I had Bunty on the phone to the Goregaon police station, to headquarters, and I was dialling and there was the busy signal again and again, and then the phones went dead, and yet the news came in, an explosion near the Rakshak headquarters, now against the abrupt, numb quiet in the street there were quick flurries of shouting. Now there were boys hurrying up and down the street, and mothers gathering their children in, a car came to a halt, and there was the sound of running feet and Bunty ran in with yet more news, fishermen had died in Mahim from an attack, bombs had fallen from the sky, there were men wading ashore with machine guns. I told everyone to get indoors, lock down, and I put my boys on guard, armed them and stood them at the peripheries of Gopalmath. By evening we knew the shape of what had happened: there were no armed marauders from the sea, but there had been grenades thrown at the Fisherman's Colony, and twelve bombs had lifted up clouds of concrete through the length of the city, twelve times in two hours a blunt, cataclysmic ringing had torn at the heads of men and women and children, had killed hundreds of them, maimed thousands. On television the torn buildings stood eviscerated, all sags and twisted metal inside, and the ministers and policemen said an investigation was being conducted, they said it again and again. But in Gopalmath, my wife huddled against me, subdued and grateful, and I knew what they were whispering in the streets outside: Bhai knew, he knew something was going to happen. Yes, I had known. Yes. I had stood on this battlefield long enough to learn its rhythms, the falling drumbeats of its narratives. We were carried along in the story's surges, and many died, and I lived. I had dug deep holes for many, but I had survived because I had come to feel the subterranean sequences of cause and consequences, I knew in my flesh where the bone-white lightning would fall next. I was awake. I was playing the game.

It made perfect sense, it fell neatly like a wheel into a muddy groove, when it was announced by the police investigators that Suleiman Isa and his people had planned and executed the bomb blasts. Of course, of course. I knew it all from our paltu policemen before it was announced on television that in the simmering and swelling of anger after the mosque was pulled down, after the riots, young Muslim boys from Bombay had been flown to Dubai and then to Pakistan, that they had been trained by Pakistanis, that greasy packets of RDX had been brought in by sea by Suleiman Isa's vastly seasoned smugglers, that the trainees had made RDX bombs complete with timing devices and planted them in cars and scooters, that they had distributed these vehicles in the most crowded and best-known parts of the city, and then the massacre had followed. This was their revenge for the riots, for the many Muslims who had been killed.

There had been one small war, my inevitable war with Suleiman Isa, the war between our companies. This combat had been long, it was eternal. Now its connections to a larger war were becoming apparent. The game was many-tendrilled, webbed and seductive and infinitely dangerous. I heard about Suleiman Isa sending the bombs and I laughed, and I said, of course. And I asked myself, where next do *I* go? Where's the next move? What's coming for me?

It took a while, many months, but it came, sure enough. It came a day after my son was born. Gopalmath was bright and noisy with celebration, and my house was full of visitors. I was a bit shaky myself from the unfamiliar gusts of joy that came from my belly, from the quite unprecedented swelling of heated, helpless emotion that I felt when I looked down at my son's wrinkled little face.

In the middle of all this commotion Bipin Bhonsle called and asked for a meeting. He was now not only an MLA but a party leader, and so we had to take precautions and double precautions, and we met at a resort on Madh Island. They had rented a private bungalow, away from all the other cabins, and were waiting when we drove up at dusk. We sat under the palm trees, under the sky that out here seemed to be choked with stars. Bipin Bhonsle drank beer, which I turned down. With him was a man he introduced as Mr Sharma. This Sharma was one of those fair-skinned UP brahmins, very soft-spoken in fancy, All-India Radio Hindi. He was dressed in a long brown kurta and sat cross-legged on his chair, very poised, like he was practising yoga.

'Sharma-ji is an associate of ours from Delhi,' Bipin Bhonsle said. He wiggled his toes and tossed kajus into his mouth and drank. For a few minutes he talked about recent political struggles, rivals he had humiliated, profits he had made. Then he waved his boys back into the shadows, and jerked his creaking aluminium chair over to me, and leaned confidentially closer. His chest was plump and bulging under the shiny shirt.

'Sharma-ji needs your help, bhai,' he said. 'He is a very close friend of mine. Not in our party, of course, but we understand each other.'

'What kind of help?'

'These Muslims, you know.'

'Yes,' I said. 'What about them?'

'This war hasn't ended, bhai,' he said. 'They are here. They are growing. They will come against us again.'

'Or you will go against them.'

'After what this bastard Suleiman Isa has done, we will have to crush them. They live here but they're maderchod Pakistanis at heart, bhai. That's just the truth.'

'What do you want from me?'

This time Sharma-ji spoke. 'We need arms.'

'The Pathans move arms through Kutch and Ahmedabad. They'll sell you what you want.'

'They're Pathans, Bhai Saab,' Sharma-ji said, and under all the soft inflections there was iron. 'We can't trust them. We want our own pipeline. We want a steady supply.'

'There must be companies in the north.'

'Nobody has an organization like yours. We want to bring in the material by sea. We need someone to move the arms in. They have Suleiman Isa.'

'And you want me?'

'Exactly.'

I lay back in the chair, stretched. Suleiman Isa was the Muslim don, so I was the Hindu bhai. It was necessary. There was a low moon over us, plump and gentle. I breathed, and took in the fragrance of jasmine. So beautiful, I thought. It is a terrible world, I thought, and it is a perfect world.

'There's a lot of money in it, bhai,' Bipin Bhonsle said. 'And you know you should be with us. We have to protect Hindu dharma. We have to.'

'Relax,' I said. 'I'll do it. I'm yours.'

408

A Woman in Distress

On Tuesday morning there were five messages waiting for Sartaj from a Mrs Kamala Pandey. Sartaj shut his eyes, and through the smooth white plane of his headache tried to remember who Kamala Pandey was. It was a whisky headache, even and narrow and persistent. The morning sounds of the station house tapped at Sartaj's skull, the constables arguing in the corridor outside, the slushing of water on concrete and the steady rasping of a jhadoo, the insistent bluster of the crows, the anguished groans of a prisoner as he was led hobbling back to the cells from an interrogation. Sartaj wanted to go home to sleep. But the day was only beginning.

'Did this Kamala Pandey say what she was calling about?' Sartaj asked Kamble.

Kamble was rooting impatiently through desk drawers. He had spoken to his contact in the Flying Squad that morning, about an opening in the squad, and he was already acting as if the humdrum business and casual chaos of a mere suburban station was beneath him. 'No, she did not say. I asked. She said it was personal. And she left only a mobile number.' Now he looked up to grin. Kamble always had time to leer. 'She sounded like a real hot item, boss. Tip-top convent accent. Your girlfriend or what?'

'No. But I remember the name from somewhere.'

Kamble slammed the drawers shut. 'Definitely some trouble over there, boss,' he said, and turned to check the shelves behind his desk. 'A woman calls five times in one day, either she's in love with you, or she's in some ghotala. I asked if I could help her, but she insisted, no, only Inspector Sartaj Singh.' He turned back, and he had found the file he had been looking for. 'This maderchod station is like a bhenchod rubbish dump,' he said. His smile was huge and happy.

'But you're leaving us soon?' Sartaj said.

'I am, absolutely,' said Kamble. 'Soon, soon.'

'What's the delay?'

'Price has gone up. I'm short. Not by a lot, but by enough.'

'I am sure you're working hard to make it up.'

Kamble shook the file at Sartaj. 'A little here, a little there. I'm off to court,' Kamble said, tucking the file into a brown rexine briefcase. 'Come out with me tonight, boss. I'll introduce you to a couple of good girls.'

'I have an appointment. You go.' Kamble spent his evenings with a changing cast of bar girls. There was always one who was getting too old, one who was in her prime and a young one he was helping to get into the business. 'Have fun. Be careful,' Sartaj said. But he knew Kamble was not going to be careful in the least. He was bouncy with confidence and daring, content with how he was raising the money to get into the Flying Squad and hungrily looking forward to swathes of action and mounds of cash. He was young, he felt strong, he had a pistol in his belt and he knew he could take life and bend her to his will.

'You look after yourself today, Sardar-ji,' Kamble said, and he was quite healthily rosy in his twill shirt and new black jeans. 'Call me on the handy if you change your mind about anything. Or if you need help with anything.' And he strutted off, his briefcase tucked under his arm.

Sartaj sank down into his chair. He didn't much mind the condescension. He was himself getting used to the idea that he was washed up, that he had reached the crest of his career and that he wouldn't advance very far past his father's rank. He knew now that he wasn't going to be the hero of any film, even the film of his own life. He had once been the promising young up-and-comer, marked for advancement. Even the fact that he was a Sikh in a department full of Marathas had been an advantage as well as a burden, a marker of his separateness. He had stood out, and was known far and wide, and journalists had loved to write about the handsome inspector. But the years had worn away the shine, and he had become just like a thousand other time-servers in the department. He had his consolations, and he plodded through the day. Maybe even his memory was failing him, a little by very little. This was true. This was the truth that Kamble no doubt saw, as he went swinging up on his upward road. The Flying Squad had been very successful lately, as well. They had been killing Suleiman Isa's men rapidly over the last three months, and not just small-time taporis either. The newspapers had been publishing the life stories of important, highly valued shooters and controllers as they had fallen one by one to the bullets of the Flying Squad. Suleiman Isa, the chief minister had proudly announced just the week before, was in retreat. The Flying Squad was going to be an exciting place for Kamble, and he was sure he was in.

But this was Sartaj's life, stretching forward and inescapable. There was nowhere to go but here, to this daily trial, to this untidy mess of a station. Still, there was work. On his current roster of investigations he had three burglaries, two missing teenagers, one case of embezzlement and fraud and one domestic murder. All the usual desolations. And now there were these calls from Mrs Kamala Pandey. Who was she?

He dialled the number. She picked up on the first ring, and she was terrified. 'Hello?' she said. 'Hello?'

'Mrs Pandey?'

'Yes. Who is this?'

'Inspector Sartaj . . .'

'Yes, yes. I need to meet you.'

'Is something wrong?'

'Listen, please . . .' She stopped herself. 'I just need to meet you.'

She was used to getting her way. Sartaj remembered her now. Her husband had thrown a puppy out of a window. Sartaj remembered the dog, poor little white thing with her skull opened on the asphalt. Mr Pandey had suspected Mrs Pandey of infidelity, so he had murdered her dog. Mrs Pandey had refused to file charges against her husband, and the husband had refused to complain about her assaults with stick and knife. Sartaj hadn't liked either of them, and Katekar had liked them less. He had wanted to put them both inside for a night or two, on charges of disturbing the peace. Or at least shove them around a little, teach the spoilt little rich snots to keep it quiet, frighten them a little. Or one of them will end up dead, Katekar had said. Maybe that's why Mrs Kamala Pandey was calling now, maybe the husband was dead already, and had been tucked and bent until he fitted into a bedroom cupboard. It had happened before. 'What about, Mrs Pandey?' Sartaj said. 'What's the trouble?'

'Not on the phone.'

'There is trouble?'

She hesitated. 'Yes,' she said. 'I can't come to the station.'

'All right,' Sartaj said. 'Do you know the Sindoor Restaurant?'

On the way from the station to the underpass, Sartaj was flagged down by Parulkar, who was convoying in the other direction in a brand-new official car. Sartaj did a U-turn and followed Parulkar, who slowed down at the next patch of empty shoulder and stopped. Parulkar's security men sprang out alertly from their jeeps and made a perimeter and held their ferocious automatic rifles at the ready. Their number had increased over the last two months, or three, ever since Parulkar had pulled off yet another of his amazing feats of survival. Whatever the dispute had been with the Rakshak government, it had been settled. Suddenly Parulkar was their grey-eyed boy, the chief minister and the home minister were consulting him every two days. The enemies had become allies, and both sides were profiting. Organized crime was retreating, bhais and controllers and shooters were being killed at such a pace that soon there would not be many left to shoot, at least until the next generation showed up. All was right with Parulkar's world. He had made it so, and once again he had proved he was amazing. The rumour was that he had paid twenty crores to the chief minister alone, and much else to various functionaries. In any case Parulkar was back, glorious and jovial again.

'Come, come,' he called. 'Quick.'

Sartaj slid in beside him. There was a new fragrance inside the car, something quite delicate.

'You like it?' Parulkar said. 'It is called Refreshing Nectar. See, from there.'

A sleek aluminium tube with fins sat on the dashboard vent, blinking a red light that Sartaj assumed signalled the release of Refreshing Nectar. 'Is it from America, sir?'

'Yes, yes. Are you well, Sartaj?'

Parulkar had just come back from a two-week visit to Buffalo, where one of his daughters was a researcher at a university. He looked rested and contented and bouncy, very much like the Parulkar of old. 'You look very healthy, sir.'

'It is the clean air over there. A morning walk, over there, revives you really. You cannot imagine.'

'Yes, sir, I cannot.'

'I brought something for you also, a portable DVD player. It is so small' – holding his squared thumbs four inches away from each other – 'and the picture is sharp, absolutely sharp. You can take it anywhere with you and watch films, you see. Very good for a policeman.'

'That is a wonderful thing, sir. There was no need . . .'

'Arre, don't tell me about need. I know what you need. You come home, tomorrow, day after, and we will talk. The player is also at home.'

'Yes, sir. Thank you, sir.'

Parulkar thumped Sartaj on his shoulder and sent him on his way. Sartaj thought about the new DVD player, and worried. Now he would have to buy or at least rent DVDs and then watch them. Parulkar was sure to ask for reports on his viewing. But maybe that was all right. Maybe Parulkar really understood better than him what he needed. Some entertainment might be exactly what would fix him up, and revive him like a good morning walk in Buffalo. Where in America was Buffalo? And why was it called Buffalo? Sartaj had no idea. Some more of life's mysteries.

Sartaj sat at his usual booth in the Sindoor Restaurant and nursed a Coke. During a recent renovation, Sindoor had gained festive new red tables and a new menu which included Bengali and Andhra food. Sartaj was reading through the Bengali desserts when Shambhu Shetty walked in. 'Hello, saab,' he said and sat. They had last seen each other a week ago, when Sartaj had come in as usual to pick up the monthly Delite Dance Bar contribution to the station. Shambhu had complained as usual about the necessity of raids and rising prices, and had told Sartaj about his dream trek, through the forests of Arunachal Pradesh. Now Shambhu had auspicious news. He was engaged. He had sampled from the revolving tray of feminine delights that his bar brought to him every day, but now he said he wanted to settle. 'Those were only trailers, boss,' he told Sartaj. 'This is the main film.' The heroine of Shambhu's life-film was a nice girl that his parents had found, of course within the Shetty community. The two families had common friends in Pune, and had known vaguely of each other for decades. The girl had a B.Ed. but was content not to work after marriage. She was a virgin, that went without saying, or asking.

'Well done, Shambhu,' Sartaj said. 'When is the date?'

'May. The cards will be printed at the end of this month. I will send you.'

It was four-thirty in the afternoon, and the restaurant was almost empty. A pair of college lovers sat next to each other, on the same side of a booth, nursing their Cokes and pressing thighs against each other. Shambhu was relaxed but brimming with energy. He had marriage plans, and also plans for another bar, this one in Borivili East. This new bar was to have a filmi theme, pictures of film stars everywhere. There would be different halls for the dancers, each with a distinct decor. There was going to be a Mughal-e-Azam room, and a DDLJ room. 'You should invest,' Shambhu said. 'I guarantee good returns. Invest for your future.'

'I am a poor man, Shambhu,' Sartaj said. 'I'm sure you're not interested in investors who come with five hundred rupees.'

'Poor, you? Even after that Gaitonde hit?'

'That wasn't a hit, Shambhu. The man shot himself.'

'Yes, yes.' Shambhu was smiling, very wise to the ways of the police. 'And how did you happen to find him?'

'Anonymous phone call. Tip-off.'

'If you get a tip-off about some ready money, saab, come straight to me. This is a good time to invest.' Shambhu uncoiled himself out of the booth. His face sloped forward to the chin, and his eyes were too close-set, but he carried himself very well. He was at ease in the world. 'I'm expecting a beer delivery,' he said.

Shambhu shook Sartaj's hand and walked briskly to the door. He stood aside then to let Mrs Pandey through. She paused to take her sleek dark glasses off, and then marched straight up to Sartaj.

'Hello,' he said. Sartaj stood up, and pointed her around a partition, to a small table near the kitchen door. Here they were quite private, alone with each other.

She was wiping at her nose with a tissue, and Sartaj saw that she was strained, exhausted, but well turned-out. Her hair was glossy, in a sweep down to the shoulders, and she was wearing white jeans and a white top with very short sleeves and a cut that exposed a bit of her toned midriff. She was smaller than he remembered, but had a spectacular chest which filled out the white top very nicely. It wasn't exactly the outfit Sartaj would have recommended for a private meeting with a seedy policeman in a very middle-class suburban restaurant, but women had their own reasons. Maybe all the jhatak and matak made her confident. Maybe she liked the fact that men always looked.

She finally spoke. 'Thank you for meeting me,' she said. Her Hindi had just that little awkwardness that came from living her life mostly in English. 'Pani,' she said sharply to a waiter who had stepped up. 'Bisleri pani.'

Sartaj waited until the waiter had poured the water and walked away. Mrs Pandey's fingers had a clear gloss on them that Megha had worn sometimes. Megha would have described her as a 'hot little number' and steered Sartaj away from her. But Sartaj felt no desire now, only curiosity. 'It is my duty,' he said. 'But what is the trouble?'

She nodded. 'Trouble,' she said. Her eyes were her best feature, large and almond-shaped and the colour of a glass of good Scotch with one or two ice-cubes melted in. Megha would have said that she wasn't classically beautiful, but had worked and polished herself into hotness. She was in some very big trouble now, and it was difficult to talk about.

'You're an air hostess,' Sartaj said.

'Yes.'

'For?'

'For Lufthansa.'

'That's a good airline.'

'Yes.'

'They pay well.'

'Yes.'

'Has something happened to your husband?'

'No, no.' The sudden question made her shrink, fold her arms across her stomach. 'Nothing like that.'

But it had something to do with the husband. Sartaj was sure of it. 'Then what is it?' he said, very gently. He was quiet, and sipped slowly at his water. He was willing to wait.

She gathered herself, and then ground it out: 'Someone is black-mailing me.'

'Someone. You don't know who?'

'No.'

'How are they talking to you?'

'They call on my mobile.'

'Is it always one person?'

'Yes. But I hear him talking to someone else sometimes.'

'Another man?'

'Yes.'

'What are they blackmailing you with?'

Her chin came up. She had made her decision, and was not going to be intimidated, or shamed. 'With a man,' she said.

'Who is not your husband?'

'Yes.'

'Tell me,' Sartaj said. She hated having to explain herself, to justify anything. 'Madam,' Sartaj said, 'if I am going to help you, I need to know the details. Everything.' He poured her some water. 'I have worked for a long time as a policeman. There is nothing I haven't seen. Nothing you can tell me will shock me. In our country we do everything and say nothing. But you have to tell me.'

So she did finally tell him. There had been a man, her husband hadn't been so wrong in his suspicions. Actually he had been rather correct. The man was a pilot, yes. Only he didn't fly for Lufthansa, and there had been no fun on stopovers in London. Kamala Pandey's pilot flew for Sahara, his name was Umesh Bindal, he was single, she had met him at a party in Versova three years ago, the affair had begun a year after their first meeting, and she had broken it off six months ago. Their assignations had all taken place in Bombay and Pune and Khandala. The blackmailers had first called a month and a half ago.

'What do they have?' Sartaj said.

'They knew a lot of details, of a hotel. And when I had gone to his house.'

'That's not enough. They must have something else.'

She was flinching now, from what she had to say. 'Videos.'

'Of what?'

'Of us. Outside our room.' It looked as if the videos had been taken with a hidden camera at a guest house in Khandala. The lovers had used this guest house often, on a regular basis, and the staff had thought they were a married couple fond of quick hill-station vacations. The videos had them going into their room, and leaving it. And also holding hands and kissing and embracing as they walked to and fro, across the hotel courtyard. The blackmailers had left the video tape on the seat of Kamala Pandey's car, in a brown envelope. Then they had called her.

'How much did you pay them?' Sartaj said.

A small shimmer of puzzlement hovered over her taut cheeks. Sartaj laughed. 'It's not so unusual, madam. Everyone pays them first. The blackmailers send over the video or photographs or whatever. Then a month later they come back with new material. So what was the amount?'

'A lakh and fifty thousand. They wanted two lakhs, but Umesh told me how to negotiate with them. Now they sent a new tape.'

'How much do they want now?'

'Two lakhs.'

'And where is the tape?'

'I burnt it.'

'Both videos? Everything they had sent?'

'Yes.'

'Madam, that is not so good. We could have learnt something from the tapes. Even from the envelope.'

She nodded. The videos would have been too frightening to keep. The mention of them had made her a little watery, a little tremulous under the sheen. But now she showed some steel. She reached into her silver handbag and pulled out a folded piece of paper. She opened it out on the table, smoothed it down. 'I kept a list of their numbers,' she said. 'Each time they called, I wrote it down. With the times.'

'That is good,' Sartaj said. 'That is very good. And now if they send you anything, keep it. Try not to touch it too much.'

'Fingerprints.'

'Yes, fingerprints. You have to help us to help you. Where is Umesh today?'

'He's flying. He would have come with me, but you didn't return my calls till today.'

'I want to talk to him.'

'I'll give you his numbers.' She wrote on the paper. 'He wanted to go to the police the first time they called. I only didn't want to come.'

'You wanted it to stop.'

'Yes.'

'They never stop. Until we stop them.'

'That's what Umesh said. But I didn't want to tell anyone then.'

'Why did you break it off with Umesh?'

'Because I realized that he wasn't interested in me really. He is a nice man, but he has too many girlfriends. He just wanted fun, and I was giving it to him. But then it wasn't fun for me any more.'

'So he's very handsome, like a hero?'

'Very.' His handsomeness still evoked a fervour in her, tinged with an aftertaste of sadness. 'Very.'

'When did the blackmailers call you last?'

'Yesterday.'

'They will call today. Start listening to them carefully. I want to know exactly what they say. Take notes. Listen for sounds from near by. Anything at all. You have to start thinking like a police-wallah. A police-walli.'

That amused her just a little, that she could ever be a lowly police-woman. 'Police-walli,' she said. 'I will try.'

'Tell them you need time to collect the money, that you're getting it together. How was it delivered last time?'

'I had to put it in a bag, a shopping bag, and drive to Apsara cin-ema in Goregaon in the evening, at six o'clock. The afternoon show was just letting out, and there were lots of crowds. I was told to wait on the road across from the gate. Then they called me. They told me that a chokra in a red T-shirt was going to come up to me, and a sec-ond later he was knocking on my window. I rolled the window down, he asked for a package, and he took the money and ran off into the crowd. That was it.'

A crowded area, a street kid sent to collect the money – just stan-dard operating procedure for the average blackmailer. 'Umesh didn't come with you for the delivery?'

'No, they don't know that he knows. They told me not to tell any-one, not a single soul. They told me that they would hurt me.'

That was unusual, that blackmailers would threaten violence. There was no need for hurt if you had photographs. 'And the chokra, what did he look like?'

Kamala Pandey was confused. 'The kid? I don't know. He was just some urchin.' A barefoot boy was just exactly like any other street sav-age, despite his red T-shirt. You could find a dozen at any street corner in Mumbai.

'Try, madam. Can you remember anything at all about him? It's very important.'

'Yes. Yes . . .' She paused. 'His T-shirt. It was a DKNY round-neck T-shirt. It had the logo on it.'

'Deekay NY jeans?' Sartaj wrote in his notebook.

'No,' she said with the amused patience of somebody dealing with the lower classes. 'The letters D, K, N, Y and then "jeans". All capi-tals, one word. Like this.' She reached for his pen, and wrote in large letters: DKNY JEANS. 'The letters were very faded.'

Witnesses had to be praised for the slightest achievement, and cajoled into further discoveries. 'That is very good, madam,' Sartaj said. 'It will help us a lot. Anything else? Please try to remember. The smallest item can solve the case.'

She made a disgusted little pout, and touched a tooth, two behind her elegant, perfect right canine. 'His tooth, this one. It was all dirty-looking. Black, grey, instead of white.'

'Excellent. On that side?'

'Yes.'

'All right,' Sartaj said. 'It's good that you wrote down the numbers of the men who called. These are probably PCOs. Once you sign a complaint we'll put a watch on some of them.'

'I can't.'

'You can't what?'

'I can't sign a complaint.'

'Madam, without a complaint, without an FIR, how can I proceed?'

'Please understand. If any of this goes into writing, people will find out. People will know.'

'Madam, I understand that you are afraid that your husband will come to know. But will you please understand that without a complaint the police have no jurisdiction. We have no reason to interfere, no grounds to act on.'

'Please.'

She was leaning into the table, both hands up by her cheeks. A practised actress, this one. 'Madam, I can't do anything,' Sartaj said. He straightened his neck, loosened his tight shoulders. He was angry at her, had been angry for a while now. It burned through his chest. He didn't know why.

'Please,' she said. 'Think about it. I'll lose everything.'

'You should have thought about that a long time ago, yes?'

'Yes.' That stopped her, cut her off in mid-flow. 'Yes.'

She covered her eyes, and when she brought away her hands she was teary. A minute passed, then two. She dabbed away the tears. Sartaj was sure that an expert application of small pressure on her eyelids had helped start the tears, but now she seemed genuinely sad. There was a weariness that he recognized, an exhaustion from losing something built over long years. You had something that you valued very little, that you maybe had slighted and abused out of familiarity. Yet you then discovered that this thing itself, this connection, this very flimsy construction had spread its roots deep under your skin, and into the bone.

Kamala Pandey gathered herself again. In preparation for a direct attack, she levelled her shoulders and straightened up a bit. Sartaj remembered the walking stick she had broken on her husband's back, and he wondered if Mr Pandey had learned to recognize her cues and guard himself.

'Look,' she said. 'I will pay you.'

Sartaj said nothing. She reached into her bag, reached deep, and brought out a long white envelope. She paused, and waited for him to react. Sartaj said nothing. She slid the envelope across the table, left it next to his water, close to his hand.

Sartaj extended his index finger, nudged open the flap. Hundred-rupee notes. Two stacks. Twenty thousand rupees.

He was now very angry. He pressed the envelope shut. He pressed until the fingernail turned white and red. 'Listen,' he rasped. 'This is not enough.'

'Yes, yes, I know. This is just a token. I would rather pay you than them. Just help me. Just stop it from happening.'

'You have so much money of your own?'

'I work. My parents help me now and then.'

She kept separate bank accounts, and she had doting parents. 'Your parents live in Bombay?'

'In Juhu.'

'Brothers and sisters?'

'No.'

She was the single, spoilt child of well-off parents, suddenly in a lot of trouble. She believed, quite completely, that she was owed her privileges. It would be a pleasure to take her money from her. But Sartaj was very angry. 'Madam, I can't help you without a complaint.'

'How much do you want?'

He shoved the envelope across the table. 'I can arrest you right now, for trying to bribe a police officer.'

That shut her up. She put a hand on her mouth and began to weep. Sartaj could see that it was real this time. He stood up and walked away.

Why had he been angry at her? It wasn't just the money. He was quite used to taking money, to being bought. Things and people were bought and sold every day in this city. Sartaj bumped down the pitted lane to Katekar's place, keeping the motorcycle as close to the centre of the

420

road as he could. The gutters were clogged, and occasionally the tides of rubbish hid serious holes in the asphalt. In this patchy dark, the khuds in the road came swiftly, and could take a man down. There was still a lingering aftertaste of indignation in Sartaj's mouth, a sour rancour that had nothing to do with what a spoilt, irritating little child she was. Was it only that she had been unfaithful, that she had done something a woman was not supposed to do? Men did it all the time, Sartaj knew this. Industrialists did it, and labourers did it. And sometimes women did it also. He knew this. He often saw, as he had done today, the aftermath. He had seen broken marriages and broken bodies, heard anguished sobs and screams. This was nothing new, in his job he had seen it all. So why had he been angry?

Sartaj coasted down the last few feet to Katekar's corner. The house was down an alley that narrowed and angled off to the left. Sartaj parked at the corner, and raised the rear seat to get at his packages. There was also a plastic bag crammed into the rear carrier. He shook away the anger, the question, and marched down the alley, turning his shoulders to slide by clumps of pedestrians. Some of them nodded at him. He had been a regular visitor for a few months, and they knew him now. He knew that some of them must still believe that he had got Katekar killed, but most of them were friendly now.

Katekar's sons were sitting near their kholi's door, studying. The tube-light inside threw their shadows out on to the road, and Sartaj knew their familiar shapes well before he saw them. Rohit sat always to the left of the doorway, his back flat against the wall and a book held well out in front of him. Mohit was always moving, his head jigging up and down even as he wrote. As Sartaj came up Mohit went from a cross-legged squat into a kneeling arc above his notebook. He was making a blue mess of the page.

'Hello, Rohit-Mohit,' Sartaj said.

'Hello,' Rohit said, grinning. Mohit kept his head down. He was writing furiously across drawings that slashed across the double spread of the notebook.

Sartaj lowered himself into the doorway and sat with his back hard against the jamb. 'Where's your Ma?'

'Aai is at her meeting.'

'What meeting?'

'There is a Family Welfare Group. She is a volunteer, so she has to go once a week.'

This was certainly new. It had been a little over two weeks since Sartaj had last visited, and Shalini had a new routine. Life moved along. 'Volunteer for what?'

'They give information. Aai goes and talks to women around here.'

'About health?'

'Yes. And I think about saving money. And cleanliness. They are planning to clean up the lanes. There are some pamphlets somewhere here if you want to see.'

'No, no.' Sartaj knew the groups, and the NGOs that worked with them, usually with government or World Bank funding. The groups were rackets for somebody or other, for the NGOs or the government or the Bank, but they did good work sometimes. And Katekar had been a great one for cleanliness, so Shalini's work was a fitting tribute. 'Here,' he said, and handed over the packets he had brought.

'Thank you,' Rohit said, in English. He had been working very hard on English recently, and planned to enrol in a beginners computer course in a month or so, immediately after his exams. Sartaj had made sure that a seat had been reserved in the Prabhat Computer Classes, which were reputed to be the best in the area. 'Learn Computer and Internet For Only Rs. 999', they advertised in multi-coloured advertisements pasted on every other wall. Rohit was going through the bags, laying down the plastic pouches of dal, and atta, and rice. 'Eh, tapori,' he said to Mohit, and tossed him two comics. 'Latest Spiderman,' Rohit said. 'Say thank you.'

Mohit couldn't take his hands off the comics, but he wouldn't say thank you. Sartaj wondered what his neighbours had told him about his father's death, who he had learned to blame. He was a strange boy, he had become a glowering little tyke, very opaque and very jerky, tightly sprung from within. 'Our Mohit likes Spiderman,' Sartaj said, 'but he is a patriotic Indian. He doesn't like saying thank-you-thank-you all the time, like those Americans.'

Rohit laughed. 'Yes, rudeness is our birthright.' He tweaked Mohit's nose, and Mohit made a spitting noise and ran past the partition into the other room. 'He really does want to be Spiderman though. For two days now he'll sleep with the books. Kartiya sala.' Rohit tapped his forehead.

Sartaj unbuttoned his breast pocket, brought out an envelope. 'Ten thousand,' he said. He handed it over, and scratched at his beard. It was getting hot, settling into the absolute grim stillness and dejection of the pre-monsoon months. His collar was soaked with sweat.

This time Rohit didn't say thank you. He got up, holding the envelope to his chest, and then Sartaj heard the metallic creak of a cupboard opening and closing. Rohit came back with a glass of water. Sartaj drank. He was a good boy, Rohit, and he was too young to be putting money in cupboards and thinking of how to raise his little brother. But then there were six-year-olds making a living on every street corner down to Colaba.

They sat for a while, talking about computers, the Middle East, and whether Kajol would do any more films. Rohit thought Kajol was the best actress since Madhubala. Sartaj hadn't seen a film for a long time, but he was glad to agree. When Rohit talked about Kajol, he grew intense and happy, and gestured emphatically with his hands at Sartaj's chest while he described Kajol's virtues. Kajol was not only a great actress, she was a good wife and mother. Sartaj found himself smiling, and was happy to listen, and agree, and let the night come on.

The next morning, Sartaj met Mary at her sister's apartment. As he had expected, it had taken several weeks to get Jojo's apartment handed over to Mary, her sole surviving relative. But now, he had been glad to report to her on the phone, he had the key, everything was ready. Tuesday was Mary's day off, and he had agreed to meet her first thing in the morning, before he went to the station. He had got himself up early, dragged himself into the shower, and was at the building punctually at six-thirty. She was waiting for him near the lift, as they had agreed. With her was a very tall, very thin woman, who was looking at Sartaj with mild amusement.

'This is my friend, Jana,' Mary said.

Sartaj had not expected friend Jana, but it certainly made sense that Mary would bring a friend. 'Namaskar, Jana-ji,' he said.

Jana took in the muted sarcasm, and grew more amused. 'Namaskar, Sartaj-ji,' she said.

Sartaj grinned, and quite unexpectedly Mary smiled. Her jaw thrust forward a little, and her eyes narrowed, and her face quite transformed. The dragging seriousness went from her, vanished. Sartaj wasn't quite sure exactly what she found funny, but it was a relief and a revelation to see that she could be diverted. 'Shall we go?' he said, pointing towards the lift.

'Yes, yes,' Mary said. 'Jana has come to look after me.'

Standing close to the two of them in the lift, Sartaj could see that Jana was very competent indeed. She wore a smear of sindoor in her carefully parted hair, and a dull red kurta over black salwars. Her shoes were sensible, and she carried a large, square shoulder-bag with wide shoulder straps. Inside it she carried a plastic bottle, no doubt full of boiled water. That was a mother's bag, nice-looking but capacious and hardy. It would carry lunch, chocolates, medicine, vegetables and school books. It was a trustworthy bag.

The lock to Jojo's apartment was tightly bandaged with coarse canvas that took in the latch as well, and the layers were secured by a drippy seal of red wax marked by the Mumbai Police. Sartaj handed Mary the key, and reached inside his gym bag for a pair of large black scissors. He had come prepared. The seal came off with a rip, and then Sartaj watched as Mary struggled with the key against the jammed lock. 'Let me,' he said, and Mary shook her head briskly and set her shoulders to the task. Jana gave Sartaj a rueful look over Mary's head: this is what she's like, let her be. They waited. Then the lock came open with a screech, and they were in.

Jana rushed around opening windows, revealing the drawing room in sections. Mary was still near the door. Sartaj reached behind her and ran his hand down the row of switches. No lights, no electricity. 'Yaar, this is a *nice* place,' Jana called from the kitchen, mingling surprise and a fat dollop of outrage.

Women were always outraged when officially bad women made money, had taste, enjoyed a little happiness, Sartaj thought. But Mary was unreadable. She walked through the apartment, paused in each room and took it in, and was very silent. Jana's commentary rolled on: in the bedroom, Jojo's lavish collection of footwear called up a moment of stunned silence, then two minutes of affronted references to Jayalalitha and Imelda Marcos, and then a long painstaking inventory. Mary was standing in the doorway, her hands by her sides.

Sartaj pushed a window open. 'There were some photo albums here,' he said. 'They must be somewhere in here.' The room was a mess, and the scattering of shoes and clothes and magazines lay under a thick slough of dust. 'Ah, there,' Sartaj said, and came around the bed to the dresser. He picked up the top album, and thumped it. A fine ash ballooned off the cover, and Sartaj was suddenly aware of how loud his voice had been, how triumphant. The direct light from the window didn't quite reach Mary, and he couldn't see her face. 'You should go to the BSES office, and have the electricity switched back on.' He put the album back on the dresser. 'There must be some outstanding bills. Okay, then, I must go.' He nodded, took a step and stopped.

Mary backed into the corridor to let him pass. Sartaj raised a hand at Jana, and she nodded, but she was watching Mary. Sartaj was all the way down the corridor when Mary spoke. 'Thank you,' she said.

'Yes, yes,' Sartaj said. 'Don't mention.'

'I haven't forgotten.'

'What?'

'About your investigation of Ganesh Gaitonde. I tried to think about Jojo, if I could remember anything.'

'Thank you.'

She smiled again, and again this time it came suddenly, without warning. She raised her left hand and did a curious little wave, holding out her hand towards him and turning it only from the wrist. Sartaj nodded, and shut the door.

An hour and a half of shifting and coiling had left Sartaj exhausted, but more awake than when he had got into bed. He had settled in just after midnight, feeling virtuous about the earliness of the hour, and clean from a long shower. But now a small and relentless agitation was working under his skin. He had drunk three whisky-and-waters. And still there was no sleep. He sat up. Shadows of wires swayed across the window-pane. He couldn't remember the name of the dog. There had been that small white dog that Kamala Pandey's husband had thrown out of the window. Sartaj remembered its stiff-legged sprawl in the car park, but he couldn't remember the name of the gaandu thing. He still had her number. He could call Kamala Pandey and ask her, what was the name of the dog your husband killed, that the two of you killed together, as you played your dirty games?

Sartaj swung his feet to the floor, rubbed at his eyes. He couldn't do that, it would be police harassment, persecution, something. But he knew who would be awake at two in the morning. He dialled, pressing at the lighted keys with a shaky finger. He listened to the ring and waited, holding up his hand. He was very tense. I need to get a blood-pressure test, he thought. There was a history in the family: Sartaj's father had struggled against hypertension and high cholesterol all his life. He had survived one heart attack, and died quietly in his sleep nine years later, of causes that the doctors said were natural.

'Peri pauna, Ma,' Sartaj said.

'Jite raho, beta,' she said. 'Did you just get home?'

'Yes. Casework.' Work was an acceptable reason for calling this late. Admitting to insomnia would occasion an enquiry into his eating habits, his consumption of alcohol and his health. He would be pre-emptive. 'Ma, you sound hoarse. Are you getting a cold?'

'A cold, me? I never get colds. Your father was the one who always got colds. He had that thin Bombay blood. We grew up in a good clean climate, we were used to good cold winters.' This was an old theme, that the north-western sardar was tougher than the Bombay sardar. The sisters were the toughest of all, and Navneet-bhenji was the eldest and the hardiest of the sisters. Here it came, the story of the stalwart and long-lost aunt. 'Navneet-bhenji used to bathe in cold water even on January mornings. At six-thirty in the morning because she had to get to early class at college. Even Papa-ji would tell her to put in a lit-tle hot water, but she never listened. And if you looked at her, you would think what a delicate, beautiful thing! She was a literature stu-dent, she looked like she should be counting pearls in a palace, but she was strong as some peasant. She used to paint really well also, you know. These scenes of the village fields, and houses, and cows. There was one she did of our new house that was wonderful, it was so exact.'

Now there was a pause. This halt was also a familiar one, as Ma mourned the dead sister. Navneet-mausi had been killed during Partition, but Ma had been talking about her for as long as Sartaj could remember. She was dead, but she had always been in Sartaj's life. All the children and grandchildren in the family knew her well, this absent mausi. They had lived with her, with the stories and the rigidity that would come over the faces of the elders as they spoke of her. Sartaj had tried now and then to press past that constriction of muscle and nerve, that freezing of emotion, to what exactly had hap-pened during those bloodstained days. But all that Ma had ever said was, 'Those were bad days, very bad days,' and that was all. And that was what they all said, all the uncles and aunts and grandparents. That, and an occasional curse against Muslims: beta, you don't know, they are bad people, very bad people.

But tonight Ma was not angry about old hurts, or bitter, she was just quiet. So Sartaj finally said, 'I don't know how you remember such old things. Exact paintings and things like that. I can't even remember the name of a dog.'

'What dog?'

So Sartaj told her the story: the husband, the wife, the dog thrown out of the window.

'What a horrible man!' Ma said. She liked dogs, and they liked her. 'Did you arrest him?'

'No.'

'Why?'

'The wife wouldn't file charges.'

'Arre, there was abuse of an innocent animal.'

'She wouldn't even say he had thrown it out of the window.'

'Maybe she was scared of him.'

'She's not so innocent either.'

'Why? You saw her again?' Ma had spent decades tussling with a policeman, two policemen, so she had developed her own skill at catching nuances and unvoiced truths. 'What's wrong with her?'

It was an ugly story to tell this late at night to his mother, but Sartaj told it. He made a quick little report on the wife, the pilot, the camera, the blackmail. He left out the bribe the wife had offered, and her tight little white top. Ma had severe opinions about shamelessness in any guise, and he didn't want to overly prejudice her against Kamala Pandey. The errant wife was surely condemned in any case. 'Of course I told her that I couldn't work on her case, without a complaint. She's a fool,' he said. 'A fool who thinks she can get whatever she wants, can do whatever she wants.'

'Yes,' Ma said. 'Her father must have done whatever his little daughter wanted, and given her no discipline. People spoil their children nowadays.'

Sartaj laughed out loud. This was why he called his mother in the middle of the night, for these sudden vaulting leaps of insight, these confirmations of his own hunches. She was quite amazing sometimes. 'Yes, she's a brat. Very irritating.' He sat up in bed, and drank a long draught of water. He was feeling better already, hearing her voice, listening to her breathing. 'Did you and Papa-ji talk much about his cases?'

'No, no. He didn't like to talk about work with me. He said a policeman's life meant that you couldn't escape from work until midnight anyway. Then to come home finally and keep thinking and

427

talking about work, that would drive you mad. So we talked about other things, and he said that relaxed him. That's what he said anyway.' She sounded dryly amused. He could see the tilt of the chin, that downward glance. 'The truth is that he was old-fashioned. He thought that I would be scared by all the murder and the dirty things they had to investigate. He thought women shouldn't be exposed to that kind of thing.'

'And you went along with that?' She loved action movies, and in recent years had developed an inexplicable taste for all the really bad, blood-dripping, moonlight-and-screams horror series on television. She read the crime columns in the papers every morning with relish and offered commentary, and the repeated observation that the world was a bad place, and getting worse.

'Beta, you adjust. *Adjust.* He didn't want to talk about work, so I didn't. That's how you go along. That's what this new generation doesn't understand.'

She meant Sartaj's generation, and Megha's. She knew that Megha was married, finally and completely out of Sartaj's reach, but occasionally she would revisit what had happened, what should have happened, what Sartaj should have done. Sartaj had long given up arguing, or even responding with anything other than the occasional 'Yes'. He lay back and listened. She was his mother, and he adjusted.

'Achcha, go to sleep now,' she said, 'or you'll be tired for your shift.'

'Yes, Ma,' Sartaj said. They said their goodbyes, and he turned towards the window so he could feel the air on his face. He fell into sleep easily, and dreamed. He dreamt of an enormous plain, a cloudless sky, an endless line of walking figures. He woke abruptly. The phone was ringing.

It was before seven, he knew that without opening his eyes. There was that stillness, in which a single bird was chittering. He waited, but the phone was not going to stop. He reached for it.

'Sartaj,' his mother said, 'you must help that girl.'

'What?'

'That woman from last night, the one you told me about. You should help her.'

'Ma, have you slept?'

'Where is she going to go? What is she going to do? She's alone.'

'Ma, Ma, listen to me. Are you all right?'

'Of course I'm all right. What would be wrong with me?'

'Fine. But why all this about that stupid woman?'

'I was just thinking this morning. You should help her.'

Sartaj kneaded his eyes, and listened to the bird. Women were mysterious, and mothers were more mysterious. Ma was quiet now, but it was her strict silence. It was a calm that tolerated no back-talk, no resistance. He wanted very much to go back to sleep. 'Yes, all right. Okay.'

'Sartaj, I'm serious.'

'I am too. Really, I will.'

'She's all alone.'

So was everyone else in the world, Sartaj wanted to say. But he mustered up obedience. 'I understand, Ma. Promise I'll help her.'

'I'm going to the gurudwara now.'

He had no idea what that had to do with calling him out of a perfectly good slumber, but he whispered, 'Yes, Ma,' and hung up the phone. Sartaj's bed was moulded to his body, the bird was not too loud, the morning was cool under his silent fan, but sleep was gone. He cursed Kamala Pandey. Saali Kamala Pandey, she is a kutiya, he said to the bird, bloody raand, and he got up.

Sartaj spent the morning writing redundant reports on small burglaries which would be perfunctorily investigated and never solved. His afternoon trickled away in court, between two magistrates and three cases. At five he drank a cup of tea in the restaurant across the road, and ate a greasy omelette. The restaurant was called Shiraz, and was full of gossiping lawyers. Sartaj hid himself away at the rear of the first-floor air-conditioned annexe, and tried to avoid meeting the lawyers' eyes as they walked to the washbasin. He chugged down a tall glass of chaas, wiped his moustache and started to feel better. He managed to get through the annexe without having to talk to anyone, and all the way down the stairs. But half-way to the entrance a weedy, pock-face rose up to intercept him.

'You're Sartaj Singh?'

This wasn't a lawyer. His grey shirt was sweat-stained, and he had the mean, foxy deference of someone used to people stepping around him. But he had a voice that made up for his build, brassy and deep. 'Who are you?' Sartaj said.

'You don't remember. I met you at the funeral. And two-three times before that.'

Of course. This voice. 'You're Katekar's . . . Shalini's sister's husband.'

'Vishnu Ghodke, saab.'

'Vishnu Ghodke, yes. Yes.' Sartaj remembered him from the funeral, but not before that. At the funeral he had been busy bringing things, organizing the mourners, directing the priests. 'Everything all right, Vishnu?'

Vishnu Ghodke touched his breastbone. 'By your blessings, saab. Although . . .'

Sartaj nodded. 'Yes. Katekar was a good man.' He waited for Ghodke to step aside. 'We'll meet again some time.'

Ghodke wasn't ready to leave Sartaj quite yet. He turned sideways to let Sartaj pass, and then followed him out on to the pavement. 'Have you seen Dada's boys?' he said into Sartaj's shoulder.

Sartaj was abruptly aware that he didn't like Vishnu Ghodke very much. He wasn't quite sure why, but he wanted to put a hand over his face and back him fast into the wall. 'Yes, I saw them yesterday. In the evening yesterday. Are they all right?'

'Of course, of course, saab. No, nothing like that.'

'Then like what?'

'Was their Aai there?'

'No, she was out.'

Vishnu Ghodke turned his head to the side, to look across the evening swell of cars towards the court house. Above his head was the red 'Shiraz' sign, with the lettering delicately arranged in four languages. 'This is what, saab?' he said, coming back to Sartaj. 'What is it? A woman should be at home. A woman should be with her family.'

'She has to work, Vishnu.'

'But this is not work, roaming about in the evening, leaving her children to go hungry.' He was making wide gestures towards the road and the courts beyond, as if Shalini was running wild among the black robes and the stained arches.

Sartaj's shoulders came up, he felt the dense throb of violence along his forearms. Maderchod. This bastard had to show up now, today. 'Those boys are fed and happy,' he said. 'Their home is well-kept. What is it that's tickling your gaand?' Vishnu Ghodke squirmed away, found the wall behind him. 'Haan? Tell me.'

'Saab, I was just saying . . .'

'Saying what?'

430

'She has started going to these meetings.' Vishnu was trying to find a quiet voice now, an intimate one. He wanted to be a man talking reasonably to another man.

'They talk about health. So?'

'Saab, health is one thing. But they tell them all these, these uncivilized things. All these things that are not fit for decent women. And they tell them to go about and talk to young girls and spread it into the community. Why does a young, unmarried girl need to know about pregnancy and nirodh and all? I have young girls, I am a father, and I tell you it is becoming very difficult. As it is, you never know what can be on television, right in the middle of the day. It is impossible for a family to sit together and watch. And then we have people like this, educated people who catch women like Shalini and turn their heads.'

Sartaj considered clouting this defender of the culture, once on each scrawny cheek. But that wouldn't smash any sense into his head, it would only make him more militant in his defence of his daughters. 'You don't worry about Shalini's head,' he said. 'And she's not talking to your daughters. If she says something to them you don't like, tell her to stop.'

'That woman won't listen to anyone, saab. Her husband is gone, so she thinks she can do what she wants.'

'So she won't listen to you. Is this why you are angry?'

Vishnu brushed at his shoulder, where the plaster from the wall had left a streak. He had grown confident as he had spoken, had forgotten some of his fear. 'Saab, I am not concerned about myself. I am only thinking of the boys, and that home. That home will suffer. We have a saying: *gharala paya rashtrala baya.*'

Sartaj reached out and put a hand on Vishnu's shoulder. He smiled. To the passing pedestrians, they were just two friends passing the time with friendly banter. But Vishnu was squirming already from the pressure of Sartaj's thumb just under his collarbone. 'So now you're worried about the country also?' Sartaj said. 'You listen to me, Vishnu. I don't like you going around talking, making trouble for her. You think you're some bhenchod saint? You wander around like some bastard loudspeaker, spewing lies.'

'But it's all true, saab.'

Sartaj squeezed, and now Vishnu was truly afraid. 'It's true that she's trying to take care of her boys. And do some good. You're a small man, Vishnu. Your brain is small, your heart is small, so you think small of people. You're a small, mean bastard, Vishnu. I don't like you. So shut up. Keep your mouth closed. Understand?'

Vishnu's eyes were sparkling with tears. He had a hand picking at Sartaj's wrist, but he couldn't get away from the pain.

'Understand?'

'Yes,' Vishnu said. But he had the persistence of a cornered rat, this Vishnu. He whispered, looking away, 'But I'm not the only one saying it. Other people are saying it as well.'

Sartaj let go of him, and leaned in close. 'Yes, other maderchods like you are always ready to say this and that about a woman who is alone. Especially when you are such a decent brother-in-law that you start these rumours yourself. So you'd better keep quiet.' Vishnu nodded, keeping his eyes down. Of course he wouldn't stop. Of course he would keep at it, add and embroider. But now he knew there would be consequences. 'If I hear you're making trouble, I'll come and look for you, Vishnu. She needs your help now. Live with her as a family should, Vishnu. Help her make that home strong, don't destroy it with your mouth.'

Vishnu was working his jaw, but was keeping his head down and his mouth shut, as instructed. Sartaj had no doubt he would open it as soon as he felt safe. Sartaj patted his cheek gently. 'I'll be watching you,' he said, and walked away.

Gharala paya rashtrala baya. So if the stability and prosperity of a house depended on its foundations, and that of a country on its women, what was Sartaj going to do about the glossy and very unreliable Kamala Pandey? He had his unambiguous instructions from Ma, and despite the distance, and his age, he did usually go along with what she wanted. For the most part. But she was a sentimentalist, wanting to rescue fallen women from their troubles. She was from another generation, and she had no idea what kind of trouble Kamala Pandey was. She could have no conception of how much Kamala Pandey annoyed Sartaj. It was easy to say, you must help that girl. Much harder to tolerate the bitch.

Sartaj let it sit in his stomach for three days. He went about his business, investigated, arrested, wrote reports, drank, slept. Kamala Pandey stayed with him, and it was pleasurable to think of her in trouble, of her wincing and cowering under the shower of abusive language that came in over her mobile phone, of her money being taken from her. Yes, she should learn that the world was not made for her delectation. Yes, she should know that she couldn't have just whatever she wanted. On the fourth day the relish ebbed, and by that evening it had been replaced by a dragging feeling of responsibility.

'What's the matter, Sartaj?' Majid Khan said.

They were standing on Majid's balcony, waiting for dinner. Sartaj was nursing his second glass of Black Label. Majid was wearing red shorts, and drinking fresh mausambi juice, and was speaking with the quiet authority of an old friend who knew exactly when Sartaj was being more morose than usual. He would press on until Sartaj talked. So Sartaj told him about Kamala Pandey, the whole story. 'She's one fancy item,' he said. 'Shows off her money. So some boys are taking some of it off her.'

Majid stroked his moustache upward. He had a spreading motion with thumb and index finger that he used when he was concentrating. 'Very interesting. I don't think there's a real problem with the case.' He meant that keeping it off the station books wouldn't be very difficult, or unusual. There was the possibility of good money, which always made discretion possible. Majid raised his glass. 'And, Sartaj, if she's so namkeen, investigating her could be fun.'

'Arre, Majid, I'm not interested in her.'

This made Majid straighten up, turn to Sartaj. 'Yaar, you said that she was sexy. She's giving it everywhere. She's got the chaska for it. So what does interest and no interest have to do with it? Take some.'

The logic was impeccable: if a woman was unfaithful once, she was therefore definitely available. Blackmailers sometimes used knowledge of an affair to take for themselves, to grab what was being distributed. Kamala Pandey's blackmailers hadn't tried that yet, but maybe they would, once she had run out of money. This was how the economy worked, there were many ways to pay. Sartaj spat over the railing. 'Ma said I should help her,' he said.

'Of course she would.'

'But . . .'

'You don't have interest in the money, you don't have interest in the woman.' Majid shrugged. 'So don't help her.'

'Yes. But what about those blackmailer bastards?'

They nodded at each other, grinning. They knew each other too well. Whatever he thought of Kamala Pandey, Sartaj was certain that he completely, unambiguously hated the blackmailers. He didn't like them operating in his zone, in his locality, in his area, in his mohalla. Maderchods, bhenchods, he wanted to squeeze their golis and see if they cried. Majid, who was scratching his thigh under his shorts, felt the same way. Sartaj could see it. Majid had a theory that all really good cops came from strong mothers. He had met Sartaj's mother, and his own Ammi was a tiny, wizened harridan who terrorized her daughters-in-law and still arranged marriages for her grandchildren without consulting anyone. Majid thought that a mother who kept an orderly house, who maintained cleanliness and had clear rules about what was right and what was wrong, actually ended up training her sons to be good policemen. He would list the names of department men he admired, and tell you about their mothers. Sartaj thought there was something to Majid's theory. Katekar's mother, for instance, had been a tough, massive-hipped matriarch. Years after her death, Katekar had spoken of her anger with awe.

'I think,' Majid said, leaning forward to clink glasses, 'Inspector Sartaj, that if your Ma tells you to, you have to put those blackmailers out of business.'

Sartaj had to agree. 'I'll call the Pandey woman,' he said. 'After dinner.'

At dinner Sartaj watched Majid and Rehana banter with each other. They argued about each other's parents, which set was more eccentric. Their own children giggled. Majid told stories about Rehana's mother that Sartaj had heard before, but he laughed again. Rehana was affectionate with her own children, with Farah and Imtiaz, and Sartaj thought that neither of these children would ever make good police. He had no doubt that Rehana was an efficient mother, and kind, but she didn't occupy her children's lives in the old-fashioned way that Majid had been talking about. She was their friend. And anyway, the kids were both too ambitious to consider a career in the force, which produced decrepit types like their father's sardar friend.

Sartaj drove home, burping loudly all the way. He went very slowly, quite aware that he was drunk. A perfectly round moon dodged behind buildings and darted out between billboards for next week's Shah Rukh Khan release, a grand love story. Sartaj tilted gently past a traffic circle, and thought that the posters had become a lot glossier than the hand-painted ones he remembered from his childhood, which had made

Dharmendra look like an alien with an inflated head. Love was altogether shinier now, or at least it had that appearance. Kamala Pandey was discovering how grimy it could be, how bare and bleak hotel rooms looked through a camera lens. Stopped at a traffic light, under another Shah Rukh poster, Sartaj considered the possibility of profits from her: did he want to take Kamala Pandey? Would he? Sartaj thought not. She was irritating, self-centred, spoilt. And anyway chodoing her would be dramatic, it would require an effort of will and force that would be exhausting, that would be anything other than pleasurable. No, if he helped her, it would be for the money, and only that.

Sartaj got home, took off his shoes and socks and dialled Kamala Pandey's number. She picked up on the first ring, and Sartaj could hear the panic in her 'Hello?'

'This is Inspector Sartaj Singh,' he said. He heard the breath that went from her then, as if someone had hit her hard under the breastbone.

'Yes,' she said. 'Yes.' Under her voice, there was conversation, music. A man was talking, close to her. They were in a restaurant, the successful young couple.

'I want to see you again. At the same place, at four o'clock.' She said nothing. 'Can you hear me?'

'Yes.'

'Don't worry. I am going to help you.'

'Okay. Thank you.' She was working hard to sound casual, as if she was speaking to a girlfriend about hair appointments.

'Did they call you again? Just say yes or no.'

'Yes.'

'We'll talk about it tomorrow. Relax. Bring that list of their numbers. Four o'clock, same place.'

'Okay, yes.'

Sartaj hung up. He put his feet up on the coffee table, loosened his belt. When he got paid on this job, maybe he would take Ma to Amritsar. He would take her to Harmandir Sahib, and watch her pray. It was comforting to feel the intensity of her devotion, it moved through him like a kind of familiar warmth. He wasn't sure if this was because he had grown up with the murmur of her prayers always sounding somewhere near, or whether within himself there was some forgotten, subterranean strand of belief that resonated into partial life when she hummed and sang. Anyway he would take her to Amritsar, and ignore her reckless remarks about this journey being her last one. If Ma wanted him to help the odious Kamala Pandey, let her profit from the job too. It was only fair, only fit.

Kamala Pandey wore a black outfit the next day at Sindoor. She was seated at the table near the kitchen when Sartaj came into the restaurant a few minutes after four. She had a bottle of mineral water in front of her, and an impossibly tiny mobile phone. Her hair was pulled back into a high ponytail, and Sartaj knew that the black blouse was definitely casual, but she still looked sleek enough to be on television, on some music channel.

'Hello,' she said. 'Thank you.' She had a way of tilting her head down when she smiled, so that she was looking up at you with very large eyes.

'Did you bring the money?' Sartaj said. He wanted short conversations with her, limited to professional requirements and concerns. She scrabbled in her bag, which was not the silver one she had carried earlier. This one was a black triangle, made out of some iridescent material. 'And the numbers?'

'The money is more today than yesterday,' she said.

There was thirty thousand in the envelope. Sartaj nodded. 'They called yesterday afternoon?'

'Yes. At one twenty-five. I told them what you said to say, that I need time to collect the money. They are not nice people.'

'They abused you?'

'They were saying very-very bad things.'

Her handwriting was full of curves and dashes and flourishes, but she had been meticulous about noting the dates and times of the calls in orderly columns with headings. 'When did you make the first payment?' Sartaj asked, and made a notation on the page. 'And when they called, did you hear anything interesting? Anything?'

'No. I tried. A car or a scooter passing by, now and then. But nothing else.'

'Keep trying. They will be very abusive, they will threaten you. Just delay. I need some time to look into this. I will call you soon.' Sartaj gathered up the envelope and pushed his chair back.

'Wait!' She held out an imperious hand, and then lowered it under Sartaj's glare. 'Please. You said you wanted to meet Umesh. He is coming.'

'Here?'

'Yes. He was supposed to be here at four. Sorry.' She was being deferential now, subdued.

'Okay,' Sartaj said. He looked at his watch, and then they sat. Sartaj had nothing to say to her. She played with her phone, pressed the keys, read a text message. Then she put it down, and looked through her bag. She peeped up at Sartaj, who kept himself very neutral, and then went back to her investigations. She was getting nervous and fidgety. This was not a woman who was used to men being silent around her. Sartaj was starting to enjoy himself. It was cruel, but he kept himself absolutely quiet, and the minutes passed.

When Kamala Pandey started to look slump-shouldered and forlorn, he took pity on her. It was too much to watch her droop. 'Is Umesh always late?'

That revived her like a bite of a tart lemon. 'He's on time for his flights, but for everything else he's late. He takes more time to get ready than me. You should see his bathroom, it looks like a chemist's shop. He has more shampoos and conditioners and scents than me and your wife and five other women put together.'

Sartaj let it pass, the little lure about his wife. He said, 'And he always calls and says he's on the way, he's in the car, he's rushing, he'll be here in fifteen minutes?'

'Yes, yes. And then two hours later he shows up, with some story. He used to drive me crazy.'

She was unable to help being just a little wistful. Sartaj was sympathetic: drama and craziness were painful, but you could miss that madness as you missed food or water. Until you settled into the dead calm of no hope, no disappointments. But Kamala Pandey still enjoyed talking about the sins of her ex, it revived her. 'Maybe he had other stops on the way?' Sartaj said.

She laughed out loud. 'Umesh always has two or three fools on his strings. He doesn't even hide it too much. He just makes you feel that he hasn't found the right one yet, that maybe you are the one where all the searching ends. He's honest enough that you believe him.'

'You saw the truth after all.'

'After a long time.'

And after all this knowledge she was still unable to cut away the yearning for him. Sartaj saw this as soon as Umesh walked in. Umesh shook hands firmly with Sartaj, and touched Kamala Pandey on the arm in greeting, on the bare skin. She kept herself stone-still, rigid. Sartaj abruptly remembered how he had fought down the vibration echoing up his arm when the estranged Megha had touched him lightly on the wrist, when she had bent towards him. He had strained with all his back and shoulders then to keep himself from tilting towards her in turn, and now he could not clench his throat shut against a warm pang of sympathy for this wandering wife.

'Hello,' Umesh said. 'I should make some excuse about being jammed in traffic, but really, I just got more and more behind this morning. Sorry.'

He certainly was beautiful. He wore dark red jeans, and a tight white T-shirt over pumped shoulders. The jeans were preposterous, but on Umesh they were perfect. He glowed golden, from his long arms up to the light brown eyes, which were very like Kamala's. She must have looked into them and seen herself. 'Sit,' Sartaj said. The man had an open, happy charm, and Sartaj wasn't going to give in to it.

'I'll just use the bathroom and come back,' Umesh said. 'It was a long ride.' He put his phone and a set of keys down on the table and hurried off. The phone was exactly the same model as Kamala's, satiny and small. His keys were attached to a model of a car, something low and fast.

'It's a Porsche,' Kamala said. 'Umesh likes cars.'

'Yes,' Sartaj said. 'And he drives too fast, right?' She nodded. That's how they must have gone up to the guest house, Sartaj thought, going too fast and weaving through the traffic, excited by the bursts of speed. 'What does he drive?'

'A Cielo.'

'A red one?'

'No, no. Those are just his pants. I told him red is not his colour, but he likes to be noticed. The car is black.'

Umesh came back into the restaurant and slid into the chair across from Sartaj. He was tall, an inch or two over six feet, and had the smallest waist Sartaj had seen on a man in a long while. He narrowed like an inverted triangle from the shoulders to the hips, and the quick travel from the gym-broadened shoulders to the absence of belly gave him the look of a cartoon figure. Kamala liked this superhero, though. She had tensed up again.

'Ah, Inspector saab,' Umesh said. 'Now I am totally at your service.'

'I know the main story,' Sartaj said. 'But I want to know about this guest house. What is it called?'

'Cozy Nook Guesthouse. On Frichley Hill, near that big Fariyas Resort. Cozy is a little place, not too crowded, nice view. It's just a cottage really, which the owners rent out. C-o-*zed*-y.'

He was looking at Sartaj's notebook, in which Sartaj had written 'Cosy Nook Guesthouse'. He was smiling warmly, and the joke was on the impenetrable English language, so it was impossible to be angry with him. He was altogether too pretty, but he was a good fellow. Sartaj could see how he would charm the ladies, he would tell them all his faults, and pay full attention with those sunlit eyes, and smile. You would have to be charmed. 'Yes,' Sartaj said. 'How did you find it?'

'A friend used to own a house near it, we used to drive past it. It's an old place.'

'Did you notice any new waiters? Any change in the staff?'

'No, not really. I wasn't paying that much attention, you see. But if I'm correct it's all the same people.'

'Any idea who could have taken those videos?'

'No, sir. There is the staff. But then also the other guests. I don't remember anybody specific, though.'

'You didn't ever recognize any of the other guests?'

'No, no. Never. If that had happened, I would have remembered.'

'Do you know which dates those videos were taken on?'

'No, you couldn't really tell. And I didn't note the dates we went up there.'

'How many times did you go to this Cozy Nook?'

'Over all those months? I don't know, maybe six, seven times?'

'More like eleven times, maybe twelve,' Kamala said. 'The last time was at the beginning of May.'

'I thought you broke up six months ago,' Sartaj said.

'We had.'

So they had gone all the way to the Cozy Nook for broken-up sex. They had probably argued all the way up there, and been silent on the way down. Judging from the bitter set of Kamala's lips, they had an argument coming now. Maybe more broken sex, although for Kamala's sake, Sartaj hoped not. There was little comfort to be gained from such transactions, especially when they involved a man like Umesh. Nice fellow, but not sturdy. Not at all like the decidedly unbeautiful but dependable Mr Pandey.

Now Sartaj asked Mrs Pandey, 'Who hates you?'

'What?' Kamala's shoulders hunched, and she curved in on herself and just a little bit towards Umesh.

'Who are your enemies?' Sartaj said evenly.

'Kamala is a very nice person,' Umesh said. He had his arm behind Kamala now, with fingertips resting on her shoulder. 'I don't think she has enemies.'

'Yes,' Kamala said. 'I mean, I've had quarrels with people, but enemies?'

'Everyone has enemies,' Sartaj said. 'It's better to know who they are.'

That silenced them for a moment, as they tried to calculate which friend or acquaintance might harbour enough secret loathing to qualify as a genuine foe. 'So you think this is personal?' Umesh said.

'Blackmail is usually about cash. But it may be worth thinking about friends and adversaries. Anybody who is in a position to have information, and who may be angry about something, or need money urgently.'

Umesh was shocked. 'Even someone connected to me? Wouldn't they have approached me as well?'

'You are not married. And you are a man.'

'And I support my parents and sisters. I don't have much cash flow. So they would go for the easy target.'

'So who can it be?'

Both the men looked at Kamala. Her cheeks were congested, flushed, and Sartaj wondered if she would weep. This time he would believe it, maybe. But she gathered herself and named her enemy. 'I had a friend named Rachel.'

'So you fought?' Sartaj said.

'Yes.'

'About what?'

Kamala laughed at his obtuseness. It was an ugly sound. 'What do you think?'

Of course. They had quarrelled over Umesh. There had once been sisterly love, maybe years of it, and then the beautiful Umesh had come between them. 'Rachel was your best friend?'

'Yes.'

'Then?'

'We met Umesh together. At a party.'

440

'And Rachel liked him?'

'Arre, boss,' Umesh interjected, a hand reaching across the table. 'I never even did anything with that woman. I met her a few times with Kamala, and God knows what all this Rachel assumed.'

What Umesh thought was not of any consequence, given the circumstances. 'What did Rachel feel?' Sartaj said to Kamala.

'She liked him.'

'From the beginning?'

'Yes. We talked about him after the first time at that party. She kept saying what a perfect man he was. Masculine, but sensitive.' This last with a roll of her eyes.

'And then?'

'What had to happen, happened.'

'When did you tell Rachel?'

She remembered exactly when. 'One Sunday two months later. I came back from a flight and went straight to her house. I just couldn't stand it any more.'

'And?'

'She told me to get out. She never spoke to me again.'

'She was that angry?'

'She had been divorced two years before that. And had never liked anyone.'

'Till Umesh.'

'Till Umesh.'

To his credit, Umesh wasn't smug about this, about his fatal charm that caused women to hate each other. He was anxious, and disbelieving. 'Still,' he said, 'it's hard to believe that someone like Rachel would come so low in the world. I mean, blackmail like this . . .'

'She is the only one who knows about us,' Kamala said dully.

Yes, Kamala knew more about anger, about the rotting remnants of friendship stored at the back of almirahs, old photographs and shirts given as gifts and souvenirs carried back from winter holidays in lovely Singapore, all of it curdling into black bitterness that burned through the day, morning and night, so that finally the only relief would be the blackmail. Not because it would yield money, but because it would cause humiliation and pain. Money was good, but healing and peace would come from elsewhere. Yes, Kamala understood. There was motive, and opportunity. Not enough to prosecute, but certainly enough to investigate.

'Give me Rachel's information, please.'

Kamala wrote swiftly, all from memory, in her pretty looping hand.

'All right,' Sartaj said. 'I will investigate. Your mobile number, please, Mr Umesh?'

'That's all?'

'It's enough for now.'

'I thought you would want to know lots of things.'

'If I have any questions, I'll call you. Number?' Sartaj wrote down Umesh's number, snapped his notebook shut. 'Remember what I told you,' he said to Kamala. 'Listen, just listen. And don't be afraid of them. They may act tough, but they need you. I'll be in touch.'

'So now you'll investigate those calls?' Umesh said. 'Follow them up at the calling numbers?' He was thrilled by the investigative process, by the potential pleasures of the story, even though it involved him directly.

'Something like that,' Sartaj said. 'You like detective movies?'

'Only Hollywood movies. Our Indian ones are so badly made.'

There was no denying that. 'That's true,' Sartaj said. 'But sometimes the Indian ones get things right also.'

Umesh plainly didn't believe this, but he let it pass. 'Why don't you just have Kamala tell them that she's going to pay, and then arrest them when they come to collect?'

'Because they expect that, and already are working against it. That's why they sent the chokra to get the money from her the first time. These boys are being careful. It's too risky. No use tipping them off.'

'They're that good?'

'Good, but not that good,' Sartaj said. 'We'll get them. Let us work on it.'

Umesh looked sceptical. Sartaj raised a hand in farewell, and left them sitting together, uncomfortable together but well-matched. Outside, he put his dark glasses on against the low late-afternoon sun. The glasses were quite out of style, he realized suddenly, by at least two years, maybe more. Maybe it was time to buy new ones. But he felt affectionate towards this old, battered black pair. They'd been through a lot together, and there was something to be said for the old and familiar and comfortable. Style was hard work, and expensive besides. He had got too old and too poor to work at it. Sartaj grinned at himself – what a boring, aged budhdha you've become – and drove on.

Kamala Pandey had a good head for detail, but the blackmailers had been very careful. The phone calls were spread out over the northern suburbs, both east and west, and there was only one call from each number. The only pattern Sartaj could pick out was that the calls came either early in the morning, between eight and ten, or after six in the evening. Which meant that the blackmailers had jobs. They were taking care of this business around the work of making a living.

'These are all PCOs,' Kamble said. 'I'm sure.'

'I know,' Sartaj said. He had recruited Kamble into the investigation that evening, once he had figured out exactly how much legwork was going to be involved. Kamble was quite willing to be recruited, for a price: forty per cent of the take. But working with Kamble also meant drinking with him at the Delite Dance Bar, and playing alibi for him with his girlfriends. Sartaj had already lied, as instructed, to two dancers about where Kamble had been earlier that evening. Sartaj said to him now, 'There's only one call from each place, so it's not likely that the operators will remember who made a call. But we'll cover the PCOs, starting with the most recent calls first. You want west or east?'

'West, boss.' Kamble was staring hungrily at the three dancers on the floor, who were spinning languidly to '*Aaja gufaon mein aa*'. The sequined blue and pink and green of their ghagras was gorgeous to watch, Sartaj had to admit. They were young. But it was early in the night, and the Delite was nearly empty, and they weren't being very energetic in their seductions. Kamble looked like he wanted to liven them up, by any means necessary. No doubt he would.

'All right,' Sartaj said. 'I'll take east. See you tomorrow.'

'Arre,' Kamble said, 'stay.'

'Tomorrow will be an early day. Extra work to do.'

'Every day is an extra-work day. Just have another drink with me.'

'Had my limit.' Sartaj got up.

'You need to get some sex in your life.'

'With whom?'

'Any of these.'

'No chance.'

'What, you think they won't like you? Boss, don't worry. They'll eat you up.'

'Exactly that.'

'Too easy? Then go for the one that doesn't want you. But you need to get back into the game, Mr Singh.'

'I do? Why?'

'What else is there?'

Indeed. What else was there? Retirement, or retreat? Ma had her religion, but that was only after a full lifetime with Papa-ji. Could you step out of the game at an early age, like some sanyasi who gave up everything and set off for the hills? No, Sartaj knew he couldn't do that. But he was going to get out of Delite for now. He was very tired, and he just wanted to go home. He raised his glass, emptied it. 'Thanks,' he said. 'Tomorrow, then.'

Kamble wasn't satisfied, but he gave in gracefully. He bared his big, toothy smile. 'Tomorrow,' he said. 'Tomorrow we'll see.'

Sartaj called Iffat-bibi that night, just before sleep. She had phoned him soon after Katekar's death, to express her condolences. She knew that they had been working together for a long time, but she also somehow knew about Katekar's young children, and had offered a nicely medium-sized sum of money to help the family. Sartaj had turned her down again, but after that they had spoken often on the phone. She was cunning, funny, and had endless stories to tell about apradhis and policemen from the past. She offered him little bits of intelligence, rumours and locations and names, and asked for nothing in return but that Sartaj make it easier, if he could, for any of her company's boys who went through his lock-up to meet their families. The information she provided was accurate and useful, but never concerned big cases or notorious apradhis. It was all comfortably small-time, and Sartaj felt their trade was fair, with no obligation left over on either side. And it was somehow restful to listen to her talk about Papa-ji. Papa-ji had talked to her about all his cases, it seemed, and Sartaj was getting a slowly emerging portrait of the old man that he could not have found anywhere else. Papa-ji, it turned out, was not so simply foppish as he may have looked, with his passion for double-breasted coats and custom-made shoes. He was vain, but without ego in the matter of his job. He knew his beat, and he had an instinct for what both apradhis and victims would do next. His arrests were not spectacular, but they were frequent, and they were steady and real, not fluff-jobs conjured up to bulk out an annual report. He was respected, despite his sartorial extravagances. But his vanity kept him mostly honest, at least in the big ways that made a difference to his career. He could not stand the thought that he, Sardar Tejpal Singh, was to be bought like a loaf of bread sitting on a shelf, like a packet of ciga-rettes. His pride kept him from being obsequious to his seniors: he was willing to ask for a favour, but he stopped at that. He found it impossible to persuade, wheedle, beg or bribe.

'Such a stubborn man,' Iffat-bibi said now, 'but he kept his head up like he wanted. Not that it did him much good.'

'Come on now, Bibi,' Sartaj said. 'Not everyone wants to earn a turnover like your Bhai's. How much is it?'

'Some newspaper said yesterday, eight thousand crores.'

'That's the newspaper. What do you think?'

She snorted. 'Bachcha, I'm an old woman, I don't do accounts. But it's enough.'

'Enough for what? What does anybody do with eight thousand crores?'

'Everyone needs a little extra. Not just for the things you need. For the things you want. Even your Sardar Saab.'

'What do you mean?'

'Arre, nothing, I was just talking like that.'

A shiver of unease moved over Sartaj's shoulders. He sat up. 'No, you were not. Tell me what you mean.'

'Nothing at all.'

'No, tell me. Iffat-bibi, don't try and fool me. What is it?'

'Beta, you are making a big noise about very little. I promised him I wouldn't tell anyone.'

'What is it? Was it a woman? Women?'

'Arre, you dirty-minded bastard, no!'

'Then what? Tell me.'

'You are making a big fuss over a very small thing.'

'What?'

'He liked to gamble.'

'Gamble?'

'Yes, yes. He loved horses. He liked to place bets on horses at the races.'

'He went to the racecourse?'

'No, never, someone might have seen and told your mother. I had one of my boys make the bets for him.'

Yes, Ma-ji, with her refugee's frugality, would never have stood for gambling in her household. She refused to buy lottery tickets because, she said, they were a complete waste of money, and anyone who thought they could get a crore by putting in one rupee was a complete jhalla. And here was Papa-ji, a regular money-scattering, gambling fool. But then, he did love horses. One of his great regrets was that he had never learned to ride. At the breakfast table, he would smooth out the newspaper with great care and point to a sports-page picture of a horse and say, 'Look, how beautiful,' and Sartaj and Ma never commented or replied or even noticed, because he had been saying it for ever. So instead, outside home, he had had a secret life, or at least a secret side. Sartaj coughed, to clear the congestion in his throat, and asked, 'Did he lose much?'

'Lose? No, he never bet that much to start with. He had a limit of fifty rupees, and then later he raised that to a hundred. But he was good at reading the racing forms. He won more than he lost. Actually a lot more.'

Papa-ji won. He had this other universe, with its own rules and systems, its particular histories and tragedies and triumphs, and here he was a winner. He had beaten the chances, he had vanquished the game. A bittersweet flood of affection and nostalgia and regret came into Sartaj's mouth and nose and eyes, and he had to hold the phone away a bit, to keep the sounds of his sentimentality from Iffat-bibi.

'Sartaj?'

'Yes, Bibi. I was just thinking, the old man was quite a character.'

'Complete namoona. But, listen, don't tell your mother, all right?'

'I won't.'

Later that night, Sartaj wondered if Ma knew already. She and Papa-ji had had their difficulties, their silences which Sartaj could never decipher. He had heard raised voices behind closed doors, and one of their quarrels had lasted three days, but Sartaj never knew why it started and how it ended. All this was normal enough for any wife and husband, and these two had been devoted to each other for more than forty years. Maybe Papa-ji had his horses, and kept quiet about them, and Ma knew but refused to know. Maybe that's how they had been happy together. But did she wonder that day, Sartaj's birthday, when Papa-ji had brought in the biggest and most expensive Meccano set that anyone had ever seen? Papa-ji had put Sartaj on his shoulders, and Sartaj had echoed Papa-ji as he went around saying his Hello-jis, and everybody had laughed and been happy. Maybe one of Papa-ji's horses had won that day. He and Sartaj sat up late that night, building a red and green house with a big wall around it, and Ma had crouched next to them, showing them where a courtyard should go in, and the proper location for the main gateway. Papa-ji wanted to put a flagpole on the roof, but Ma said that would make it look like a government building, not a home. Papa-ji and Sartaj worked hard, putting in the final touches, an actual swinging gate, a small shed for the chowkidar, and Ma let Sartaj finish the whole thing before she took him off to sleep.

The next morning, there was a message waiting at the station house for Sartaj. It was from Mary: 'Come to the Yari Road apartment tomorrow evening.' And that was all. Sartaj turned the note over, puzzled, then folded it carefully in half and put it into his pocket. He was glad that Kamble hadn't seen it, or he would have had to endure at least half a day of smirking jokes about ghochi and merry Mary and private trysts.

Sartaj spent the afternoon driving from one PCO to another, reaping the expected harvest of blank looks and bafflement. An orange-haired, sixtyish owner of a shop near Film City put a paan in her mouth and gave it to him straight: 'Baba, I know the call was just the day before yesterday. But you see how many people I get making calls in one day. I don't sit here looking at their faces. They come in, they make their calls, they give me their money. Bas. I don't even remember the ones who came today.' She bent to the electronic meter on her desk, squinted at it. 'Already today there have been a hundred and thirty calls. And the busiest time is the evening.' Her hair was appallingly hennaed, but she was telling the truth.

'You have a good turnover,' Sartaj said.

'Everyone needs to ring home,' she said.

There was a small queue of carpenters waiting for her two phones, pretending that they weren't listening to the policeman's questioning. They were Punjabis, stubbled and brawny. They had walked over from the shop three doors down, where they were building shelves. They were interested in the fact of a Sikh policeman in Bombay, but they were too scared of police inspectors to talk to him. Their families were probably in Gurdaspur, or Amritsar, and they had learnt caution.

Sartaj went on to the next PCO. He went to nineteen in all, and at all of them there were the same men and women, making calls across the city and across the country. None of the owners or cashiers could remember two men among these thousands. At seven Sartaj called a halt and veered off to Yari Road. The traffic was dense, and by the time Sartaj got across the subway, the twilight was losing its fantastic range of orange hues. The bulb in the lift was fused, and Sartaj had to grope for the buttons. But Mary had light. She opened the door into a well-lit drawing room and grinned up at Sartaj. She had a duster in her hand, and a chunni tied around her hair, giving her something of a Rani-of-Jhansi air. 'Hello, hello,' she said. 'And sat-sri-akal. Come in.'

'Hello,' Sartaj said. The drawing room was crowded with card-board boxes, but had been scrubbed clean. Mary had put in a day of work all right, but she seemed relaxed, buoyant. 'You have electricity.'

'Jana has a friend at BSES. I paid the past bills, and her friend got it all switched on.'

Jana was the kind of practical woman who would of course have a friend who could get electricity from BSES in a few days, instead of in a month or two. There was loud filmi music sweeping down the hall, from the bedroom. 'Jana's taking care of the shoes?'

Mary nodded, twinkling. 'And the clothes. She gets upset every two minutes because Jojo was too small for anything to fit her. Come on.' She stepped past Sartaj, calling, 'Jana! Jana!'

Jana also had a chunni tucked behind her ears, and the rapt look of a woman absorbed in her work. She greeted Sartaj with a quick nod and 'Hello,' and led the way into the study. 'We started cleaning in here first,' she said. 'Because mostly we were going to throw all these papers and files away.'

'We were throwing,' Mary said. 'And then Jana noticed one thing.'

They were pleased with themselves, for being able to tell Sartaj that they had noticed. But they were pleasured also by the knowledge itself, by the pleasure of detection. Sartaj said, with exactly the right degree of eagerness, 'What did she notice?'

From the top of the filing cabinet, Jana snatched up an envelope. From it she pulled out a photograph, and held it up with a flourish. 'This.' And another photograph. 'And this.'

Sartaj put out a hand to steady the picture she was holding up. A girl. A girl in a model pose, looking over her shoulder. She wasn't an especially attractive girl.

'The photograph was in the bottom drawer of Jojo's desk,' Mary said. 'Under some bills.'

'Yes.' Sartaj was trying to remember if he had examined these pho-tographs himself when he and Katekar had searched the study. There was nothing distinctive about them, nothing to remember. 'And so?'

Jana was astonished. 'You don't recognize her?' She held up another photograph.

Sartaj took it from her. This one was a portrait, with the hair falling forward and a wistful look. He turned it over. The name was noted in a neat hand, 'Jamila Mirza'. Which meant nothing to Sartaj. 'Who is she?'

Both Jana and Mary were looking at him with that tolerant, motherly patience that women practised when faced with male stupidity. Jana held up another piece of paper. 'This is a list of monies. I think they're payments, and they go on over months and years. Copies of passport pages, see, same girl. And copies of plane tickets, to Singapore. She went lots of times, see, sometimes every month. This wasn't a casual thing. This one was a regular girlfriend.'

'But we know that Jojo sent girls to Gaitonde. This girl is just one of those.'

'But do you know who this girl is?' Jana said.

'Jamila Mirza?'

'She was that. Then she became Zoya Mirza.'

'Miss India? The actress?'

'Yes. That one.'

Sartaj could see a resemblance, but he was doubtful. He pointed to Jamila Mirza's waist. 'This one's too fat.'

'Liposuction,' Jana said. 'Maybe the last ribs were taken out.'

Mary ran her finger over the portrait. 'Definitely had her nose done. And the hairline's been taken up.'

'There was work on the chin too,' Jana said. 'See how it's longer. And the jaws have been narrowed. So now that we've found this early Zoya, we give you to her. You have to tell us what happens with her, okay? Whatever you find out, you have to tell us. Promise?' She was an old-time and very regular *Stardust* reader for sure, this Jana, she was ravenous for nippy star natter.

'But are you sure this is her?'

'Yes,' they both said together.

They spoke with the certainty of experts, and they were very sure. This was their work. Sartaj had to believe them. 'Amazing,' he said. 'I could never have seen it.'

Mary laughed, and touched his hand, near the wrist. She said, 'That's all right. Men never do.'